Books by Margaret Atwood

Fiction
The Edible Woman
Surfacing
Lady Oracle
Life Before Man
Bodily Harm
The Handmaid's Tale
Cat's Eye
The Robber Bride

Short Fiction
Dancing Girls
Bluebeard's Egg
Wilderness Tips
Good Bones and Simple Murders

Poetry
The Circle Game
The Animals in That Country
The Journals of Susanna Moodie
Procedures for Underground
Power Politics
You Are Happy
Two-Headed Poems
Selected Poems
True Stories
Interlunar
Selected Poems II
Morning in the Burned House

Nonfiction
Survival: A Thematic Guide to Canadian Literature
Second Words

BODILY HARM

MARGARET ATWOOD

BANTAM BOOKS

New York • Toronto • London • Sydney • Auckland

This edition contains the complete text
of the original hardcover edition.
NOT ONE WORD HAS BEEN OMITTED.

BODILY HARM

A Bantam Book / published by arrangement with Simon & Schuster
PUBLISHING HISTORY
Simon & Schuster edition / March 1982
Bantam Windstone edition / April 1983
Bantam trade edition / January 1996

Acknowledgment is made for permission to quote from *Ways of Seeing* by John Berger, published in 1973 by The Viking Press, Inc. Reprinted by permission of Viking Penguin Inc.

An excerpt from *Bodily Harm* was previously published in the *Paris Review,* October 1981

Library of Congress Catalog Card Number: 95-80240

ISBN 0-553-37789-2

PRINTED IN THE UNITED STATES OF AMERICA

BVG   10 9 8 7 6 5 4 3 2 1

For Jennifer Rankin, 1941–1979
For Graeme, James and John

ACKNOWLEDGEMENTS

The author would like to thank the Canada Council and the Guggenheim Foundation for making it easier to complete this book. She would also like to thank Nan Talese, Donya Peroff, Phoebe Larmore, Michael Bradley, Jennifer Glossop, Jack McClelland, Carolyn Moulton, Rosalie Abella, Dan Green, Susan Milmoe, Carolyn Forché, and the others who are not named but whose help has been essential.

A man's presence suggests what he is capable of doing to you or for you. By contrast, a woman's presence . . . defines what can and cannot be done to her.

John Berger
Ways of Seeing

I

This is how I got here, says Rennie.

It was the day after Jake left. I walked back to the house around five. I'd been over at the market and I was carrying the shopping basket as well as my purse. There wasn't as much to carry now that Jake wasn't there any more, which was just as well because the muscles in my left shoulder were aching, I hadn't been keeping up the exercises. The trees along the street had turned and the leaves were falling onto the sidewalk, yellow and brown, and I was thinking, Well, it's not so bad, I'm still alive.

My next-door neighbour, an old Chinese man whose name I didn't know, was tidying up his front yard. The yard in front of my house had been covered over with paving stones so you could park a car on it. That meant the street was going up rather than down, and in a few years I'd have to move; though I'd stopped thinking in years. My neighbour had pulled up the dead plants and was raking the earth into a raised oblong. In the spring he'd plant things I didn't know the names for. I remember thinking it was time I learned the names, if I was going to live there.

I did notice the cruiser, which they'd left beside a meter like any other car, no flashing lights, but it was a few doors away so I didn't pay much attention to it. You see more police cars down there than you might farther north.

The front door was open, which wasn't out of place on such a warm day. The downstairs neighbour, an old woman who isn't the landlady but behaves like one, has cats and likes to leave the outside door ajar so they can get in and go through the cat door. "Cat hole," Jake calls it; used to call it.

My own door at the top of the stairs was open too. There were people inside, men, I could hear them talking, and then a laugh. I couldn't think who it could be, it wasn't Jake, but whoever it was didn't seem to care who knew they were there. The key was under the mat where I always leave it, but the edge of the doorframe was splintered, the lock was shoved right out of it. I went into the livingroom, which was still piled with the boxes of books Jake had packed but not collected. Nothing had been moved. Through the kitchen doorway I could see feet and legs, shining feet, pressed legs.

Two policemen were sitting at the table. I had that quick rush of fear, late for school, caught on the boys' stairs, caught out. The only thing I could think of was that they were after the pot, but there were no drawers pulled open and the tea and coffee canisters were where they should be. Then I remembered that Jake had taken the whole stash with him. Why not? It was his. Anyway, surely they'd stopped worrying about that, everyone does it now, even the police, it's almost legal.

The younger one stood up, the older one didn't. He stayed sitting down, smiling up at me as if I'd come for a job interview.

You Miss Wilford? he asked. He didn't wait. You're damn lucky. He had a massive head, with the hair clipped short like a punker's. His was left over though, from sometime in the fifties: no green highlights.

Why? I said. What's the matter?

You've got good neighbours, the younger one said. He looked like a high-school gym teacher or a Baptist, about twenty-two, earnest and severe. The one downstairs. She was the one who phoned.

Was it a fire? I said. There was no sign of it, no smell.

The older one laughed. The other one didn't. No, he said. She heard footsteps up here and she knew it wasn't you, she saw you go out, and she didn't hear anyone go up the stairs. He jimmied open your kitchen window.

I put the shopping basket on the table; then I went and looked at the window, which was open about two feet. The white paint was scratched.

You could do it with a jackknife, he said. You should get those safety locks. He heard us coming and went back out through the window.

Did he take anything? I said.

You'll have to tell us that, said the older one.

The young one looked uneasy. We don't think he was a burglar, he said. He made himself a cup of Ovaltine. He was just waiting for you, I guess. There was a cup on the table, half full of something light brown. I felt sick: someone I didn't know had been in my kitchen, opening my refrigerator and my cupboards, humming to himself maybe, as if he lived there; as if he was an intimate.

What for? I said.

The older one stood up. He took up a lot of space in the kitchen. Take a look, he said, pleased with himself, in charge. He had a present he'd been saving up. He walked past me into the livingroom and then into the bedroom. I was glad I'd made the bed that morning: lately I hadn't always.

There was a length of rope coiled neatly on the quilt. It wasn't any special kind of rope, there was nothing lurid about it. It was off-white and medium thick. It could have been a clothesline.

All I could think of was a game we used to play, Detective or Clue, something like that. You had to guess three things: Mr. Green, in the conservatory, with a pipewrench; Miss Plum, in the kitchen, with a knife. Only I couldn't remember whether the name in the envelope was supposed to be the murderer's or the victim's. *Miss Wilford, in the bedroom, with a rope.*

He was just waiting for you, the younger one said behind me.

Drinking his Ovaltine, the big one said. He smiled down at me, watching my face, almost delighted, like an adult who's just said *I told you so* to some rash child with a skinned knee.

So you were lucky, the younger one said. He came past me and picked up the rope, carefully, as if it had germs. I could see now that he was older than I'd thought, he had anxious puckers around the eyes.

The big one opened the closet door, casually, as if he had every right. Two of Jake's suits were still hanging there.

You live alone, that right? the big one said.

I said yes.

These your pictures? said the big one, grinning.

No, I said. They belong to a friend of mine. The pictures were Jake's, he was supposed to take them away.

Quite a friend, said the big one.

He must've been watching you for a while, said the young one. He must've known when you'd get home. Any idea who it might be?

No, I said. I wanted to sit down. I thought of asking them if they wanted a beer.

Some nut, the big one said. If you knew what was walking around loose out there you'd never go out. You close the curtains in the bathroom when you take a shower?

There aren't any curtains in the bathroom, I said. There aren't any windows.

You close the curtains when you get dressed at night?

Yes, I said.

He'll be back, the young one said. That kind always comes back.

The big one wouldn't let up. You have men over here a lot? Different men?

He wanted it to be my fault, just a little, some indiscretion, some provocation. Next he would start lecturing me about locks, about living alone, about safety.

I close the curtains, I said. I don't have men over. I turn out the lights. I get undressed by myself, in the dark.

The big one smirked at me, he knew about single women, and suddenly I was angry. I unbuttoned my blouse and pulled my left arm out of the sleeve and dropped the slip strap over my shoulder.

What in hell are you doing? the big one said.

I want you to believe me, I said.

There's a two-hour stopover in Barbados, or so they tell her. Rennie finds the women's washroom in the new Muzak-slick airport and changes from her heavy clothes to a cotton dress. She examines her face in the mirror, checking for signs. In fact she looks quite well, she looks normal. Her dress is a washed-out blue, her face isn't too pale, she wears only enough makeup so she won't seem peculiar, a leftover hippie or a Plymouth Brethren or something like that. This is the effect she aims for, neutrality; she needs it for her work, as she used to tell Jake. Invisibility.

Take a chance, said Jake, during one of his campaigns to alter her, what was it that time? Purple satin with rhinestone spaghetti straps. Make a statement.

Other people make statements, she said. I just write them down.

That's a cop-out, said Jake. If you've got it, flaunt it.

Which God knows you do, said Rennie.

You're putting me down again, said Jake, affable, showing his teeth, flawless except for the long canines.

You're impossible to put down, said Rennie. That's why I love you.

In the washroom there's a blow-dryer for your hands,

which claims to be a protection against disease. The instructions are in French as well as English, it's made in Canada. Rennie washes her hands and dries them under the blow-dryer. She's all in favour of protection against disease.

She thinks about what's behind her, what she cancelled or didn't bother to cancel. As for the apartment, she just shut the door with its shiny new lock and walked out, since out was where she needed to be. It gets easier and easier, dishes in the sink for two weeks, three weeks, only a little mould on them, she hardly even feels guilty any more; one of these days it may be permanent.

Rennie's lucky that she can manage these sidesteps, these small absences from real life; most people can't. She's not tied down, which is an advantage. It's a good thing she's versatile, and it helps to know people, in this case Keith. Keith has recently come across to *Visor* from *Toronto Life*. He's a contact of hers, which is not the same as a friend. While she was in the hospital she decided that most of her friends were really just contacts.

I want to go somewhere warm and very far away, she said.

Try the Courtyard Café, he said.

No, seriously, said Rennie. My life is the pits right now. I need a tan.

Want to do The Restless Caribbean? he said. So does everyone else.

Nothing political, she said. I can do you a good Fun in the Sun, with the wine lists and the tennis courts, I know what you like.

You finked out on the last piece I wanted you to do, said Keith. Anyway, you just came back from Mexico.

That was last year, she said. Come on, we're old buddies. I need some time out.

Keith sighed and then agreed, a little too quickly. Usually he haggled more. He must have heard about the operation;

maybe he even knew about Jake leaving. He had that faint sick look in his eyes, as if he wanted to give her something, charity for instance. Rennie hates charity.

It's not a total freebie, she said. It's not as if I don't produce.

Pick an island, he said. Only it has to be someplace we haven't done. How about this one? A friend of mine went there, sort of by mistake. He says it's off the beaten track.

Rennie had never heard of it. Sounds great, she said. Ordinarily she would have done some homework, but she was in too much of a hurry. This time she's flying blind.

Rennie repacks her bag, stuffing her pantyhose into an outside pocket, the one with the clock. Then she goes to the restaurant, where everything is wicker, and orders a gin and tonic. She does not look long at the distant sea, which is too blue to be believable.

The restaurant isn't full. There are a few women alone and more in clutches, and a couple of families. There are no men by themselves. Men by themselves usually go to the bar. She knows, she's learned since Jake left, that if she spends much time gazing around the room with that slightly defiant stare adopted by women alone to indicate that they don't have to be, one of the other solitaries might join her. So instead she watches her hands and the ice cubes in her glass, which despite the air conditioning are melting almost at once.

When she goes to the gate she's told the plane is late. Lugging her bag and her camera bag, she walks among the kiosk shops: small black hand-sewn dolls, cigarette boxes and mirrors encrusted with shells, necklaces made from the teeth of sharks, porcupine fish, inflated and dried. A miniature five-piece steel band, mounted on a slab of driftwood, in which the players are toads. Looking more closely, she sees that the toads are real ones that have been stuffed and varnished. A long time ago she would have bought this monstrosity and sent it to someone for a joke.

• • •

Rennie is from Griswold, Ontario. Griswold is what they call her background. Though it's less like a background, a backdrop—picturesque red Victorian houses and autumn trees on a hillside in the distance—than a subground, something that can't be seen but is nevertheless there, full of gritty old rocks and buried stumps, worms and bones; nothing you'd want to go into. Those who'd lately been clamouring for roots had never seen a root up close, Rennie used to say. She had, and she'd rather be some other part of the plant.

In an earlier phase, Rennie used to tell jokes about Griswold to amuse her friends. Such as: How many people from Griswold does it take to change a lightbulb? The whole town. One to change it, ten to snoop, and the rest of them to discuss how sinful you are for wanting more light. Or: How many people from Griswold does it take to change a lightbulb? None. If the light goes out it's the will of God, and who are you to complain?

People from bigger places, Jake in particular, think that Griswold has an exotic and primitive charm. Rennie doesn't think this. Mostly she tries to avoid thinking about Griswold at all. Griswold, she hopes, is merely something she defines herself against.

Though it's not always so easy to get rid of Griswold. For instance: When Rennie saw the piece of rope on her bed, she knew what Griswold would have had to say about it. This is what happens to women like you. What can you expect, you deserve it. In Griswold everyone gets what they deserve. In Griswold everyone deserves the worst.

The night before the operation Jake took Rennie out to dinner, to cheer her up. She didn't feel like going, but she knew she had been boring recently and she'd vowed, a long time ago, when she was still in her early twenties, never to be boring; a vow that had been harder to keep than she'd expected.

Rennie was an expert on boredom, having done a piece on it for *Pandora*'s "Relationships" column in which she claimed that there were two people involved in boredom, not just one: the borer and the boree. Out-and-out boredom of the jaw-stiffening kind could be avoided by small shifts in attention. *Study his tie,* she recommended. *If you're stuck, make an imaginary earlobe collection and add his. Watch his Adam's apple move up and down. Keep smiling.* The assumption was that the active principle, the source of the powerful ergs of boredom, was male, and that the passive recipient was female. Of course this was unfair, but who except women would read a *Pandora* "Relationships" column? When writing for male-oriented magazines such as *Crusoe* or *Visor* she offered self-help hints: "How To Read Her Mind." *If she's looking too hard at your earlobes or watching your Adam's apple go up and down, change the subject.*

Jake took her to Fentons, which used to be more than he could afford, and they sat under one of the indoor trees. At first he held her hand, but she felt he was doing it because he thought he ought to and after a while he stopped. He ordered a bottle of wine and urged her to drink more of it than she wanted to. Perhaps he thought she would be less boring if she got drunk, but this was not the case.

She didn't want to talk about the operation but she couldn't think about anything else. Maybe it would turn out to be benign; on the other hand, maybe they would open her up and find that she was permeated, riddled, rotting away from the inside. There was a good chance she'd wake up minus a breast. She knew she ought to be thinking about how to die with dignity but she didn't want to die with dignity. She didn't want to die at all.

Jake told stories about people they knew, gossipy stories with a malicious twist, the kind she used to enjoy. She tried to enjoy them but instead she started to think about Jake's fingers: he was holding the stem of his wineglass with his left hand, lightly, but the knuckles were absolutely white. He had a habit of never throwing out empty containers; that morning she'd taken down the Shreddies box and there was nothing in it. How could she know when it was time to get more if he kept leaving empty peanut butter jars and honey jars and cocoa tins on the shelves? She refrained from mentioning this. She felt that Jake's eyes kept slipping away from her face, down to the top button of her blouse; then, as if he'd reached a line, a taboo, back up to her face again. He's fascinated, she thought.

They walked home with their arms around each other, as if they were still in love. While Jake took a shower, Rennie stood in the bedroom with the closet door open, wondering what she should put on. Two of her nightgowns, the black one with the see-through lace top and the red satin one slit up the sides, had been presents from Jake. He liked buying her things like that. Bad taste. Garters, merry widows, red bikini pants with gold spangles, wired half-cup hooker brassieres that squeezed and pushed up the breasts. The real you, he'd say, with irony and hope. Who'd ever guess? Black leather and whips, that's next.

She wanted to make it easy for him, she wanted to help him along with the illusion that nothing bad had happened to her or was going to happen. Her body was in the mirror, looking the same as ever. She couldn't believe that in a week, a day, some of it might have vanished. She thought about what they did with the parts.

In the end she wore nothing. She waited in bed for Jake to come out of the shower. He would smell of body shampoo and he would be damp and slippery. She used to like it when he slid into her wet like that, but tonight she was only waiting for a certain amount of time to be over, as if she were in a dentist's office, waiting for something to be done to her. A procedure.

At first he couldn't. It had been too sudden; she'd been told, she'd told him, the operation had been scheduled, all in the same day. She could understand his shock and disgust and the effort he was making not to reveal them, since she felt the same way. She wanted to tell him he didn't have to, not if it was too much of an effort, but he wouldn't take that well, he'd think she was being critical.

He ran his hand over her breast a couple of times, the bad one. Then he began to cry. This was what she'd been afraid she herself would do. She hugged him, stroking the back of his head.

After that he made love to her, painfully and for a long time. She could hear his teeth grinding together, as if he were angry. He was holding back, waiting for her to come. He thought he was doing her a favour. He was doing her a favour. She couldn't stand the idea of anyone doing her a favour. Her body was nerveless, slack, as if she was already under the anaesthetic. As though he could sense this he gathered skin and muscle, wrenching, twisting, he bit her, not gently, shoving himself into her, trying to break through that barrier of deadened flesh. At last she faked it. That was another vow she'd made once: never to fake it.

By the time the flight is called it's already dark. They stand at the gate, a dozen or so of them, watching the plane land. The gate isn't even a gate but an opening in the cement wall with a chain across it. The airline officials, two kids, a light-brown girl who looks about sixteen and a boy with a set of earphones, can't decide which gate they should be standing at, so the whole group straggles back and forth several times between one hole in the wall and another. A man in tinted glasses offers to carry her camera bag for her, but Rennie refuses politely. She doesn't want anyone sitting beside her on the plane, especially a man who would wear a safari jacket. She didn't like safari jackets even when they were still possible. He's the only white man in the group.

When the hole is finally unchained, Rennie follows the others toward the plane, which is tiny and looks alarmingly homemade. Rennie tells herself that you stand a better chance in a small plane like this than in a jumbo jet. Jake has a joke about planes. He says they can't really fly, it's absurd to think a heavy piece of metal like that can fly; what keeps them up is the irrational belief of the passengers, and all plane crashes can be explained by loss of faith.

He'd have a job with this one, she thinks, anyone can see it'll never get off the ground. St. Antoine isn't a rich country, they probably buy their planes fourth-hand from other countries, then stick them together with Band-Aids and string until they fall apart irreparably. It's like the fat trade in restaurants. Rennie knows a lot about the fat trade in restaurants: the good ones selling their used fat to the second-rate ones, and so on down the line until the fat reaches the chipworks of cheap hamburger stands. Rennie's piece on the fat trade was called, "By Their Fats Ye Shall Know Them." The editor's title, not hers. She wanted to call it "Fat City."

She climbs the wobbling metal steps through the dark heat, which is doubled by the heat of the plane. The camera bag strap cuts into her shoulder and the flesh above her left breast; the scar is pulling again. When it feels like this she's afraid to look down, she's afraid she'll see blood, leakage, her stuffing coming out. It isn't a very big scar as such things go; worse things happen to other people. She's lucky. Why then doesn't she feel lucky?

I don't want to have the operation, she said. She believed two things at once: that there was nothing wrong with her and that she was doomed anyway, so why waste the time? She had a horror of someone, anyone, putting a knife into her and cutting some of her off, which was what it amounted to no matter what they called it. She disliked the idea of being buried one piece at a time instead of all at once, it was too much like those women they were always finding strewn about ravines or scattered here and there in green garbage bags. Dead but not molested. The first time she'd seen that word, in a Toronto newspaper when she was eight, she'd thought a molester was someone who caught moles. A molester is someone who is indecent, said her grandmother. But since that was what her grandmother said about almost everyone, it wasn't much help. Rennie still used that word sometimes, for fun, where other people would use *gross*.

Daniel, who at that point was still Dr. Luoma, looked at her as if he was disappointed in her: other women no doubt said similar things. This embarrassed her, since even such a short time ago she still assumed she was unique.

You don't have to, he said. Or, well, you don't *have* to do anything. Nobody's forcing you, it's your own decision. He paused here, letting her remember that the alternative he offered her was death. *Either/or.* Multiple choice: which was not what it said.

During the morning of the day on which she had her routine, once-a-year appointment at the gynecologist's, Rennie was working on a piece about drain-chain jewellery. You could get it for pennies at your local Woolworth's, she wrote. Buy as many lenghts as you need, make the chains as long as you like with those cunning little peanut-shaped connectors, wear them on any part of your anatomy: wrists, neck, waist, even ankles, if you wanted the slave-girl effect. It was the latest Queen Street thing, she wrote, a New Wave sleaze put-on of real jewellery. Or beyond New Wave even: *nouveau wavé.*

In fact it wasn't the latest Queen Street thing. It wasn't a thing at all, it was an embellishment Rennie had spotted on one of her friends, Jocasta, who ran Ripped Off, a second-hand store on Peter Street that specialized in violently ugly clothes from the fifties, springolator pumps, tiger-stripe pedal pushers, formals with jutting tits and layers of spangles and tulle.

Jocasta was five foot nine, with the cheekbones of an ex-model. She went in for fake leopard-skin shortie coats. The women who hung out at Ripped Off were half Jocasta's age and wore a lot of black leather. They had hair dyed green or bright red, or they shaved their heads with an Iroquois fringe running down the middle. Some of them had safety pins in their ears. They looked up to Jocasta, who was right over the edge in the creative sleaze line and could carry it off, too. In her display window she made arrangements that she called Junk Punk: a stuffed lizard copulating with a mink collar in a child's rocking chair, motorized, a cairn of false teeth with a born-again tract propped against it: "How Can I Be Saved?" Once she hung a coat tree with blown-up condoms sprayed with red enamel and a sign: NATIONAL LOVE A REFUGEE WEEK.

Of course it's gross, said Jocasta. But so's the world, you know what I mean? Me, I'm relaxed. A little deep breathing, mantras of one syllable, bran for breakfast. Can I help it if I'm the wave of the future?

Jocasta wasn't Jocasta's name: her real name was Joanne. She changed it when she was thirty-eight because, as she said, what can you do with a name like Joanne? Too *nice*. She didn't dye her hair green or wear a safety pin in her ear but calling herself Jocasta was the equivalent. Good taste kills, said Jocasta.

Rennie met Jocasta when she was doing a piece on the Queen Street renaissance for *Toronto Life,* all about the conversion of hardware stores and wholesale fabric outlets into French restaurants and trendy boutiques. She did not necessarily believe that a trendy boutique was any improvement over a wholesale fabric outlet, but she knew enough to avoid such negative value judgements in print. At first she thought Jocasta was a lesbian, because of the way she dressed, but later she decided Jocasta was merely bizarre. Rennie liked Jocasta because Jocasta was much more bizarre than Rennie felt she herself could ever be. Partly she admired this quality, partly she felt it was dangerous, and partly, being from Griswold after all, she had a certain contempt for it.

Jocasta wore drain chains because she was miserly and they were cheap. She hadn't even bought her chains, she'd raided the sinks of neighbouring restaurants for them: "All I did was take the plug off with a pair of pliers, and *voilà.*" But sometimes Rennie liked to write pieces about trends that didn't really exist, to see if she could make them exist by writing about them. Six to one she'd see at least ten women with bathplug chains looped around their necks two weeks after the piece came out. Successes of this kind gave her an odd pleasure, half gleeful, half sour: people would do anything not to be thought outmoded.

Usually her articles on fake trends were just as plausible as the ones on real trends; sometimes more so, because she tried harder with them. Even the editors were taken in, and when they weren't they'd go along anyway, half-believing that what Rennie had to say on subjects like this would eventually come true, even if it wasn't true at the moment. When she wasn't fooling around she was uncanny, they told each other: as if she could see into the future.

If I could see into the future, Rennie said to one of them (a man, who kept suggesting that they should have drinks sometime soon), do you think I'd waste my time on this sort of thing? The colour of women's lipstick, the length of their skirts, the height of their heels, what bits of plastic or gilt junk they choose to stick on themselves? I see into the present, that's all. Surfaces. There's not a whole lot to it.

Rennie became a quick expert on surfaces when she first moved away from Griswold. (On a university scholarship: the only other respectable way out of Griswold for a young single woman, she used to say, is straight down.) Surfaces determined whether or not people took you seriously, and what was mandatory in Griswold was, more often than not, ludicrous in the real world. Griswold, for instance, was an early convert to polyester knit.

At first she'd looked in order to copy; later on she'd looked in order not to copy. After that she just looked. When Marxist college professors and hard-line feminists gave her a rough time at parties about the frivolity of her subject matter she would counter with a quote from Oscar Wilde to the effect that only superficial people were not concerned with appearances. Then she would tactfully suggest certain alterations to their wardrobes that would improve their own appearances no end. They were usually vain enough to be interested: nobody wanted to be in bad taste.

Most of the people she knew thought Rennie was way out ahead of it, but she saw herself as off to the side. She preferred it there; she'd noted, many times, the typical pose of performers, celebrities, in magazine shots and publicity stills and especially on stage. Teeth bared in an ingratiating smile, arms flung wide to the sides, hands open to show that there were no concealed weapons, head thrown back, throat bared to the knife; an offering, an exposure. She felt no envy towards them. In fact she found them embarrassing, their eagerness, their desperation, for that was what it was, even when they were successful. Underneath it they would do anything; they'd take their clothes off if there was no other way, they'd stand on their heads, anything, in that frenzied grab for attention. She would much rather be the one who wrote things about people like this than be the one they got written about.

Rennie finished the first draft of her piece on drain-chain jewellery and spent some time thinking about the title. Eventually she discarded "The Chain Gang" in favour of "Chain Reaction." The pictures would be easy to get, but she'd leave that to the magazine. She never shot high-gloss fashion, she wasn't good enough.

At eleven-thirty Jake surprised her by coming home, "for a lunchtime quickie," he said. That was fine, since she liked being surprised by him. At that time he was still inventive. Sometimes he would climb up the fire escape and in through the window instead of coming through the door, he'd send her ungrammatical and obscene letters composed of words snipped from newspapers, purporting to be from crazy men, he'd hide in closets and spring out at her, pretending to be a lurker. Apart from the first shock, none of these things had ever alarmed her.

So they had the lunchtime quickie and afterwards Rennie made grilled cheese sandwiches and they ate them in bed, which wasn't as pleasant as she'd thought it would be because some of the crumbs and melted cheese got on the sheets, and Jake went back to his office. Rennie had a bath, because her background was still with her and she felt it would be inconsiderate to go to the gynecologist right after making love without having had a bath.

Ready to have babies yet? the doctor asked, his standard opening joke as he snapped on his prophylactic gloves. You're heading for the cutoff point. He'd been saying this for six years. Half and hour later, everything ceased to be funny.

Though as she walked home she was still thinking in the ways she was used to. For instance, she could do a piece on it. "Cancer, The Coming Thing." *Homemakers* might take it, or *Chatelaine*. How about "The Cutoff Point"?

This is a fact, it's happened to you, and right now you can't believe it, she would begin. *You've been used to thinking of yourself as a person, but all of a sudden you're just a statistic.* Dying was in bad taste, no doubt of that. But at some point it would be a trend, among the people she knew. Maybe she was way out ahead on that one too.

On the plane they serve warm ginger ale in paper cups and sandwiches wrapped in plastic film. The sandwiches are made of slices of white bread, with slightly rancid butter and a thin piece of roast beef between them. Rennie picks out the lettuce: she's been to Mexico, she knows about amoebic dysentery.

The seats are hard and covered with scratchy maroon plush, like those on ancient buses. The stewardesses, two of them, one with straightened upswept hair like Betty Grable's, one with cornrows and beaded Rasta braids, wear hot-pink satin outfits with tiny white aprons. They teeter up and down the narrow aisles on high-heeled sandals, open-toed with multiple straps, magenta: fuck-me shoes, Jake would call them. When the plane bumps they grab for the back of the nearest seat, but they seem used to it.

Though the plane is just half full, there's a man beside Rennie. It isn't the white man in the safari jacket, who's sitting at the very front reading a newspaper, but an older man, brown. He's wearing a dark suit, despite the heat, and a tie in which a small pin shines. She notices that he's taken only one bite of his sandwich. When the remains of the sandwiches are being collected he speaks to Rennie, throwing his voice above the drone of the engines.

"You are from Canada," he says, stating it rather than asking. He's about sixty, spare-faced and tall, with a high-bridged nose; he looks vaguely Arabian. His jaw is undershot, his bottom teeth close slightly over the top ones.

"How did you know?" says Rennie.

"We get mostly Canadians," he says. "The sweet Canadians."

Rennie can't tell whether or not this is meant as irony. "We're not all that sweet," she says.

"I trained in Ontario, my friend," he says. "I was once a veterinarian. My specialty was the diseases of sheep. So I am familiar with the sweet Canadians." He smiles, speaking precisely. "They are famous for their good will. When we had our hurricane, the sweet Canadians donated a thousand tins of ham, Maple Leaf Premium. It was for the refugees." He laughs, as if this is a joke, but Rennie doesn't get it. "The refugees never see this ham," he says, explaining patiently. "Most likely they never eat ham in their lives before. Well, they miss their chance." He laughs again. "The ham turn up, surprise, at the Independence Day banquet. To celebrate our freedom from Britain. For the leading citizens only. Many of us were very amused, my friend. There was a round of applause for the sweet Canadians."

Rennie doesn't know what to say to this. She feels he's making fun of her in some obscure way, but she isn't sure why. "Was it a bad hurricane?" she says. "Was anyone killed?"

He ignores this question entirely. "Why are you coming to St. Antoine?" he says, as if it's an odd thing to be doing.

"I'm writing a piece on it," she says. "A travel piece."

"Ah," he says. "To entice the sweet Canadians."

Rennie is becoming irritated with him. She looks at the pocket in the seatback in front of her, hoping there's something she can pretend to read, an airline magazine, barf-bag mags as they're known in the trade, but there's nothing in it but the card illustrating emergency procedures. On the 707 to Barbados she had a thriller she bought at the airport, but she finished it and left it on the plane. A mistake: now she's bookless.

"You must visit our Botanic Gardens," he says. "The British made very good ones, all over the world. For medicinal purposes, you understand. Ours is one of the oldest. It is still in good repair; they have only been gone a month. Now that we are free, we have to pull out the weeds ourselves. We have a small museum there, you must see that. Broken pots made by the Carib Indians and so forth. They did not make very accomplished pottery. We still have a few of them in our country, we have not fully modernized."

He reaches into his jacket pocket and takes out a bottle of aspirin. He taps two into his palm and offers the bottle to Rennie, as if offering a cigarette. Rennie doesn't have a headache, but feels she should take one anyway, it's the polite thing to do.

"There is a fort also," he says. "The British were proficient at that, too. Fort Industry. Under the British it was called Fort George, but our government is renaming everything." He signals the stewardess and asks for a glass of water.

"We just have ginger ale," she says.

"It will have to do," he says. His teeth clamp together in a bulldog grin. "In my country that is a very useful phrase."

The ginger ale comes and he swallows his aspirins, then

offers the Styrofoam cup to Rennie. "Thank you," says Rennie. "I'm saving mine for later." She holds the aspirin in her hand, wondering if she's just been rude, but if so he doesn't seem to notice.

"I have many statistics you might find useful," he says. "Those on unemployment, for instance. Or perhaps you would prefer the Botanic Gardens? I would be happy to escort you, I take an interest in plants."

Rennie decides not to ask him about restaurants and tennis courts. She thanks him and says she'll have a better idea of what she's looking for once she gets there.

"I think we are approaching." he says.

The plane dips. Rennie peers out the window, hoping to see something, but it's too dark. She glimpses an outline, a horizon, something jagged and blacker than the sky, but then the plane goes down at a forty-five degree angle and a moment later they hit the ground. She jolts forward against the seat belt as the plane brakes, much too fast.

"We have a very short runway here," he remarks. "Before I tendered my regrets to the present government I attempted to have something done about it. I was at that time the Minister for Tourism." He smiles his lopsided smile. "But the Prime Minister had other priorities."

The plane taxis to a stop and the aisle jams with people. "It's been nice meeting you," Rennie says as they stand up.

He holds out his hand for her to shake. Rennie transfers the aspirin. "I hope you will have a pleasant stay, my friend. If you need assistance, do not hesitate to call on me. Everyone knows where I can be found. My name is Minnow, Dr. Minnow, like the fish. My enemies make jokes about that! A small fish in a small puddle, they say. It is a corruption of the French, Minôt was the original, it was one of the many things they left behind them. The family were all pirates."

"Really?" Rennie says. "That's wild."

"Wild?" says Dr. Minnow.

"Fascinating," says Rennie.

Dr. Minnow smiles. "They were common once," he says.

"Some of them were quite respectable; they intermarried with the British and so forth. You have a husband?"

"Pardon?" says Rennie. The question has caught her by surprise: nobody she knows asks it any more.

"A man," he says. "Here we do not bother so much with the formalities."

Rennie wonders if this is a sexual feeler. She hesitates. "Not *with* me," she says.

"Perhaps he will join you later?" Dr. Minnow says. He looks down at her anxiously, and Rennie sees that this isn't an advance, it's concern. She smiles at him, hoisting her camera bag.

"I'll be fine," she says. Which is not what she believes.

When Rennie floated up through the anaesthetic she did not feel anything at first. She opened her eyes and saw light green, then closed them again. She did not want to look down, see how much of herself was missing. She lay with her eyes closed, realizing that she was awake and would rather not be. She also realized, though she had not admitted it before, that she had expected to die during the operation. She'd heard stories about people going into shock or being allergic to the anaesthetic. It was not out of the question.

Her left arm was numb. She tried to move it and couldn't. Instead she moved her right hand, and not until then did she understand that someone was holding it. She turned her head, forced her eyes to open, and saw, a long distance away, as if she were looking through the wrong end of a telescope, the image of a man, a head surrounded by darkness, glassy and clear. Daniel.

It's all right, he said. It was malignant but I think we got it all.

He was telling her that he had saved her life, for the time being anyway, and now he was dragging her back into it, this life that he had saved. By the hand. *Malignant,* Rennie thought.

Now what, she said. Her mouth felt thick and swollen. she looked at his arm, which was bare from the elbow down and was lying beside hers on the white sheet; hair licked along the skin like dark flames. His fingers were around her wrist. She did not see hands but an odd growth, like a plant or something with tentacles, detachable. The hand moved: he was patting her.

Now you go to sleep, he said. I'll be back.

Rennie looked again and his hand attached itself to his arm, which was part of him. He wasn't very far away. She fell in love with him because he was the first thing she saw after her life had been saved. This was the only explanation she could think of. She wished, later, when she was no longer feeling dizzy but was sitting up, trying to ignore the little sucking tubes that were coming out of her and the constant ache, that it had been a potted begonia or a stuffed rabbit, some safe bedside object. Jake sent her roses but by then it was too late.

I imprinted on him, she thought; like a duckling, like a baby chick. She knew about imprinting; once, when she was hard up for cash, she'd done a profile for *Owl Magazine* of a man who believed geese should be used as a safe and loyal substitute for watchdogs. It was best to be there yourself when the goslings came out of the eggs, he said. Then they'd follow you to the ends of the earth. Rennie had smirked because the man seemed to think that being followed to the ends of the earth by a flock of adoring geese was both desirable and romantic, but she'd written it all down in his own words.

Now she was behaving like a goose, and the whole thing put her in a foul temper. It was inappropriate to have fallen in love with Daniel, who had no distinguishing features that Rennie could see. She hardly even knew what he looked like, since, during the examinations before the operation, she hadn't bothered to look at him. One did not look at doctors; doctors were functionaries, they were what your mother once hoped you would marry, they were fifties, they were passé. It wasn't only inappropriate, it was ridiculous. It was expected. Falling in love with your doctor was something middle-aged married women did, women in the soaps, women in nurse novels and in sex-and-scalpel epics with titles like *Surgery* and nurses with big tits and doctors who looked like Dr. Kildare on the covers. It was the sort of thing *Toronto Life* did stories about, soft-core gossip masquerading as hard-nosed research and exposé. Rennie could not stand being guilty of such a banality.

But there she was, waiting for Daniel to appear (out of nowhere, she never knew when he would be coming, when she was having a sponge bath or struggling to the toilet, leaning on the large wattled nurse), hooked like a junkie on those pats of the hand and Rotarian words of cheer and collective first-person plurals ("We're coming along nicely"), and in a feeble rage because of it. *Shit.* He wasn't even that handsome, now that she had a good look: his proportions were wrong, he was too tall for his shoulders, his hair was too short, his arms were too long, he gangled. She sniffled with anger into the wad of Kleenex the nurse held out to her.

A good cry will do you good, said the nurse. But you're lucky, they say there's none anywhere else, some of them are full of it, they cut it out and it just pops up somewhere else. Rennie thought of toasters.

Daniel brought her a pamphlet called *Mastectomy: Answers to Down-To-Earth Questions.* Down to earth. Who wrote these things? Nobody in her position would want to think very hard about *down* or *earth. Are there any restrictions on sexual activity?* she read. The pamphlet suggested that she ask her doctor. She considered doing this.

But she didn't. Instead she asked him, How much of me did you cut off? Because she was in love with him and he hadn't noticed, her tone of voice was not all it should have been. But he didn't seem to mind.

About a quarter, he said gently.

You make it sound like a pie, said Rennie.

Daniel smiled, indulging her, waiting her out.

I guess I should be relieved, said Rennie. That you didn't hack off the whole thing.

We don't do that any more unless there's massive involvement, said Daniel.

Massive involvement, said Rennie. It's never been my thing.

He follows up, said the nurse. A lot of them, they just do their number and that's that. He likes to know how things work out, in their life and all. He takes a personal interest. He says a lot of it has to do with their attitude, you know?

Jake brought champagne and pâté and kissed her on the mouth. He sat beside her bed and tried not to look at her wrapped chest and the tubes. He spread pâté on crackers, which he'd also brought, and fed them to her. He wanted to be thanked.

You're a godsend, she said. The food here is unbelievable. Green Jell-O salad and a choice of peas or peas. She was happy to see him but she was distracted. She didn't want Daniel to walk in, trailing interns, while Jake was still there.

Jake was restless. He was healthy and healthy people are embarrassed by sickness, she could remember that. She was convinced also that she smelled peculiar, that there was a faint odour of decay seeping through the binding: like an off cheese. She wanted him to go quickly and he wanted to go.

We'll get back to normal, she told herself, though she could not remember any longer what *normal* had been like. She asked the nurse to adjust her bed so she could lie back.

That's a fine young man, the nurse said. Jake was a fine young man. He was all in place, a good dancer who hardly ever bothered to dance.

● ● ●

Rennie climbs down the steps of the plane and the heat slips over her face like thick brown velvet. The terminal is a low shed with a single turret. It looks grey under the weak lights of the runway, but as Rennie walks toward it she sees that it's really yellow. Over the doorway there's a bronze plaque thanking the Canadian government for donating it. It's odd to see the Canadian government being thanked for anything.

The immigration officer is wearing a dark-green uniform, like a soldier's, and there are two actual soldiers leaning against the wall beside him, in crisp blue shirts with short sleeves. Rennie assumes they're soldiers, since they have shoulder holsters with what look like real guns in them. They're young, with skinny innocent bodies. One of them is flicking his swagger stick against his pantleg, the other has a small radio which he's holding against his ear.

Rennie realizes she's still clutching the aspirin in her left hand. She wonders what to do with it; somehow she can't just throw it away. She opens her purse to put it with her other aspirins, and the soldier with the swagger stick saunters towards her.

Rennie feels a chill sweep down her. She's about to be singled out: perhaps he thinks the bottle she's holding contains some kind of illegal drug.

"It's aspirin," she says, but all he wants is to sell her a ticket to the St. Antoine Police Benefit Dance, Semi-formal, Proceeds For Sports Funds. So they're only police, not soldiers. Rennie makes this out by reading the ticket, since she hasn't understood a word he's said.

"I don't have the right kind of money," she says.

"We take anything you got," he says, grinning at her, and this time she understands him. She gives him two dollars, then adds a third; possibly it's the price of admission. He thanks her and strolls back to the other one, and they laugh together. They haven't bothered with anyone else in the line.

In front of Rennie there's a tiny woman, not five feet tall.

She's wearing a fake-fur shortie coat and a black wool jockey cap tilted at a rakish angle. She turns around now and looks up at Rennie.

"That a bad man," she says. "Don't you have nothin' to do with that one." She holds out to Rennie a large plastic bag full of cheese puffs. From under the brim of her jockey cap her eyes peer up out of her dark wrinkled face, she must be at least seventy but it's hard to tell. The eyes are bright, candid, sly, the eyes of a wary child.

"This my grandson," she says. She opens the coat to reveal an orange T-shirt. PRINCE OF PEACE, it says in large red letters.

Rennie has never seen a religious maniac up close before. When she was at university an economics student was rumoured to have run through his dormitory one night, claiming to have given birth to the Virgin Mary, but that was put down to pre-exam tension.

Rennie smiles, as naturally as possible. If this woman thinks she's Ste. Anne or whoever, it would be best not to upset her, not in the immigration line at any rate. Rennie accepts some cheese puffs.

"It my grandson, all right," says the woman. She knows she's been doubted.

Then it's her turn, and Rennie hears her say to the immigration officer in a shrill, jocular voice, "You give me trouble, my grandson blaze your arse good for you." This seems to have the desired effect, for the man stamps her passport immediately and she goes through.

When he comes to Rennie he feels he has to be extra severe. He flips through her passport, frowning over the visas. He wears thick bifocals, and he pushes them further down on his nose and holds the passport away from him, as if it smells funny.

"Renata Wilford? That you?"

"Yes," Rennie says.

"It don't look like you."

"It's a bad picture," Rennie says. She knows she's lost weight.

"Let her in, man," one of the policemen calls, but the immigration clerk ignores him. He scowls at her, then at the picture. "What the purpose of your visit?"

"Pardon?" Rennie says. She has to strain to understand the accent. She looks around for Dr. Minnow, but he's nowhere in sight.

"What you doin' here?" He glares at her, his eyes enlarged by the lenses.

"I'm a writer," Rennie says. "A journalist. I write for magazines. I'm doing a travel piece."

The man glances over at the two policemen. "What you goin' to write about here?" he says.

Rennie smiles. "Oh, the usual," she says. "You know, restaurants, sight-seeing, that sort of thing."

The man snorts. "Sight-seein'," he says. "No pretty lights here." He stamps her passport and motions her through.

"Write it good," he says to her as she goes past. Rennie thinks he's teasing, as such a man at Heathrow or Toronto or New York would be. They would say, "Write it good, honey." Or *love,* or *sweetheart.* They would grin. But when she turns to give the required smile he's staring straight ahead, through the plateglass window to the tarmac, where the plane has already turned in the darkness and is taxiing again for take-off between the rows of white and blue lights.

Rennie changes some money, then waits while a tired uniformed woman pokes through her purse and her bags. Rennie says she has nothing to declare. The woman scrawls a chalk mark on each of her bags, and Rennie walks through a doorway into the main room. The first thing she sees is a large sign that says, THE BIONIC COCK: IT GIVES YOU SPURS. There's a picture of a rooster; it turns out to be an advertisement for rum.

•   •   •

There's a crowd outside the door, taxi drivers, and Rennie goes with the first one who touches her arm. Ordinarily she would talk with him, find things out: beaches, restaurants, shops. But it's too hot. She sinks into the marshmallow-soft upholstery of the car, some derelict from the fifties, while the driver goes far too fast through the winding narrow streets, honking at every bend. The car is on the wrong side of the road, and it takes Rennie a moment to remember that this is in fact the British side.

They wind up a hillside, past houses she can make out only dimly. The headlights shine on massive bushes over-hanging the road, with flamboyant red and pink flowers dangling from them like Kleenex flowers at a high-school dance. Then they're in the lighted part of town. There are crowds of people on the streetcorners and in front of the shops but they aren't walking, they're just standing or sitting on steps or chairs, as if they're inside a room. Music flows through the open doorways.

Some of the men wear knitted wool caps, like tea cosies, and Rennie wonders how they can stand it in the heat. Their heads turn as the taxi goes by, and some wave and shout, at the driver rather than Rennie. She's beginning to feel very white. Their blacks aren't the same as our blacks, she reminds herself; then sees that what she means by *our blacks* are the hostile ones in the States, whereas *our blacks* ought to mean this kind. They seem friendly enough.

Nevertheless Rennie finds their aimlessness disturbing, as she would at home. It's too much like teenagers in shopping plazas, it's too much like a mob. She discovers that she's truly no longer *at home*. She is away, she is *out*, which is what she wanted. The difference between this and home isn't so much that she knows nobody as that nobody knows her. In a way she's invisible. In a way she's safe.

When Jake moved out, naturally there was a vacuum. Something had to come in to fill it. Maybe the man with the rope hadn't so much broken into her apartment as been sucked in, by the force of gravity. Which was one way of looking at it, thought Rennie.

Once she would have made this man into a good story; she would have told it at lunch, with the strawberry flan. She wasn't sure what stopped her, from telling anyone at all. Perhaps it was that the story had no end, it was open-ended; or perhaps it was too impersonal, she had no picture of the man's face. When she was outside, walking along the street, she looked at the men who passed her in a new way: it could be any one of them, it could be anyone. Also she felt implicated, even though she had done nothing and nothing had been done to her. She had been seen, too intimately, her face blurred and distorted, damaged, owned in some way she couldn't define. It wasn't something she could talk about at lunch. Anyway, she didn't want to become known as a man-hater, which was what happened when you told stories like that.

The first thing she did after the policemen had gone was to get the lock fixed. Then she had safety catches put on the windows. Still, she couldn't shake the feeling that she was being watched, even when she was in a room by herself, with the curtains closed. She had the sense that someone had been in her apartment while she was out, not disarranging anything, but just looking into her cupboards, her refrigerator, studying her. The rooms smelled different after she'd been out. She began to see herself from the outside, as if she was a moving target in someone else's binoculars. She could even hear the silent commentary: Now she's opening the bean sprouts, now she's cooking an omelette, now she's eating it, now she's washing off the plate. Now she's sitting down in the livingroom, nothing much going on. Now she's getting up, she's going into the bedroom, she's taking off her shoes, she's turning out the light. Next comes the good part.

She began to have nightmares, she woke up sweating. Once she thought there was someone in the bed with her, she could feel an arm, a leg.

Rennie decided she was being silly and possibly neurotic as well. She didn't want to turn into the sort of woman who was afraid of men. It's your own fear of death, she told herself. That's what any armchair shrink would tell you. You think you're dying, even though you've been saved. You should be grateful, you should be serene and profound, but instead you're projecting onto some pathetic weirdo who's never going to bother you again. That scratching you heard at the window last night wasn't coming from the outside at all.

Which was all very well, but the man existed; he was an accident that had almost happened to her; he was an ambassador, from some place she didn't want to know any more about. The piece of rope, which was evidence, which the police had taken away with them, was also a message; it was someone's twisted idea of love. Every time she went into her bedroom she could see it, coiled on the bed, even though it was no longer there.

In itself it was neutral, and useful too, you could use it for all kinds of things. She wondered whether he'd intended to strangle her with it or just tie her up. He hadn't wanted to be drunk, there had been beer and half a bottle of wine in the refrigerator, she was sure he'd looked, and he'd chosen Ovaltine. He'd wanted to know what he was doing. When he got as far as the scar perhaps he would have stopped, apologized, untied her, gone home, to the wife and children Rennie was certain he had. Or perhaps he knew, perhaps that's what turned him on. *Mr. X, in the bedroom, with a rope.*

And when you pulled on the rope, which after all reached down into darkness, what would come up? What was at the end, *the end*? A hand, then an arm, a shoulder, and finally a face. At the end of the rope there was someone. Everyone had a face, there was no such thing as a faceless stranger.

Rennie is late for dinner. She has to wait at the front desk while they set a table for her in the diningroom. Around the corner, where she can't see, a tray of silverware hits the floor and there's an argument in low voices. After fifteen minutes a waitress comes out and says sternly that Rennie can go in now, as if it's a trial rather than a meal.

As Rennie walks towards the diningroom, a woman with a tan the colour of clear tea walks out of it. She has blonde hair braided and wound around her head, and she's wearing a sleeveless magenta dress with orange flowers on it. Rennie feels bleached.

The woman smiles at her with fluorescent teeth, looking at her with round blue china-doll eyes. "Hi there," she says. Her friendly, glassy stare reminds Rennie of the greeting perfected by hostesses in the restaurants of Holiday Inns. Rennie waits for her to say, "Have a good day." The smile lasts a little too long, and Rennie gropes, wondering if she knows this woman. She decides with relief that she doesn't, and smiles back.

The tables are covered with starched white tablecloths and the wineglasses have linen napkins tucked into them, pleated into fans. Propped against the flower vase, one hibiscus per table, is a small typewritten card which isn't exactly a menu, since there's no choice. The food is brought by three waitresses, in light-blue full-skirted dresses and white aprons and mobcaps. They are totally silent and do not smile; perhaps they've been called away from their own dinners.

Rennie begins to compose, from habit and to pass the time, though she doesn't think the Sunset Inn will find its way into her piece:

The décor is nondescript, resembling nothing so much as an English provincial hotel, with flowered wallpaper and a few prints of hunting and shooting. The ceiling fans add a pleasant touch. We began with the local bread, and butter of perhaps a questionable freshness. Then came (she consulted the menu) *a pumpkin soup, which was not the bland version most*

North Americans may be used to. My companion . . .

But there is no companion. It's necessary to have a companion for these excursions, always, if only a paper one. The readers would find the suggestion that you would go to a restaurant and sit there all by yourself, just eating, far too depressing. They want gaiety and the possibility of romance and a mention of the wine list.

Rennie gives up anyway when the roast beef arrives, leathery and khaki and covered with a gravy that tastes like mix. It's garnished with a cube of yam and something light green that has been boiled too long. This is the kind of food you eat only when very hungry.

Rennie is reminded of the put-on piece she did, months ago, on fast-food outlets. It was for *Pandora*'s "Swinging Toronto" section. She'd once done a piece for them on how to pick men up in laundromats, unobtrusively and safely, with addresses of the good laundromats. *Check their socks. If they ask to borrow your soap flakes, forget it.* The food franchise piece was called "Sawdust Yummies" and the subtitle (not hers) read, "You better take a good thou, 'cause the bread and the wine are nowhere."

She'd covered every McDonald's and Kentucky Fried Chicken spot in the downtown core for it, dutifully taking one bite of everything. *My companion had the Egg McMuffin, which he found a trifle runny. My buns were chilly.*

Rennie picks at the alien vegetables on her plate, gazing around the room. There's only one other diner, a man, who's sitting on the far side of the room reading a paper. In front of him is a dish of what looks like whipped lime Jell-O. If this were a laundromat, would she pick him up? He turns the page of his newspaper and smiles at her, a half-smile of complicity, and Rennie looks down at her plate. She likes to stare but she doesn't like to be caught doing it.

Eye contact, that was one hint. She's not surprised when he folds the paper, gets up, and heads towards her table.

"It's kind of dumb, sitting across the room from each other like that," he says. "I think this place is empty except for us. Mind if I join you?"

Rennie says no. She has no intention of picking this man up. She never actually picked men up in laundromats, she just went through the preliminaries and then explained that she was doing research. That's what she can always say if necessary. Meanwhile, there's no reason not to be polite.

He goes to the kitchen door and asks for another cup of coffee, and one of the waitresses brings it. She also brings a dish of the green substance for Rennie, and then, instead of returning to the kitchen, sits down at the man's vacated place and finishes off his dessert, staring balefully at him as she does so. The man has his back to her and can't see.

"I wouldn't eat that if I were you," he says.

Rennie laughs and looks at him more carefully. Before the operation, there was a game she used to play with Jocasta, on the street and in restaurants. Pick a man, any man, and find the distinguishing features. The eyebrows? The nose? The body? If this man were yours, how would you do him over? A brush cut, a wet suit? It was a rude game and Rennie knew it. Jocasta, for some reason, didn't. Listen, she'd say. You'd be doing them a favour.

Rennie thinks this man would resist being done over. For one thing, he's too old: he's past the Silly Putty stage. Rennie decides he must be at least forty. His tan is leathery, there are permanent white creases around his eyes. He has a light moustache and post-hippie-length hair, bottom of the ear-lobes in front, top of the collar in back; it's a little ragged, as if he does it himself with kitchen scissors. He's wearing shorts and a yellow T-shirt without anything written on it. Rennie approves of this. She liked T-shirts with mottoes on them when they first came out, but now she thinks they're jejune.

Rennie introduces herself and mentions that she's a journalist. She always likes to get that in first, before people mistake her for a secretary. The man says his name is Paul and he's from Iowa. "Originally," he says, implying travel. He's not staying at the hotel, he says, just eating there. It's one of the better places.

"If this is better, what's worse?" says Rennie, and they both laugh.

Rennie asks him where home is. It's all right to ask such questions, since Rennie has already decided this does not have the flavour of a pickup. File it under *attempt at human contact*. He just wants someone to talk to, he's killing time. Which is fine, that's all she's doing herself. If there's anything she doesn't need in her life right now, it's another one of what Jocasta would call *those*. Nevertheless, she's conscious of a desire to stick her head down under the tablecloth, to see what his knees look like.

"Home?" says Paul. "You mean, where the heart is?"

"Was that a personal question?" says Rennie. She starts to eat the dessert, which appears to be made of sweetened chalk.

Paul grins. "Most of the time I live on a boat," he says. "Over at Ste. Agathe, the harbour's better there. I'm just here for a couple of days, on business."

Rennie feels she's expected to ask what sort of business, so she doesn't. She's decided he will be boring. She's met people with boats before and all they ever talk about is boats. Boats make her seasick. "What sort of boat?" she says.

"Quite a fast one. Actually I have four of them," he says, watching her. Now she's supposed to be impressed.

"I guess that means you're filthy rich," she says.

This time he laughs. "I charter them out," he says. "They're all out now. It's a pain in the ass in some ways. I don't like tourists. They're always complaining about the food, and they throw up too much."

Rennie, who is a tourist, lets this pass. "How did you get four?" she says.

"You can pick them up cheap around here," he says, "from the dead or the disgusted, retired stockbrokers who have heart attacks or decide it's too much trouble scraping off the barnacles. There's a bit of owner piracy too."

Rennie doesn't want to give him the satisfaction of her ignorance, but he smiles at her with his tan folding into pleats around his eyes, he wants her to ask, so she relents and asks.

"People stealing their own boats," he says. "They collect the insurance. Then they sell the boat."

"But you would never do a thing like that," says Rennie. She's paying more attention. No gold earring, no wooden leg, no hooks on the ends of the arms, no parrot. Still, there's something. She looks at his hands, square-fingered and practical, carpenter's hands, on the tablecloth, not doing anything.

"No," he says. "I would never do a thing like that."

He smiles a little, his eyes are light blue, and she recognizes something about him, a deliberate neutrality. He's doing what she does, he's holding back, and now she's really curious.

"Do you have a job?" she says.

"If you have four boats you don't exactly need a job, around here," he says. "I make enough on the charters. I used to have one, I was an agronomist with the U.S. Department of Agriculture. They sent me as an adviser. I was supposed to be telling them what else they can grow here besides bananas. I was pushing red kidney beans. The catch is, nobody really wants them to grow anything here besides bananas. But they wouldn't send me anywhere else, so I kind of retired."

"Where were you before that?" says Rennie.

"Here and there," he says. "A lot of places. I was in Viet Nam, before the war, the official one that is. After that I was in Cambodia." He says this still smiling, but looking at her straight on, a little belligerently, as if he's expecting her to react with horror or at least disgust.

"What were you doing there?" says Rennie pleasantly, putting down her spoon.

"Advising," he says. "I was always advising. It's not the same as having people do what you say."

"What about?" says Rennie; she feels now as if they're on the radio.

There's a small pause, another crinkled smile. "Rice," he says, watching her closely.

She's being asked for something, but she's not sure what it is. Not admiration, not absolution. Maybe she's not being asked for anything at all, which is just as well, since she doesn't have a whole lot of handouts left. "That must have been interesting," she says. She hasn't done profiles for nothing, she isn't stupid, she knows how to add, she knows there's an X factor. Ten years ago she would have felt entitled to moral outrage, but it's no skin off her nose. People get trapped in things that are beyond their control, she ought to know that by now.

He relaxes, leans back in his chair. She's passed the test, whatever it was. "I'll tell you about it sometime," he says, assuming the future; which is more than she can do.

Rennie's room at the Sunset Inn is papered with a small floral print, pink and blue; there are several pale-orange watermarks near the ceiling, which is fifteen feet high. At the end of the bed, which is single and narrow and covered with a white chenille spread, hangs a picture of a green melon cut open to reveal the seeds. Over the bed itself is a knotted mosquito net, not quite as white as the bedspread. On the night table beside the bed are a Bible, a mosquito coil in a saucer, a box of matches, Three Star, made in Sweden, and a lamp with a pleated paper shade. The lamp is a mermaid with her arms over her head, holding up the bulb. Her breasts aren't bare, she's wearing a harem jacket open at the front, its edges grazing the nipples. In the drawer of the night table are two more mosquito coils in a box labelled *Fish Mosquito Destroyer, Blood Protection Co. Ltd.*

On the pale-green bureau there's a thermos jug of water, a glass and a hand-printed card warning visitors not to drink the tap water. Rennie opens the drawers. In the centre one is a lime-green blanket, in the bottom one a safety pin. Rennie feels momentarily that she may be spending the rest of her life in rooms like this. Not her own.

She lights the mosquito coil, turns on the mermaid lamp and puts her travelling alarm clock on top of the Bible. She unpacks her cotton nightgown and the zipper bag in which she keeps her toothbrush and the other pieces of cleaning and sterilizing equipment people use on their bodies. She's ceased to take such things for granted; "Prevention of Decay" is no longer just a slogan. She closes the Venetian blind on the narrow window, turns off the overhead light and undresses. The mirror over the bureau is small, so she isn't reflected anywhere.

She takes a shower, in water that refuses to become more than lukewarm. When she comes out of the tiny bathroom, there's a green lizard sticking to the wall beside the window.

She turns down the chenille spread and the sheet and looks carefully in the bed and under the pillow, checking for wildlife. She untwists the mosquito net and tucks it around the bed. Then she crawls into the white tent, turns off the light, and moves to the centre of the bed so that no part of her body is touching the net. She can see the oblong of the window, grey against the darkness, and the glowing end of the mosquito coil. The air is warm and damp, warmer and damper on her skin now than before she took the shower, and the bed smells faintly of mildew.

There are sounds from outside the window, a high cricket sound and a repeated note like a bell or a waterglass being struck, some kind of insect or frog perhaps, and beyond that the insistent syncopated music. Several minutes after she turns out the light a car backfires, or maybe it's firecrackers, and a woman screams with laughter; but that stops and the music keeps going.

Despite the heat Rennie lies with her arms folded, left hand on her right breast, right hand on the ridge of skin that slants across the side of her breast up towards her armpit. This is how she always sleeps now.

She runs the fingers of her left hand over the skin of her breast, the good one, the one she hopes is good, as she does every night. From the surface you can feel nothing, but she no longer trusts surfaces. She brushed her teeth and cleaned them with dental floss, prevention of decay, and rinsed out her mouth with water from the thermos, which smells like melted ice cubes, like the inside of a refrigerator, like cloth in a trunk. Nevertheless she can still taste the airplane sandwich, slightly rancid butter and roast beef, rotting meat.

She sleeps and wakes fitfully, listening to the music and, occasionally, a car going past in what always sounds like the wrong gear. She feels clogged and furry; she's convinced she's been snoring, though it hardly matters. At last she sinks into a heavy damp sleep.

She wakes up suddenly. She can feel something like moist cloth, webbing, pressing down over her eyes and mouth. Her face is against the net. Through it she can see the figures on her digital clock, the dot pulsing like a tiny heart. It's six in the morning. She was dreaming that someone was climbing in through the window.

She remembers where she is and hopes she hasn't bothered anyone in the hotel by screaming. She's too warm, she's sweating, and despite the mosquito net she has several bites, from where she's rolled against the net. The muscles of her left shoulder are aching again.

There's a rooster crowing nearby and beyond that a dog, dogs. The room is growing light. Close to her ear, on the other side of the wall, there are sounds it takes her a moment to recognize, unfamiliar, archaic, the rhythmic creak of a bed and a woman's voice, wordless and mindless. Before she places it she hears it as agony. Once this intrusion would merely have irritated her, or, if she was with someone, amused or even excited her. Now it's painful to her, mournful, something lost, a voice from the past, severed from her and going on beside her in another room. Get it over, she thinks through the wall.

Oh please.

II

One of the first things I can remember, says Rennie, is standing in my grandmother's bedroom. The light is coming in through the window, weak yellowish winter light, everything is very clean, and I'm cold. I know I've done something wrong, but I can't remember what. I'm crying, I'm holding my grandmother around both legs, but I didn't think of them as legs, I though of her as one solid piece from the neck down to the bottom of her skirt. I feel as if I'm holding on to the edge of something, safety, if I let go I'll fall, I want forgiveness, but she's prying my hands away finger by finger. She's smiling; she was proud of the fact that she never lost her temper.

I know I will be shut in the cellar by myself. I'm afraid of that, I know what's down there, a single light bulb which at least they leave on, a cement floor which is always cold, cobwebs, the winter coats hanging on hooks beside the wooden stairs, the furnace. It's the only place in the house that isn't clean. When I was shut in the cellar I always sat on the top stair. Sometimes there were things down there, I could hear them moving around, small things that might get on you and run up your legs. I'm crying because I'm afraid, I can't stop, and even if I hadn't done anything wrong I'd still be put down there, for making a noise, for crying.

Laugh and the world laughs with you, said my grandmother. *Cry and you cry alone.* For a long time I hated the smell of damp mittens.

I grew up surrounded by old people: my grandfather and my grandmother, and my great-aunts and great-uncles, who came to visit after church. I thought of my mother as old too. She wasn't, but being around them all the time made her seem old. On the street she walked slowly so they could keep up with her, she raised her voice the way they did, she was anxious about details. She wore clothes like theirs too, dark dresses with high collars and small innocuous patterns, dots or sprigs of flowers.

As a child I learned three things well: how to be quiet, what not to say, and how to look at things without touching them. When I think of that house I think of objects and silences. The silences were almost visible; I pictured them as grey, hanging in the air like smoke. I learned to listen for what wasn't being said, because it was usually more important than what was. My grandmother was the best at silences. According to her, it was bad manners to ask direct questions.

The objects in the house were another form of silence. Clocks, vases, end-tables, cabinets, figurines, cruet sets, cranberry glasses, china plates. They were considered important because they had once belonged to someone else. They were both overpowering and frail: overpowering because threatening. What they threatened you with was their frailty; they were always on the verge of breaking. These objects had to be cleaned and polished once a week, by my grandmother when she was still well enough and afterwards by my mother. It was understood that you could never sell these objects or give them away. The only way you could ever get rid of them was to will them to someone else and then die.

The objects weren't beautiful, most of them. They weren't supposed to be. They were only supposed to be of the right kind: the standard aimed at was not beauty but decency. That was the word, too, among my mother and my aunts, when they came to visit. "Are you decent?" they would call gaily to one another before opening bedroom or bathroom doors. Decency was having your clothes on, in every way possible.

If you were a girl it was a lot safer to be decent than to be beautiful. If you were a boy, the question didn't arise; the choice was whether or not you were a fool. Clothes could be decent or indecent. Mine were always decent, and they smelled decent too, a wool smell, mothballs and a hint of furniture polish. Other girls, from families considered shoddy and loose, wore questionable clothes and smelled like violets. The opposite of decent wasn't beautiful, but flashy or cheap. Flashy, cheap people drank and smoked, and who knew what else? Everyone knew. In Griswold, everyone knew everything, sooner or later.

So you had your choice, you could decide whether people would respect you or not. It was harder if your family wasn't respectable but it could be done. If your family was respectable, though, you could choose not to disgrace it. The best way to keep from disgracing it was to do nothing unusual.

The respectability of my family came from my grandfather, who had once been the doctor. Not a doctor, the doctor: they had territories then, like tomcats. In the stories my grandmother told me about him, he drove a cutter and team through blizzards to tear babies out through holes he cut in women's stomachs and then sewed up again, he amputated a man's leg with an ordinary saw, knocking the man out with his fist because no one could hold him down and there wasn't enough whisky, he risked his life by walking into a farmhouse where a man had gone crazy and was holding a shotgun on him the whole time, he'd blown the head off one of his children and was threatening to blow the heads off the other ones too. My grandmother blamed the wife, who had run away months before. My grandfather saved the lives of the remaining children, who were then put in an orphanage.

No one wanted to adopt children who had such a crazy father and mother: everyone knew such things ran in the blood. The man was sent to what they called the loony bin. When they were being formal they called it an institution.

My grandmother worshipped my grandfather, or so everyone said. When I was little I thought of him as a hero, and I guess he was, he was about the closest you could get in Griswold unless you'd been in the war. I wanted to be like him, but after a few years at school I forgot about that. Men were doctors, women were nurses; men were heroes, and what were women? Women rolled the bandages and that was about all anyone ever said about that.

The stories my mother and aunts told about my grandfather were different, though they never told these stories when my grandmother was there. They were mostly about his violent temper. When they were girls, whenever they skirted what he felt to be the edges of decency, he would threaten to horsewhip them, though he never did. He thought he was lenient because he didn't make his children sit on a bench all Sunday as his own father had. I found it very difficult to connect these stories, or my grandmother's either, with the frail old man who could not be disturbed during his afternoon nap and who had to be protected like the clocks and figurines. My mother and my grandmother tended him the same way they tended me, efficiently and with a lot of attention to dirt; only more cheerfully. Perhaps they really were cheerful. Perhaps it made them cheerful to have him under their control at last. They cried a lot at his funeral.

My grandmother had been amazing for a woman of her age; everyone told me that. But after my grandfather's death she began to deteriorate. That's how my mother would put it when her sisters would come to visit. They were both married, which was how they'd got away from Griswold. I was in high school by then so I didn't spend as much time hanging around the kitchen as I used to, but one day I walked in on them and all three of them were laughing, stifled breathless laughs, as if they were in a church or at a funeral: they knew they were being sacrilegious and they didn't want my grandmother to hear them. They hardly saw me, they were so intent on their laughter.

She wouldn't give me a key to the house, my mother said. Thought I'd lose it. This started them off again. Last week she finally let me have one, and I dropped it down the hot air register. They patted their eyes, exhausted as if they'd been running.

Foolishness, said my aunt from Winnipeg. This was my grandmother's word for anything she didn't approve of. I'd never seen my mother laugh like that before.

Don't mind us, my aunt said to me.

You laugh or you cry, said my other aunt.

You laugh or you go bats, said my mother, injecting a little guilt, as she always did. This sobered them up. They knew that her life, her absence of a life, was permitting them their own.

After that my grandmother began to lose her sense of balance. She would climb up on chairs and stools to get things down, things that were too heavy for her, and then she would fall. She usually did this when my mother was out, and my mother would return to find her sprawled on the floor, surrounded by broken china.

Then her memory began to go. She would wander around the house at night, opening and shutting doors, trying to find her way back to her room. Sometimes she wouldn't remember who she was or who we were. Once she frightened me badly by coming into the kitchen, in broad daylight, as I was making myself a peanut-butter sandwich after school.

My hands, she said. I've left them somewhere and now I can't find them. She was holding her hands in the air, helplessly, as if she couldn't move them.

They're right there, I said. On the ends of your arms.

No, no, she said impatiently. Not those, those are no good any more. My other hands, the ones I had before, the ones I touch things with.

My aunts kept watch on her through the kitchen window

while she wandered around in the yard, prowling through the frost-bitten ruins of the garden which my mother didn't have the time to keep up any more. Once it had been filled with flowers, zinnias and scarlet runner beans on poles where the hummingbirds would come. My grandmother once told me heaven would be like that: if you were good enough you would get everlasting life and go to a place where there were always flowers. I think she really believed it. My mother and my aunts didn't believe it, though my mother went to church and when my aunts visited they all sang hymns in the kitchen after supper when they were doing the dishes.

She seems to think it's still there, said my aunt from Winnipeg. Look. She'll freeze to death out there.

Put her in a home, said my other aunt, looking at my mother's caved face, the mauve half-moons under her eyes.

I can't, my mother would say. On some days she's perfectly all right. It would be like killing her.

If I ever get like that, take me out to a field and shoot me, said my other aunt.

All I could think of at that time was how to get away from Griswold. I didn't want to be trapped, like my mother. Although I admired her—everyone was always telling me how admirable she was, she was practically a saint—I didn't want to be like her in any way. I didn't want to have a family or be anyone's mother, ever; I had none of those ambitions. I didn't want to own any objects or inherit any. I didn't want to cope. I didn't want to deteriorate. I used to pray that I wouldn't live long enough to get like my grandmother, and now I guess I won't.

Rennie wakes up finally at eight. She lies in bed and listens to the music, which seems to be coming from downstairs now, and decides she feels much better. After a while she gropes her way through the mosquito netting and gets out of bed. She leans on the windowsill, looking out at the sunlight, which is very bright but not yet ferocious. Down below is a cement courtyard, she seems to be at the back of the hotel, where a woman is washing sheets in a zinc tub.

She considers her wardrobe. There isn't a lot of choice, since she packed the minimum.

She remembers picking out the basic functional sunbreak mix 'n' match, wrinkle-free for the most part. That was only the day before yesterday. After she'd packed, she had gone through her cupboard and her bureau drawers, sorting, re-arranging, folding, tucking the sleeves of her sweaters care-fully behind their backs, as if someone would be staying in her apartment while she was away and she needed to leave things as tidy and manageable as possible. That was only the clothes. The food in the refrigerator she'd disregarded. Who-ever it was wouldn't be eating.

Rennie puts on a plain white cotton dress. When the dress is on she looks at herself in the mirror. She still looks normal.

Today she has an appointment with the radiologist at the hospital. Daniel made it for her weeks ago, he wants more tests. A work-up, they call it. She didn't even cancel the ap-pointment before taking off. She knows that later she will regret this lack of courtesy.

Right now she only feels she's escaped. She doesn't want the tests; she doesn't want the tests because she doesn't want the results. Daniel wouldn't have scheduled more tests unless he thought there was something wrong with her again, though he said it was routine. She's in remission, he says. *But we'll have to keep an eye on you, we always will. Remission* is the good word, *terminal* is the bad one. It makes Rennie think of bus stations: the end of the line.

She wonders whether she's already become one of those odd wanderers, the desperate ones, who cannot bear the thought of one more useless hospital ordeal, pain and deathly sickness, the cells bombarded, the skin gone antiseptic, the hair falling out. Will she go off on those weird quests too, extract of apricot pits, meditation on the sun and moon, coffee enemas in Colorado, cocktails made from the juice of cabbages, hope in bottles, the laying on of hands by those who say they can see vibrations flowing out of their fingers in the form of a holy red light? Faith healing. When will she get to the point where she'll try anything? She doesn't want to be considered crazy but she also doesn't want to be considered dead.

Either I'm living or I'm dying, she said to Daniel. Please don't feel you can't tell me. Which is it?

Which does it feel like? said Daniel. He patted her hand. You're not dead yet. You're a lot more alive than many people.

This isn't good enough for Rennie. She wants something definite, the real truth, one way or the other. Then she will know what she should do next. It's this suspension, hanging in a void, this half-life she can't bear. She can't bear not knowing. She doesn't want to know.

She goes into the bathroom, intending to brush her teeth. In the sink there's a centipede, ten inches long at least, with far too many legs, blood-red, and two curved prongs at the back, or is it the front? It's wriggling up the side of the slippery porcelain sink, falling back again, wriggling up, falling back. It looks venomous.

Rennie is unprepared for this. She's not up to squashing it, what would she use anyway? And there's nothing to spray it with. The creature looks far too much like the kind of thing she's been having bad dreams about: the scar on her breast splits open like a diseased fruit and something like this crawls out. She goes into the other room and sits down on the bed, clasping her hands together to keep them from shaking. She waits five minutes, then wills herself back into the bathroom.

The thing is gone. She wonders whether it dropped from the ceiling in the first place, or came up through the drain, and now where has it gone? Over the side onto the floor, into some crack, or back down the drain again? She wishes she had some Drano and a heavy stick. She runs some water into the sink and looks around for the plug. There isn't one.

There's a lounge where you can have afternoon tea; it's furnished with dark green leatherette chairs that look as if they've been hoisted from an early-fifties hotel foyer in some place like Belleville. Rennie waits on one of the sticky chairs while they set a table for her in the diningroom, grudgingly, since she's half an hour late. In addition to the chairs there's a glass-topped coffee table with wrought-iron legs on which there are copies of *Time* and *Newsweek* eight months old, and a mottled plant. Gold tinsel is looped around the tops of the windows, left over from Christmas; or perhaps they never take it down.

The tablecloths from the night before have been removed; underneath, the tables are grey formica with a pattern of small red squares. Instead of the pleated linen fans there are yellow paper napkins. Rennie looks around for Paul but there's no sign of him. The hotel seems fuller, though. There's an older woman, white, thin-faced, by herself, who stares perkily around the diningroom as if expecting to be charmed by everything, and an Indian family, the wife and grandmother in saris, the little girls in frilled sundresses. Luckily, Rennie is placed one table away from the older woman, who looks unpleasantly Canadian. She doesn't want to have a conversation about scenery or the weather. The three little girls parade the room, giggling, being chased and pinched playfully by the two waitresses, who smile for them in a way they do not smile for adults.

The older woman is joined by another like herself, plumper but with hair as tight. Listening to them, watching them consult their little books, Rennie discovers that they aren't Canadian but German: one of that army of earnest travellers that is everywhere now on the strength of the

Deutschmark, even in Toronto, blue-eyed, alert, cataloguing the world. Why not? thinks Rennie. It's their turn.

The waitress comes and Rennie orders yoghurt and fresh fruit.

"No fresh fruit," says the waitress.

"I'll take the yoghurt anyway," says Rennie, who feels she's in need of some friendly bacteria.

"No yoghurt," says the waitress.

"Why is it on the menu then?" says Rennie.

The waitress looks at her, straight-faced but with her eyes narrowing as if she's about to smile. "Used to be yoghurt," she says.

"When will there be some again?" Rennie says, not sure why this should all be so complicated.

"They got Pioneer Industries for dairy now," the waitress says, as if reciting a lesson. "Government thing. Dairy don't make no yoghurt. Yoghurt need powder milk. Powder milk outlaw, you can't buy it. The yoghurt place shut down now."

Rennie feels that there are connections missing here, but it's too early in the morning to have to deal with this. "What can I have then?" she says.

"What we got," says the waitress, very patiently.

This turns out to be orange juice made from instant powder of some sort, an almost-cooked egg, coffee from a jar with tinned milk, bread with margarine, and guava jelly, too sweet, dark orange, of the consistency of ear wax. Rennie wishes she could stop reviewing the food and just eat it. Anyway, she isn't at the Sunset Inn because of the food. She's here because of the price: this time the deal isn't all-expenses. She can do the other, flossier places for lunch or dinner.

The waitress comes and takes away her plate, the runny egg in its custard cup, the pieces of bread and jam lying beside it. Like a child, she's eaten the centres and left the crusts.

After breakfast comes the rest of the day, which will surely be too long, too hot and bright, to be filled with any activity that will require movement. She wants to go to sleep in the sun on a beach, but she's prudent, she doesn't want to come out like crispy chicken. She needs suntan lotion and a hat. After that she can start going through the motions: places of interest, things to do, tennis courts, notable hotels and restaurants, if any.

She knows you become exhausted in the tropics, you lose momentum, you become comatose and demoralized. The main thing is to keep going. She has to convince herself that if she doesn't manage to complete a well-researched and cheerfully written piece on the pleasures of St. Antoine the universe will be negatively affected.

Maybe she could fake the whole article, concoct a few ravishing little restaurants, some Old World charm in the New World, throw in some romantic history, tart the whole thing up with a few photos from the lesser-known corners of, say, St. Kitts. She pictures legions of businessmen descending on St. Antoine and then, in outrage, on the editorial offices of *Visor*. It won't do, she'll have to come up with something, she's overdrawn at the bank. She can always talk about development potential.

What I need is a pith helmet, she thinks, and some bearers, or are they beaters, to carry me around in a hammock, and some of what those people in Somerset Maugham are always drinking. Pink gin?

Rennie does what she does because she's good at it, or that's what she says at parties. Also because she doesn't know how to do anything else, which she doesn't say. Once she had ambitions, which she now thinks of as illusions: she believed there was a right man, not several and not almost right, and she believed there was a real story, not several and not almost real. But that was 1970 and she was in college. It was easy to believe such things then. She decided to specialize in abuses: honesty would be her policy. She did a piece for the *Varsity* on blockbusting as practised by city developers and another on the lack of good day-care centres for single mothers, and she took the nasty and sometimes threatening letters she received as a tribute to her effectiveness.

Then she graduated and it was no longer 1970. Several editors pointed out to her that she could write what she liked, there was no law against it, but no one was under any obligation to pay her for doing it, either. One of them told her she was still a southern Ontario Baptist at heart. United Church, she said, but it hurt.

Instead of writing about the issues, she began interviewing the people who were involved in them. Those pieces were a lot easier to sell. The *in* wardrobe for the picket line, the importance of the denim overall, what the feminists eat for breakfast. The editors told her she was better at that anyway. Radical chic, they called it. One day she found herself short of petty cash and did a quick piece on the return of hats with veils. It wasn't even radical, it was only chic, and she tried not to feel too guilty about it.

Now that she no longer suffers from illusions, Rennie views her kind of honesty less as a virtue than a perversion, one from which she still suffers, true; but, like psoriasis and hemorrhoids, those other diseases typical of Griswold, it can be kept under control. Why make such things public? Her closet honesty is—there's no doubt about it—a professional liability.

Other people have no such scruples. Everything is relative, everything is fashion. When a thing or a person has been too widely praised, you merely reverse the adjectives. No one considers this perverse, it's simply the nature of the business, and the business runs on high turnover. You write about something until people become tired of reading about it or you become tired of writing about it, and if you're good enough or lucky enough it's the same thing. Then you write about something else.

Rennie is still close enough to Griswold to find this attitude irritating at times. Last year she went into the office of the *Toronto Star* when some of the younger staff members were making up a list. It was close to New Year's and they were drinking gallon white wine out of Styrofoam coffee cups and killing themselves laughing. The list was a regular feature. Sometimes it was called "In and Out," sometimes "Plus and Minus"; such lists reassured people, including those who wrote them. It made them think they could make distinctions, choices that would somehow vindicate them. She had once composed such lists herself.

This time the list was called "Class: Who Has It, Who Doesn't." Ronald Reagan didn't have class, Pierre Trudeau did. Jogging didn't have class, contemporary dance did, but only if you did it in jogging pants, which did, for that but not for jogging, but not in stretchy plunge-back leotards, which didn't for that but did if you went swimming in them, instead of in bathing suits with built-in bra cups, which didn't. Marilyn's didn't, the Lickin' Chicken on Bloor, which didn't sell chicken, did.

"What else for the No list?" they asked her, giggling already, anticipating her answer. "What about Margaret Trudeau?"

"What about the word *class*?" she said, and they weren't sure whether that was funny or not.

Which is a problem she has. The other problem is the reputation she's getting for being too picky. She's aware of this, she listens to gossip; people are beginning to think she won't finish assignments. There's some truth to this: increasingly there are things she can't seem to do. Maybe it isn't *can't,* maybe it's *won't.* What she wants is something legitimate to say. Which is childish. Loss of nerve, she's decided. It started before the operation but it's getting worse. Maybe she's having a mid-life crisis, way too soon. Maybe it's Griswold squeezing her head: *If you can't say anything nice, don't say anything at all.* Not that its own maxims ever stopped Griswold.

Two months ago she was offered a good piece, a profile in *Pandora*'s "Women of Achievement" series. A ballet dancer, a poet, a female executive from a cheese food company, a judge, a designer who specialized in shoes with glitter faces on the toes. Rennie wanted the designer but they gave her the judge, because the judge was supposed to be hard to do and Rennie was supposed to be good.

Rennie was not prepared for the panic that overtook her the first day out. The judge was nice enough, but what did you say? What does it feel like to be a judge? she asked. What does it feel like to be anything? said the judge, who was only a year older than Rennie. She smiled. It's a job. I love it.

The judge had two wonderful children and an adoring husband who didn't at all mind the time she spent being a judge, because he found his own job so satisfying and re-warding. They had a charming house, Rennie couldn't fault the house, filled with paintings by promising young artists; the judge decided to be photographed in front of one of them. With each question Rennie felt younger, dumber and more helpless. The judge had it all together and Rennie was beginning to see this as a personal affront.

I can't do it, she told the editor at *Pandora*. The editor's name was Tippy; she was a contact of Rennie's. She opens her mouth and out comes this ticker tape.

She's a control freak, Tippy said. She's controlling the interview. You've got to turn it around, get an angle on her. Our readers want them to be human too, a few cracks in the armour, a little pain. Didn't she have to suffer on her way up?

I asked her that, said Rennie. She didn't.

What you have to do, said Tippy, is ask her if you can just sort of hang out with her. Follow her around all day. There's a real story in there somewhere. How she fell in love with her husband, did you ask that? Look in the medicine cabinet, go for the small details, it matters what they roll on under their arms, Arrid or Love, it makes a difference. Stick with them long enough and sooner or later they crack. You've got to dig. You're not after dirt, just the real story.

Rennie looked across the desk, which was messy, at Tippy, who was also messy. She was ten years older than Rennie, her skin was sallow and unhealthy, there were pouches under her eyes. She chain-smoked and drank too much coffee. She was wearing green, the wrong colour for her. She was a good journalist, she'd won all sorts of awards before she became an editor, and now she was telling Rennie to peer into other people's medicine cabinets. A woman of achievement.

Rennie went home. She looked at what she'd already written about the judge and decided that it was, after all, the real story. She tore it up and started a new page.

A profile used to mean a picture of somebody's nose seen from the side, she wrote. *Now it means the picture of somebody's nose seen from the bottom.* Which was as far as she got.

Rennie takes her camera, on the off chance. She's not very good, she knows that, but she forced herself to learn because she knew it would increase her scope. If you do both the pictures and the text you can go almost anywhere, or so they say.

She picks up a mimeographed map of Queenstown and a tourist brochure from the registration desk. "St. Antoine and Ste. Agathe," the brochure says. "Discover Our Twin Islands In The Sun." On the front is a tanned white woman laughing on a beach, sheathed in one-piece aqua Spandex with a modesty panel across the front. A black man in a huge straw hat is sitting on the sand beside her, handing up a coconut with a couple of straws sticking out of it. Behind him is a machete propped against a tree. He's looking at her, she's looking at the camera.

"When was this printed?" Rennie asks.

"We get them from the Department of Tourism," says the woman behind the desk. "That's the only kind there is." She's British and seems to be the manager, or perhaps the owner. Rennie is always slightly cowed by women like this, women who can wear thick-soled khaki shoes and lime-green polyester jersey skirts without being aware of their ugliness. This woman's no doubt responsible for the lounge chairs and the scabby plant. Rennie envies people who are unaware of ugliness: it gives them an advantage, they can't be embarrassed.

"I understand you're a travel writer," the woman says severely. "We don't usually have them here. You ought to be at the Driftwood."

For a moment Rennie wonders how she knows, but then remembers that it says "freelance journalist" on her disembarkation card, which is in the office safe. Not a hard deduction. What she probably means is that Rennie can't expect special treatment because there isn't any, and in particular she's not supposed to ask for a discount.

The hotel is on the second floor of an old building. Rennie goes down the outside stone staircase, the steps worn concave in the centres, to an inner courtyard that smells of piss and gasoline, then under an archway into the street. Sunlight hits her like a wind, and she rummages in her purse for sunglasses. She realizes she's stepped over a pair of legs, trousers with bare feet at the ends, but she doesn't look down. If you look they want something. She walks along beside the wall of the hotel, patchy stucco that was once white. At the corner she crosses the main street, which is pocked with holes; thick brown sludge moves in the gutters. There aren't many cars. On the other side of the street is an overhang supported by columns, a colonnade, like the ones bordering the *zócalos* in Mexican towns. It's hard to tell how old things are, she'll have to find out. The tourist brochure says the Spaniards were through here, once, along with everyone else. "Leaving a charming touch of Old Spain" is how they put it.

She walks in the shade, looking for a drugstore. Nobody bothers her or even looks at her much, except for a small boy who tries to sell her some spotty bananas. This is a relief. In Mexico, whenever she left Jake at the hotel and ventured out by herself, she was followed by men who made sucking noises at her with their mouths. She buys a straw hat, overpriced, in a shop that sells batiks and shellwork necklaces made from the vertebrae of fish. It also sells bags, and because of that it's called Bagatelle. Not bad, thinks Rennie. There are familiar signs: The Bank of Nova Scotia, The Canadian Imperial Bank of Commerce. The bank buildings are new, the buildings surrounding them are old.

In the Bank of Nova Scotia she cashes a traveller's cheque. A couple of doors down there's a drugstore, also new-looking, and she goes into it and asks for some suntan lotion.

"We have Quaaludes," the man says as she's paying for the lotion.

"Pardon?" says Rennie.

"Any amount," the man says. He's a short man with a gambler's moustache, balding, his pink sleeves rolled to the elbows. "You need no prescription. Take it back to the States," he says, looking at her slyly. "Make you a little money."

Well, it's a drugstore, Rennie thinks. It sells drugs. Why be surprised? "No thank you," she says. "Not today."

"You want the hard stuff?" the man asks.

Rennie buys some insect repellent, which he rings up half-heartedly on the cash register. Already he's lost interest in her.

Rennie walks uphill, to the Church of St. Antoine. It's the oldest one left, says the tourist brochure. There's a graveyard surrounding it, the plots enclosed by wrought-iron fences, the gravestones tipping and overgrown with vines. On the lawn there's a family planning poster: KEEP YOUR FAMILY THE RIGHT SIZE. No hints about what that might be. Beside it is another poster: ELLIS IS KING. There's a picture of a fattish man, smiling like a Buddha. It's been defaced with red paint.

Inside, the church is completely empty. It feels Catholic, though there are no squat guttering red candles. Rennie thinks of the Virgins in Mexico, several of them in each church, dressed in red or white or blue or black; you chose one and prayed to it according to your needs. Black was for loss. The skirts of the Virgins had been studded with little tin images, tin arms, tin legs, tin children, tin sheep and cows, even tin pigs, in thanks for what had been restored, or perhaps only in hope that it might be. She'd found the idea quaint, then.

There's an altar at the front, a table at the back with a slotted box where you can buy postcards, and a large picture on the west wall, "by an early unknown local artist," says the brochure. It's St. Anthony, being tempted in the desert; only the desert is bursting with tropical vegetation, vivid succulent red flowers, smooth fat leaves bulging with sap, brightly coloured birds with huge beaks and yellow eyes, and St. Anthony is black. The demons are noticeably paler, and most of them are female. St. Anthony is on his knees in an attitude of prayer, his eyes turned up and away from the scaly thighs, the breasts and pointed scarlet tongues of the demons. He isn't wearing one of those bedspreads she remembers from the Griswold Sunday school handouts but an ordinary shirt, white and open at the throat, and brown pants. His feet are bare. The figures are flat, as if they've been cut from paper, and they cast no shadows.

There are postcards of the painting on the table, and Rennie buys three. She has her notebook with her but she doesn't write anything in it. Then she sits down in the back pew. What part of herself would she pin on the skirt of the black Virgin now, if she had the chance?

Jake went to Mexico with her. It was their first trip together. He didn't like the churches much: churches didn't do a whole lot for him, they reminded him of Christians. Christians have funny eyes, he said. Clean-minded. They're always thinking about how you'd look as a bar of soap.

I'm one, said Rennie, to tease him.

No, you're not, said Jake. Christians don't have cunts. You're only a *shiksa*. That's different.

Want to hear me sing "Washed in the Blood of the Lamb"? said Rennie.

Don't be perverted, said Jake. You're turning me on.

Turning? said Rennie. I thought you were on all the time.

It was a whole week. They were euphoric, they held hands on the street, they made love in the afternoons, the wooden louvres of the old windows closed against the sun, they got flea bites, there was nothing that didn't amuse them, they bought dubious cakes and strange fried objects from roadside stands, they ate them recklessly, why not? They found a sign in a little park that read, *Those found sitting improperly in the park will be punished by the authorities.* It can't mean that, said Rennie. We must've translated it wrong. What is *sitting improperly?* They walked through the crowded streets at night, curious, fearless. Once there was a fiesta, and a man ran past them with a wickerwork cage balanced on his head, shooting off rockets and Catherine wheels. It's you, Rennie said. Mr. General Electric.

She loved Jake, she loved everything. She felt she was walking inside a charmed circle: nothing could touch her, nothing could touch them. Nevertheless, even then, she could feel the circle diminishing. In Griswold they believed that everything evened out in the end: if you had too much good luck one day, you'd have bad the next. Good luck was unlucky.

Still, Rennie refused to feel guilty about anything, not even the beggars, the women wrapped in filthy *rebozos,* with the fallen-in cheeks of those who have lost teeth, suckling inert babies, not even brushing the flies away from their heads, their hands held out, for hours on end it seemed, in one position as if carved. She remembered stories she'd heard about people who mutilated themselves and even their children to make tourists feel sorry for them; or was that in India?

At the end of the week Jake got a case of Montezuma's Revenge. Rennie bought a bottle of sweet pink emulsion for him at the corner *farmacia*, running the gauntlet of sucking mouths, and he allowed himself to be dosed. But he wouldn't lie down. He didn't want her to go anywhere without him, he didn't want to miss anything. He sat in a chair, clutching his belly and limping to the bathroom at intervals, while Rennie consulted him about her piece. "Mexico City On Less Than You'd Think."

I'm supposed to be doing this other piece too, she said, for *Pandora*. It's on male pain. How about it? What's the difference?

Male what? Jake said, grinning. You know men don't feel pain. Only when they cut themselves shaving.

It's just been discovered that they do, she said. Tests have been done. Papers have been presented. They wince. Sometimes they flinch. If it's really bad they knit their brows. Come on, be a nice guy, give me a few hints. Tell me about male pain. Where do you feel it the most?

In the ass, Jake said, during conversations like this. Enough with the instant insight.

It's a living, she said, it keeps me off the streets. Where would I be without it? You wouldn't feel so much pain in the ass if you'd take the poker out.

That's not a poker, it's a backbone, he said. I got it from pretending to be a *goy*. Girls can never tell the difference.

Only between the backbone and the front bone, she said. She sat down on his lap, one leg on either side of him, and began to lick his ear.

Have a heart, he said, I'm a sick man.

Beg for mercy, she said. Do boys cry? We have ways of making you talk. She licked his other ear. You're never too sick, she said. She undid the buttons on his shirt and slid her hand inside it. Anyone as furry as you could never be too sick.

Enough with the voracious female animalistic desires, he said. You should all be locked in cages.

He put his arms around her and they rocked slowly back and forth, and outside the wooden shutters a bell rang somewhere.

Rennie walks back on the shadow side. After a few blocks she realizes she's not entirely sure where she is. But she came up to get to the church, so now all she has to do is head down, towards the harbour. Already she's coming to some shops.

Someone touches her on the shoulder, and she stops and turns. It's a man who has once been taller than he is now. He's wearing worn black pants, the fly coming undone, a shirt with no buttons, and one of the wool tea-cosy hats; he has no shoes on, the trouser legs look familiar. He stands in front of her and touches her arm, smiling. His jaw is stubbled with white hairs and most of his teeth are missing.

He makes his right hand into a fist, then points to her, still smiling. Rennie smiles back at him. She doesn't understand what he wants. He repeats the gesture, he's deaf and dumb or perhaps drunk. Rennie feels very suddenly as if she's stepped across a line and found herself on Mars.

He runs the fingers of his right hand together, he's getting impatient, he holds out his hand, and now she knows, it's begging. She opens her purse and gropes for the change purse. It's worth a few cents to be rid of him.

But he frowns, this isn't what he wants. He repeats his series of gestures, faster now, and Rennie feels bewildered and threatened. She gets the absurd idea that he wants her passport, he wants to take it away from her. Without it she could never get back. She closes her purse and shakes her head, turning away and starting to walk again. She's being silly; in any case, her passport is in the safe back at the hotel.

Wherever that is. She can feel him behind her, following her. She quickens her pace; the slip-slop of his bare feet speeds up too. Now she's almost running. There are more people on the street, more and more as she runs downhill, and they notice this little procession of two, this race, they even stop to watch, smiling and even laughing, but nobody does anything to help her. Rennie is close to panic, it's too much like the kind of bad dream she wishes she could stop having, she doesn't know why he's following her. What has she done wrong?

There are crowds of people now, it looks like a market, there's a widening that in Mexico would be a square but here is an amorphous shape, the edges packed with stalls, the centre clogged with people and a few trucks. Chickens in crates, fruit stacked into uneasy pyramids or spread out on cloths, plastic pails, cheap aluminum cookware. It's noisy, dusty, suddenly ten degrees hotter; smells engulf her. Music blares from tiny shops crammed with gadgets, the spillover from Japan: cassette players, radios. Rennie dodges among the clumps of people, trying to lose him. But he's right behind her, he's not as decrepit as he looks, and that's his hand on her arm.

"Slow down," says Paul. And it is Paul, in the same shorts but a blue T-shirt, carrying a string bag full of lemons. The man is right behind him, smiling again with his gaping jack-o'-lantern mouth.

"It's okay," says Paul. Rennie's breathing hard, her face is wet and must be red, she probably looks demented and certainly inept. "He just wants you to shake his hand, that's all."

"How do you know?" says Rennie, more angry now than frightened. "He was chasing me!"

"He chases women a lot," says Paul. "Especially the white ones. He's deaf and dumb, he's harmless. He only wants to shake your hand, he thinks it's good luck."

Indeed the man is now holding out his hand, fingers spread.

"Why on earth?" says Rennie. She's a little calmer now but no cooler. "I'm hardly good luck."

"Not for him," says Paul. "For you."

Now Rennie feels both rude and uncharitable: he's only been trying to give her something. Reluctantly she puts her hand into the outstretched hand of the old man. He clamps his fingers around hers and holds on for an instant. Then he lets her go, smiles at her again with his collapsing mouth, and turns away into the crowd.

Rennie feels rescued. "You need to sit down," says Paul. He still has his hand on her arm, and he steers her to a store-front café, a couple of rickety tables covered with oilcloth, and inserts her into a chair next to the wall.

"I'm all right," says Rennie.

"It takes a while for your body to adjust to the heat," says Paul. "You shouldn't run at first."

"Believe me," says Rennie, "I wasn't doing it on purpose."

"Alien reaction paranoia," says Paul. "Because you don't know what's dangerous and what isn't, everything seems dangerous. We used to run into it all the time."

He means in the Far East, he means in the war. Rennie feels he's talking down to her. "Those for scurvy?" she says.

"What?" says Paul.

"On your pirate boats," Rennie says. "The lemons."

Paul smiles and says he'll go inside and order them a drink.

It isn't just a market. Across from the café they've set up a small platform: orange crates stacked two high, with boards across the top. A couple of kids, fifteen or sixteen at the oldest, are draping a bedsheet banner on two poles above it: PRINCE OF PEACE, it says in red. A religious cult of some kind, Rennie decides: Holy Rollers, Born Againers. So the woman in the airport with the Prince of Peace T-shirt wasn't a maniac, just a fanatic. She knows about those: Griswold had its lunatic fringe, women who thought it was a sin to wear lipstick. Then there was her mother, who thought it was a sin not to.

There's a man sitting on the edge of the platform, directing the kids. He's thin, with a riverboat moustache; he slouches forward, dangling his legs. Rennie notices his boots, riding boots, cowboy boots almost, with built-up heels. He's the first man she's seen here wearing boots. Why would anyone choose to? She thinks briefly of his feet, stifled in humid leather.

He sees her watching him. Rennie looks away immediately, but he gets up and comes towards her. He leans his hands on the table and stares down at her. Up close he looks South American.

Now what? thinks Rennie. She assumes he's trying to pick her up, and she's stuck here, wedged in between the table and the wall. She waits for the smile, the invitation, but neither comes, he just frowns at her as if he's trying to read her mind or impress her, so finally she says, "I'm with someone."

"You come in on the plane last night?" he says.

Rennie says yes.

"You the writer?"

Rennie wonders how he knows, but he does, because he doesn't wait for her to answer. "We don't need you here," he says.

Rennie's heard that the Caribbean is becoming hostile to tourists, but this is the most blatant sign she's seen of it. She doesn't know what to say.

"You stay around here, you just mess things up," he says.

Paul is back, with two glasses full of something brown. "Government issue," he says, putting them down on the table. "Something the matter?"

"I don't know," says Rennie. "Ask him." But the man is already sauntering away, teetering a little on the uneven ground.

"What did he say to you?" says Paul.

Rennie tells him. "Maybe I'm offending someone's religion," she says.

"It's not religion, it's politics," says Paul, "though around here it's sometimes the same thing."

"Prince of Peace?" says Rennie. "Politics? Come on."

"Well, his name's Prince, really, and the one you just met is Marsdon. He's the campaign manager," says Paul, who doesn't seem to find any of this odd. "They're the local excuse for communists, so they stuck the *Peace* on for good measure."

Rennie tastes the brown drink. "What's in it?" she says.

"Don't ask me," says Paul, "it's all they had." He leans back in his chair, watching not her but the space in front of them. "They're having an election, the first since the British pulled out," he says. "This afternoon they'll make speeches, all three parties, one after the other. Prince, then Dr. Minnow, that's his corner over there. After that the Minister of Justice. He's standing in for Ellis, who never goes outside his house. Some say it's because he's always too drunk; others, say he's been dead for twenty years but no one's noticed yet."

"Dr. Minnow?" says Rennie, remembering the man on the plane. With a name like that there can't be two of them.

"The fish," says Paul, grinning. "They use pictures here, it gets around the illiteracy."

The signs and banners are going up everywhere now. ELLIS IS KING. THE FISH LIVES. Everything looks homemade: it's like college, like student elections.

"Will there be trouble?" says Rennie.

"You mean, will you get hurt?" says Paul. "Yes, there will be trouble. No, you won't get hurt. You're a tourist, you're exempt."

There's a truck making its way through the crowd now, slowly; in the back is a man wearing a white shirt and mirror sunglasses, barking at the crowd through a bullhorn loudspeaker. Rennie can't understand a word he's saying. Two other men flank him, carrying placards with large black crowns on them. ELLIS IS KING. "The Minister of Justice," says Paul.

"What sort of trouble?" says Rennie, wondering if she can get a refund on her excursion ticket if she goes back early.

"A little pushing and shoving," says Paul. "Nothing to get excited about."

But already people are throwing things at the truck; fruit, Rennie thinks, they're picking it up from the stacks on the sidewalk. A crumpled beer can hits the wall above Rennie's head, bounces off.

"They weren't aiming at you," says Paul. "But I'll walk you back to the hotel. Sometimes they get into the broken glass."

He moves the table to let her out, and they push their way through the crowd, against the stream. Rennie wonders if she should ask him about tennis courts and restaurants but decides not to. Her image is fluffy enough already. Then she wonders if she should ask him to have lunch with her at the hotel, but she decides not to do that either. She might be misunderstood.

Which is just as well, considering the lunch. Rennie has a grilled cheese sandwich, burned, and a glass of grapefruit juice out of a tin, which seems to be all there is. After the Jell-O pie she takes out the map of Queenstown and pores over it with vague desperation; she has the unpleasant feeling that she's already seen just about everything there is to see. There's a reef, though, on the other side of the jetty that marks off the harbour; you can go out in a boat and look at it. The picture in the brochure shows a couple of murky fish. It doesn't look too promising, but it might yield a paragraph or two.

The map shows a shortcut to the sea. Rennie envisioned a

road, but it's only a rudimentary path; it runs behind the hotel, beside something that looks like a sewage pipe. The ground is damp and slippery. Rennie picks her way down, wishing her sandals had flat soles.

The beach isn't one of the seven jewel-like beaches with clean sparkling iridescent sand advertised in the brochure. It's narrow and gravelly and dotted with lumps of coagulated oil, soft as chewing gum and tar-coloured. The sewage pipe runs into the sea. Rennie steps over it and walks left. She passes a shed and a hauled-up rowboat where three men are cutting the heads off fish, gutting them and tossing them into a red plastic pail. Bladders like used condoms litter the beach. One of the men grins at Rennie and hold up a fish, his finger hooked through the gills. Rennie shakes her head. She might take their picture and write something about the catch fresh from the sea and down-to-earth lifestyles. But then she would have to buy a fish, and she can't carry a dead fish around with her all day.

"What time you meet me tonight?" one of the men says behind her. Rennie ignores this.

In the distance there are two boats with awnings, more or less where the map says they should be. She plods along the beach; when she's well past the fish heads she takes off her sandals and walks on the wet packed sand near the water. To the left she can now see the mountains, rising steeply behind the town, covered with uniform nubbled green.

The boats don't leave until high tide. She buys a ticket from the owner of the nearest and newest-looking one, *The Princess Anne,* and sits on the raspy grass in the shade of a bush. The other boat is called *The Princess Margaret.* There's hardly a lineup: a grey-haired couple with binoculars and the ingenuous, eager-to-be-pleased look of retired Americans from the Midwest, and two girls in their teens, white and speckled. They're both wearing T-shirts with mottoes: TRY A VIRGIN (ISLAND), PROPERTY OF ST. MARTIN'S COUNTY JAIL. There's half an hour to wait. The girls peel off their T-shirts and shorts; they're wearing bikinis underneath. They sit out on the filthy beach, rubbing oil on each other's parboiled backs. Skin cancer, thinks Rennie.

Her own dress comes up to her neck. Although it's sleeveless she's already too warm. She gazes at the deceptively blue sea; even though she knows what kind of garbage runs into it nearby, she longs to wade in it. But she hasn't been swimming since the operation. She hasn't yet found a bathing suit that will do: this is her excuse. Her real fear, irrational but a fear, is that the scar will come undone in the water, split open like a faulty zipper, and she will turn inside out. Then she would see what Daniel saw when he looked into her, while she herself lay on the table unconscious as a slit fish. This is partly why she fell in love with him: he knows something about her she doesn't know, he knows what she's like inside.

Rennie takes the three postcards out of her purse, "St. Anthony by an early unknown local artist." She addresses one of them to her mother in Griswold. Her mother still lives in Griswold, even though her grandmother is dead and there's no reason at all why her mother can't move, travel, do something else. But she stays in Griswold, cleaning the red brick house that seems to get bigger and both emptier and more cluttered every time Rennie visits it. Where else would I go? says her mother. It's too late. Besides, my friends are here.

One of Rennie's less pleasant fantasies about the future, on nights when she can't sleep, is that her mother will get some lingering disease and she'll have to go back to Griswold to take care of her, for years and years, for the rest of her life. She'll plead illness, they'll have a competition, the sickest one will win. That's how it's done in Griswold, by the women at any rate. Rennie can remember her mother's church group in the front parlour, drinking tea and eating small cakes covered with chocolate icing and poisonous-looking many-coloured sprinkles, discussing their own and each other's debilities in hushed voices that blended pity, admiration and envy. If you were sick you were exempt: other women brought you pies and came to sit with you, commiserating, gloating. The only thing they liked better was a funeral.

On the card Rennie writes that she's well and is having a nice relaxing time. She hasn't told her mother about Jake leaving, since it was hard enough to get her to accept the fact that he'd moved in. Rennie would have dodged that one if she could, but her mother was fond of phoning her early in the morning, at a time when she thought everyone ought to be up, and the phone was on Jake's side of the bed. It would have been better if Jake weren't in the habit of disguising his voice and saying things like "The White House" and "Fiedlefort's Garage." Rennie finally had to explain to her mother that it was only one male voice she was hearing, not several. Which was only marginally acceptable. After that, they didn't discuss it.

Rennie hasn't told her mother about the operation, either. She stopped telling her mother bad news a long time ago. As a child, she learned to conceal cuts and scrapes, since her mother seemed to regard such things not as accidents but as acts Rennie committed on purpose to complicate her mother's life. What did you do *that* for, she would say, jabbing at the blood with a towel. Next time, watch where you're going. The operation, too, she would see as Rennie's fault. Cancer was a front-parlour subject, but it wasn't in the same class as a broken leg or a heart attack or even a death. It was apart, obscene almost, like a scandal; it was something you brought upon yourself.

Other people think that too, but in different ways. Rennie used to think it herself. *Sexual repression. Couldn't act out anger.* The body, sinister twin, taking its revenge for whatever crimes the mind was supposed to have committed on it. Nothing had prepared her for her own outrage, the feeling that she'd been betrayed by a close frined. She'd given her body swimming twice a week, forbidden it junk food and cigarette smoke, allowed it a normal amount of sexual release. She'd trusted it. Why then had it turned against her?

Daniel talked about the importance of attitude. It's mysterious, he said. We don't know why, but it helps, or it seems to.

What does? she said.

Hope, he said. The mind isn't separate from the body; emotions trigger chemical reactions and vice versa, you know that.

So it's my fault if there's a recurrence? I have cancer of the mind? said Rennie.

It isn't a symbol, it's a disease, said Daniel patiently. We just don't know the cure yet. We have a few clues, that's all. We're looking for the X factor. But we'll get it sooner or later and then people like me will be obsolete. He patted her hand. You'll be fine, he said. You have a life to go back to. Unlike some. You're very lucky.

But she was not fine. She was released from the hospital, she went back to the apartment, she still wasn't fine. She longed to be sick again so that Daniel would have to take care of her.

She constructed a program for herself: schedules and goals. She exercised the muscles of her left arm by lifting it and pressing the forearm against the wall, she squeezed a sponge ball in her left hand twenty times a day. She went to movies with Jake to cheer herself up, funny movies, nothing heavy. She began to type again, a page at a time, reworking her drain-chain jewellery piece, picking up where she'd left off. She learned to brush her hair again and to do up buttons. As she did each of these things, she thought of Daniel watching her and approving. Good, he would say. You can do up buttons now? You can brush your own hair? That's right, go to cheerful movies. You're doing really well.

She went for an examination and to get the stitches out. She wore a red blouse, to show Daniel what a positive attitude she had, and sat up straight and smiled. Daniel told her she was doing really well and she began to cry.

He put his arms around her, which was what she'd wanted him to do. She couldn't believe how boring she was being, how stupid, how predictable. Her nose was running. She sniffed, blotted her eyes on Daniel's pocket, in which, she noted, he kept several cheap ballpoint pens, and pushed him away.

I'm sorry, she said. I didn't mean to do that.

Don't be sorry, he said. You're human.

I don't feel human any more, she said. I feel infested. I have bad dreams, I dream I'm full of white maggots eating away at me from the inside.

He sighed. That's normal, he said. You'll get over it.

Stop telling me I'm fucking *normal,* she said.

Daniel checked his list of appointments, looked at his watch, and took her down for a swift coffee in the shopping arcade below his office, where he delivered an earnest lecture. This was the second part of her life. It would be different from the first part, she would no longer be able to take things for granted, but perhaps this was a plus because she would see her life as a gift and appreciate it more. It was almost like being given a second life. She must stop thinking of her life as over, because it was far from over.

When I was a student I used to think I would be able to save people, he said. I don't think that any more. I don't even think I can cure them; in this field you can't afford to think that. But in a lot of cases we can give them time. A remission can last for years, for a normal lifespan even. He leaned forward slightly. Think of your life as a clean page. You can write whatever you like on it.

Rennie sat across the table from him, white formica with gold threads in it, thinking what a lot of facile crap he was talking and admiring his eyes, which were an elusive shade between blue and green. Where does he get this stuff, she thought, *The Reader's Digest?*

How many times have you used that one? she said. Are

you just saying that because I'm a journalist? I mean, if I were a dentist, would you say, Your life is like an empty tooth, you can fill it with whatever you like?

Rennie knew you weren't supposed to say things like this to men you were in love with, or to men in general, or to anyone at all for that matter; making fun was rude, especially when the other person was being serious. But she couldn't resist. He would have had a right to be angry, but instead he was startled. He looked at her for a moment almost slyly; then he began to laugh. He was blushing, and Rennie was entranced: the men she knew didn't blush.

I guess you think that's pretty corny, he said.

Corny. My God, thought Rennie, I'm caught in a time warp, it's nineteen fifty-five again. He's from another planet.

I'm sorry, she said. I get pretty surly at times. It's just that, what am I supposed to do with it? All this time I've got. Sit around waiting till it gets me? You know it's going to, sooner or later.

He gazed at her sadly, disappointed again, as if she were talking like a spoiled child. Do what you want to, he said. What you really want to.

What would you do? she said. She fought the impulse to interview him. "When Doctors Get Sick."

He looked down at his hands. What I'm doing now, I guess, he said. That's about all I know anything about. But you have an interesting life.

This was the first clue Rennie had that Daniel thought she was interesting.

Rennie looks at the other two postcards. She addresses one to Jake, it would be a courtesy to let him know where she is, but she doesn't write anything on it because she can't think of anything she wants to say to him. The third one she leaves empty. Empty is not the same as clean. She bought the third one for Daniel but she decides not to send it. She'll send it later, when she can say, *I'm fine.* That's what he would like to hear: that she's fine, that everything is fine, that he's done no damage.

Rennie feels a darker shadow fall over her. "Hi there," says a flat nasal voice, mildly familiar. It's the woman who passed her in the hotel last night. She now sits down beside Rennie uninvited and takes a pack of cigarettes out of her bag. Rennie puts away her postcards.

"You smoke?" says the woman. The fingers holding the cigarette are bitten to the quick, stub-tipped, slightly grubby, the raw skin around the nails nibbled as if mice have been at them, and this both surprises Rennie and repels her slightly. She wouldn't want to touch this gnawed hand, or have it touch her. She doesn't like the sight of ravage, damage, the edge between inside and outside blurred like that.

"No, thanks," says Rennie.

"My name's Lora," says the woman. "With an *o*, not the other way. Lora Lucas. *L*'s run in our family, my mother's name was Leona." Now that she's talking, the illusion shatters: "Hi there" is about the only thing she's learned to fake, the rest is natural. She's not as young as she looked in the dim light of the hotel. Her hair is down today, flower-child length, dry as hay. She's wearing an above-the-knee oblong of orange knotted across her large breasts.

Her eyes are scanning, all the time, back and forth, taking everything in. "You just come in, eh?" she says, and Rennie thinks, *Canadian.*

"Yes," says Rennie.

"You got to watch it around here," says Lora. "People see you don't know what you're doing, they rip you off. How much he soak you from the airport last night?"

Rennie tells her and she laughs. "You see?" she says.

Rennie immediately resents her, she resents the intrusion. She wishes she had a book; then she could pretend to read.

"You should watch your stuff, that camera and all," says Lora. "There's been some break-ins around here. A girl I know, she woke up in the middle of the night and there was this black guy in a bathing suit holding a knife to her throat. Nothing sexual, he just wanted her money. Said he'd kill her if she told anyone. She was afraid to go to the police."

"Why?" Rennie says, and Lora grins at her.

"She figures he *was* the police," she says.

In response to some signal Rennie hasn't caught, she stands up and brushes the sand from her orange tie dye. "Boat time," she says. "If that's what you're here for."

It seems they're expected to wade out to the boat. The old couple with the matching binoculars go first. They're both wearing wide-legged khaki shorts, which they roll up even farther, exposing stringy whitish legs which are surprisingly muscular. Even so, the drooping bottoms of their shorts are wet through by the time they reach the boat's ladder. The two speckled pink girls make it with a lot of shrieking. Lora unties her tie dye, under which she's wearing a black bikini half a size too small, and drapes it around her neck. She holds the purple cloth bag she's carrying at shoulder height and surges into the water; surf breaks around her thighs, which bulge out of the bikini like caricatures of thighs, like the thighs on humorous cocktail napkins.

Rennie considers her options. She can either hitch up her dress and tuck it into her underpants, with everyone watching her, or get it wet and smell like seaweed for the rest of the day. She compromises, hiking her skirt halfway up and draping it through the sash tie. It gets wet anyway. The man who appears to own the boat smiles widely as the swell hits her. He reaches out a long ropy arm, a hand like a clamp, to help her up. At the last moment, when the motor is already running, five or six children come screaming and laughing out through the waves and swarm onto the boat, clambering up onto the awning, which Rennie now sees is wooden rather than cloth.

"Mind yourself, you fall off," the owner yells at them.

Rennie sits on the wooden bench, dripping, while the boat goes up and down and the exhaust blows into her face. Lora has gone up on top where the kids are, probably to work on her tan. The two girls are flirting with the man running the boat. The old couple are looking at sea birds through their binoculars, murmuring to each other in what sounds like a secret language. "Booby," the old woman says. "Frigate," the man replies.

In front of Rennie is a raised ledge bordering an oblong piece of glass almost the length of the boat. Rennie leans forward and rests her arms on it. Nothing but greyish foam is visible through the glass. She's doing this, she reminds herself, so she can write about how much fun it is. *At first you may think you could get the same effect for a lot less money by putting a little Tide in your Jacuzzi. But wait.*

Rennie waits, and the boat stops. They're quite far out. Twenty yards from them, surf crashes over an invisible wall, each wave lifting the boat. In the furrows between the waves they sink down until they're only a foot from the reef. It's an illusion, Rennie thinks. She prefers to believe that people who run things know what they're doing, and these people surely would not do anything so dangerous. She doesn't like the idea of a prong of coral suddenly bursting through the glass.

Rennie looks, which is her function. The water is clouded with fine sand. At the edges of the glass oblong, dark shapes flit and are hidden. Below her, so encrusted in purplish coral that its shape is almost obscured, is a soft-drink bottle. A tiger-striped fish swims near it.

"It's not so great today, it's been too windy, and this one's not such a great one anyway," Lora says to her. She's come down from the roof and is kneeling beside Rennie.

"The reef's getting all messed up by the oil and junk from the harbour. What you need is a snorkel and stuff, over at Ste. Agathe. That's where I live, you'd like it a lot better than here."

Rennie doesn't say anthing; she doesn't seem expected to. Also she doesn't want to start a conversation. Conversations lead to acquaintances, and acquaintances are too easy to make on these trips. People mistake them for friendships. She smiles and turns back to the glass oblong.

"You write for the magazines, eh?" the woman says.

"How did you know that?" Rennie asks, a little annoyed. This is the third time today.

"Everyone knows everything around here," the woman says. "Word of mouth, the grapevine you might say. Everyone knows what's happening." She pauses. She looks at Rennie, scanning her face as if trying to see through the blue lenses of her sunglasses. "I could tell you stuff to write about," she says darkly. "The story of my life, you could put it in a book all right. Except no one would believe it, you know?"

Rennie is instantly bored. She can't remember how many people have said this to her, at parties, on airplanes, as soon as they've found out what she does. Why do they think their own lives are of general concern? Why do they think that being in a magazine will make them more valid than they are? Why do they want to be *seen*?

Rennie switches off the sound and concentrates only on the picture. Lora could definitely be improved. She would benefit greatly from a good cut and shape, for instance, and she should grow her eyebrows in, just a little. Plucking them fine like that broadens her face. Rennie arranges her into a Makeover piece, before and after, with a series of shots in between showing the process, Lora being tweezed and creamed and coloured in and fitted with a Norma Klein sweater. After that you could take her to lunch at Winston's and all you'd have to teach her would be how to keep her mouth shut.

•   •   •

They're sitting under a metal umbrella at one of the round white tables on the patio at the Driftwood, Lora with the sun on her back, Rennie in the shade. The other tables are thinly scattered with white people in various phases of hot pink, and one couple who seems to be Indian. The waiters are black or brown; the architecture is roadside modern, the balconies have plastic panels, green and blue. At the edge of the patio there's a tree covered with red flowers, huge lobed blossoms like gigantic sweet peas; a dozen hummingbirds swarm around them. Below, on the other side of the curving stone wall, the surf crashes against the rocks just as it is supposed to, and a fresh wind blows off the Atlantic. To the right is a wide beach devoid of fish heads. There's nobody on it.

Lora orders another piña colada. Rennie is only halfway through hers, but she orders another one anyway.

"Who's paying for this?" Lora asks, too innocently.

"I will," says Rennie, who has always known she would.

"You can put it on your whatchamacallit," Lora says. "Don't they pay for everything, those magazines?"

"Not always," says Rennie, "but I can write it off as an expense. We can pretend I was interviewing you."

"Write it off," says Lora. "Jesus." Rennie can't tell whether she's impressd or disgusted.

"This is where people like you stay, most of the time," says Lora.

Rennie dislikes having these kinds of assumptions made about her, she dislikes being lumped in with a fictitious group labelled *people like you*. She can't stand the self-righteousness of people like Lora, who think that because they've had deprived childhoods or not as much money as everybody else they are in some way superior. She feels like using one of her never-fail ploys. She'll lean across the table, take off her sunglasses, gaze into Lora's round blue-china eyes, eyes that manage to look at the same time aggrieved and secretly delighted, and say, "Why are you being so aggressive?" But she has a feeling this wouldn't work on Lora.

She thinks about unbuttoning her dress and displaying her scar. If they're having a poor-me contest, that should be good for a few points; but she doesn't want to turn into one of those people who use their physical disabilities for social blackmail.

She knows she shouldn't have allowed herself to be picked up on the reef boat, she shouldn't have expressed interest in seeing the other hotels, she should have insisted on a taxi instead of listening to Lora, who said she knew people and why get ripped off when you could get a free ride? "Free rides, that's my motto," she said. Rennie's mother used to say there was no such thing as a free ride.

The free ride turned out to be a battered pickup truck with two yellow eyes painted on the hood. It was delivering toilet paper, and they had to sit on the boxes in the back, perched up there like float queens; groups of people waved and yelled at them as they went past. Outside the town the road got steadily worse, dwindling finally into a two-wheel track of cracked and disintegrating concrete. The driver went as fast as possible, and every time they hit a gap in the concrete Rennie could feel the top of her spine being rammed up into her skull.

She doesn't want to face the ride back, but she doesn't want to stay here either. If she isn't careful she'll be trapped into having dinner. Lora, she's decided, is one of those women you meet in bars in foreign countries, who seem not to have chosen anything but merely ended up wherever they happen to be, and it's too much effort for them to go home. Rennie can't imagine why Lora has been so insistent about coming with her. They have nothing in common. Lora says she has nothing else to do at the moment so she might as well show Rennie around, but Rennie doesn't believe this. She resolves to finish her drink and then go. If she's lucky it will rain: promising clouds are already piling up.

Now Lora opens her purple bag and rustles through it, and suddenly everything falls into place. What she takes out is a poly bag of grass, about an ounce, Rennie guesses. She wants Rennie to buy it. The price, by Toronto standards, is ridiculously low.

"The best," she says. "Colombian, it just came in."

Rennie of course refuses. She's heard about dope laws in foreign countries, she knows about being set up, she has no intention of spending any time at all growing fungus in the local jail while the local bureaucrats try, unsuccessfully, to put the squeeze on her mother. Her mother is a firm believer in taking the consequences for your actions. And who else would get her out? Who would even try?

Lora shrugs. "It's cool," she says. "No harm in asking."

Rennie looks around to see what has become of Lora's drink, and feels herself turn cold.

"My God," she says.

There are two policemen in the bar, they're going from table to table, it looks as if they're asking questions. But Lora stares calmly over at them, she doesn't even put the dope away, she just moves her cloth bag so it's covered. "Don't look so weird," she says to Rennie. "It's cool. I wouldn't say it was cool if it wasn't."

And it turns out after all that they're just selling tickets to the Police Benefit Dance. Rennie thinks she recognizes them from the airport, but she's not sure. One sells, the other stands behind him, dangling his swagger stick and checking out the scene. She produces her own ticket from her purse. "I already have one," she says, a little too smugly, because the one selling grins at her and says, "You need two, man. One for your boyfriend. Some things you can't do by yourself."

The second one laughs, a high giggle.

"That's a real good idea," says Lora, smiling a little tightly, her Holiday Inn smile; so Rennie pays.

"We see you there," says the first policeman, and they saunter off.

"If there's one thing I hate it's cops," says Lora, when they're hardly out of earshot. "They're all in the business if you ask me, one way or another, I've got nothing against that but they take advantage. It's unfair competition. You ever been stopped by a cop? For speeding or anything? Back home I mean, around here they don't bother that much about speeding."

"No," says Rennie.

"They look at your driver's licence. Then they use your first name. Not Miss or Mrs. or anything, your first name, and you've got no way of knowing any of their names at all. You ever have that happen to you?"

In fact Rennie hasn't. She's having trouble paying attention, there's too much rum in the drinks. Lora, however, has just signalled for another one, it's not bothering her.

"That's where it begins," says Lora. "Where they can use your first name and you can't use theirs. Then they think they've got you, they can look down on you, like. Sometimes they give you a choice, fork out or put out."

"Sorry?" says Rennie.

"You know, pay the fine or go down on them. They always know where the vacant lots are, eh?"

Lora looks at her slyly and Rennie knows she's supposed to be shocked. "Really," she says, as if she's been through it herself, dozens of times.

The Women's Movement would have loved Lora, back in the old days, back in the early seventies when they were still doing pieces about the liberating effects of masturbation. They'd have given her ten out of ten for openness, a word that always made Rennie think of a can of worms with the top off. Nevertheless, Rennie did several pieces on the movement back then, until its media potential burnt out. Then she did a piece called "Burned Out": interviews with eight women who'd explained why they'd gone into weaving placemats and painting miniature landscapes on bottles, instead. It was the infighting, they said. The bitching. The trashing. Other women were just so difficult to work with, you never knew where you stood with them. And it all went on behind your back. At least with men it was out on the table, they said; and Rennie busily wrote it all down.

Great stuff, said the editor. It's about time someone had the courage to speak out.

Lora smiles but she's not fooled; she can tell this is one of the things Rennie doesn't know. But she's generous, she's willing to share. Ten out of ten for sharing.

"Listen," she says, "at least you have the choice. You can always say you're worth more than a speeding ticket. I don't know which is worse though, no choice at all or just a lot of bad ones. At least when you don't have a choice you don't have to think, you know? The worst times in my life I had choices all right. Shit or shit."

Rennie doesn't want to hear about the worst times in Lora's life, so she doesn't say anything.

"Anyway, why dwell on it?" says Lora. "That's what my mother used to say. There's enough bad things in the world, there's no shortage, so why dwell on it, there's better things to talk about."

Rennie wonders what these may be, since Lora can't seem to think of any. She slurps at the bottom of her glass with the two plastic straws. "You like maraschino cherries?" she says. "I can't stand them."

Rennie hesitates. She does like maraschino cherries, but she isn't sure she wants to eat the one Lora is now poking around for at the bottom of the glass with her bitten fingers. However, she's about to be rescued, because Paul has just stepped out onto the patio and is standing there scanning the tables as though he's looking for someone.

Rennie knows it's her. She waves, and he strolls over to their table.

"What have you been up to?" he says, smiling at her.

"Research," says Rennie, smiling back.

"You're late," Lora says to him. "I've been here for hours."

"I'll get myself a drink," he says, and walks over to the bar.

"Just a sec," says Lora. "Would you mind keeping an eye on my bag?" She stands up, pushes back her hair, straightens up so her breasts stick out more, and walks over to join Paul. They stand there talking, for a lot longer than Rennie wants them to.

The third piña colada comes, the one for Lora, and Rennie drinks some it, for something to do.

Lora comes back from the bar and sits down. Her drink is there but she doesn't touch it. Something has happened, her face is no longer a dollface. Rennie notices the skin under her eyes, too much sun, in a few years she'll shrivel up like an apple. She looks at Rennie, dolefully as a spaniel.

"What's wrong?" says Rennie, knowing as she says it that she shouldn't have asked. To ask is to get involved.

"Look," says Lora, "can you do me a big favour?"

"What?" says Rennie, on guard.

"Elva's sick," she says, "that's Prince's grandmother. Over on Ste. Agathe."

"Prince?" says Rennie. There can't be two of them.

"The guy I live with," Lora says.

"The one in the election?" says Rennie, who can't quite put it together.

"That's why he can't go over to Ste. Agathe," says Lora, "he's making a speech today, so I have to, she sort of lives with us. She's eighty-two, it's her heart, and there's no doctors over there and nobody to, you know. So I have to get over there right away." Is it possible she's almost crying?

"What can I do?" says Rennie. In Griswold it would be cupcakes or a pumpkin pie. This is familiar ground. She's friendlier towards Lora now that she knows Lora's living with someone. Who is not Paul.

"There's this box coming into the airport tomorrow," says Lora, "you think you can pick it up for me?"

Rennie is immediately suspicious. "What's in it?" she says.

Lora looks at her and manages a grin. "Not what you think," she says. "There's one thing around here you don't have to get mailed in from New York, that's for sure. It's her heart medicine. She's got this daughter there sends it to her all the time. You can't get stuff like that here. She ran out of it, that's why she got sick."

Rennie does not want the death of an eighty-two-year-old grandmother on her hands. What can she say but yes? You're too distrustful, Jake used to tell her. Try the benefit of the doubt, for once in your life.

Paul walks over, he's taking his time, he never seems to move very fast. He puts his half-empty drink on the table and sits down. He smiles, but Lora doesn't even look at him.

"What you need to do," Lora says, "you need to go there tomorrow morning around eight, the window that says Customs. Here, you need this thing here. It has to be around eight." She rummages in her purple bag, she can't seem to find it. Finally she takes out a creased and folded piece of paper. "Right," she says. "Just say she sent you and give them this. You ask for this fellow called Harold, he should be there; if he's not you have to wait."

Rennie takes the paper; it's a simple customs notice. There's nothing to pay, no complications. "Why can't I just hand it in at the window?" she says. "Anyone should be able to deal with this."

Lora gives her a patient but exasperated look. "You don't know how they do things around here," she says. "He's the one I gave the bribe to. If you don't do that, they just open it up and keep half the stuff. Or they might keep all of it and never tell you it got here, you know? Sell it on the black market."

"Really?" says Rennie.

"Every place has a different system," says Lora. "But they've all got one. You just need to figure out how it works." She's more relaxed now, she siphons up the rest of her piña colada and stands, scraping back the metal chair. "I got to go to the can," she says, and disappears into the main building.

Rennie and Paul are left sitting together. "Can I get you another?" Paul says.

"No thanks," says Rennie. She's on the edge of being quite drunk. "How do I get back from here?" She realizes this sounds like a request. "I'll call a taxi," she says.

"Taxis don't like to come out here," Paul says. "The roads are too bad, they don't like to wreck their springs. Anyway, you'd have to wait for hours. I'll give you a lift, I've got a jeep out front."

"Only if you're going back anyway," says Rennie.

He stands up, he's ready to leave right now. "What about Lora?" says Rennie. She doesn't want to ride back with Lora, but it would be rude to leave her stranded.

"She'll get back on her own all right," Paul says. "She knows a lot of people."

On the way out Rennie sees Lora, who isn't in the can after all but is standing near the kitchen door, talking with one of the waiters. Rennie goes over to say goodbye.

"Have a nice time," Lora says, with her Holiday Inn smile. She presses something into Rennie's hand; it feels like a wad of Kleenex. "It's a gift," she says. "You're doing me a favour."

"Is Lora a friend of yours?" Rennie asks when they're outside, walking across the Driftwood's thick lawn.

"How do you mean?" says Paul.

Rennie founders. She doesn't want to reveal jealousy or even interest, though she suddenly realizes that she feels both. "I mean, do you know her very well?"

"Well enough," says Paul. "She's been around for a while."

"She seems to be living with some man, over on Ste. Agathe," Rennie says.

"Prince?" Paul says. "Not exactly. Off and on, the way they do. He's into politics, she's not."

"She seems to be into just about everything else," says Rennie.

Paul doesn't say anything, he's staying completely neutral. Rennie's real question hasn't been answered and she can see it won't be.

They reach the driveway and find the jeep, which is small and battered, with open sides and a canvas top. "Is it yours?" Rennie says.

"Friend of mine's," says Paul. He doesn't open the door for her and it takes her a while to get it open for herself. She's definitely had too much to drink. Paul takes out a pair of mirror sunglasses and puts them on. Then he turns the key. The jeep scoots backwards into the ditch, which seems to be the only way to turn around, then accelerates forward, wheels spinning in the mud. Rennie clamps her right hand to the metal frame at the top, her left to the seat, which is also metal. There are no safety belts.

They drive through the forest that surrounds the Driftwood, huge hothouse trees draped with creepers, giant prehistoric ferns, obese plants with rubbery ear-shaped leaves and fruit like warts, like glands. Some of the trees have toppled over, tearing up swaths of earth, their thick snarled roots in the air now.

"Allan," Paul yells over the noise of the jeep.

"What?" says Rennie.

"The hurricane."

Now they're in a coconut plantation. It seems to be abandoned, some of the trees are dead, the coconuts are everywhere, on the road even, the road is worse here, they're hitting every pothole. Rennie's hands are cold, she's sweating, she no longer feels drunk but she thinks she's going to be sick.

"Could you stop?" she shouts.

"What?" says Paul.

"Stop!" she says. "Please stop!"

He looks over at her, then pulls the jeep off to the side of the road. Rennie puts her head down on her knees; she'll be all right if she can just stay like this for a minute. It's a drag, stopping like this, she feels silly, but it's better than vomiting on him. "Throwing Up In The Sun," she thinks briefly. Tippy would say everything's raw material, you just have to know how to work it in.

Paul touches her back. "Any better?" he says. "I guess I was driving too fast for you."

With her head down Rennie listens, she can hear birds, thin shrill voices like fingernails, raucous croaks, insects, her heart going too fast. After a while, she doesn't know how long, she lifts her head. Paul is looking at her, his face is right there, she can see two little faces, white and tiny, relfected back at her from his sunglasses. Without his eyes his face is expressionless, he's a faceless stranger. She's aware of his arm lying across the back of the seat.

"Could you take off your sunglasses, please?" she says.

"Why?" he says, but he does.

Rennie turns her head away from him. It's late, the sun is slanting down through the long spokes of the palm trees, the coconuts lie rotting in their husks; here and there something, an animal, has made large burrows in the ground.

"What lives in the holes?" says Rennie.

"Landcrabs," Paul says. "Big white buggers. They only come out at night, you hunt them with a flashlight and a big stick. You shine the light in their eyes, that stops them, and then you pin them down with the stick."

"Can you eat them?" Rennie says. She's still not connecting very well: the outlines are too clear, the sounds too sharp.

"Sure, if you want to," Paul says. "That's why you hunt them."

He turns her around to face him, he's smiling, he kisses her, more exploration than passion. After a minute Rennie puts her hand on the back of his neck; the hair is soft, she can feel the muscles under it, the ropes, the knots. His hand moves towards her breast, she takes hold of it, slides her fingers between his own. He looks at her and nods a little. "Right," he says. "Let's go back." The rest of the way he drives slowly; it's dark by the time they reach the town.

Rennie wants everything to be easy, why not? Once it would have been, there would have been nothing to it. She likes him, well enough but not too well, she knows nothing about him, she doesn't need to know anything, he knows nothing about her, it's perfect. She walks down the wooden corridor, past the chilly eyes of the Englishwoman, he's just behind her, this is something she wants to do, again, finally, she wants it so much her hands are shaking.

But at the door of her room she turns, without unlocking the door, she can't do it. She can't take that risk.

"I take it I'm coming in?" he says.

She says no, but there's nothing more she can say.

He shrugs. "Up to you," he says. She has no idea what he thinks. He kisses her on the cheek, a peck, and walks away down the green corridor.

Rennie goes into her room, locks the door, and sits down on the edge of the bed. After a while she opens her purse. From the zipper compartment at the back she takes out the Kleenex package Lora handed her and unwraps it. Inside, there's what she knew there would be, five joints, tightly and expertly rolled. She's grateful.

She picks one and lights it with a wooden Swedish match. She smokes a little of it, just enough to relax, puts it out and slides the remaining half and the other four joints between the folds of the green blanket in the middle drawer of the bureau. She lies down on the bed again, hearing the blood running through her body, which is still alive. She thinks of the cells, whispering, dividing in darkness, replacing each other one at a time; and of the other cells, the evil ones which may or may not be there, working away in her with furious energy, like yeast. They would show up hot orange under one kind of light, hot blue under another, like the negative print of the sun when you close your eyes. Beautiful colours.

They use it now in hospitals for terminal cases, it's the one thing that can stop the nausea. She pictures all those Baptists and Presbyterians, no longer sitting in their upright pews but laid out in rows in clean white crank-up beds, stoned to the gills. Of course they call it something else, some respectable Latin name. She wonders how much pain she could take before she would give herself up, give herself over again to the probers, the labellers and cutters. *Doctored,* they say of drinks that have been tampered with, of cats that have been castrated.

You just feel this way about me because I'm your doctor, Daniel said. I'm a fantasy for you. It's normal.

I don't mean to be rude, said Rennie, but if I was going to have a fantasy why would I pick you?

It would be nice to have someone on the bed with her. Almost anyone, as long as he would keep still. Sometimes she wanted just to be still.

You're using me for a teddy bear, Jake said. Why don't you go back to sucking your thumb?

You wouldn't like the substitution, she said. Is there something wrong with quiet companionship?

No, he said, but not every night.

Sometimes I think you don't like me very much, she said.

Like? he said. Is that all you want to be? Liked? Wouldn't you rather be passionately and voraciously desired?

Yes, she said, but not every night.

• • •

That was before. After, he said, You're cutting yourself off.

That's a bad pun, she said.

Never give a sucker an even break, he said. What can I do if you won't let me touch you? You don't even want to talk about it.

What aspect of it would you like to discuss? she said. Instances of recurrence? My chances of survival? You want statistics?

Stop talking like a sick joke, he said.

It may be a sick joke but it's what I'm stuck with, she said. That's why I don't want to discuss it. I *know* it's a sick joke. So I'd rather not, if you don't mind.

How you feel, he said. Try that.

How I feel? Great. I feel great. I feel like the body beautiful. How do you want me to feel?

Come on, he said. So it's the end of the world?

Not yet, she said. Not for you.

You're relentless, Jake said.

Why? she said. Because I don't feel like it in the same way any more? Because I don't believe you do either?

She used to think sex wasn't an issue, it wasn't crucial, it was a pleasant form of exercise, better than jogging, a pleasant form of communication, like gossip. People who got too intense about sex were a little *outré*. It was like wearing plastic spikes with rhinestones and meaning it, it was like taking mink coats seriously. What mattered was the relationship. A good relationship: that was what she and Jake were supposed to have. People commented on it, at parties, as if they were admiring a newly renovated house.

That was what it had been at first: no mess, no *in love*. By the time she met Jake she'd decided she didn't much like being in love. Being in love was like running barefoot along a street covered with broken bottles. It was foolhardy, and if you got through it without damage it was only by sheer luck. It was like taking off your clothes at lunchtime in a bank. It let people think they knew something about you that you didn't know about them, it gave them power over you. It made you visible, soft, penetrable; it made you ludicrous.

There was no question about love with Jake, at first. Not that he wasn't attractive, not that he wasn't possible. He wasn't deformed or a fool and he was good at what he did, he was even good enough to have started his own small company by the time he was thirty. This was how she'd met him: she'd been doing a piece for *Visor* on men who had started their own small companies by the time they were thirty. "The Young and The Solvent," it was called. They'd used Jake for the full-page picture facing the title, and when she thought about him that was the first image she always saw: Jake, "saturnine" she'd called him in the piece, with his dark skin and white teeth and narrow muzzle, grinning like a fox, perched with jaunty irony at his drawing board, wearing a navy blue three-piece suit to prove you didn't have to be afraid of suits. That was about the year the tide was turning, on suits.

A prick, the photographer said to Rennie. He was an old pro, that's what he called himself, the mournful kind, balding and a little seedy. He wore vests with no jacket and his shirt sleeves rolled up. They used him a lot for indoor shots, but only the black and white ones that were supposed to be the subject's real life. For the colour they used a fashion photographer.

How can you tell? asked Rennie.

I can just tell, the photographer said. Women can't tell.

Oh, come on, said Rennie.

Or maybe they can tell, said the photographer. The thing about women is they prefer guys who treat them like shit. A nice guy like me never gets a chance. There's only two kinds of guys, *a prick* and *not a prick*. Not counting fags.

You're jealous, Rennie said. You wish you had teeth like that. He's good at what he does.

Watch out, said the photographer. He's still a prick.

What Jake did was design. He was a designer of labels,

not just labels but the total package: the label, the container, the visuals for the advertising. He was a packager. He decided how things would look and what contexts they would be placed in, which meant what people would feel about them. He knew the importance of style, so he didn't sneer at Rennie for doing pieces on the return of the open-toed spike-heel sandal.

Better than that, he liked her body and said so, which Rennie found refreshing. Most of the men she knew used the word *person*, a little too much, a little too nervously. *A fine person*. It was a burden, being a fine person. She knew she was not as fine a person as they wanted her to be. It was a relief to have a man say, admit, confess, that he thought she had a terrific ass.

What about my mind? she said. Aren't you going to tell me I have an interesting mind?

Screw your mind, Jake said. Both of them laughed. No, he said, I couldn't screw your mind even if I wanted to. You're a tough lady, you've got your legs crossed pretty tight. You can't rape a woman's mind without her consent, you know that.

You can try, Rennie said.

Not me, Jake said. I'm not a mind man. I'm more interested in your body, if you want the truth.

When they'd moved in together, they'd agreed to keep their options open. That was another phrase she'd had to translate for Daniel; by that time she'd had trouble explaining what it meant.

It took her more time than it should have to realize that she was one of the things Jake was packaging. He began with the apartment, which he painted several shades of off-white and filled with forties furniture, chrome for the kitchen and a deep-pink bulgy chair and sofa for the livingroom, "like thighs," he said, with a real trilight he'd picked up at the Sally Ann. Wicker and indoor plants had been done, he said, and he got rid of the benjamina tree, Rennie suspected, by pouring his leftover coffee into it when she wasn't looking.

Then he started on her. You have great cheekbones, he said. You should exploit them.

Oppressed cheekbones? said Rennie, who was slightly embarrassed by compliments; they'd been rare in Griswold.

Sometimes I feel like a blank sheet of paper, she said. For you to doodle on.

Screw that, said Jake. It's all there underneath. I just want you to bring it out. You should enjoy it, you should make the most of it.

Aren't you afraid packs of ravening, lustful other men will storm in and snatch me away from you? said Rennie. If I make the most of it.

Not a chance, said Jake. Other men are wimps. He believed this, which was one of the things Rennie liked about him. She didn't have to stroke his ego, he did that for himself.

He decided she should wear nothing but white linen jumpsuits, with shoulder pads. The Rosie the Riveter look, he said.

They make my ass look big, she said.

That's the point, he said. Small asses have been done.

Rennie drew the line at *nothing but*—Let's not be absolutist, she said—but she got one, to please him, though she refused to wear it out on the street. In the livingroom he hung blowups of Cartier-Bresson photographs, three Mexican prostitutes looking out of wooden cubicles, their eyebrows plucked thin and drawn into exaggerated bows, their mouths clown-mouths, an old man sitting in a field of deserted chairs.

That was the daytime. When he had that arranged, he started on the night. In the bedroom he hung a Heather Cooper poster, a brown-skinned woman wound up in a piece of material that held her arms to her sides but left her breasts and thighs and buttocks exposed. She had no expression on her face, she was just standing there, if anything a little bored. The picture was called *Enigma*. The other picture in the bedroom was a stylized print of a woman lying on a 1940's puffy sofa, like the one in their own livingroom. She was feet-first, and her head, up at the other end of the sofa, was tiny, featureless, and rounded like a doorknob. In the foreground there was a bull.

These pictures made Rennie slightly nervous, especially when she was lying on their bed with no clothes on. But that was probably just her background.

Put your arms over your head, Jake said, it lifts the breasts. Move your legs apart, just a little. Raise your left knee. You look fantastic.

A secure woman is not threatened by her partner's fantasies, Rennie told herself. As long as there is trust. She'd even written that, or something like it, in a piece on the comeback of satin lingerie and fancy garter belts. And she was not threatened, not for some time.

You're so closed, Jake said once. I like that. I want to be the one you open up for.

But she could never remember afterwards what he had actually said. Perhaps he'd said, I want to be the one who opens you up.

III

My father came home every Christmas, says Rennie. He always spoke of it as coming home, though it became obvious at last, even to me, that his home was elsewhere. He'd gone to Toronto soon after I was born, he'd been in the war and got university free as a veteran. He studied chemical engineering. He stayed there, everyone said, because the jobs were there. We couldn't go because my grandfather got sick and my grandmother needed the help, that's what they said, and after my grandfather died my grandmother could not be left alone. People in Griswold had a great fear of being left alone. It was supposed to be bad for you, it made you go funny, it drove you bats. Then you had to be put in the loony bin.

So my father would turn up every Christmas. He would stay in one of the guest bedrooms, we had a lot of them, bedrooms that had once been for children and now stood empty, dustless and smelling of lavender and dead air. These visits of his, I was told later, were for my sake. My father and I would be bundled up and sent for walks on the icy streets; both of us would be told not to fall down. He would ask me how I was doing at school and tell me that soon I would be able to come and visit him. Neither of us believed this. On the main street people's heads would turn, not too abruptly, as we went past, and I would know that we were being looked at and discussed.

When I was in Grade Six, two girls, the kind from loose families, spread the story that my father was living with another woman in Toronto, and that was the real reason my mother didn't go to join him. I didn't believe this, but I didn't ask my mother about it either, so I probably did believe it after all. Just as well, because it was true, and when my mother finally told me I wasn't surprised. She waited until my thirteenth birthday, two weeks after my first period. She must have felt I was ready for pain.

I think she wanted sympathy, she felt that at last I would understand what a hard life she had led and what sacrifices she had been forced to make. She hoped I would blame my father, see him in his true light. But I was unable to feel what I was supposed to; instead I blamed her. I was angry with him, not for leaving—I could see why he would have wanted to do that—but for leaving me behind.

By that time he'd stopped coming back for Christmas, though he still sent cards, to me but not to her, and I didn't see him again until I moved to Toronto to go to university. For years he'd been married to someone I thought of only as *her,* because that's what my mother called her. I'd forgotten what he looked like.

I visited them at their apartment. I had never been in an apartment before. That was the first time I'd ever seen a house plant that wasn't an African violet or a poinsettia. They had a lot of plants, hanging all over the southern windows, things I didn't know the names for. There was space between the furniture in their apartment, a lot more space than I was used to. The first thing he said to me was *You look like your mother.* And that was the end of him.

When I was growing up, says Lora, we lived in cellars. We lived in the cellars of apartment buildings; they were always dark, even in summer, and they smelled like cat piss, partly because of Bob's cats, he never emptied the litter box even though they were his cats, and partly because those kinds of places always smell like cat piss anyway. Bob got the apartments for next to nothing, they were the caretaker's apartments, he was supposed to take out the garbage and mop the floors and fix people's toilets, but he was never much good at that, or maybe he didn't want to, which is why we were always moving.

His war buddy Pat used to say that wasn't how Bob really made his money anyway. He said Bob made his money by catching things that fell off the backs of lorries. I didn't figure out for a while that *lorry* was the English word for truck, Pat was from England, and then I didn't believe it, because I knew Bob didn't chase after trucks waiting for stuff to fall off them. He was home most of the time, sitting at the kitchen table in his old grey cardigan, and besides he couldn't run because of his limp. This was lucky for me: if I could keep him from grabbing me I could always outrun him, but he was fast with the hands, he'd pretend he was looking the other way and then snatch, and when I was small he could keep hold of me with one hand while he got his belt off with the other. I guess that's partly what made me so quick on my feet.

He said he got the limp in the war and it was typical of the government that they wouldn't give him a pension. He was against the government, whoever was in, he said it didn't matter a tinker's piss, but don't get the wrong idea, he was death on communism too. He couldn't stand the idea of welfare, that was communism as far as he was concerned. Bob's war buddy Pat used to talk about the working class, he used to say that's what they were, the both of them, but that was always a big joke to me. Working class my ass. Bob worked as little as he could. His whole thing was how you could avoid working, he thought anyone with a steady job was the world's number-one dummy. He was dead against the unions too, he had no sympathy for them at all, he said they just made things more expensive for everybody else. When there were strikes on the TV he would cheer on the police, which was something, because the rest of the time he was dead against them too.

Anyway, it took me a long time to figure out why we would suddenly have five television sets, then none, then eight radios, then only one. Sometimes it was toasters, sometimes it was record players, you never knew. Things appeared and disappeared around our place like magic. I got the belt for bragging at school that we had five television sets, I brought one of the kids over to see, which made Bob mad as hell. This'll teach you to keep your fuckin' lip zipped, he said.

A lot of things made him mad as hell. It was like he spent the whole day sitting at that table, smoking Black Cat cigarettes the way he did and waiting for something to come along and make him mad, and my mother spent the whole day trying to guess what it would be so she could stop it from happening.

Go *around* him, she told me. Why do you have to walk right into him all the time? Pretend he's a closed door. You wouldn't walk right into a door if you could help it, would you? I thought when she said stuff like this she was taking his side, but now I see she was just trying to keep me from getting beat up too much.

I hated him more than anything. I used to lie awake at nights thinking up bad things that could happen to him, like falling down a sewer or getting eaten by rats. There were rats in our apartments too, or anyway mice, and Bob wouldn't let my mother put out poison because the mice might eat it and then his cats might eat the mice, though his cats never ate any mice that I ever saw. When he wasn't there, which wasn't all that often, I used to step on the cats' tails and chase them around with the broom. I couldn't do anything to him but I sure could make life miserable for his bloody cats. I still can't stand to have a cat near me.

It was mean on the cats, but I think I did stuff like that so I wouldn't have to be so scared of him. Remember that story in the papers, six, seven years ago? It was about this woman with a little boy, who married this man, and after a while the two of them killed the little boy, out in the woods. They said they were taking him on a picnic. There was a picture of the little boy that broke my heart. The man just didn't want him around, I guess, and the mother went along with it. I was grown up by the time I read that, I was almost thirty, but it put me in a cold sweat and I dreamed about it off and on for weeks. It was like something that almost happened to me and I didn't even know it at the time, like you're sleepwalking and you wake up and you're standing on the edge of this cliff. I was always more scared of Bob when he was trying to be nice than when he was mad. It's like knowing there's someone in the closet waiting for you but not being able to see in.

My mother married Bob after my father died, that would be when I was around four. I don't know why she married him. My mother wasn't religious or anything, we didn't go to church, but she had this belief that things were ordered, *meant to be* she would say. When I asked her why she married Bob she would say it was meant to be. I don't know who by, somebody with a pretty poor sense of humour if you ask me. She never did figure out that some things are just accidents. When I was twelve or so I decided that was about the best way to think of Bob: he was an accident that happened to me, like getting run over by a truck, I was just in the way. I had to live with him, but like a broken leg, not like a person. I stopped trying to work out in advance what would make him happy or not or mad or not, because I never would be able to work it out, and I stopped thinking it had a whole lot to do with me. If he hit me it was like the weather, sometimes it rains, sometimes it doesn't. He didn't hit me because I was bad, like I used to think. He hit me because he could get away with it and nobody could stop him. That's mostly why people do stuff like that, because they can get away with it.

My mother was full of schemes. She was always reading the back pages of magazines, those ads that tell you how to start your own business in your home and make thousands of dollars. She tried a lot of them too, she addressed envelopes, she sold magazine subscriptions and encyclopedias and stuff like that door to door, she even tried arts and crafts, putting together dried flower arrangements out of the raw materials they'd send to her. Once she even rented a knitting machine. That one died a quick death.

But it was no use, she never did get rich the way they promised, you'd have to work forty-eight hours a day anyway on most of those things just to break even, and she'd lose interest pretty fast. She didn't have the business sense to handle things that really would work, like Tupperware parties. Not that we lived in Tupperware country, no way she could've had one of those parties in any of our apartments, with the cat litter box in the kitchen and the lightbulbs with no shades and the red stains down the backs of the toilets and that smell, and Bob sitting there in his cardigan with the ravelly cuffs and his cigarette cough, like his insides were going to come up any minute. That and chip dip and salads with baby marshmallows in them don't mix, you know?

She was more interested in reading the ads anyway, and sending off the first letter. That always excited her. For her it was like gambling, she wanted to believe in fate, she wanted to believe that some day the wheel would come around and it would be her turn, not for anything she'd done that would make her deserve it, but just because it was her turn. She never said so, she used to say we should make the most of what we had and be thankful for our blessings, but underneath it I think she hated those cellars and the smell of cat piss and maybe even Bob as much as I did. But she didn't know what else to do, she didn't know how to get out.

Where there's life there's hope, that's what my mother would say. She had to believe good luck was out there somewhere and it was waiting for her. All those years I didn't see her I used to send her a Loto Canada or a Wintario ticket for her birthday, sometimes a book of them when I had the money, but she never won.

Rennie's dreaming, she knows it, she wants to wake up.

She's standing in her grandmother's garden, around at the side of the house, she knows this garden disappeared a long time ago, I can't take care of everything, said her mother, but here it is, back in place, everything is so bright, so full of juice, the red zinnias, the hollyhocks, the sunflowers, the poles with scarlet runner beans, the hummingbirds like vivid bees around them. It's winter though, there's snow on the ground, the sun is low in the sky; small icicles hang from the stems and blossoms. Her grandmother is there, in a white cotton dress with small blue flowers on it, it's a summer dress, she doesn't seem to mind the cold, and Rennie knows this is because she is dead. There's an open window, through it Rennie can hear her mother and her aunts singing hymns in the kitchen while they do the dishes, three-part harmony.

Rennie puts out her hands but she can't touch her grandmother, her hands go right in, through, it's like touching water or new snow. Her grandmother smiles at her, the hummingbirds are around her head, lighting on her hands. Life everlasting, she says.

Rennie struggles to wake up, she doesn't want to be in this dream, and finally she makes it. She's lying in her bed, the sheet's twisted around her, she thrashes and untangles herself and pushes herself upright. Outside the window it's grey, the room is dim, perhaps it's not yet morning. There's something she has to find. She stands up, in her bare feet, she's wearing a long white cotton gown, it ties at the back, but this is not a hospital. She gets to the other side of the room and pulls open her bureau drawers, one after another, rummaging through her slips, scarves, sweaters with their arms tucked carefully behind them. It's her hands she's looking for, she knows she left them here somewhere, folded neatly in a drawer, like gloves.

Rennie opens her eyes; this time she's really awake. It's dawn, the noises are beginning, the mosquito netting hangs around her in the warm air like mist. She sees where she is, she's here, by herself, she's stranded in the future. She doesn't know how to get back.

What do you dream about? Rennie asked Jake, a month after they'd started living together.

You sound like my mother, Jake said. Next thing you'll want to know about my bowel movements.

Jake was in the habit of making Jewish-mother jokes, which Rennie felt was just a way of not really talking about his mother. She resented all jokes about mothers, even the ones she made about her own. Mothers were no laughing matter. You don't have a monopoly on mothers, she said. And I'm not yours. You should be flattered that I'm even interested.

Why does every woman in the world need to know that? said Jake. A few good fucks and they have to know what you dream. What difference does it make?

I just want to know you better, said Rennie. I want to know everything about you.

I'd have to be crazy to tell you anything at all, said Jake. You'd use it against me. I've seen those notebooks of yours. You'd keep lists. I bet you go through the trash can when I'm out.

Why are you so defensive? said Rennie. Don't you trust me?

Do chickens have lips? said Jake. Okay, here's what I

dream about. I dream about your bum, a hundred times life-size, floating in the sky, covered with neon lights and flashing on and off. How's that?

Don't put me down, said Rennie.

I like you down, said Jake. Flat on your back. He rolled over on top of her and started biting her neck. I'm uncontrollable, he said. I'm an animal in the dark.

Which one? said Rennie. A chipmunk?

Watch it, pussycat, said Jake. Remember your place. He got hold of her two hands, held her wrists together, shoved himself in between her thighs, squeezing her breast harder than he needed to. Feel that, he said. That's what you do to me, the fastest erection in the West. Pretend I just came through the window. Pretend you're being raped.

What's pretend about it? said Rennie. Stop pinching.

Admit it turns you on, said Jake. Admit you love it. Ask for it. Say please.

Fuck off, said Rennie. She kicked him on the backs of his legs with her heels, laughing.

Jake laughed too. He liked it when she swore; he said she was the only woman he knew who still pronounced the *g* in "fucking." This was true enough: swearing was one of the social graces Rennie hadn't learned early in life, she'd had to teach herself.

You have a dirty mouth, Jake said. It needs to be washed out with a tongue.

What do you dream about? Rennie asked Daniel.

I don't know, said Daniel. I can never remember.

Last night Rennie set her alarm for seven. She lies in bed, waiting for it to be seven. When the alarm goes off she claws her way through the mosquito netting and pushes the OFF button.

If it weren't for Lora and the grandmother with the bad heart, she wouldn't have to get up at all. She considers staying in bed, she could always say she slept in. But Griswold is ingrained in her. If you can't keep your word, don't give it. Do unto others. She struggles out through the cocoon of mouldy-smelling gauze, feeling not virtuous but resentful.

She wants to have breakfast before taking a taxi to the airport, but the Englishwoman says breakfast isn't ready yet, it won't be for another hour. Rennie can't wait. She decides to have coffee and a doughnut at the airport. She asks the English-woman to call for a taxi for her and the Englishwoman points to the phone. "You don't need to call for one," she says, "they're always hanging around down there." But Rennie calls anyway.

The car's interior is upholstered in mauve shag, the kind they use for bedroom slippers and toilet seat covers. A St. Christopher doll and a pair of rubber dice swing from the mirror. The driver is wearing purple shorts and a T-shirt with the sleeves ripped off, and a gold cross on a chain around his neck. He's young, he turns the music up as loud as it can go. It's a noxious capon-like rendering of "I Saw Mommy Kiss-ing Santa Claus," and Rennie wonders what month they're in; already she's lost track. She's far too cowardly to ask him to turn it down, and she clenches her teeth against the ade-noidal soprano as they drive into town, much too fast, he's doing it on purpose. They pass a clump of people, gathered outside a store for no discernible purpose, and he honks the horn, a long drawn-out blare, drawing attention to them as if it's a wedding.

At the airport Rennie wrestles with the door, gets it open and climbs out. The driver makes no move, so she goes around to his side.

"How much?" she says.

"You leavin' us?" he says.

"No, I'm just picking up a package," says Rennie, and realizes immediately that she's made a mistake, because he says, "I wait for you here."

"That's all right," says Rennie. "I may be a while."

"Nothin' else to do," he says cheerfully.

The airport is almost empty. Rennie looks around for the snack bar and finds it, but it's closed. The customs window is closed too. There's a large poster Scotch-taped to the glass: ELLIS IS KING.

It's a quarter to eight. Rennie sits down on a bench to wait. She hunts through her purse, looking for Lifesavers, cough drops, anything she could eat, but there's nothing. Beside the bench is a photo machine, a booth with a curtain and a slot for the coins. Rennie considers this, but it takes only American quarters. She stares across at the poster, the one with the rooster on it. THE BIONIC COCK. IT GIVES YOU SPURS. *Prince of Peace,* someone has scrawled across it.

At eight-thirty the window slides up, there's someone behind it. Rennie digs the crumpled customs form out of her purse and goes over.

"I'm looking for Harold," she says, feeling very silly, but the man behind the counter isn't surprised.

"Yeah," he says. He disappears into a back room. Rennie thinks he's gone to find Harold, but he returns with a large oblong box.

"Are you Harold?" she says.

He regards this as a stupid question and doesn't answer it. "That must be one fat old lady," he says. "She get six parcel this month. From New York. Food, it say. What she needin' all this food for?"

He looks at her slyly, smiling as if he's told a joke. The box is too big to go through the window, so he unlocks the door at the side.

Rennie was expecting something more like a package. "Isn't that the wrong box?" she says. "I'm looking for a smaller one. It's just some medicine."

"That in here too," he says airily, as if he's been through the contents himself. "This the one, ain't no other box I see."

Rennie is dubious. She reads the label, which indeed has the right name on it. "You forgot this," she says, handing him the customs form. He glances at it with contempt, then tears it in two.

"Shouldn't I sign something?" says Rennie, whose sense of correct procedure is being violated. He scowls at her.

"You tryin' to get me in trouble?" he says. "You take that and go on out of here." He locks himself in his cubicle and turns his back on her.

The box weighs a ton. Rennie has to drag it. It occurs to her that she has no idea where Lora lives or where the grandmother lives, or how she's supposed to deliver the box to either of them. The address is typed clearly enough, but all it says is ELVA, *Ste. Agathe.* There isn't any last name. What next? She feels she has been either duped or used, but she isn't sure which or how. She makes it through the front door and looks for her taxi. It's nowhere in sight and there isn't another; probably they come to the airport only when there's a plane. There's a single car parked across the street but it isn't a taxi, it's a jeep. There's a policeman sitting in it, smoking a cigarette and talking with the driver, and Rennie realizes with a small shock that the driver is Paul. He doesn't see her, he's facing straight ahead, listening to the policeman. Rennie thinks of asking him for a lift; he could carry the box up those stairs for her and then they could have breakfast together. But she's embarrassed, she can't ask him to do that. After the way she's behaved. Chickening out on friendly sex with no explanation at all is socially gauche, inexcusable really: she treated him as if she thought he had genital wens. He'd be right to be angry.

She'll have to lug the box back into the terminal building and phone for another taxi; then she'll have to wait for it to arrive. While she's sifting through her purse for pay-phone change, a taxi pulls up, the original. The driver is eating a huge roti; filling drips down his wrist, meat sauce. The smell reminds Rennie that she's nearly faint with hunger, but she can hardly ask for a bite. That would be borderline familiar.

The box is too big to fit into the trunk. The driver tosses the remains of his roti on the sidewalk, wipes his hands carefully on his shorts so as not to damage his mauve upholstery, and helps Rennie slide the box into the back seat. Rennie sits beside him in the front. This time the music is Nat King Cole, singing "I'm Dreaming of a White Christmas," which is better.

"How much?" Rennie asks again, outside the hotel.

"Twenty E.C.s," he says promptly. Rennie knows this is outrageous.

"It's only seven one-way from the airport," she says.

"The extra for waitin'," he says, grinning at her.

Before, on a trip like this, Rennie would have haggled; once she prided herself on her haggling. Now she doesn't have the energy, and he knows it, they all know it, they can smell it on her. She gives him twenty-three and goes around to haul out the box.

To her surprise, the driver gets out of the car, though he doesn't help her, he just watches.

"You a friend of Miss Lora's?" he says. "I see you with her. Everyone know Miss Lora."

"Yes," says Rennie, to avoid explanations. She's grappling with the box; the end slides off the back seat and hits the street.

"She a nice lady," he says softly. "You a nice lady too, like her?" Two other men, also with the sleeveless T-shirts, have stopped and are leaning against the wall.

Rennie decides to ignore this. There's an innuendo but she can't interpret it. She smiles, politely she hopes, and retreats toward the inner courtyard, dragging the box with what she hopes is dignity. Laughter trails her in.

At the foot of the stairs the deaf and dumb man is curled,

asleep and snoring, drunk most likely. His fly is open, revealing torn cloth, grey; there's a recent cut across his cheek, the white stubble on his face is now half an inch long. Rennie can't get the box up the stairs without moving his legs, so she moves them. When she's setting down his feet, bare and crusted with drying mud, he opens his eyes and smiles at her, a smile that would be innocent, blissful even, if it weren't for the missing teeth. She's afraid he will want to shake her hand again, but he doesn't. Maybe he thinks she has enough good luck already.

Rennie negotiates the stairs, hugging the box, lifting it one stair at a time. It's too hot to be doing this; she's an idiot for getting herself into it, for saying she would.

When she reaches the front desk the Englishwoman informs her that it's now too late for breakfast.

"What can I have then?" says Rennie.

"Tea and biscuits," says the Englishwoman crisply.

"Can't I have some toast?" says Rennie, trying not to whine.

The Englishwoman gives her a contemptuous look. "You might find something else," she says, "out there." Her tone implies that anything eaten out there will result in cholera or worse.

Rennie orders the tea and biscuits and pulls the box along the hall to her room. By now it's almost like another person, a body, a dancing partner who's passed out cold. There's no place to put it, it won't fit into the bureau and there's no closet. Rennie slides it under the bed, and she's still on her knees when one of the waitresses brings the tea and biscuits, on a plastic tray with a picture of Windsor Castle on it.

Rennie clears the Bible and her clock off the night table so the waitress can set the tray down. The bed hasn't been made. When the waitress has gone Rennie bundles the mosquito netting into a loose knot and sits down on the twisted sheets.

The tea is made with a Tetley's teabag, and water that was

obviously not boiling. The biscuits are arrogantly English, flat beige ovals with the edges stamped into a Victorian-ceiling design and the centres dabbed with putty-like red jam. They look like enlarged corn plasters. Rennie bites into one. It's uncompromisingly stale, it tastes like a winter foot, like a cellar, like damp wool. Rennie wants to go home.

Rennie sits by the window, staring at her notebook, in which she's managed to write four words: *Fun in the Sunspots.* But why worry? The editors always change her titles anyway.

There's a knock at the door. A man, says the maid, is waiting for her at the front desk. Rennie thinks it must be Paul; she checks her face in the small mirror. Now she will have to explain.

But it's Dr. Minnow, in a khaki shirt and immaculate white shorts, looking even neater than he did on the plane.

"You are enjoying your stay?" he asks, smiling his crooked smile. "You are learning about local customs?"

"Yes," says Rennie, wondering what he wants.

"I have come to take you to the Botanic Gardens," he says. "As we arranged."

Rennie can't remember having arranged any such thing, but perhaps arrangements are more casual here. She also can't remember having told him where she's staying. The English-woman is looking at her from behind the desk. "Of course," says Rennie. "That would be very nice."

She collects her camera, just in case, and Dr. Minnow ushers her to his car. It's a maroon Fiat with an ominous dent in the left fender. When Rennie is strapped in, Dr. Minnow turns to her with a grin that verges on slyness. "There are things more useful for you to see," he says. "We will go there first."

They drive, alarmingly fast, along the main street, away from the bankers' end. The road ceases to be mostly paved and becomes mostly unpaved; now they're in the market. The

signs are still up here and there but the orange-crate plat-
forms are gone.

Dr. Minnow hasn't slowed down as much as Rennie
thinks he ought to. People stare at them, some smile. Dr.
Minnow has rolled down his window and is waving. Voices
call to him, he answers, everyone seems to know who he is.

Palms press flat against the windshield. "We for you,"
someone shouts. "The fish live!"

Rennie's beginning to be worried. The crowd around the
car is too thick, it's blocking the car, not all of these people
are smiling. Dr. Minnow honks his horn and revs the engine
and they move forward.

"You didn't tell me you were still in politics," Rennie
says.

"Everyone is in politics here, my friend," says Dr. Minnow. "All the time. Not like the sweet Canadians."

They turn uphill, away from the centre of the town. Rennie
grips the edge of the seat, her hands sweating, as they careen
along the road, barely two lanes and switchbacked up a steep
hill. She looks at the ocean, which is below them now, too far
below. The view is spectacular.

They bump at a forty-five degree angle through an
arched stone gateway. "Fort Industry," says Dr. Minnow.
"Very historical, built by the English. You will want to take
some pictures." There's a field of sorts, rutted partially dried
mud with a little grass growing on it, and a number of tents,
not tents really, pieces of canvas held up by poles. Dr. Minnow parks the car on the near side of the tents and gets out,
so Rennie gets out too.

Even outside there's a smell of bodies, of latrines and
lime and decaying food. There are mattresses under the canvas roofs, most without sheets. Clothing is piled on the beds
and hangs from ropes running from pole to pole. Between the
tents are cooking fires; the ground around them is littered

with utensils, pots, tin plates, pans. The people here are mostly women and young children. The children play in the mud around the tents, the women sit in the shade in their cotton dresses, talking together and paring vegetables.

"They from the hurricane," says Dr. Minnow softly. "The government have the money to rebuild their houses, the sweet Canadians send it to them. Only it has not yet happened, you understand."

An old man comes over to Dr. Minnow, an older woman, several younger ones. The man touches his arm. "We for you," he says gently. They look sideways at Rennie. She stands awkwardly, wondering what she's supposed to do or say.

Across the field, walking away from them, there's a small group of people, white, well dressed. Rennie thinks she recognizes the two German women from the hotel, the old couple from the reef boat, binoculars pointed. That's what she herself must look like: a tourist. A spectator, a voyeur.

Near her, on a mattress that's been dragged out into the sun, a young girl lies nursing a baby.

"That's a beautiful baby," Rennie says. In fact it isn't, it's pleated, shrivelled, like a hand too long in water. The girl says nothing. She stares woodenly up at Rennie, as if she's been looked at many times before.

Should we have a baby? Rennie said to Jake, only once.

You don't want to limit your options too soon, said Jake, as if it was only her options that would be limited, it had nothing to do with him. Maybe you should postpone it for a while. You want to get the timing right.

Which was true enough. What about you? said Rennie.

If you don't like the road, don't go, said Jake, smiling at her. I'm not too good at lifetime goals. Right now I like the road.

. . .

Can I have a baby? Rennie said to Daniel, also only once.

Little boys say *Can I,* said her grandmother. Little girls are more polite. They say *May I.*

Do you mean right now? said Daniel.

I mean ever, said Rennie.

Ever, said Daniel. *Ever* is a pretty big word.

I know. Big words get you in trouble, said Rennie. They told me that at school.

It's not a question of whether you can or not, said Daniel. Of course you can, there's nothing physical that would stop you. You could probably have a perfectly normal, healthy baby.

But? said Rennie.

Maybe you should give yourself some time, said Daniel. Just to adjust to things and consider your priorities. You should be aware that there are hormonal changes that seem to affect the recurrence rate, though we don't really know. It's a risk.

God forbid I should take a risk, said Rennie.

The girl pulls the baby off her breast and switches it to the other side. Rennie wonders if she should give her some money. Would that be insulting? Her hand moves towards her purse, but now she's surrounded by a mob of children, seven or eight of them, jumping excitedly around her and all talking at once.

"They want you to take their pictures," says Dr. Minnow, so Rennie does, but this doesn't seem to satisfy them. Now they want to see the picture.

"This isn't a Polaroid," says Rennie to Dr. Minnow. "It doesn't come out," she says to the children. It's hard to make them understand.

It's noon. Rennie stands under the violent sun, rubbing lotion on her face and wishing she had brought her hat. Dr. Minnow seems to know everything there is to know about this fort, and he's going to tell it all to her, brick by brick, while she dehydrates and wonders when she'll faint or break out in spots. What does he want from her? It must be something. "You shouldn't take the time," she's protested, twice already. But he's taking it.

The number of things Rennie thinks ought to happen to her in foreign countries is limited, but the number of things she fears may happen is much larger. She's not a courageous traveller, though she's always argued that this makes her a good travel writer. Other people will want to know which restaurant is likely to give you the bends, which hotel has the cockroaches, she's not the only one. Someday, if she keeps it up, she'll find herself beside a cauldron with an important local person offering her a sheep's eye or the boiled hand of a monkey, and she'll be unable to refuse. The situation has not reached that point. Nevertheless she's a captive; though if worst comes to worst she can always get a lift back with the other tourists.

Now Dr. Minnow is speculating on the methods of sanitation used by the British. It's almost as if they're extinct, a vanished tribe, and he's digging them up, unearthing their broken Queen Anne teacups, exhuming their garbage dumps, exclaiming with wonder and archaeological delight over their curious customs.

The fort itself is standard Georgian brickwork, falling into decay. Although it's listed in the brochure as one of the chief attractions, nothing has been done to improve it or even to keep it in repair. Below is the muddy open space cluttered with tents, and beyond that a public toilet that's ancient and wooden and looks temporary. The only new structure is a glassed-in cubicle with an antenna of some sort on top.

"They have a high-power telescope in there," Dr. Minnow tells her. "They can see everything that comes off the boats. When it is not so hazy you can see Grenada." Beside the cubicle is a square hut that Dr. Minnow says is the prison bakery, since the fort is used as a prison. A goat is tethered beside the toilets.

Dr. Minnow has scrambled up the parapet. He's remarkably active for a man of his age. He seems to expect Rennie to climb up there too, but it's a sheer drop, hundreds of feet to the sea. She stands on tiptoe and looks over instead. In the distance, there's a blue shape, long and hazy, an island.

Dr. Minnow jumps down and stands beside her.

"Is that Grenada?" says Rennie.

"No," says Dr. Minnow. "Ste. Agathe. There, they are all sailors."

"What are they here?" says Rennie.

"Idiots," says Dr. Minnow. "But then, I am from Ste. Agathe. The British make a big mistake in the nineteenth century, they put us all together in one country. Ever since then we have trouble, and now the British have got rid of us so they can have their cheap bananas without the bother of governing us, and we have more trouble."

He's watching something below them now, his head with its high-bridged nose cocked to one side like a bird's. Rennie follows his gaze. There's a man moving among the refugees, from group to group, children following him. He's handing something out, papers, Rennie can see the white. He's wearing boots, with raised heels, cowboy boots: when he pauses before a trio of women squatting around their cooking fire, a small child runs its hands up and down the leather.

Dr. Minnow is grinning. "There is Marsdon," he says. "That boy always busy, he's working for the Prince of Peace. They're making the leaflets in the People's Church, there is a machine. They think they have the one true religion and you go to hell if you don't believe, they be glad to send you. But with these people they will not get far. You know why, my friend?"

"Why?" says Rennie, humouring him. She's tuning out, it's too much like small-town politics, the tiny feuds in Griswold, the grudges, the stupid rivalries. Who cares?

"Always they hand out papers," says Dr. Minnow.

"They say it explain everything, why the sun shine, whose arse it shine out, not mine I can assure you of that." He chuckles, delighted with his own joke. "But they forget that few can read."

The children caper in Marsdon's wake, holding the squares of paper up in the air by their corners, waving them, white kites.

Another car drives into the muddy space and parks in front of the bakery; there are two men in it but they don't get out. Rennie can see their upturned faces, the blank eyes of their sunglasses.

"Now we have the whole family," says Dr. Minnow. "This kind does not hand out papers."

"Who are they?" says Rennie. His tone of voice is making her jumpy.

"My friends," he says softly. "They follow me everywhere. They want to make sure I am safe." He smiles and puts his hand on her arm. "Come," he says. "There is more to see."

He steers her down some steps to a stone corridor, where at least it's cooler. He shows her the officers' quarters, plain square rooms with the plaster falling away from the walls in patches.

"We wanted to have a display here," he says. "Maps, the wars between the French and English. And a gift shop, for the local arts and culture. But the Minister for Culture is not interested. He say, 'You can't eat culture.' " Rennie wants to ask what the local arts and culture are, but decides to wait. It's one of those questions to which she's already supposed to know the answer.

They go down more stone stairs. At the bottom there's a line of fresh washing, sheets and flowered pillowcases hung out to dry in the sun. Two women sit on plastic-webbed chairs; they smile at Dr. Minnow. One of them is making what looks like a wallhanging from shreds of material in pastel underwear colours, peach, baby-blue, pink; the other is crocheting, something white. Perhaps these are the local arts and culture.

A third woman, in a brown dress and a black knitted hat, comes from a doorway.

"How much?" Dr. Minnow says to the woman who's crocheting, and Rennie can see that she's expected to buy one of the white objects. So she does.

"How long did it take you to make it?" Rennie asks her.

"Three days," she says. She has a full face, a pleasant direct smile.

"That if your boyfriend not around," says Dr. Minnow, and everyone laughs.

"We here to see the barracks," Dr. Minnow says to the woman in brown. "This lady is from Canada, she is writing about the history here." He's misunderstood her, that's why he's showing her all this. Rennie doesn't have the heart to correct him.

The woman unlocks the door and ushers them through. She has a badge pinned to her shoulder, Rennie sees now. MATRON.

"Do those women live here?" she asks.

"They are our women prisoners," Dr. Minnow says. "The one you buy the thing from, she chop up another woman. The other one, I don't know." Behind her the matron stands beside the open door, laughing with the two women. It all seems so casual.

They're in a corridor, with a row of doors on one side, a line of slatted windows on the other, overlooking a sheer drop to the sea. They go through a doorway; it leads to another corridor with small rooms opening off from it.

The rooms smell of neglect; bats hang upside down in them, there are hornets' nests on the walls, debris rotting in the corners. DOWN WITH BABYLON, someone has scrawled across one wall. LOVE TO ALL. The rooms farthest from the sea are damp and dark, it's too much like a cellar for Rennie.

They go back to the main corridor, which is surprisingly cool, and walk towards the far end. Dr. Minnow says she should try to imagine what this place was like with five hundred men in it. Crowded, thinks Rennie. She asks if this is the original wood.

Dr. Minnow opens the door at the end, and they're looking at a small, partly paved courtyard surrounded by a wall. The courtyard is overgrown with weeds; in a corner of it three large pigs are rooting.

In the other corner there's an odd structure, made of boards nailed not too carefully together. It has steps up to a platform, four supports but no walls, a couple of crossbeams. It's recent but dilapidated; Rennie thinks it's a child's playhouse which has been left unfinished and wonders what it's doing here.

"This is what the curious always like to see," Dr. Minnow murmurs.

Now Rennie understands what she's being shown. It's a gallows.

"You must photograph it, for your article," says Dr. Minnow. "For the sweet Canadians."

Rennie looks at him. He isn't smiling.

Dr. Minnow is discoursing on the Carib Indians.

"Some of the earlier groups made nose cups," he says, "which they used for taking liquid narcotics. That is what interests our visitors the most. And they took drugs also from behind. For religious purposes, you understand."

"From behind?" says Rennie.

Dr. Minnow laughs. "A ritual enema," he says. "You should put this in your article."

Rennie wonders whether he's telling the truth, but it's too grotesque not to be true. She's not sure the readers of *Visor* will want to hear about this, but you never know. Maybe it will catch on; for those who cough when smoking.

Dr. Minnow has insisted on taking her to lunch, and Rennie, hungry enough to eat an arm, has not protested. They're in a Chinese restaurant, which is small, dark, and hotter than the outside sunlight. Two ceiling fans stir the damp air but do not cool it; Rennie feels sweat already wetting her underarms and trickling down her chest. The table is red formica, spotted with purplish brown sauce.

Dr. Minnow smiles across at her, kindly, avuncular, his bottom teeth clasped over the top ones like folded hands. "There is always a Chinese restaurant," he says. "Everywhere in the world. They are indefatigable, they are like the Scots, you kick them out in one place, they turn up in another. I myself am part Scottish, I have often considered going to the Gathering of the Clans. My wife say this is what makes me so pig-headed." Rennie is somewhat relieved to hear that he has a wife. He's been too attentive, there must be a catch.

A waiter comes and Rennie lets Dr. Minnow order for her. "Sometimes I think I should have remained in Canada," he says. "I could live in an apartment, or a split-level bungalow, like all the sweet Canadians, and be a doctor of sheep. I even enjoy the snow. The first time it snowed, I ran out into it in my socks, without a coat; I danced, it made me so happy. But instead I come back here."

The green tea arrives and Rennie pours it. Dr. Minnow takes his cup, turns it around, sighs. "The love of your own country is a terrible curse, my friend," he says. "Especially a country like this one. It is much easier to live in someone else's country. Then you are not tempted."

"Tempted?" says Rennie.

"To change things," he says.

Rennie feels they're heading straight towards a conversation she doesn't really want to have. She tries to think of another topic. At home there's always the weather, but that won't do here, since there is no weather.

Dr. Minnow leans across the table towards her. "I will be

honest with you, my friend," he says. "There is something I wish you to do."

Rennie isn't surprised. Here it comes, whatever it is. "What's that?" she says warily.

"Allow me to explain," says Dr. Minnow. "This is our first election since the departure of the British. Perhaps it will be the last, since it is my own belief that the British parliamentary system will no longer work in this place. It works in Britain only because they have a tradition, there are still things that are inconceivable. Here, nothing is inconceivable." He pauses, sips at his tea. "I wish you to write about it."

Whatever Rennie's been expecting, it isn't this. But why not? People are always coming on to her about their favourite hot topic. She feels her eyes glaze over. *Great*, she should say. *Good idea.* Then they're satisfied. Instead she says, "What on earth could I write about it?"

"What you see," says Dr. Minnow, choosing not to pick up on her exasperation. "All I ask you to do is look. We will call you an observer, like our friends at the United Nations." He gives a small laugh. "Look with your eyes open and you will see the truth of the matter. Since you are a reporter, it is your duty to report."

Rennie reacts badly to the word *duty*. Duty was big in Griswold. "I'm not that kind of reporter," she says.

"I understand, my friend," says Dr. Minnow. "You are a travel writer, it is an accident you are here, but you are all we can turn to at the moment. There is no one else. If you were a political journalist the government would not have been happy to see you, they would have delayed your entry or expelled you. In any case, we are too small to attract the attention of anyone from the outside, and by the time they are interested it will be too late. They always wait for the blood."

"Blood?" says Rennie.

"News," says Dr. Minnow.

The waiter brings a platter of tiny corncobs and some things that look like steamed erasers, and another of greens and squid. Rennie picks up her chopsticks. A minute ago she was hungry.

"We have seventy-percent unemployment," says Dr. Minnow. "Sixty percent of our population is under twenty. Trouble happens when the people have nothing left to lose. Ellis knows this. He is using the foreign aid money from the hurricane to bribe the people. The hurricane was an act of God, and Ellis thinks that too. He hold out his hands to heaven and pray for someone up there to save his ass for him, and bang, all that money from the sweet Canadians. This is not all. He is using threats now, he says he will take away the jobs and maybe burn down the houses of those who do not vote for him."

"He's doing this openly?" says Rennie.

"On the radio, my friend," says Dr. Minnow. "As for the people, many are afraid of him and the rest admire him, not for this behaviour, you understand, but because he can get away with it. They see this as power and they admire a big man here. He spends their money on new cars and so forth for himself and friends, they applaud that. They look at me, they say, 'What you can do for us?' If you have nothing you are nothing here. It's the old story, my friend. We will have a Papa Doc and after that a revolution or so. Then the Americans will wonder why people are getting killed. They should tell the sweet Canadians to stop giving money to this man."

Rennie knows she's supposed to feel outrage. She remembers the early seventies, she remembers all that outrage you were supposed to feel. Not to feel it then was very unfashionable. At the moment though all she feels is imposed upon. Outrage is out of date.

"What good would it do, even if I wrote it?" says Rennie. "I couldn't get it published here, I don't know anyone."

Dr. Minnow laughs. "Not here," he says. "Here there is one paper only and Ellis has bought the editor. In any case, few can read. No, you should publish it there. This will be of help, they pay attention to the outside, they are sensitive about their foreign aid. They would know they are being watched, that someone knows what they are doing. This would stop excesses."

Rennie wonders what an excess is. "I'm sorry," she says, "but I can't think of anyone who would touch it. It isn't even a story yet, nothing's happened. It's hardly of general interest."

"There is no longer any place that is not of general interest," says Dr. Minnow. "The sweet Canadians have not learned this yet. The Cubans are building a large airport in Grenada. The CIA is here, they wish to nip history in the bud, and the Russian agents. It is of general interest to them."

Rennie almost laughs. The CIA has been done to death; surely by now it's a joke, he can't be serious. "I suppose they're after your natural resources," she says.

Dr. Minnow stares across at Rennie, smiling his cramped smile, no longer entirely kind and friendly. "As you know, we have a lot of sand and not much more. But look at a map, my friend." He's no longer pleading, he's lecturing. "South of St. Antoine is Ste. Agathe, south of Ste. Agathe is Grenada, south of Grenada is Venezuela with the oil, a third of U.S. imports. North of us there is Cuba. We are a gap in the chain. Whoever controls us controls the transport of oil to the United States. The boats go from Guyana to Cuba with rice, from Cuba to Grenada with guns. Nobody is playing."

Rennie puts down her chopsticks. It's too hot to eat. She feels as if she's stumbled into some tatty left-liberal journal with a two-colour cover because they can't afford three colours. She's allowed this conversation to go on too long, a minute more and she'll be hooked. "It's not my thing," she says. "I just don't do that kind of thing. I do lifestyles."

"Lifestyles?" says Dr. Minnow. He's puzzled.

"You know, what people wear, what they eat, where they go for their vacations, what they've got in their livingrooms, things like that," says Rennie, as lightly as she can.

Dr. Minnow considers this for a moment. Then he gives

her an angelic smile. "You might say that I also am concerned with lifestyles," he says. "It is our duty, to be concerned with lifestyles. What the people eat, what they wear, this is what I want you to write about."

He's got her. "Well, I'll think about it," she says limply.

"Good," says Dr. Minnow, beaming. "This is all I wish." He picks up his chopsticks again and scrapes the rest of the squid into his bowl. "Now I will give you a good piece of advice. You should be careful of the American."

"What American?" says Rennie.

"The man," says Dr. Minnow. "He is a salesman."

He must mean Paul. "What does he sell?" says Rennie, amused. This is the first she's heard of it.

"My friend," says Dr. Minnow. "You are so very sweet."

There's a small stationery shop across the street from the hotel, and Rennie goes into it. She passes over the historical romances, imported from England, and buys a local paper, *The Queenstown Times,* which is what she's come to the shop for. Guilt impels her: she owes at least this much to Dr. Minnow.

Though it's becoming clear to her that she has no intention of doing what he wants her to do. Even if she wanted to, she could hardly run all over the place, talking to men in the street; they don't understand the convention, they'd think she was trying to pick them up. She can't do proper research, there are no books in the library here; there's no library. She's a hypocrite, but what else is new? It's a Griswold solution: if you can't say anything nice, don't say anything at all. I'm dying, she should have told him. Don't count on me.

She orders tea and biscuits and takes the paper into the leatherette lounge. What she really wants is to lie down and sleep, and if she goes back to her room she knows she will. She's trying to resist that; it would be so easy here to do nothing but eat and sleep.

The Englishwoman brings the tea tray herself and slams

it down in front of Rennie. "I don't know where *they've* gone to," she says.

Rennie expects her to go away, but instead she hovers. "There's no water," she says. "They should have it fixed in a few hours." Still she lingers.

"May I offer you some advice?" she says at last. "Don't have anything to do with that man."

"What man?" says Rennie. The Englishwoman's voice suggests some violation of sexual morality, and Rennie wonders what she's done to deserve this.

"That man," says the Englishwoman. "Calls himself a doctor."

"He just wanted to show me the Botanic Gardens," says Rennie, conscious of a slight lie. She waits for the woman to tell her that Dr. Minnow is really a notorious sexual molester, but instead she says, "The trees have signs on them. You can read them yourself, if that's what you want."

"What's the matter with him?" says Rennie. Now she expects racial prejudice.

"He stirs people up for nothing," says the Englishwoman.

This time the biscuits are white and sprinkled with sand. The tea is lukewarm. Rennie fishes the teabag out by its string. She doesn't want to leave it on her saucer, it's too much like a dead mouse, so after some thought she conceals it in the earth around the mottled plant.

The editorial is about the election. Dr. Minnow, it seems, is almost as bad as Castro, and Prince Macpherson is worse. If anyone at all votes for either of them, they are likely to combine forces and form a coalition, and that will be the end of the democratic traditions that St. Antoine has cherished and protected for so long, says the editor.

On the front page there's a story about the new sugar factory Prime Minister Ellis is planning, and an article about road repairs. There's a picture of Ellis, the same picture that's everywhere on the posters. The Canadian High Commissioner has recently paid a visit from his base in Barbados, and a reception was given for him at Government House. Canada is sponsoring a diver training program for lobster fishermen on Ste. Agathe, where most of the fishermen live. The inhabitants of Songeville will be pleased to learn that the United States has contributed an extra five hundred thousand dollars to the hurricane relief fund, which will be used to repair roofs and fix the schoolhouse. Those still living in temporary camps and in churches will soon be able to return to their homes.

The Englishwoman comes back in, white-faced, tight-lipped, dragging an aluminum step ladder which screeches on the wooden floor. "If you want it done, do it yourself," she announces to Rennie. She sets the ladder up, climbs it, and starts taking down the tinsel festoons, her solid white-marbled calves two feet from Rennie's head. There's a strong smell of women's washrooms: tepid flesh, face powder, ammonia. Rennie tries to read a story about the sudden increase in petty thievery, but the Englishwoman is making her feel lazy and selfish. In a minute she'll offer to help and then she'll be stuck, catching those fuzzy fake poinsettias as the Englishwoman tosses them down and putting them away in that tatty cardboard box. She folds up her newspaper and retreats to her room, carrying her cup of cold tea.

"WHAT TO DO IF THE THIEF VISITS YOU," she reads. "1. Have a flashlight by your bed. 2. Have a large can of Baygon or other insect spray. 3. Shine the flashlight into his face. 4. Spray the Baygon into his face. 5. Go to the police, make a statement." Rennie wonders what the thief is supposed to do while you're spraying the Baygon into his face, but doesn't pursue this further. Like everything else she's been reading, the instructions are both transparent and impenetrable.

She skips the column entitled "Spiritual Perspectives," toys with the idea of doing the crossword puzzle but discards it; the answers are on page 10 and she knows she'll cheat. The

Housewives' Corner has nothing in it but a recipe for corn fritters. The Problem Corner is by Madame Marvellous.

Dear Madame Marvellous:

I am in love with a boy. Both of us are Christians. Sometimes he asks me for a kiss, but I have read that kissing before marriage is not right because it arouses passions that lead to sex. But he does not believe that sex before marriage is wrong. The Bible says fornication is wrong, but he says fornication is not sex. Please explain this in a clear way.

                                                    Worried.

Dear Worried:

My dear, love is the full expression of oneself. As long as you remember this you will not go wrong. I do hope I have helped you.

                                        Madame Marvellous.

Rennie closes her eyes and pulls the sheet up over her head. She doesn't have the strength to untangle the mosquito netting.

Oh please.

Rennie lies in bed and thinks about Daniel. Which is hopeless, but wasn't it always? The sooner she stops the better. Still, she keeps on.

It would be easier if Daniel were a pig, a prick, stupid or pompous or even fat; especially fat. Fat would be a big advantage. Unfortunately Daniel is thin. Also he loves Rennie, or so he said, which is no help at all. (Though what did it amount to? Not much, as far as Rennie could see. She isn't even sure what it meant, this love of his, or what he thought it meant; which may not be the same thing.)

Rennie once spent a lot of time trying to figure out what Daniel meant. Which was difficult, because he wasn't like any of the people she knew. The people she knew spoke of themselves as bottoming out and going through changes and getting it together. The first time she'd used these phrases with Daniel, she'd had to translate. Daniel had never bottomed out, as far as she could tell, and apparently he'd never felt the need to get it together. He didn't think of himself as having gone through changes. In fact he didn't seem to think of himself much in any way at all. This was the difference between Daniel and the people she knew: Daniel didn't think of himself.

This sometimes made it hard for Rennie to talk to him, since when she asked him questions about himself he didn't know the answers. Instead he acted as if he'd never even heard the questions. Where have you been for the past twenty years? she wanted to ask him. Etobicoke? It was more like Don Mills, but Daniel didn't seem to care where he lived. He didn't care what he ate, he didn't care what he wore: his clothes looked as if they'd been picked out by his wife, which they probably had been. He was a specialist, he'd been immersed, he knew only one thing.

He thought Rennie knew things he didn't know but ought to; he thought she lived in the real world. It pleased him to believe this, and Rennie wanted him to be pleased, she liked to amuse him, though she was afraid that sooner or later he would decide that the things she knew weren't really worth knowing. Meanwhile he was like a Patagonian in Woolworth's, he was enthralled by trivia. Maybe he's having a mid-life crisis, thought Rennie. He was about that age. Maybe he's slumming.

Sometimes they had lunch together, but not very often because most of Daniel's life was spoken for. At lunch Rennie did tricks, which was easy enough with Daniel: he could still be surprised by things that no longer surprised anyone else. She deduced the customers from their clothes, she did them over for him in front of his very eyes. This one, she said. A receptionist at, let's see, Bloor and Yonge, but she'd like you to think she's more. Overdid it on the eyeshadow. The man with her though, he's a lawyer. At the next table, middle management, probably in a bank. I'd redo the cuffs on the pants, the lawyer's, not the other one. On the other one, I'd redo the hair.

I don't see anything wrong with his hair, said Daniel.

You don't understand, Rennie said. People love being redone. I mean, you don't think you're finished, do you? Don't you want to change and grow? Don't you think there's more? Don't you want me to redo you? It was one of Rennie's jokes that the perfect magazine title would be "Sexual Makeovers." People thought of their lives as examinations they could fail or pass, you got points for the right answers. Tell them what was wrong, preferably with them, then suggest how to improve it. It gave them hope: Daniel should approve of that.

How would you redo me? said Daniel, laughing.

If I could get my hands on you? said Rennie. I wouldn't, you're perfect the way you are. See how good I'd be for your ego, if you had one?

Daniel said that he did have one, that he was quite selfish in fact, but Rennie didn't believe him. He didn't have time for an ego. During lunch he looked at his watch a lot, furtively but still a lot. "Romance Makes a Comeback," thought Rennie. She kept hoping she'd see enough of him so she'd begin to find him boring; talking with Daniel was a good deal like waltzing with a wall, even she knew that. But this failed to happen, partly because there wasn't a whole lot of him to see. When he wasn't at the hospital he had family obligations, as he put it. He had a wife, he had children, he had parents. Rennie had trouble picturing any of them, except the parents, whom she saw as replicas of American Gothic; only Finnish, which was what they were. They didn't have a lot of money and they were very proud of Daniel, who wasn't any more Finnish than she was except for the cheekbones. Sundays the parents got him; Saturdays were for the kids, evenings for the wife. Daniel was a dutiful husband, a dutiful parent, a dutiful son, and Rennie, who felt she had given up being dutiful some time ago, found it hard not to sneer and hard not to despise herself for wanting to.

She wasn't jealous of his wife, though. Only of his other patients. Maybe I'm not the only one, thought Rennie. Maybe there's a whole lineup of them, dozens and dozens of women, each with a bite taken out of them, one breast or the other. He's saved all our lives, he has lunch with us all in turn, he tells us all he loves us. He thinks it's his duty, it gives us something to hold on to. Anyway he gets off on it, it's like a harem. As for us, we can't help it, he's the only man in the world who knows the truth, he's looked into each one of us and seen death. He knows we've been resurrected, he knows we're not all that well glued together, any minute we'll vaporize. These bodies are only provisional.

At the beginning, when she still believed she could return to normal, Rennie thought that they would see each other a certain number of times and then they would have an affair; naturally; that's what people did. But this also failed to happen. Instead, Daniel spent one whole lunch explaining, earnestly and unhappily, why he couldn't go to bed with her.

It would be unethical, he said. I'd be taking advantage of you. You're in an emotional state.

What is this, thought Rennie, Rex Morgan, M.D.? People she knew prided themselves on taking emotional risks. She couldn't decide whether Daniel was being wise, principled or just a coward.

Why is it such a big deal? she said. Once wouldn't kill you. Behind a bush, it would only take five minutes.

It wouldn't be once, he said.

Rennie felt suspended; she was waiting all the time, for something to happen. Maybe I'm an event freak, she thought. The people she knew, Jocasta for instance, would have regarded it all as an experience. Experiences were like other collectables, you kept adding them to your set. Then you traded them with your friends. Show and tell. But Rennie had trouble thinking of Daniel as just an experience; besides, what was there to tell?

What do you get out of this? she said. What do you want?

Does there have to be something? he said. I just want it to go on the way it is.

But what *is* it? she said. It isn't anything. There's nothing to it.

He looked hurt and she was ashamed of herself. What he probably wanted was escape, like everyone else; a little but not too much, a window but not a door.

I could ask you the same thing, he said.

I want you to save my life, thought Rennie. You've done it once, you can do it again. She wanted him to tell her she was fine, she wanted to believe him.

I don't know, she said. She didn't know. Probably she didn't really want him to go to bed with her or even touch her; probably she loved him because he was safe, there was absolutely nothing he could demand.

Sometimes they held hands, discreetly, across the table in the corners of restaurants; which, in those weeks and then those months, was about as much as she could stand. Afterwards she could feel the shape of his hand for hours.

There's someone knocking at the door. The room is dark. Whatever sings at night is singing outside her window, and there is the same music.

The knocking goes on. Perhaps it's the maid, coming far too late, to make up the bed. Rennie pulls off the damp sheet, walks to the door in her bare feet, unlocks it, opens it. Paul is there, one shoulder leaning against the wall, looking not at all like a salesman.

"You shouldn't unlock your door like that," he says. "It could be anyone." He's smiling though.

Rennie feels at a disadvantage without her shoes on. "I'm lucky this time," she says. She's glad to see him: he's the closest facsimile here to someone she knows. Maybe they can just skip yesterday and start again, as if nothing at all has happened. Which is true enough, since nothing has.

"I thought you might like dinner," he says, "some place with real food."

"I'll put on my shoes," says Rennie. She turns on the mermaid lamp. Paul comes into the room and closes the door, but he doesn't sit down. He just stands, gazing around as if it's an art gallery, while Rennie picks up her sandals and purse and goes into the bathroom to see what she looks like. She brushes her hair and sticks on a little blue eyeliner pencil, not too much. She thinks about changing her dress but decides against it; it might look anxious. When she comes out he's sitting on the edge of her bed.

"I was having a nap," says Rennie, feeling she has to explain the unmade bed.

"I see you got Lora's box for her all right," he says. "Any problems?"

"No," says Rennie, "except it was a little bigger than I thought, and now I don't know what to do with it." It occurs to her that she may be able to fob the box off on Paul, since he knows Lora. "I don't know where this woman lives," she says, as helplessly as she can.

"Elva?" says Paul. "You just take it over to Ste. Agathe, there's a boat every day at noon. Once you get there anyone can tell you." He doesn't offer to take it himself.

Rennie turns off the mermaid lamp and locks the door and they walk out past the front desk and the Englishwoman's laser-beam gaze, and Rennie feels she's sneaking out of the dorm.

"The dinner's part of the plan," says the Englishwoman behind them.

"Pardon?" says Rennie.

"If you don't eat it you pay for it anyway. It's part of the plan."

"I realize that," says Rennie.

"We lock up at twelve," says the Englishwoman.

Rennie's beginning to understand why she dislikes this woman so much. It's the disapproval, automatic and self-righteous, it's the ill-wishing. Rennie knows all about that, it's part of her background. Whatever happens to Rennie the Englishwoman will say she was asking for it; as long as it's bad.

They go down the stone steps and through the damp little courtyard and step out into the musical night. Paul takes hold of Rennie's arm above the elbow, his fingers digging in. "Just keep going," he says. He's steering her.

Now she sees what he's talking about. A little way up the street, in the dim light over by the stationery store, two of the blue-shirted policemen are beating a man up. The man is on his knees in the pot-holed road and they're kicking him, in the stomach, on the back. All Rennie can think of is that the two policemen are wearing shoes and the man isn't. She's never seen anyone being beaten up like this before, only pictures of it. As soon as you take a picture of something it's a picture. Picturesque. This isn't.

Rennie has stopped, though Paul is pushing her, trying to keep her moving. "They don't like you to stare," he says. Rennie's not sure who he means. Does he mean the policemen, or the people they beat up? It would be shaming, to have other people see you so helpless. There are other people on the street, the usual clumps and knots, but they aren't staring, they're looking and then looking away. Some of them are walking, nobody is doing anything, although the walking ones deflect themselves, they go carefully around the man, who is now doubled over.

"Come on," says Paul, and this time Rennie moves. The man is struggling onto his knees; the policemen are standing back, watching him with what seems like mild curiosity, two children watching a beetle they've crippled. Perhaps now they will drop stones on him, thinks Rennie, remembering the schoolyard. To see which way he will crawl. Her own fascination appals her. He lifts his face and there's blood streaming down it, they must have cut his head, he looks directly at Rennie. Rennie can remember drunks on Yonge Street, men so drunk they can't stand up, looking up at her like that. Is it an appeal, a plea for help, is it hatred? She's been seen, she's being seen with utter thoroughness, she won't be forgotten.

It's the old man. He can't be totally mute because there's a sound of some kind coming out of him, a moaning, a stifled reaching out for speech which is worse than plain silence.

They reach the jeep and this time Paul opens the door and helps her in, he wants her in there as fast as possible. He closes the door carefully, tests it to make sure it's really shut.

"Why were they doing that?" Rennie says. She's pressing her hands together, she refuses to shake.

"Doing what?" says Paul. He's a little sharp, a little annoyed. She stalled on him.

"Come on," says Rennie.

Paul shrugs. "He was drunk," he says. "Or maybe they caught him thieving. He was hanging around the hotel when I came in, they don't like people bothering the tourists. It's bad for business."

"That was horrible," says Rennie.

"Up north they lock them up, down here they just beat them up a little. I know which I'd choose," says Paul.

"That wasn't a little," says Rennie.

Paul looks over at her and smiles. "Depends what you think a lot is," he says.

Rennie shuts up. She's led a sheltered life, he's telling her. Now she's annoyed with herself for acting so shocked. Squealing at mice, standing on a chair with your skirts hitched up, that's the category. *Girl*.

Paul drives through the darkness with elaborate slowness, for her benefit. "You can go faster," she says. "I'm not about to throw up." He smiles, but he doesn't.

The Driftwood at night is much the same as the Driftwood by day, except that it's floodlit. There's a half-hearted steel band and two couples are dancing to it. The women are wearing shirts made from fake flour sacks; the blonde is taking pictures with a flashcube camera, the brunette is wearing a captain's cap, backwards. One of the men has a green shirt with parrots on it. The other one is shorter, fatter, with the fronts of his legs so badly burned that the skin is peeling off in rags. He's wearing a red T-shirt that says BIONIC COCK. It's the usual bunch, from Wisconsin Rennie decides, dentists and their wives fresh off the plane, their flesh like uncooked Dover sole, flying down to run themselves briefly under the grill. The dentists come here, the dental assistants go to Barbados, that's the difference.

Rennie and Paul sit at a metal table and Rennie orders a ginger ale. She's not going to get sick in the jeep again, once was enough. She's thinking about the man on his knees in the dark road, but what is there to think? Except that she's not hungry. She watches the awkward stiff-legged dancers, the steel-band men, who are supple, double-jointed almost, glancing at them with a contempt that is almost but not quite indifference.

"Dentists from Wisconsin?" she says to Paul.

"Actually they're Swedes," he says. "There's been a rash of Swedes lately. Swedes tell other Swedes, back in Sweden. Then all of a sudden the place is swarming with them."

"How can you tell?" says Rennie, impressed.

Paul smiles at her. "I found out," he says. "It's not hard. Everyone finds out about everyone else around here, they're curious. It's a small place, anything new or out of the ordinary gets noticed pretty fast. A lot of people are curious about you, for instance."

"I'm not out of the ordinary," says Rennie.

"Here you are," he says. "You're at the wrong hotel, for one thing. It's mostly package tours and little old ladies who stay there. You should be at the Driftwood." He pauses, and Rennie feels she has to supply an answer.

"Pure economics," she says. "It's a cheap magazine."

Paul nods, as if this is acceptable. "They wonder why you aren't with a man," he says. "If you'd come on a boat they'd know why, they'd figure you're just boat-hopping. Girls do that quite a bit here, it's like hitchhiking, in more ways than one. But you don't seem the type. Anyway, they know you came in on the plane." A smile, another pause. It occurs to Rennie that it may not be *they* who want to know these things about her, it may only be Paul. A small prickle goes down her spine.

"If they know so much, they must know what I'm doing here," she says, keeping her voice even. "It's business. I'm doing a travel piece. I hardly need a chaperone for that."

Paul smiles. "White women have a bad reputation down here," he says. "For one thing, they're too rich; for another they lower the moral tone."

"Come on," says Rennie.

"I'm just telling you what they think," says Paul. "The women here think they spoil the local men. They don't like the way white women dress, either. You'd never see a local woman wearing shorts or even pants, they think it's degenerate. If they started behaving like that their men would beat the shit out of them. If you tried any of that Women's Lib stuff down here they'd only laugh. They say that's for the white women. Everyone knows white women are naturally lazy and they don't want to do a woman's proper work, and that's why they hire black women to do their work for them." He looks at her with something between a challenge and a smirk, which Rennie finds irritating.

"Is that why you like it here?" she says. "You get your grapes peeled for you?"

"Don't blame it on me," Paul says, with a little shrug. "I didn't invent it."

He's watching her react, so she tries not to. After a minute he goes on. "They also think you aren't only a journalist. They don't believe you're really just writing for a magazine."

"But I am!" says Rennie. "Why wouldn't they believe that?"

"They don't know much about magazines," says Paul. "Anyway, almost nobody here is who they say they are at first. They aren't even who somebody else thinks they are. In this place you get at least three versions of everything, and if you're lucky one of them is true. That's if you're lucky."

"Does all this apply to you?" says Rennie, and Paul laughs.

"Let me put it this way," he says. "For ten thousand dollars you can buy a St. Antoine passport; officially, I mean, unofficially it costs more. That's if you've got the right connections. If you want to, you can open your own private bank. The government even helps you do it, for a cut of the action. Certain kinds of people find it very convenient."

"What are you telling me?" says Rennie, who senses increasingly she's been asked out to dinner for a reason, which is not the same as the reason she had for accepting. She looks into his light-blue eyes, which are too light, too blue. They've seen too much water. Burned out, she thinks.

Paul smiles, a kindly threatening smile. "I like you," he says. "I guess I'm trying to tell you not to get too mixed up in local politics. That is, if you really are writing a travel piece."

"Local *politics*?" says Rennie, taken by surprise.

Paul sighs. "You remind me of a certain kind of girl back home," he says. "The kind who move to New York from the Midwest and get jobs on magazines."

"In what way?" says Rennie, dismayed.

"For one thing you're nice," says Paul. "You'd rather not

be, you'd rather be something else, tough or sharp or something like that, but you're nice, you can't help it. Naïve. But you think you have to prove you're not merely nice, so you get into things you shouldn't. You want to know more than other people, am I right?"

"I don't have the faintest idea what you're talking about," says Rennie, who feels seen through. She wonders if he's right. Once he would have been, once there were all kinds of things she wanted to know. Now she's tired of it.

Paul sighs. "Okay," he says. "Just remember, nothing that goes on here has anything to do with you. And I'd stay away from Minnow."

"Dr. Minnow?" says Rennie. "Why?"

"Ellis doesn't like him," says Paul. "Neither do some other people."

"I hardly know him," says Rennie.

"You had lunch with him," says Paul, almost accusingly.

Rennie laughs. "Am I going to get shot, for having *lunch*?"

Paul doesn't think this is funny. "Probably not," he says. "They mostly shoot their own. Let's go get something to eat."

Under an open-sided hut with fake thatching there's a buffet laid out, bowls of salad, platters of roast beef, lime pies, chocolate cakes with hibiscus flowers stuck into them. As much as you can eat. There are more people now, piling food high on their plates. To Rennie, they all look Swedish.

She takes her plate back to the table. Paul is silent now and absent. It's almost as if he's in a hurry to get away. Rennie sits across from him, eating shrimp and feeling like a blind date, the comic-book kind with buck teeth and pimples. In situations like this she reverts to trying to please, or is it appease? Maybe he's with the CIA, it would all fit in, the warning and the neo-hippie haircut, camouflage, and the time in Cambodia, and the boats he shouldn't be able to afford. The more she thinks about it the more sense it makes. She's innocent, she doesn't want him to get the wrong impression, he might end up putting some kind of weird drug into her guava jam. Does he think she's a dangerous subversive because she had lunch with Dr. Minnow? She wonders how she can convince him that she is who she is. Would he believe drain-chain jewellery?

Finally she asks him about tennis courts. She wants things to return to normal; she wants the situation to normalize, as they say on the news. "Tennis courts?" Paul says, as if he's never heard of them.

Rennie feels that she's been investigated and dismissed, she's been pronounced negligible, and this is either because Paul believes her or because he doesn't. Which is worse, to be irrelevant or to be dishonest? Whichever it is has erased her as far as he's concerned. As for her, all she can think of is how to recapture his interest, now that it's no longer there. She's almost forgotten there's some of her missing. She realizes she was looking forward, though to what she doesn't know. An event, that's all. Something. She's had enough blank space recently to last her for a long time.

Rennie and Jocasta were trying on used fur coats in the Sally Ann at Richmond and Spadina. According to Jocasta this was the best Sally Ann in the city. It was really Jocasta who was trying them on, since Rennie didn't have much interest in used fur coats, she stuck to her classic down-fill from Eddie Bauer's. They were supposed to be shopping for Rennie; Jocasta thought it would make her feel better if she went out and bought something. But she should have known. With Jocasta you always ended up in the Sally Ann.

I won't wear seal though, said Jocasta. I draw the line. Look at this, what do you think it is?

Dyed rabbit, said Rennie. You're safe.

Jocasta turned the pockets inside out. There was a stained handkerchief in one of them. What I'm really looking for, she said, is a black hat with a pheasant feather, you know those curved ones? Gloria Swanson. How's everything?

I'm having a thing with this man, said Rennie, who had resolved many times never to discuss this with anyone, especially Jocasta.

Jocasta looked at her. The pause was just a little too long, and Rennie could hear Jocasta wondering how much of her was gone, chopped away; under all that, you couldn't tell really. A thing with a man. *Bizarre.* Possibly even gross.

That's wizard, said Jocasta, who liked resurrecting outmoded slang. Love or sex?

I'm not sure, said Rennie.

Love, Jocasta said. Lucky you. I can't seem to get it up for love any more. It's such an effort.

She slipped her arms into a late forties lantern-sleeve muskrat, while Rennie held it for her. A little tatty around the collar, but not bad, said Jocasta. So it's walking-on-air time, a little pitty-pat of the heart, steamy dreams, a little how-you-say purple passion? Spots on the neck, wet pits? Buying your trousseau yet?

Not exactly, said Rennie. He's married.

Before Daniel, Rennie had never paid much attention to married men. The mere fact that they were married ruled them out, not because they were off-limits but because they had demonstrated their banality. Having a married man would be like having a Group of Seven washable silkscreen reproduction in your livingroom. Only banks had those any more, and not the best banks, either.

Lately, though, she'd been seeing it from a different angle. Maybe Daniel wasn't an afterglow from the past; maybe he was the wave of the future. As Jocasta said about her wardrobe, save it up. Never throw anything away, because time is circular and sooner or later it all comes round again. Maybe experiments in living, trying it out first, and infinitely renegotiable relationships were fading fast. Soon Daniel would be *in*, limited options would be *in*. No way out would be *in*. Group of Seven silkscreens were coming back too, among the ultra *nouveau wavé*, but they had to be washable.

Sometimes married is better than not married, Jocasta said. They've got their own lives, they don't need to muck up yours. You can do it in the afternoon, have a nice fuck, hear all about how important you are in their life, listen to their little troubles, their mortgage, the way their kid grinds chewed-up caramels into the shag, how they had to get the clutch on the Volvo replaced, and then you can go out with someone fun at night. I used to like stoles, but you know those little shortie jackets they used to wear with formals? With the handkerchief pocket. They're better.

You don't quite see it, said Rennie. He's *really* married. He thinks of himself as married.

You mean he says stuff like his wife doesn't understand him, Jocasta said. That can be boring. Usually their wife understands them backwards, that's the problem. I went through all that ten years ago, when I was still a junior buyer for Creeds. Every time I had to go to New York; it was the goddamn supervisor. He thought I was so *dirty*, you know? *Turkey*ville! I must have been desperate, I hadn't discovered cucumbers then. What they usually mean is that their wives won't go down on them, as far as I can figure out. Kids? Let me guess. Two.

Three and a half, Rennie said.

You mean one's brain-damaged? said Jocasta, looking over her shoulder in the mirror. Waltz length. Remember waltz length?

No, said Rennie. His wife's pregnant again.

And he loves his wife, of course, said Jocasta. And she loves him. Right?

I'm afraid so, said Rennie.

Daniel had not said *I'm afraid so*. He'd said *I think so*.

You mean you don't know? said Rennie.

We don't talk about it, he said. I guess she does. She does.

So sit back and enjoy it, said Jocasta. What do you have to worry about? Except Jake, but he's cool.

Rennie wondered how cool Jake actually was. She hadn't told him about Daniel. Daniel, however, asked about Jake almost every time they saw each other. How's Jake? he would say hopefully, and Rennie would always say, Fine. She knew about bookends, she knew that one wouldn't work without the other. Any damage to Jake, and Daniel would be off and running. He wouldn't want to be stuck with the whole package. She might be the icing on his cake but she sure as hell wasn't the cake.

Jake's a grownup, she said. *Open-ended* is one of his favourite words.

Well, there you go, said Jocasta. Nifty. Two's better than one any day, as long as you don't go all soft and grubby and Heartbreak Hotel.

You still don't see it, said Rennie. Nothing's happening.

Nothing? said Jocasta.

Unless you count some pretty frantic hand-holding, said Rennie. She was embarrassed to have to admit this, she knew how abnormal it was, but she wasn't as embarrassed as she would have been once. The fact was that she wasn't sure whether she wanted it or not, an affair with Daniel. It would not be what you would call relaxed, it wouldn't be very much fun. Pulling the plug on all that repression. It would be like going over Niagara Falls in a spin-dryer, you could get injured that way.

Why not? said Jocasta.

I told you, said Rennie. He's too married.

They looked at one another. Nothing, said Jocasta. Weird. She put her hand on Rennie's shoulder. Listen, she said, it could be worse. Look at it this way. I mean, an affair's just another affair, what else is new? It's like one chocolate bar after another; you start having these fantasies about being a nun, and you know what, they're enjoyable. But nothing, that's kind of romantic; he must think a lot of you. There's something to be said for nothing.

After the chocolate cake they drive back, straight back, no stopping in the woods this time. Rennie sits jolting in the front seat, trying not to feel disappointed. What does she need it for anyway? It's foolishness, as her grandmother would say. Her mother too. They all have the category, it gets passed down like a cedar chest, though they each put different things into it.

When they reach the hotel Paul doesn't touch her, not even a peck on the cheek. He opens his door and gets out, whistling through his teeth. He doesn't take her hand to help her down, he takes her arm, and he doesn't go as far as her room. He waits at the bottom of the stone stairs until she reaches the top, that's all.

Rennie walks down the green wooden corridor, feeling very tired. What is she supposed to make of all this? Why is she trying to make anything? He asked her for dinner and dinner is what she got. She remembers seeing a film, years ago, about the effects of atomic radiation on the courtship instincts of animals: birds ignoring each other or attacking instead of dancing, fish going around in lopsided circles instead of spawning, turtles leaving their eggs to fry in the sun, unfertilized anyway. Maybe this is what accounts for the New Chastity: a few too many deadly rays zapping the pineal gland. The signals are all screwed up and nobody understands any more what they used to mean.

What she remembers most clearly about the evening is not even Paul. It's the deaf and dumb man on his knees in the street, the two men kicking at him, then watching him with that detachment, that almost friendly interest.

A long time ago, about a year ago, Jocasta said, I think it would be a great idea if all the men were turned into women and all the women were turned into men, even just for a day. Then they'd all know exactly how the other ones would like to be treated. When they got changed back, I mean. Don't you think that's a great idea?

It's a great *idea,* said Rennie.

But would you vote for it? said Jocasta.

Probably not, said Rennie.

That's the problem with great ideas, said Jocasta. Nobody votes for them.

Jocasta thinks it would be a great idea if all the men were changed into women and all the women were changed into men for a week. Then they'd each know how to treat the other ones when they got changed back, said Rennie.

Jocasta's full of crap, said Jake. And too bony. Bony women shouldn't wear V-necks.

What's the matter with it? said Rennie. Wouldn't you like to know how women want to be treated? Wouldn't it make you irresistible?

Not if everyone else knew it too, said Jake. But first of all, that isn't what would happen. The women would say, Now I've got you, you prick. Now it's my turn. They'd all become rapists. Want to bet?

What would the men say? said Rennie.

Who knows? said Jake. Maybe they'd just say, Oh shit. Maybe they'd say they don't feel like it tonight because they're getting their periods. Maybe they'd want to have babies. Myself, I could do without it. Feh.

That would take more than a week, said Rennie.

Anyway, said Jake, do you really know how you want to be treated? You ever met anyone who does?

You mean any women, don't you, said Rennie.

Skip the semantics, said Jake. Tell the truth. Tell me how you want to be treated. In twenty-five words or less. You say it, I'll do it.

Rennie began to laugh. All right, she said. Is that a promise?

Later she said, It depends who by.

* * *

Rennie unlocks the door of her room. The mermaid lamp is on, and for a moment she can't remember whether or not she turned it off when she left. She could swear she did. There's a smell in the room that wasn't there before.

She sees her notebook, laid out on the bed, with the material she's been collecting, maps and brochures, neatly beside it. Someone's been in here. Rennie senses an ambush. She had her purse with her, the camera and lenses are at the front desk, there's nothing anyone would want. Is there? She opens the bureau drawer and hunts for the joints but they're safely in place.

In the bathroom her cosmetic bag has been emptied into the sink: toothbrush, toothpaste, Love deodorant, dental floss, bottle of aspirins, the works. Two of the glass louvres have been slid out of the metal frame that holds them in place. They're nowhere in sight, they must be outside somewhere, on a balcony, a fire escape, the ground, who knows what's out there, and there's no way of putting them back. That is how he got in, sliding himself into the bathroom like an anonymous letter. The man in the bathing suit. She thinks of herself standing there with a flashlight and a can of insect spray. God knows what he'd do, she's glad she wasn't here.

But it's only a thief, there are worse things. Whatever he wanted, which was probably only money, he didn't get: nothing is missing. She moves her notebook, *Fun in the Sunspots*, and sits down on the bed. Then she looks under it.

The box is there all right, but it's been opened, the packing tape slit neatly. Styrofoam beads leak out onto the floor. Perhaps he's made off with the heart medicine. She slides the box out, lifts the flap, and thrusts her hand into the fake snow.

At first there's nothing. Then there are two tins of smoked oysters, which Rennie sets on the floor, and after that her hand hits something that is in no way like a tin of anything at all, except that it's hard and metallic. Rennie pulls and it comes towards her, scattering Styrofoam beads. This is something else she's only seen pictures of. It's the front end of a small machine gun.

Rennie shoves it back, replaces the smoked oysters and the Styrofoam beads, and closes the flap. She wonders if the Englishwoman has any Scotch tape. She pushes the box as far under the bed as it will go and re-arranges the chenille coverlet, spreading it so it hangs to the floor.

This, thinks Rennie, is an exceptionally tacky movie. What next, what now? It's not even a good lunchtime story, since the main point of it would have to be her own stupidity. Dumb, gullible, naïve, to believe people; it came from drinking too much. Now she must try not to panic.

Everything, especially this room, is now unsafe, but it happens to be the middle of the night and there's no way she can move. She can't report the break-in to the police or even to the Englishwoman: she may be naïve but it's not terminal. No one would believe she didn't know what was in the box when she picked it up at the airport. Lora knows, of course: that's why she sent Rennie instead of picking it up herself. Who else knows? Whoever sent the box. Harold the customs official, maybe. And now another man, possibly in a bathing suit. A faceless stranger. Mr. X, in the bedroom, with a knife.

Rennie goes to the bathroom door, closes it, tries to lock it. She doesn't want anyone else coming in through the bathroom window while she's asleep. The lock is broken. She opens the bureau drawer again, takes out Lora's joints, crumbles them into the toilet and flushes them down. She refolds her mix 'n' match wardrobe and packs it into her bag. She cleans her things out of the bathroom. Then she lies down on the bed in her clothes and turns out the light. She wants somebody to be with her, she wants somebody to be with. A warm body, she doesn't much care whose.

IV

In the summer, soon after she'd come out of the hospital, Rennie called up Jocasta and asked if they could have lunch. She wanted some support. *Support* was what the women she knew said to each other, which had once made Rennie think of stretch stockings for varicose veins. Firm support, for life crises or anything else you could mention. Once Rennie had not intended to have life crises and she did not feel in need of support. But now she did. Jocasta was a little too surprised to hear from her, a little too pleased.

Rennie made it to the restaurant in the usual way, one foot in front of the other on a sidewalk that wasn't really there; but it was important to keep your balance, it was important to behave normally. If you did that enough, Daniel said, sooner or later you would begin to feel normal.

Jocasta drank red wine and Perrier and gobbled up her spinach salad in no time flat. Then she started on the bread. She didn't ask Rennie how she was, she didn't ask her anything. Politely, elaborately, she avoided the subject of Rennie. If anyone brought it up it wouldn't be her.

Rennie picked at her quiche, watching Jocasta's angular

face with the huge mime's eyes. She wondered whether she herself would be that odd at forty. She wondered whether she would ever be forty. She wanted Jocasta to reach across the table, past the breadbasket and the blue silk rose in the bud vase, and put her hand on top of Rennie's and say that everything was going to be fine. She wanted to tell Jocasta she was dying.

Jocasta had just moved in with someone, or was it out on someone? Go with the flow, said Jocasta. She did a lot of moving. She was talking much too fast, Rennie embarrassed the hell out of her. Rennie concentrated on behaving normally. If she drank just enough but not too much, she could do it.

Who knows what goes on in their heads? said Jocasta. They were well into the second carafe of wine. Not me, I've stopped even trying. It used to be women that were so mysterious, remember? Well, not any more, now it's men. Me, I'm an open book. All I want is a good enough time, no hassle, a few laughs, a little how-you-say romance, I'll take the violins if they're going around, dim lights, roses, fantastic sex, let *them* scrape the pâté off the rug in the morning, is that too much to ask? Are they afraid of my first name or something, is that it? Remember when we all batted our eyes and pretended not to know what dirty jokes meant and crossed our legs a lot and they chased around like pigs after a truffle and God did they complain. Frigid, cock teaser, professional virgin, remember those? Remember panty girdles, remember *falsies,* remember Peter Pan brassieres in the front seat after the formal, with your wires digging into his chest?

Rennie didn't remember these things too well. But she didn't say so, she didn't want to remind Jocasta about her age.

There's probably men still around who don't think a woman's a woman unless she feels like a car grille or the insides of a toaster, said Jocasta. Not the back seat though,

God forbid the word should get around you were an easy out.

Well, so two months ago this man, a nice enough man, nice shoulders, said why didn't we go out for dinner. I've known him a while, I like him okay, he's fine, nothing wrong with him, not ultra bright but not a nylon stocking murderer either, and I've always felt I wouldn't mind, you know. If the occasion should arise. Well, it looked as if it was arising, pardon the pun, so I tarted myself up, nothing too obvious, I just bought this fabulous black knitted sheath for the store, remember bat wings?

So out we go, he was paying it seems, though I did offer, it's a new place over on Church, not too many of those damn asparagus ferns shedding down your back, I had the quails, which was a mistake, gnawing those tiny bones and trying to look soignée. But everything was going fine, a lot of eye contact, we talked about his career, he's into real estate, doing up downtown houses. All he has to do is beat off the Marxists, the ones that rent rather than owning. The ones that own don't care, it jacks up their property values.

So I admire him some and he asks me back to his place, and we sit on the broadloom drinking white wine, and he puts on a record, Bartok, which I thought was a little heavy for the occasion but never mind, and he wants to talk about himself some more. Okay, I don't mind listening, but all this time he doesn't touch me. What's the matter, you think I have vaginal warts, I want to ask him, but I'm doing some serious listening, it's all about his two business partners and how they can't express anger. I personally think it's just dandy when people can't express anger, there's enough of it in the world already.

So nothing happens and finally I say, I'm really tired, this certainly has been nice but I've got to get home, and he says, Why don't you stay the night? Funny you should ask, I think, though I don't say it, so we go into the bedroom and I swear to God he turns around so his *back* is to me and he takes off all his clothes. I can't believe it, I stand there with my mouth open, and before you know it he's all tucked into his side of the bed, he was practically wearing striped flanellette pyjamas if you know what I mean. He asks if I want the light on or off, and by this time I'm so freaked I say *off,* so he turns it off and there I am, taking my clothes off all by myself in the dark. If I was smart I'd have left them on and headed fast for the Down elevator, but you know me, Little Mary Sunshine, ever hopeful, so I climb into the bed, expecting to be embraced passionately, maybe he's just afraid of the light, but he says good night and turns over and goes to sleep!

Talk about feeling like an asshole. Now if a girl did that, what would she be called? There I was, horny as hell from looking at his *shoulders* for about five hours, and he's sleeping away like a baby. So I got up and spent the night on his sofa.

So in the morning he waltzes in, all bright and shiny in his brown velour dressing gown with the monogram on the pocket, with two glasses of fresh orange juice, and he says, Where did *you* go last night? When I woke up this morning you weren't there.

He hadn't even noticed, he hadn't noticed all night that I was gone.

I'm sorry, I said, but I think we have a semantic problem. A problem in communications, or maybe it's linguistics. What does *spending the night* usually mean to you? I mean, I'm not knocking the orange juice but I don't have to spend the night on the sofa to get it, I can squeeze it myself, you know what I mean?

Well, it turns out he's having an identity crisis, boy, am I sick of those. Before this he's only made it with younger, dumber chicks, women who're easy to impress, he says, and he's never tried it with someone like me, notice he meant old and wise, like an owl maybe. If you have to be a bird, which would you rather be, a chick or an owl? He's not sure someone like me would think he has anything to offer besides sex, and he wants to be valued for himself, whatever that is. Chin*ese*! He wants a long-term meaningful relationship. I can tell he was a bedwetter as a child. Maybe still is for all I know.

I'm sitting there with my hair not brushed and I really have to pee, but I don't want to interrupt him because he obviously finds this important, and I'm thinking, I've heard this before, only it used to be women saying it to men. I can't believe it! And I'm thinking, do I want a long-term meaningful relationship with this guy? And then I'm thinking, *does* he have anything to offer besides sex?

Well, the answer was no. But that didn't used to matter, did it? How come it matters all of a sudden? Why do we have to start respecting their *minds*? Who keeps changing the rules, them or us? You know how many times that's happened to me since then? Three more times! It's an epidemic! What do they *want*?

My theory is that when sex was such a big deal, above the waist, below the waist, with stages of achievement marked on it like the United Appeal thermometer, they wanted it that way because you could measure it, you could win, scoring, you know? Our team against their team. Getting away with it. One in the teeth for Mummy. So we said, you want it, fine, we want it too, let's get together, and all of a sudden millions of pricks went limp. Nation*wide*! That's my theory. The new scoring is *not* scoring. Just so long as you keep control. They don't want love and understanding and meaningful relationships, they still want sex, but only if they can *take* it. Only if you've got something to lose, only if you struggle a little. It helps if you're eight years old, one way or another. You follow me?

Jocasta paid for Rennie's lunch. That meant she thought Rennie was in terrible shape, on the brink of death in fact, since ordinarily she never paid for anything if she could help it.

I'm hardly dead yet, Rennie wanted to say. But she was touched by this gesture, it was support after all, Jocasta had done what she could. She had paid for the lunch, which was a big thing, and she'd been as amusing as possible, a cheerful bedside visit in the terminal ward. Talk about your own life, life after all goes on, shun morbid subjects. A positive attitude does wonders for out-of-control cell division.

Rennie walked back to the apartment, unsupported, one foot in front of the other, keeping her balance. When she got there Jake was sitting in the livingroom. There were two beer bottles, Carlsberg, on the floor beside the plump pink chair. Ordinarily he never drank from the bottle. He didn't get up.

Once Rennie would have known why he was there, in the middle of the day. But he would not have been sitting in a chair, he would have been hiding behind the door, he'd have grabbed her from behind.

What's wrong? she said.

Jake looked up at her. His eyes were puffy, he hadn't been sleeping well lately. Neither had Rennie, as far as that went, but every time she mentioned it it turned out he'd slept even worse than she had. They were competing for each other's pity, which was too bad because neither of them seemed to have a lot of it lying around, they'd been using it up on themselves.

Rennie went over and kissed Jake on the top of the head. He looked so awful.

He took her hand, held on to it. We should try again, said Jake.

If I could do it over again I'd do it a different way, says Lora, God knows. Except maybe I wouldn't, you know? Look before you leap, my mother used to say, not that she ever did, she never had the time. When they're right behind you you don't look, you only leap, you better believe it, because if you don't leap that's fucking it, eh? Just keep moving, is my motto.

The year I turned sixteen my mother got a job selling Avon door to door, so she wasn't there in the afternoons when I got home. I didn't like being there in the cellar with just Bob, he gave me the creeps, so I used to hang out after school with Gary, that's my boyfriend. Sometimes we'd skip after lunch, and we'd have a few beers in his car, he sure loved that car, and then we'd neck afterwards. We never went all the way. Everyone thought it was the girls like me and Marie who went all the way, but mostly it was the nice girls. They figured it was okay if you were going with the guy and you were in love with him. Sometimes they'd get caught, that was before the Pill was a big thing or abortions either, and Marie and me would kill ourselves laughing, because we were the ones always getting accused of it.

At that high school they thought we were the tough girls and I guess we thought that too. We wore this heavy eye makeup and white lipstick, I guess we were something. But I never let myself get too drunk or carried away or anything. When the nice girls got in trouble their parents bought them trips to the States to get fixed up, but I knew what happened to you if you couldn't afford it. Somebody's kitchen table. There was one girl a couple of grades ahead of us at school, she tried it herself with a knitting needle only it didn't work. The teachers told us it was some kind of a rare disease but everyone knew the truth, it got around. As for me, I knew Bob would make sure I'd be out on my ass just as soon as he could throw me out, and that would be it.

Gary liked me to stop him, he said he respected me for it. He wasn't the motorcycle type, he had a job too on weekends. It was the other kind you had to look out for, the ones with money. No one at our school was a millionaire or anything but some had more money than others and they thought they were the cat's ass. I never went out with them, they'd never ask me anyway except to somewhere like the back of the field hut. It was all how much money you had. If you had enough you could get away with anything, you know?

Whenever I'd come in late Bob would be there, sitting at the kitchen table with his cardigan sleeves coming unravelled, and he'd look at me like I was dirt. He didn't slap me around any more though; I was too big for that. I used to get Gary to park right in front of the kitchen window, it was half below street level because we lived in a cellar, and we'd neck away like crazy right where Bob could hear us and maybe see us too if he looked out.

Then I quit school and started working full-time, at the pizza takeout, it was no great hell but it was money. I figured I'd have enough soon to move into my own place, and Gary said, Why don't we get married. That was what I wanted then, I wanted to get married, have kids; only I wanted to do it right, not like my mother.

It was pretty soon after that I let him go all the way, it was okay because we were getting married anyway. It just happened that way, we didn't have a safe or anything. It was in the back seat of his car, right in broad daylight behind this reservoir where we used to go. It was uncomfortable as hell, and I kept thinking someone would come along and look in the window. There wasn't all that much to it, except it hurt, not a lot though, and I couldn't figure out what they were always making so much fuss about. It was like my first cigarette, I was sick as a dog, though I ended up smoking in a big way.

We didn't have any Kleenex or anything so we had to use this old undershirt he had in the trunk, to polish the car with, he made some joke about running me through the car wash. When he saw the blood though he stopped laughing, he said everything would be okay, he'd take care of me. What he meant was we were still getting married.

I had to go to work that night, I was working three evenings with two afternoons off, so I got Gary to drop me off at the apartment so I could change into my uniform. After I did that I went into the kitchen to make myself some dinner, I could get free pizza at the shop but by that time I couldn't stand the sight of it. You don't like it so much once you know what they put into it. Bob was in there as usual, smoking and finishing off a beer. I guess by that time my mother was supporting him because he didn't seem to be in the television business any more.

His damn cats came over right away and began rubbing on my legs, they must've smelled it, like I was a raw steak or a fish or something. It was the same when I got the curse, when I started using Tampax they'd fish the used ones out of the garbage and go around with the strings hanging out of their mouths, the first time Bob saw that he was so proud, he thought they'd finally caught a mouse and those were the tails. When he found out what it really was he was mad as hell.

I kicked one of the cats away from my legs and he said, Cut that out. I started opening a can of soup, like nothing was happening, Campbell's Chicken Noodle, and I could feel Bob looking at me and all of a sudden I was scared of him again just like when I was little.

Then he stood up and took hold of my arm and pulled me around, he hadn't tried the belt routine for a while, he hadn't put a hand on me for years, so I wasn't expecting it. I slammed into the refrigerator and this bowl on top of it fell off, my mother was keeping the used lightbulbs in it, she had this idea she was going to paint them and make Christmas tree ornaments out of them and sell them but she never did, it was the same as her other ideas. Anyway the lightbulbs broke and the bowl too. I thought he was going to slap me around but he didn't. He just smiled down at me with those grey teeth of his with the fillings showing and the black gums around the edges. If there's anything I can't stand it's bad teeth. Then he put his other hand right on my tit. He said, Your mother won't be home till six, and he was still smiling. I was really scared, because I knew he was still stronger than me.

I thought about screaming, but there was a lot of screaming around there and people had this thing about minding their own business. I reached behind me and picked up the can opener from the kitchen table, it was that kind with the prong, you know? And I shoved it into him as hard as I could, and at the same time I brought my knee up right into his balls. So it wasn't me that screamed. He fell onto the floor, right onto the lightbulbs and the dish of cat food, I heard that sound of glass breaking, and I ran like hell out of there, I didn't care if I'd killed him or not.

I phoned my mother the next day and told her why I wasn't coming back. She was really mad, not at him but at me. It wasn't that she didn't believe me, she did and that was the trouble. You're asking for it, she said, you flaunt it around enough, it's a wonder every man in the city didn't do the same thing a long time ago. Later on I thought maybe I shouldn't of told her. She didn't have that much in life and God knows he wasn't much either but at least she had him. You won't believe this, but I guess she thought I was trying to take him away from her. She wanted me to apologize for sticking the can opener into him, but I wasn't sorry.

There's a line between being asleep and being awake which Rennie is finding harder and harder to cross. Now she's up near the ceiling, in the corner of a white room, beside the air-conditioning unit, which is giving out a steady hum. She can see everything, clear and sharp, under glass, her body is down there on the table, covered in green cloth, there are figures around her, in masks, they're in the middle of a performance, a procedure, an incision, but it's not skin-deep, it's the heart they're after, in there somewhere, squeezing away, a fist opening and closing around a ball of blood. Possibly her life is being saved, but who can tell what they're doing, she doesn't trust them, she wants to rejoin her body but she can't get down. She crawls through the grey folds of netting as if through a burrow, sand in her eyes, blinking in the light, disoriented. It's far too early. She takes a shower, which helps a little, and gets dressed. Routines are calming.

The box under her bed is making her very nervous. She

doesn't want to let it out of her sight, but she can hardly take it to breakfast with her. She locks it in the room, convinced that once she's around the corner it will hatch and something unpleasant will emerge. All the time she's eating, watery scrambled eggs, she worries about it. She could check out of the hotel and leave it behind in the room, she could try for the next flight out, but that would be risky. The English-woman would be into it before she was down the stairs, and there's no doubt about it, she's the police-phoning type. She'd make sure Rennie got arrested at the airport. The only thing to do with it is to get the box to Elva as quickly as possible and then forget about it.

After breakfast she walks across the street to the stationery store and buys a roll of packing tape. She goes back to her room and tapes the box shut, trying to make it seem as much as possible like the original job. If the box doesn't look opened she can always plead ignorance. She orders tea and biscuits in her room and puts in some time looking at her watch. Then she goes to the front desk and tells the English-woman she'll be over at Ste. Agathe tonight but she wants the room held for her.

"You have to pay for it, you know," the Englishwoman says. "Even if you're not in it."

Rennie says she's aware of this. She considers haggling about the meals, but drops the idea. It's what the English-woman is expecting her to do, she's tapping her pencil on the edge of the desk, waiting for it. Rennie's not up to that goose-berry stare.

She lugs the box out of her room and props it against the front desk. She goes back for her bags and checks her camera out of the safe; she leaves the passport, it's safer here. Then she goes down the stone stairs to look for a taxi.

There are no taxis, but there's a boy with a wheelbarrow. He looks about eight, though he's probably older, and after hesitating a moment Rennie hires him. She sends him upstairs for the box, which she doesn't want to touch any more than she has to. The boy is shy and doesn't talk much. He loads all her things, even her purse, into the wheelbarrow and sets off along the pockmarked road in his bare feet, almost running.

At first Rennie thinks he's going this fast because he has some notion of making off with her possessions. She hurries behind him, sweating already and feeling not very dignified. But then she notes his thin arms and decides that he's like rickshaw drivers, he had to go this fast to keep up the momentum. He takes her a back way, between two ramshackle wooden buildings, along a rutted path too narrow and muddy for cars, cluttered with discarded cardboard boxes. Then there's a tiny house with a family of chickens scratching around it, then a storage warehouse piled with sacks, and they come out onto the pier.

The boy, who has not looked back once, speeds up on the level ground, heading for the boat, which must be the one at the end. Rennie sees the virtue of arriving at the same time he does. Even if he's honest the others may not be, and there are several of them now, a whole group of young boys, running beside the wheelbarrow, calling out things she can't understand, grinning back at her as she jogs, puffing now, the edges of her straw hat flapping, chasing her own purse as it flees ahead of her down the pier, around piles of wooden crates, parked trucks covered with tarpaulins, small mounds of fruit and unknown vegetables discarded and rotting. Opposite the boat the boy stops and waits for her with a smile she can't interpret, and the other boys draw back into a circle, leaving a gap for her to enter. Is he making fun of her?

"How much?" she says.

"What you wish," he answers. Of course she overpays him, she can tell by his grin and those of the other boys, delighted and mocking. They want to put things on the boat for her, they're grabbing for the purse, the camera bag, but she fends them off, she's had enough of that. She piles her things on the dock and sits down on top of them, feeling like a hen. Now, of course, there's no way she can leave the pile to ask about the fare and the departure time, and the boy has already run off with his wheelbarrow. She sees why he was going so fast: he wants to get in as many trips as possible before the boat leaves.

Rennie catches her breath. Nobody is watching her, she's avoided suspicion. She remembers the time Jake got pulled over for speeding, with some hash in the glove compartment. Act normal, he said to her quickly before rolling down the window, and Rennie had to think about that. Normal for her would be getting out of the car and walking as fast as possible in any direction as long as it was away. But she sat there without saying anything at all, and that was acceptable enough, though she'd felt guilt shining around her like a halo.

As she does now. She decides to act like a journalist, for the benefit of anyone watching but also for her own. If she goes through the motions, takes a few pictures, a few notes, maybe she'll convince herself. It's like making faces: her mother used to say she shouldn't do that or her face would grow that way permanently. Is that what happened to you? she'd said once, when she was thirteen, the backchat age her mother called it. But she said it under her breath.

She looks around her for possible subjects, takes out her camera, fiddles with the lens. There's the boat, for instance, which is tied to the pier with looped ropes thick as a wrist. It was black once but is now mottled with rusty brown where the paint has weathered. The name is fading on the bow: *Memory*. Rennie feels about it much as she felt about the plane she came on: can it really float? But it makes the trip, twice a day, to the blue shape in the distance, there and back. Surely people would not use it if it weren't safe.

The deck is a jumble of wicker hampers, suitcases and bundles. Several men are tossing cardboard boxes aboard and stowing them through the open hatchway and under the outside benches. Rennie takes a picture of them, shooting into the sun, catching a box in midair with two pairs of outstretched arms framing it, thrower's and catcher's. She hopes the picture will look dramatic, though she knows that when she tries for such effects they usually don't turn out. Overexposure, Jake says. On Ste. Agathe she'll take pictures of the restaurants, if any, and of old women sitting in the sun peeling lobsters, or peeling anything within reason. She knows there will be old women peeling things but she's not dead certain about the lobsters.

There's a hand on her shoulder and Rennie freezes. She's been watched, they know, she's been followed. But then she hears the voice, "Hi there," and it's Lora, in cerise today with blue orchids, smiling away as if she's supposed to be here.

Rennie stands up. "I thought you were over on Ste. Agathe," she says. It will take a moment but very soon she'll be angry.

"Yeah, well, I got held up," says Lora. She's glancing around, down, she's already checked out the box, swiftly and casually. "I missed the boat. Anyway, Elva got better."

Both of them know this is a lie. But what should she do now? One question too many may take her somewhere she definitely doesn't want to go. There's no way she wants Lora to find out that she knows what's in the box, that she knows she's been used. The less she admits to knowing the better. When people play with guns, sooner or later they go off, and she would rather be somewhere else at the time.

Lora's scanning the pier now, noting who's there, who isn't. "I see you got Elva's box okay," she says.

"No problem," says Rennie, amiably, neutrally. "I guess we can just have it put down there in the hold?"

"Keep it with you," says Lora. "Things disappear around here. Anyway Elva always comes down for her box, she gets impatient if she has to wait around for them to unload all that stuff. She hates standing out in the sun."

Lora doesn't offer to take charge of the box. She does however get it lifted on board and stowed under the seat, Rennie's seat, the wooden bench running along the side. Upwind, says Lora, and outside. That way you don't get wet and it's not so smelly. "Never sit in the cabin," she says. "You just about choke to death. If we're lucky they'll only use the sails."

"Where do we pay?" says Rennie.

"They collect once you're on," says Lora. She's looking around the pier again.

Without any signal people begin to board. They wait until the boat rocks towards them, then jump the gap of water where seaweed washes out from underneath the pier, swatches of rubber hair. When it's Rennie's turn, one of the men grabs her purse, wordlessly, then grips her arm to pull her across.

The deck fills with people, most of them brown or black. They sit on the benches, on the crates and canvas-covered baggage, anywhere, and Rennie begins to remember stories about overloaded boats capsizing. The two German women from the hotel appear, looking around for seats. The retired American couple from the reef boat climb on board too, still wearing their baggy wide-legged shorts, but they choose to stand. Already they're peering up into the sky.

"Is it usually this crowded?" Rennie asks.

"This is extra," Lora says. "They're going home to vote. The election's tomorrow."

The men are casting off, there are legs and feet beside Rennie's head, the thick ropes come aboard. A pink-faced fattish man in a greasy white hat and a dark blue jacket has come up through the hatchway, which they're now closing, pulling a tarp over it; he shoves himself among the people, squeezing past legs, climbing over bodies, collecting the money. Nobody is giving orders, least of all him, though suddenly there are about ten men all undoing knots. The edge of the pier is crowded, everyone's shouting. Water grows between the boat and the shore, a split, a gap.

Behind the line of people a maroon car is driving slowly out onto the pier. It stops, a man gets out, then another; their mirror sunglasses are turned towards the boat. Lora bends down, scratching at her ankle. "Damn fleas," she says. The motor starts and the cabin immediately fills with smoke.

"See what I mean?" says Lora.

Ste. Agathe emerges out of the blue hazy sky or sea, rising slowly, sinking slowly, at first only an indistinct smudge, then clearer, a line of harsh vertical cliffs flat-topped and scrubby past the glassy slopes of waves. It looks dry, not like St. Antoine, which from this distance is a moist green, its outline a receding series of softly rounded cones. Queens-town is now just a sprinkling of white. Rennie decides the pale oblong on the hill above it must be Fort Industry. From here the whole place looks like a postcard.

They've turned off the motor and are coasting, the three sails bellying out like old sheets on a line, patched and stained, revealing too many secrets, secrets about nights and sick-nesses and the lack of money. They remind Rennie of the lines of washing seen from trains, the trains she used to take for Christmas visits home during university, since no planes go to Griswold. Dryers were invented not because they were easier but because they were private. She thinks about her mother's red knuckles and her phrase for disreputable stories: *dirty laundry*. Something you weren't supposed to hang out in public. Her mother's red knuckles were from hanging the sheets out on the line, even in winter, to get the sun she said, but of course her sheets were always very clean.

Lora says this is a calm day, but Rennie feels queasy anyway; she wishes she'd had the foresight to take some-thing, there must be a pill. The people sitting on the down-wind side get the occasional bucketful of spray as the boat creaks and lurches heavily into a trough.

Lora is sitting beside her; she's taken a small loaf of bread out of her purple bag and is breaking pieces off of it and chewing them. At their feet four men are lying on the floor, half on top of the canvas-covered suitcases, passing around a bottle of rum. They're already quite drunk and they're getting drunker, they're laughing a lot. The bottle sails past Rennie's head into the sea, they've already got another one. Lora offers the bread silently to Rennie, who says no thanks.

"It'll help you out," says Lora. "If you're not feeling too good. Don't look down, look out at the horizon."

Right beside them there's a small boat, no bigger than a rowboat it seems to Rennie, with a reddish-pink sail; two men are on it, fishing. The boat rolls and tips, it looks very unsafe.

"It's boats like that they hunt the whales in," Lora says.

"You're joking," says Rennie.

"Nope," says Lora. She tears another piece off the loaf. "They have a lookout, and when they see a whale they get into those boats and row like shit. Sometimes they even catch one, and then there's a big feast." Rennie doesn't want to think about anyone eating anything.

Down by their feet there's more laughter. One of the men, Rennie sees now, is the deaf and dumb man, the man they were beating up. He has a cut on his forehead, but apart from that he doesn't seem any worse off than the others, he's drunk as a skunk and grinning away, no teeth at all now. The old American couple in their wide-legged shorts step carefully over the bodies on their way to the stern. "Careful, Mother," says the man, gripping the thin freckled elbow. Laughter rises around their four white chicken-shank legs. Rennie tugs at her skirt, pulling it down over her knees.

And then Paul comes out of the cabin. He too pushes past the knees, picks his way over the lolling bodies. He nods to Rennie and Lora but keeps on going, he's in no hurry, he wanders back to the stern, ducking under the mainsail boom. Rennie didn't see him get on. He must have been down there all the time, when the boat was tied up at the pier.

Suddenly she's hungry, or at least the rocking emptiness, the absence of a centre of gravity, feels now like hunger. She never liked roller coasters either. "I'll take you up on the bread," she says.

"Have the rest," says Lora, handing her the heel of the loaf. "It swells up inside, you know?" She gets out her cigarettes and lights one, tossing the match over the side.

"Can I ask you something?" says Rennie. She's almost finished the bread. It works, already she feels better.

"Sure," says Lora, looking at her with what Rennie is almost sure is amusement. "You want to know if I'm making it with Paul, right? The answer is, Not any more. Help yourself, be my guest."

This is not what Rennie thought she wanted to know, nor does she appreciate Lora's generosity; nor is Paul a buffet casserole or a spare room, Occupied or Vacant as the case may be. "Thanks," she says, "but really I wanted to ask you something quite different. Is he working for the CIA?"

"The CIA?" says Lora. "Him?" She begins to laugh, throwing her head back, showing all her white teeth. "Hey, that's great! Wait'll he hears that! Is that what he told you?"

"Not exactly," says Rennie, who now feels foolish, and annoyed because of it. She turns away, watching the scrubby cliffs as they slide too slowly past the boat.

"Listen, if that's what he told you," says Lora, "who am I? Hey, maybe he thinks it turns you on!" She laughs some more, until Rennie is ready to shake her. Then she stops. "You want to know who the CIA really is around her?" she says. "Look down there." She points to the old American couple standing in the stern, harmless and implausible in their khaki shorts. They're flipping through their bird book now, heads together, like eager children. "They are," says Lora. "Both of them."

"I can't believe that," says Rennie, who can't. Surely these people are the embodiment of midwestern innocence, not at all the kind; though she's no longer sure what the kind is. After all, she was willing to beleive Paul was; and if him, why not anyone?

Lora laughs again. She's delighted, as if the whole thing is a joke she's telling. "It's great," she says. "I love it. It's them all right, everyone knows. Prince always knows which one's the CIA. When you're in local politics you have to know."

"Aren't they too old?" says Rennie.

"They don't have much of a budget for down here," says Lora. "Listen, who's complaining? Everyone tells them stuff just to keep them happy; if they didn't have anything to put in their reports someone up there might get the idea they're senile or something and send down somebody heavy. Of course they're supposed to support Ellis, that's the official line, so Ellis loves them, and Prince loves them because they're so dumb; even Minnow doesn't mind them all that much. Sometimes he takes them out to lunch and tells them all this stuff about what the U. S. should be doing to avoid a revolution, and they write it all down and send it off, it keeps them busy. As for them, they haven't had so much fun since they got to go through the wastebaskets in Iceland, that was their last posting. They tell everyone he's a retired bank manager."

Maybe he is, thinks Rennie. Lora is laughing too much. "So who is he really?" she says. Paul, she means, and Lora picks that up too quickly, she's been waiting for it, the shrug and the answer are right there. "A guy with four boats and some money," she says. "Guys with boats and some money are a dime a dozen down here. It's the ones with boats and no money you've got to look out for."

Rennie eats the rest of the bread, slowly, feeling more and more dim-witted. She may not have asked the wrong question, but she's asked the wrong person. She knows she should pretend to believe the answer, that would be clever, but she just can't manage it.

Lora must sense this; she lights another cigarette from the butt of the first and leans forward, resting her elbows on her spread knees. "I didn't mean to laugh," she says, "except it's so funny, when you really know."

The boat is pulling around into the harbour, out of the wind, and they turn on the smelly motor. Around Rennie people are stirring, gathering up small parcels, stretching their legs out. The harbour seems crowded, small fishing boats, a police launch, yachts at anchor, sails furled, bright flags fluttering from their masts. The *Memory* threads through them, trailing grey smoke. Ahead the pier swarms with people, waving, calling.

"They come down for the eggs," Lora says. "And the bread. There's never enough eggs and bread here. You'd think someone would get a bright idea and start a bakery or something."

"When you know what?" says Rennie.

Lora looks at her with that posed smile, then leans over and forward, getting into the right position for the truth, the confidence. "Who he really is," she says. "Really, he's the connection."

The *Memory* hits with a soft thud; there's a line of tractor tires nailed along the dock to keep it from scraping. Already there are men roping the boat to the shore. Rennie's caught in the scramble, legs around her head, it's like a football team walking across her. There's a lot of shouting, friendly she thinks. In self-defence she stands up, then feels it will be safer sitting down; but Lora's pulling at her arm and there's a man on his knees in front of her, digging for the box. She stands up again and hands reach for her, she makes the leap, she's been landed.

Right in front of her there's a small woman, not five feet tall. She's wearing a pink cotton skirt with red flamingoes on it and a black jockey cap, and a red T-shirt with PRINCE OF PEACE on it in white. Now Rennie remembers her.

"You got my food?" she says, not to Lora but directly to Rennie herself. She says nothing at all about heart medicine. It's an old face, but her black hair is in pigtails today; they stick out sideways from under the jockey cap.

"It's here," says Lora, and it is, she's holding the box upright, steadying it with one hand.

The woman ignores her. "Good," she says, to Rennie alone. She takes the box by its sides and lifts it onto her head, much more easily than Rennie could have done, balancing it on the woolly jockey cap. She steadies it with one hand and marches off without another word to either of them. Rennie, who's been expecting a cross between Aunt Jemima and a basket case, watches her go. What will happen when she opens the box? Rennie can hardly believe she knows what's in it. But if Rennie can believe the geriatric CIA she can believe anything. Possibly this woman's the local gun runner.

Still, Rennie can't quite imagine her opening the box, unpacking the gun, assembling it if it needs assembling, and then what? Does she sell them, and if so, who's buying? What are they used for, here? But these questions are not ones Rennie needs the answers for. Yesterday she would have asked; today she knows it's safer not to. The box is off her back, which is where it should be: off.

She looks around for Paul but he's gone already; she spots him up on the road, getting into a jeep, with another man and the driver. Elva's on the beach, walking along with the machine-gun box on her head, as if that's the most normal thing in the world.

"She's amazing," Rennie says to Lora. "That's a heavy box. I thought you said she had a heart condition," she adds. Now that she's safe she can risk it.

"That's the other grandmother," says Lora, lying without much energy.

"And they're both called Elva," says Rennie.

"Yeah," says Lora, "this place is crawling with grandmothers. The old bitch, you see the way she didn't speak to me? She hates it that I'm living with Prince, but she also hates it that we don't have kids. Around here, if you don't have kids you're nothing, that's what she keeps telling me. She wants me to have a son for Prince, so she can have a great-grandson. *For* Prince, that's what she says. 'You too smart to make babies?' she says. At the same time she hates it that I'm white; but she thinks she's practically related to the Royal

Family, *my* Princess Margaret, *my* Prince Charles, last time I heard they were all white, eh? You figure it out."

"Maybe she's just old," says Rennie.

"Sure," says Lora. "Why not. Where you staying?"

Rennie hasn't considered this. She's just assumed there would be a hotel.

"But it's the election," says Lora. "They might be full up. I can ask for you, though."

When they step onto the beach Lora takes off her shoes, so Rennie does too. Lora's carrying her camera bag for her. They walk along the packed sand, under the trees, palm trees. The beach is wider than the one on St. Antoine and it's fairly clean. Boats are hauled up on it, turned over. Above the beach the town begins, one main road, a couple of foreign banks, a couple of stores, all two-storey and white; a church, then square houses, white and pastel, scattered up the hillside.

They come to a cliff jutting into the sea and wade around it, hitching up their skirts. Then there's more beach and more palm trees, and finally a stone wall and some steps. There's a sign, sea-shells glued on wood: THE LIME TREE. The hotel's hardly bigger than a house.

"The food's not bad here," Lora says. "Only, Ellis is trying to squeeze them out. He wants to buy it and put in his own people. Funny thing, their electricity keeps going off."

"Why?" says Rennie. "Why would he want to do that?"

"Politics, is what they say," says Lora. "They're for Minnow. What I figure is, he hates anyone making money. Except him, of course."

"If this man is so terrible," says Rennie, "why does he keep getting elected?"

"Search me," says Lora. "I'll see about the room." She walks off towards the main building.

Rennie's standing in a beach bar, surrounded by low wooden tables and chairs with people in them. She sits down and piles her bags on the chair beside her and orders a rum and lime. She drinks it, looking out at the boats in the harbour, the flags: Norway, she thinks, Germany, France for sure, and some others.

The rum is going right into her, smoothing her down from the inside. She can relax now, she's off the hook. One hook at any rate.

At the table beside her there's a young couple, the girl brown-haired, lightly tanned, in a white dress, the man in jogging shorts, his nose peeling. The man is fooling with his camera, expensive enough but jammed. "It's the light meter," he says. They're people like her, transients; like her they can look all they want to, they're under no obligation to see, they can take pictures of anything they wish.

There's a small dock in front of the Lime Tree, and on it there's a man, shouting and waving his arms. Rennie watches him for a moment and decides that he's teaching three girls to wind-surf: there they are, out in the harbour. "Upright!" the man shouts, lifting both arms like an orchestra conductor. "Bend the knees!" But it's no use, the sail collapses and the girls topple almost in unison into the sea. In the distance the two German women from the hotel are wading around the cliff, their skirts hitched up, carrying their suitcases. One of their sunhats has blown off into the water.

Rennie wonders where Lora is. She orders a cream cheese and banana bread sandwich from the bar, and another rum and lime. She goes back to her chair and moves it so it's out of the sun.

"May we sit here?" says another voice, a woman's. Rennie looks up. It's the old American couple, in their adventurous shorts, their binoculars hanging like outsized talismans around their necks. Each of them is carrying a glass of ginger ale. "There don't seem to be any other chairs."

"Of course," Rennie says. "I'll move my things for you."

But the old man insists on doing it himself. "My name is Abbott," he says, "and this is Mrs. Abbott." He holds the chair for his wife, who sits down and fixes Rennie with eyes round as a baby's.

"That's very nice of you, dear," she says. "We saw you on the reef boat. Disappointing, we thought. You're Canadian, aren't you? We always find the Canadians so nice, they're almost like members of the family. No crime rate to speak of at all. We always feel quite safe when we go up there. We go to Point Pelee, for the birds. Whenever we can, that is."

"How did you know?" says Rennie.

Mrs. Abbott laughs. "It's a very small place," she says. "You hear things."

"Nice though," says her husband.

"Oh yes. The people are so lovely. So friendly, not like a lot of places." She sips her ginger ale. "So independent," she says. "We have to go back soon, we're getting too old for it. It's a little primitive down here, on Ste. Agathe especially, they don't have many of the conveniences. It's all right for younger people but it's sometimes difficult for us."

"When you can't get toilet paper," says Mr. Abbott.

"Or garbage bags," says his wife. "But we'll be sorry to leave it."

"You don't see many beggars," says Mr. Abbott, who is looking at something in the harbour through his binoculars. "Not like India."

"Do you travel a lot?" says Rennie politely.

"We love to travel," says Mrs. Abbott. "It's the birding, but we like the people too. Of course with the exchange rate these days it's not as easy as it used to be."

"You're right about that," says her husband. "The U.S. borrowed too much money. That's the whole problem in a nutshell. We should stop living beyond our means."

"He ought to know," says Mrs. Abbott, proudly and fondly. "He's a retired bank manager." Mr. Abbott now has his head tilted back and is looking straight up.

Rennie decides that Lora must be wrong. Surely two such innocuous, kindly, boring people cannot possibly be CIA agents. The question is, how can she get rid of them? They appear to have settled in for the afternoon. Rennie waits for the pictures of the grandchildren to make their appearance, out of Mrs. Abbott's sensible canvas shoulder bag.

"Do you see that man over there?" says Mrs. Abbott, pointing towards the bar, which is more crowded than when Rennie first arrived. Rennie isn't sure which one, but she nods.

"He's an international parrot smuggler," says Mrs. Abbott, dropping her voice.

"A parrot smuggler?" says Rennie faintly.

"Don't laugh," says Mrs. Abbott. "It's a big business. In Germany you can get thirty-five thousand dollars for a mated pair."

"The Germans have too much money," says Mr. Abbott. "It's coming out of their ears. They don't know what to do with it."

"It's the St. Antoine parrot," says Mrs. Abbott. "They're very rare, you know. You don't find them anywhere but on St. Antoine."

"It's disgusting," says Mr. Abbott. "They give them drugs. If I ever caught him with one of those little parrots I'd wring his neck."

From the horror in their voices, they could be talking about a white-slave ring. Rennie concentrates on taking this seriously.

"How do they smuggle them?" she says.

"On the yachts," says Mr. Abbott, "like everything else around here. We made it our business to find out about him. He's not from here, he's from Trinidad."

"Then we reported him to the association," says Mrs. Abbott, pleased. "It didn't stop him but it slowed him down. He didn't know it was us, though. Some of them are dangerous and we really aren't equipped to deal with that sort of thing."

"Not at our age," says Mr. Abbott.

"Which association?" says Rennie.

"The International Parrot Association," says Mrs. Abbott. "They're quite good, but they can't be everywhere at once."

Rennie figures she'd better have another drink. If surrealism is taking over the world, she might as well enjoy it. She asks the Abbotts if they would like another ginger ale, but they say they're quite happy. In any case it will soon be dusk.

"Roosting time," says Mr. Abbott happily, as he stands up.

This is Rennie's third rum and lime. She's fuzzy, but not too fuzzy. It's occurred to her several times that there's no boat back and she doesn't have a place to stay. She supposes there's always the beach.

It isn't dark yet, but beneath the overhanging porch roof the waitresses are setting the tables for dinner, lighting the candles inside the little red glass chimneys. The tables outside are full now, with yacht people, and the bar is lined with men, brown and black mostly. Some of them look familiar, but maybe they aren't. She spots a pair of boots, that one she knows anyway, the man with the South American moustache. This time he's ignoring her. There are a few white men with the leathery dull skin and the dry albino hair of those who spend constant time in the sun.

While she's walking back from the bar, Dr. Minnow steps onto the patio. He hasn't come along the beach but down through the garden behind the hotel. He's with three other men; two of them are wearing T-shirts that say THE FISH LIVES, with a picture of a whale, and, underneath, VOTE JUSTICE PARTY. The third man is white and thin; he's wearing a safari jacket and tinted glasses. He stays a little behind.

Dr. Minnow spots Rennie and comes over to her at once. The two men head for the bar, but the third hesitates a moment and then comes over too.

"Well, my friend," says Dr. Minnow. "I see you are covering the election after all." He smiles his crooked smile.

Rennie smiles back. She thinks he's treating it as a joke now, and she can handle that. "From a bar," she says. "All good journalists cover elections from bars."

"I'm told it is the best place," says Dr. Minnow. His accent is broader here, he's less controlled. Rennie thinks he's had a few himself. "Everyone is here. For instance, that is our Minister of Justice over there. He is preparing himself for his defeat." He laughs. "You will excuse me for talking sedition," he says to the white man with him. "This is a compatriot of yours, my friend. He is with the Canadian High Commissioner in Barbados; he come here to see why no one attend the diving program sponsored by the sweet Canadians."

Rennie doesn't catch the name, it's something Middle European, she thinks. A multiculturalism functionary. The man shakes her hand.

"I understand you're a journalist," he says. He's nervous.

"I just do food," says Rennie, to make him feel better. "Things like that."

"What could be more important?" he says politely. They both sit down.

"I tell you why, my friend," Dr. Minnow says. "The sweet Canadians wish to teach the fishermen how to dive so they don't get the bends and come up crippled. What do they do? They hire an expert who comes just at the lobster season when the fishermen all have to be out fishing. That's the money they live on. There is no conspiracy, it is all very simple. Tell them next time they should ask first. Ask someone who knows."

The man smiles and takes out a cigarette, a brown one, and screws it into a black holder. Rennie decides this is pretentious. It embarrasses her that her country's representative is wearing a safari jacket. Where does he think he is, Africa? He could at least have chosen a different colour: the beige should not wear beige.

"You know what they're like," he says. "Governments have to deal with governments in power, which does not always produce the most accurate information."

"Are you going to win?" Rennie says to Dr. Minnow.

"Yesterday," Dr. Minnow says conversationally, his eye on the Canadian, "the government offer me a large sum of money to go over to their side. Minister of Tourism, they offer me."

"I take it you didn't accept," says Rennie.

"Why cut your own throat?" says Dr. Minnow, who seems very pleased. "I have not read Machiavelli for nothing. If they offer, it means they are scared, they think they could lose. So I turn them down, and today they are slandering me in a new way. Before it was Castro, now they say I am in the pocket of the Americans and the plantation owners. They should make up their minds, one way or the other. It confuses the people: they may think I am neither, which would be the truth. If we begin to believe the truth here, that would be the end of Ellis, and also of the Prince of Peace, as he calls himself. He think he got the true religion, all right." He stands up.

"Tomorrow I will make a speech on the problems of garbage collection, among other things," he says. "It is one of our most urgent problems on these islands, what to do with the garbage. You should attend, my friend." He bestows one more smile upon Rennie and moves away towards the bar, the neutral-coloured Canadian trailing.

As she's coming back from the bar again, Rennie sees the two German women climbing the stone steps. The bottoms of their dresses are dripping wet and their hair has come unglued and is hanging in wisps and strands; their faces are dangerously pink. They seem to have abandoned their suitcases. One of them is supporting the other, who is limping and uttering little shrieks of pain. Both have been crying, but as they enter the bar and the ring of curious faces that quickly surrounds them, they pull themselves together. Someone offers a chair.

"What on earth?" says Rennie, to no one in particular. Everyone in the place is peering at the German woman's foot, plump and white and pink-toed, stuffed-looking, which her friend holds up like a trophy.

"She stepped on a sea urchin," says Lora, who's back again. "They always do it, they should watch where they're going. It hurts at first but it's no big deal."

The woman is lying back with her eyes closed; her foot sticks straight out. After a few minutes Elva comes through the doorway that leads to the kitchen; she no longer has the box, she's wearing a red and white checked apron and carrying a lime and a candle. She kneels in front of the outstretched foot, appropriates it, peers at the toes. Then she begins rubbing with the cut lime. The German woman screams.

"Keep still," says Elva. "It nothin'. This will be gone tomorrow."

"Can you not take them out?" says the other woman. She's anxious, she's almost incoherent. This is not according to schedule.

"They break off and poison you," Elva says. "You got matches?"

There's no doubt who's in charge. Someone from the circle produces a box of matches and Elva lights the candle. She tilts it and drops the hot wax over the toes, rubbing it in. "You should of pee on it," she says to the other woman. "When this happen here, the boy pee on the girl's foot or the girl pee on the boy's. That take away the pain."

The German woman opens her eyes and gazes at Elva. Rennie recognizes the look, it's a look you can give only to a foreigner, a look of hope, a desperate clinging to the illusion that it's all a translation problem and you haven't really heard what you know you've just heard.

Several people laugh, but not Elva. She's got the other foot now, the uninjured one, she's digging her thumbs into it. The German woman gasps and looks around for help: she's been invaded, this is the wrong foot. She has the controlled, appalled expression of a visiting duchess who knows she must not openly disparage the local customs, however painful or revolting.

Elva digs harder. She's smug now, she has an audience, she's enjoying herself. "Your veins block," she says. "I unblock your veins, the blood carry the poison away."

"I wouldn't let her near me," says Lora. "She's got thumbs like hammers. She'll total your back as soon as look at you. She says she can cure just about anything but I'd rather be sick, thank you very much."

There's an audible snapping sound; the tendons, Rennie thinks. The German woman's face is twisted, her eyes are screwed up, she's not going to yell or moan, she's determined to preserve her dignity. "You hear the veins cryin' out?" says Elva. "That the gas, movin' in them. You feel lighter?"

"There's no rooms," Lora says to Rennie. "It's full up, it's the election."

"Maybe I should phone the other hotels," says Rennie, who is still watching Elva.

"Phone?" says Lora. "Other hotels?" She laughs a little.

"There aren't any other hotels?" says Rennie.

"There used to be," says Lora, "but they're closed down now. There's one for the locals, but I wouldn't stay there. A girl could get seriously misunderstood. I'll try somewhere else for you."

"It in the hands," says Elva to the onlookers. "It a gift, I have it from my grandmother, she give me that when I small. She pass it to me. You feel this lump?"

The German woman nods. She's still wincing, but not as much.

"Your mama give you a blow when you small," Elva says. "You too small that time, you don't remember. The blood lie down, it make a lump. Now it have to move or the poison grow into a cancer." She digs in both thumbs again. "The pain is your youth, risin' up now."

"The old fake," says Lora. "Give her a tourist and she's happy as a pig in shit. Even if they don't believe her they have to act like they do. There's no doctor around here anyway, so they don't have a whole lot of choice; if you sprain your ankle it's her or nothing."

"I think this is maybe enough," says the other woman, who's been hovering around like a concerned parent.

Elva gives her a look of contempt. "I say when I done," she says. The foot cracks, bends in her hands like rubber.

"Now," Elva says, sitting back on her heels. "Walk on it."

Tentatively the German woman puts both feet on the ground. She stands up.

"The pain gone," says Elva, looking around the circle.

The German woman smiles. "It is remarkable," she says.

Rennie, watching, wants to hold out her own foot, even though there's nothing wrong with it, even though it will hurt. She wants to know what it feels like, she wants to put herself into the care of those magic hands. She wants to be cured, miraculously, of everything, of anything at all.

Paul is standing in the kitchen doorway, looking without hurry; Rennie sees him, but decides not to wave. He comes over anyway.

"Taking it easy?" he says to Rennie. "Lora says you don't have a place to stay. I've got space, if you like."

"On a boat?" Rennie says dubiously. She ought to have said thank you first.

"I have a house too," Paul says, smiling. "Two bed-rooms. Two beds."

Rennie's not sure what is being offered, but suspects it's not much. There's some room in this world for face value.

"Well," she says. "If you're sure it's all right."

"Why wouldn't it be?" says Paul.

. . .

They walk back through the garden. It's full of trees, flowering, overgrown, limes and lemons and something else, odd reddish-orange husks split open to show a white core and three huge black seeds like the eyes of insects. There are a lot of things here that Rennie has no names for.

At the back of the garden there's a five-foot stone wall. Paul lifts her camera bag and her other bag to the top, hoists himself up, and reaches down for her. She takes hold of his hands; she doesn't know where they're going.

Rennie and Daniel were sitting in Daniel's car, which was an unusual thing for them to be doing. It was night, which was also unusual, and it was raining, which was par for the course. When they were together it always seemed to be raining.

They'd just had dinner, dinner, not lunch. Rennie wondered whether Daniel was about to do something out of character.

Well, how about it? she said to him. A little reckless handholding? Want to roll around on the gear shift?

I know I can't offer you much, he said.

He looked so miserable that she felt she ought to express compassion, she ought to comfort him, she ought to tell him everything was fine. Instead she said, You're right. You can't offer me much.

Daniel looked at his watch, then out the window at the rain. There were cars going by but nobody walking on the street. He took hold of Rennie's shoulders and kissed her gently on the mouth. He ran the ends of his fingers over her lips.

I'm very fond of you, he said.

Flamboyant adjectives will be your downfall, said Rennie, who couldn't resist.

I know I don't express myself very well, Daniel said. Rennie wasn't sure she could take that much sincerity all at once. He kissed her again, quite a lot harder. Rennie put her face against his neck and the collar of his shirt. He smelled like laundry. It was safe enough, he could hardly take off her clothes or his in a parked car on a street with two-way traffic.

She wanted him to though, she wanted to lie down beside him and touch him and be touched by him; at the moment she believed in it, the touch of the hand that could transform you, change everything, magic. She wanted to see him lying with his eyes closed, she wanted to see him and not be seen, she wanted to be trusted. She wanted to make love with him, very slowly, she wanted it to last a long time, she wanted the moment just before coming, helplessness, hours of it, she wanted to open him up. There was such a gap between what she wanted and where she was that she could hardly stand it.

She pulled back. Let's go home, she said.

It's not that I don't want to, he said. You know that.

His face for a moment was like a child's looking up, he was so sweet it hurt, and Rennie felt brutal. He had no right to appeal to her like that, to throw himself on her mercy. She wasn't God, she didn't have to be understanding, which was a good thing because she was rapidly understanding less and less about this and soon she wouldn't understand anything at all. Rennie liked to know the names for things and there was no name for this.

What do you do afterwards, she said, go home and jerk off? Or maybe you go home and stick your hand into the job jar. Don't tell me you haven't got one, I know you do. What else would you do with your spare time?

He put his hand gently on the back of her neck. What would you like to do? he said. If you really want to, we'll check into a hotel somewhere. I can only stay an hour, that's all I've got, and then what? Would that be love? Is that what you want?

No, said Rennie. As usual she wanted everything, which was in short supply.

I'm not good at that sort of thing, Daniel said. I'd resent

you for it and I don't want that. I care about you, I care what happens to you. I guess I think I can do more for you as your doctor; I'm better at it. He looked down at his hands, which were on the steering wheel now.

Why not both? said Rennie.

That's the way I am, said Daniel. There are some things I just can't do.

It struck Rennie that Daniel was a lot like Griswold, not as it was but as it would like to be. Ordinary human decency, a fine decent man they would say, with a list of things you just couldn't do. This insight did not fill her with joy. He was normal, that was what she'd fallen in love with, the absolutely ordinary raised to the degree of X. What you were supposed to be. He did make his living cutting parts off other people's bodies and patting their shoulders while they died, he used the same hands for both, but nobody considered that unusual. He was a good man, a mystery, Rennie wanted to know why. Maybe it was habit.

What do you believe in? she said to him. I mean, what keeps you ticking over? What makes you get up in the mornings? How do you know what kinds of things you can do and what kinds you can't do? Don't tell me it's God. Or maybe you've got those things in the job jar, along with the jobs. Saying this, she felt like a troll, but Daniel took it straight.

I don't know, said Daniel. I've never thought that much about it.

Rennie felt cold, she felt she was dying and Daniel knew it, he just hadn't told her about it yet. But making love for an hour in a hotel room with Daniel would not work, she could see that now. They would go in and close the door and take off their damp coats and he would sit down on the edge of the bed. Seeing him with his head bent, dutifully undoing his shoelaces: this would be too much for her, it would be too sad. You don't have to, she would say. She would hold on to his hands and cry and cry.

She no longer expected Daniel to save her life. She no

longer expected Daniel. Maybe that was the right way to do it, never to expect anything.

Let's go home, she said.

Rennie lay on the bed, their bed, stiff as plaster, waiting for Jake to come out of the shower. They'd talked about it enough. The truth was she didn't want him to touch her and she didn't know why, and he didn't really want to touch her either but he wouldn't admit it.

You have to try, he said. You won't let me try.

You sound like the little engine that could, she said. I think I can, I know I can.

You really are relentless, he said.

So they were going to try. She'd stood in front of her open closet, wondering what you should wear to try, to a trial. A trial of strength. She wanted to wear something and knew she had to; these days she always wore something to bed. She didn't want to be seen, the way she was, damaged, amputated.

Once he'd given her a purple one-piece number that snapped together at the crotch and they'd got very high on some top-grade Colombian, and at the crucial moment neither of them could get the snaps undone. They'd hugged each other, rolling around and laughing so much they almost fell off the bed. So much for sexy underwear, she'd said.

She decided on black, two pieces, he'd given that to her a while ago. He could leave the top part on if he wanted to. She lit some candles and lay down on the bed, raising one knee, arranging herself. It was no good.

She tried to think about Daniel, lying here beside her instead, hoping that would make her feel better, softer, but she couldn't. She could hardly imagine him without clothes. All she could imagine were his hands, hands with thin fingers and with the marks of a slow dark burning on their backs. In the Middle Ages they'd painted pictures of souls, the souls of the dying leaving their bodies, and for a long time they'd argued about what part of the body the soul inhabited when you were alive. There was no doubt about Daniel at all: his soul was in his hands. Cut them off and he'd be a zombie.

One man I'm not allowed to touch, she thought, and another I won't allow to touch me. I could write a piece on it: "Creative Celibacy." "Sexual Abstinence, the Coming Thing." Except it's been done. What's supposed to come next? Sublimation? Ceramics? Devotion to a good cause?

Jocasta would have advised her to try masturbation. That too was once supposed to be the wave of the future. *Listen, when all else fails let your fingers do the walking.* But masturbation didn't interest her, it would be like talking to yourself or keeping a journal. She'd never been able to understand women who kept journals. She already knew what she would be likely to say. Unlikely things could only be said by other people.

Jake came in from the shower with a blue towel tucked around his waist. He sat down on the bed beside her and kissed her gently on the mouth.

I'd like the candles out, she said.

No, he said, leave them on. I want to see you.

Why? she said.

You turn me on, he said.

She didn't answer. He ran his hand up her right leg, across her belly, down the left thigh, over the bent knee. He did that again, moving the black cloth down. He didn't go above the waist. Upsidedown high school, Rennie thought. He moved his hand between her legs, bent to kiss her navel.

Maybe we should smoke some dope, he said.

To help me relax? she said, watching him from her head, which was up there on the pillow at the other end of her body. She felt her eyes sparkling like those of some small malicious animal, a weasel or a rat. Red, intelligent, in a sharp little face with tiny incisors. Cornered and mean.

That's right, he said. He brought the tea canister in and opened it and rolled a joint and lit it and passed it to her. I love you, he said, but you can't believe it.

What's the difference between a belief and a delusion? she said. Maybe you just think you ought to. Maybe I make you feel guilty. You've always told me guilt was a big thing with Jewish mothers.

You aren't my mother, he said. A good thing, too.

How could I be? she said. I'm not Jewish.

Nobody's perfect, he said. You're my golden *shiksa*. We all have to have at least one, it's obligatory.

So that's what I am, said Rennie. I guess that's it for my identity crisis. It's nice to know who you are. But I'm hardly golden.

Gilt-edged security, anyway, said Jake.

Is that a pun? said Rennie.

Don't ask me, said Jake, I'm a functional illiterate and proud of it.

But up and coming, said Rennie.

As often as possible, said Jake. You think we could set this to music?

This isn't a forties movie, said Rennie.

You could have fooled me, said Jake.

Rennie felt she was going to cry. What she couldn't bear was the effort he was making to pretend nothing was different, the effort she was making to help him pretend. She wanted to say, I'm dying, but that would be melodrama, and anyway she probably wasn't.

Jake began rubbing her left thigh, slowly up and then down. I feel awkward, he said. I feel you don't want me to be doing this.

She was watching him but she didn't know how to help him. I can't believe, she thought. Why not? The words in her head came one at a time, as if they were being spoken by someone else. She watched them form, rise, burst. It was strong grass.

You don't have to be perfect, he said.

He bent down and kissed her again, supporting himself with his arms so his torso didn't touch her. He's doing this for me, she thought. It's not for him, he doesn't want to.

He lifted her and slid the black satin shorts down and put his mouth on her.

I don't want that, she said. I don't need charity. I want you inside me.

Jake paused. He raised her arms, holding her wrists above her head. Fight me for it, he said. Tell me you want it. This was his ritual, one of them, it had once been hers too and now she could no longer perform it. She didn't move and he let go of her. He put his face down on her shoulder; his body went limp. Shit, he said. He needed to believe she was still closed, she could still fight, play, stand up to him, he could not bear to see her vulnerable like this.

Rennie knew what it was. He was afraid of her, she had the kiss of death on her, you could see the marks. Mortality infested her, she was a carrier, it was catching. She lay there with his face against her neck, thinking of something she'd seen written in a men's washroom once when she was doing a piece on graffiti. *Life is just another sexually transmitted social disease.* She didn't blame him. Why should he be stuck with it? With her.

After a while he raised his head. I'm sorry, he said.

So am I, said Rennie. She waited. You're having a thing with someone else, aren't you?

It's not important, said Jake.

Is that what you say about me? Rennie said. To her?

Look, said Jake, it's either that or a warm wet washcloth. You won't let me touch you.

Touch, said Rennie. Is that all? Does it matter that much? Isn't there any more to it than that?

· · ·

She stroked the back of his neck and thought of the soul leaving the body in the form of words, on little scrolls like the ones in medieval paintings.

Oh please.

They walk inland, uphill. Rennie tries to think of something neutral to say. He's carrying her camera bag and the other bag. It's the minimum, but she shouldn't have brought so much.

It's about five-thirty and although the asphalt road is hot it's not too hot, the trees cast shadows. There are little houses set back from the road, people are sitting out on their porches, the women wear print dresses, some of the older ones have hats on, and Paul nods to them, they nod back, they don't stare but they look, taking note. A group of girls passes, going down the hill, fifteen- or sixteen-year-olds in white dresses, some with bows or flowers in their hair, which is braided and pinned up; they look oddly old fashioned, costumed. They're singing, three-part harmony, a hymn. Rennie wonders if they're going to church.

"It's up here," Paul says. The house is concrete block like the others and only a little bigger, painted light green and raised on stilts above the rainwater tank. There's a rock garden covering the hill, cactus and rubbery-looking plants. The shrubs at the gateway are dying though, there's a many-stranded yellow vine covering them like a net, like hair.

"See that?" Paul says. "Around here they break pieces of that off and throw it into the gardens of the people they don't like. It grows like crazy, it strangles everything. Love vine, they call it."

"Are there people here who don't like you?" Rennie says.

"Hard to believe, isn't it?" he says, grinning at her.

Inside, the house is neat, almost blank, as if no one is actually living in it. The furniture is noncommittal, wood-frame chairs of the kind Rennie has seen in the beach bars. Beside one of the chairs there's a telescope on a tripod.

"What do you watch through it?" says Rennie.

"The stars," says Paul.

On the wall above the sofa there's a map, on the wall facing it another, island after island, navigational maps with the soundings marked. There are no pictures. The kitchen is an open counter with appliances behind it, a stove, a refrigerator, no clutter. Paul takes ice cubes from the refrigerator and fixes two drinks, rum and lime. Rennie looks at the maps; then she goes out through the double doors, there's a porch with a hammock, and leans on the railing, looking down over the road to the tops of the trees and then the harbour. There's a sunset, as usual.

The bed is expertly made, hospital corners firmly tucked in. Rennie wonders where he learned to do that, or maybe someone comes in to do it for him. Perhaps this is the spare bedroom, it's empty enough. There are two pillows, though nobody lives with him. He untwists the mosquito net, spreads it over the bed. "We can go for dinner, if you like," he says.

Rennie's wearing a white shirt and a wrap skirt, also white. She wonders which she should take off first. What will happen? Maybe there's no point to taking off anything, maybe she should offer to sleep in the other bed. All he said was that he had room.

Nevertheless she's afraid, of failure. Maybe she should be fair, maybe she should warn him. What can she say? I'm not all here? There's part of me missing? She doesn't even have to do that, failure is easy to avoid. All you have to do is walk away.

Then she realizes she doesn't care. She doesn't care what he thinks of her, she never has to see this man again if she doesn't want to. She never has to see anyone again if she doesn't want to. She's been hoping for some dope, he's in the business, he must have some; it would help, she thought, she'd be able to relax. But she doesn't need it; already she feels light, insubstantial, as if she's died and gone to heaven and come back minus a body. There's nothing to worry about, nothing can touch her. She's a tourist. She's exempt.

He's standing in front of her, in the half-light, smiling a little, watching her to see what she'll do.

"I thought you didn't want that," he says.

He doesn't touch her. She undoes the buttons on the blouse, he's watching. He notes the scar, the missing piece, the place where death kissed her lightly, a preliminary kiss. He doesn't look away or down, he's seen people a lot deader than her.

"I was lucky," she says.

He reaches out his hands and Rennie can't remember ever having been touched before. Nobody lives forever, who said you could? This much will have to do, this much is enough. She's open now, she's been opened, she's being drawn back down, she enters her body again and there's a moment of pain, incarnation, this may be only the body's desperation, a flareup, a last clutch at the world before the long slide into final illness and death; but meanwhile she's solid after all, she's still here on the earth, she's grateful, he's touching her, she can still be touched.

Jake liked to pin her hands down, he liked to hold her so she couldn't move. He liked that, he liked thinking of sex as something he could win at. Sometimes he really hurt her, once he put his arm across her throat and she really did stop breathing. Danger turns you on, he said. Admit it. It was a game, they both knew that. He would never do it if it was real, if she really was a beautiful stranger or a slave girl or whatever it was he wanted her to pretend. So she didn't have to be afraid of him.

A month before the operation Rennie had a phone call from *Visor.* Keith, the managing editor, thought it would be sort of fun to do a piece on pornography as an art form. There had already been a number of anti-porno pieces in the more radical women's magazines, but Keith thought they were kind of heavy and humourless. They missed the element of playfulness, he said. He wanted a woman to write it because he thought they'd crack the nuts of any guy who tried to do it. Rennie tried to find out who he meant by "they," but he was vague. Tie it in with women's fantasy lives, if you can, he said. Keep it light. Rennie said she thought the subject might have more to do with men's fantasy lives, but Keith said he wanted the woman's angle.

Keith fixed it up for her to interview an artist who lived

and worked in a warehouse down off King Street West and did sculptures using life-sized mannequins. He was making tables and chairs from the mannequins, which were like store mannequins except that the joints had been filled in and plastered over to make them smooth. The women were dressed in half-cup bras and G-string panties, set on their hands and knees for the tables, locked into a sitting position for the chairs. One of the chairs was a woman on her knees, her back arched, her wrists tied to her thighs. The ropes and arms were the arms of the chair, her bum was the seat.

It's a visual pun, said the artist, whose first name was Frank. He had one woman harnessed to a dogsled, with a muzzle on. It was called *Nationalism is Dangerous.* There was another one with a naked mannequin on her knees, chained to a toilet, with a Handy Andy between her teeth like a rose. It was called *Task Sharing,* said Frank.

If a woman did that, said Rennie, they'd call it strident feminism.

That's the breaks, said Frank. Anyway, I don't just do women. He showed her a male figure sitting in a swivel chair with a classic blue pinstripe business suit on. Frank had glued nine or ten plastic dildoes to the top of his head, where they stood out like pigtails or the rays of a halo. *Erogenous Zone Clone Bone,* it was called.

You're going to find this boring, said Rennie, but your work doesn't exactly turn me on.

It's not supposed to turn you *on,* said Frank, not offended. Art is for contemplation. What art does is, it takes what society deals out and makes it visible, right? So you can *see* it. I mean, there's the themes and then there's the variations. If they want flower paintings they can go to Eaton's.

Rennie remembered having read these opinions already, in the file on Frank given to her by *Visor.* I guess I see your point, she said.

I mean, said Frank, what's the difference between me and Salvador Dali, when you come right down to it?

I'm not sure, Rennie said.

If you don't like my stuff, you should see the raw material, he said.

That was the other part of Keith's plan, the raw material. The Metro Police had a collection of seized objects, Keith said; it was called Project P., P for pornography, and it was open to the public. Rennie took Jocasta with her, not because she didn't think she could get through it on her own, she felt she was up to almost anything. Still, it didn't seem like the kind of thing you would do by yourself if you could help it. Someone might see you coming out and get the wrong idea. Besides, it was Jocasta's kind of thing. Bizarre. Human ingenuity, that's what you should stress, said Keith. Infinite variety and that.

The collection was housed in two ordinary rooms at the main police building, and this was the first thing that struck Rennie: the ordinariness of the rooms. They were rectangular, featureless, painted government grey; they could have been in a post office. The policeman who showed them around was young, fresh-faced, still eager. He kept saying, Now why do you think anyone would want to do *that*? Now what do you think *that* could be for?

Rennie made it through the whips and the rubber appliances without a qualm. She took notes. How do you spell the plural of *dildo*? she asked the policeman. With or without an *e*? The policeman said he didn't know. Probably like *tomatoes*, Rennie thought. Jocasta said it all looked very medical to her and she understood that in England it was the truss shops that used to sell under-the-cover bondage magazines, before sex supermarkets came in. The policeman said he wouldn't really know about that. He opened a cupboard and took out something even the police hadn't been able to figure out. It was a machine like a child's floor polisher, with an ordinary-looking dildo on the handle. He plugged it into a wall socket and the whole machine scooted around the floor, with the handle plunging wildly up and down.

But what's it *for*? Jocasta said, intrigued.

Your guess is as good as mine, the policeman said. It's too short for anyone standing up, and there's no place on it to sit down. Anyhow, the way it runs around the room like that you couldn't keep up with it. We've got a private bet on here. Anyone comes up with some use for it that wouldn't take your guts out, we give them a hundred dollars.

Maybe it's for very active midgets, Jocasta said.

Maybe the police made a mistake, Rennie said. Maybe it really is just a floor polisher, with kind of a strange handle. Next thing you know you'll be raiding General Electric and seizing pop-up toasters.

Fifty percent of fatal accidents occur at home and now we know why, said Jocasta.

The policeman somehow did not like them laughing. He disapproved of it. He took them into a third room, which was set up with black-out windows and a video viewer and showed them some film clips, a woman with a dog, a woman with a pig, a woman with a donkey. Rennie watched with detachment. There were a couple of sex-and-death pieces, women being strangled or bludgeoned or having their nipples cut off by men dressed up as Nazis, but Rennie felt it couldn't possibly be real, it was all done with ketchup.

This is our grand finale, the policeman said. The picture showed a woman's pelvis, just the pelvis and the tops of the thighs. The woman was black. The legs were slightly apart; the usual hair, the usual swollen pinkish purple showed between them; nothing was moving. Then something small and grey and wet appeared, poking out from between the legs. It was the head of a rat. Rennie felt that a large gap had appeared in what she'd been used to thinking of as reality. What if this is normal, she thought, and we just haven't been told yet?

Rennie didn't make it out of the room. She threw up on the policeman's shoes. Sorry, she said, but he didn't seem to mind. He patted her on the back, as if she'd passed a test of some sort, and took her arm, leading her from the darkened room. Politely, he did not look down at his shoes.

I thought that one would get to you, he said. A lot of women do that. Look at it this way, at least it's not for queers.

You need your head repaired, said Jocasta, and Rennie said she thought maybe it was time to leave. She thanked the policeman for being so cooperative. He was annoyed with them, not because of his shoes but because of Jocasta.

I can't do this piece, Rennie told Keith.

Why not? he said, disappointed in her.

It's not my thing, she said. I'll stick to lifestyles.

Maybe it is a lifestyle, he said.

Rennie decided that there were some things it was better not to know any more about than you had to. Surfaces, in many cases, were preferable to depths. She did a piece on the return of the angora sweater, and another one on the hand-knit-look industry. That was soothing. There was much to be said for trivia.

For a couple of weeks after that she had a hard time making love with Jake. She didn't want him grabbing her from behind when she wasn't expecting it, she didn't like being thrown onto the bed or held so she couldn't move. She had trouble dismissing it as a game. She now felt that in some way that had never been spelled out between them he thought of her as the enemy. Please don't do that any more, she said. At least not for a while. She didn't want to be afraid of men, she wanted Jake to tell her why she didn't have to be.

I thought you said it's okay if you trust me, he said. Don't you trust me?

It's not you, she said. It's not you I don't trust.

Then what is it? he said.

I don't know, she said. Lately I feel I'm being used; though not by you exactly.

Used for what? said Jake.

Rennie thought about it. Raw material, she said.

Later on, she said, If I had a rat in my vagina, would it turn you on?

Dead or alive? said Jake.

Me or the rat? said Rennie.

Feh, said Jake. You sound like my mother. Always worrying about the dustballs under the bed.

No, seriously, she said.

El sleazo, he said. Come on, don't confuse me with that sick stuff. You think I'm some kind of a pervert? You think most men are like that?

Rennie said no.

I ran into Paul in Miami, says Lora. At first he told me he was in real estate. I was down there with some guy, that was after me and Gary split up, and around that time if there was a free weekend going I took it. It wasn't the sex, I couldn't have cared less if a man ever touched me again or not, that's how I felt then. With Gary it was never that great anyway, it was a lot like going through a revolving door, in and out before you know it and if you sneezed it was all over except for washing the sheets.

Maybe I wanted it that way, maybe I wanted to be able to take it or leave it. Maybe I thought if I got to like it too much I'd be stuck. I wanted to think, Chuck you, Farley, there's nothing much I need *you* for, if I want to I can turn around and walk right through that door and the only one who'll be missing a thing is you. I thought it was just something you let men do to you. I don't think most of them even liked it very much either. They only did it because you were supposed to.

I guess I just wanted to be with someone. It wasn't the nights that were bad, it was the mornings. I didn't like to wake up in the morning and have nobody there. After a while you just want someone to like you. You want someone to maybe have breakfast with, go to the movies with, stuff like that. I used to say there's only two things that matter, is he nice or is he rich. Nice is better than rich but take it from me, you can't have both, and if you can't get nice take rich. Sometimes I said it the other way around. Not that there's a whole lot of either one hanging out there on the trees, you know?

At first I thought Paul was only nice. He wasn't mean like a lot of them, he was easy to be with, he wasn't a pain in the ass, you know? Then I figured it out that he was rich, too. He had this boat, he only had the one then, and he said why didn't I come down here for a couple of weeks, get a tan, relax, and there wasn't any good reason not to. Once I got down here I couldn't see any good reason to leave. Around that time I found out what he really did.

I worked on the boats for a while. Most of these boats have two or three crew and a cook, they really do run charters on the boats, it would look funny if they didn't, and the crew all knew what he was doing, they were in for a percentage, he had people he could trust. I was supposed to be the cook, what I knew about cooking on a boat you could stick in your ear, it's not like cooking in a real kitchen, but I picked it up. I was seasick as hell at first, I puked my guts out, but I figure you can get used to almost anything if you have to and when you're out in the middle of the ocean there's only one way off the boat, eh?

A lot of girls work the boats here, the straight boats as well, though you never really know if the boat's straight or not, you learn not to ask what they've got in the hold. Whoever runs the boat expects you to make it with them; if you don't like it you can always get off the boat. I never made it with the charters though, that wasn't part of the deal. It's always them that get the maddest about it too. They think if they're renting the boat they're renting everything on it.

Maybe I'm for sale, I'd tell them, but I'm sure as hell not for rent. How much? one of them said, an asshole. Hot-shot lawyer or something. You couldn't afford it, I said. Funny, you look pretty cheap to me, he said. I may be pretty but I'm not cheap, I said. I'm like a lawyer, what you're paying for is the experience.

Anyway you only had to do a few charters, maybe once a month, you could survive on that. The rest of the time I was living with Paul. Or anyway that's what it was called. We slept in the same bed and all, but there was something missing in him, it was like being with someone who wasn't there, you know? He didn't care what I did, anything I wanted to do was okay with him, other men, anything, as long as it didn't interfere with him. Deep down inside he just didn't give a shit. You know what the locals say about him? *He does deal.* With the devil, is what they mean, they don't mean the business. It's what they say about loners.

About the only thing that really turned him on was danger, as far as I could figure out. Once in a while he'd do this really dangerous stuff.

Like, a couple of months after I came down here there was this thing with Marsdon. That was before Marsdon went to the States. He was living with this woman, and he came home one day and caught her in the sack with one of his cousins, I forget which one. It could be anybody, sooner or later they all turn out to be cousins if you study it hard enough.

Of course Marsdon beat her up. If he hadn't beat her up, the other men would have laughed at him and so would the women. They expect it, for being *bad,* which is what they call it. But he went too far, he made her take off all her clothes, not that she had that many on when he found her, and then he covered her with cow-itch. That's like a nettle, it's what you do to people you really don't like a whole lot. Then he tied her to a tree in the back yard, right near an ant hill, the stinging kind. He stayed in the house, drinking rum and listening to her scream. He left her there five hours, till she was all swollen up like a balloon. A lot of people heard her but nobody tried to untie her, partly because he had a mean reputation and partly because it was a man-woman thing, they don't think that's anyone else's business.

Paul heard about it and he walked into the back yard and cut the rope. You just don't do that. Everyone waited to see what Marsdon would do, but he didn't do anything. He's hated Paul ever since. It was after that he went to the States and got into the army, or that's what he said he was doing. I wish he'd stayed there.

Paul didn't know the woman, he wasn't being noble as far as I could tell. He did it because it was dangerous; he did it because it was fun. Some fun if you ask me. You'd never know when he was going to pull one of those, you'd be washing your hair and you'd look out the window and there he'd be swinging from some goddamn tree, like Tarzan. He was like a little boy that way. He always said he knew what he was doing, but I knew some day he'd try it once too often and that would be that.

That's one of the reasons I stopped working on his boats. He was taking too many chances.

The stuff comes from Colombia, on the freighters. For the government there it's just another cash crop. Nobody can do anything about the freighters and once they're out in the ocean nobody can do anything about that either, except maybe hijack the boat. People have tried that but it's not too safe any more, they're shooting back. The U.S. knows which boats it's on, they follow everything by satellite, they can track the big boats by the sound of the motors; so they can't get it into the States that way. They bring it here, to one of these islands, and they split it up and put it onto yachts or private planes, they're using those more now, and they take it up to Miami or maybe in through the Virgin Islands. It's not just the U.S. and Cuba trying to control it here. The third group is the mob, and they're spending more money. It's a guaranteed multi-million-dollar business, so they can afford a top-level lobby in Washington, to keep them from legalizing it. Nobody wants it legalized, then you could grow it right there in your own back yard, the bottom would fall out of the market.

Ellis never stopped them, they were paying him off, but that may be changing, he may want in on the ground floor. He just made a big bust in the harbour over at St. Antoine. It seems some locals were growing it up there behind the bananas and smuggling it out on the fishing trawlers. A medium-sized operation but the big ones don't want any competition, and Ellis doesn't want the peasants marketing it themselves, he'd lose his cut. I'd guess it was the mob who put Ellis up to making the bust. Two to one he'll resell it himself.

At first they were just hiring Paul's boats, piecework, to make the run up from here to Miami. But then he went down there himself and bought his own army general. He figured why should he be the middleman when he could buy whole-sale himself and sell retail, which makes sense except that then he had them all down his back, the CIA, the mob, Ellis, the works. No thanks, I said, I like my skin the way it is, only the holes God gave me. I told him I'd do the tourists, they'd trust me more because I was white and a woman, as long as he bought a few local cops for me, I'd do retail, but none of that other stuff.

The second reason I stopped was Prince. I just met him in a beach bar and it was love at first sight, that never happened to me before. I know you think it's weird because he's so much younger than me but that's the way it happened. I don't know what it was, maybe it was the eyes. He looked at you straight on, you felt that everything he was saying just had to be the truth. It wasn't always, I found that out, but he always believed it was. He even believed all that communist stuff, he really believed he could save the world. He couldn't tell you something and not believe it himself. He was so sweet. I was a real sucker for that.

He didn't want me going out on the boats with Paul, he

didn't want me having anything to do with Paul in that way any more, he was jealous as hell. I guess I was a sucker for that, too. He wanted me all to himself, nobody else ever wanted that. He wanted us to have a baby. I never felt that important before.

As for Paul, you know what he did? He shook hands with me. That was all. I thought I was going to cry but instead I laughed. And I thought, that's what it's been like all along, sleeping with him and everything, there's been nothing more to it than that. Shaking hands.

Rennie wakes up in the middle of the night and Paul is still there, she can hardly believe it; he's even awake, he's a shape in the darkness, above her, resting on one elbow; is he watching her?

"Is that you?" she says.

"Who else would it be?" he says. She doesn't know. She reaches out for him and he's tangible, he doesn't go away.

It's early morning. Rennie can hear a sound outside the window, a bleating. She gets out of bed and looks: it's a goat, right beside the house, with a chain around its neck attached to a stone so it can't wander off. She wishes it would shut up. Two men are nearby, hacking at the shrubs with machetes. Gardeners. One of them has a transistor radio, which is thinly playing a hymn. Paul is still asleep, he must be used to it. She was dreaming there was another man in the bed with them; something white, a stocking or a gauze bandage, wrapped around his head.

When she wakes again Paul is gone. Rennie gets up and puts on her clothes, then wanders through the house looking for him. It's nobody's house, it could be a motel, it's empty space and he's left no footprints. It occurs to her that she's just spent the night with a man about whom she knows absolutely nothing at all. It seems a foolhardy thing to have done.

She goes outside. There's a tree beside the porch, covered with pink flowers, a swarm of hummingbirds around it. It looks arranged. The too-bright sunshine, the rock garden, the road below it along which two women are walking, one carrying a large tree limb balanced on her head, the foliage and then the blue harbour dotted with postcard boats, the whole vista is one-dimensional this morning, a scrim. At any moment it will rise slowly into the air and behind it will appear the real truth.

There's a noise coming from behind a clump of trees to the east, a desolate monotonous wail, a child. It goes on and on, as if this is a natural form of speech, almost like breathing. A woman's voice rises, there are thumps; the child's howling changes in intensity but not in rhythm.

Rennie looks through the telescope, which is focused on one of the yachts. There's a woman in a red bikini, lowering herself into the water; the telescope is so strong that even the roll of fat above the bikini bottom, even the striations on her belly are visible. Is this Paul's hobby, peering at distant flesh? Surely not. Yet the telescope confers furtive power, the power to watch without being watched. Rennie's embarrassed by it and turns away. She swings herself in the hammock, trying not to think. She feels deserted.

When Paul still doesn't come back, she goes into the house. She checks out the refrigerator for something to eat, but there's not much. Ice cubes in the ice cube tray, a tin of condensed milk with holes punched in the top, a small paper bag full of sugar, some yellowing limes, a pitcher of cold water. Noodles in the cupboard, a bottle of rum, a packet of coffee, some Tetley's teabags, a tin of Tate & Lyle golden syrup with a string of ants undulating around the lid. They skipped dinner last night and she's starving.

The logical explanation is that Paul has gone for food, since there isn't any. She wishes he'd left a note for her, but he doesn't seem like the note-leaving type. The house is very empty. She walks through the livingroom again; there aren't even any books or magazines. Maybe he keeps his personal things on the boat, the boats. She goes into the bedroom and looks into the closet: a couple of shirts, a spear gun and a mask and flippers, jeans folded on a hanger, that's it.

In the bureau there are some T-shirts, neatly stacked, and stuck at the back of the top drawer a couple of photos: colour snapshots, a white colonial house with a double garage, a green lawn, a yellow-haired woman in a shirtwaist dress, smiling to reveal slightly buck teeth; hair short and close to the head, an unsuccessful permanent growing out, two little girls, one blonde, one reddish-brown, both in pigtails with ribbons, it must have been a birthday. The mother's hands on their shoulders. The sun casts shadows under their eyes so that even though they're smiling they look slightly disappointed, the disappointment of ghosts. In the other picture Paul is there too, much younger, a crewcut but it must be him: a shirt and tie and pants with sharp creases, and beneath his eyes the same shadows.

Rennie feels she's prying but she's into it now, she might as well go on. It's not as if she'll use it for anything: she just wants to know, she wants to find something that will make Paul real for her. She goes into the bathroom and looks through the medicine cabinet. The brand names are unrevealing: Tylenol in a large bottle, Crest toothpaste, Elastoplast, Dettol. Nothing unusual.

There's another bedroom, or she assumes it's a bedroom. The door's closed but not locked: it opens as easily as all the other doors. It is a bedroom, or at least there's a bed in it. There's also a table, with what looks like a radio on it, a complicated-looking one, and some other equipment she can't identify. In the closet there's a large cardboard box standing on end. The address label's been torn off. It's full of Styrofoam packing beads, but otherwise empty. It looks very familiar.

There's someone in the house, walking across the

wooden floor. She feels as if she's been caught in a forbidden room, though Paul hasn't forbidden anything. Still, it isn't nice to snoop in other people's houses. She comes out, closing the door behind her as quietly as she can. Luckily there's a hallway: she can't be seen.

But it's not Paul, it's Lora, in a fresh pink dress with bare shoulders. "Hi there," she says. "I brought you some stuff." She's at the kitchen counter, taking it out of a straw basket: bread, butter, a carton of long-life milk, even a tin of jam. "He never has anything in the house. I'll make us some coffee, okay?"

She gets out the electric kettle, the coffee, the sugar; she knows exactly where everything is. Rennie sits at the wooden table, watching her. She knows she should feel thankful for all this attention, thoughtfulness, but instead she's irritated. This isn't her kitchen and she doesn't live here, so why should it bother her that Lora is acting as if she owns the place? And how did Lora know she'd be here? Maybe she didn't know it. Maybe she's in the habit.

"Where's Paul?" says Lora.

"I don't know," Rennie says. She's on the defensive: shouldn't she know, shouldn't he have told her?

"He'll turn up," says Lora lightly. "Here today, gone tomorrow, that's Paul."

Lora brings the coffee, a cup for each of them, and sets it down on the table. Rennie doesn't want to ask for food, though she's ravenous; she doesn't want to tell Lora about missing dinner. She doesn't want to tell Lora anything. She would like Lora to vanish, but instead Lora sits down at the table, settling in. She sips her coffee. Rennie watches her hands, the squat fingers, the rough gnawed skin around the nails.

"I wouldn't get too mixed up with Paul if I was you," she says. Here it comes, thinks Rennie. She's going to tell me something for my own good. In her experience, things that people told you for your own good were always unpleasant.

"Why not?" she says, smiling as neutrally as possible.

"I don't mean you can't," says Lora. "Hell, why not, it's a free country. Just, don't get mixed up, is all. Not that he gets that mixed up with most people anyway. Easy come, easy go. Around here there's a high turnover."

Rennie isn't sure what she's being told. Is she being warned off or just warned? "I guess you've known him a long time," she says.

"Long enough," says Lora.

Now there are footsteps and a shadow falls on the front window, and this time it is Paul, coming across the porch. He walks through the door smiling, sees Lora, blinks but keeps on smiling.

"I went for eggs," he says to Rennie. "I thought you'd be hungry." He sets a brown paper bag down on the table, proud of himself.

"Where in hell did you get any eggs, at this time of day?" says Lora. "The eggs aren't in yet." She's getting up, to go Rennie hopes, she sets down the coffee mug.

Paul grins. "I've got connections," he says.

Paul scrambles the eggs, quite well, they're not too dry; Rennie gives him three and a half stars for the eggs. They eat them with jam and toast. There's a toaster, though the only way you can get it to work, says Paul, is by short-circuiting it with a paring knife. He keeps meaning to get a new one, he says, but new toasters are smuggled in and none have come in lately.

After breakfast Rennie thinks she should offer to wash the dishes, since Paul did the cooking. "Forget that," says Paul. "Someone comes in." He takes her hands and pulls her to her feet and kisses her, his mouth tasting of buttered toast. Then he leads her into the bedroom. This time he takes off her clothes, not too quickly, without fumbling. She takes his hands with their blunt practical fingers, guides him, they slide onto the bed, it's effortless.

Rennie comes almost at once, they're both slippery with sweat, it's luxurious, indulgent, gleeful as rolling around in warm mud, the muscles of her thighs are aching. He pauses, goes on, pauses, goes on until she comes again. He's skilled and attentive, he's good at it. Maybe she's just a quick fuck for him, a transient, maybe they're both transients, passing through, is that what Lora was trying to say? But she can live with that, it's something, and something is better than nothing after all.

After a long time they get up and take a shower; together, but Paul is absent-minded as he soaps her back and then her breasts, carefully enough but he's already thinking about something else. She passes her hands over his body, learning him, the muscles, the hollows. She's looking for something, his presence in his own body, the other body beneath the tangible one, but she can't reach him, right now he's not there.

Paul takes Rennie's arm above the elbow as they step out into the white light. She wants to ask what they're going to do now, but she doesn't, because it doesn't seem to matter. Go with the flow, Jocasta would say, and she's going. She feels lazy and unhurried; the future, which contains among other things an overdraft at the bank, seems a long way from here. She knows she's fallen right into the biggest cliché in the book, a no-hooks, no-strings vacation romance with a mysterious stranger. She's behaving like a secretary, and things must be bad, because it isn't even bothering her. As long as she doesn't fall in love: that would be more than secretarial, it would be unacceptable. Love or sex? Jocasta would ask, and this time Rennie knows. Love is tangled, sex is straight. High-quality though, she'd say. Don't knock it.

They walk down to the sea and along the beach. By now he's remote but friendly, like a tour guide. Part of a package.

"See that building?" he says. He's pointing to a low shed-like structure. It's painted green and has three doors. "That made a lot of trouble here a couple of years ago. Ellis built it, it was supposed to encourage the tourists."

"What is it?" Rennie asks, unable to see why it would be encouraging.

"Now they use it to store fishnets in," says Paul, "but it used to be a can. A public can; Men, Women and Tourists. The idea was that the tourists would get off the boat and need a place to shit, and it would be right there handy for them. But the people here didn't think a thing like that should be down on the beach, out in the open like that. They thought it was indecent. They filled it up with stones, Tourists first." He smiles.

"They don't like tourists?" says Rennie.

"Let's put it this way," says Paul. "When the tourists come in, the prices go up. The big election issue this year is the price of sugar. They say it's getting too high, the people can't afford it."

"Just as well, it's bad for you," says Rennie, who believes in roughage, more or less.

"That depends on what else you have to eat," says Paul.

There's music, coming along the beach, wooden flutes and a drum. It's a parade of some sort, a mob of people walking along on the sand. Even though it's morning they have torches, cloth wrapped on sticks and soaked in kerosene, Rennie can smell it. Behind the adults in the crowd, around the edges, children are jumping and dancing in time to the music. Two kids are carrying a banner made from an old sheet: PRINCE OF PEACE: HE WORKS FOR YOU NOT YOU FOR HIM. Out front is Elva, chin up, strolling rather than marching. She has a white enamel potty in one hand and an unfurling roll of toilet paper in the other. She holds these objects high, as if they're trophies.

Rennie and Paul stand to the side as the parade goes past. At the very end comes Marsdon, still in his boots; the heels sink into the sand, it's hard for him to walk. He sees the two of them but does not acknowledge them.

"What does it mean?" says Rennie. "The toilet paper."

"It's aimed at the government," says Paul. "It's what they'll need after the election."

"I don't understand," says Rennie.

"They'll be so scared they'll shit their pants," says Paul. "Roughly translated." He's indulging her again.

They walk up the beach to the main road of the town. The parade has turned around now and is coming back; people have stopped to watch it. There's a car parked also, with two men in mirror sunglasses in the front and a third in the back. He's wearing a black suit, like an undertaker.

"The Minister of Justice," says Paul.

Paul says a lot of the stores are closed because of the election. Knots of men are gathered here and there; sun glints on the bottles as they pass from hand to hand. Some of the men nod to Paul. Not to Rennie: their attention slides over her, around her, they see her but only from the corners of their eyes.

They go up the hill and along a back street. There's a persistent hum; as they walk north it becomes a throb, a steady heartbeat. Metal, a motor of some kind.

"The power plant," says Paul. "It runs on oil. That's the poor end of town."

They go into a store called The Sterling Emporium. Paul

asks for some long-life milk, and the woman gets it for him. She's about forty-five, with huge muscled arms and a small neat head, the hair screwed into lime-green plastic curlers. She brings out a brown paper bag from under the counter. "I save it for you," she says.

"Eggs," Paul says. He pays. Rennie can't believe how much they cost.

"If they're that hard to get," she says, "why doesn't someone start a chicken farm?"

"You'd have to ship in the feed," says Paul. "They don't grow it here. The feed weighs more than the eggs. Besides, the eggs come in from the States."

"What's that got to do with it?" says Rennie. Paul only smiles.

"They catch the thief," the woman says to Paul as they're heading for the door. "The police take him on the boat today."

"He's lucky then," Paul says to her.

"Lucky?" says Rennie, when they're outside.

"He's still alive," says Paul. "They caught another man, last month, stealing pigs up at one of the villages; they pounded him to death, no questions asked."

"The police?" says Rennie. "That's terrible."

"No," says Paul. "The people he was stealing the pigs from. It's a good thing for this one he only stole from tourists. If it was locals they'd have kicked his head in or taken him out and dumped him into the sea. As far as they're concerned, stealing's worse than murder."

"I can't believe that," says Rennie.

"Look at it this way," says Paul. "If you get angry and chop up your woman, that's understandable; a crime of passion, you might say. But stealing you plan beforehand. That's how they see it."

"Is there a lot of that?" says Rennie.

"Stealing?" says Paul. "Only since the tourists came in."

"Chopping up your woman," says Rennie.

"Less than you might think," says Paul. "Mostly they beat or slice rather than chop." Rennie thinks of cookbooks. "There's no shooting at all. Not like in, say, Detroit."

"Why is that?" says Rennie, hot on the sociological trail.

Paul looks at her, not for the first time, as if she's a charming version of the village idiot. "They don't have any guns," he says.

Rennie is sitting on a white chair in the beach bar of the Lime Tree, where Paul has left her. Parked her. Stashed her. He has a boat coming in in a few days, he said, there are some things he has to take care of. Rennie feels peripheral.

Is there anything you need? he asked before he went off.

I thought most of the stores were closed, she said.

They are, he said.

Something to read, she said, with a touch of malice. If he's so good at it let him try that.

He didn't miss a beat. Anything in particular?

Anything you think I'd like, said Rennie.

Which will at least make him think about her. She sits at the wooden table, eating a grilled cheese sandwich. What could be nicer? What's wrong anyway? Why does she want to go, if not home, at least away? Paul doesn't love her, that's why, which ought to be irrelevant.

Don't expect too much, he said last night.

Too much of what? said Rennie.

Too much of me, said Paul. He was smiling, calm as ever, but she no longer found this reassuring. Instead she found it a symptom. Nothing could move him. He kissed her on the forehead, as if she were a child, as if he were kissing her goodnight.

Next you're going to tell me there isn't very much, said Rennie. Right?

Maybe there isn't, said Paul.

Rennie didn't know she was expecting anything until she was told not to. Now they seem vast, sentimental, grandiose, technicolour, magical, ridiculous, her expectations.

What am I doing here? thinks Rennie. I should take my body and run. I don't need another man I'm not supposed to expect anything from.

She's a tourist, she can keep her options open. She can always go somewhere else.

"I am disturbing you?" It's a statement, with the force of a question. Rennie looks up: it's Dr. Minnow, in a white shirt open at the throat, balancing a cup of coffee. He sits down without waiting for an answer.

"You are enjoying yourself at the home of your American friend?" he says slyly.

Rennie, who believes in personal privacy, is annoyed. "How did you know I'm staying there?" she says. She feels as if she's been caught by a high-school teacher, necking under the boys' gym stairs. A thing she never did.

Dr. Minnow smiles, showing his skewed teeth. "Everyone knows," he says. "I am sorry to interrupt you, but there are some things I must tell you now. For the article you are writing."

"Oh yes," Rennie says. "Of course." Surely he doesn't still believe she's going to do this, now or in the future; but apparently he does, he's looking at her with candour and assurance. Faith. "I don't have my notebook with me," she says, feeling more and more fraudulent.

"You can remember," says Dr. Minnow. "Please, continue with your lunch." He's not even looking at her, he's glancing around them, noting who's there. "We are seeing how the election is going, my friend," he says.

"Already?" says Rennie.

"I do not mean the results," says Dr. Minnow. "I mean the practices of this government. Ellis is winning, my friend. But not honestly, you understand? This is what I wish you to make clear: that Ellis will not have the support of the people." It's the same measured tone of voice he's always used, but Rennie can see now that he's far from calm. He's enraged. He sits with his thin hands placed one on the other, on top of the wooden table, but the hands are tense, it's as if he has to hold on to them to keep them from moving, lifting, striking out.

"The only votes Ellis is getting are the ones he buys. First they bribe the people with the foreign aid money from the hurricane," he says. "This I can prove to you, I have witnesses. If they are not afraid to come forward. He give out the roofing materials too, the sewage pipes, the things donated. On St. Antoine this bribery is effective, but here on Ste. Agathe it does not work. Here the people take the money from Ellis but vote for me anyway; they think this is a good joke. Ellis knows this trick will not work here on Ste. Agathe, he knows the people are for me. So he has been playing with the voters' list. When my people go to vote today, they find they are not recorded. Even some of my candidates have been removed, they cannot cast a vote in their own favour. 'Sorry,' they tell them. 'You cannot vote.' You know who he put on? Dead people, my friend. Half the people on the voters' list are dead. This government is being elected by corpses."

"But how could he do that?" says Rennie. "Didn't your party see the lists before the election?"

Dr. Minnow smiles his crooked smile. "This is not Canada, my friend," he says. "It is not Britain. Those rules no longer apply here. Nevertheless I will do what the sweet Canadians would do. I will challenge the results of the election in the courts and demand another vote, and I will call for an independent inquiry." He laughs a little. "It will have the same results here as it has there, my friend. None at all. Only there it takes longer."

"Why do you bother?" Rennie says.

"Bother?" says Dr. Minnow.

"If it's as rotten as you say," says Rennie, "why do you bother trying to do anything at all?"

Dr. Minnow pauses. She's shaken him a little. "I agree with you that it seems illogical and futile for me to do so," he says. "But this is why you do it. You do it because everyone tell you it is not possible. They cannot imagine things being different. It is my duty to imagine, and they know that for even one person to imagine is very dangerous to them, my friend. You understand?" He's about to say something else, but there are screams, from over near the kitchen door, the yacht people at the tables are looking, getting up, already there's a cluster of them.

Rennie stands up, trying to see what it is. It's Lora. She has one arm around Elva, whose eyes are closed, who's silently crying. There are red splotches on her PRINCE OF PEACE T-shirt. Her face is streaked, mapped, caked, dark red.

Lora sits at a table, one leg crossed, ankle on her knee. In front of her is a rum and lime and a glassful of ice cubes and a white enamel basin full of dark pink water. Elva is sitting beside her, still crying, her hands in her lap. Lora is washing away the blood with a blue washcloth from the hotel.

"Maybe I should lie her down," she says to Rennie. "What do you think?"

"God," says Rennie. "What happened?"

"I don't really know," says Lora. "I hardly saw it, it was too fast. One minute Prince was outside this polling station, just talking to the people, and the next thing there was all this shouting. It was two policemen with guns and the Minister of Justice. They just pushed in and started hammering Prince. Don't ask me why."

"Is he all right?" says Rennie.

"I don't even know that," says Lora. "I don't know where he went. He'll turn up, he usually does."

"Did she get knocked down by accident or something?" Rennie says.

"Her?" says Lora. "Hell no. She had her hands around the Justice Minister's neck, she damn near strangled him.

They hit her on the head with a pistol butt to make her let go."

"Is there anything I can do?" says Rennie, who isn't too comfortable: the sight of the blood in the white basin is making her feel sick. Maybe she can go for Band-Aids and then she'll be off the hook.

"Get me some cigarettes," says Lora. "Over at the bar, Benson and Hedges. Maybe we should take her home."

"Marsdon," says Elva. "Some time I kill that boy."

"What?" says Lora. "What's she saying?"

"Marsdon start it," says Elva. She stops crying and opens her eyes. "I hear him. He call the Justice Minister a bad name. Why he need to do that?"

"Shit," says Lora. "Marsdon thinks everybody has to die for the revolution. *His* revolution, is what he means. He'll do just about anything to make sure they do. I wish he'd take off those stupid cowboy boots, I bet he sleeps in them. He thinks he's God's gift, ever since he came back from the States. He was in the army up there, it did something to him. He saw too many movies and now he thinks he's a hero. If Prince gets elected, Marsdon gets to be the Minister of Justice. Shit, can you picture that?"

"I better now," says Elva. She takes an ice cube out of the glass and pops it into her mouth.

"She's still bleeding," says Rennie, but Elva's already walking away, steadily, as if there's nothing wrong with her. "Shouldn't you go with her?"

Lora shrugs. "What makes you think she'd let me?" she says. "She does what she likes. When you get to be her age around here nobody can tell you a thing."

"Does she have somewhere to go?" Rennie says. "Someone who can take care of her?"

"She has daughters," Lora says. "She has grandchildren. Not that she needs taking care of, mostly she takes care of them. This whole place runs on grandmothers."

A girl from the hotel comes and takes away the basin.

Rennie feels a little better, now that there's no actual blood. The people are back in their chairs, voices are normal, the sun shines on the boats in the harbour. Lora has her cigarettes now; she lights one, blowing the smoke out through her nostrils in a long grey sigh.

"The whole thing was Marsdon's idea," she says. "Prince running in the election. He never would've thought it up himself. Marsdon would run for God if it was open, except who would vote for him? Nobody likes him, everybody likes Prince, so he had to talk Prince into doing it for him. Prince thinks the sun shines right out of Marsdon's ass and nobody can tell him any different, so what can you do?"

"Do you think he'll win?" Rennie says.

"Christ, I hope not," Lora says. "I hope he loses. I hope he loses so bad he never even thinks of doing it again. Then maybe we can get back to some kind of a normal life."

Rennie trudges up the road towards Paul's house, because where else is there? She wishes Paul had told her when he was coming back, but she's hardly in a position to demand it. She's only a sort of house guest. A visitor.

There's no cool side of the road, and the asphalt is so hot it's almost melting. No one is sitting on the porches at this time of day; nevertheless, Rennie feels she's being watched. Halfway up the hill she's overtaken by a crowd of schoolgirls, ten or twelve of them, different sizes but all in heavy black skirts and white long-sleeved blouses, white bows in their hair, bare feet for the most part. Without asking or saying anything two of them take her hands, one on either side. The rest of them laugh and mill around her, examining her dress, her sandals, her purse, her hair.

"Do you live near here?" she asks one of them, the one holding her right hand. She's about six, and now that Rennie's speaking directly to her she's shy; but she doesn't let go of the hand.

"You have a dollar?" says the one on the left. But an older girl puts a stop to that. "Don't be so bold," she says.

"Are you cousins?" asks Rennie. One of them attempts to explain: some are sisters, others cousins, others cousins of some but not of others. "Her daddy the same, her mother different." When they reach Paul's gateway they let go of her hands without being told: they already know she's staying there. They watch as she goes up the steps, giggling behind her.

Rennie has no key, but the door isn't locked. Until recently, Paul said, you never had to lock your door, and he's still not in the habit. She goes out to the hammock and rocks herself, waiting for time to pass.

Half an hour later a short brown woman in a green print dress with large yellow butterflies walks in through the door. She nods at Rennie but takes no notice of her after that. She wipes off the table, washes the dishes and dries them and puts them away, cleans off the top of the stove, and sweeps the floor. Then she goes into the bedroom and brings the sheets out. She carries them into the garden at the side of the house, where she washes them, by hand, in a big red plastic pail, using water from a small tap that comes out of the water tank. She rinses them and wrings them out and hangs them up. She disappears into the bedroom again, to make up the bed, Rennie assumes. Rennie swings herself in the hammock, watching. She ought to pretend to be doing something important, but she can't, she's too uneasy, she can almost smell what it feels like to be cleaning up after other people's feeding and sex. She feels superfluous and both invisible and exposed: something so much there that nobody looks at it. The woman comes out of the bedroom with Rennie's pink bikini underpants from the day before. Presumably she's going to wash them.

"I'll do that," says Rennie.

The woman gives her a sideways glance, of contempt,

puts the underpants on the kitchen counter, nods again, and goes down the steps to the road.

Rennie gets up and locks the doors of the house and mixes herself a drink. She lies down on the bed, under the mosquito net, meaning to take only a short nap. Then someone is touching her neck. Paul. A faceless stranger.

It's raining; heavy drops like tacks patter on the tin roof. The huge leaves outside the window move in the wind, making a sound like the dragging of thick cloth across a floor. Something's loose out there.

Rennie's both avid and melancholy, as if it's the last time. More and more the emptiness of this house reminds her of a train station. Terminal, the place where you go to say goodbye. Paul is being too tender, it's the tenderness of a man boarding a troop ship. A man who can hardly wait. *Wait for me* would be the proper thing for him to say; he'd have no intention of doing the same himself. But she doesn't know where he's going. He's not giving anything away.

"If I were noble," says Paul, "I'd tell you to get the next boat out to St. Antoine and get the next plane out to Barbados and get the hell back home."

Rennie's kissing him beside the ear. His skin is dry, salty, the hair greying there. "Why would you do that?" she says.

"Safer," says Paul.

"Who for, you or me?" says Rennie. She thinks he's talking about their relationship. She thinks he's admitting something. This cheers her up.

"You," he says. "You're getting too involved, it's bad for you."

Rennie stops kissing. *Massive involvement,* she thinks. He smiles at her, looking down at her with his too-blue eyes, and she wonders whether she can believe a word he says.

"Take the plane, lady," he says, very sweetly.

"I don't want to go back," Rennie says.

"I'd like you to," says Paul.

"Are you trying to get rid of me?" says Rennie, smiling, fearing it.

"No," says Paul. "Maybe I'm just being stupid. Maybe I want there to be something good I've done."

Rennie feels she can make her own choices, she doesn't need to have them made for her. In any case she doesn't want to be something that Paul has done. Good or otherwise.

She thinks about going back. There will be the hedgehopper to Barbados, the wait in the steamy airport among the secretaries, just-arrived or in transit, lonely and hopeful, with their vague expectations; then the monotonous jet and then the airport, sterile and rectilinear. It will be cold outside and grey, and the wind will smell of diesel fuel. In the city people will be hunched into their winter coats, scuttling heads-down along the sidewalks, their faces not flat and open like the faces here but narrow and pallid and pushed into long snouts, like the snouts of rats. No one will even glance at anyone else. What does she have to look forward to?

Jake came over to pick up his suits and his books and pictures. He had his new lady's car downstairs, his own was on the fritz. He didn't say whether or not the new lady was in it, and Rennie didn't ask. *Lady* was his own term, a recent one. He had never called Rennie his lady.

He made several trips, up the stairs and down again, and Rennie sat at the kitchen table and drank coffee. From the hooks above the stove there were now things missing, pots, frying pans, which had left round haloes of lighter yellow on the wall, penumbras of grease. From now on she would have to decide what to eat. Jake decided before: even when it was her turn to cook he decided. He brought home all kinds of things: bones, wrinkled old sausages filmed with powdery mould, rank and horrible cheeses which he insisted she had to try. Life is an improvisation, he said. Exploit your potential.

Rennie's potential had been exploited, she didn't have any left. Not for Jake, who stood awkwardly in the doorway, holding a dark blue sock, asking if she'd seen the other one. Domesticity still hung in the air around them, like dust in sunlight, a lingering scent. Rennie said she hadn't, but he might try the bathroom, behind the laundry hamper. He went out and she could hear him rummaging. She should have gone somewhere else, not been here, they should have arranged things differently.

She tried not to think of the new lady, of whom it was not right to be jealous. She didn't know what the new lady looked like. To Rennie she was just a headless body, with or without a black nightgown. As perhaps she was to Jake. What is a woman, Jake said once. A head with a cunt attached or a cunt with a head attached? Depends which end you start at. It was understood between them that this was a joke. The new lady stretched out before her, a future, a space, a blank, into which Jake would now throw himself night after night the way he had thrown himself into her, each time extreme and final, as if he was pitching himself headlong over a cliff. It was for this she felt nostalgia. She wondered what it was like to be able to throw yourself into another person, another body, a darkness like that. Women could not do it. Instead they had darkness thrown into them. Rennie couldn't put the two things together, the urgency and blindness of the act, which had been urgent and blind for her too, and this result, her well-lit visible frozen pose at the kitchen table.

Jake was in the doorway again. Rennie did not want to look at him. She knew what she would see, it would be the same thing he saw when he looked at her. Failure, of a larger order than they would once have thought possible. But how could there be failure, since failure had been outside their terms of reference? No strings, no commitments, that's what they'd said. What would *success* have been?

Rennie thought of telling him about the man with the rope. Meanly, since it would only make him feel guilty and that was why she would be doing it. What would Jake make of it, the sight of one of his playful fantasies walking around out there, growling and on all fours? He knew the difference between a game and the real thing, he said; a desire and a need. She was the confused one.

Rennie did not say anything, nor did she stand up and throw her arms around Jake's neck, nor did she shake hands with him. She didn't want charity so she didn't do anything. She sat with her hands clenched around the coffee cup as if it was a bare socket, live electricity, and she couldn't move. Was this *open*, was it grief? What had become of them, two dead bodies, what could you do without desire, without need, what was she supposed to feel, what could be done? She pressed her hands together to keep them still. She thought of her grandmother, hands together like that, head bowed over the joyless Christmas turkey, saying grace.

Keep well, said Jake, and that was the whole problem. He could not admit she wasn't. No fun playing games with the walking wounded. Not only no fun, no fair.

The day after Jake was gone, for good, Rennie did not get up in the morning. There did not seem to be any point. She lay in bed thinking about Daniel. It was true he was a fantasy for her: a fantasy about the lack of fantasy, a fantasy of the normal. It was soothing to think of Daniel, it was like sucking your thumb. She thought about him waking up in the morning, rolling over, turning off the alarm clock, making love with his pregnant wife, whose face Rennie did not picture, carefully and with consideration but somewhat quickly because it was morning and he had other things to do. His wife didn't come but they're both used to that, they love each other anyway. She'll come later, some other day, when Daniel has more time. Taking a shower, drinking a cup of coffee, black, no sugar, which is handed to him by his wife through the bathroom door, looking in the mirror while he shaves and not seeing at all what she saw when she looked at him. Daniel getting dressed, in those mundane clothes of his, tying his shoelaces.

At three in the afternoon Rennie called Daniel, at the office, where she thought he would be. She left her number with the nurse: she said it was an emergency. She had never done such a thing before. She knew she was being wicked, but thinking about Daniel brought out in her whatever notions of wickedness were left over from her background. Daniel himself had such clean fingernails, such pink ears, he was so *good*.

Daniel called her back fifteen minutes later, and Rennie did her best to give the impression of someone on the verge of suicide. She never actually said it, she could not go so far, but she knew the only way she could entice Daniel over would be to give him a chance to rescue her. She was crying though, that was real enough.

She wanted Daniel to hold her hand, pat her on the back, comfort her, be with her. That was what he was good at. She had given up expecting anything else. She got dressed, made the bed, brushed her teeth and hair, being a good child at least to this extent. When Daniel came he would give her a gold star.

He knocked at the door, she opened it, he was there. What she saw was not someone she knew. Anger and fear, and something else, a need but not a desire. She'd pushed it too far.

Don't do that again, he said, and that was all for the time being.

She thought he knew what was inside her. No such luck.

After a while Rennie was lying on her own bed, which was still more or less made, and Daniel was putting on his shoes. She could see the side of his head, the bent back. The fact was that he had needed something from her, which she could neither believe nor forgive. She'd been counting on him not to: she was supposed to be the needy one, but it was the other way around. He was ashamed of himself, which was the last thing she'd wanted. She felt like a vacation, Daniel's, one he thought he shouldn't have taken. She felt like a straw that had been clutched, she felt he'd been drowning. She felt raped.

This is what *terminal* means, she thought. Get used to it.

After they make love Rennie wraps a towel around herself and goes out to the kitchen. There's a lizard, sand-coloured, with huge dark eyes, hunting the ants that file towards the cupboard where the golden syrup is kept. Rennie eats three pieces of bread and jam and drinks half a pint of long-life milk. Paul says some people here think that because it says LONG LIFE on the carton, you'll have a long life if you drink it.

She goes back to the bedroom and steps over the clothes entwined on the floor. Paul is lying with his hands behind his head, legs flung out, looking up at the ceiling. Rennie climbs in under the mosquito net and curls beside him. She licks the hollow of his stomach, which is damp and salty, but he hardly twitches. Then she runs her hand over him, stroking. He blinks and smiles a little. The hair on his chest is grey, and Rennie finds it comforting, this sign of age: it's possible after all for people to grow older, change, weather. Without deteriorating; up to a point. It's the past, it's time that's stained him.

She wants to ask about his wife. It must be a wife, the house and the lawn and the shirtwaist dress wouldn't go with anything else. But she doesn't want to admit she's been going through the bureau drawers.

"Were you ever married?" she asks.

"Yes," says Paul. He doesn't volunteer anything else, so Rennie keeps on going. "What happened?"

Paul smiles. "She didn't like my lifestyle," he says. "She said there wasn't enough security. She didn't mean financial. After the Far East, I tried to go back and settle down, but when you've been living that way, day to day, never knowing when someone's going to blow you into little pieces, that other kind of life seems fake, you can't believe in it. I just couldn't get too excited about taking the car in for the winter tune-up or any of that. Not even my kids."

"So you're a danger freak," says Rennie. "Is that why you run dope?"

Paul smiles. "Maybe," he says. "Or maybe it's the money. It beats selling real estate. Second biggest dollar import commodity in the States; oil's the first. I don't take unnecessary risks though." He takes her hand, moves it down, closes his eyes. "That's why I'm still alive."

"What do you dream about?" says Rennie after a while. She wants to know, which is dangerous, it means she's interested.

Paul waits before answering. "Not a hell of a lot," says Paul finally. "I think I gave it up. I don't have time for it any more."

"Everyone dreams," says Rennie. "Why don't men ever want to say what they dream about?"

Paul turns his head and looks at her. He's still smiling, but he's tightened up. "That's why I couldn't hack the States," he says. "When I went back there, the women were talking like that. That's how they began all their sentences: *Why don't men.*"

Rennie feels she's been both misinterpreted and accused. "Is there something wrong with saying that?" she says. "Maybe we want to know."

"There's nothing wrong with saying it," says Paul. "They can say it all they like. But there's no law that says I have to listen to it."

Rennie continues to stroke, but she's hurt. "Sorry I asked," she says.

Paul puts a hand on her. "It's not that I've got anything against women," he says. Rennie supplies: *In their place.* "It's just that when you've spent years watching people dying, women, kids, men, everyone, because they're starving or because someone kills them for complaining about it, you don't have time for a lot of healthy women sitting around arguing whether or not they should shave their legs."

Rennie's been outflanked, so she retreats. "That was years ago," she says. "They've moved on to other issues."

"That's what I mean," says Paul. "*Issues.* I used to believe in issues. When I first went out there I believed in all the issues I'd been taught to believe in. Democracy and freedom and the whole bag of tricks. Those gadgets don't work too well in a lot of places and nobody's too sure what does. There's no good guys and bad guys, nothing you can count on, none of it's permanent any more, there's a lot of improvisation. Issues are just an excuse."

"For what?" says Rennie. She leaves her hand on him but stops moving it.

"Getting rid of people you don't like," says Paul. "There's only people with power and people without power. Sometimes they change places, that's all."

"Which are you?" says Rennie.

"I eat well, so I must have power," says Paul, grinning. "But I'm an independent operator. Freelance, same as you."

"You don't take me very seriously, do you?" says Rennie sadly. She wants him to talk to her, about himself.

"Don't start that," says Paul. "You're on vacation." He rolls over on top of her. "When you go back home, I'll take you seriously."

Once upon a time Rennie was able to predict men; she'd been able to tell exactly what a given man would do at a given time. When she'd known that, when she was sure, all she had to do was wait and then he would do it. She used to think she knew what most men were like, she used to think she knew what most men wanted and how most men would respond. She used to think there was such a thing as most men, and now she doesn't. She's given up deciding what will happen next.

She puts her arms around him. She's trying again. She should know better.

From the refrigerator Paul takes two fish, one bright red, the other blue and green, with a beak like a parrot's. He cleans them with a large black-handled knife, kneeling by the tap in the garden. Rennie can smell the fish from where she lies in the hammock; it's not her favourite smell. It strikes her that she hasn't yet been to the beach here. She would like to lie on the sand and let the sun wash out her head so that nothing is left in it but white light, but she knows the consequences, a headache and skin like a simmered prune's. She's gone so far as to put on a pair of shorts though.

There's a vine over the porch, large cream-white flowers, cup-shaped and unreal. From the porch railing two blue-green lizards watch her. The road below is empty.

Paul leaves the fish on the porch and shinnies up a nearby tree, coming down with a papaya. Rennie can't help it, but all this activity reminds her of Boy Scouts. Next thing you know he'll be showing her how well he can tie knots.

There's a sunset, a quick one; it's getting dark. Rennie goes inside. Paul is cooking the fish, with onions and a little water, but he won't let her help.

They sit across from each other at the wooden table. Rennie gives him four out of five on the fish. He's even got candles; a huge green locust has just singed itself in one of them. Paul picks it up, still jerking, and throws it out the door.

"So you thought I was with the CIA," he says, as he sits down again.

Rennie is not so much embarrassed as startled. She isn't ready for it, she drops her fork. "I suppose Lora told you that," she says.

Paul is having fun. "It's a strange coincidence," he says, "because we thought you were, too."

"What?" says Rennie. "You must be crazy!" This time it's not surprise, it's outrage.

"Look at it from our point of view," says Paul. "It's a good front, you have to admit. The travel piece, the camera. This just isn't the sort of place they do a lot of travel pieces about. Then the first person you connect with happens to be the man who has the best chance of defeating the government in the election. That's Minnow. Nobody watching would call that an accident."

"But I hardly know him," says Rennie.

"I'm just telling you what it looks like," says Paul. "Spot the CIA, it's a local game; everybody plays it. Castro used tourists a lot, and now all kinds of people are using them. The CIA is using non-Americans a lot; it's a better cover. Locals and foreigners. We know they're sending someone else in; they may be here already. There's always one or two here, and in my business you like to know who it is."

"So it wasn't the Abbotts after all," says Rennie. "I didn't think so, they were just too old and nice."

"As a matter of fact it was," says Paul. "But they've been recalled. Whoever comes in next will be taking a more active role. It could be anyone."

"But *me*," says Rennie. "Come on!"

"We had to check it out," says Paul.

"Who is *we*?" she says. "Lora, I suppose." Things are coming clear. They picked her up almost as soon as she was off the plane. First Paul in the hotel diningroom; so much for eye contact. Then Lora, the next day on the reef boat. Between the two of them they'd hardly let her out of their sight. There must have been someone following her around and reporting back to them so they'd know where she was heading.

"Lora comes in handy," says Paul.

"Who went through my room?" says Rennie. It couldn't

have been him, since he was having dinner with her at the Driftwood.

"Did someone go through your room?" asks Paul. Rennie can't tell if his surprise is real or not.

"Everything," she says. "Including the box. The one in your spare bedroom."

"I don't know who it was," says Paul. "I'd like to though."

"If you thought I was the CIA, why did you send me to pick up the box?" says Rennie.

"First of all," says Paul, "they don't care that much about the dope trade. They like to know what you're up to so they can maybe use it on you to get you to do something for them, but apart from that they don't care. It's the political stuff they care about. But the police hanging around the airport are something else. They'd seen Lora too many times, that was the sixth box we'd run through. We needed someone else and I didn't want it to be me. It's always better to use a woman, they're less likely to be suspected. If you weren't an agent, no harm done; unless you got caught, of course. If you were, you'd already know what was in the box but you'd pick it up anyway, you wouldn't want to lose contact by refusing. Either way, I'd have the gun."

"It was for you?" says Rennie.

"In my business you need them," Paul says. "People shoot at you and you have to be able to shoot back. I had some coming up from Colombia, you can often pick them up down there, serial numbers filed off but they're U.S. Army equipment, military aid, you get them from crooked generals who want to make a little money on the side. But I lost that boat and I lost the connection at the same time. Elva's the contingency plan. She really does have a daughter in New York, so it was easy enough to fly her there with the money. Those people like cash. She didn't know what it was for though. She didn't know what was in the boxes."

"Lost?" says Rennie.

"The boat got sunk, the general got shot," says Paul. "I've just replaced both of them but it took me a while."

"Who's shooting at you?" says Rennie, who is trying very hard not to find any of this romantic. Boys playing with guns, that's all it is. Even telling her about this is showing off; isn't it? But she can't help wondering whether Paul has any bullet holes in him. If he has, she'd like to see.

"Who isn't?" says Paul. "I'm an independent. They don't like people like me, they want a monopoly."

Rennie picks up her fork again. She lifts her fish, separating the bones.

"So that's what all this was about," she says.

"All what?" says Paul.

"All this fucking," says Rennie, pronouncing the g despite herself. "You were checking me out."

"Don't be stupid," says Paul. "It was mostly Marsdon's idea anyway, he's paranoid about the CIA, it's like a monomania with him. He wanted us to get you out of here as fast as possible. I never believed it myself."

This isn't the answer Rennie wants. She wants to be told she's important to him. "Why not?" she says.

"You were too obvious," Paul says. "You were doing everything right out in the open. You were too nice. You were too naïve. You were too easy. Anyway, you wanted it too much. I can tell when a woman's faking it."

Rennie puts her fork down carefully on her plate. Something is being used against her, her own desire, she doesn't know why. "I'll do the dishes," she says.

Rennie fills the sink with hot water from the teakettle. Paul is in the second bedroom, with the door closed. He says he's trying to find out who's winning the election. Local politics, he's told her. Nothing to do with her. She can hear blurred voices, the crackle of static.

She's scraping the fishbones off the plates when she hears footsteps on the porch. There are a lot more footsteps than she's prepared to deal with. Wiping her hands on the dish-towel, she goes to the second bedroom and knocks at the door. "Paul," she says. Feeling like a wife. Incapable.

Rennie's in the bedroom, which is where she wants to be and where Paul wants her to be. Out there, in the livingroom, there's a loud meeting going on. The results of the election are in, Ellis has seven seats, Minnow has six and Prince has two, and Rennie can add. So can everyone in the livingroom, but so far six and two still only make six and two.

It's nothing to do with her though. Paul said that and she believes it. She's reading the books he got for her somewhere, God knows where since they're museum pieces, Dell Mysteries from the forties, with the eye-and-keyhole logo on the cover, the map of the crime scene on the back, and the cast of characters on the first page. The pages are yellowed and watermarked and smell of mould. Rennie reads the casts of characters and tries to guess who gets murdered. Then she reads up to the murder and tries to guess who did it, and then she turns to the back of the book to see if she's right. She doesn't have much patience for the intricacies of clues and deductions.

"You goin' to let that bastard win?" It's Marsdon, almost a shriek. "You let him fool you? So many years he betray the people, you goin' to betray the people too?"

Dr. Minnow is making a speech; his voice rises and falls, rises and falls. He, after all, has more experience as well as more seats, he will be the leader of the opposition, if nothing else. Why should he back down in favor of Prince? He cannot let the Justice Party swing in the direction of Castro.

"Castro!" Marsdon yells. "All you tell me is Castro! Prince no Castro!"

Why here? Rennie asked. I'm the connection, Paul told her. Rennie wishes they would turn down the volume. She's not doing too well with the murderers, but she's eighty percent on the victims: two blondes with pale translucent skin, mouths like red gashes and swelling breasts bursting through their dresses, two tempestuous redheads with eyes of green smouldering fire and skin like clotted cream, each carefully arranged on floor or bed like a still life, not quite naked, clothing disheveled to suggest rape, though there was no rape in the forties, finger-marks livid around the throat—they loved *livid*—or a wound still oozing, preferably in the left breast. Dead but not molested. The private eyes finding them (two hot-tempered Irishmen, one Greek, two plain Americans) describe each detail of the body fully, lushly, as if running their tongues over it; all that flesh, totally helpless because totally dead. Each of them expresses outrage at the crime, even though the victim provoked it. Rennie finds it curiously innocent, this hypocritical outrage. It's sweetly outmoded, like hand-kissing.

After a while Rennie hears the sound of chairs being scraped back, and then it's quiet. Then Paul comes into the room and starts taking off his clothes, as if nothing at all has happened. He peels the T-shirt off first, drops it to the floor. Already it seems to her a familiar gesture. Rennie counts: she's known him five days.

"What happened?" she says. "What were they doing?"

"Dealing," says Paul. "Minnow won. As of fifteen minutes ago, he's the new prime minister. They've all gone off to have a party."

"Marsdon backed down?"

"No," says Paul. "He didn't exactly back down. He said he was doing it for the good of the people. There was some disagreement about who *the people* were, but you have to expect that."

"Did Prince just sort of abdicate?" says Rennie.

"Prince didn't do anything," Paul says. "Marsdon did it for him. Marsdon's going to be Minister of Tourism, and they sawed off at Justice Minister for Prince. That's why Marsdon didn't struggle too hard. He wants to see the look on the face of the current Justice Minister. They hate each other like shit."

He disappears into the bathroom and Rennie can hear him brushing his teeth. "You don't seem too happy," she calls.

Paul comes out again. He walks flat-footed, heavily towards the bed. He's older than she thought. "Why should I be?" he says.

"Dr. Minnow's a good man," says Rennie. This is true, he is a good man, and it's not his fault that goodness of his kind makes her twitchy. It's like being with someone on a diet, which always makes her lust for chocolate mousse and real whipped cream.

"Good men can be a pain in the ass," says Paul. "They're hard to deal with. He's a politician so he's a user, they have to be, but he's less of a user than most. He believes in democracy and fair play and all those ideas the British left here along with cricket, he really does believe that shit. He thinks guns are playing dirty."

"What do you think?" says Rennie. She's back to interviewing him.

Paul's sitting on the edge of the bed, as if reluctant to get into it. "It doesn't matter what I think," he says. "I'm neutral. What matters right now is what the other side thinks. What Ellis thinks."

"What does Ellis think?" says Rennie.

"That remains to be seen," says Paul. "He's not going to like it."

"What about Prince?" says Rennie.

"Prince is a believer," says Paul. "He supplies the belief. He thinks that's all you need."

Now at last he does get into the bed, crawling under the mosquito net, tucking it in before turning to her. He's tired, no doubt of that, and Rennie suddenly finds this very suburban. All he needs are some striped pyjamas and a heart attack and the picture will be complete. He's not the one who's giving that impression though. It's her own solicitude, faked. She knows something he doesn't know, she knows she's leaving. She'll be on the afternoon boat tomorrow, and everything in between is just filler. Maybe she'll tell him she has a headache. She could use some sleep.

Still, doubt is what you should give other people the benefit of, or that's the theory. She owes him something: he was the one who gave her back her body; wasn't he? Although he doesn't know it. Rennie puts her hands on him. It can be, after all, a sort of comfort. A kindness.

"What do you dream about?" Rennie says. It's her last wish, it's all she really wants to know.

"I told you," Paul says.

"But you lied," says Rennie.

For a while Paul doesn't say anything. "I dream about a hole in the ground," he says finally.

"What else?" says Rennie.

"That's all," says Paul. "It's just a hole in the ground, with the earth that's been dug out. It's quite large, there are trees around it. I'm walking towards it. There's a pile of shoes off to the side."

"Then what?" says Rennie.

"Then I wake up," says Paul.

Rennie hears it before she realizes what it is. At first she thinks it's rain. It is rain, but something more. Paul is out of the bed before she is. Rennie goes into the bathroom for a large towel, which she wraps around her. The pounding at the door goes on, and the voice.

When she gets to the livingroom what she sees is Paul, stark naked, and Lora with her arms around him. She's dripping wet.

Rennie stands with her mouth open, holding her towel

around her, while Paul grapples with Lora, pushing her away from him, holding her at arms' length, shaking her. She's crying. "Oh God, oh Christ," she says.

"What is it?" says Rennie. "Is she sick?"

"Minnow's been shot," Paul says, over the top of Lora's head.

Rennie goes cold. "That's incredible!" she says. She feels as if someone's just told her the Martians have landed. It must be a put-on, an elaborate joke.

"They shot him from behind," says Lora. "In the back of the head. Right out on the road and everything."

"Who would do it?" Rennie says. She thinks of the men, the followers, the ones with mirror sunglasses. She tries to focus on something useful she could do. Maybe she should make some tea, for Lora.

"Get your clothes on," Paul says to her.

Lora starts to cry again. "It's so crummy," she says. "The fuckers. I never thought they'd go that far."

Dr. Minnow is in a closed coffin in the livingroom. The coffin is dark wood, plain; it rests on two kitchen chairs, one at either end. On top of the coffin there's a pair of scissors, open, and Rennie wonders whether they are part of some ritual, some ceremony she doesn't know about, or whether someone's just forgotten them.

The coffin is like a stage prop, an emblem out of some horrible little morality play; only they've forgotten to say what the moral is. At any moment the lid will pop up and Dr. Minnow will be sitting there, smiling and nodding, as if he's pulled off a beautiful joke. Only this does not happen.

Rennie is in the livingroom with the women, who sit on chairs or on the floor, children sleeping in their laps, or stand against the wall. It's one o'clock at night. There are other women in the kitchen, making coffee and setting out plates for the food that the women have brought: Rennie can see them through the open doorway. It's a lot like Griswold, it's a lot like her grandmother's funeral, except in Griswold you ate after the burial, not before, and you did the hymn-singing in church. Here they do it whenever they feel like it: one starts, the others join in, three-part harmony. Someone's playing the mouth-organ.

Dr. Minnow's wife has the place of honour beside the coffin; she cries and cries, she makes no attempt to hide it, nobody disapproves. This, too, is different from Griswold: sniffling was all right, into a handkerchief, but not this open crying, raw desolation, this nakedness of the face. It wasn't decent. If you went on like that they gave you a pill and told you to go upstairs and lie down.

"Why this happen?" the wife says, over and over again. "Why this happen?"

Elva is sitting beside her, holding her hand, which she rubs gently between her own two hands, massaging the fingers. "I see him into this world," she says. "Now I see him out of it."

Two women come out of the kitchen, carrying a tray with mugs of coffee. Rennie takes one, and some banana bread and a coconut cookie. It's her second mug of coffee. She's sitting on the floor, her legs are going to sleep beneath her.

She feels guilty and useless, guilty because useless. She thinks of all the history that's lying there in the coffin, wasted, a hole blown through it. It seems to her a very tacky way to die. Now she knows why he wanted her to write about this place: so there would be less chance of this happening, to him.

"Should we be doing anything?" she whispers to Lora, who's sitting beside her.

"Who knows?" says Lora. "I never went to one of these before."

"How long does it go on?" says Rennie.

"All night," says Lora.

"Why this happen?" says the wife again.

"It was his time," says one of the women.

"No," says Elva. "A Judas here."

The women stir uneasily. Someone begins to sing:

> *"Blessed assurance, Jesus is mine,*
> *Oh what a foretaste of Glory divine,*
> *Perfect salvation, sent from above,*
> *Washed in his goodness, lost in his love."*

Rennie is uneasy. It's hot in the room and too crowded, it smells of cinnamon and coffee and sweat, a sweet, stuffy, unhealthy smell, clogged with emotion, and it's getting so much like Griswold she can't bear it. *What did she die of? Cancer, praise the Lord.* That was the kind of thing they said. She stands up, as unobtrusively as she can, and edges towards the porch, out the door that stands mercifully open.

The men are outside, on the concrete porch that runs around three sides of the house. The drink here is not coffee; in the dim porch light the bottles gleam, passing from hand to hand. There are more men, down below in the garden, there's a crowd, gathering, some of them have torches, there are voices, tense, rising.

Paul is out there, a conspicuous white face, standing to one side. He spots Rennie and pulls her back against the wall beside him. "You should be in with the women," he says.

Rennie chooses to take this not as a put-down but as a social hint. "I couldn't breathe," she says. "What's going on down there?"

"Nothing yet," says Paul. "They're mad as hell though. Minnow was from Ste. Agathe. A lot of people here are related to him."

Someone's carrying a chair over to the porch railing. A man climbs up on it and looks down at the upturned faces. It's Marsdon. The voices quiet.

"Who kill this man?" he says.

"Ellis," someone calls, and the crowd chants, "Ellis, El-lis."

"Judas," says Marsdon, almost a shout.

"Judas. Judas."

Marsdon raises his hands and the chanting stops.

"How many more times?" he says. "How much more, how many more dead? Minnow a good man. We are going to wait till he kill all of us, every one? We been asking, many times, we get nothing. Now we gonna take."

There's shouting, an enraged cheer, then one clear voice: *"Tear down Babylon!"* In the dark below, bodies begin to move. Marsdon bends, stands up again; in his hands is a compact little machine gun.

"Shit," says Paul. "I told them not to do that."

"Do what?" says Rennie. "What are they going to do?" She can feel her heart going, she doesn't understand. *Massive involvement.*

"They don't have enough guns," says Paul. "It's as simple as that. I don't know where Prince is, he'll have to stop them."

"What if he can't?" says Rennie.

"Then he'll have to lead them," says Paul. He pushes off from the wall. "Go back to the house," he says.

"I don't know the way," says Rennie. They came in a jeep.

"Lora does," says Paul.

"What about you?" says Rennie.

"Don't worry," says Paul. "I'll be fine."

They go by the back streets, Lora first, then Rennie. The only place to be, in Lora's opinion, is out of the way. It's muddy here from the rain but they don't bother to pick their way around the water-filled potholes, there's no time and it's hard to see. The only light comes from the small concrete-block houses set at intervals back from the road. The road is deserted, the action is a couple of streets farther down towards the sea. They hear shouting, the smash of glass.

"Bank windows," says Lora. "I bet you anything."

They cross a side street. For a moment there's a glimpse of torches. "Don't let them see you is my motto," says Lora. "In the dark anyone's fair game. They can apologize afterwards but who cares, eh? There's going to be a few old scores settled, no matter what else they do."

Now they can hear gunfire, irregular and staccato, and after a minute the feeble lights in the houses flicker and go out, the underlying hum in the air shudders and cuts. "There goes the power plant," says Lora. "They'll take over that and the police station, there's only two policemen on Ste. Agathe anyway so it shouldn't be that hard. There isn't a hell of a lot else to take over around here. Maybe they'll smash up the Lime Tree and get drunk on the free booze."

"I can't see," says Rennie. Her sandals are muddy, the bottom of her skirt is dripping; she's more disgusted than frightened. Window-breaking, juvenile delinquency, that's all it is, this tiny riot.

"Come on," says Lora. She gropes for Rennie's arm, pulls her along. "They'll be up here in a minute, they'll be after Ellis's people. We'll take the path."

Rennie stumbles after her. She's disoriented, she has no idea where they are, even the stars are different here. It's slow going without a moon. Branches heavy with damp flowers brush against her, the smells are still alien. She pushes through the leaves, slipping on the wet earth of the path. Below them is the road. Through the undergrowth she can see moving lights now, flashlights, torches, and hurrying figures. It's almost like a festival.

When they finally reach the house it's completely dark.

"Damn," says Rennie. "We locked it when we went out and Paul's got the key. We'll have to break in."

But Lora's already at the door, pushing. "It's open," she says.

As soon as they're inside the door there's a sharp glare, sudden, against their eyes. Rennie almost screams.

"It's only you," says Paul. He lowers the flashlight.

"How in shit did you get back here ahead of us?" says Lora.

"Took the jeep," says Paul. To Rennie he says, "Get your things."

"Where's Prince?" says Lora.

"Down there being a hero," says Paul. "They've got the two policemen tied up with clothesline, and they're declaring an independent state. Marsden's writing a proclamation and they want to send it out over my radio. They're asking Grenada to recognize them. There's even some talk of invading St. Antoine."

"You've got to be kidding," says Lora. "How the shit would they do that?"

"In the fishing boats," says Paul, "plus whatever other boats they can grab. They've got a bunch of Swedish tourists in the police station, and those two German women who are making one hell of a fuss. They've requisitioned them. Hostages."

"Can't you stop them?" says Lora.

"You think I haven't tried?" says Paul. "They won't listen to me any more. They think they've won. It's way out of control. Go into the bedroom," he says to Rennie," and get your stuff. There's a candle in there. I'm taking you over to St. Antoine, you can get the morning plane out. If you were smart," he says to Lora, "you'd go with her. You've still got your passport." Rennie lets herself be ordered. This is his scene after all, his business; he's the one who's supposed to know what to do next. She hopes he does.

She feels her way along the hall into the bedroom. There isn't much to pack. It might as well be a hotel room; it has the same emptiness, the same melancholy aura of a space that has been used but not lived in. The bed is tangled, abandoned. She can't remember having slept in it.

The jeep is parked on the road in front of the house. They go down the stone steps, hurrying, their feet in the strong beam of the flashlight.

Paul has one of the small machine guns; he carries it casually, like a lunch pail. To Rennie it looks like a toy, the kind you aren't supposed to give little boys for Christmas. She doesn't believe it could go off, and surely if it did nothing would come out of it but rubber bullets. She's afraid, but even her fear seems inappropriate. Surely they are not in any real danger. She tries hard for annoyance: perhaps she should feel interrupted.

Just before they climb into the jeep Paul heaves something overarm into the darkness of the rock garden.

"What was that?" says Lora.

"I killed the radio," says Paul. "I called my boats first. They're staying away. I don't want anyone calling St. Antoine, I don't want any welcoming committees in the harbour when we get there."

"Who'd do that?" says Lora.

"I've got a few ideas," says Paul.

The motor catches and the headlights go on and they drive down the road, which is empty. Paul doesn't go all the way into the town. Instead he parks beside a stone wall.

"Go down to the shore and wait beside the pier," he says. "I'll pick you up there in about fifteen minutes. I'll get us a boat."

"Your boats are all out," says Lora.

"I didn't say mine," says Paul. "I'll jump the motor."

He's younger, alive in a way he hasn't been before. He loves it, thinks Rennie. That's why we get into these messes: because they love it.

He helps them over the stone wall and passes Rennie's

bags down to her. She feels stupid lugging her camera: what is there to take pictures of now?

"Don't talk," says Lora. Rennie sees where they are: they're in the garden at the back of the Lime Tree. They find the path and feel their way down it. The hotel is dark and silent; behind a few of the windows candles flicker. The bar is deserted, the patio littered with broken glass. Along the beach, towards the town, they can hear singing. It's men, it's not a hymn.

The tide's going out, there are several yards of wet beach. The waves are strangely luminous. Rennie wants to look at this, she's heard about it, phosphorescence.

"Crawl under the dock," Lora whispers.

"For heaven's sake," says Rennie, who doesn't like the idea of crabs and snails.

"Do it," Lora says; it's almost a hiss. This, apparently, is serious.

The dock is built on a foundation of split rocks that have not yet been smoothed by the sea; the space between the rocks and the wooden slats of the dock is only two feet high. They crouch together, doubled over. Rennie's still clutching her bags and her purse. She doesn't know who they're supposed to be hiding from.

The moon comes up, it's almost full; the grey-white light comes through the slats of the dock, throwing bars of shadow. Rennie thinks how nice it would be to have a warm bath and something to eat. She thinks about having lunch with someone, Jocasta maybe, and telling this story. But it's not even that good a story, it's about on the level of being stopped at customs, since nothing more than inconvenience has happened to her.

At last they can hear a motor, turning over, starting up, moving towards them.

"That's him," says Lora, and they back out from under the dock.

Marsdon is sitting in one of the wooden chairs up on the

patio, one leg bent, the ankle resting on his knee to show off his boots. He's got his machine gun pointed right at them. Two men stand silently behind him.

"Where you think you goin'?" he says.

The St. Antoine police motor launch is tied at the end of the Lime Tree pier, where it bobs gently up and down in the swell. Paul sits at the round wooden table facing Marsdon. He's soaking wet, from swimming out to the launch. Between them there's a bottle of rum. Each of them has a glass, each of them has a machine gun; the machine guns are on the ground under the table, but within reach. The two other men are over at the bar. There's a woman with them, very drunk, she's lying on the patio near them, in the broken glass, humming to herself, her skirt up over her thighs, opening and closing her legs. Rennie and Lora sit in the other two chairs.

Paul and Marsdon are arguing about them. Paul wants to take Rennie to St. Antoine, Marsdon doesn't want him to. Marsdon doesn't want anyone leaving the island. Also, Marsdon wants more guns. Paul promised him more, says Marsdon, they've been paid for; now he should deliver. He's the connection.

"I told you about the problem," Paul said. "You should have waited. Next week I have some coming."

"How can we wait?" Marsdon says impatiently. "When they hear on St. Antoine that Minnow is shot, they goin' to blame us anyway." Slyly, he offers to trade Paul's own machine gun for a safe exit. Slyly Paul refuses.

Rennie can see what she is now: she's an object of negotiation. The truth about knights comes suddenly clear: the maidens were only an excuse. The dragon was the real business. So much for vacation romances, she thinks. A kiss is just a kiss, Jocasta would say, and you're lucky if you don't get trenchmouth.

She listens, trying to follow. She feels like a hostage, and, like a hostage, strangely uninvolved in her own fate. Other people are deciding that for her. Would it be so bad if she stayed here? She could hole up in the Lime Tree, call herself a foreign correspondent, send out dispatches, whatever those are. But maybe Paul just wants to leave, get out; maybe she's just the occasion.

"You think I'm more important than I am," she says to Marsdon.

"Don't bug him," Lora says in a low voice. Marsdon looks at Rennie, seeing her this time. His movements are slow enough, outwardly calm, but he's excited, his eyes gleam in the moonlight. Fragmentation, dismemberment, this is what he sees when he looks at her. Then he's ignoring her once more.

"You bring the guns, you can take her," he says.

"No deal," says Paul.

There are more men now, coming along the beach from the town; several carry torches. One of them comes over to the table and puts his hand on Marsdon's shoulder.

"I am ready to make the broadcast now," he says, and Rennie realizes that this must be Prince. She's never seen him before. His face is in shadow, but the voice is young, younger than she thought, he sounds about nineteen.

"I wouldn't do that yet," says Paul, "if I were you."

Prince's head turns towards him in the shadows. "Why?" he says.

"Have you any idea of what's going to happen next?" Paul says.

"We have won the revolution," says Prince, with the placid confidence of a child reciting a lesson. "Grenada has recognized us. They are sending men and guns, in the morning."

"Where did you hear that?" says Paul.

The outline of Prince's head turns towards Marsdon.

"The radio," Marsdon says.

"Did you hear it yourself?" Paul says to Prince.

Marsdon pushes his chair back. "You calling me a liar,"

he says. There are more men now, a circle; tension draws them in.

"Take a boat to Grenada," Paul says to Prince. "Anything you can get. Right now, before morning. If you're lucky they'll let you stay there."

"You an enemy of the revolution," says Marsdon.

"Bullshit," says Paul. "You just want an excuse to blow my head off the way you blew off Minnow's."

"What you tellin' me?" says Prince.

"Put it together," says Paul. "He's the new agent. You've been set up, right from the beginning."

There's a pause. Rennie closes her eyes. Something with enormous weight comes down on them, she can hardly breathe. She hears the night sounds, the musical waterdrip, the waves, going on as usual. Then everything starts to move.

Oh God, thinks Rennie. Somebody change the channel.

Rennie walks along the pier at St. Antoine. She's safe. It's almost dawn. The power plant here isn't on the fritz and there's a string of feeble bulbs to see by. She feels dizzy and nauseated, an hour and a half in the launch, not rolling with the waves but smashing into them, a collision, a sickening lurch downwards, then up like a roller coaster, thud, crunch of her bones, backbone against backbone, stomach lurching inside her with its own motion. She'd hung on, trying to think of something serene, keeping her head up, eyes on the moon, on the next wave, the water glowed when it moved, phosphorescent, sweating all over her body despite the wind, wondering when she was going to throw up, trying not to. After all she was being rescued.

Can't you slow down? she called to Paul.

It's worse that way, he called back, grinning at her. Even now he found her funny.

At the dock he idled the motor and practically threw her onto the shore, her and her luggage, before backing the boat out and turning towards the sea. No goodbye kiss and just as well, she didn't want anything against her mouth just now. They touched hands for a moment, that was all. What bothers her is that she forgot to thank him.

He's not going back to Ste. Agathe, he's heading south. He'll meet one of his boats, he says. There are other harbours.

What about Lora? said Rennie.

She had the chance, said Paul. She wanted to stay with Prince. I can't fight off the entire St. Antoine police force just for Lora. She can take care of herself.

Rennie doesn't understand anything. All she knows is that she's here and there's a plane at six and she wants to be on it, and she can't keep walking. She sits down on the pier with her head between her knees, hoping that the rolling under her feet will stop.

She can hear the sound of the motor launch, receding, no more significant than the drone of a summer insect. Then there's another sound, too loud, like a television set with a cop show on it heard through a hotel room wall. Rennie puts her hands over her ears. In a minute, when she's feeling better, she'll go to the Sunset Inn and pick up her passport and see if she can get a cup of coffee, though there's not much chance of that. Then she'll take a taxi to the airport and then she'll be gone.

She sits there until she's ready enough; then she starts walking again. There are a few people about, men; only one of them tries to stop her, a simple request for fornication, and he's pleasant enough when she says no. There's no war on here, possibly they haven't heard anything about it yet, everything seems normal. Then there are more men, running past her towards the end of the pier.

It's light; close by there are roosters. After what seems a very long time she reaches the Sunset Inn and goes in through the archway. She climbs the stairs; now she will have to sign her name for all the time she hasn't spent here, all the meals she hasn't eaten. She won't even argue, she'll put it on her charge card. Enjoy now, pay later.

The Englishwoman is up and dressed, in an avocado-green shirtwaist, behind the counter as usual. Possibly she never sleeps.

"I'd like to check out," says Rennie, "and I'd like my passport, please, it's in the safe. And I'd like to call a taxi."

The Englishwoman looks at her with the gloating, almost possessive stare of one who enjoys giving unwelcome news. "Are you thinking of taking that morning plane?" she says.

Rennie says yes.

"It's been cancelled," says the Englishwoman. "All the planes have been cancelled. The airport's been shut down."

"Really?" says Rennie, cold within.

"We're in a state of emergency," says the Englishwoman proudly. "There's been an uprising on Ste. Agathe. But you must know all about that. Didn't you just come from there?"

Rennie lies on her bed. At least it's a bed. She's fallen on it without even taking off her clothes but she's too exhausted to sleep. Now she will have to stay here, at the Sunset Inn, home of beige gravy, until they start the planes again. She feels marooned.

Then it's full of daylight and the door, which was shut and locked, is open. Two policemen are standing in the doorway. Grins, drawn guns. Behind them is the Englishwoman, her arms folded across her chest. Rennie sits up. "What?" she says.

"We arrestin' you," says one of the policemen, the pinkish one.

"What for?" says Rennie. She feels she ought to act like an outraged tourist.

"Suspicion," says the other policeman.

"Suspicion of what?" says Rennie, who is still half asleep. "I haven't done anything." It can't be the box with the gun, they haven't mentioned it. "I'm writing a travel piece. You can phone the magazine and check," she adds. "In Toronto, when they're open. It's called *Visor.*" This sounds improbable even to her. Does Toronto exist? They won't be the first to wonder. She thinks of her blank notebook, no validation there.

The two policemen come forward. The Englishwoman looks at her, a look Rennie remembers from somewhere, from a long time ago, from a bad dream. It's a look of pure enjoyment. *Malignant.*

VI

"I thought it was dumb," says Lora. "I always thought it was dumb. Anyone who'd die for their country is a double turkey as far as I'm concerned. I mean any country, but this one, well, that would make you a triple one. Shit, it's only three miles long. I thought they were all nuts, but what can you tell them, eh?

"You may think Ellis is an old drunk, I told Prince, you may think he's harmless because nobody's seen him for twenty years, but if you think he's just going to let you take over without a squeak, you're out of your mind. But then Marsdon would start talking about sacrifice for the good of all, and that stuff would get to Prince every time. He's a sweet guy, he's soft-hearted, it appealed to him, and though I wouldn't want to be part of a country Marsdon was the leader of, he's no dummy, he knew he was making me look like a selfish white bitch who didn't care and only wanted Prince to screw around with.

"Maybe I should've left, but the truth is I thought they were just having a good time, sneaking around at night, having secrets, sort of like the Shriners, you know? I never thought they'd *do* anything.

"Change the system, Marsdon used to say. Why would I want to do that? I said. It's working just fine for me. Stuff politics, I'd tell him. As far as I'm concerned the world would be a lot better off if you took the politicians, any kind at all, and put them in the loony bin where they belong. You can tell that junk to Prince if you want to but don't tell it to me, because I know what you really want. You want to shoot people and feel really good about it and have everyone tell you you're doing the right thing. You'd get a kick out of that. You make me sick.

"I always knew Marsdon would shove a knife in me as soon as look at me if he got the chance, or in anyone else for that matter, he's a mean bugger but I guess if you want to start a war you have to have someone who doesn't give that much of a piss about killing people, you can't make an omelette without breaking eggs.

"There just weren't enough of them and they weren't ready. They wouldn't of been ready in a month of Sundays. Paul used to tell Marsdon he just wanted to be Castro without putting in the time, and it would get to him because that was about the size of it. They wouldn't of even had any guns if Paul hadn't brought some in for them. That was Marsdon's idea too, the guns. Paul didn't know he was an agent. I don't think he knew, not until Minnow got shot.

"If you're thinking of hiding out in the hills, forget it, Paul said. Two helicopters and that's it, this is a dry island, you know there's no cover up there, it's just scrub. But they seemed to think it was enough for them to be right. Getting rid of Ellis, that was the point. Nobody's denying it would've been nice, but there's real life, you know? I mean, I used to think I'd like to fly like a bird but I never jumped off any roofs. I once heard of a man who blew himself up in the toilet because he was sitting on the can and he lit a cigarette and he threw the match in, except his wife had just dumped some paint remover into it. I mean, that's what it was like. Though once in a while I thought, well, they might just do it. You know why? They're crazy enough. Sometimes crazy people can do things other people can't. Maybe because they believe it."

Rennie wonders where her passport is. She feels naked without it, she can't prove she is who she says she is. But she believes that other people believe in order, and in the morning, once they find out she's in here, once they realize who she is, they'll let her out.

Lora slaps at herself. "Fucking bugs," she says. "They like some people and not others. You think you'd get used to them, but you never do. Anyway, we've got a roof over our head. There's lots worse things."

Rennie decides not to think about what these may be.

"There was a little shooting at the police station," says Lora, "but not that much, and the power plant was empty. The police did a sweep of the island, it's not that hard because it's not that big, and they picked up anyone they found hiding or running or even walking on the road. They had the names of the main ones and they wanted everyone related to them too but that would've been everyone on the island, everyone's related to everyone else around here.

"They tied the men up with ropes, those yellow nylon ropes they use a lot around here for boats and stuff, they tied them together in bundles of three or four and threw them on top of each other in the ship, down in the hold, like they were cargo. The women they just tied their hands together, behind their backs, two together, they let them stand up. When we got over to St. Antoine there was a big crowd at the dock already, the radio had been full of it all morning, communists and all that, they hauled the bundles of men off the boat and the people in the street were screaming *Hang them! Kill them!* It was like wrestling.

"The police took us to the main station, down in the cellar where there's a cement floor, and they tied the men together in a long line, there must've been fifty or sixty people, and they beat them up, sticks and boots, the works. The women they beat up some too but not as much. I wasn't there for that part of it, they had me in another room, they were asking me questions about Prince. They've got him in here somewhere.

"Then they threw buckets of cold water over them and locked them up, they were wet and cold, nowhere to piss, nothing to eat, and then they brought them here. They didn't lay any charges because they hadn't figured out what charges to lay. The Justice Minister went on the radio and said there hadn't been any violence, the people got the cuts and bruises from falling down when they were running away. And then they declared a state of emergency, which made everything legal. They can take anything of yours they want to, your car, anything, and there's a curfew too. Nobody knows for how long.

"They said Minnow was shot by the rebels, they said Prince killed him. People believe what they hear on the news and who's going to tell them any different? They'll believe Ellis because it's easier to believe Ellis.

"It's perfect for Ellis: now he's got an excuse to do it to everybody he doesn't like, plus nobody's going to say anything against him, for years. And think of all the foreign aid he'll get now. The hurricane was all right but this is a lot better.

"We're lucky. The others are all seven or eight to a cell. Some of these people have no idea why they're here, all of a sudden these police with guns just bashed into their houses and grabbed them. They didn't know what was happening, they don't have a clue, they were just in the way."

The room they're in is about five feet by seven feet, with a high ceiling. The walls are damp and cool, the stone slick to the touch as if something's growing on it, some form of mildew. The back of Rennie's shirt is damp, from the wall. This is the first time she's been cold since coming down here.

The floor is stone too and wet, except for the corner they've been sitting in. There's a barred metal door fitted into the end wall and opening onto the corridor, which is lighted;

the light shines in on them through the bars. Someone has written on the walls: DOWN WITH BABYLON. LOVE TO ALL. In the wall opposite the door, higher up, there's a small window with a grating. Through this window they can see the moon. There's nothing in the room with them except a bucket, red plastic, new, empty. Its use is obvious but neither of them has used it yet.

"How long do you think they'll keep us in here?" says Rennie.

Lora laughs. "You in any hurry?" she says. "If you are, don't tell them. Anyway it's not how long you're in, it's what they do to you." She inhales, then blows the smoke out. "Well, this is it," she says. "Tropical paradise."

Rennie wonders why they've left Lora her cigarettes and especially the matches. Not that there's anything here that could burn down, it's all stone.

Rennie wishes they had a deck of cards or a book, any book at all. It's almost bright enough to read. She can smell the smoke from Lora's cigarette and beneath that a faint after-smell, stale perfume, underarm deodorant wearing off; it's from both of them. She's starting to get a headache. She'd give anything for a Holiday Inn. She longs for late-night television, she's had enough reality for the time being. Popcorn is what she needs.

"You got the time?" says Lora.

"They took my watch," says Rennie. "It's probably about eleven."

"That all?" says Lora.

"We should get some sleep, I guess," Rennie says. "I wish they'd turn out the lights."

"Okay," says Lora. "You sleepy?"

"No," says Rennie.

They're scraping the bottom of the barrel. Rennie thinks of it as the bottom of the barrel, Lora thinks of it as the story of her life. This is even what she calls it. "The story of my life,"

she says, morosely, proudly, "you could put it in a book."
But it's one way not to panic. If they can only keep talking,
thinks Rennie, they will be all right.

Lora takes out her cigarettes, lights one, blows the smoke
out through her nose. "You want a cigarette? I've got two
left. Oh, I forgot, you don't smoke." She pauses, waiting for
Rennie to contribute something. So far most of the contributing has been done by Lora. Rennie is having a hard time
thinking up anything about her life that Lora might find interesting. Right now, her life seems like a book Jocasta once
lent her, very *nouveau wavé*, it was called *Death By Washing
Machine* although there were no washing machines in the
book. The main character fell off a cliff on page sixty-three
and the rest of the pages were blank.

Rennie tells Lora about the man with the rope. She's certain that Lora will be able to produce something much
heavier, a multiple axe murder at the least.

"Sick," Lora says. "They shouldn't even put those guys
away, they should just hang a few cement blocks around their
legs and drop them in the harbour, you know? Let them out
in twenty years and they just do it again. I once knew this
guy who wanted to tie me to the bedpost. No way, I said.
You want to tie somebody up, I've got a few suggestions, but
you're not starting with me. Try a sheep and a pair of rubber
boots and work your way up. He come back?"

"No," says Rennie.

"I'd rather be plain old raped," says Lora, "as long as
there's nothing violent."

Rennie feels there's been a communications breakdown.
Then she realizes that Lora is talking about something that
has actually happened to her. Without any warning at all.

"God," she says, "what did you do?"

"Do?" says Lora. "He had a knife. I was just lucky he
didn't mess anything up, including me. I could've kicked myself for not having a better lock on the window."

Rennie sees that Lora is pleased to have shocked her.

She's enjoying the reaction; it's as if she's displaying something, an attribute somewhere between a skill and a deformity, like double-jointedness; or a mark of courage, a war wound or a duelling scar. The pride of the survivor.

Rennie knows what she's supposed to feel: first horror, then sympathy. But she can't manage it. Instead she's dejected by her own failure to entertain. Lora has better stories.

Rennie watches Lora's mouth open and close, studies the nicotine stains on her once perfect teeth, it's a movie with the sound gone. She's thinking that she doesn't really like Lora very much; she never has liked her very much; in fact she dislikes her. They have nothing in common except that they're in here. There's nobody here to look at but Lora, nobody to listen to but Lora. Rennie is going to like her a whole lot less by the time they get out.

"But, Jesus, will you listen to me," says Lora. "Here we are, just sitting around on our asses talking about men, fucking men, pardon my French, like at high school only then it was boys."

"What else do you suggest we do?" says Rennie, with sarcasm; after all, it's Lora's fault they're in here. But it's lost on Lora.

"If it was two guys in here," she says, "you think they'd be talking about women? They'd be digging a tunnel or strangling the guards from behind, you know? Like at the movies." She stands up, stretches. "I need to pee," she says. "At least we don't have to do it on the floor, though ten to one somebody already has, it smells like it." She slips off her underpants, spreads her purple skirt over the red bucket like a tent, squats down. Rennie stares at the wall, listening to the patter of liquid against plastic. She doesn't want to know what Lora will wipe herself with; there are only two choices, hands or clothing.

●　　●　　●

Rennie has her knees drawn up, she's cold. If they lie down they'll be wet, so they're still sitting, backs against the wall. The light comes through the door, endlessly, it's impossible to sleep. She puts her forehead on her knees and closes her eyes.

"I bet you could see out the window," says Lora, "if I gave you a leg up."

Rennie opens her eyes. She fails to see the point, but it's something to do. Lora bends and cups her hands, Rennie puts her right foot into them and Lora hoists, and Rennie manages to reach up and grab the bars. She pulls herself up, she can raise her head to the opening.

It's a courtyard of sorts, with a wall around it and another building on the other side. Her eyes are almost at ground level; it's overgrown with weeds, a white jungle in the moonlight. The gallows platform rises out of the weeds, a derelict tower. Rennie knows where they are. On three sides of the courtyard it's a sheer drop to the sea, and the building they're in is the fourth side. There's a faint smell of pigs. No one is out there.

"There's nothing to see," she says when she's back down.

Lora rubs her hands together. "You're heavier than I thought," she says.

They sit down again. After five minutes or half an hour there's a sound above them, outside the window. A scuttling, a squeak.

"Rats," says Lora. "Around here they call them coconut rodents. Mostly they just eat coconuts."

Rennie decides to concentrate on something else. She closes her eyes: she knows that there are some things she must avoid thinking about. Her own lack of power, for instance; what could be done to her.

She can feel Lora's arm against her own, it's comforting. She thinks about refrigerators, cool and white, stocked with the usual things: bottles, cartons of milk, packets, coffee beans in fragrant paper bags, eggs lined up quietly in their shells. Vacuum cleaners, chromium plated taps, bathtubs, a whole store full of bathtubs, soap in pastel wrappers, the names of English herbs, the small routines.

Lora's still talking. But Rennie can't concentrate, she's getting hungrier and hungrier. She wonders when it will be morning. Surely they will bring something to eat, they'll have to, her stomach is cramping and she hopes it's only the hunger.

Her eyes feel gritty, she's irritated because she hasn't slept more, it's Lora's fault, she needs more sleep and she's thirsty too. It's like the time she was trapped all night in a bus station, by a blizzard, on her way home for Christmas, some town halfway there, the snack bar isn't open and the toilets don't work, there's a bad smell and no prospect of a bus out until dawn, maybe not even then, they have to wait for the wind to go down before they can plough the roads, people yawning and dozing, a few grumpy children, the coffee machine out of order. But it would be tolerable if only the woman packed beside her on the bench would quit talking, in a maroon coat and curlers, no such luck, it goes on and on, triplets, polio, car crashes, operations for dropsy, for burst appendixes, sudden death, men leaving their wives, aunts, cousins, sisters, crippling accidents, a web of blood relationships no one could possibly untangle, a litany at the same time mournful and filled with curious energy, glee almost, as if the woman is childishly delighted with herself for being able to endure and remember so much pointless disaster. *True Confessions.* Rennie tunes out, studies the outfit on the woman asleep on the bench across from them, her head sideways: the corsage with the Christmas bells and silver balls and the tiny plastic Santa Claus held captive on her large woollen breast.

"You aren't listening," says Lora accusingly.

"Sorry," says Rennie. "I'm really tired."

"Maybe I should shut up for a while," says Lora. She sounds hurt.

"No, go on," says Rennie. "It's really interesting."

Maybe soon they will come to question her, isn't that what happens? And then she can explain everything, she can tell them why it's a mistake, why she should not be here. All she has to do is hang on; sooner or later, something is bound to happen.

Rennie is walking along a street, a street with red-brick houses, the street she lives on. The houses are big, square, solid, some with porches, some with turrets and gingerbread trim painted white. These people take care of their houses, they are proud of their houses. Houseproud, says Rennie's grandmother, who is.

Her mother and her grandmother are with her. It's Sunday, they've been to church. It's fall, the leaves have turned, yellow, orange, red, a few drift down on them as they walk along. The air is cool, cold almost, she's so glad to be back, she feels safe. But nobody's paying any attention to her. Her hands are cold, she lifts them up to look at them, but they elude her. Something's missing.

Here we go, says her mother. Here are the steps. Easy, now.

I don't want to die, says her grandmother. I want to live forever.

The sky has darkened, there's a wind, the leaves are falling down, red on her grandmother's white hat, they're wet.

The window above them gets brighter and brighter, now it's a square of heat. Rennie thinks she can see mist rising from the floor and walls and from the red bucket. The lights in the corridor are still on. Lora's asleep, her head thrown back into the corner where she's propped, her mouth is open a little, she's snoring. Rennie has found out she talks in her sleep, nothing intelligible.

Finally there's a shuffle in the corridor, the clink of metal. A policeman is here, unlocking the door; in two-tone blue and a shoulder holster. Rennie shakes Lora's arm to wake her up. She wonders if they're supposed to stand at attention, as they used to in public school when the teacher came in.

There's another man with the policeman, dressed in shoddy grey. He's carrying a bucket, red, identical to the one that's fermenting by the door, and two tin plates stacked one on the other and two tin cups. He comes in and sets the bucket and the plates and cups down on the floor beside the first bucket. The policeman stays outside in the corridor.

"Hi there, Stanley," Lora says, rubbing her eyes.

The man grins at her, shyly, he's frightened, he backs out. The policeman with him locks the door again, acting as if he hasn't heard.

On each of the plates there's a slice of bread, thinly buttered. Rennie looks into the bucket. The bottom is covered with a brownish liquid that she hopes is tea.

She scoops some out in a tin cup, takes that and a plate over to Lora.

"Thanks," says Lora. "What's this?" She's scratching her legs, which have red dots on them, bites of some kind.

"Morning tea," says Rennie. It's the English tradition, still.

Lora tastes it. "You could've fooled me," she says. "You sure you got the right bucket?" She spits the tea out onto the floor.

The tea is salty. They've made a mistake, Rennie thinks, they've put salt in it instead of sugar. She pours the tea back into the bucket and chews the bread slowly.

The cell heats up. Rennie begins to sweat. The stench from the bucket is overpowering now. Rennie wonders when she'll stop noticing it. You can get used to almost anything.

She's wondering when someone in authority will arrive, someone she can talk to, someone she can inform of her presence. If they only realize she's here, who she is, they'll get her out. The policeman did not look like someone in authority.

She's convinced of her right to be released, but she knows that not everyone will see it exactly that way.

About midmorning, judging by the sun, two other policemen arrive outside the door. One is black, one brownish pink. They seem friendlier than the first one, they grin as they unlock the door.

"Take the bucket and come with us," says the pink one. Rennie thinks they're talking to her. She comes forward.

"I wonder if I could see the supervisor," she says.

"We not talking to you," the black one says rudely. "She the one."

"Hi there, Sammy," Lora says. "Hold your horses."

She goes out with them, carrying the bucket of piss.

Lora is gone a long time. When she comes back she has a clean bucket. Rennie, who's been imagining atrocities, says, "What happened?"

"Nothing to it," says Lora. "You just empty out the bucket. There's a hole in the ground out there. I saw some of the others, they were doing the same thing." She sets the bucket down in its old place and comes over to the dry corner to sit down.

"Prince is on the floor above us," she says. "They're fixing it up for me to see him, maybe in a couple of days." She's happy about this, she's excited. Rennie's envious. She would like to feel like that.

"Guess what?" says Lora. "They got Marsdon."

"Oh," says Rennie. "Is he in here?"

"I mean he's dead," says Lora. "Somebody shot him."

"The men on Ste. Agathe?" says Rennie. She thinks of Marsdon running through the scrub, up the hill in his slippery leather boots, nine or ten men after him, while the police boat comes into the harbour, they'd want to get him while they still had time.

"No," says Lora. "The story is it was the cops. Ellis."

"I thought he was working for the CIA," says Rennie. "I thought he was an agent."

"There's a lot of stories," says Lora. "The CIA, Ellis, what's the difference? Anyway Ellis didn't want him talking about how he set it up, Ellis wants everyone to believe it was real. Nothing like a revolution to make the States piss money, and they've done it already, Canada just gave a great big lump of cash to Ellis, they told me, it said on the radio. Foreign aid. He can use it to finance his dope trade." She pauses, keeping an eye on Rennie. "Some of them are saying that Paul shot Minnow," she says.

"You don't believe that," says Rennie.

"Who knows?" says Lora.

"Why would he do that?" says Rennie.

"CIA," says Lora. "He was the one bringing in the guns for Marsdon, eh?"

"Come *on*," says Rennie.

Lora laughs. "You believed it once," she says. "I'm just telling you what they're saying. Guess what else?"

"What?" says Rennie, not wanting to.

"They think you're a spy," says Lora. She chuckles, a little insultingly.

"Who does?" says Rennie. "The police?"

"Everyone," says Lora, grinning. "Just, they haven't figured out who for yet."

"How did you hear all this?" Rennie says. "It's ridiculous."

Lora looks at her and smiles. From the pocket of her skirt she takes out a fresh package of cigarettes, Benson and Hedges, and a box of Swedish matches. "Same place I got these," she says. "I told you I had my ass covered."

Rennie's tired of guessing games. "How?" she says.

"I'm a dealer, remember?" says Lora. "So I made a deal."

"Who on earth with?" says Rennie, who can't imagine it.

"Those two cops, the ones who came just now?" says Lora. "Morton and Sammy. I knew they'd be here sooner or later; it took them a while to work it out but now they're in charge of us. They don't want us in with the others. They were selling for me on St. Antoine, they were my protection. Nobody knew except Paul. They sure as hell don't want anyone else around here finding out about that." She lights one of her new cigarettes, tosses the match onto the damp floor. "They were in on the shipments. They knew what was coming in and when, they knew the guns were coming up from Colombia along with the grass, they knew what was in Elva's boxes, they didn't know all about it but they knew enough, and they didn't tell, how could they without blowing their own act wide open? Ellis wouldn't like that. He'd think that was treachery. A little dealing he could understand but not that. Dealing they'd just get canned. That, they'd get offed. So I've got them by the nuts."

"Can they get us out?" Rennie says.

"I don't want to push it," says Lora. "I don't want to make them jumpy, they're jumpy enough already. Anyway they want me here, they can keep an eye on me better. They don't want anyone else to get hold of me and start squeezing; who knows, the first hot cigarette on the foot and everything might come squirting out. They'll take good care of me though, they know I won't go down alone, I told them that. If I go I take somebody with me."

"What's to stop them from just burying you quietly in the back yard?" says Rennie.

"Nothing at all," says Lora. She finds this funny. "Pure bluff. I told them I had someone on the outside who's checking up on me."

"Do you?" says Rennie.

"Well," says Lora, "there's always Paul. Wherever he is."

Neither of them wants to talk about that.

They're eating, lunch, cold rice and chicken backs, boiled, Rennie thinks, but not enough. Pink juice runs out. Lora gnaws with relish, licking her fingers. Rennie doesn't feel too well.

"You can have the rest of mine," she says.

"Why waste it?" says Lora.

"Maybe we could ask them to cook it more," says Rennie.

"Ask who?" says Lora.

Rennie hasn't thought about it. Surely there must be someone to ask.

"It could be a lot worse, is what I always say," says Lora. "Where there's life there's hope. It's better than a lot of the people get at home, think of it that way."

Rennie tries to but without much success. Lora is eating the rest of Rennie's chicken back now. She aims a bone at the bucket, misses, wipes her hands on her skirt. The nails are grey, the skin around them nibbled. Rennie looks away. Now they will have stale chicken to smell, as well as everything else.

"We could ask them about the tea," says Rennie.

"What?" says Lora, her mouth full.

"The salt in the tea," says Rennie. "You could tell them they made a mistake."

"Hell, no," says Lora. "That wasn't a mistake, that was orders. They're doing it on purpose."

"Why would they do that?" says Rennie. The poor food she can understand, but this seems gratuitous. Malicious.

Lora shrugs. "Because they can," she says.

It's dusk. They've had supper, a piece of bread, the salty tea, water which tastes like rancid butter, a cupful each. The mosquitoes are here. Outside the grated window they can hear the pigs, up there in the yard; as Rennie watches, a curious snout pokes through.

Neither of them is saying anything. Rennie can smell their bodies, unwashed flesh, and the putrid smell from the bucket, Lora is out of cigarettes for the time being, she's picking at her fingers, Rennie can see her out of the corners of her eyes, it's an irritating habit, they've both run out, run down. She's having trouble remembering which day this is, they should have begun when they got here, scratches on the wall, perhaps this is the day her ticket expires, her twenty-one-day excursion. Maybe now someone will come looking for her, maybe she will be rescued. If she can only keep believing it, then it will happen.

She hopes they'll do it soon, she's deteriorating, she knows this because right now she's daydreaming about food, not even real food, not spinach salads with bacon and mushrooms and a glass of dry white wine, but Colonel Sanders chicken, McDonald's hamburgers, doughnuts filmed with ersatz chocolate and shreds of stale coconut, thick nasty cups of ancient coffee, the dregs, her mouth's watering at the thought of it, potato chips, candy bars from subway magazine stands, Mars, Rowntree's coated raisins, silently and voluptuously she repeats the names, how can she? She sleepwalks along Yonge Street, into one franchise after another. *No-frills Snak Pak.* Maybe she's delirious.

She switches to a jigsaw puzzle, in her head, the top border, the ones with the flat edges, it's always the sky, one piece fits into another, fits into another, interlocking, pure blue.

"Try getting a comb for us," says Rennie. "If you can."

"I tried before," says Lora. "People slash their wrists with them. They don't want any funny deaths in here, not if they can help it. Some church or other is poking around."

"How about a brush?" says Rennie.

"You got any money?" says Lora, with a small laugh.

Rennie looks at her, she's thinner now and filthy, there's no other word for it, the white blouse is grey, the purple skirt is damp and greasy, dark moons under the eyes, they both smell, there's a sore on Lora's leg that won't heal, her hair is matted. Rennie knows how she herself must look. She thinks they should do exercises, but when she suggested it, Lora said, "What for?" and Rennie doesn't have the strength to do them by herself. What she really wants is a toothbrush. A mirror. Someone who could get them out.

"I could braid it," she says.

"What?" says Lora. It's harder and harder to keep her attention.

"I could braid your hair," says Rennie. "At least that would untangle it."

"Okay," says Lora. She's restless, she's out of cigarettes again, the flesh around her nails is raw. "I wish we could get some news in here," she says. "You can't trust what they tell you. I'm tired of this place."

Rennie doesn't remember hearing her complain before. It seems like a bad omen. She begins on the hair, it's like pulling strands of wool apart.

"Go easy," says Lora. "At least we don't have lice."

"Yet," says Rennie. Now they're laughing, it's idiotic, they can hardly stop. There's no reason for it. When they finish, Rennie keeps going with the hair. She's making it into two long frizzy braids. "What do you dream about?" she says to Lora.

"Lots of stuff," says Lora. "Being on a boat. My mother. Sometimes I dream about having a baby. Except I never know what to do with it, you know? I think I'd like it though. When I get out of here and I get Prince out maybe that's what we'll do. They think it's funny here if you have a baby after you're about twenty-five though. For them that's old. But I don't care, let them laugh. Elva will like it, she's always bugging me to have a son for Prince."

Rennie finishes with one of the braids and stars on the other. "If we had some beads," she says, "I could do you up like a Rasta."

"Tinfoil," says Lora. "Some of the girls use that on the ends. When you get out, can you do something for me?"

"What makes you think I'll be out any sooner than you?" says Rennie.

"Oh, you will," says Lora. She says this wistfully, fatalistically, as if it's just a fact of life that everyone knows about.

Instead of cheering Rennie up this makes her anxious. She winds the two braids around Lora's head. "There," she says. "You look like a German milkmaid. Except I've got nothing to pin them with."

"Tell someone I'm here," says Lora. "Tell someone what happened."

Rennie lets go of the braids. "Who should I tell?" says Rennie.

"I don't know," says Lora. "Someone."

Lora's face is streaked with dirt. Perhaps later they can take turns wiping off each other's faces with the salty tea.

Rennie can't remember what people are supposed to think about. She tries to remember what she herself used to think about, but she can't. There's the past, the present, the future: none of them will do. The present is both unpleasant and unreal; thinking about the future only makes her impatient, as if she's in a plane circling and circling an airport, circling and not landing. Everyone gripping the arms of the seat, trying not to imagine the crash. She's tired of this fear, which goes on and on, no end to it. She wants an end.

She wants to remember someone she's loved, she wants to remember loving someone. It's hard to do. She tries to conjure up a body, Jake's body, as she has before, but she can hardly remember what he looks like. How does she know he ever existed? There's no proof. Acts of the body, of love, what's left? A change, a result, a trace, hand through the sea at night, phosphorescence.

Of Paul, only the too-blue eyes remain. They don't talk about Paul much; nothing has been heard, according to Lora, nothing has been said on the radio. He's disappeared, which could mean anything. Rennie does not want to think about the noises behind her in the harbour, the machine-gun fire, the explosion. She doesn't want to think of Paul as dead. That would rule out the possibility of rescue. She would rather know nothing. Possibly she is the last person he touched. Possibly he is the last person who will ever touch her. The last man.

She switches to a yoga class she once went to with Jocasta. *Feel the energy of the universe. Now relax. Start with the feet. Tell your feet, Feet, relax. Now send your mind into your ankles. Tell your ankles, Ankles, relax.* Go with the flow.

She thinks about Daniel, Daniel eating his breakfast while listening to the news, which he doesn't really seem to hear, since his knowledge of world affairs is more or less nil, Daniel caught in rush hour, Daniel getting his feet wet because he didn't listen to the weather forecast. Daniel in surgery, a body spread before him, his hands poised for incision. Daniel leaning across his desk, holding the hand of a blonde woman whose breasts he has recently cut off. Who wants to cure, who wants to help, who wants everything to be fine. You're alive, he says to her, with kindness and duplicity, compelling as a hypnotist. You're very lucky. Tears stream silently down her face.

Daniel moves through the day enclosed in a glass bubble, like an astronaut on the moon, like a rare plant in a hothouse: a fluke. Inside the bubble his life is possible. Normal. Outside, what would become of him? Without food or air. Ordinary human decency, a mutation, a freak. Right now she's on the outside looking in.

From here it's hard to believe that Daniel really exists: surely the world cannot contain both places. He's a mirage, a necessary illusion, a talisman she fingers, over and over, to keep herself sane.

Once she would have thought about her illness: her scar, her disability, her nibbled flesh, the little teethmarks on her. Now this seems of minor interest, even to her. The main thing is that nothing has happened to her yet, nobody has done anything to her, she is unharmed. She may be dying, true, but if so she's doing it slowly, relatively speaking. Other people are doing it faster: at night there are screams.

Rennie opens her eyes. Nothing in here has changed. Directly above her, up on the high ceiling, some wasps are building a nest. They fly in through the grating, up to the nest, out through the grating again. Jack Spaniards, Lora calls them. In memory of what war?

Pretend you're really here, she thinks. Now: what would you do?

It's another morning, time has a shape even here. When the guards come, they have names, Sammy and Morton, and she knows now which name belongs to which, Morton's the pink one, Rennie stays in the background. She still has difficulty understanding what's being said, so she lets Lora deal with it. They have a hairbrush now, though not a comb; which is better than nothing. Rennie would like a nail file, but she knows better than to ask, it's too much like a weapon. Lora doesn't need one, her nails are bitten down to the quicks anyway.

"Try for some chewing gum," Rennie says to Lora. Where there are cigarettes there must be gum. It will give the illusion of toothpaste; her mouth feels as if it's rotting. Lora goes out with the bucket.

She's gone longer than usual, and Rennie begins to worry. At the back of her mind is the fear that Lora won't be able to restrain herself, her temper, that she'll do something or say something that will tip the balance, put them both in jeopardy. She herself, she feels, would have more control.

But when Lora comes back she's the same, there are no cuts or bruises, nothing has been done to her. She sets the empty pail on the ground and squats over it. Rennie knows that smell, the smell of bloodheat, seaweed, fishegg. Lora wipes with a corner of her skirt, stands up.

"I got your chewing gum," she says. "Next time I'll try for some toilet paper."

Rennie is disgusted. She thinks Lora should have more self-respect. "No thanks," she says coldly.

Lora looks at her for a moment. "What the shit's eating you?" she says.

"You're worth more than a package of gum," Rennie says. How many of them, she wants to ask, one or both? One at a time, or both? Lying down or standing up? It isn't decent.

Lora is bewildered for an instant. Then she laughs. "Goddamn right I am," she says. "Two packages. I got one for myself too."

Rennie doesn't say anything. Lora sits down and opens the gum. "Women like you make me sick," she says. "Tight-ass. You wouldn't put out to save your granny, would you?"

"Let's not talk about it," says Rennie. There's no point. They're in this room and it's a small one and there's no way out. All she can do is try to avoid a fight.

"Why in hell not?" says Lora, chewing. "What's wrong with talking about it? What makes you think it's any different from having some guy stick his finger in your ear?"

"It is," says Rennie.

"Only sometimes," says Lora.

Rennie turns her head away. She feels sick to her stomach. She doesn't want to watch Lora's grubby hands, her bitten fingers as they strip open the pack of cigarettes, the cigarette between the drying lips, the corner of her mouth.

But Lora is crying, Rennie can't believe it, convulsive sounds from her throat, her eyes clenched. "Fuck it," she says. "They've got Prince in here. They won't let me see him, they keep promising. What'm I supposed to do?"

Rennie is embarrassed. She looks down at her hands,

which ought to contain comfort. Compassion. She ought to go over to Lora and put her arms around her and pat her on the back, but she can't.

"I'm sorry," she says. *Women like you.* She deserves it. It's a pigeonhole, she's in it, it fits.

Lora sniffles, stops now, wipes her nose on the back of her hand. Grudging, resentful, forgiving, a little. "How would you know?" she says.

Rennie doubles over, stumbles for the bucket, crouches. It's sudden, she can feel the sweat dripping down her back, she's dizzy, she hates pain. She's been invaded, usurped, germs taking over, betrayal of the body.

She lies down on the floor, even though it's wet. She closes her eyes, her head is the size of a watermelon, soft and pink, it's swelling up, she's going to burst open, she's going to die, she needs water, even water tasting of chlorine, Great Lakes poisons, her sense of irony has deserted her, just when she needs it, any kind of water, an ice cube, sugar and fizz from a machine. What has she done, she's not guilty, this is happening to her for no reason at all.

"You okay?" says Lora. She's touching Rennie's forehead, her fingertips leave dents. Her voice comes down from a great distance.

Rennie tries hard. "Make them get a doctor," she manages to say.

"For that?" says Lora. "It's only *turistas.* Montezuma's Revenge, the tourists call it. Everyone gets it sooner or later. Take it from me, you'll live."

It's night again. Someone is screaming, quite far away, if you tune it down it sounds like a party. Rennie tunes it down. She can sleep now in the light from the corridor, she goes to sleep quite peacefully, no one has done anything to her yet, she goes to sleep hugging herself. The screaming is worse when it stops.

Rennie is dreaming about the man with the rope, again, again. He is the only man who is with her now, he's followed her, he was here all along, he was waiting for her. Sometimes she thinks it's Jake, climbing in the window with a stocking over his face, for fun, as he once did; sometimes she thinks it's Daniel, that's why he has a knife. But it's not either of them, it's not Paul, it's not anyone she's ever seen before. The face keeps changing, eluding her, he might as well be invisible, she can't see him, this is what is so terrifying, he isn't really there, he's only a shadow, anonymous, familiar, with silver eyes that twin and reflect her own.

Lora is shaking her, trying to wake her up. "For Christ's sake," says Lora. "You want every cop in the place down our necks?"

Rennie says she's sorry.

It's noon, Rennie can tell by the heat and the angle of the light, and then the rice arrives. How much she's come to depend on it, that tin plate. The day ends when it's empty and another day of waiting begins, right then, with the scrape of the bones into the red bucket. Her life is shrinking right down to that one sound, a dull bell.

Outside in the courtyard there's something going on; all of a sudden there are harsh voices, shouts, a shuffle and clank. Then there's a scream. Lora gets up, her plate drops and spills. "Christ," she says, "they're shooting people."

"No," says Rennie. There haven't been any shots.

"Come on," says Lora. She bends, holds out her cupped hands.

"I don't think we should look," says Rennie. "They might see us."

"Maybe it's Prince," says Lora.

Rennie places her tin plate carefully on the ground. Then she puts her foot in Lora's hands, is lifted, clutches the bars.

There are people in the courtyard, five or six men in uniform, the two blues of the police, then another group, they seem to be tied together, arm to arm, they're being pushed down, to their knees, among the dry weeds and snarls of wire, the police have sticks, cattle prods? The ones kneeling have long hair, long black hair standing out from their heads; at first Rennie thinks they're women, then she sees they are naked from the waist up, they have no breasts.

One man still wears a woolly tea-cosy hat; a policeman snatches it off and the hair tumbles out. A pig runs in panic through the archway, it zigzags among the men, standing and kneeling, the policmen laugh, two of them chase it with cattle prods while the others watch, it dashes under the gallows platform and then back through the archway again. The kneeling men turn their heads, follow it with their eyes.

Now Rennie sees that one of the policemen has a rifle, he's raising it, for a minute she thinks he's going to shoot them all, the whole line of them. He hesitates, letting them believe this, do they? But he detaches the bayonet and walks slowly around to the back of the line with it, strolling, hips rolling, taking his time, luxuriating. He's not doing this just because he's been ordered to: he's doing it because he enjoys it. *Malignant.*

"What's going on?" says Lora, whispering. Rennie doesn't answer.

The policeman grasps the hair of the first man in the line, gathers it almost lovingly into a bunch, a handful, then suddenly jerks the man's head back so that the throat is taut, it's going to be worse than shooting. Butchery.

But all he does is saw at the hair, he's cutting the hair off; that's all he's doing. Another man follows him with a green garbage bag, for the hair. It's chilling, this tidyness.

"What is it?" says Lora. "What're they doing?"

He's at the second man now, the courtyard is oddly silent, the noon sun beats down, everything is bright, the men's faces glisten with sweat, fear, the effort of keeping in the hatred, the policemen's faces glisten too, they're holding themselves back, they love this, it's a ceremony, precise as an operation, they're implementing a policy, he pulls the head back like a chicken's, the hair is grey, he slices again with the bayonet but he's not careful enough, the man howls, a voice that is not a voice, there are no teeth in his opened mouth, blood is pouring down his face. The man with the bayonet stuffs the handful of hair into the bag and wipes his hand on his shirt. He's an addict, this is a hard drug. Soon he will need more.

The kneeling man continues to howl. As if they've been waiting for it, two others come over and one of them kicks the howling man in the stomach. A third throws water over him from a red plastic bucket. The man falls forward, he's kept from hitting the pavement by the ropes that link him to the other men, one of the policemen jams the cattle prod in between his legs, he's flung back, now it's a scream. Not human.

"Pull him up," says the man in charge, and they do. They continue along the line, the hurt man's face is on a level with Rennie's own, blood pours down it, she knows who it is, the deaf and dumb man, who has a voice but no words, he can see her, she's been exposed, it's panic, he wants her to do something, pleading, *Oh please.*

"Let me down," says Rennie. The best they can do is avoid calling attention to themselves. She leans against the wall, she's shaking. It's indecent, it's not done with ketchup, nothing is inconceivable here, no rats in the vagina but only because they haven't thought of it yet, they're still amateurs. She's afraid of men and it's simple, it's rational, she's afraid of men because men are frightening. She's seen the man with the rope, now she knows what he looks like. She has been turned inside out, there's no longer a *here* and a *there*. Rennie understands for the first time that this is not necessarily a place she will get out of, ever. She is not exempt. Nobody is exempt from anything.

"Good God, what is it?" says Lora. She's still whispering, her hands on Rennie's shoulders.

"Prince isn't there," says Rennie. "They're cutting their hair off."

She kneels, picks up the chicken back Lora spilled, wipes the dirt from it with her fingers, puts it on Lora's plate. "You should eat it," she says. "We need to eat."

In the middle of the morning, at the usual time, the two guards come again. Today one of them is new, he's too young, skinny body, thin wiry arms, face smooth as a plum, eyes innocent. Rennie takes one look at him and sees that he knows nothing at all. Morton is frightened, he's got his arm across his chest, almost touching his pistol, things are no longer under his control. It's the innocence of the other one that frightens him.

They unlock the door. Lora's watchful but she bends over anyway to pick up the smelly red bucket.

"Her turn today," says Morton, pointing at Rennie with the other hand. "You been doin' it every time."

Rennie isn't prepared for this, she knows what will be expected of her and she's not ready for it, but Lora steps in front of her, she's going to dare him. "Why?" she says. "Where's Sammy?"

"I don't mind which one," says the boy. He's heard something then, he wants part of it, he knows what but not what for.

"Shut your mouth," says Morton. He's afraid of being caught out, the young kid's smart enough to figure it out but he's a fool, he'll tell, maybe not deliberately but one way or another. He wants Rennie to go rather than Lora because it's safer, that's what he thinks. "Sammy's grandmother got sick," he says to Lora.

"Yeah," says the young boy. "She sick bad." He has a high nervous giggle. "What you need Sammy for? I just as good."

"I'll go," says Rennie. She doesn't want a squabble, something's about to go wrong.

"No," says Lora. The barred door's partly open, she yanks it and pushes out into the corridor. "What's happened to Prince? Is that it? You don't want me to know, you don't want to tell me. Oh shit. Where did you put him?"

She's got Morton by the arm but he's the one who's sweating, it's not her, she's tight and cold. The young boy's looking at both of them, trying to untangle this. He giggles again. "Prince?" he says. "The big man, Prince of Peace? He never in here at all, man."

"Shut your damn mouth," Morton says to him.

"You tell her he still alive?" says the boy. "He dead a long time ago, man." He thinks this is a joke. Rennie wonders whether he's stoned, it's a possibility.

"When?" Lora says quietly, to him alone, not to Morton. She's dropped her hands down, she's no longer holding Morton's arm.

"What you need to tell her that for?" Morton says with disgust. The boy has completely blown it.

"He caught in the crossfire," the boy says. He giggles some more. "That what it say on the radio. You tell her you got him in here, make her work hard for you, eh? Get some for your own self. You are a bad man." He's laughing now, not just giggling, this is the funniest thing he's heard in a long time.

"You pig," Lora says to Morton. "You knew all along. You were just afraid I'd crack up if I heard about it, right, and then they'd find out what you were up to. They shot him in the back, right?"

Morton puts his hand on her arm, soothingly, like a doctor almost. "You go back in," he says. "I doin' the best I can for you. You lucky you alive."

"Fuck you!" Lora screams. "I'll tell everyone about you,

nobody screws me around like that, they can shoot you too for all I care!"

Tears are running down her face. Rennie heads towards her. "Lora," says Rennie, "there's nothing you can do," but Lora is beyond her. Morton is pushing her now, back towards the door.

"Fucking pig," she says, "take your fucking hands off me!" She kicks at Morton, aiming for the groin, but he's too fast for her. He catches the raised leg, lifts, tips her backwards towards the boy, who's quick enough, he's not stoned after all, he catches her and jerks her arms behind her. Morton knees her in the belly, he's knocked the air out of her. Now nobody needs to hold her arms and after the first minute she's silent, more or less, the two of them are silent as well, they don't say anything at all. They go for the breasts and the buttocks, the stomach, the crotch, the head, jumping, *My God,* Morton's got the gun out and he's hitting her with it, he'll break her so that she'll never make another sound. Lora twists on the floor of the corridor, surely she can't feel it any more but she's still twisting, like a worm that's been cut in half, trying to avoid the feet, they have shoes on, there's nothing she can avoid.

Rennie wants to tell them to stop. She wants to be strong enough to do that but she isn't, she can't make a sound, they'll see her. She doesn't want to see, she has to see, why isn't someone covering her eyes?

This is what will happen.

Rennie will be taken to a small room, painted apple green. On the wall there will be a calendar with a picture of a sunset on it. There will be a desk with a phone and some papers on it. There will be no windows.

Behind the desk there will be a policeman, an older man, with short greying hair. In front of the desk there's a chair.

Rennie sits down in the chair when the policeman tells her to. The policeman who's brought her here will stand behind her.

She is asked to sign a release form saying that while in custody she has not been harmed in any way and has not witnessed any other detainee being so harmed. She thinks of Lora, her pulped face. She understands that unless she makes a mark on this paper they may not let her out. She feels that she has forgotten how to write. She signs her name.

They have her suitcase here, from the hotel, and her purse. The older man says that perhaps she would like to change her clothes before meeting the gentleman from the Canadian government who is here to see her. Rennie feels this would be a good idea. She's taken to another small room, much like the first except that the calendar is different, it's a white woman in a blue bathing suit, one piece, again no windows. She knows the young policeman is standing outside the door. She opens her suitcase and sees her own clothes, the clothes that used to be hers. Alien reaction paranoia. She starts to cry.

Rennie knocks on the inside of the door, which opens. She walks out. She's just as dirty but she feels less dirty now, she feels decent, she's wearing a cotton dress, faded blue, and her hair is combed, as well as she could do it in the mirror from her purse. She's carrying the suitcase in her right hand, the purse is over her left shoulder. Her passport isn't in the purse or the suitcase either. So she's not really out, not yet. She's decided not to ask where her camera bag is.

She is taken up some stairs, along a stone hallway, then into a much larger room, one with windows. She can hardly remember what it's like to be in such a large room, to look out of windows that are so huge. She looks out. What she sees is the muddy field where the tents were; now it's empty. She understands that this is one of the rooms that are usually shown to tourists, the room where they were going to sell the local arts and crafts, a long time ago. There are two wooden chairs in the corner, and a man is standing beside them waiting for her. He's still got the tinted glasses and the safari jacket.

He shakes hands with Rennie and they sit down on the wooden chairs. He offers her a cigarette, a black one with a gold band, which she refuses. He smiles at her, he's a little nervous. He says she certainly has given them some uneasy moments. There wasn't a lot they could do when the region was destabilized and the government here was so panicky, overreacting he says, but the situation is normalizing now.

The government can't make a public apology of course but they would like her to know unofficially that they consider it a regrettable incident. They understand that she is a journalist and such things should not happen to journalists. It was an error. They hope she's prepared to consider it in the same light.

Rennie nods and smiles at him. Her heart is beating, she's beginning to think again. Of course, she says.

To tell you the truth, says the man, they thought you were an agent. Of a foreign government. A subversive. Isn't that absurd? It's the common charge though, in countries like this.

The man is uneasy, he's leading up to something, here it comes. He says he realizes she's a journalist but in this instance things are very delicate, getting her out of here has been more difficult than she may suppose, she doesn't know how these small southern countries operate, the people who run them are quite temperamental. Irrational. For instance, the Prime Minister was very angry because the Americans and the Canadians didn't send in their armies and their navies and their air forces to support him, over, let's face it, a completely minor insurrection, doomed even before it started. The Prime Minister seemed to feel that Rennie should be kept in a cell because these armies had failed to materialize. As a kind of hostage. Can she imagine that?

Rennie says she can. I suppose you're telling me not to write about what happened to me, she says.

Requesting, he says. Of course we believe in freedom of the press. But for them it's a matter of saving face.

For you too, thinks Rennie. Have you any idea of what's going on in here? she says.

The Council of Churches made an inspection and was satisfied with the conditions, he says, too quickly. In any case we can't interfere in internal matters.

I guess you're right, says Rennie. She wants her passport back, she wants to get out. Anyway it's not my thing, she says. It's not the sort of piece I usually do. I usually just do travel and fashion. Lifestyles.

He's relieved: she understands, she's a woman of understanding after all.

Of course we don't make value judgements, he says, we just allocate aid for peaceful development, but *entre nous* we wouldn't want another Grenada on our hands.

Rennie looks out the window. There's a plane, coming down at a sharp angle across the oblong of sky, it flashes, silver, up there in the viciously blue air. It must be the afternoon flight from Barbados, the one she came in on, only now it's on time. The situation is normalizing, all over the place, it's getting more and more normal all the time.

Actually I'd like to forget the whole thing as soon as possible, she says. It's not the sort of thing you want to dwell on.

Of course not, he says. He stands up, she stands up, they shake hands.

When they're finished, when Lora is no longer moving, they push open the grated door and heave her in. Rennie backs out of the way, into the dry corner. Lora hits the floor and lies there, limp, like a bundle of clothing, face down, her arms and legs sprawled out. Her hair's all over, her skirt's up, her underpants ripped and filthy, bruises already appearing on the backs of her legs, the heavy flesh of her thighs, massive involvement, or maybe they were there already, maybe they were always there. There's a smell of shit, it's on the skirt too, that's what you do.

The older one throws something over her, through the bars, from a red plastic bucket.

"She dirt herself," he says, possibly to Rennie, possibly to no one. "That clean her off."

They both laugh. Rennie's afraid it isn't water.

They go away, doors close after them. Lora lies on the floor, unmoving, and Rennie thinks *What if she's dead?* They won't be back for hours, maybe not until the next morning, she'll be alone here all night with a dead person. There should be a doctor. She picks her way carefully around the outline of Lora, the puddle on the floor, blood mixing with the water, it was only water after all. She looks out through the bars, down the corridor, as far as she can see in either direction. No one's there, the corridor is empty and silent, the light-bulbs hang along the ceiling with loops of wire in between, at regular intervals. One of them is burnt out. I should tell someone, thinks Rennie.

Rennie is in the kitchen, making herself a peanut butter sand-wich. There's a radio on somewhere, a soft blur of noise, or maybe it's the television, a blue-grey oblong of mist in the livingroom where her grandmother sits propped in front of it, seeing visions. Rennie cuts the sandwich in four and puts it on a plate, she likes small neat ceremonies like this, she pours herself a glass of milk.

Her grandmother comes through the doorway between the diningroom and the kitchen. She's wearing a black dress printed with white flowers.

I can't find my hands, she says. She holds out her arms to Rennie, helplessly, her hands hanging loose at the ends of them.

Rennie cannot bear to be touched by those groping hands, which seem to her like the hands of a blind person, a half-wit, a leper. She puts her own hands behind her and backs away, into the corner and along the wall, maybe she can make it to the kitchen door and go out into the garden.

Where is everybody? says her grandmother. She starts to cry, screwing up her eyes like a child, scant tears on the dry skin of her face.

Rennie's mother comes in through the kitchen door, carrying a brown paper bag full of groceries. She has on one of her shopping dresses, navy blue.

What's going on? she says to Rennie.

I can't find my hands, says her grandmother.

Rennie's mother looks with patience and disgust at Rennie, at her grandmother, at the kitchen and the peanut butter sandwich and the groceries she's carrying. She sets the bag down carefully on the table. Don't you know what to do by now? she says to Rennie. Here they are. Right where you put them. She takes hold of the grandmother's dangling hands, clasping them in her own.

The sunlight is coming in through the little window, it falls on the floor in squares, in one of the squares is Lora's left hand, the dirty blunt fingers with their bitten cuticles curled loosely, untouched, they did nothing to her hands, shining and almost translucent in the heavy light. The rest of the body is in darkness, in water, the hand is in the air. Rennie kneels on the wet floor and touches the hand, which feels cold. After a moment she takes hold of it, with both of her hands. She can't tell from holding this hand whether or not Lora is breathing, whether or not her heart is still moving. How can she bring her back to life?

Very carefully, this is important, she turns Lora over, her body is limp and thick, a dead weight. Dead end. She hauls Lora over to the dryest corner of the room and sits with her, pulling Lora's head and shoulders onto her lap. She moves the sticky hair away from the face, which isn't a face any more, it's a bruise, blood is still oozing from the cuts, there's one on the forehead and another across the cheek, the mouth looks like a piece of fruit that's been run over by a car, pulp, Rennie wants to throw up, it's no one she recognizes, she has no connection with this, there's nothing she can do, it's the face of a stranger, someone without a name, the word *Lora* has come unhooked and is hovering in the air, apart from this ruin, mess, there's nothing she can even wipe this face off with, all the cloth in this room is filthy, septic, except her hands, she could lick this face, clean it off with her tongue, that would be the best, that's what animals did, that's what you were supposed to do when you cut your finger, put it in your mouth, clean germs her grandmother said, if you don't have water, she can't do it, it will have to do, it's the face of Lora after all, there's no such thing as a faceless stranger, every face is someone's, it has a name.

She's holding Lora's left hand, between both of her own, perfectly still, nothing is moving, and yet she knows she is pulling on the hand, as hard as she can, there's an invisible hole in the air, Lora is on the other side of it and she has to pull her through, she's gritting her teeth with the effort, she can hear herself, a moaning, it must be her own voice, this is a gift, this is the hardest thing she's ever done.

She holds the hand, perfectly still, with all her strength. Surely, if she can only try hard enough, something will move and live again, something will get born.

"Lora," she says. The name descends and enters the body, there's something, a movement; isn't there?

"Oh God," says Lora.

Or was that real? She's afraid to put her head down, to the heart, she's afraid she will not be able to hear.

Then the plane will take off. It will be a 707. Rennie will sit halfway down, it will not be full, at this time of year the traffic is north to south. She will be heading into winter. In seven hours she'll be at the airport, the terminal, the end of the line, where you get off. Also where you can get on, to go somewhere else.

When she's finally there, snow will be on the ground, she'll take a taxi, past the stunted leafless trees, the slabs of concrete, the shoebox houses, they'll stop and she'll give the driver the correct amount of money and she'll walk up the stairs and through her own front door, into the unknown. She doesn't know who will be waiting for her, who will be there, in any sense of the word that means anything. Perhaps nobody, and that will not be fine but it will be all right. Wherever else she's going it will not be quietly under.

She's drinking a ginger ale and thumbing through the inflight magazine, which is called *Leisure*. On the front, up at the top, there's a picture of the sun, orange, with a smiling face, plump cheeks and a wink. Inside there are beaches, the sea, blue-green and incredible, bodies white and black, pink-brown, light brown, yellow-brown, some serving, others being served, serviced. A blonde in a low-riding tie-dye sarong, the splotches reddish. She can feel the shape of a hand in hers, both of hers, there but not there, like the afterglow of a match that's gone out. It will always be there now.

The ginger ale tastes the same as it used to, the ice cubes are the same, frozen with holes in them. She notes these details the way she has always noted them. What she sees has not altered; only the way she sees it. It's all exactly the same. Nothing is the same. She feels as if she's returning after a space trip, a trip into the future; it's her that's been changed but it will seem as if everyone else has, there's been a warp. They've been living in a different time.

There's a man sitting beside her. Although there's an empty seat between them he moves over, he says he wants to see out the window, one last glimpse as he puts it. He asks if she minds and she says she doesn't. He's standard, a professional of some sort, he's wearing a suit and drinking a Scotch and soda, he's selling something or other.

He asks how long she was down for and she says three weeks. He says she doesn't have much of a tan and she says she's not all that fond of lying around in the sun. She asks what he does and he says he represents a computer company.

She wonders if he really is who he says he is; she'll wonder that about everybody now.

Vacation? he says.

She could pose as a tourist but she chooses not to. Working, she says. She has no intention of telling the truth, she knows when she will not be believed. In any case she is a subversive. She was not one once but now she is. A reporter. She will pick her time; then she will report. For the first time in her life, she can't think of a title.

He asks her if she's a secretary. "I'm doing a travel piece," she says, and gets the usual reaction, a little surprise, a little respect, she's not what she looks like. She tells him where.

Where they had the trouble? he says. He says he's been there and it doesn't have a tennis court worth mentioning, and she agrees that it doesn't.

He asks her if she travels alone much and she says yes, she does, her work requires it. He asks her to dinner and she wonders what to say. She could say that her husband is meeting her at the airport or that she's a lesbian or that she's dying, or the truth. She says unfortunately she doesn't have enough time, she has to meet a deadline, and that's the end of him, he feels rejected, he's embarrassed, he moves back to his own seat and opens up his briefcase, it's full of paper.

She looks out the window of the plane, it's so bright, the sea is below and there are some islands, she doesn't know which ones. The shadow of the plane is down there, crossing over sea, now land, like a cloud, like magic. It's ordinary, but for a moment she can hardly believe she's here, up here, what's holding them up? It's a contradiction in terms, heavy metal hurtling through space; something that cannot be done. But if she thinks this way they will fall. *You can fly,* she says to no one, to herself.

There's too much air conditioning, wind from outer space blowing in through the small nozzles, Rennie's cold. She crosses her arms, right thumb against the scar under her dress. The scar prods at her, a reminder, a silent voice counting, a countdown. Zero is waiting somewhere, whoever said there was life everlasting; so why feel grateful? She doesn't have much time left, for anything. But neither does anyone else. She's paying attention, that's all.

She will never be rescued. She has already been rescued. She is not exempt. Instead she is lucky, suddenly, finally, she's overflowing with luck, it's this luck holding her up.

Margaret Atwood has published over thirty books, including novels, poetry, and literary criticism; they have been published in more than twenty-five countries and have been translated into more than twenty languages. Her most recent novels are *Cat's Eye* and *The Robber Bride,* both bestsellers. *The Handmaid's Tale,* also a bestseller, was made into a major motion picture. She lives in Toronto with novelist Graeme Gibson and their daughter, Jess.

Homer

Poet of
the
Iliad

Mark W. Edwards

Homer

Poet of the *Iliad*

THE JOHNS HOPKINS UNIVERSITY PRESS   BALTIMORE AND LONDON

This book has been brought to publication with the generous assistance
of the David M. Robinson Publication Fund and the Andrew W. Mellon
Foundation.

The Johns Hopkins University Press
701 West 40th Street, Baltimore, Maryland 21211
The Johns Hopkins Press Ltd., London

Originally published in hardcover, 1987
Johns Hopkins Paperbacks edition, 1990

LIBRARY OF CONGRESS CATALOGING-IN-PUBLICATION DATA
Edwards, Mark W.
    Homer, poet of the *Iliad*.
    Bibliography: p.
    Includes index.
  1. Homer. *Iliad*.   2. Trojan War in literature.
  3. Achilles (Greek mythology) in literature.   I. Title.
PA4037.E39   1987   883'.01   86-21134
ISBN 0-8018-3329-9 (alk. paper)
ISBN 0-8018-4016-3 (pbk.)

Title page illustration: Poet, youth, and dog, from an Attic red-figure cup of
490–480 B.C. attributed to Douris. From The Metropolitan Museum of Art,
Gift of Dietrich von Bothmer, 1976, and loan Musee du Louvre. (1976.181.3)
Used by permission.

Contents

Acknowledgments

The origins of this book go back to 1955, when I began teaching the *Iliad* to freshmen at Brown University in the Identification and Criticism of Ideas program, at that time in its third year. We met for a full year, in small seminars, discussing a single major work and the ideas it presented, together with associated readings. It was, I think, the best general introduction to literature and to university-level study I have known. This course on the *Iliad*, together with another I taught later in the same program based on Thucydides, influenced all my later teaching. I am happy to acknowledge here the debt I owe to the late Herbert Newell Couch and the late John Rowe Workman, two master teachers who had the courage and confidence to entrust their students to someone totally inexperienced in the American university system, and by their example showed me the importance of classical studies as an instrument for general education and personal development. Since that time I have learned much more about Homer, but my old files show that my basic ideas were formed during those years at Brown. They also recall to mind the names and faces of many Brown (and Pembroke) students to whom I owe a great deal.

In addition, this book is full of the insights of generations of scholars, from antiquity to the present. It contains the ideas I think best—some absorbed from others, some developed by me in thirty years of research and teaching. In this volume I generally cannot present in detail the arguments on which my views are based, and this may give the false impression that my views are the accepted opinion; those who turn to the further readings appended to each chapter will soon learn otherwise. In the text I have tried to give credit to a scholar responsible for a particular insight when it is especially identified with him or her, and when the work is recent; but to attribute every idea to its original source would be impossible because of the vast quantity of bibliographical references that would be required. This book overlaps little with other general books on Homer, because my emphasis, my basic approach, and the arrangement of the book are significantly different.

I am grateful to Daniel Blickman and Virginia Jameson for their helpful comments on the chapters on Book 9 and Book 3, respectively. The arrangement of Part One owes much to the perceptive and constructive criticisms of the anonymous reader appointed by the Press. Above all, I thank Marsh H. McCall, Jr., who read the entire manuscript and drew my attention to many obscurities in exposition and infelicities of expression.

I would also like to acknowledge especial debts to the late Richmond Lattimore for his translation of the *Iliad*, which I have used in classrooms for thirty years; and to Dean Wessells, of the School of Humanities and Sciences at Stanford, whose well-designed program for painlessly introducing humanities faculty to the word processor brought this book to completion several years sooner than would otherwise have been possible.

The translations of *Iliad* 16.666–75 by Christopher Logue and of *Iliad* 18.39–49 by William Arrowsmith appeared in *Arion* 1, no. 2 (Summer 1962): 23, and ibid. 6, no. 3 (Autumn 1967): 347–48, respectively, © The Trustees of Boston University.

Introduction

The Purpose and Plan of This Book

This book attempts to combine the advantages of a general introduction to Homer and a commentary on the *Iliad*. The ideal at which it aims is an up-to-date union of the virtues of two excellent old books: S. E. Bassett's *The Poetry of Homer* (1938), a survey of the poetic qualities of the two epics, and E. T. Owen's book-by-book companion, *The Story of the Iliad as Told in the Iliad* (1946). The second section of this Introduction sets out certain basic features of the Homeric poems that I think are essential for their proper appreciation, but that may be misinterpreted by readers familiar mainly with other kinds of literature. The third section explains the scale of the works and briefly analyzes their structure.

Part One contains essays on the poetic characteristics of the epic, in which I set out to show both what the traditional style seems to be and how the poet has used, adapted, or ignored it in specific instances. The last four essays outline the religious ideas depicted in the poems (both the *Iliad* and the *Odyssey*) and some aspects of the poet's social background that may have affected his work. Part Two consists of commentaries on the most important books of the *Iliad*, with brief linking passages explaining important points in books not included here. There is a good deal of cross-referencing between Parts One and Two and, for simplicity, I have occasionally repeated information in more than one place. A final Afterword sums up my general view of the meaning and significance of the *Iliad*.

This book need not be read in sequence; those already familiar with the poems may prefer to do so, but others may find it best to begin with the commentary on a book in which they are interested and refer later to the fuller details on particular points given in Part One. The *Odyssey* is included in the material of Part One, but it was impractical to include commentaries on its books in Part Two.

The approach and the emphasis are my own; the chief aim being to identify the poet's original ideas by understanding the regular conventions that he manipulated for particular effects. Of course, I make frequent use of the discoveries of others, and indeed I hope to make accessible to nonspecialists the results of important recent research on Homer, which they are unlikely to read in the original publications. A number of scholars have recently enlarged our understanding of Homer's use of formulaic expressions and standard type-scenes, but much of the work is scattered in learned journals and made inaccessible to many humanists by the use of ancient Greek and modern foreign languages. For many years Milman Parry's work was unappreciated even by classicists; there are signs that the same may occur with some of the recent pioneering ideas, and I hope this book may help avoid this. Classical scholars who are not Homerists will, I think, find the book informative, but it does not attempt to cover in detail all the recent contributions that studies in anthropology, religion, sociology, and history have made.

At the end of every section I have listed works for further reading, with brief comments; I included both standard authorities and recent significant studies, giving preference to those in English. Full details of these and other works referred to in the text are given in the Bibliography. The translations are my own, and in keeping with the purpose of the book often bring out the emphasis and word order of the original at the expense of contemporary English style and idiom. All Homeric references are to the *Iliad* unless the *Odyssey* is specified.

Homeric Style: Some Basic Features

A thoughtful reader who comes to the Homeric poems for the first time, or one who knows them superficially and for the first time approaches them seriously as literature, often brings preconceptions that can prevent proper appreciation of the works. One may unconsciously apply standards that are not valid for this orally composed but highly sophisticated poetry. The battle scenes may seem wearisome, the conventional adjectives meaningless; there may seem to be little symbolism, little care in the placing of words; descriptions of places or scenery are few; plots may seem slow-moving and delayed by purposeless digressions; the frequent interventions of the gods may seem to remove all responsibility and much of the interest from the human characters. However, a clearer knowledge of the principles and techniques of Homeric poetry should lead to an appreciation of the poet's mastery of the conventions of his art and his power over an audience familiar with those conventions. The major characteristics of Homeric style and content will be examined in detail in Part One. First, however, some preliminary observations about basic features of the poems, including their structure.

Scholars still disagree on when, where, how, and why the *Iliad* and the *Odyssey* were first written down, and on how these first written versions may have differed from our standard text (see pp. 23–28). But it is clear that before Homer there were centuries of epic song, centuries in which singers developed techniques that simplified composition within a strict meter and made it possible to render a poem at greater or lesser length, according to the immediate circumstances of delivery and the skill of the particular singer. These techniques are highly visible in the *Iliad* and the *Odyssey*, and so—no matter how they were composed and written down—they must be considered "oral" poems.

Homer, however, is completely the master of his inherited techniques, and can use them, ignore them, violate them for specific effect, or transcend them as he wishes. It is likely that, just as Virgil constantly imitates Homeric scenes, modifying them to produce quite different effects, so Homer adapted the standard scenes and phraseology developed by his predecessors. A common type-scene is sometimes expanded and given enormous emotional effect; two examples are the supplication scene of Lycaon and Achilles, in which Achilles states in unforgettable terms his acceptance of his own coming death (21.34ff.), and that of Priam and Achilles, which occupies most of the final book and brings the thought of the whole poem to its magnificent conclusion. Sarpedon's famous speech to Glaucus about the roots of honor and the reasons men go to face death in battle (12.310ff.) is basically a *parainesis*, a standard encouragement to one's troops, but Homer turns it into a thoughtful justification of heroic behavior.

Sometimes the deeper implications of a scene are so important that the superficial purpose makes little sense; if too much attention is paid to this, the poet may be unfairly censured for improbabilities in the story. The short catalogue of Greek leaders recounted to Priam by Helen in Book 3 has no practical plausibility—it would not take a king nine years to identify the leader of the army besieging his city—but the poet turns it into a brilliant means of portraying Helen's emotions (see pp. 191–93). The motif of divinely made armor probably originated in a magical device given by a helper to the hero to make him invulnerable, like the herb moly that Hermes gives to Odysseus (*Odyssey* 10.275ff), and like the fantastic mechanical devices prepared for James Bond. But this aspect of the armor inherited by Achilles from his father, Peleus, is carefully avoided in the *Iliad*, and even the use of the armor to disguise Patroclus when he leads Achilles' troops into battle is not exploited (see pp. 255–56). Instead, the armor given by the gods to Peleus and that made by Hephaestus for Achilles (which may well be Homer's innovation) are used as a vivid and visible connection between the deaths of Patroclus, Hector, and Achilles himself, and as an ironic symbol of the gulf between the immortal gods, who fashion the armor and present it to their favorites, and the mortal heroes whom it cannot save from death (see pp. 115–16).

Homer also often modifies the standard phraseology, especially the use of conventional fixed epithets with proper names and common nouns (see pp. 49–53). A good example of this occurs in the heart of the moving farewell scene between Hector and his wife, Andromache. When the hero takes his infant son in his arms, the child cries in fright at the bronze helmet his father is wearing, with its great nodding horsehair plume. Hector laughs, takes off the helmet, and lays it on the ground; instead of the conventional epithet for "ground," the poet uses the adjective "all-glittering," which describes the helmet, further explains the child's fear, and adds to the visual effect (see p. 209). It is very common in Homer for a conventional epithet to be left out, so that a new sentence or phrase can begin in mid-verse, and thus give increased variety of phrasing.

A major part of Homer's technique is expansion, which he uses for emphasis; a lengthy description of a scene or a long-winded speech must not be passed over as an irrelevant display of the poet's powers or the uncontrolled love of detail, but accepted as the poet's method of dignifying the present or future action, and allowed its full impact. "Where the drama is most intense the digressions are the longest and the details the fullest" (Austin 1966.306). This kind of amplification is normal in ancient rhetoric, but Austin was the first to realize and demonstrate it in Homer, and his refutation of Auerbach's argument on this point (in the first chapter of Auerbach's influential book, *Mimesis*) is of the greatest importance.

The principle can be seen in type-scenes, as in the enormous expansion of the preparations for Priam's supplication to Achilles in Book 24. It can be seen in the speeches, especially in the paradigms (examples from the past that justify a claim to be heard and a proposed course of action; see pp. 98–99). Nestor is prolix not because he is old but because what he has to say is always important, and his longest monologue (following a protracted refreshment scene) leads up to the vital suggestion that Achilles lend his armor to the impatiently listening Patroclus (Book 11). Agamemnon's long lecture to Diomedes on the achievements of Diomedes' father prepares for Diomedes' mighty victories in Books 4 to 6. Episodes are built up to proper scale; the truce will be broken and Menelaus wounded by the otherwise unimportant Trojan Pandarus, but Pandarus's bowshot is introduced by a long conversation of the gods, a vividly described journey by Athena, her suggestion to him that he shoot off an arrow, and descriptions of the construction of his bow and his action in drawing it (Book 4). The battles of Books 11 to 15 are long–drawnout because the eventual defeat of the Greeks and the entry of Patroclus into the combat are immensely important; the book-long battle over the body of Patroclus (Book 17) builds up the grief of Achilles; the visit of Thetis to Hephaestus is described in detail not simply for its charm but as a fitting preparation for the immense account of the making of Achilles' shield (Book 18), itself of fitting length for the grandeur of the hero and the magnificence of his return to the battle.

Occasionally in the *Odyssey* an episode or speech may be unnecessarily lengthy, but usually this same principle applies. Hermes' journey to Calypso's island is described at length because it frees Odysseus after so many years of detention, and the building of his raft is performed in detail before our eyes to emphasize how much his escape means to him (*Odyssey* 5). As the commentary will indicate, it is a measure of Homer's quality as a poet that the material for these expansions is not mere decorative description, but also contributes greatly to the emotional effect.

The *Iliad* and *Odyssey* are long stories intended to be recited (or possibly sung) to an audience; they combine some features of a novel with some of those of a play (see pp. 20–21). The poet can exploit the possibilities inherent in both forms and can also avail himself of the liberties permitted within each genre. The large proportion of both epics that is presented as direct speech must have been rendered as a kind of drama, and many scenes read almost like a dramatic script (for example, in *Iliad* 6 and 9). On the other hand, realism is often suspended in a way that would be impossible in a movie and difficult on the stage. The battle raging around two combatants is often ignored while they converse (as in the case of Diomedes and Glaucus; 6.119ff.), and all other actions stop while a suppliant speaks. When Achilles finally enters the battle, all the other Greeks vanish for nearly three books (20–22), then reappear after his victory to stab the dead Hector.

Like a skillful novelist, the poet often produces a powerful effect by a vivid description of a scene, arising from a powerful visualization. A fine brief example of this occurs early in the *Iliad*, where the Greeks' sufferings from the plague are summarized in a single verse: "Continually the pyres of the dead were burning, everywhere" (1.52). The success of the Trojans in Achilles' absence, which allows them for the first time to encamp on the plain for the night instead of withdrawing inside the safety of the city walls, is conveyed by the famous description of the scene around their twinkling campfires (8.553ff.). Achilles' interminable pursuit of Hector around the walls of Troy is drawn out, not by speeches from the watching Trojans and Greeks, still less by an account of their emotions, but by repeated descriptions of the visible scene interspersed with similes and other techniques of expansion (see pp. 293–94).

Modern readers easily accept the existence of the Greek gods, but usually resent their interference in the affairs of mortals. In order not to distort the effect of the poems, we must realize that for the Greeks, divine support for a hero is a strongly positive sign, showing that the gods take an interest in him; accordingly he must be worthy of their regard and ours. The idea is well expressed in a quotation from Hesiod in one of the victory songs of Bacchylides: "Whomever the gods honor, him should fame amongst men follow also" (Hesiod, fragment 344, Merkelbach and West). Any hero who wins a contest with a god's help has *increased* his merit, not (as we would tend to take it) *reduced* it. Achilles waves off the Greeks who attempt to help him against Hector for fear they might diminish his glory, but he welcomes the arrival of Athena (22.205–7, 224). Athena returns Achilles' spear in his duel with Hector (22.276–77) and Diomedes' whip in the chariot race (23.390), and these interventions, like the inspiration she gives Diomedes in Book 5, add glory to the hero.

On the other hand, the important actions in the poems, such as the quarrel of Agamemnon and Achilles (Book 1), are usually caused by purely human character and motivation. Achilles holds back, on the advice of Athena, from killing Agamemnon (Book 1), and restores Hector's corpse on the order of Zeus (Book

24), but both actions are presented as resulting from a mighty effort of self-control on Achilles' part; the hero was free to refuse to follow the gods' will, though at his own cost (see pp. 180–81).

The Scale and Structure of the Poems

The length of the *Iliad* and the *Odyssey* is remarkable, much exceeding (as far as we know) that of other epics of the period. More remarkable still, and worthy of immense credit (as Aristotle saw; *Poetics* 23), is that this size was attained not by chronological extension, not by adding exploit to exploit and generation to generation, but by *contracting* the time frame to a much shorter period than other epics, thus bringing about the unity of each poem. Let us consider some other poems in the cycle of epics about Troy. The eleven books of the *Cypria* carried the story from the gods' decision to cause the Trojan War down to the beginning of the *Iliad*; in its four books the *Little Iliad* covered events from the death of Achilles to the fall of Troy and the departure of the Greeks. (The plots of these and other early Greek epics are conveniently summarized in the introduction to Lattimore's translation of the *Iliad*; the evidence is printed and translated in Evelyn-White 1936.)

The *Iliad*, however, covers a period of fifty-three days; Books 2 to 22 cover only five days and most of the others pass in a verse or two (nine days for the plague, twelve for the gods' visit to the Ethiopians, eleven for Achilles' mistreatment of Hector's body, nine for Hector's funeral; see Camps 1980.78–79). The *Odyssey* covers forty days in all; the only ones recounted in detail are the six days of Telemachus's adventures in Books 1 to 4 and the six that pass between Odysseus's landing in Ithaca and his triumph over the suitors (Books 13 to 23). The expansion of the poem by the *Decameron*-like tales of the hero's exciting encounters since he left Troy is carried out in Odysseus's own words, and thus is strictly confined and unified in both time and place.

Kirk has suggested that the huge scale of the poems is not the culmination of gradual growth, but the direct result of the enormous reputation of a particularly accomplished singer. He drew an analogy from the huge Geometric-style amphorae of this time: "The evidence of archaeology does not suggest that pots became systematically larger and larger until eventually one was made that was seven feet tall, but rather that there was a leap from the largeish pot to the perfectly colossal one, a leap which must have been made for the first time by a particular potter who suddenly had a flash of ambition and the inspiration of sheer size, and at the same time realised that he possessed the necessary materials and technique" (Kirk 1962.281). On such a scale the mighty catalogue of ships in Book 2 is a fitting introduction of the armies; the almost surrealistic disappearance of all the Greeks but Achilles once he returns to the battle is no longer surprising; and one can understand how the poet can be original enough to conceive a massive poem that ends with neither the sack of Troy nor the death of its hero Achilles.

However straightforward it may appear, the main plot of the *Iliad* consists of several themes skillfully and unobtrusively linked together. First comes the main "withdrawal-devastation-return" structure (see pp. 62–63); Agamemnon unwisely rejects a priest's offer of ransom and insults Achilles, Achilles "withdraws" from the battle, and Zeus agrees that the Greeks shall be defeated in his absence. But before their actual defeat in Book 8, the poet contrives to enlarge the scope of the work by inserting five elements: (1) the history of the expedition (the poet's device is the omen, predicting victory in the tenth year, which appeared to the Greeks as they mustered at Aulis, and the catalogue of the forces that embarked there; see Book 2: the Greeks thought of Homer as their first historian as well as their supreme poet); (2) a recapitulation of the cause of the war, in the form of a reenactment of the seduction of Helen by Paris and a new affront to the gods by the Trojans (Books 3 to 4); (3) Diomedes' exploits as a substitute for the absent Achilles, to show Greek fighting power before the defeat Zeus has decreed for them, and to drive home the distinction between mortals and immortals (Books 5 to 6); (4) an introduction of the Trojan leader Hector and his family (Book 6); and (5) a formal duel between Hector and Ajax as a forerunner of his final duel with Achilles (Book 7).

Disheartened by their "devastation" in Book 8, the Greeks send to Achilles and offer him a huge recompense if he will return (Book 9), but he rejects three appeals, binding himself not to return until his own ships are endangered. So the troubles of the Greeks continue. After a rather irrelevant nighttime scouting expedition (Book 10), the next major turn in the plot is prepared for by five books describing the varying fortunes of battle around the Greek's defensive wall (Books 11 to 15), interspersed with some diverting byplay among the gods (Book 14). Early in this part of the story the way is prepared for the next big theme, the "revenge," as Nestor suggests to Achilles' great friend, Patroclus, that he return to battle in Achilles' place (Book 11). At the height of the Greeks' danger, as their ships are being set afire, Achilles yields to further supplication from Patroclus, though because of his earlier commitment Achilles will not return to battle himself; Patroclus must go in his stead, wearing Achilles' own armor. So the first "return" of the hero is carried out by a surrogate (Book 16). After many victories, Patroclus is killed by Hector.

After a long struggle (Book 17), Patroclus's body is recovered by the Greeks. Achilles swears to avenge him, but before he can do so (1) new armor for him must be made and described (Book 18), and (2) the gifts promised at the first supplication (in Book 9) must be handed over, together with the prize of honor Agamemnon had taken from him, and the insult repudiated (Book 19). When the hero at last "returns" to the battle, all the other Greeks vanish and the only diversion amid his exploits is a mock battle among the gods (Books 20 to 21). Achilles kills Hector (Book 22) and gives honorable burial to Patroclus's body (Book 23).

The "withdrawal" and "revenge" themes are now complete, but the final "consolation" theme has already been introduced by Achilles' continued maltreatment of Hector's body. The consolation is double: when old Priam comes to ransom the body of his son, Achilles not only consoles him for his grief and hands over the corpse for burial, but at last overcomes his own grief for his friend, which had not been appeased by his revenge (Book 24). The poem is thus formally concluded not by the hero's triumph, his revenge, or his death (as is, for instance, *Beowulf*), but by his acceptance of an honorable ransom for a dead enemy, his compassion for the griefs of others, and his mastery of his sorrow. The final understanding of mortal limits is much like that which the hero experiences at the end of *Gilgamesh*.

The joining of the "withdrawal" and "revenge" themes is skillfully done by the use of Patroclus as a surrogate for the returning Achilles, a surrogate who can be killed and must then be avenged. Also, the device of his taking Achilles' armor gives a plausible reason for the hero's not storming out immediately to seek revenge (as well as opening up many possibilities for powerful symbolism: see pp. 115–16). However, Achilles returns to battle not because his anger with Agamemnon has been assuaged, but because it has been overwhelmed by his passion for vengeance on Hector. The final "consolation" theme may appear to be rather awkwardly linked on at the beginning of Book 24 by the description of Achilles' still inconsolable grief, despite his courteous supervision of the magnificent funeral games in Book

23. It can, however, be formally considered a grand enlargement of the struggle over the corpse of a victim (Hector), which normally concludes a hero's mighty exploits (see pp. 79–81).

This beautifully contrived arrangement of the themes allows for multiple effects. Achilles both rejects the plea to help his suffering fellow Greeks (Book 9), and then accepts it (Book 16), adding greater depth to his character. Hector first flees in terror before Achilles, then stands to face him with hope still in his heart, and finally loses all hope but still attacks his enemy courageously (Book 22). This is similar to the double effect in the *Odyssey*, where Odysseus finds his wife both faithful and (in a sense) unfaithful, for she leads him to suspect someone has tampered with his marital bed (*Odyssey* 23), and in the *Song of Roland*, where the hero both splendidly refuses to blow his horn to summon help and finally does so.

The *Odyssey*, too, though it appears straightforward, is artfully constructed; it is not simply a series of adventures of a particular hero—which Aristotle declared would not make a unified story (*Poetics* 8)—but a well-designed whole, with a single theme, which manages to cover many years of wanderings within the scope of a few days' actual time. The starting point of the tale is not (as it might have been) Penelope's final enforced completion of the famous tapestry, but the coming to maturity of Odysseus's son, Telemachus, amid the host of suitors for his mother's hand. In folk-tale manner, with a supernatural guide (Athena), he sets off to seek his fortune, or (more specifically) to try to find news of his lost father (Books 1 to 2). His adventures include meetings with the legendary figures of Nestor, Menelaus, and Helen (Books 3 to 4). The advantage of this beginning is that the poet can present to us the wicked misdeeds of Penelope's suitors in Ithaca and the difficult situation Odysseus will face on his return, long before the hero triumphs and our sense of justice is finally satisfied.

Then Odysseus's present situation on Calypso's island is presented, introduced (as was that of Telemachus) by a council of gods—effectively the same one, though for simplicity Homer presents two consecutive councils. By divine order, Odysseus leaves Calypso's island at last, and after the wrecking of his craft by the aggrieved Poseidon (whose son, the Cyclops, Odysseus has wounded), he is received hospitably by the Phaeacians (Books 5 to 8). To them he recounts the tale of his past miraculous adventures before he reached the point at which we found him with Calypso (Books 9 to 12). These traveler's tales could easily have lapsed into the episodic events of a weekly series, but the structure of the *Odyssey* binds them together by the device of having the hero recount them himself, at a single sitting, to his Phaeacian hosts.

Odysseus is then conveyed to Ithaca and stays at the farm of the faithful swineherd, Eumaeus; the two strands of the tale come together as he is joined there by the returning Telemachus (Books 13 to 16). He reveals his identity to his son, and the two plot the overthrow of the suitors. This pattern of revelation and conspiracy is repeated as Odysseus makes his way in disguise back to his own palace, is insulted by the suitors, reveals himself to the swineherd and another faithful servant, and induces them to join the plot. A *tête-à-tête* meeting with Penelope seems set to follow the same pattern, but veers aside in an exciting postponement of our expectations (Book 19). Finally, Odysseus is recognized by the suitors when he successfully passes the tests of stringing his old bow and performing his old feat of shooting through the row of axheads. The recognition device also conveniently provides the hero with the weapon for slaying his opponents (Books 20 to 22). This triumph is followed by another superbly handled recognition, that by his wife Penelope, and their reunion in their marital bed—the folk-tale marriage with the beautiful princess (Book 23). The tale is extended—perhaps not altogether happily—by yet another recognition, that by the hero's father, further plotting, and the final improbably rapid and unconvincing settlement of the disputes in Ithaca by the intervention of Athena.

The complete plot thus depicts not merely a string of adventures linked only by the identity of the hero, but the eventual triumph of the rightful king and the long-awaited and well-deserved punishment of the wicked suitors. Aristotle thought this double reversal of fortunes characteristic of comedy (*Poetics* 13).

Further Reading

ON HOMER AND HIS BACKGROUND. The best general survey is still Kirk 1962 (abbreviated version, Kirk 1965). Bowra 1972 sums up a traditional view of most aspects. Whitman 1958 and Beye 1966 are good on the poet's art and include chapters on his background. Nagy 1979 places the poems against the framework of Indo-European and early Greek poetry and ideas. The relevant chapters in the new *Cambridge Ancient History* vol. II part 2 are quite accessible, and Wace and Stubbings 1963 is still serviceable though sometimes outdated. Clarke 1981 gives an interesting history of the way Homer has been interpreted and appreciated, and is especially good on the modern period. The most recent survey of Homeric bibliography, with references to earlier bibliographies, is by Holoka in *Classical World* 73 (1979): 65–150.

ON THE POETRY. Griffin 1980 is concerned primarily with characterization, pathos, death, and the gods. Vivante 1985 seems to me very subjective. There are excellent sections on Homer in the works of two of the most eminent classicists of this century, Fränkel 1973 and Lesky 1966, and Bassett 1938 is still very good on most aspects. There are good articles on specific topics in Kirk 1964 and 1976 and Wright 1978. On the significance of expansion, see Austin 1966 and Edwards 1980b.

ON THE "ILIAD" IN PARTICULAR. Schein 1984 deals with the poetic tradition, the gods, and the heroic portrayal of Achilles and Hector, and is very good on previous bibliography; Mueller 1984 treats the structure of the *Iliad*, the battle scenes, similes, and the gods. MacCary 1982 approaches the poem from the psychoanalytical angle. On the structure of the *Iliad*, Heubeck 1958 is still good.

ON THE "ODYSSEY" IN PARTICULAR. Clarke 1967 is very good generally; Austin 1975 takes a provocative and perhaps controversial view of the poetics of the poem. Kitto 1966.116–52 is very good on the structure. Clay 1983 makes many fine observations and (implausibly, to me) finds the anger of Athena at the heart of the poem.

COMMENTARIES. There are running commentaries on the *Iliad* by Owen 1946 (still very good indeed), Willcock 1976 (based on Lattimore's translation; no introduction), Hogan 1979 (based on Fitzgerald's translation, with a good general introduction), and Kirk 1985 (based on the Greek text, with general introduction).

HOMER AND VIRGIL. Teachers of ancient epic may find useful several excellent books that compare Homer and Virgil and illuminate both: Otis 1964, Johnson 1976, Lee 1979, Williams 1983, Gransden 1984. Beye 1966 is good on all three epics.

Characteristics of Homeric Poetry

The Bard, Oral Poetry, and Our Present Text

Helen, to cheer her young visitors Telemachus and Peisistratus after the whole gathering has been weeping for the heroes lost at Troy, casts a tranquilizing drug into the wine and suggests they tell stories as they dine; she herself begins with the tale of Odysseus's visit to Troy in disguise (*Odyssey* 4.238ff.). In the *Iliad* she similarly juxtaposed grief and storytelling, saying that Paris's follies and her own would become the songs of the future (6.356ff.). As he sits with the disguised Odysseus and the other men in his hut after the evening meal, the swineherd Eumaeus, after having told of past events on Ithaca, introduces the story of his life by drawing a picture of an age-old yarn-swapping session: "Listen in silence and enjoy yourself; sit there and drink your wine. / These nights are endless. A man can sleep, / or enjoy listening to stories; no need for you / to go to bed before it is time. A lot of sleep is a bore." And in fact they talk almost until dawn (*Odyssey* 15.391–94, 493–95). King Alcinous of Phaeacia, enraptured by his guest's tall stories, is eager to listen to him all night long until dawn comes (*Odyssey* 11.373ff.), and Telemachus could listen to Menelaus for a year (*Odyssey* 4.594ff.). Though the tales are of strenuous adventures and the loss of loved ones, listening to them brings release and pleasure; the paradox is beautifully symbolized in the first account of the singing of the bard Demodocus, which delights the Phaeacians so that they urge him to continue, whilst Odysseus, the actual participant in the tale, cannot restrain his tears (*Odyssey* 8.83ff.).

A good deal of the *Odyssey* consists of stories told by the characters; Helen, Menelaus, Demodocus and Odysseus tell tales of Troy (4.240ff., 8.499ff., 14.468ff.), the shade of Agamemnon tells of Achilles' funeral (24.36ff.), Menelaus and Nestor tell of journeys home (3.254ff. and 4.351ff.; 3.103ff.), and in addition to Odysseus's mighty narrative in Phaeacia (Books 9 to 12), we hear the tale of the boar hunt that was the origin of his scar (19.392ff.) and the three false accounts he gives of his life (13.256ff., to Athena; 14.191ff., to Eumaeus; 19.165ff., to Penelope). The *Iliad* includes the tale of the omen at Aulis as the troops gathered (2.301ff.), Nestor's accounts of his youthful exploits (1.260ff.,

7.124ff., 11.670ff., 23.629ff.), Phoenix's autobiography (9.447ff.), and a number of shorter tales told as paradigms (see pp. 98–99).

This is all natural enough in any society, real or fictitious. But besides amateur storytelling there is also professional work, and bards who earn their living singing songs to entertain an audience are portrayed in detail in the *Odyssey*. How much does the picture resemble the circumstances of the actual singer of the epics, and what kind of feelings does the poet show toward his art? Since both pictured and real bard are singing to an audience, not writing for readers, what techniques were developed to make composition and memorization of lengthy songs possible? And if the *Iliad* and the *Odyssey* were sung, not read, when, where, how, and why were they written down, eventually to reach us? The following four sections will deal with these questions.

The Bard in Homer

The two major bards are Demodocus, "received by the people," who sings in the palace of Alcinous and is described in *Odyssey* 8.62ff., and Phemius, "prophetic utterance," the bard of Odysseus who unwillingly entertains the suitors in his absence (*Odyssey* 22.330ff.). They are not slaves, but have the standing of free and independent craftsmen; like prophets, healers, carpenters, and heralds, they are summoned to one's house when necessary (*Odyssey* 17.383–86, 19.135). Demodocus is not a retainer or employee of Alcinous, but is brought to the palace by a herald (*Odyssey* 8.43–45, 62–83); Phemius is more closely associated with Odysseus's palace, perhaps as a kind of retainer with status similar to Medon the herald; the two are spared by Odysseus on the word of Telemachus (*Odyssey* 22.356f.). A similar in-house status seems to attach to the unnamed bard who was unsuccessfully set by Agamemnon to keep watch over his wife and was deported by Aegisthus (*Odyssey* 3.267ff.; Page 1972 suggested that this highly responsible assignment recalls an era when a minstrel would also be high priest and spokesman for the gods).

Besides singing to the lyre, the bards also play the lyre for dancing (*Odyssey* 4.17–19, 8.261–64, 23.143–45, and perhaps *Iliad* 18.604–5; see p. 283). Singers also appear singing a dirge at the funeral of Hector (24.720–22, see p. 313). The only nonprofessional said to sing to the lyre is Achilles (9.186–91), who sings of the great deeds of heroes while Patroclus waits, either to take over in his turn or simply as audience. Achilles can hardly be expected to control the elaborate compositional techniques of the oral composer, and so either these must be memorized songs, or the poet is ignoring realism for the sake of the special effect he wishes to produce (see p. 220). One mythical singer is also mentioned: Thamyris, who boasted he would surpass the Muses, who in anger took away his voice and his lyre-playing (2.594–600).

Singers are treated with great respect, a characteristic one cannot resist associating with the desires of the real-life poet. Demodocus is "cherished by the people," and Odysseus personally sends him a gift of meat, praises him lavishly, and declares that singers must be cherished and revered, because the Muse has taught them and loves them (*Odyssey* 8.470ff.). Phemius is spared by Odysseus because he sang for the suitors only under constraint (*Odyssey* 22.331ff.). A singer is essential for a festive occasion; before he begins his melancholy tale of his wanderings, Odysseus paints a cheerful picture of feasting in a king's palace, with the bard singing amongst the throng (*Odyssey* 9.2–11), and Alcinous refers to the lyre as "the companion of the generous feast" (*Odyssey* 8.99).

A good singer enraptures his audience. Eumaeus praises Odysseus as a storyteller who enchanted his heart like a singer inspired by the gods, so that men yearn insatiably to hear him (*Odyssey* 17.518–21), and silence follows Odysseus's tale to the Phaeacians as all are "held in thrall" (*Odyssey* 13.1–2 = 11.333–34). The most detailed description of this spell comes from the mouth of another singer, Hesiod (*Theogony* 96–103):

Happy is the man whom the Muses
love, and sweetly flows the voice from his mouth.
For if a man, even one who has sorrows and fresh grief in his
   mind
and is pining away with the distresses in his heart, yet when
   a singer,
the servant of the Muses, sings of the glorious deeds of men of
   old
and of the blessed gods who inhabit Olympus,
at once that man forgets his heavy-heartedness and remembers
nothing of his sorrows; the gifts of the goddesses soon turn his
   mind away from them.

The enchantment is almost like that of the Sirens, who offer Odysseus knowledge of all that happens over the earth (*Odyssey* 12.39ff., 184ff.). In true tragic vein, it is the sorrows of mankind that are the subject of song (6.358, *Odyssey* 8.580). It is noteworthy that nothing is said of the bard inspiring men to glorious deeds.

The lyre is essential for the singer, and he needs periods of rest during his song (*Odyssey* 8.87); we remember the *gusle* of the Yugoslavian singers whose songs were recorded by Parry and Lord, and their need for occasional rest (Lord 1960.17). His songs, as Hesiod declared in the passage quoted above, are of the glorious deeds of men—not necessarily "men of old," as Hesiod said, but also men of his own day: Telemachus says that the latest song is always the most popular (*Odyssey* 1.351–52). So Demodocus sings of the quarrel of Odysseus and Achilles during the Trojan War, the adventure of the wooden horse, and another unspecified tale (*Odyssey* 13.27–28). He sings of the gods, too: the notorious affair of Ares and Aphrodite in Hephaestus's absence (*Odyssey* 8.266ff.), which has a humorous inappropriateness for an audience that includes another long-absent husband. Phemius, in the palace of Odysseus, sings (more appropriately) of the harsh homecomings that Athena inflicted upon the Greeks (*Odyssey* 1.325ff.), and Circe refers to the story of the Argonauts "which all men care about" (*Odyssey* 12.70). The *truth* of the song is important, perhaps better expressed as the ability to carry conviction, or (in our terms) to suspend disbelief. Odysseus praises Demodocus for giving the story "properly [*kata kosmon*], as if you had been there or heard it from one who was" (*Odyssey* 8.489ff.). Similarly, Alcinous compliments Odysseus as "one who knows [his tale] well, like a bard" (*Odyssey* 11.363ff.)—with perhaps some humor, since Odysseus usually lies about himself, and the poet is indirectly praising his own superior performance as bard.

It is the inspiration of the Muses that gives the bard his power over men and allows him to know the truth about the past; "you know all things, but we have heard only the report [*kleos*] of it and know nothing" (2.485–86). Without them he is powerless (2.488–92), but with their help his song reaches down far into the future (6.357–58). So Demodocus owes his knowledge to the Muses (*Odyssey* 8.488), and his ability to tell the truth about the wooden horse is a test of the Muses' inspiration working upon him: "If you can tell me this [tale of the wooden horse] accurately [*kata moiran*], I will at once tell all men that the goddess has willingly given you her sacred song," says Odysseus to him (*Odyssey* 8.496–98). It is the Muse who stirs him to start his song (*Odyssey* 8.73), and the motif is worked up in Hesiod into an actual meeting with them in which they give him a staff (not a lyre, which perhaps belongs to the tales of heroes rather than to theogonies: *Theogony* 22–34). The Muses are daughters of Mnemosyne ("Memory"), and memory retains information, gives the poet his skill in composition, and immortalizes the subjects of his song. They do not send the poet into an ecstasy or frenzy like a prophet; Phemius can say, with the usual Homeric "double motivation" (see pp. 134–35), that he is self-taught, but the goddess has implanted all kinds of songs in him (*Odyssey* 22.347–48). Invoking them establishes the poet's authority and guarantees the truth of his song, and is used to focus attention upon an important moment. The motif is not overworked: besides the proems to each poem, the Muse is invoked only four times in the *Iliad* (before the catalogue of ships [2.761ff.], before Agamemnon's victories [11.218ff.], when the great battle turns in favor of the Greeks [14.508ff.], and when fire is hurled on the Greek ships [16.112ff.]).

The power that song exerts over men and gods alike, and its comprehension of the world and the fates of men and gods, must have a divine origin. Such a gift from the gods might make a man feel too fortunate if it were not counterbalanced by some evil; Demodocus is blind (*Odyssey* 8.63–64), so is the poet of the Delian *Hymn to Apollo* (172), and so too was Homer himself in later legend. The gift of prophecy evoked similar disabilities, sometimes explained as punishments: examples are the blindness of Teiresias (*Odyssey* 10.492–93), the maiming of Phineus (Hesiod frag. 157 M.-W.), and the odd tale of Evenus (Herodotus 9.93–94). Of course, in real life handicapped men were likely to turn to vocations such as these.

Homer the Singer

In Hesiod's *Works and Days* the singer includes a great deal of personal information about his relations with his brother Perses, and in the *Theogony* he recounts his personal meeting with the Muses. This may be fact, real at least to the poet, or a conventional motif acceptable in the genres of didactic and genealogical poetry. In epic there is nothing of this. The poet Homer does not introduce himself. Perhaps the difference arises because Hesiod is teaching and exhorting his audience, and therefore must strongly assert his claim to authority; whereas the epics are presented as history, as the facts of the past, which the singer (with the Muse's help) has only to relate with knowledge and truth, which as we saw above are the qualities praised in Demodocus. So nothing is known of Homer himself; what we can deduce of the circumstances of his life will be mentioned below (see pp. 160–62).

Already in antiquity it was debated if the *Iliad* and the *Odyssey* were composed by one poet or two, and the question remains open, for though there are obvious differences in tone (and some in language) they may be the result of the different aims of the two poems. Who could prove that *King Lear* and *As You Like It* are by the same poet, on internal evidence alone? For Simonides, writing in the last quarter of the sixth century and first quarter of the fifth, Homer is "the poet of Chios" and famous enough to need no further identification (frag. 8 West), and in the passage that links the Delos-inspired and Delphi-inspired parts of the *Homeric Hymn to Apollo* (165–77), perhaps datable to 522 (see Burkert 1979), the "sweetest singer of all . . . whose songs will always hereafter be the best," is "the blind man who lives in rocky Chios."

But great as his fame already was, Homer's life was so little known that other places besides Chios could claim him as their son. His personal experience can often be glimpsed in the similes (see pp. 103–4), perhaps even in the swift thoughts of a man who "has travelled widely over the earth, and remembering in the depths of his mind, often thinks 'I wish I were there, or there'" (15.80–82), or in those of the hero who "saw the cities of many men and learned their thoughts" (*Odyssey* 1.3).

Of the performance of the poems, we can safely conjecture only that it *was* a performance; not an individual reading to himself from a text, nor one person reading it to others, but a recitation, perhaps close to a dramatic performance. The immense size of the *Iliad* and the *Odyssey* almost certainly set them apart from other epics, though others also were too long for a single continuous recitation, and we just cannot tell how, or even if, they were performed in their entirety. In later times, perhaps already in the sixth century, they were sung in Athens by relays of singers (see p. 25). We cannot tell if the poet accompanied himself on the lyre, as singers do in the poems. If he did not—and even if he did, though perhaps to a lesser extent—he must have become an actor as well as reciter, for the amount of direct speech, especially the four books of Odysseus's own narrative, must have placed the epic genre somewhere between narrative and drama. Perhaps Demodocus's lengthy song of Ares and Aphrodite, though containing direct speech of the characters, is itself presented in the form of indirect speech so that there can be no confusion between Homer the singer of the *Odyssey* (who invokes the Muse and occasionally addresses his audience) and Demodocus the singer of this episode, whose song has no formal proem, invocation, or conclusion. The singer must have been tempted to impersonate the characters whose direct speech he was repeating; one wonders, frivolously, what the voice of Xanthus the horse sounded like (19.408ff.).

The poet's pride in his creation, his awareness of the immortality it will bring him and his characters, is sometimes openly expressed. Helen laments, "Upon [Paris and myself] Zeus has laid a hard lot, so that even afterwards we may become subjects of song for men still to be born" (*Iliad* 6.357–58), similar to the thought Shakespeare gives his Cleopatra: "Antony / Shall be brought drunken forth, and I shall see / Some squeaking Cleopatra boy my greatness / I' the posture of a whore" (*Antony and Cleopatra* 5.2.215ff.). Alcinous says the gods destroyed the heroes at Troy "for the singing of men hereafter" (*Odyssey* 8.579–80), and the shade of Agamemnon declares, "The fame of [Penelope's] virtues shall not die, for the gods will make a song for mortals, a lovely one for prudent Penelope" (*Odyssey* 24.196–98)—a positive note like that of Cassius: "How many ages hence / Shall this our lofty scene be acted o'er / In states unborn and accents yet unknown!" (*Julius Caesar* 3.1.111ff.). Telemachus's remark that men always prefer the newest song (*Odyssey* 1.351–52), the praise of Demodocus by Odysseus and the others (see above), and the praise of Odysseus himself by the Phaeacians are fairly overt allusions by the poet to the greatness of his work. In the *Iliad*, the superb description of the craftsmanship of Hephaestus, as he depicts by his artistic skill the circumstances of human life on the shield of Achilles, may well be thought a conscious parallel between divine smith and Muse-inspired poet (see p. 285).

The Techniques of Oral Poetry

The craft of Homer the poet was that of a performing bard. It comprised not only knowledge of stories and the ability to adapt them (see pp. 61–70) but also mastery of the techniques of composition (and perhaps of memorization) developed by past generations of singers. Homer himself possessed the quality of genius that enabled him to exploit, master, and transcend his predecessors, his contemporaries, and most of his successors in literary history. Oral techniques make composition easier in a rigid meter, without the aid of writing to stabilize the text immediately, and probably also facilitate memorization. The actual writing down, if done at all, is irrelevant. The blind Milton waited to dictate to a daughter the lines he had composed and memorized; but he did not use oral techniques, and so *Paradise Lost* is not an oral poem. On the other hand, the *Battle of Frogs and Mice*, a parody of a Homeric battle composed perhaps in the fifth century B.C., begins with an appeal to the Muses to visit the poet for the sake of the song "which I have newly placed upon the tablets on my knees," a clear reference to written composition, expressed, like the rest of the poem, in formulae derived from oral poetry. The poem declares itself composed in writing, but still copies oral techniques.

The essential characteristic of true oral poetry is that each performance is different, shaped to suit its particular circumstances, including the caliber of the singer. The time available, the reactions and nature of the audience shape the form of each presentation. The structure and plot of the story may remain the same, but the expansiveness and perhaps the emphasis will vary every time; the quality of the song, too, will vary according to the singer's genius. In this sense, every performance is extemporaneous; but this does not mean that every line, every passage will be different. Each singer has individual expressions and scenes that are carefully polished and unique to him — until someone else admires them and takes them over.

To make possible the immediate production of a version of a song, and perhaps to facilitate memorization of verses and even scenes, special techniques developed, and these are still an essential feature of the Homeric poems, no matter what were the actual circumstances of their production and recording. Among these techniques are: a special dialect, including characteristics of different periods and different areas, which provides synonyms of different metrical shapes (see pp. 42–44); formulaic expressions adapted to fit various parts of the verse (see pp. 46–51); type-scenes, enabling the poet to structure the basic components of a scene (see pp. 71–77); perhaps too the standardization of certain plot patterns (see pp. 62–66). Complete mastery of these conventional aids, so that he can exploit them or ignore them as he chooses, is characteristic of the genius of Homer.

It is therefore possible that Homer, the creator of our *Iliad* and *Odyssey*, had only the conception of performances of a story that varied at each presentation, and no notion of a fixed text, intended to be repeated as it stood (in whole or in part) on every occasion. It is possible that the knowledge of writing first provided not only the possibility, but the very idea, of a stable, unchanging version of a tale. There are, however, some indications that verbatim repetition of a text was not unfamiliar to Homer. Messenger speeches are often repeated verbatim (sometimes with small required grammatical changes), including the lengthy recitation of the recompense Agamemnon promises to Achilles in *Iliad* 9; even after four books have intervened, Nestor's important suggestion to Patroclus is still repeated in virtually the same words (11.794–803; 16.36–45). These word-for-word repetitions contrast with the verbal differences that occur in instances of any one type-scene, and are perhaps a recent development in the oral epic. Again, the song of the heroic deeds of men that Achilles is singing when the embassy arrives implies a memorized song rather than spontaneous composition on his part, for which he could hardly have had the expertise (9.189).

But if Homer was so close to an era in which songs were not recorded, perhaps not even memorized, how was it that these mighty epics were written down at all? It was, after all, a lengthy and expensive undertaking, unlikely to profit either the composer or other bards who made their living by singing such songs. This problem must next be faced.

The Establishment of the Text

The first firm and generally accepted fact is that the text we have, which is essentially the same as that of Roman and medieval times, did not become the standard or "vulgate" text until about the middle of the second century B.C. Before this time, as ancient scholars attest and surviving papyri prove, there were a number of different texts, differing from each other often in a word or two and sometimes in a sequence of three or more verses. In the century preceding the appearance of this vulgate text, the scholars Zenodotus, Aristophanes, and Aristarchus had each established a preferred text based on their revision of texts collected in the great library at Alexandria, but it is not clear which principles they followed in deciding which readings to accept or even if they always had authority in the manuscripts before them for the readings they preferred. The vulgate text is not identical with the preferred text of any of the Alexandrian scholars (S. West 1967.16 says, "It is notorious that comparatively few of the readings which Aristarchus preferred are preserved in the Vulgate"), but its emergence is likely to be due in some way to their work.

Evidence for the nature of the texts before the establishment of this standard vulgate comes mainly from three sources: the remarks of commentators of the Roman and Byzantine periods (the "scholiasts") about the methods and decisions of the Alexandrian scholars; papyri surviving from the period before the mid-second century B.C. ("Ptolemaic" papyri, edited by S. West 1967); and quotations from Homer in writers of the classical period.

The old scholars name a variety of early texts of Homer, sometimes referring to "ordinary" texts (koinai), which they often call "better" or "worse," sometimes to texts attributed to individuals (such as the poet Antimachus of Colophon in Asia Minor, perhaps some fifteen years older than Plato, and the younger Euripides, nephew of the dramatist), sometimes to those of cities from which copies were acquired (or perhaps for which texts were prepared). Athens is not included among these cities (though Atticisms in the text suggest Athenian influence at some point), and none of the texts—not even that from Homer's supposed birthplace, Chios—is said to have any special authority or antiquity. One estimate of their relative value is attributed to the third-century B.C. philosopher Timon, who when questioned about how to find a reliable text of Homer, said, "If you get hold of an old copy, not one of the 'corrected' copies of nowadays" (Diogenes Laertius 9.113). This is reminiscent of the sarcastic remark attributed to Alcibiades, Socrates' pupil, when a schoolmaster offered him a copy of Homer corrected by himself: "Are you teaching boys to read when you know how to edit Homer? Why aren't you teaching *men*?" (Plutarch, *Alcibiades* 7.1).

These divergent versions must be represented in our papyrus texts. Some of the Ptolemaic papyri differ in details from our vulgate, generally in a word or two or by the insertion of additional verses that occur in similar contexts elsewhere in Homer; or one occurrence of a type-scene may be enlarged by adding verses that occur in other examples of it. Some verses are new to our text, and may be unique or may come from epic poetry now lost. In the words of the most recent editor, "Few of these interpolations add anything very significant to the narrative: Iliad pap. 121 and 342 have a slightly different version of the battle scene at [*Iliad* 12] 183ff. [line-numbering marks indicate several additional verses were present]. But no new episodes or changes in the plot are introduced. The relatively minor scale of the interpolations argues against the view that there is a connection between the eccentricities of the early texts and the long oral tradition of the poems, except in so far as the rather discursive style suitable for oral technique attracted interpolation" (S. West 1967.13).

In the first six books of the *Iliad*, for example, the most significant changes introduced by various early papyri are: a few verses of expansion are added to the landing after the expedition to return Chryseis (1.484ff.); an ancient quotation adding an extra tribe to the Trojan catalogue (2.855a–b) is confirmed; thundering from Zeus is added after the armies' prayer during the oath-taking (improperly, since the prayer will not be fulfilled; 3.302a–d); Paris is given two spears instead of one at his arming (3.338); and Menelaus's arming is also described, in a weirdly muddled order which has him picking up his shield and donning his helmet before he puts on his greaves and sword strap (3.339a–c).

Quotations from Homer in Plato and Aristotle are fairly numerous and frequently show verbal changes from our own text, usually affecting the sense only in very minor ways. Both writers probably quoted often from memory, and it is impossible to know where the divergencies indicate a different written text and where a simple slip of the philosopher's memory is responsible; such slips are all the more probable where the two writers quote different versions of the same verse. In the first six books of the *Iliad*, Plato's quotations show a few different readings, none of them altering the sense at all, and the omission of 4.219. The only significant divergence in Plato's quotations is in Achilles' description of the jars of Zeus (24.528), on which see p. 310. Aristotle, who is said to have compiled a collection of *Homeric Problems*, edited the text of Homer for his famous pupil, Alexander, but it is not known whether this text (called "the cylinder edition," from its storage place) survived in other copies; it is never mentioned as a source for the Alexandrian scholars. His quotations are numerous; he quotes (according to La Roche 1866) twenty-seven verses from the first six books of the *Iliad*, twenty of them in agreement with our text; of the variants, the only one of much significance is at 2.15, where he replaces "and evils have been laid upon the Trojans" (the wording is repeated at 2.32) by "We grant that he win glory" (found in our text at 21.297).

So by the fifth century B.C. written texts were available, differing from each other and from our vulgate in minor ways. At this time there were also public recitations of Homer by "rhap-

sodes"—performers who recited from memory—of the kind depicted in Plato's *Ion*. Recitations of this kind are attested for
Athens in the late fourth century and may perhaps have been
instituted there as early at the late sixth century, and Herodotus
records (5.67.1) that Cleisthenes, tyrant of Sicyon about 600–570
B.C., put an end to public competitions of rhapsodes declaiming
Homer because Argos and the Argives, his enemies, were so
much glorified in them. In a passage in Xenophon (*Memorabilia*
4.2.10) the suggestion is made to someone that he might become
a rhapsode because he owns a complete Homer, an idea he
scorns on the grounds that rhapsodes know the epics perfectly
but are otherwise fools. So rhapsodes at this time are considered
reproducers, not makers of new poems. How they acquire their
repertoire is not stated, but it should not be assumed from Xenophon's tale that it could only have been from written texts.

A professional guild of Homeridae or "descendants of Homer"
(Plato's Ion is not one of them, because he declares they should
give him a golden crown; *Ion* 530d), based in Chios, the birthplace of Homer, is attested for the sixth century. An ancient
report runs: "Homeridae they called in ancient times those of
Homer's race, who also used to sing his poetry by right of suc-
cession; after this rhapsodes too, no longer tracing their line
back to Homer [were called Homeridae?]" (see Burkert 1972). Presumably, though it is not certain, they recited the poems verbatim, not in varying oral versions, and learned them by ear, not
by reading. It is unknown if they possessed a written version,
and if so, what relation it bore to the attested Chian text (see
above).

What is the relationship between Plato's written text, the
other written versions, and the version(s) recited by the Homeridae? How, when, where, and why did the first established version intended for verbatim repetition appear (whether written
down or not)? Was there one such fixed text, or more than one?
Here we must resort to speculation; and probability is an unhelp-
ful criterion, for it is not easy to find reasons for undertaking, at
any time, such a laborious and expensive task as writing down
epics of such length. Homeridae and rhapsodes would have no
obvious reason for writing down a text; it is easier to find reasons
why they should *not* relinquish their exclusive control over the
poems.

The earliest evidence for a written text is the record that The-
agenes of Rhegium, who was active in the last half of the sixth
century B.C., "first wrote on Homer" (see Pfeiffer 1968.10f.). A

written text may have been established at Athens in the time of the strongman Peisistratus (third quarter of the sixth century) if it is true (the evidence is weak) that he set up recitations of Homer at his newly established Panathenaic festival. Polycrates, from 532 to 522 tyrant of Samos, which claimed a close connection with Homer, is said to have possessed a large library (Athenaeus 1.3a), and this may well have included a text of Homer.

If there is any truth in these reports, one can only guess how the written text was acquired: Was it copied from an earlier written text, perhaps one provided by the Homeridae? Or was it taken down by dictation from a singer? The occasion of the Panathenaea provides a motive for so doing, and the resources of a ruler remove problems of expense. If this occurred, was the dictation done by a singer who had memorized a verbatim version, or a bard who composed a special "oral" one on the spot? Or was it (as Dihle 1970 has suggested) a matter of combining oral composition with written versions of parts of the poems? Since we know of no specially authoritative Athenian version, why did it disappear? The most economical hypothesis is to suppose one early written version (since either dictation or composition in writing must have been difficult for works of such length), which was recopied for various purposes, while singers continued to learn the songs by ear (which is much simpler than reading from a text that would have no word divisions and might be in an unfamiliar alphabet). The variants in later texts might be either the additions of copyists (since most of the additional verses occur elsewhere in the texts), or (less probably) the result of expansions inserted when small portions of the poems were sung in isolation. Further publications and study of papyri may help us to form more firmly based views.

One thing gives us comfort. There is no hint whatever of versions of the *Iliad* or the *Odyssey* widely different from our own, or even different in more than the most minor details of wording and expansions of type-scene. There never seems to have been an established *Iliad* without Helen and Priam on the wall of Troy, the parting of Hector and Andromache, Achilles' rejection of the embassy, or the ransoming of Hector's body. More than this; the evidence we do have does not indicate any tendency toward standardization of type-scenes or uniformity of the text in parallel passages, still less any pressure to reduce the individual elaboration of a particular scene. So we need not feel that we have lost much of the distinctive hand of the great poet. Expansion by repetition of recurrent verses, by minor variation in expression of the same idea, is the characteristic of the variants in the divergent texts, and this has little effect on our understanding or appreciation.

The storytelling in the *Iliad* covers not just the anger, withdrawal, and return of Achilles, but events from the marriage of Peleus and Thetis to the death of Achilles himself; and the *Odyssey* includes the death of Achilles, the conquest of Troy by means of the wooden horse, and the death of Odysseus. Many other tales are explicitly referred to: tales of Heracles, Thebes, the Argonauts, and others. The bards knew a huge corpus of song and legend. Our *Iliad* and *Odyssey* derive from many patterns of story, and their formation may well have been a matter of many years, the final accomplishment of a poet of unusual genius who sang these stories and many others in different shapes until the huge final, monumental versions of each poem were created. What part writing played in the establishment of a fixed version we do not yet know; but it happened, and something very much like that first written version was preserved for the world.

Further Reading

ON BARDS AND ORAL POETRY. Thalmann 1984.113–33, 157–86 has an excellent account of the bards in Homer, including Odysseus's tale. Lord 1960 is the basic work on Homer and Yugoslavian oral poetry, arguing that Homer must have dictated his poems to a scribe; Finnegan 1977 covers a wide range in modern song. P. Murray 1981 and 1983 discusses Homer and ancient bards. Several of Kirk's articles dealing with oral poets and the oral tradition are reprinted in Kirk 1976. Burkert 1972 and 1979 is good on the Homeridae. Walsh 1984 has interesting chapters on truth and the psychology of the audience in Homer and Hesiod.

ON THE WRITING DOWN OF THE TEXT. Parry 1966 gives a fine account of the problems, with an assessment of the arguments of Lord and Kirk. Dihle 1970 presents a different view. The basic facts are given in Davison 1963 and Jeffery 1963.

ON THE EARLY TRANSMISSION. Kirk 1985.38–43 gives a good short account of the Alexandrian scholars; Apthorp 1980 and Pfeiffer 1968 discuss their work on the text in greater detail, and Richardson 1980 gives a good view of their literary criticism. Turner 1968 and S. West 1967 and 1981 give an account of the papyrus texts.

Narrative: The Poet's Voice

A good deal of both the *Iliad* and the *Odyssey* takes the form of direct speech by the characters; as Aristotle observed, "Homer, with little prelude, leaves the stage to his men and women, all with characters of their own" (*Poetics* 1460a9). Even the thoughts of the general mass of soldiers are given in direct speech (for example, 3.297ff.). Because the poem was recited by a professional bard, rather than read to oneself, the use of so much direct speech was even more effective (see pp. 20–21). But besides the descriptive passages (on which see pp. 82–87), there remains a great deal of narrative in poems of such length, and many of the more memorable passages are in the poet's own voice. What position does he take toward his audience, and what techniques does he control?

Much interesting work has recently been done on narrative theory, but the advances and techniques of analysis have not yet been thoroughly carried over into Homeric studies, and the theorists usually fail to investigate the narrative practices of the old epics. In any case, oral epics like those of Homer, intended to be declaimed by a bard to a listening audience, and including both direct speech and narrative, combine the effects of the novel (bard as narrator), drama (bard as actor), and oratory (bard as public speaker), and analyses developed mainly or entirely from works intended to be read instead of heard are likely to be incomplete. However, the categories used by Seymour Chatman (1978) in his analysis of "discourse, the means through which the story is transmitted," are useful in clarifying the different relationships between author and audience, and the analogies and examples he draws from cinema and comic strip often provide insights into Homeric techniques.

Chatman (1978.147) distinguishes six "parties to the narrative transaction," which may be identified in the Homeric epics as:

1. The "real author," a Greek (or possibly Greeks) living in Ionia about 750 B.C., who composed the *Iliad* in virtually the same form in which we know it now. Nothing more is known of his life, and he may not have been named Homer. For our present purpose the only significant facts are his approximate date

(he was not an eyewitness of the events he describes) and the existence of a long tradition of tales and highly formalized poetic composition of which he could avail himself.

2. The "implied author," the picture that the audience forms of the person telling the story. In the *Iliad* and the *Odyssey* the "implied author" combines both human and divine knowledge, and can tell both the thoughts and words of the gods and the resentment of humans at their mortal nature. Thanks to his immortal divine inspirer, he can also pass beyond the constraints of time and know of events before and after the time of his story. He is moral and sympathetic, not overtly a Greek or a Trojan (neither nation is "our side"), and we like his company. This last quality, the attitude the audience develops toward the storyteller, is important, and is one of the advantages epic retains over drama. Booth (1961.213) quotes from Salinger's *Catcher in the Rye:* "What really knocks me out is a book that, when you're all done reading it, you wish the author that wrote it was a terrific friend of yours and you could call him up on the phone whenever you felt like it." Many lovers of Jane Austen must feel that the implied author of *Pride and Prejudice* has much in common with Elizabeth Bennet, whereas in *Emma* (as Booth points out, 264f.) the implied author is a good deal wiser and nicer than Emma Woodhouse. (Jane Austen herself, of course, may or may not have resembled her implied author.)

3. The "narrator," a speaker presented by the author, like Huck Finn, or Marlowe in *Lord Jim*. In our case the "narrator" is Odysseus recounting his adventures in *Odyssey* 9 to 12, Menelaus and Helen telling their stories to Telemachus in *Odyssey* 4, and in shorter forms Nestor's tales of his youth, Eumaeus's life-story (*Odyssey* 15.403–84), Odysseus's lying accounts of his life, and the many mythical examples or paradigms in the poems (see pp. 98–99). (Demodocus's song about Ares and Aphrodite [*Odyssey* 8.266ff.] does *not* fall into this category; see below.) In these cases the audience feels itself in the hands not of the author but of the character who is telling the story, with results that, in the case of Homer, have not yet been fully worked out.

4. On the receiving end of the tale, there is the "narratee," the fictional audience of the "narrator," represented for us by the Phaeacians who hear Odysseus's adventures, Telemachus the listener in Pylos and Sparta, and so on. This category becomes important if the narrator adapts his tale to suit the narratee, which in Odysseus's case is a question awaiting further study.

5. The "implied audience," the audience presupposed by the

narrative as a whole. In our case this is Greeks who are living at a later period than the Trojan War but know a good deal about the legends of their ancestors; they must know, for instance, the identities of the major characters, the outcome of the war, the fate of Priam, Andromache, and Hector's son Astyanax at the sack of the city, and they must know that Achilles never returned home. Several times the poet identifies himself with the audience ("Diomedes took up a stone, a great weight which two men could not lift, such as men are nowadays"; 5.302–4), and the everyday life presented in the similes also links implied author and implied audience. (For comparison, it may be noted that Thucydides' implied audience is different; he writes for posterity and often, though not always, remembers to explain things with which his readers may no longer be familiar.)

6. Finally, the "real audience," unknown to Homer—yourself and myself, whose attitudes toward religion, warfare, slavery, gender distinctions, and so on must also affect the impact of the poems. Sometimes we are obliged to remember the differences between us and the "implied audience"; we must not, for instance, be revolted if Zeus fails to behave as we expect a deity to, any more than we are perturbed by Hector's fighting with a spear rather than with a rifle. But unless our reactions to the major human issues involved in the poem are much the same to those of the implied audience, the work will no longer for us be an effective work of art. However, the experience of more than a hundred generations has shown that differences of language, civilization, and time do not destroy the value of these poems as presentations of universal human situations and emotions. For appreciation of the poet's technique, the most interesting of these categories are the second and third, the implied author and the narrator.

As implied author, Homer is omniscient. However, the present time of the implied author and audience is seldom mentioned. That the events described took place long ago is implicit, and occasionally the heroes at Troy are contrasted with those of the present, as when Diomedes and Aeneas hurl rocks that present-day men could not lift (5.303–4, 20.286–87, cf. 12.383). This familiar exaggeration of the past happens occasionally even in the speeches of the heroes themselves, as when Nestor says the men at Troy would be no match for the opponents he faced in his distant youth (1.271–72) and Odysseus defers to Heracles and others of generations past (Odyssey 8.223ff.). In only one passage of any length, the account of the destruction of the Greeks' wall by Poseidon in later days (12.10–35; see p. 239), does the poet himself speak explicitly of events later than his narrative.

The omniscient narrator has the immense advantage, denied to most of us, of knowing the future; and Homer often shares this knowledge with his audience for pathetic effect. Characters may predict the future, either because they are gods, with special knowledge, or because they correctly interpret the omens the gods send. In many instances the poet in his own voice comments on the future outcome of an action, or sets the present action against a future unknown to his characters. The predicted future may fall within the limits of the poem, in which case we wait in suspense to see it come true—the suspense arising, as is usual in Greek literature, not from ignorance of the outcome, but from the agony of waiting for it to happen. Or the event predicted may occur beyond the conclusion of the poem, in which case the audience must be familiar enough with the story to realize its truth and react with the proper emotion.

Most of this foreshadowing is done through the mouths of the characters. The fall of Troy, obviously known to the audience in advance, is predicted early in the poem (and at impressive length) in Odysseus's tale of the omen at Aulis (2.301–30). The prediction is often repeated, most powerfully in the words of Agamemnon when infuriated by the oath-violating attack on Menelaus (4.163ff.), words later repeated even more poignantly by Hector himself (6.447ff.). Both Hector and Priam describe the agonizing events of the sack of the city (6.454ff., 22.59ff.), and the audience's knowledge of the fate of the infant Astyanax gives a deep emotional irony to Hector's proud prayer for him (6.476ff.). Andromache paints a dismal picture of the future her son will actually never see (22.485ff.), and finally realizes what will happen to him in her last lament over her husband's corpse (24.734ff.). Achilles' death is constantly lamented by Thetis, from her first appearance to her last, with special effect in Book 18 (see p. 271). It is reaffirmed as he sets off to kill Hector by his immortal horse Xanthos (19.404ff.), by the words of the hero himself to his victim Lycaon (21.108ff.), and in the last prophetic words of Hector (22.355ff.).

The events of the poem itself are carefully foreshadowed, sometimes by the gods but often in the poet's own voice. Zeus, after his attention has been distracted by Hera from human affairs, swings back into action with a major account of the future plot of the poem (15.53–71). It is less usual for the poet himself to announce Zeus's intentions, but he does so at the

height of the Trojan success, perhaps to excuse the defeat of the
Greeks (15.592ff.). The death of Patroclus is foreshadowed as he
first enters the main action ("He came out from the dwelling,
and this was the beginning of his trouble"; 11.604), reasserted as
his main (and final) scene begins with his prayer to Achilles ("It
was his own death he was praying for"; 16.46–47), and confirmed
by the report that Zeus rejected that part of Achilles' prayer
(16.250–52). A remarkable and emotional final direct prophecy to
the hero by the poet comes just before his end: "But when for the
fourth time he rushed on, like a god, / then for you, Patroclus,
appeared the end of your life" (16.786–87). On the other side,
Hector's death is anticipated in his own words (6.367–68, 464–65),
and predicted—at the times of his greatest triumph—by his
victim Patroclus (16.852–54) and by Zeus as he watches him put
on the divinely made armor of Achilles (17.192–208).

It is normal for the poet to tell us a deity's reaction to the
character's prayer, for example Athena's to the expansively described prayer of the Trojan women (6.311) and that of the gods in
general to the massive Trojan sacrifice after their victorious day
(8.550–52), which has a foreshadowing effect. Similarly, he tells
us that the duel of Paris and Menelaus will not end the war,
despite the hopes of both sides (3.302).

However, the most characteristic kind of foreshadowing comment is an ejaculation by the poet himself after a character has
performed some action: "Foolish man [or woman], who did not
know. . . ." Memorable instances come as Andromache, ignorant
of Hector's death, prepares his bath (22.445ff.), and as Patroclus
blindly pursues the Trojans in disregard of Achilles' warnings
(16.686ff.; see also p. 263). Often the pitiable futility of a doomed
character's actions is emphasized in this way: Asios refuses to
leave his horses, not knowing that he will never drive them back
to Troy (12.113ff.); Tros makes his supplication, not knowing he
has no hope of placating the furious Achilles (20.466ff.); and the
wicked suitor Antinous hopes to string the bow, not knowing he
will be the first to be killed by an arrow from it (Odyssey
21.96ff.). Similar to these in their omniscience, though referring
to the present rather than the future, are the poet's remarks
about the bereaved parents and wife of a dying hero (see pp. 156–
57), and his comment, after Helen has expressed her concern
about the absence of her brothers from the Greek army, that
they lie dead at their home in Sparta (3.243–44; see p. 193 and
Parry 1966.197).

Homer as implied author has complete freedom of movement,

and he takes us from Greek camp to Troy, from Ithaca to Calypso's island, and from Olympus to the underworld at his will. In the *Iliad* the narrative normally provides a link when there is a change of location; we follow a character who travels from one place to another, or move from a scene to the position of someone watching it, or we see some connection in thought that associates one location with another. For instance, after the long description of Chryseis's restoration to her father and the joyful return of the Greek ship, there is an abrupt change of scene to the lonely and grieving Achilles on the seashore, but the contrast in tone is exactly the effect the poet desires and the connection in thought is close (1.488ff.; see p. 184). Similar, though less moving, is the link made by one character who remains awake while the rest sleep, which bridges Books 1 and 2, 9 and 10, and 23 and 24. In the *Odyssey* such a close connection might not be expected because of its widely divergent scenes of action (the suitors in Ithaca, Telemachus in Sparta, Odysseus in Phaeacia), but nevertheless only twice is there an abrupt change of scene, once from Sparta to Ithaca (*Odyssey* 4.620–21) and once from Ithaca to Olympus (*Odyssey* 14.533–15.1).

The poet does not, however, allow himself freedom in time. The narrative line always moves forward; simultaneous events are narrated as if one followed another, and when the scene changes, time continues uninterrupted. This sometimes leads to the duplication of an action. The council of the gods at the beginning of the *Odyssey*, which results in the dispatch of Athena to Telemachus and his adventure in the next three books, is repeated in Book 5 in order to send Hermes to Calypso with the message that frees Odysseus. The delivery of Zeus's messages to Iris and Apollo (15.157ff., 220ff.) and to Thetis and Iris (24.120ff., 142ff.) are similarly handled. The past, in the sense of the time before the action of the poem, is narrated by the characters rather than by the poet; for instance, the capture of Chryseis and her presentation to Agamemnon are recounted by Achilles (1.366–69), the gathering at Aulis and the portent there by Odysseus (2.301ff.). An apparent exception, the history of Odysseus's scar (*Odyssey* 19.393–466), may perhaps be explained as being the thoughts of Eurycleia. This restriction to forward movement in time makes it easier for the audience to keep track of the story, but occasionally causes minor awkwardness in the structure of the narrative; it explains, for instance, Telemachus's month-long stay in Sparta (despite his desire for haste; *Odyssey* 4.594) while Odysseus builds his boat, endures his eighteen-day

voyage from Calypso's island to Phaeacia and subsequent shipwreck, returns home to Ithaca, and reaches Eumaeus's hut, so
that the two may meet there immediately on Telemachus's
return.

Psychologically, the poet does not exploit his omniscience. He
will explain a character's intention or his mood, often to prepare
us for what the character is going to say before he says it and so
ease the audience's comprehension; but if a person's thoughts are
to be given at length, it is done by direct speech in a soliloquy—
he "speaks to his own heart." Homer does not describe his characters; there is nothing like "Mr. Bennet was so odd a mixture
of quick parts, sarcastic humour, reserve, and caprice. . . . His
wife . . . was a woman of mean understanding, little information, and uncertain temper" (*Pride and Prejudice* 1). Even in the
case of Thersites, who receives more personal description than
anyone else, it is his physique and his abusive language that are
described, not his character or motives (2.212ff.). We deduce character for ourselves from speech and action.

Homer does, however, often present his own opinions in the
form of explicit comments on the action (see Chatman 1978.228),
which may take a number of different forms (though not that of
aphorism). A judgment on the actions of a character may be combined with foreshadowing of events or results to come, as
already mentioned. The poet may voice reproach to the gods: his
comment on the abuse of Hector's dead body is "Zeus abandoned
Hector to his enemies, to be defiled in his own country" (22.403–
4). Moral disapproval of human actions is less common; it is not
quite clear if Achilles' killing of twelve Trojan captives at the
pyre of Patroclus is an "evil action" or "an action evil for them"
(23.176), though I think the former probable. The comment on
Glaucus's foolishness in exchanging bronze armor for gold is unusual and almost humorous, particularly since Glaucus got
away with his life and doubtless thought he came off well (6.234–
36; see p. 206).

Two particularly noteworthy comments by the poet should be
mentioned. When Achilles' divinely made helmet is struck from
Patroclus's head and rolls under the horses' feet, the poet says,
"The crest was befouled / with blood and dust; before that time
it had not been allowed / to befoul the horsehair-crested helmet
in the dust, / but of a godlike hero the head and handsome
brow / it had guarded, Achilles'. But then Zeus granted to Hector / to wear it on his head, and disaster was close to him"
(16.795–800). The poet's eye is caught by an object, as it was by

Hector's helmet at his farewell to Andromache (see p. 211), and he gives full rein to his sympathy for his doomed characters. In another place Homer seems again to wonder at the sorrows and heroism of the character he has created: as the Phaeacian ship brings Odysseus to his homeland at last, returning from land of wonder to the realities that await him on Ithaca, the poet describes the rowers, the sleeping hero, and the progress of the ship, and then in four verses seems to stand back with us and gaze on the scene: "Bearing a man of intelligence like that of the gods, / who before this had suffered many griefs in his mind [the phrase is repeated from the proem] / and had been tested in the wars of men and on the cruel seas / but now he slept at peace, oblivious of all he had suffered" (*Odyssey* 13.89–92).

Occasionally the poet speaks of himself in the first person. At the beginning of each poem he calls upon the Muse to inspire him, and the invocation is repeated at much greater length as a part of the buildup toward the climax of the catalogue of ships in the second book (2.484–93; see also pp. 18–19). Without her aid he could neither know his theme nor rise to its mighty challenge. This has been called the first occurrence of the "inexpressibility topos," the "emphasis upon inability to cope with the subject," which has enormously wide ramifications in the poetry and oratory of later ages (Curtius 1953.159). Shorter invocations signal the turning of the tide of battle as Poseidon rallies the Greeks while Zeus's attention is otherwise engaged (14.508–9), and the long-delayed climax of the Trojans throwing fire on the Greek ships (16.112–13). At one point in the struggle before the Greek wall, the poet ignores the Muse and says, in apparent despair, "It is hard for me to tell all this, as if I were a god" (12.176).

The poet's self-consciousness is again allowed to emerge in an occasional direct address to the audience, in "gentle reader" style. It is noteworthy that Finnegan, without special reference to Homer, remarks, "Direct address to the audience is again peculiarly appropriate to oral literature. It is surprising that it does not occur more often" (1977.118). A rhetorical question may be used to focus attention on the situation, as for instance during Hector's flight before Achilles ("How could Hector have escaped death, had not . . . ?" 22.202ff.), or to explain a character's ignorance ("For who would think that one man alone could . . . ?" *Odyssey* 22.12ff.), or to dramatize the poet's task ("Who could tell all the names [of the Greeks who rallied to Menelaus]?" 17.260ff.). A special form of this is the conventional "Whom first, whom last did [X] slay?" Sometimes the hearer is addressed directly, but

in a rather impersonal and perhaps conventional way: when the
Greeks march to battle silently, *"you* [singular] would not think
so many could be silent" (4.429–30); when Agamemnon inspects
his troops, *"you* would not have seen him asleep" (4.223). The
same convention also occurs in the direct speech of the characters (for example, at 3.220 and 14.58). This uniting of audience
and author as they view the scene is occasionally found in other
techniques, such as "No-one might recognize Sarpedon" (16.638–
39), "no-one might blame" (4.539), or the intensified "not even
Ares or Athena might blame" (17.398).

Another very striking appearance of the poet's own voice is his
occasional use of apostrophe, a direct address to one of his characters. With a few exceptions (to be mentioned below) the usage
is confined to Patroclus, Menelaus, and the swineherd Eumaeus,
three sympathetic characters for whom the poet has been
thought to have a special regard. In the case of Eumaeus,
Odysseus's loyal old swineherd, little can be made of the direct
address, for thirteen of the fifteen examples are in the same
formulaic line "And in answer, Eumaeus, you said," and the remaining two use the same phrase modified to include an adverb.
The poet cannot form a nominative formula including Eumaeus's name that will fit metrically with this phrase (see pp. 48–
49), and instead of using the available "excellent swineherd"
(*dios huphorbos*, which occurs fourteen times in nominative
and accusative, once even in a parallel "he answered" formula),
he may for some reason prefer to use the vocative form and the
direct address. Whatever the reason, in Eumaeus's case the expression seems to be too fossilized to have any great effect; Fitzgerald's rendering, "O my swineherd!" regrettably overtranslates
the Greek.

Patroclus, too, lacks a nominative name-formula of one particular length, though it would not be hard to create one (*Patroklos
amumôn* has been suggested), but in his case it is quite certain
that the personal address by the poet, found eight times (all in
Book 16) has an intentional emotional effect, because the variety
of usages is much greater and some of them cannot be explained
by the absence of a formula. In one place (16.692–93) the conventional expression "Whom first, whom last did [X] slay?" is pur-
posely adapted to the second person and followed by "Patroclus,
as the gods called you to your death?" This is clearly not done
for metrical reasons, but to increase the poignancy. To introduce
Apollo's fatal advance, the poet says, "Then, Patroclus, the end
of your life appeared" (16.787); it was Euphorbus "who first struck

you with his spear, Patroclus, horseman" (812), and the hero's dying words are introduced by a final "feebly you spoke to him, Patroclus, horseman" (843). No other hero is addressed with such sympathy. The poet is using a technique that was almost certainly developed for handling metrically intransigent proper names, but using it to increase our emotional involvement not only with the doomed man but with his bereaved friend, Achilles.

Menelaus, too, is addressed in this way seven times by the poet, three times when he is in special danger (after his wounding by Pandarus, 4.127ff.; after the simile that dramatizes his wound, 4.146; and after he valiantly offers to take on a duel against Hector, which all know would be fatal for him, 7.104); three times when he is displaying special concern for others (for the dead Patroclus, 17.679ff. and 702; and for Antilochus, 23.600); and at 13.603, where he begins a duel, after which he will make an unusually powerful speech (13.620ff.). He, too, is a character whom the poet obviously likes.

There are a few other instances of this kind of direct address. Apollo is twice addressed in the second person and called *ēïe Phoibe*, a title used to hail the god at his birth in the *Homeric Hymn* (120), presumably an old religious style. The usage occurs once after the vivid sandcastle simile (15.365ff.), which contrasts the ease of the god's destruction after the long toil of men (see 12.29ff.), and a second time as he leads one team in the Battle of the Gods (20.152); it is likely that in both cases the direct address is intended to emphasize the god's immortal power. Achilles is once so addressed, at the climactic point as the Greeks prepare at last to follow him into battle (20.2). And once Hector's cousin Melanippus (one of three Trojans of that name) is treated in the same way, after his slaying by Antilochus (15.582). He may receive this distinction merely because his name is metrically similar to Menelaus's (Matthews 1980.98), but Homer has given him a detailed biography a little earlier (15.547–51) and some special attentiveness is possible.

Though interpretation of particular passages may vary, there can be no doubt that in the cases of Patroclus and Menelaus at least, the poet uses direct address, a technique probably developed primarily for metrical convenience, to indicate his special sympathy.

When a character becomes the narrator, his thoughts take the place of those of the implied author, who disappears from view, and verisimilitude places limits on his knowledge. His viewpoint may be different from that of the implied author, especially since he is both an actor in his tale and the teller of it. Present time may intrude, though in Odysseus's tale it is only allowed to do so at beginning and end and before and after the intermission that falls within his account of the underworld (11.333–77). In addition the audience always has the comforting feeling that the hero must somehow have survived the dangers he recounts. The alterations produced in narrative viewpoint, formulaic usage, structure, and content in *Odyssey* 9 to 12 by the changeover to first-person narrative by Odysseus have still not been fully studied, and only an outline can be given here.

The questions are complicated by the fact that Odysseus in his own story is a less mature man than in the rest of the poem (though he does not say so). Instead of the utterly self-controlled hero who can endure insults in his own house and a meeting with his wife in which he does not reveal his identity, Odysseus by his own account is brutal in his treatment of the Cicones, rash in his approach to the Cyclops (as Eurylochus complains; *Odyssey* 10.435ff.), dangerously inquisitive in his desire to hear the Sirens, and so on. Since he is the main actor in his own tale, and is telling it after it is over, he can be allowed a good deal of the poet's usual foreknowledge. He can guess, when a storm arises, that Zeus has sent it (*Odyssey* 9.67ff. and elsewhere). He can (with hindsight) know that Zeus was planning destruction of his companions all the time that Odysseus was sacrificing to him (*Odyssey* 9.553ff.), just as Achilles can know that the priest Chryses complained to Apollo (1.380–81; de Jong 1985) and Glaucus knows that the gods hated Bellerophon because of what happened to him (6.200ff.). And on two occasions he can tell what his men said and did while he himself was asleep (10.34ff., 12.339ff.). But often he cannot be sure which god is involved in an action ("some god" guided him to a landing on Circe's island, "some god" sent him a stag; *Odyssey* 10.141, 157), and of course he cannot describe a scene on Olympus.

The conversation between Helios and Zeus, important because it testifies that it is the wickedness of Odysseus's men that leads to their disaster, has to be specially explained in a way some have found jarring (*Odyssey* 12.374–90). In fact the poet seems almost to draw attention to the handicap he has given himself: he makes Odysseus acknowledge his limitation and say, "Who can see a deity going here or there unless the god wills it?" (*Odyssey* 10.573–74), and complain that Athena did not stand by him in his adventures (*Odyssey* 13.316ff.), when in his own storytelling he could not have related her concerns and actions as the poet himself can do. Nor can the poet himself comment on the action in the same ways as he does in the *Iliad*.

Perhaps, however, the poet is not displeased that the use of Odysseus as narrator allows him to distance himself from all the traveler's tales of fantastic monsters and beautiful immortal seductresses, quite different from the very human characters of the main returning-hero tale. From the mouth of the notorious liar, Odysseus, we may believe them or not at our own choice. There may be a conscious irony in Alcinous's complimentary words to his guest that he is "not one of those men, widely scattered over the earth, telling lies made up from who knows what" (*Odyssey* 11.364–66). Whether Homer or his predecessors ever sang the Cyclops tale or the Circe tale in his own voice cannot be known with certainty. Finnegan says, "In heroic narratives the action is commonly in the third person, but it is also sometimes presented as if the singer/poet was himself the hero" (1977.116–17); she gives a number of examples. Whatever the precedents were, the device adds excitement, immediacy, and reality to subject matter that might otherwise have appeared rather incongruous with the more familiarly human concerns of the rest of the two great poems.

It is worth noting that the three songs of the Phaeacian bard Demodocus (*Odyssey* 8.73–82, 266–366, 499–520) are not given in his direct speech but reported by the implied author, despite the considerable length of the Ares and Aphrodite tale and the large amount of direct speech it contains. Since, however, in all three tales most of the verbs are in the normal indicative mood of narrative (the indirect-speech construction of 515–18 is the exception), a listening audience would hardly be aware of any difference. The reason may be that by retaining the narrative in his own voice, the poet avoids the need to have Demodocus sing a full song, with initial invocation to the Muses, direct address to the audience in his own voice, comment on the action, and so on. When sung to an actual audience by an actual bard, a poem narrated by an implied author that contained a narrator who was himself a bard (Demodocus) might become confusing for the audience. Odysseus's account of his adventures to Penelope when they are in bed together (*Odyssey* 23.310–41) is placed firmly in indirect speech, with constant reminders of the grammatical construction ("He began by telling how . . . and how . . . and how . . . " etc.).

Homer is objective in the sense that the Trojan characters are as real and attractive as the Greeks, but not at all objective in the sense of dispassionate or detached. Though he does not tell us his name, and though as narrator he sees and hears man and god alike, free from constraints of time and place, the poet sometimes allows his personal feelings to appear in the various ways described in this section. In *Gilgamesh* the poet's voice is almost totally absent; in *Beowulf* it is openly Christian and sometimes critical of the heathen ways of the characters; in Homer and Virgil its occasional direct intimacy with the hearer conveys a powerful sensation of our common humanity.

Further Reading

ON NARRATIVE THEORY. Booth 1961; Chatman 1978; and the works of J. Culler, G. Genette, W. Iser, G. Prince, R. Scholes, and T. Todorov (among many others). Lang 1984 deals with narrative in Herodotus, with a chapter discussing Homeric influence. Gransden 1984.9–30 has perceptive remarks on the *Iliad* from this viewpoint. Homer's techniques for describing simultaneous events are examined in detail in Latacz 1977.77ff., Krischer 1971.91ff., and Helwig 1964.

ON FORESHADOWING. Duckworth 1966 is the standard work.

ON THE POET'S SUBJECTIVITY AND USE OF PATHOS. Griffin 1976 and 1980.103–43.

ON APOSTROPHE (DIRECT ADDRESS TO CHARACTERS). In general, Culler 1981.135–54 (without reference to Homer). Parry 1972.9–22 discusses the Homeric examples (omitting two of those for Patroclus), holding that they do have significant meaning; Matthews 1980 decides that in many of the examples metrical reasons are predominant. Block 1982 covers apostrophe and other types of address to the reader in Homer and Virgil.

ON FIRST-PERSON NARRATIVE. Suerbaum 1968 is the most comprehensive study of Odysseus's narrative. De Jong 1985 applies current narratological theories of a "mirror story," comparing Achilles' account of his quarrel with Agamemnon with the poet's account, with very interesting results.

3

Language

The form of Greek that appears in the Homeric poems is a standardized, artificial amalgam, combining forms from different dialects and from different stages in the history of the spoken language. Like Greek religion, the legendary past, and the big festivals, this poetic language was a strong unifying force in Greek culture. The Greeks recognized four dialects in their everyday language, mutually intelligible but clearly distinct: Ionic, spoken on the coast of Asia Minor; Aeolic, spoken on many of the islands (including Sappho's Lesbos) and in Hesiod's Boeotia on the mainland; Attic, the dialect of Athens, closely related to Ionic; and Doric, the dialect of Sparta and Corinth, which came to Greece later than the others and had no part in the epic diction. But the epic language was used for poetry by Homer on the coast of Asia Minor, by Hesiod in Boeotia on the Greek mainland, by Eumelus for his epic about Corinth in southern Greece, and by a (probably) Athenian poet for the *Hymn to Demeter*. Transcending the separate local dialects, it strongly influenced early nonepic poets such as Sappho, Alcaeus, and Archilochus, and there are still many reminiscences of it in fifth-century Athenian tragedy.

The poetic language is based primarily on the Ionic dialect spoken in the Ionian settlements on the coast of Asia Minor in the eighth century, but it includes a large number of forms used in the Aeolic dialect and some that may go back as far as Mycenaean times. There is no Doric admixture, which has always been considered a sign of the late arrival of the Dorians in Greece, and very little Attic, most of it almost certainly added to the text after the time of the main composition. This mixture of forms added to the universality of the language for the Greeks but is probably largely the result of metrical convenience. As dialects changed with the course of time, some old forms that were metrically useful survived in the poetic diction, whereas others were replaced by newly developed forms; linguistic changes opened up new metrical possibilities, which became part of the technique of composition.

The Homeric poet has at his disposal, for instance, four

metrically different forms of the ending of the infinitive (*-menai, -men, -nai, -ein*), several different forms of the personal pronouns ("your" [singular] can be *seio, seo, seu, sethen, teoio*), and a number of variations in the declension of nouns and adjectives. Several sound changes that had taken place in Ionic itself a few generations before the composition of the poems may be admitted to the language, or the older forms may be retained; so the old *w* sound, dropped by Ionic, could for metrical purposes either retain the force of a consonant or be ignored (*erga* beside *werga, idein* beside *widein*, from the same roots as English "work" and "wit" respectively). Many words ending in a vowel either could drop the vowel from the metrical count before a following initial vowel, or could add a final *n* to retain the vowel and syllable; the prefix *e*, which indicates the past tense of a verb, may or may not be used; and there are other possible variations of this nature. There are also abundant synonyms with different metrical forms. For instance, there are four common words for "house" (*domos, dôma, oikos, oikia*), and the names of both Achilles and Odysseus have alternative forms, with a single *l* or *s*, giving different metrical values.

The result is a language that is metrically flexible, archaic, dignified, and international, set apart from the ordinary spoken dialects and combining the prestige and archaism (to us) of the King James version of the Bible with the unfamiliar, dignified Latinity of Milton and the enormous vocabulary of Shakespeare. Throughout the Greek world it would be remote from common talk but easily intelligible (except for a few fossilized, ultradignified words in formulae), the accepted language of high culture and ancient national tradition.

The first line of the *Iliad* provides a good example. The first word, "anger" (*mênin*), is normal Greek, but lacks the Greek definite article, which developed only around Homer's own time and is normally absent from epic diction. The second word, "sing" (*aeide*), has an Ionic form, unfamiliar to Attic and other dialects but easily recognizable. Next, the word for "goddess" (*thea*, in the vocative, the case of direct address) has a feminine form, which survived only in religious formulas—the masculine form (*theos*) served for both sexes in normal Greek—so there would be a strongly religious flavor to the word, befitting an invocation. Then Achilles' name is preceded by his patronymic "son of Peleus" (*Pêlêïadeô*); its ending appears in our texts in an Ionic form, which mildly violates the meter (*-eô* must be pronounced as one syllable, and causes a hiatus before the initial vowel of Achilles' name). This form has been substituted for a metrically correct older form (-*âo*) from which the Ionic developed through two sound changes; the spoken Ionic form prevailed despite the metrical solecism. Finally, the last two syllables of Achilles' name (*Achilêos*) represent a non-Ionic, archaic genitive ending that could not be completely Ionicized without unacceptable metrical violation and so has suffered only a minor change (*êos* for *âos*); it is a form remote from any contemporary spoken dialect. Pope's version of the first two lines—"Achilles' wrath, to Greece the direful spring / Of woes innumerable, heavenly goddess, sing!"—is less "poetic" to our ears than Homer's Greek would sound to Greeks of any period. Fitzgerald's powerful rendering retains much of the effective word order of the Greek, without the archaism: "Anger be now your song, immortal one, / Akhilleus' anger, ... "

There are no significant differences in diction between the *Iliad* and the *Odyssey*, or between the parts of the poems in narrative and direct speech (though sometimes unusually short sentences or interrupted syntax may suggest a speaker's strong emotion). The similes, however, include a considerably higher proportion of Ionic forms that are contemporary with the composition of the poems, which in view of their uniqueness and everyday content is not surprising (see p. 103). The diction is uniformly stately, inescapably remote and "poetic," and immediately identifiable. It is the conventional language of culture, regularly used by the Delphic oracle, and it continued to be imitated for special purposes throughout the history of Greek poetry.

Further Reading

The best treatment of Homeric language is now *Cambridge Ancient History* II 2B chapter 39a and III 1 20d. More briefly, see Kirk 1962.142–50 and 192–203 and 1964.90–118. A detailed analysis of the dialect is given by Palmer 1963. Shipp 1972 studies the distribution of "late" forms, finding them particularly in the similes.

4

Meter and Formulae

In Homeric verse the meter and the recurrent formulaic expressions that fit within it are essentially interconnected, and neither can be understood without the other. For those unfamiliar with Homer's dactylic hexameters, a very rough parallel to both his meter and his use of formulae of set length can be seen in Longfellow's *Hiawatha*. In this poem Longfellow uses a verse composed of two four-syllable units separated by a break between words; in each of the units the first and third syllables are stressed. If these verses are printed in pairs, as in the example below, the result is a sixteen-syllable line, roughly equivalent in length to the Homeric line, and usually falling into four parts:

Thus it was they | journeyed homeward; | thus it was that | Hiawatha
To the lodge of | old Nokomis | brought the moonlight, | starlight, firelight,
Brought the sunshine | of his people, | Minnehaha, | Laughing Water,
Handsomest of | all the women | in the land of | the Dacotahs.

The effect is monotonous, because usually the units are sharply divided by the word end and have an identical pattern of stress. Rarely do the words overrun the metrical divisions:

Striding over | moor and meadow | through intermin | able forests,
Through uninter | rupted silence | with his mocca | sins of magic.

The French classical alexandrine is somewhat shorter than the Homeric line (twelve syllables, not counting the final mute *e* in alternate couplets) and falls into two halves, each with two accented syllables; so each of these halves may also be divided into two parts after the accented syllable:

Noble | et brillant auteur | d'une triste | famille
Toi, | dont ma mère osait | se vanter | d'être fille,

Qui peut-être | rougis | du trouble | où tu me vois,
Soleil, | je te viens voir | pour la dernière | fois!

(Racine, *Phèdre* I.3)

Here the mid-verse break is fixed, but the number of syllables falling between the accented syllables varies a great deal and avoids monotony. In alexandrines of the Romantic period, even the mid-verse break was sometimes abandoned and the verse fell into three sections instead of two (or four), an effect that is also common in Homer:

Une nuit claire, | un vent glacé. | La neige est rouge.

(Leconte de Lisle, "Le coeur de Hialmar" 1)

The Homeric verse consists of six heavy syllables bearing a metrical accent; the first four are each followed by either another heavy unaccented syllable or two light unaccented syllables; the fifth is usually followed by two light syllables, less often by a single heavy one; the last heavy accented syllable is followed either by another heavy one or by *one* light syllable. This gives a line of between twelve and seventeen syllables. There is usually a break between words, and often a pause in the sense, close to the midpoint of the verse, after either the third heavy accented syllable or after the first light syllable following it. Each of the resulting half verses usually has a pause in sense within it; in the first half verse the pause has a wide range of positions, but in the second the pause is usually before the fifth heavy accented syllable, or less commonly after the fourth.

The verse thus tends to fall into four blocks of varying length and metrical shape. Because of the pause in sense normally occurring about halfway through, and the limited choice of positions for the pause in the last half of the verse, the line has both an easily recognizable order and an unmistakable ending cadence; because of the different positions possible for each pause, it also has great flexibility, the flexibility found in good English blank verse. Some idea of the movement may be conveyed by the following roughly isometric translation (16.667–75), in which the English stressed syllable (marked só) stands for the accented heavy Greek syllable and the vertical bar marks the pauses in sense:

"Gó if you wíll, | my dear Phoébus; | and wásh from his
    woúnds | the dark bloódstain,
  dráwing | óut of the fíght | Sarpédon; | Phoébus, thereáfter

beáring him fár, far awáy | cleanse hím | in the streáms | of
the ríver;
sméar him with | heávenly oíl | and clóthe him with |
gárments immórtal.
Sénd him on thén | in ćare of | a swíft-footed éscort | to
béar him,
Sléep and | lóvely-winged Deáth, | the two bróthers who |
swíftly will láy him
Dówn in | Lýcian lánd, | that wíde, rich | lánd of his
péople.
Thére will they | móurn and buíld him, | his ówn dear
fólk | and his kínsmen,
gráve and | tómb and bárrow; for thís is the hónor | of
mórtals."

(Logue's much more musical translation is on p. 263.)
Here is the Greek in transliteration, with accented heavy syllables marked:

eí d' age nún | phile Phóibe | keláinephes | háima kathéron
élthôn ék beleón | Sarpédona, | kaí min epeíta
póllon apópro pherón | lousón | potamoío roéisi
chríson t' | ámbrosiéi, | peri d' ámbrota | heímata hésson;
pémpe de mín | pompoísin (||) hamá kraipnoísi (||)
pherésthai
Hýpnôi kaí Thanatói | didumáosin, | hoí ra min óka
thésous' (||) én Lukiés (||) eureiês | píoni démôi,
éntha he tárchusousi | kasígnêtoí te etaí te
túmbôi té (||) stêlé te; | to gár geras (||) ésti thanóntôn.

As in the Romantic alexandrine, the mid-verse break is often
suppressed and the line falls into three parts. The first example
comes early in the *Iliad* (1.7):

Átreus' són | the lórd of mén | and gódlike Achílles.

An impressive example comes as the old men of Troy talk
about Helen (3.159):

Bút even só | as faír as she ís, | let her gó to her hómeland.

In the few lines of *Hiawatha* quoted at the beginning of this
section, we see that many of the characters' names fit neatly into
one of the four-syllable units of the verse: Hiawatha, Minne-
haha, Laughing Water. If the name is not long enough, an adjective (always the same one) is added to fill it out: *old* Nokomis,

lazy Kwasind. Or a name may be expanded to cover two units: Gitche Manito the mighty, Chibiabos the musician. Longfellow also uses a number of recurrent set phrases and repeated patterns of sentence construction:

> Down the river o'er the prairies
> Came the warriors of the nations,
> Came the Delawares and Mohawks,
> Came the Choctaws and Camanches,
> Came the Soshonies and Blackfeet,
> Came the Pawnees and Omawhas
>
> I have given you lands to hunt in,
> I have given you streams to fish in,
> I have given you bear and bison,
> I have given you roe and reindeer,
> I have given you brant and beaver
>
> None could run so fast as he could,
> None could dive so deep as he could,
> None could swim as far as he could;
> None had made so many journeys,
> None had seen so many wonders

Occasionally a few verses are repeated verbatim, or with minor adaptations:

> You shall hear how Hiawatha
> Prayed and fasted in the forest,
> Not for greater skill in hunting,
> Not for greater craft in fishing,
> Not for triumphs in the battle,
> And renown among the warriors,
> Bur for profit of the people,
> For advantage of the nations

A little farther on the later verses are repeated after "For you pray not like the others; / Not for . . . . "

Longfellow does this because he is imitating an old oral epic, the Finnish *Kalevala*. Homeric epic has these and other features of oral poetry developed to an immensely high degree. As in *Hiawatha*, proper names are the most obvious instance of fitting a word into a unit of the verse, but because of the variety of Homeric names and the greater complexity of the pattern of units, the development is much more complicated. The names of most characters can be combined with an adjective to fit into the five syllables of the last unit of the verse, and the major characters each have their own individual adjective. Using English stress to match the accented heavy syllables of the Greek, one might suggest as syllabic equivalents "gódlike Achílles," "glórious Héctor," "Pállas Athéna," "quícksilver Hérmes," "Zéus the allseéing." A slightly longer phrase fits after an earlier break in the verse: "swift-foóted Achílles," "bright-hélmeted Héctor," "blue-greén-eyed Athéna." Another fills the entire second half of the verse: "the swíft-foot gódlike Achílles," "the greát bright-hélmeted Héctor," "the góddess gréy-eyed Athéna," "the rúler of mén Agamémnon," "the fáther of góds and of mórtals." Often there are alternative expressions beginning either with a consonant or a vowel, to suit the metrical needs, and if desired the phrase can be expanded to fill a whole verse for formal titles of address.

The major characters, as indicated above, have individual adjectives defining constant qualities, and these never change under given metrical conditions (the very rare exceptions will be discussed later). This "economy" has been claimed as a characteristic development of a long tradition of oral composition. Lesser characters share a variety of adjectives ("splendid," "great-hearted," "spear-famous" and the like) depending on the metrical shape of their names. It is noticeable, however, that a few of the individual adjectives have spread to lesser heroes with metrically equivalent names; even Agamemnon's "lord of men" is borrowed by his subordinate Eumelus (23.288), as well as the Trojans Aeneas, Anchises, and Euphetes, and Nestor's old enemy Augeias (11.700). A few major characters have two interchangeable adjectival phrases, one obviously older than the other; Hera, for instance, may be—uniquely—"ox-eyed mistress Hera" or simply "goddess white-armed Hera," sharing the epithet with many others. One adjective, "godlike" (dios), is used regularly for Achilles, Odysseus, and some thirty other heroes. These are signs that the highly complex system of individual adjectives is breaking down, and more commonplace (and less interesting) adjectives are taking over.

In addition to the proper names, common nouns also have similar systems of combination with adjectives so that the expression will fit conveniently in different parts of the verse; the qualities of ships, the sea, horses, helmets, and many other objects vary according to metrical and not narrative circumstances. These expressions occur on every page and need not be illustrated here. Often the adjective must have sounded archaic even in Homer's time, and sometimes even unintelligible, like some words in Shakespeare or the King James version are in our own day. (Lattimore's "single-foot [horses]" renders the obscure by the bizarre; the Greek adjective means "with uncloven hoofs," distinguishing horses from cattle, though the audience may not have realized this. "Ungulate" would be a better—and similarly obscure—modern equivalent.)

Homer has many recurrent verses that allow the inclusion of standard-sized name or noun phrases; the same can be seen in some of the Longfellow examples above. Probably the commonest is the system for the concept "he answered," which can accommodate not only the name of the person speaking (in various lengths, for some names, such as Agamemnon's, are too long or too awkward to be fitted within the final five-syllable unit) but also a pronoun designating the person addressed (singular or plural, male or female), or that person's name, or an adverb ("angrily," for example). Beyond this, there are an almost infinite number of common phrases that fit within the units of the verse, often adaptable to mesh with the different shapes of other units.

As an example, consider the verses in which the verb form *ek-ekleto*, "he shouted," occurs (though this system is of unusual regularity). *Ekekleto* always occurs immediately after the mid-verse break and just fills the third unit of the verse. One of the verses in which it occurs (16.268) may be isometrically rendered (with a false stress on Patroclus's name): "Pátroclús | to his cómrades | then shoúted out | loúdly and cleárly." Where Patroclus's name stands, in the first unit, other verses substitute the names of Hector, Nestor, Antilochus, Autolycus, Aeneas, Ajax; or the phrase "so speaking," connecting with what precedes; or "but he," "she then," "to the Trojans," and "terribly" are used. The second unit is usually filled by the persons shouted at, including (as well as "comrades") Greeks, Trojans, Lycians, horses, sons, and male or female servants; or when these are placed in a different unit, the adverb *heterôthen*, "from the other side" is inserted. The third unit contains our verb, "shouted." Then the fourth, besides a padding phrase as in the example quoted above, may contain the subject of the sentence ("gódlike Achílles," "goódhearted swíneherd"), a padding complimentary phrase for the subject ("nóblest of héroes," "lóveliest of wómen"), the names of the persons called to, a significant phrase qualifying the horses of the second unit ("théy were his fáther's"), a padding phrase reintroducing the direct speech to come ("sáying what fóllows"), and even a new and complete sentence, "Ánd they obéyed him." With the exception of the last, all these phrases occur elsewhere with different verbs.

It is almost certain that these formulaic usages were developed to facilitate rapid, perhaps extemporaneous, composition in a complex meter. The repeated phrases and standard adjectives also convey a strong effect of regularity, permanence, and stability, reassuring the audience by their familiarity. It is hard to parallel this in modern English, except perhaps in children's tales; there are superb examples in Kipling's *Just So Stories*, with their constant reiteration of the "great grey-green greasy Limpopo River, all set about with fever trees," and the "bi-coloured-Python-Rocksnake with the scalesome flailsome tail" (the parallel is suggested by Wender 1977.342–44). On a very small scale, Hemingway's invariable use of his hero's full name, Robert Jordan, in *For Whom the Bell Tolls* has a similarly formal effect; so have the careful verbatim repetitions describing the three attempts to return the sword Excalibur at the climax of Tennyson's *Passing of Arthur*. The effect is stately and comforting, not at all that of an irritating cliché.

It might be thought that the highly conventional nature of the formulaic expressions deprives the poet of originality in his choice of words. To some extent it certainly takes from him the free choice of attributive adjectives and the power of suggestive repetition of key words and phrases, since in most cases parallel usages must be attributed to metrical convenience rather than conscious intent. Undeniably, the same expression is used more than once without any association intended, even with very different impact, depending on the context of each occurrence. "So he spoke; and the old man was afraid, and obeyed him" is used both for Chryses' reaction to Agamemnon's brutal rejection of his request to ransom his daughter (1.33) and for Priam's meek submission after Achilles' warning to him to step carefully (24.571), where the tone is totally different. The same phrase decorates the footstool that Hera promises to have Hephaestus make as a bribe for Sleep and the one that Antinous threatens to throw at the disguised Odysseus (14.241, *Odyssey* 17.410); the same phrase describes the din of a marching army and Telemachus's sneeze (2.466, *Odyssey* 17.542); and Eumaeus's fifty pigs dwell in sties described in phraseology that recalls the houses of Priam's fifty sons (*Odyssey* 14.14–15, *Iliad* 6.243–44). These peculiarities would not be noticed by an experienced audience.

Sometimes, however, a repetition *can* be intentional, for instance when the same phrases are used of Patroclus's death and Hector's (see p. 297).

The poet rarely claims the freedom to substitute a metrically equivalent adjective for the one tradition supplies; only, in fact, when the usual adjective would be extremely inappropriate or otiose, as when Zeus "the cloud-gatherer" is called "the thunderer" when he is *dispersing* the clouds (16.297), "seven-gated" Thebes (when even its walls are still unbuilt) is called "wide-spaced," (*Odyssey* 11.265), and Penelope, when being explicitly complimented on her good sense, is called "noble" instead of her normal "sensible" (*Odyssey* 24.194). In most cases the usual adjective, describing some general quality of the object, is retained, even if the particular circumstances make it illogical. Nausicaa's dirty laundry is still "shining" as garments regularly are (*Odyssey* 6.26), Eumaeus's dogs are "ever-barking" when they *don't* bark at the familiar Telemachus (*Odyssey* 16.4–5), Antilochus's horses are still "swift-footed" even when described as very slow (23.304, 309–10), Priam on his sad journey to Achilles, preceded by a muledrawn wagon full of treasures and followed by a lamenting throng, still "whips up his horses swiftly" (24.326–27). In the most famous case, where the seducer and murderer Aegisthus is called "noble" (*amumôn, Odyssey* 1.29), it may be significant that the adjective, normal for any aristocrat, is used only *before* we have heard the tale of his guilt; the same is true of "godlike" Pandarus the truce-breaker (4.88).

But the poet has the freedom to apply to a person or thing a specific and emphatic adjective or participle standing at the beginning of the following verse, often expanded in the rest of that verse. "Hands" are formulaically "heavy," "invincible," or "strong," but at the climax of the ransom scene between Priam and Achilles the poet amplifies the regular phrase "and kissed his hands" by adding in the following verse "*terrible, murderous* [hands], which had killed many of his sons" (24.478–79)—the adjective "murderous" gaining all the more power here because it is regularly attached to the name of Hector himself. The other adjective, "terrible" (*deinos*), is often effectively placed like this, for instance when Achilles charges against Hector "brandishing Peleus' spear over his right shoulder, / the *terrible* [spear], and the bronze shone around him" (22.133–34), or when Apollo advances through the battle toward the doomed Patroclus "*terrible*; and Patroclus did not see him come" (16.789).

Careful study of the usage of formulae makes it clear that

Homer is completely master of the techniques that the tradition
supplied, so much a master that he not only controls them for
considerable emotional effect but often declines the aid to
versification they offer. The tradition embraced a large number
of five-syllable words and phrases designed to fill the last unit of
the verse and conveniently complete it, many of them adding
dignity and color but not much special effect; besides the two
hundred or more different adjectives found here, there are such
common phrases as "shépherd of péople," "líke unto Áres," "gódlike in áspect," and so on. Homer, however, instead of using one
of these devices, often varies the rhythm by ending the sense before this last unit and then beginning a new sentence that will
run over into the following verse, or sometimes be completed
within the five syllables of the unit (as in the last example
quoted under the usage of *ekekleto* above). As an example—one
of many, and not necessarily representative—the phrase
"Achaiôn chalkochitônôn" ("of Árgives brónze in their ármor")
ends the verse twenty-four times in Homer, but the noun
Achaiôn in this position (without *chalkochitônôn*) is followed
eighteen times by a different conventional phrase, eight times by
the start of a new sentence that runs over into the next verse,
and three times by a new sentence or clause that is complete at
the end of the verse. Nietzsche spoke of Homer "dancing in
chains." So to some extent does any artist, but few have exploited, or ignored, a rigid convention with such individual
artistry as Homer.

Further Reading

There are accessible accounts of Homeric meter, formulae, and
verse structure in Kirk 1985.18–30, Schein 1984.2–13, Hogan 1979.19–
29, and Bowra 1962.19–37. On the use of formulae in an illogical context see Bowra 1962 and Combellack 1965. The origins of the Greek
hexameter meter have long been debated; recent contributions,
putting forward contrasting views, can be found in Nagy 1974,
Peabody 1975, and M. L. West 1973.

Adam Parry's introduction to Milman Parry's collected works
(Parry 1971) gives a fine outline of Parry's work, both on Homeric
formulae and in collecting modern South-slavic oral songs; Parry's
monographs and articles are excellent reading even for those without a knowledge of Greek.

On the general concept of the formula as a means of poetic expression, see the very clear approach in Kiparsky 1976 and the first two
chapters (in particular) of Nagler's fundamental work (1974). On the

replacement of individual by more general epithets, see Hainsworth 1978. Adaptations of formulae for aesthetic reasons in *Iliad* 18 are examined in Edwards 1968.

A survey of recent scholarship on Homeric formulae is due to appear in the new journal *Oral Tradition* in 1986.

5

Word Order and Emphasis

The clarity and directness of Homeric verse is much greater in the Greek than in any translation. This is so partly because of the word order and the ability of an inflected language to place important words in prominent positions, and partly because of the sentence structure, which first makes clear the major ideas of the sentence and then elaborates and develops them while the sentence progresses. An inferior poet might have been to some extent overpowered by the strength of traditional formulaic usages and the strong tendency of words of a certain metrical shape to fall at certain preferred places in the network of long and short syllables and word breaks that make up the hexameter line (see pp. 46–47). Though passages can be found in Homer that show no special composition skill, there are many where the possibilities of word position and sentence structure are exploited for powerful poetic effects.

Two main characteristics make Homeric verse easier for the hearer to follow, and probably easier for the poet to compose. The first is the "padding" effect of the regular formulaic expressions, which add purely ornamental details or repeat an idea already established. Removal of these takes away much of the color but leaves the factual content of the narrative quite clear; it has been shown (by Bassett 1938.152–53) that in some passages half of each verse can be ignored and the basic sense remains intact, though much of the poetic impact has vanished. (He also showed that the same can be done with the initial stanzas of Gray's *Elegy*.) This amplitude of language, or to be more precise the limiting of new content within any one verse, gives color to the bare narrative just as expansion gives color to the type-scenes.

The other feature helpful for the listener is *parataxis*—placing the subject, verb, and predicate first (in any order), so that the main thought is complete and understood before any qualifications and color, in the form of adjectives, adverbs, and participial or subordinate clauses, are added. Long periodic sentences, in which the outline of the thought becomes complete only when the end of the sentence is reached, and the complex interweaving and postponement of essential words, which is frequent in Latin verse, are foreign to Homer. It is rare, for instance, to find an adjective, or a genitive noun dependent upon another noun, that is not preceded by the noun it qualifies; its grammatical attachment is never obscure. Hector's picture of what people will say of his captive wife, "*Hector's* wife that is" (6.460) shows a word order as unusual in Homer as it is effective in this special instance. Milton's "Of man's first disobedience" followed by several coordinate phrases and two subordinate clauses before its controlling verb "sing" appears (in line 6), is totally un-Homeric in style.

The normal Homeric usage can be seen in the first sentence of the *Iliad*. The construction and main ideas become clear after the second or third word ("Anger sing, goddess"). Next the particular case is specified ("of Peleus' son Achilles"), and the basic sense is complete. The second verse begins with the emphatic participle "accursed," its ending showing that it qualifies "anger," and this additional idea is characteristically amplified in succeeding coordinate relative clauses "which caused ... and sent ... and made ...." Next comes the parenthetical "Zeus' will was fulfilled," and finally the temporal clause further defining the theme of the poem, "from when first they quarrelled." Subordinate and qualifying ideas are added only after the main outlines are clear.

This style is not often apparent in *Hiawatha*, because of the shortness of Longfellow's line and the overwhelming repetitions ("Ye who love the haunts of Nature, / Love the sunshine of the meadow, / Love the shadow of the forest, / Love the wind among the branches"), but can sometimes be found: "From the full moon fell Nokomis, / Fell the beautiful Nokomis, / She a wife, but not a mother. / She was sporting with her women / Swinging in a swing of grape-vines, / When her rival, the rejected, / Full of jealousy and hatred, / Cut the leafy swing asunder, / Cut in twain the twisted grape-vines." There is an effective small-scale example of postponed elaboration in the Homeric style in Tennyson's *Passing of Arthur* (denoted here with italics): "But ere he dipt the surface, rose an arm / *Clothed in white samite, mystic, wonderful*, / And caught him by the hilt, and brandish'd him / *Three times*, and drew him under in the mere."

Long periodic sentences do, however, occur in Homer, but only when the complete main clause is placed early and subordinate clauses or phrases follow it. There is a good example at 15.53–64, which begins with the protasis of a conditional clause (with two coordinate verbs), then gives the main verb (a command) and a coordinate verb that has an object-clause dependent upon it, goes on to two coordinate purpose clauses (the second of which again has an object clause dependent upon it; 58) and three further purpose clauses (one of them amplified by a relative clause; 61), and concludes with two further purpose clauses. Since all this describes the purpose and outcome of Zeus's order, given in the second line of the sentence, there is no difficulty in immediately grasping the structure of the sentence. A long sentence may, however, ramble on inconclusively as one's thoughts do, the best example being in Hector's soliloquy as he awaits Achilles and casts about for ways of escape. "If I should . . . " he thinks, and the sentence wanders on for eleven verses until he pulls himself together and breaks it off with "But why do I think like this?" (22.111–22). There is a similar effect, in similar circumstances, in Agenor's soliloquy a little earlier (21.556–62). For special effect the main clause may be held back, as in Achilles' powerful statement "Not if he were to give me . . . , or . . . , or . . . , not even then would he . . ." which continues for seven verses before the main clause is reached (9.379–87). There is, however, no obscurity, as it is obvious from the start what the point of the sentence is going to be.

Sometimes short, choppy sentences may convey a character's emotion. Achilles' great speech in answer to Odysseus (9.308ff.) contains a number of explosive sentences overrunning the end of the verse (9.334–41):

"He gave many other prizes to the chiefs and kings;
they still have them; me alone of the Greeks
he has robbed, he keeps my beloved woman; let him lie with
  her
enraptured! Why must fight with Trojans
Greeks? Why has he collected and led here this host
Atreus' son? Was it not for lovely Helen?
Alone do they love their wives among mortal men
Atreus' sons?"

There are similar effects, in incoherent grammar, in Agamemnon's furious outburst in response to Achilles (1.131–34; see p. 179). The poet can, however, when he wishes, construct sentences of short clauses in a quite complex structure. A good example occurs in Andromache's first lament for Hector: "The boy is still a baby, / who was born to ill-fated you and me; not to him can you / be, Hector, a help, since you are dead, nor he to you"

(22.484–86). Often words are artistically balanced (see pp. 122–23).

Enjambment, running a sentence over from one verse to the next, is very common in Homer, but usually sense units are not split by the enjambment and so easy understanding of the meaning is not impaired. Though the sentence is not finished before the verse end, one or more grammatical components will be complete (subject, object, or verb, or combinations of these) as explained above, and often the enjambment takes the form of appending subordinate or participial clauses after the main sentence. Even after a new sentence has begun at the start of the final five-syllable unit of the verse (see pp. 49–51) the poet usually manages to avoid dividing a sense unit at verse end. This technique of keeping sense units together means that the poet, without making his verse hard to follow for the listening audience, can begin a sentence at any of the three usual sense-pause positions within the line, and so avoid the monotony of verses in which sentence end and verse end constantly coincide. (Taking at random the first one hundred lines of *Iliad* 6, with Allen's rather lavish punctuation, a break marked by period, semicolon, or comma falls fifty-six times at verse end and fourteen, twenty-eight, and thirteen times respectively at the first, second, and third breaks in the verse). Sequences of end-stopped lines seem, in fact, to be reserved for special effect, as in the case of the first, perhaps hardly distinguishable words of Patroclus's ghost (23.69–71), Achilles' yell to Patroclus that the ships are blazing and there's no time to waste (16.126–29), and his gloomy, aphoristic reflections on the world's unfairness (9.318–20).

The beginning of the verse can be an emphatic position, and a word placed there in enjambment with the preceding verse and followed by a pause (a "runover" word) is often specially effective. This is the case with Achilles' "accursed" anger in the second line of the *Iliad* (see above), in his violent condemnation of Agamemnon (9.334–41, translated above), and—the most obvious case of all—in the drawing lots for Hector's opponent in the duel, where "out leapt the lot from the helmet, the one they had hoped for, / *Ajax's*" (7.182–83). These runover words are a characteristic feature of Homer's Greek, but are often obscured in translation into a noninflected language. Adjectives and participles are commonly used in this way; among the great number of examples may be picked out the many occurrences of *nêpios* followed by an explanation: "Foolish! for he . . ." Other powerful uses are *schetlios*: "Cruel! for he . . ."; and *deinos*: "Terrible!"

especially when Priam kisses Achilles' hands, "terrible, murderous, which had killed so many of his sons" (24.479), and when
Apollo advances unseen through the battle toward the doomed
Patroclus (16.789). *Gumnos*, "stripped," is often used in this position to stress the pathos of a corpse after the victor has taken the
armor, most notably when Antilochus brings to Achilles the report of Patroclus's death and the loss of the divine armor lent to
him by Achilles (18.21).

Sometimes a conventional formulaic adjective appears in this
runover position, if it cannot be fitted with its noun into the preceding verse. In many such cases the adjective seems to bear no
emphasis, but occasionally stressing its meaning produces a
strong poetic effect, and it is very likely that this was the poet's
intention. Achilles strips the armor from Hector's corpse, and
the runover word is *haimatoent'*, "bloodied as it was"—contrasting Hector's death and the divinely made armor of Peleus, which
could not save him (22.369); the oil with which Aphrodite
anoints Hector's corpse is *ambrosiôi*, "immortal, so that the
dragging should not tear it" (23.187). Adverbs may be so used here
("today; later on") and also verbs; some monosyllabic forms appear with especially dramatic force (*ball'*, "shot," of Apollo's
plague arrows, 1.52; *kopt'*, "struck," of the Cyclops beating out
the brains of Odysseus's men, *Odyssey* 9.290; *lamp'*, "flashed," of
Agamemnon's spearheads in his splendid arming scene, 11.45).

The initial word may carry a stress even if it is not followed,
as runover words are, by a pause. "Now against oath- / *breakers*
we fight," says Antenor (7.351–52); "he struck . . . / *heel* of right
foot" (11.376–77); "Don't, Achilles, . . . / *hungry* Greeks drive on
against Troy" (19.155–56); "If Hector captures our ships, / *on foot*
do you hope to reach home?" asks Ajax (15.504–5). The pauses or
word breaks between the units of the verse (see pp. 46–47) do not
have quite as much emphasis as the beginning and end of the
verse, but their existence means that words within the verse can
sometimes be powerfully effective. Two examples must suffice.
As the helmet is struck from Patroclus's head by Apollo and rolls
beneath the horses' feet, the poet pauses to describe its befouling
in the blood and dust; such a disgrace had never happened before,
"for of a godlike man the head and handsome brow / it had
guarded, *Achilles*'" (16.798–99)—the name of Patroclus's mighty
avenger introduced in the second unit of the verse. The third
unit of the verse, often filled by an adjective or adverb of little
significance, is the place of perhaps the most heavily weighted
word in all the *Odyssey*, in the verse (19.209) that describes how

Penelope, immensely moved by the disguised Odysseus's fictitious account of how he met her husband years ago as he was journeying to Troy, bursts into tears, "weeping for her husband *as he sat beside her,*" the Greek participle *parêmenon* conveying all the poignant meaning of the italicized phrase.

Other usages show the poet's exploitation of the interrelationship of sentence and verse. *Anaphora,* repetition of a word, is particularly common with a word standing at the beginning of the verse and sentence and at the last pause in the verse, especially with "sometimes . . . , sometimes . . . ," or "someone . . . , someone [else]." There are neat expressions such as "A brave man would have killed, a brave man been slain" (21.280). More striking are instances where an emphatic word stands at the beginning of successive verses; "*Skill,* not brute force, makes a good woodcutter; / *skill* keeps a ship on course . . . ; / *skill* makes one charioteer beat another" (23.315ff.). The angry Achilles changes the emphatic word without losing the powerful effect: "*Seize* I can cattle and sheep, / *win* I can tripods and horses, / *man's life* cannot be seized again" (9.406ff.). The formulaic quality of the language and the rigorous meter must not be thought of as preventing the poet from using the usual poetic devices of word positioning for emphasis. On the contrary, they provide opportunities for him to exploit.

Further Reading

Bassett 1938 (chapter 6) gives an interesting but somewhat tendentious account of sense and meter in Homer. Kirk 1966 and Edwards 1966 examine sentence and verse structure in detail. Edwards 1968 deals with Homer's handling of formulae in *Iliad* 18. Hoekstra 1981.81–89 has a full treatment of the nature and origins of *amplitudo* (fullness of expression) in Homer.

Story Patterns and Use of Myth

It is obvious to anyone that the plots of the *Iliad* and the *Odyssey* share common features with other well-known tales; it is easy to find striking parallels between Odysseus's adventures with villains, monsters, and beautiful females and those of Sindbad the Sailor, James Bond, or Captain James T. Kirk, and between Achilles' revenge for the killing of his best friend and the plot of many a western movie. The fact that the tales were already placed in the legendary past for Homer's audience gave them the remoteness that brings added appeal and makes the fantastic possible; modern fantasies like Tolkien's *Ring* tales also use the distant past for this purpose or, more commonly, the future, as in the science fiction and space fiction genres. Besides similarities in plot, small motifs with immediate appeal constantly recur in literature and life; Odysseus's journeying until he finds someone who mistakes the oar he carries for a winnowing fan (*Odyssey* 11.119ff.) finds a parallel in the weary Yukon resident who longs to "tie a snow shovel to the hood of my car and drive south until nobody had the faintest idea what the damn thing was" (*San Francisco Chronicle*, 31 December 1982).

Modern scholarly analyses of the structure of folk tales have made it possible to identify common features in stories, and a good deal of work has also been done in comparing the parallels between the Homeric epics and other ancient Greek tales. In recent years we have also reached a better understanding of how Homer uses plot motifs in different ways and how he modifies the shape of myths, or even invents new ones, to suit his purpose. Structural analyses and comparisons of this kind not only offer the delights of taxonomy and theorizing, but assist our understanding of the poet's methods and can sometimes explain features of a plot or episode that have led to misapprehensions in the past.

The following discussion will deal first with large-scale structures of the plots of the two epics; then, by a rather arbitrary but practical division, with smaller-scale repeated motifs; and finally with the ways in which Homer can be seen to manipulate or invent the material of myth for his own purposes.

Perhaps the commonest of all basic story patterns is the absence
or loss of a person or persons, the troubles that result, and the
eventual return of the person or recovery of the loss and the ending of the problems. In more abstract terms, a state of order is
thrown into disorder and eventually returned to order. This is
generally called the "withdrawal, devastation, and return" pattern, or the "eternal return" (see especially Lord 1960 ch. 9 and
Nagler 1974 ch. 5). This obviously forms the main plot of the
Odyssey: the initial scenes in Ithaca show the evils resulting
from Odysseus's absence, then the young son Telemachus sets
off to find his father, and the eventual return of both brings
about the punishment of the wicked and the end of the troubles.

The more detailed analysis of the elements of such a basic
story, as described by Propp (conveniently summarized in
Scholes 1974.62ff.), appear even more clearly in the Circe episode
in Odyssey 10.203ff. Odysseus is told that his men have been
overcome by Circe (Propp's functions 8–8a) and sets out to find
them (9–11), meets the divine helper Hermes (12–13), and is given
the magical agent, the herb moly, which will make him immune
to Circe's magical powers (14). He confronts Circe (15–16) and is
touched by her wand (17), but defeats her (18) and recovers his
men (19). He and Circe then go to bed together (31?), but this
"marriage" of the hero, which appears in full form in the reunion
of Odysseus and Penelope, is in the Circe episode more likely to
be an adaptation of the motif of the fairy seductress who unmans
or destroys her lovers, as do Ishtar (in Gilgamesh), Eve, la Belle
Dame sans Merci, the Lorelei, and many others. Divine helpers
with gifts, like Hermes here, also appear to rescue Menelaus
when he is stranded off Egypt (Eidothea, who gives him not only
counsel but also sealskins for disguise; Odyssey 4.435ff.) and
Odysseus himself when he is shipwrecked by Poseidon (Leucothea, who gives him her garment for protection; Odyssey 5.351ff).
The pattern recurs in the divinely made armor given by Hephaestus to Achilles, the gifts of Medea to Jason and Ariadne to
Theseus in Greek legend, and of course in the marvelous devices
given to James Bond in the opening scenes of his adventures and
to Frodo in Tolkien's Ring cycle. The many other folk tale parallels in the Odyssey have been identified in the work of Woodhouse (1930) and Page (1955; 1973).

The "withdrawal-devastation-return" structure is the obvious
foundation of the Iliad plot, too, with revenge and consolation

tales added at the end (see pp. 8–10). In fact it is repeated several times in that poem, for besides Achilles' loss of Briseis, which is the motive for his withdrawal and the defeat of the Greeks, and the paradigm of Meleager that Phoenix relates (see pp. 226–29), it is Agamemnon's loss of Chryseis that leads to the plague and begins the plot; and of course the loss of Helen is the reason for the entire Trojan War. This special form of the structure, the abduction of women and consequent troubles, is very common in myth—Persephone, Ariadne, and Medea are famous instances—and its popular appeal shows up in Herodotus's account of the origin of the conflict of Greeks and Persians (1.1–5). He blames it on the successive abductions of Io by the Phoenicians and Europa and Medea by the Greeks, until Paris was inspired by the impunity of the offenders in these tales to steal a wife from Greece. Aristophanes' lighthearted account of the origins of the Peloponnesian War of his own time in successive reprisals for the abduction of whores by the Athenians and Megarians (*Archarnians* 523ff.) confirms the popular appeal of such tales.

Another familiar pattern in the plot of the *Iliad* is the loss of the hero's best friend, which is repeated later in the Trojan War cycle in the case of Antilochus, who is killed by Memnon and avenged by Achilles in the *Aethiopis* (*Odyssey* 4.187–88). It also appears in *Gilgamesh* (associated with the mortality of the hero himself, since it is as a result of Enkidu's death that he sets off to find the secret of everlasting life), in the David and Jonathan tale in *Samuel*, in the part of Oliver in the *Song of Roland*, and in the Greek myths of Castor and Pollux, Theseus and Pirithous.

The quarrel of Achilles and Agamemnon in *Iliad* 1 is also modelled on a standard pattern. There are references to a quarrel between Agamemnon and Menelaus (*Odyssey* 4.134–50), to one between Achilles and Odysseus (sung by Demodocus, *Odyssey* 8.73–80; see Nagy 1979), to one between Ajax and Odysseus over the armor of Achilles (*Odyssey* 11.543ff.), and perhaps others lie behind the hints of Paris's resentment against the Trojans (6.326) and Aeneas's against Priam (13.459ff.).

Some of these patterns occurred in much the same form in other epics of the Trojan cycle (the evidence is most conveniently summarized and assessed by Fenik 1968.231ff.). The clearest examples are the rescue of Nestor by Diomedes (8.80ff.), which is similar to the much more poignant rescue of the old man by his son Antilochus in the *Aethiopis*, in which the younger man lost his life to the hero Memnon; and the scene in which Diomedes is wounded in the foot by Paris (11.369ff.), which recalls the scene in the *Aethiopis* where Achilles himself is struck in the heel and killed by Paris. Such parallel scenes may well be examples of standard patterns of story, rather than proving a dependence of one poem upon the other. But of course Homer, like other bards, must have known and sung a much wider range of songs than the *Iliad* and the *Odyssey*, and the influence of one song upon another must have been considerable.

Small-Scale Patterns

The most obvious among the repeated small-scale patterns in the *Odyssey* are the recognition scenes, which also serve as a good example of the poet's use of the pattern in various ways for different effects. The recognition of Odysseus by his old dog Argus (*Odyssey* 17.290ff.) does not further the plot in any way, but it intensifies the emotion of his return to his palace, disguised as an abject beggar; it may reflect the common feature of the death of a parent or close relative at the hero's return (see Lord 1960.177); and it represents the usual appearance of dogs at the door of a dwelling (*Odyssey* 14.29ff.; Alcinous's are of gold and silver, *Odyssey* 7.91). The scar Odysseus bore from his youth leads to his recognition by old Eurycleia, which again does not further the plot but forms a long, exciting interlude in the hero's conversation with his wife, in which there is *no* overt recognition and our expectations are frustrated (*Odyssey* 19.343–505). The clothing and brooch given to the departing hero by his wife are not used to identify him in this scene, but to validate the disguised Odysseus's false tale (19.221ff.).

The famous tapestry Penelope has been forced to complete does not lead to her husband's return in the nick of time, as one would expect, but is used to demonstrate her cleverness and fidelity in her talk with Odysseus (19.137ff.) and to contrast her with the murderous Clytemnestra (*Odyssey* 24.129–202). Even the stringing of the hero's own bow and his shooting through the axes (*Odyssey* 21.404ff.) are used not only to reveal his true identity to his enemies but to place in his hands the weapon with which he will destroy them. Finally, the most emotionally significant recognition of all, that by the hero's wife, is contrived by means of the secret of their marriage bed, which not only beautifully symbolizes the physical union of husband and wife that began and confirms their marriage, but shows Odysseus deceived and caught off his guard for the first time in the poem, outwitted by his wife. The poet has superbly contrived that not only can Penelope confirm that he is not a god in disguise (a very real fear; cf. *Odyssey* 23.63ff., 81ff., and 16.183ff., 194ff.) who might know the secret of the bed, she can also recognize her true husband's outrage at the implied violation of his marriage bed (*Odyssey* 23.205–6). The final recognition by Odysseus's father, by the motif of the orchard trees (*Odyssey* 24.336ff.), involves the sentiment of childhood memories.

Another story used many times is the contest for a bride. The climax of the *Odyssey* is the contest between Odysseus and the suitors for Penelope, which is spread over Books 18 to 23. Penelope appears formally to receive the admiration and the gifts of the suitors in a long scene soon after Odysseus has reached the palace (*Odyssey* 18.158–303), and Telemachus explicitly describes her as the prize when he sets up the archery competition ("Come, you suitors, here the prize appears, / a woman like no other in all Greece"; *Odyssey* 21.106–7). Normally the bride would watch the contest, but because of the battle that will immediately follow its conclusion, the poet rather ostentatiously removes her from the scene before it begins (*Odyssey* 21.350–58). It has been pointed out that the games in Phaeacia in which Odysseus finally triumphs are not unlike a competition for the hand of Nausicaa (see Woodhouse 1930 and Lattimore 1969). In the *Iliad*, the duel for Helen between Paris and Menelaus (after she has been admired by the old men, and in her presence) is used brilliantly by the poet to recapitulate her seduction and reaffirm the cause of the war (see pp. 195–97). The scene between Andromache and Hector in *Iliad* 6 can be regarded as a similar kind of preparation for his challenge and duel with Ajax in the following book, and after Hector's slaying by Achilles and the sack of the city it will be Achilles' son who bears off Andromache as a prize of victory. There are many other tales of contest for a bride in Greek legend, among them that for Helen (described by Hesiod, frag. 197 M.-W.), the chariot-race of Pelops and Oenomaus for the hand of Hippodameia, the race of Hippomenes for Atalanta (Hesiod frags. 73–76 M.-W.), Oedipus's vanquishing of the sphinx to win Jocasta, Perseus's killing of the sea monster to rescue Andromeda, and Herodotus's account of the wooing of the daughter of Cleisthenes of Sicyon (Herodotus 6.126–30). Pausanias (3.12.1) even reports a tale from Sparta that Odysseus won Penelope in a footrace there.

Many motifs of less significance than these are repeated within the poems. Several times a character remembers too late a

prophecy of a coming disaster: Polyphemus and Circe, after being defeated by Odysseus, recall predictions of his coming (*Odyssey* 9.507ff., 10.330ff.); after sending Odysseus home Alcinous remembers Poseidon's threat of vengeance on his city for its help
to the shipwrecked (*Odyssey* 13.172ff.); and, more poignantly,
Achilles recalls a sinister prediction immediately before he
hears of the death of Patroclus (18.10ff.). Three times objects are
thrown at the disguised Odysseus (*Odyssey* 17.462ff.; 18.394ff.;
19.299ff.); three times a guest dissolves in tears, to his host's embarrassment (*Odyssey* 4.113ff., 8.83ff., 521ff.); three times a perplexed host is rescued by someone with quicker reactions (*Odyssey* 4.120ff., 7.155ff., 15.169ff.). Before his landing on Scheria after
his shipwreck, Odysseus delivers a monologue to himself, clambers on to the wreckage of his raft, and is aided by Leucothea
(*Odyssey* 5.297ff.); then he delivers a second monologue to himself, clambers a second time back on to the wreckage, and is
aided again, this time by Athena (*Odyssey* 5.354ff.; see Fenik
1974.143). Such repetitions are natural in poems of such a size,
and must not be taken as an indication of multiple authorship.

Of much greater importance is the recent demonstration by
Fenik (1974.133ff.) that Homer has a habit of doubling roles, a
"tendency . . . to use two persons of a single type where he might
conceivably have used one" (172). The old palace servants
Eurycleia and Eurynome can be distinguished—the former is the
more important character and is associated with Telemachus
and Odysseus, the latter with Penelope—but they appear together only in the final preparation of the marriage bed (*Odyssey*
23.289ff.) and one wonders whether both are necessary to the
plot. Eumaeus and Philoetius, the faithful swineherd and cow-
herd, grieve for their lost master in similar fashion when they
meet with him and participate in the final killing of the suitors,
and their careers match in other details; though here, too, one of
them, Eumaeus, is dominant. Among the suitors, Antinous and
Eurymachus are the most vicious, Amphinomus and Leodes the
least guilty; and in both instances one of the pair is considerably
more important. Amongst the major characters, Odysseus is per-
secuted mainly by Poseidon, to a lesser extent by Helios.

It is pointless to speculate *why* the poet works in this way, but
it is clear that he has a habit of doing so. Recognition of this
habit removes the temptation to consider that the presence of a
doublet pair betrays the hand of an interpolator.

Like the Athenian tragedians, Homer allowed himself a good deal of freedom in adapting myths to suit his purpose and his context. The clearest case perhaps is the Niobe *paradeigma* (24.602–17; see Willcock 1964 and p. 311), where Achilles, urging Priam to eat, declares that even Niobe is said to have eaten despite her grief. Why was that tale chosen for the paradigm? Partly because of Niobe's reputation as the example of extreme grief, but mainly because of the familiar story that Niobe boasted she had many children, whereas the goddess Leto had only two; whereupon those two killed all Niobe's brood. Priam has been lamenting his many slain sons; Achilles, on the other hand, has described old Peleus's sorrows while his *only* son is far away in Troy (24.538ff.). The fact that Niobe ate, even though grieving, was invented by the poet to fit the myth to the situation; the underlying parallel of many killed by few subtly reinforces the emotion of the situation. In this same paradigm, the feature of the bodies of Niobe's children lying unburied until the gods took care of the burial, since the local people had been turned to stone by the gods, has been invented to correspond to Achilles' denying burial to Hector, the care of the gods for his burial (24.23ff.), and the old tale that Niobe herself was turned to stone by the gods in sympathy and survives as a cliff face with trickling streams.

In the same way Nestor, to give him dignity, has been added to the legendary battle of Centaurs and Lapiths (1.259ff.); they are even said to ask him for counsel, though he was only a youth at the time and presumably had as yet no reputation for wisdom, to better justify Nestor's offer of counsel to the Greeks (see Lang 1983).

In several instances the poet may have actually invented a myth in order to provide a deity who is seeking a favor with a previous favor to trade upon as a *quid pro quo*. The story of Thetis's aid to Zeus when he was set upon by an unlikely alliance of Hera, Athena, and Poseidon, which gives her a ploy to use in seeking Zeus's aid (1.396ff.); Hephaestus's gratitude to Thetis for saving him after his fall from Olympus, which moves him to make the shield for Achilles (18.395ff.); Phoenix's upbringing of Achilles, which gives him a claim upon the hero (9.438ff.; usually he is brought up by Chiron the Centaur, 11.831–32)—all these are unsupported by other evidence and may well have been invented by the poet for purposes of their immediate context (see Braswell 1971, Lang 1983, Willcock 1964). A recent study (Lang 1983) suggests very plausibly that the hostility between Zeus and Hera in the *Iliad* indicates that there were other tales of divine discords, and that mutual influence between such mythic tales and the *Iliad* plot continued for some time and shaped both the myth and the *Iliad* itself.

One further aspect of Homer's use of myth should be stressed. Though the gods are ever-present in both epics, the supernatural, in the sense of the fantastic and the miraculous, is rarely found; neither are the more sordid elements of human villainy and suffering. The divinely made armor presented to Peleus and worn by Patroclus and Hector, and that given to Achilles by Thetis, are *not* said to be invulnerable, and Patroclus and Hector die despite their protection. No hint is given of the tale that Achilles was invulnerable, or that he or any other hero, even Sarpedon, will become immortal (Menelaus is an exception [*Odyssey* 4.561] but for the unheroic reason of his wife's family connections, and the statement is made by him, not by the poet). Though Helen is daughter of Zeus, one is never reminded that she hatched out of an egg laid by Leda.

This reticence about the more miraculous parts of mythology is of course in accord with the seriousness of these epics, but contrasts with what is known of other epics about Troy (as has recently been documented by Griffin 1977). In these, for instance, the army was fed for nine years by Anius's daughters, Oeno, Spermo, and Elais ("Winy, Grainy, and Oily"), who could provide at will the products after which they were named; Troy could not fall until the magic image of Athena, the Palladium, was removed, or until Philoctetes and his bow joined the Greek army; the exotic Amazons and the Aethiopian Memnon appear.

There are no cowards on either side in the *Iliad*, and no place for the tales of how heroes tried to evade their draft calls — Achilles hidden among women, Odysseus pretending to be mad. Homer's conception of the dignity of epic is much above that of his successors. Some idea of the extent to which he was selecting his material from widely different tales can be gained from reading the medieval Troy-tales of Dares and Dictys, though there is no evidence that they are derived from an early period (see Frazer 1966, Clarke 1981).

Understanding the common structures that underlie the stories in Homer brings at least three advantages. In the first place, it helps us to avoid errors in interpretation when a part of the motif does not fit or two motifs do not properly join. For instance, Odysseus's account of his visit with the dead in *Odyssey* II is difficult to follow topographically: at the beginning of the account the ghosts come to Odysseus on the seashore and drink the blood of the sacrifices, but later (at least from *Odyssey* 11.568 onward) it is clear that he is deep in the underworld. There is no account of how he manages to return to the daylight.

These discrepancies are accounted for, and hence cease to matter, when we realize that the poet is combining two separate story patterns. The first is a *nekyiomanteia,* or calling up of the dead for consultation, which occurs also in Aeschylus's *Persians* (and very nearly in his *Choephoroe*) and is described by Herodotus (5.92ê.2). The famous account of Saul and the witch of Endor (*I Samuel* 28.7–20) is another parallel. This necromancy merges into a *katabasis,* the descent of a hero into the underworld, usually to recover someone lost, a theme that occurs in the tales of Gilgamesh, Theseus, Heracles, Orpheus, and others. (It has been pointed out that Priam's journey to recover Hector's body has certain elements of a *katabasis;* Whitman 1958.217ff., Nagler 1974.184ff.) Secondly, a knowledge of parallel tales enables us to see where the poet has altered a story for a particular purpose, and hence to appreciate more fully his craft and his intent. Finally, the universal appeal of the *Odyssey* in particular can be better understood in the light of the enormously wide range of parallel tales.

Further Reading

ON GREEK MYTH GENERALLY. Kirk 1970 and 1974; Nilsson 1932 is still useful. The contemporary anthropological approach, which is not covered in the above essay, can be seen in the works of M. Detienne, L. Gernet, J.-P. Vernant, and P. Vidal-Naquet (a selection can be found in R. L. Gordon, *Myth, Religion and Society,* Cambridge 1981).

ON THE STRUCTURE OF MYTH. Propp 1968, summarized in Scholes 1974.

ON THE "ILIAD." The "withdrawal-devastation-return" pattern is examined especially by M. L. Lord 1967 and Nagler 1974 ch. 5. Nethercut 1976 has some excellent ideas on folk tale elements in the story of Achilles in the *Iliad.* Damon 1980 compares the "pedimental" structure of the *Iliad* with the structures of *Roland* and *Beowulf.*

ON THE "ODYSSEY." Page 1955 and 1973 has many folk tale parallels from other cultures, and Powell 1977 discusses the poet's handling of the tales. The older work by Woodhouse 1930 is still worth reading. Hölscher 1978 discusses the relationship between folk tale and epic.

Mondi 1983 has a good account of the Cyclopes tale.

ON HOMER'S ADAPTATION OF MYTH. The ideas of Willcock 1964, 1977, and 1976 (Appendix C and D) on Homer's adaptation of myth are important, together with those of Braswell 1971. The older work of J. T. Kakridis 1949 and 1971 is still fundamental. Fenik 1964 deals with the use of the Rhesus tale in *Iliad* 10. Lang 1983 has very interesting ideas on the interaction of mythic stories and the epic plots. Griffin 1977 illustrates the differences between Homer's use of myths and that of the poets of the epic cycle. On Achilles' invulnerability see Young 1979. Sowa 1984 analyzes story patterns in the *Homeric Hymns*.

7

Type-scenes and Expansion

Any reader of Homer notices not only the recurrent formulaic adjectives but also the repeated scenes of performing a sacrifice, preparing and eating a meal, fighting a single combat in the midst of the general battle, receiving a visit from a deity, and so on. Actually these type-scenes, as they are called, are all-pervasive, and as important a tradition of epic composition as the formulae that make up the verses. Of course any human social activity, any ritual, committee meeting, or dinner party, will have a standard form and will be composed of a number of distinguishable elements occurring generally in the same sequence. But in Homer the standardization goes beyond simple representation of repeated human actions. It probably developed as an aid to oral composition or memorization. Familiarity with a uniform sequence of elements in a scene reduces the danger of omitting some important action; and the possibility of presenting a scene at greater or lesser length, by elaborating the set elements (rather than by adding new elements), enables the poet to dwell on a scene if necessary for the purpose of emphasis, and also to shape the expansion to suit the circumstances without losing track of the scene as a whole. Like the secretary of a committee, Homer can report an event in two or three words or in two or three pages.

The sacrifice scene is the most complex (not, of course, the most expanded) of type-scenes, no doubt because it describes the actions of a major religious ritual. Twenty-one different elements have been counted (by Arend 1933), and the list could be extended. The longest example is Nestor's magnificent display for the eyes of the inexperienced Telemachus, which begins with catching the sacrificial beast and gilding its horns, and includes the only example of the cry of the womenfolk (*Odyssey* 3.418–76). In the *Iliad*, the longest examples are the sacrifice by Agamemnon before the great march to battle, which is additionally extended by the gathering of the army's chief commanders (2.402–31), and that performed by the priest Chryses in order to request Apollo to end the plague, likewise a most significant occasion (1.447–74). A shorter description, with some elements omitted and no elaboration, can be seen when Agamemnon sacrifices in honor of Ajax after his duel with Hector (7.314–25). The disastrous sacrifice to Helios of his own cattle is accompanied by unique and sinister features, the meat on the spits bellowing like live cattle (*Odyssey* 12.353–65, 395–96); and Eumaeus's sacrifice of a pig has the unique features of stunning the animal before it is slaughtered and singeing off its bristles (*Odyssey* 14.413–38). On two occasions when the connotations of formal hospitality to guests are of major importance, a meal is prepared in some detail without explicit mention of a sacrifice: at the tense and immensely important meeting of Achilles and the Greek envoys (9.205–21) and at Achilles' reconciliation with Priam (24.621–27).

It cannot be too much emphasized that although a number of verses may be repeated in several different examples of the type-scene, no description is identical with any other; though it might seem natural that long, standard blocks of verses might develop to describe the repeated rituals of sacrifice (just as a messenger usually delivers his message in the same words in which it was entrusted to him), this in fact does not occur; each occurence is unique and often specifically adapted to its context. Like Greek temples, instances of a type-scene are similar in structure but always different in scale and in details.

Even more variety occurs in the type-scene of a warrior putting on his armor before entering battle—the archetype of the equally conventional preparations before the final shootout in a western movie. There are four major instances, which use much of the same phrasing for the donning of the equipment (see Armstrong 1958). The first is that of Paris before his duel with Menelaus (3.330ff.); of the nine verses, eight are standard and the single item of elaboration is the note that the corselet he puts on belonged to his brother Lycaon. This is not simply padding, but a reminder that Paris is normally an archer who needs no heavy defensive armor; in fact the poet has mentioned specifically at Paris's first entrance that he is wearing a leopardskin in place of armor (3.17). The next is that of Agamemnon (11.17ff.) as he leads his troops back to battle again after the unsuccessful embassy to Achilles and the night expedition of Odysseus and Diomedes; to do him honor, the poet devotes nine verses to a description of his corselet and another eight to his shield, besides an extra verse or two about sword, helmet, and spears, and concludes with a special thunderclap from the gods. Patroclus, disguising himself in Achilles' divinely made armor (16.130ff.), is given slightly more elaboration than Paris received, but the main expansion is the five verses explaining that he did *not* take Achilles' mighty spear, which Chiron had given to Peleus, his father; no one but Achilles can wield this, and the audience realizes that Patroclus is not the equal of his master. Finally, the formal arming of Achilles himself (19.369ff.) is decorated with similes for the glitter of golden shield and helmet and a further account of Peleus's spear, and completed by a detailed preparation of the chariot. The previous description of the making of the armor by Hephaestus could be considered a further expansion of the scene.

Such arming scenes, expanded to a greater or lesser extent, are probably a part of the epic tradition. In some cases, however, details are heavily modified to suit a particular occasion. When Odysseus and Diomedes equip themselves for their night foray (10.254ff.), both put on inconspicuous leather helmets in place of the usual glittering bronze, and the occasion is dignified by the history of this famous boar's-tusk helmet of Odysseus; the Trojan Dolon does much the same (10.333ff.). The swineherd Eumaeus, as he sets out to protect his herd on a cold night, prepares himself with a heavy "windbreaker" (*alexanemon*) cloak and thick goatskin as well as sword and javelin (*Odyssey* 14.528ff.). Athena arms herself before she and Hera begin their fruitless attempt to enter the battle before Troy (5.733ff.; a shorter version at 8.384ff.), and puts on Zeus's terrible *aegis*, decorated with dreadful forms of violence, and a golden helmet; the tunic that she dons in place of her woman's dress reaches to her feet, as in artistic representations, and modesty prevents her putting the usual greaves on her legs.

Sometimes an expected arming scene is replaced by a kind of surrogate. In spite of his eminence, Hector is never given a regular arming scene, but after he has put on—in half a verse (17.194b)—the glorious armor he has taken from Patroclus, the poet replaces the account of his arming with the ill-omened history of the armor and the grim forebodings of Zeus (17.195–209). Ajax similarly arms himself in a mere half a verse (7.206b) before his duel with Hector, but is then honored by nearly twenty verses made up of a simile, an account of the reactions of the Greeks, Trojans, and Hector, and a description of his mighty shield (7.207–23). Sarpedon's famous lecture on honor (12.310ff.) is technically a *parainesis*, an exhortation to his friend Glaucus to charge into the battle, but the preceding description of his shield (294–97) turns it into something like the arming scene that he does not otherwise have. The description of Pandarus's bow (4.105ff.) before he looses his arrow against Menelaus similarly fills the honorific place of an arming scene. Diomedes is already armed when his mighty deeds begin in book 5—his buildup came in the form of Agamemnon's account of his father's prowess (4.370ff.)—so to glorify him the poet substitutes the fire Athena makes blaze from his shield and helmet (5.3–8). Before the unarmed Achilles utters his terrifying cry to drive back the Trojans from Patroclus's body, Athena encircles his shoulders with the *aegis* and his head with a golden cloud (18.203ff.) as substitutes for corselet and helmet. It is hard not to think that these alternatives to regular arming scenes are Homer's own variations on the standard pattern.

Other type-scenes, too, show the same range in scale, between a bald statement made in a verse or two and an expanded version that covers several pages; and it is in such amplifications of length, each unique in content though usually standard in form, that we can be sure the individual choice of the poet, not the force of his convention, is at work. In Homer, elaboration is inserted for a purpose—to emphasize an action or scene—and its content is usually not simple background information but something of interest and relevance in itself. (One may contrast the leisurely descriptions of garments and weapons in the first few hundred lines of Mededović's *The Wedding of Smailagić Meho*, which add impressiveness and dignity but are much less closely connected to the narrative than Homeric elaboration; see Lord 1974.)

For example, the supplication scene of Chryses to Agamemnon at the beginning of the *Iliad* is very brief, but includes a mention of his holy regalia to dramatize his standing with Apollo. There is, however, no listing of the gifts he brings as ransom, as there is when Priam prepares a ransom for Hector (24.228ff.), since the poet is getting his story under way and does not desire much expansion here. The supplication scene of the young Trojan Lycaon to Achilles is enlarged by the preliminary account of his history and by his attempt to dodge under the uplifted spear, and the episode is extended to more than a hundred verses (21.34–135) to match the importance of Achilles' unforgettable words about the inevitability of death.

Greater still is the extension of Priam's supplication to Achilles at the end of the poem, which might be considered to begin with the council of the gods and the dispatch of Iris to bring Thetis to Olympus to hear Zeus's instructions to Achilles (24.23ff.). Even if we consider it to begin with the dispatch of the message to Priam that brings about his departure, the scene begins at 24.142 and continues through the preparation of the ransom, the discussion with Hecuba, the harnessing of wagon and chariot, the prayer to Zeus, the omen, the meeting with Hermes, the arrival in Achilles' dwelling, the supplication and Achilles' response, and concludes with Achilles' announcement that the body lies in Priam's wagon (24.599)—some 450 verses in all. During all this time the tension has been mounting and the immense importance of the scene between the two mourners has been built up—and the details themselves have been of absorbing interest.

The reader should be aware of the underlying structure of type-scenes and of the elaboration which the poet is using; where appropriate, attention is drawn to this in Part Two, but of course it is impossible to indicate every interesting instance. As has been well pointed out (by Austin 1966), much of what has been called digression in the poems is really amplification for the purpose of emphasis (see p. 4).

An interesting example of what type-scenes can be like when they are *not* elaborated occurs on the last page or two of the *Odyssey*, which show a breathless speed, the causes of which we can only speculate on. Odysseus has revealed himself to his father, a meal (which Odysseus had ordered in advance, 24.214ff.) has been prepared, and all sit down to eat (24.386). A further reunion interrupts the meal, which then continues with the newcomers included (24.412). While it is going on, Rumor tells the Ithacans of the deaths of their relatives the suitors, they gather at Odysseus's house, carry out the corpses, bury the local men (presumably with washing, oiling, and clothing of the dead, lamentations, and so on) and send the others back to their kinsfolk, hold an assembly, go home and don their armor, and take up their positions in front of the city—all in just fifty-six verses (*Odyssey* 24.413–68). After a short colloquy between Athena and Zeus, the poet returns us to Odysseus and his companions, who have just concluded their meal. At least all this frenzied activity by the Ithacans takes place offstage; but the poet continues at the same frantic speed, and in the final fifty verses covers the approach of the Ithacans, the arming of Odysseus and his companions, a divine visitation, an exhortation to battle and two responses, a prayer, the duel of Laertes and Eupeithes, a description of the general battle, the calling of a truce (by Athena), flight, pursuit, an omen (Zeus's thunderbolt), and the oath-taking for the unconvincing peacemaking that ends the poem. Even the direct speeches are reduced to a couple of lines or so each.

All the type-scenes are standard (Hainsworth 1966 points out that the gathering, arming, and parade of both the Ithacans and Odysseus's men are similar to those in the *Iliad*), but piling them up without elaboration is fortunately unique in Homer. The longest surviving fragment of the *Little Iliad* is in this same style (see Griffin 1977), and possibly it was common in contemporary epics now lost to us. The conclusion of the *Odyssey*, unsatisfactory as it is artistically, may be a valuable example of the work not perhaps of an inferior poet, but of one who knows the techniques but is in an enormous hurry to finish off the tale, because he is dead tired, or has lost his audience, or is utterly weary of dictating to the stenographer who some scholars think must be the source of our text.

Finally, two particular characteristics of Homer's use of type-scenes should be mentioned. One is his habit of employing two instances of a scene in fairly close proximity, as in the successive confrontations of Agenor and Hector with Achilles (see pp. 290–92). Another is his way of using occurrences of a type-scene, or part of one, for different purposes, just as the successive recognitions of Odysseus are employed for different emotional effects (see pp. 64–65).

For example, compare the significance given to the dogs that regularly guard a dwelling. When Odysseus arrives at Eumaeus's hut, he is threatened by dogs, and Eumaeus's rescue of him introduces us to the swineherd's good principles, his hospitality to strangers, and his grief for his lost master (*Odyssey* 14.29ff.). When Telemachus arrives there, the dogs recognize him and make a fuss, which announces his arrival to Odysseus (16.4ff.). When Athena herself shows up, the dogs are not forgotten but are said to draw back in fear of the divinity (16.160ff.). When Odysseus stands admiring Alcinous's palace in Phaeacia, it would be unfitting for him to be accosted by watchdogs in such a luxurious and peaceful setting, but in front of the golden doors and silver pillars and lintel he observes the gold and silver immortal watchdogs made by Hephaestus, affirming the opulence of the king and his friendship with the gods (*Odyssey* 7.91–94; presumably these are not thought of as statues, but as thinking and moving "cynoids," similar to Hephaestus's robot attendants at *Iliad* 18.418–20). And the most superb instance of modified use of the same element, of course, occurs in the famous scene when the disguised Odysseus approaches his own house again after his twenty-year absence and is recognized only by the aged guardian, the dog Argus; here the regular element becomes an emotional and pathetic addition to the impact of the wanderer's return (*Odyssey* 17.291ff.). This kind of varied usage of a common motif can with some confidence be attributed to the original genius of the poet.

Further Reading

The pioneering work, Arend 1933, is still the best treatment of some of the most clearly identifiable type-scenes; published in the same year, Calhoun 1933 is also still important, especially on the aesthetic side. Lord 1951 compares some type-scenes ("themes") in Homer and Southslavic epic, and expands on this in Lord 1960 ch. 4. Armstrong 1958 makes an Arend-like analysis of arming scenes, and Lang 1969 examines (in particular) arrival and entertainment scenes. Gunn 1970 shows how minor inconsistencies arise from a poet's slips in handling a type-scene; Gunn 1971 compares examples of certain type-scenes from *Iliad* and *Odyssey* and draws the very important conclusion that they are indistinguishable in form. Fenik 1968 and Krischer 1971 give excellent and detailed treatments of various battle type-scenes. Fenik 1974 is a most important survey of type-scenes and other repeated motifs in the *Odyssey*. Nagler 1974 ch. 3 and 4 contains a most interesting theoretical examination of type-scenes ("motifs") as compositional units. Edwards 1974 attempts to explain some problems in type-scenes of hospitality; Edwards 1980a examines examples of the catalogue type-scene, Edwards 1980b the type-scenes in *Iliad* 1, and Edwards 1982 the ending of the *Odyssey*. Krischer 1979 (a brief but brilliant article) discusses Virgil's alterations of Homeric type-scenes, makes many very acute observations on Homer, and casts new light (based on his analysis of Virgil's compositional habits) on the remarkably abrupt ending of the *Aeneid*. A survey of bibliography on Homeric type-scenes is being prepared for publication in the journal *Oral Tradition*.

8

Battle Scenes

Eight books of the *Iliad*, one-third of the entire poem, consist mainly of battle scenes; and that is not including the big duels in Books 3 and 7 and the rampages of Patroclus in Book 16 and Achilles in Books 20–22. "The named casualties of officers total 238, and unnamed 26. Other ranks are not recorded. Of these 24 seem to have been wounded only, though in some cases it is left uncertain whether a man was only wounded, and not killed. To the wounded must be added Ares and Aphrodite" (C. B. Armstrong 1969.30). How is all this slaughter to be described by a poet? How can he even keep track of the names? In recent years the structure and narrative techniques of the battle scenes have been examined in a number of excellent studies, especially those of Beye (1964), Fenik (1968), Krischer (1971), and Latacz (1977); the following account depends heavily on their researches.

The most comprehensive and detailed analysis of the subtle structures of the battle scenes is that of Latacz (1977). He identifies two main components, which repeatedly succeed each other: continuous combat, eventually interrupted by a breakthrough, a divine intervention, or nightfall; and a flight and pursuit, ended by an exhortation and recovery. The combat scenes can be subdivided into two types: the descriptions of general battle (see pp. 85–87); and the individual duels. Latacz identifies three main forms of these individual duels: balancing series of duels in which Greek kills Trojan, Trojan kills Greek, and so on, with a great variety of different treatments; a major duel between two characters; and a series of exploits by one hero, an *aristeia* (see below). The poet skillfully weaves together these different structures, moving over the field of battle and focusing now on the long-range picture, now on closeups of one duel after another, to present a living and varied picture of the course of the struggle.

The duels, the actual hand-to-hand fighting of two or more combatants, are over very quickly and are very limited in scale, usually not exceeding two or three exchanges of blows. (For an account of the combatants' weapons and armor, see pp. 167–68.) The separate actions that make up the combat constantly recur—for example, A throws something at B but misses; B strikes A but fails to wound him; A kills B—though as with other type-scenes, no two instances of conflict are exactly alike. (The few pages of Introduction to Fenik 1968 list the common features of these encounters.) The brevity of the episodes of actual duelling is remarkable; perhaps the tradition developed in this way to avoid tedium, though one would think that much longer descriptions could be enjoyed.

The short duels are constantly diversified with a great variety of descriptive techniques. As one of the combatants dies, the poet tells us something about him and what his death means to his family (see pp. 156–57); men are wounded, and are assisted by their friends; for a period one hero will sweep everything before him, usually with the aid of a god (for instance, Diomedes in Books 5 and 6); attention shifts from Greeks to Trojans and back; there is a great deal of speech-making, both between opponents (the challenges to battle, the vaunts over a victim) and between colleagues (exhortations, conferences, rebukes, calls for help; see pp. 92–94); there are general descriptions of the movements of the armies, studded with similes (see pp. 85–87); and of course the gods continually intervene and the scene constantly shifts from the struggle on the battlefield to the quarreling on Olympus. The commentary on Book 13 analyzes in detail a typical account of a battle.

There are five major *aristeiai*, series of exploits of an important hero: those of Diomedes (Books 4 to 6), Agamemnon (Book 11), Hector (Book 15), Patroclus (Book 16), and finally the immensely amplified victories of Achilles himself (Books 19 to 22). Krischer (1971) has shown that these accounts follow the same basic pattern. They begin with an arming scene, a key element of which is the shining of the hero's armor. After the fighting begins, the hero kills several opponents in duels, charges against the opposing army, and starts a rout among them. Then he is wounded, and the pursuit comes to an end. He prays to a god for help, and his strength is restored. He then returns to the battle, engages in a duel with the leader of the enemy, and kills him. Finally there is a fight over the corpse, which is eventually recovered by the dead man's friends with the help of the gods.

The exploits of all five major warriors follow this basic pattern but, in usual Homeric style, show interesting adaptations in detail. Diomedes has no formal arming scene, but as a substitute the shining of his armor is heavily elaborated by Athena's help at the beginning of Book 5. After winning several duels, he storms against the enemy (5.84ff.), but the rout is omitted; he is next wounded by Pandarus and healed by Athena. He returns to battle and kills Pandarus, and after several interruptions the wounding element is recapitulated (5.793ff.) and he is again reinvigorated by Athena. He returns again to the battle and engages in a duel with Ares himself, whom he defeats. There is, of course, no corpse to fight over, but the scene between Ares and Zeus takes its place. It is even possible that the exchange of armor between Diomedes and Glaucus before he drops out of view (6.232–36) is a reflection of stripping the armor from the corpse of a defeated enemy, a part of Krischer's final element.

Agamemnon's triumphs are introduced by a fairly long arming scene, including the glitter of his spearhead (11.44); after killing a number of Trojans (in pairs), he leads a charge and pursues the enemy as far as the Scaean gate of Troy (11.170). The next stage is his wounding (11.232ff.), but instead of being reinvigorated by a god and returning to the fray, he withdraws entirely, and his exploits end at this point; it is Hector who receives the divine encouragement, in the form of Iris's message from Zeus (11.181ff.), and it is Hector who takes over the brunt of the battle (11.284). Though he has not received an arming scene (it is postponed until he dons the armor of Achilles, 17.192ff.), Hector's armor glittered grandly at the beginning of this battle like an ominous star (11.62–66). His charge and pursuit follow immediately upon Agamemnon's retreat (11.284–309), his wounding and reinvigoration by Apollo follow later (14.409ff., 15.220ff.), and his triumph over Patroclus and the struggle over the body of his victim come in Books 16 and 17.

In the case of Patroclus, the structure begins normally, except that his armor, divinely made though it is, does not glitter as he puts it on, perhaps a sign that he will not return from this battle. His main victory over Sarpedon occurs earlier than usual, and the usual fight over the victim's body is ended by Apollo's rescue of it. The wounding element follows, in the form of his repulsion by Apollo from the wall of Troy (16.698ff.), and then the final triumph of Hector takes over and Patroclus is killed.

For Achilles himself the component parts of the structure spread from Book 18, the making of his armor, to the end of the struggle over his enemy's corpse in Book 24. Apart from this giant scale, the poet has brilliantly adapted some of the standard components of the structure. When Achilles enters the battle, all other Greeks vanish and he fights the Trojan army alone. Instead of being wounded by a Trojan, he is overwhelmed by the river god Scamander (21.233ff.), and his divine reinvigoration takes the form of his rescue by Hephaestus. Finally, the concluding element, the struggle over the body of his victim, Hector, is expanded into the mighty consolation theme that ends the poem.

Occasionally descriptions of the killings degenerate into a mere list of names (at 8.274–76, for example), but such lists are rare and short. Here one of the poet's few slips results; the Trojan Melanippus is killed in proper style at 15.546ff., but because his name is so convenient for ending such a list, the unfortunate man is killed again at 8.276 and 16.695 (or has he two name-sakes?). A few other such slips are summed up by Beye 1964.360–61: "Of the nine Greeks whom Hektor kills in a list (11.301–3), five appear again. . . . Of the thirteen slain (16.569–696) seven appear only here; four have been slain before; two will be slain again." Often the same names occur for Greeks and Trojans; many of them are formed from those of towns, and occasionally euphony seems to play some part (see Beye 1964.354ff.). To what extent all these names were inherited or invented by the poet of the *Iliad* is quite unknown. The *Iliad* contains few examples of the kind of playing with the meanings of names that sometimes occurs in the *Odyssey* (see p. 121). It is noteworthy, as Beye has pointed out (1964.354), that although many of the names are identical in metrical shape, there is remarkably little confusion between them in our manuscripts.

Further Reading

Latacz 1977 is a full and intensive study of the historicity of the battle descriptions and the kind of poetic techniques used. Fenik 1968 on the structure of the battle scenes, and Krischer 1971 (and briefly in 1979.149–50) on the exploits of the main heroes, are also of the greatest importance. Mueller 1984 ch. 3 gives an account of the structure of duels, the kinds of injuries inflicted, the death descriptions, and the exploits. Kirk 1968 discusses the realism of Homeric descriptions in the light of archaeological knowledge, epic standards of behavior, the historicity of the Trojan War, and the practicality of the siege tactics. Beye 1965 deals thoroughly with the names of the heroes killed and the structure of the brief comments or obituaries (in the poet's voice) that often follow deaths in battle. Hainsworth 1966 examines the descriptions of joining battle. C. B. Armstrong 1969 sums up the casualty lists.

9

Description

Direct descriptions of the appearance or the personality of characters are not common in Homer. It is an old and familiar observation that Helen's beauty, as she appears on the wall of Troy, is conveyed not by a description, but by the effect it has on the old men who watch her and talk among themselves. Athena improves Odysseus's stature and good looks, but it is the effect on Nausicaa that matters (*Odyssey* 6.229ff.); the same is true when the suitors admire the shoulders, chest, and huge limbs of the disguised hero (*Odyssey* 18.66–74). The fullest descriptions of physical appearance are that of Thersites, who before his one and only appearance is memorably (though briefly) characterized by his quarrelsome nature, his unheroic physique, and the attitudes of leaders and men toward him (2.211–23), and the unlovely details of Athena's disguising Odysseus as an old beggar (*Odyssey* 13.430–38). Of the appearance of the chiefs on both sides we hear little besides the accounts (in a character's voice, not Homer's) of Odysseus's short stature and his style of speaking, and the tallness of Ajax, as Helen and the Trojans look at them from the wall (3.192–227). Usually we must imagine the appearance of a warrior from the recurrent hints conveyed by the fixed epithets ("swift-footed Achilles," "loud-voiced Diomedes") and the impact of the similes.

The general topography of the city, the plain, the two rivers that cross it, and the Greek encampment on the seashore is also rather vague; no one draws a map to illustrate the action of the *Iliad*. Troy stands a little inland, with Mount Ida not far away, and has a Scaean Gate with an oak tree beside it; before it are springs, washing troughs and a fig tree, and some way off is the Tomb of Ilus. This is about all Homer tells us (see Camps 1981.105–6), though he, or some predecessor, knew something about this district, for he tells us carefully that the wall built by the Greeks no longer stood in his time (7.448–63, 12.10–33), and he knows that the plain can be seen from the highest point of Samothrace over the top of the interposed island of Imbros (13.12–14).

Nevertheless there is a great deal of description in Homer: description of actions, scenes, and objects, often vivid and colorful like the similes. But the descriptions are not simply ornament. Like other techniques of expansion (see p. 4), a descriptive passage is usually a means of emphasis. Sometimes the simple length of the description makes it important. The eight-verse description of Agamemnon's shield in his arming scene (11.33–40) builds up his superiority in the coming battle; the inventory of the ransom prepared for Hector, and the twice-repeated account of the enormous compensation offered to Achilles by Agamemnon, in each case demonstrate the importance of the situation (24.229–37, 9.121–56, 262–93). Much attention has been paid to the account of Nestor's cup (11.631–36) and the boar's-tusk cap worn by Odysseus for the night foray against the Trojans (10.256–71), because both can be matched with articles in Mycenaean graves; but it is less often observed that the first passage is part of the expansion leading up to Nestor's vitally important proposal to Patroclus (see p. 239), and the second elaborates the arming of Odysseus before the following detailed account of his exploits.

The connection with the context is often very close. When the priest Chryses approaches Agamemnon to ransom his daughter at the beginning of the poem, the exposition moves quickly and there is no real expansion—for instance, no details of the gifts that make up the ransom are given—but the priest is said to be bearing the insignia of the god Apollo, a clear indication that he has the power of the god behind him and his request should be respected. The robe that Hecuba picks out to offer to Athena (6.289ff.) is chosen for its beauty, but it is described as a treasure that Paris brought back with Helen, and so it is a reminder of the past wrongdoing of the Trojans and unlikely to appease the goddess who favors the Greeks. The washing pools beside the springs before Troy prolong the narrative of Hector's flight before Achilles, but also evoke (as a simile might) the women laughing as they worked there in the past and the contrasting prospect of capture and slavery that now lies before them.

In one of the most obvious of all Homeric type-scenes, a sacrifice, the description takes the form of an account of the successive actions of the characters. In the same way, action and movement are also a characteristic feature of the descriptions of physical objects. The most famous example is the bow of Pandarus the Trojan, carefully brought before our eyes before he looses the arrow that wounds Menelaus and breaks the truce (4.105ff.). Shooting the wild goat and crafting the bow from its horns depict not only the actual object but Pandarus's pride in it, which explains his foolishness in shooting at that time; Athena's persuasion is secondary. The craftsman of the bow is anonymous, but in the description of the making of Odysseus's raft, Odysseus and Calypso figure very largely, since the implied— and very different—emotions of the two characters are more important than the object itself (*Odyssey* 5.228–62). The emotion of a character is also brilliantly depicted through action when Achilles anxiously prays to Zeus for Patroclus's safe return, for his immense anxiety is conveyed not by a description of the cup, precious though it is, but by the hero's immense concern in unwrapping and cleansing it (16.220f.). The pictures that appear on Achilles' mighty shield are described in great detail by the poet, but he still reminds us from time to time that we are watching the actions of Hephaestus in crafting them by the repeated phrase "and on it he fashioned . . ." (18.483 and elsewhere). It is significant that when Achilles describes the speakers' staff, to emphasize Agamemnon's violation of civilized order, he tells of its fashioning from raw trunk to symbol of justice (1.234ff.); it is equally significant that when Agamemnon holds it, the expansion takes the form of an account of its descent to him from the hands of Zeus himself (2.101ff.), reminding us that though Agamemnon may be weak and foolish he is still "the scepter-bearing King to whom Zeus gives honor" (Nestor's words, 1.279).

The actions described above link an object or scene with a human character. A similar link occurs in the common technique of picturing a scene as one of the characters is looking at it; we see it through his eyes. The major examples are in the *Odyssey*: the view of Calypso's fertile island through the admiring eyes of Hermes (*Odyssey* 5.63ff.), or of Alcinous's magnificent palace and lovely orchard (*Odyssey* 7.84ff.) through Odysseus's eyes. The palace storeroom is described as Telemachus enters it (*Odyssey* 2.337ff.), and Eumaeus's farm as Odysseus approaches for his first encounter in his own country (*Odyssey* 14.5ff.). In the *Iliad*, Achilles' shelter is described in detail for the first time as Priam approaches it (24.448ff.; see p. 307), and Hector's meetings with the women of his family are preceded by an account of Priam's magnificent palace (6.243ff.). It is an effective technique, often used in modern movies, for the audience to look at a scene as a character steps into it. Cleanth Brooks has observed (1947.108f.) that in Gray's *Elegy* the descriptions are similarly centered on humanity: "What the attention is focused on, even in the first stanzas, is not the graveyard itself, but what can be seen by a man standing in the graveyard."

Vividness and immediacy are often given by spotlighting one particular item in a scene, "a single external detail which vouches for the reality of the whole" (Bassett 1938.231–32; see also Andersson 1976.34ff.). Hector's huge shield, slung across his back, taps against his neck and ankles as he hastens back to Troy (6.117–18), and he holds a long spear in his hand when he addresses the Trojans after their victory (8.493–95). (These same lines also appear when Hector enters Paris's house and finds the delinquent there [6.318–20], although, as a reader pointed out to me, a twenty-foot-long spear would be unmanageable indoors; perhaps they were inserted on the initiative of a scribe, or perhaps the poet slipped unthinkingly into a phrase associated with Hector.) As with the similes, all readers find their own favorites among these intimate details. The sweaty shield strap chafes Diomedes' shoulder (5.796–97); Hector, pondering whether to flee or to stand and face Achilles, leans his shield against a buttress of the wall (22.97); Apollo, encouraging Agenor, leans casually against an oak tree (21.549).

Distinct from all the above are the passages of general description of the course of battle. Battle scenes regularly open with such passages, and they often occur as the bridge between two sections of single combats (see Fenik 1968.79ff.). They are made up by grouping together a number of different motifs. The commonest motif is a simile (often more than one in a passage). Others are a mention of the thoughts of the men on each side, or those of an imaginary spectator ("One would say that . . ."), or those of the poet himself ("Neither side could . . ."). There may be a vivid detail (Hector foaming at the mouth, 15.607), correlative temporal clauses ("As long as . . . so long did . . ."), or a reference to the purpose of Zeus.

One of the longest and most splendid of these passages occurs during the fight over the body of Patroclus, bridging the exploits of Ajax and those of Automedon (17.352–459). The poet holds the action stationary, with the charge led by Asteropaeus stubbornly resisted by Ajax (352–59); then he describes the men falling on both sides, addresses the audience directly ("You would not have thought . . ."; 366), and contrasts the mist over this part of the battlefield with the sunlight elsewhere. Then he uses the motif "But [X] did not know . . ." (377ff.), a vivid detail (the sweat running down the fighters), a simile, and the thoughts of men on both sides (395–97). He makes another comment in his own voice ("Not even Ares could have found fault"), repeats the "But [X] did not know" motif at greater and more effective length (401–11), and then repeats the thoughts of both sides, again at greater length than formerly (414–23). Then, after a startling double metaphor ("The iron tumult rose to the bronze sky"), he reveals Zeus's intention, brilliantly shaping and amplifying it into the pathetic scene of the immortal horses mourning their dead driver and the god's reflection on the sadness of man's wretched mortality (426–58). After this, the normal motifs of battle resume with the charge of Automedon. Many of the same techniques are used to expand the flight of Hector before Achilles (see pp. 292–94).

Perhaps the most famous descriptive scene of all is the picture that concludes the Trojans' day of victory and shows them making their camp outside the city walls (8.543ff.). Only Achilles' absence from the battle has allowed them this confidence, and the poet wishes to expand the scene to draw our attention to it. The usual techniques are used. First he gives a vivid detail (the unharnessing of the horses), a brief sacrifice (significantly, it is rejected by the gods; 550–52), and a mention of the Trojans' thoughts and their watch fires. A simile stresses the brightness of the fires twinkling like stars through the clear air, and the happiness of the successful troops (559). Finally the fires and men sitting around them are mentioned again, and the scene closes with a last shot of the patient horses, returning to the first item of description (564–65; cf. 543–44). Beautiful as it is, the scene is not mere decoration, but climaxes the successes of the Trojans during Achilles' absence (while he fought they never dared to encamp outside the walls) and prepares for the embassy to him in the following book.

In the last scene mentioned above there are signs of a feature that occasionally occurs in a more obvious form: a gradual narrowing of focus, a "zoom" from a distant view of a scene to a closeup. Watch fires were first pictured twinkling in the distance, then we see the circles of men sitting around them, and finally there is a closeup view of the chomping horses. The finest example of this is the great cluster of similes that introduces the catalogue of ships (2.455–83), where with gradually increasing detail the advancing army is observed. First it is seen as a single blaze of gleaming bronze, then as a noisy flock of migrating birds, then as an innumerable swarm of flies about a milk pail; next, as the captains come more clearly into view, it looks like a great herd of goats divided up by shepherds; and finally, as the field narrows to the supreme commander of the host, Agamemnon is seen as a bull standing proudly over his herd of cattle. Similar, on a smaller scale, is the march out to battle at the end of Book 4 (422ff.), where the first view of the silently advancing waves of men gives way to the thoughts in their minds (expressed by personifications of Fear and Strife), then to the clash of weapons and the shouting of victors and vanquished, and finally to the individual duels.

One cannot resist seeing parallels between the pictures Homer draws and the techniques of modern filmmaking. Innumerable scenes, between the long shot of the burning pyres that represent the results of Apollo's plague (1.52) and the final receding view of Hector's tomb (24.804), inescapably suggest the modern analogy. Besides his eye for an evocative and often unusual simile, the poet must constantly have visualized both the small-scale and the large-scale pictures his words present.

Further Reading

There is a good account of most aspects in Andersson 1976 ch. 1; his second chapter deals with Virgil. Griffith 1985 prefaces his account of Virgil's description of Aeneas with an excellent paragraph on Homer (perhaps slightly overstressing Homeric effects). Camps 1980.17–21, 105–8 discusses descriptions of action and the facts of the topography; Bassett 1938.50–51 has a brief account. General battle descriptions are examined by Fenik 1968 in several places, especially pp. 19, 79, 177–80, 215–16, and by Latacz 1977.78ff. Among the many shorter passages in which Homer's use of his various descriptive techniques can be seen are 4.422ff., 11.47ff., 12.413ff., 15.592ff., 15.696ff., 16.632ff., 16.756ff.

Speeches, Soliloquies, and Characterization

"Homer deserves to be commended on many grounds, but mainly because he alone among the poets knew what his own role should be. The poet himself ought to say very little; for it is not by virtue of what he says himself, that he is an imitator. The other poets play a part themselves throughout their works and imitate only a little and rarely; but after a short introduction, Homer at once introduces a man or a woman or some character; and these are not characterless either, they all really do have characters." So Aristotle (*Poetics* 1460a, trans. Bambrough; quoted by Owen 1946.4).

Homer does not describe his characters (see p. 82), but lets them speak for themselves. The frequent and often lengthy speeches, besides allowing the character's feelings and motives to emerge, also serve as one of the commonest means of expanding and elaborating a scene and thus giving it the proper weight (see p. 4). In fact, about two-thirds of the *Iliad* and the *Odyssey* consists of direct speech, and the little we know of other ancient Greek epics supports Aristotle's statement that this ratio is unique. In other cultures, however, there are many examples of first-person presentation of oral heroic narratives (Finnegan 1977.116–17, 124).

Like Aristotle, Plato was interested in the difference between narrative and "imitation" (the direct speech of a character); such direct speech would be allowed in Plato's ideal state only under very strict limits, as it is fitting for a good citizen to "imitate" only good characters when they are behaving properly. In one passage (which Aristotle may have had in mind) Plato paraphrases the first scene of the *Iliad* as it would be without the dialogue (*Republic* 392d). Though he does not explicitly point it out, these first scenes provide a good example of the use of speeches for expansion and characterization; when Achilles describes to Thetis what has happened, he omits the direct speech of Agamemnon and the old priest Chryses and repeats (almost verbatim) only the narrative lines of the poet, which are sufficient to convey the essentials of the story (1.370–82; see p. 183). In the long scenes of massive importance in the epic, like the quarrel

in Book 1, the parting of Hector and Andromache in Book 6, the
embassy in Book 9, and the encounter of Achilles and Priam in
Book 24, the entire weight of the meaning is presented through
the words of the characters, and the poet recedes almost totally
into the background, permitting himself only the conventional
one-line introduction of the speaker without even an adverb
(such as the common "grimly") as a stage direction.

Speeches in Homer can easily be grouped into categories: examples are hortatory speeches persuading someone to a course
of action, prayers and supplications, laments, messages, and the
various kinds of battlefield oratory (especially exhortations,
challenges, vaunts, conferences, and rebukes). As in the case of
type-scenes, comparison of various examples of speeches within
each of these genres throws into relief the poet's methods and
intentions. The first section below makes such comparisons. In
the second section the special case of soliloquies will be examined, and finally some aspects of Homeric characterization
will be summarized. (The four books of the *Odyssey* that are in
the hero's direct speech have been discussed above [see p. 38], and
the paradigms that often occur in a dialogue will be treated
below [pp. 98–99].)

Speeches

Proficiency in public speaking is required of the Homeric warrior. The young Achilles must be taught to be a speaker in words
as well as a man of action (9.443), the assembly as well as the battlefield brings glory to heroes (*agorên . . . kudianeiran*, 1.490),
and Odysseus says the people look upon a good speaker as upon
a god (*Odyssey* 8.171–73). There is delight in listening to Nestor,
who is "fair-spoken, the clear orator, from whose mouth speech
flowed sweeter than honey" (1.248–49), and an interest in comparing different kinds of oratory (3.212–24).

Often the attempt at *persuasion* reveals a great deal of the
character of the speaker, for example in Hector's three encounters with the women who try to persuade him not to return
to the battlefield. Hecuba, like any proud mother, is worried
about how thirsty he must be after his exertions, and offers to
fetch him wine (6.254ff.); Helen, thinking as usual of herself,
speaks of what he is suffering for her sake and presses him to remain with her (6.343ff.); and Andromache reminds him of what
his death would mean to her and to their son (6.407ff.). Helen's
scornful speech to Paris urging him to challenge Menelaus

again—"No, don't; or he'll kill you!" (3.428ff.)—is close to a parody of the others.

The three major persuasive speeches in the *Iliad* are those of Odysseus, Phoenix, and Ajax in Book 9. They all have the same purpose—to persuade Achilles to a certain course of action—but they differ enormously in style and content. Odysseus's speech is a display of rhetoric: his delineation of the existing situation, smoothly introducing the name of the hated Agamemnon, includes a vivid word picture of Hector praying for the morrow to come and let him set fire to the Greek ships, and after a challenge to Achilles to come and face him, Odysseus goes on to a moving impersonation (the rhetorical figure *prosopopoeia*) of Achilles' old father sending him off to Troy with final words of wisdom. His polished eloquence makes Achilles feel sure he has something to hide (9.312–13). The speech of old Phoenix, the longest in the poem, is a complete contrast, consisting mainly of three successive paradigms (see pp. 98–99 and 224–29). The first, technically justifying his right to give advice, reminds Achilles of Phoenix's care for him since his childhood; the second presents advice in the form of personifications of Prayers and Disaster; and the third draws further advice from the tale of Meleager. Together the paradigms make up 85 percent of this speech, and represent a very simple, but very effective, type of persuasive oratory. Ajax's speech is comparatively short (though the longest the taciturn Greek ever makes; Hector once calls him "you tongue-tied, bull-headed Ajax," 13.824), but has the unique feature of beginning as an address to Odysseus, referring to Achilles as though he were not there (and in terms he might hesitate to use to him directly), and then switching to an emphatic "you" as he suddenly turns toward his host (9.636ff.). Achilles' own speeches in this book are masterpieces of theater and of character portrayal (see pp. 231–36).

Prayers to a deity, as might be expected, are a particularly formal kind of speech. They normally begin with an invocation of the deity by his titles, and go on to remind him of favors the suppliant has done for him or which he has done for the suppliant; for example, Chryses' "If ever I built you a temple . . ." (1.39ff.) and "If you ever heard my prayer before . . ." (1.453). Then comes the specific request, often including a reference to the deity's particular sphere of activity. Sometimes a promise of future sacrifice if the request is granted is included; for example the Trojan women offer Athena twelve oxen if she will stop Diomedes' attacks (6.308ff.). A special case occurs in Odysseus' resentful appeal to Athena, "Since you *didn't* help me in the past" (*Odyssey* 6.325ff.; see Lang 1975.313).

Supplications between equals have a similar shape: a formal address, a specific request, and an offer of some kind of recompense if the request is granted. The brief but important supplication by the priest Chryses to Agamemnon at the beginning of the poem is in the regular form, with an appeal to the gods preceding the request for the return of his daughter and the offer of ransom. Priam's concluding speech of supplication to Achilles also contains the normal elements, but because of the unusually powerful emotions of the situation, they are almost overwhelmed by the evocation of Priam's sorrows and those of Achilles' old father. Supplications on the battlefield are always denied in the *Iliad*, and often the most interesting element is the negative response of the person supplicated. Agamemnon's rejection of Adrestus's supplication to Menelaus shows his brutality, like his response to Chryses at the beginning of the poem (though with more excuse; 6.55ff.), and Achilles' magnificent reply to Lycaon is a moving acceptance of human mortality (21.74ff.). Among the divinities, Thetis's supplication to Zeus on behalf of Achilles is remarkable for the delay of the response, obviously intended to increase the contrast between the magnificence of Zeus's power and the god's fear of his wife (1.511ff.; see p. 185); and Hera is at first unsuccessful in her request to Sleep and is obliged to increase her offer until he can no longer refuse (14.267ff.), another means of expanding and enlivening the episode.

Lamentations are frequent in the later books of the *Iliad*, and the differences in the content movingly depict the different emotions of the speakers. Three people speak immediately after Hector's death (22.416ff.): Priam tells of his overwhelming desire to recover the corpse, in preparation for the ransoming in book 24; Hecuba laments the loss of the splendid son who was her pride; and Andromache speaks mainly of her son and Hector's. When the body is returned and the funeral lamentations begin (24.725ff.), Andromache again speaks of her son, and also of her own grief at being unable to be with her husband at his death, a poignant reminder of the love we saw between them at their parting in Book 6; Hecuba again shows her pride in the son she bore, handsome even in death; and Helen, from her usual self-centered viewpoint, tells of Hector's kindness to her. The repeated laments for Patroclus also differ considerably in content and effect.

A striking feature of Homeric speeches is the often verbatim repetition by a messenger of the *message* given to him to deliver. This both increases the importance of the message and assists the audience's comprehension by giving a duplicate prediction of what is to come. Occasionally the messenger is granted personality enough to modify the instructions; Dream adds a couple of verses telling Agamemnon not to forget what he has heard (2.33–34), and Iris delivers a message to Poseidon verbatim but (like a good secretary) demurs at his indignant response and is complimented for it when her superior recovers his equanimity (15.201–4).

Homeric heroes, though strong, are far from silent, and the battle scenes are full of their eloquence. The occasions for speeches fall into well-defined categories (see especially the index to Fenik 1968, and the summary of recent work in Latacz 1975). Amongst the commonest is the *parainesis*, the *exhortation* to battle, which is found some sixty-five times (so Latacz 1975.419), and is usually short (about six verses). The usual shape is a reproachful address, often in the form of one or more indignant rhetorical questions ("How long will you let your men be killed by the Greeks?" says Ares, 5.465), followed by a final call to action. But as always with Homer, each *parainesis* is different and most add significantly to the effect of their immediate surroundings.

A splendid example of a matching pair comes from Hector on one side and Ajax on the other, at the height of the Trojan drive to the Greek ships (15.486ff.; 502ff.). Hector assures his Trojans that Zeus is with them (*Gott mit uns*) and that death in battle for country, wife, and children is an honorable thing—a close equivalent to Horace's *dulce et decorum est pro patria mori*. Ajax in response asks the Greeks in colorful language if they are hoping to walk home to Greece if the ships are destroyed, and adds that Hector is not inviting them to dance, but to fight. Ajax has another good *parainesis* a little later (15.733ff.), in which he repeats that they are isolated in a foreign land with no city to take refuge in and concludes with the epigrammatic (but unformulaic) "*In your hands* is the light, not in lukewarmness in battle" (15.741).

Sometimes there is a topical reference. Achilles' exhortation to his long-inactive Myrmidons (16.200ff.) mentions that reproaches have been made against him for holding them back from the battle so long, and declares that the time for fighting has come at last; Patroclus's later encouragement (16.269ff.) with similar topicality calls on them to bring honor to Achilles after the insult he has received from Agamemnon. Similarly Menelaus, during the struggle over Patroclus's body, calls on the others to remember the gentleness and kindliness of the dead man (17.669ff.). Hector's speech to Glaucus and the other allied chiefs seems to express an unexpected resentment at their presence at Troy and the costs of maintaining them (17.220ff.), perhaps because of the many rebukes he receives in this and the former book.

The most individual of all the *paraineseis* is Sarpedon's famous speech to his friend Glaucus (12.310ff.), which examines the roots of honor and the reasons men should risk their lives in battle. Here above all it is what the *poet* wishes to say that matters, and his desire to impress the character of Sarpedon on our minds before his death at the hands of Patroclus, not any significance of the speech in its immediate context.

Other frequent occasions for battlefield speeches include the *challenge* before a duel begins, the most interesting example of which is Diomedes' lecture to Glaucus about not fighting against gods, after which the encounter is eventually aborted (6.123ff.; see pp. 201–6). There is no challenge before the fights between Patroclus and Sarpedon or Hector and Patroclus, but before the final duel between Hector and Achilles, Hector turns the challenge into an attempt to bargain for the return of the loser's body, which harks back to his duel with Ajax in Book 7 and forward to Achilles' maltreatment of his corpse. An unsuccessful attack is often followed by a scornful remark by the intended victim, the most important, of course, being Hector's exultant cry after Achilles' first spearcast has missed, especially moving because of its irony (22.279ff.). Another powerful speech of this type is Diomedes' biting insult to Paris after being wounded by him with an arrow, the coward's weapon (11.385ff.).

The victorious combatant often celebrates his triumph with a *vaunt*. Often this chest-thumping includes boasts about the speaker's eminent ancestors (for instance, 13.446ff.), or mockery of his defeated enemy, as when Idomeneus taunts his dead opponent Othryoneus, who joined the Trojan side in the hope of marrying Priam's daughter Cassandra, and is now offered one of Agamemnon's daughters instead if he will come and talk it over by the ships (13.374ff.). Diomedes has a short but remarkable vaunt over the wounded Aphrodite (5.348–52). Even the gentle Patroclus in the heat of the moment mockingly congratulates Hector's charioteer Cebriones, who has fallen headfirst from his chariot in death, on his skill in diving and suggests he take up oyster gathering (16.745ff.). Three other important vaunts, with a significance beyond the immediate context, are (1) that by Menelaus over Peisandros (13.620ff.), in which he blames first the Trojans for outrage to Zeus by abduction of his wife and possessions, then Zeus for supporting them now and prolonging their insatiable lust for battle; (2) a short but touching one by Achilles' man Automedon, who having killed the nonentity Aretos says, "Now indeed, just a little, for Patroclus' death / I have freed my heart from sorrow, though it was a poorer man I killed" (17.538–39); and (3) that of Hector over Patroclus (16.830ff.), in which he wildly misconceives Achilles' instructions in sending Patroclus to battle and shows his lack of judgment by suggesting he might be able to kill Achilles. It is a mark of the greatness of the poet that Achilles is given three successive vaunts over Hector, which sum up the themes of the latter part of the poem; the first celebrates his revenge for Patroclus's death, the second predicts his defiling of Hector's body and looks forward to the eventual ransom by denying the possibility of it, and the third acknowledges that his own death is now close at hand (22.331ff., 345ff.; 365ff.).

Conferences between leaders, *rebukes* by one leader to another, and *calls for help* are also common, and often act as part of the basic structure of the swaying fortunes of battle. They are not considered in detail here, but can be seen in the commentary on Book 13 (pp. 241–44).

Soliloquies

In some circumstances an important means of characterization for the major characters is the soliloquy. There are eleven of these in the *Iliad* and ten in the *Odyssey*, all but one introduced by a normal verb of speaking, indicating that they are thought of as uttered aloud rather than as simply the unspoken thoughts of the character; the exceptional instance is the account of Odysseus's thoughts as he is awakened by the cries of Nausicaa's maidens, where a spoken soliloquy in their hearing would be too unrealistic (*Odyssey* 6.119ff.). Soliloquies are found as a reaction to some observed occurrence, often a crisis, and fall into two groups: those that lead to a decision about what action should be taken, and those that simply arouse reflections in the observer. Both take us more deeply into the mind and motivation of the character.

The four soliloquies in which a decision is made occur in similar circumstances: a hero faces danger alone, deliberates on resistance or flight, is dignified by a simile, and escapes (though Hector's flight does not save him). All follow much the same pattern and use the same phrase to introduce the final decision ("But why do I think about all this?"), but reveal different motivation and character (see especially Fenik 1978). Odysseus, left alone amid the enemy, firmly states the heroic code that forbids retreat, and manages to hold his ground (11.404ff.). Menelaus, on the other hand, sensibly realizes it is foolish for him to oppose Hector while he has Zeus behind him, despite his reluctance to abandon the corpse of Patroclus, who died fighting in his cause, and he goes for reinforcements (17.91ff.). Agenor sees no rational hope of safety in flight and comforts himself with the thought that even Achilles is mortal; fortunately for him, Apollo intervenes (21.553ff.). Hector, whose soliloquy is the longest of the four and the most poignant, reflects on his own responsibility for the Trojans' disaster, considers the possibility of surrender, and at last decides ("falteringly," says Fenik 1978.85) that there is no alternative to standing his ground (22.99ff.; see p. 292). The form of the scenes and even of the speeches is similar, but the poet portrays realistically different emotions in the character who makes the decision.

Of the soliloquies not involving a decision, the most interesting is that of Achilles as he observes the approach of Antilochus (18.6ff.; see p. 270), and in a few lines thinks of the ominous flight of the Greeks, dreads bad news, recalls his mother's sinister prophecy, faces the fact that Patroclus must be dead, and yet remembers the careful instructions he gave for his safety. Hector's last words to himself as he realizes his death is at hand are similarly intimate and moving (22.297ff.; see p. 296). Two very reflective soliloquies by Zeus deepen the emotional tone of the battle for Patroclus's corpse (17.201ff.; 403ff.), and Achilles has three during his lonely battles with the Trojans (20.344ff., 425ff., 21.54ff.). In the *Odyssey*, four soliloquies in Book 6 present the hero's perplexity and fear during and after his shipwreck, and two others the angry planning and later satisfaction of his persecutor Poseidon; others depict the hero's perplexity as he wakes to hear Nausicaa's maidens (the unspoken one, 6.119ff.), finds himself deserted on the disguised Ithaca (13.200ff.), and lies sleepless as a beggar in his own palace wondering how to deal with the suitors (20.18ff.). Finally, a soliloquy gives Penelope's thoughts as she awakens after her beautification by Athena, before her appearance to the suitors and to Odysseus (18.201ff.). The poet uses the device of the soliloquy sparingly and at vital moments, and every instance has an important effect.

Characterization

"They [the characters] say what fits their situation and attitude, not what is objectively true" (Willcock 1978.17); nor is what they say necessarily what the poet himself believes. This must be emphasized, because sometimes a character's words about the gods, or fate, or *Atê* ("Blind Folly"), or love of violence, have been taken as the poet's view or that of his society as a whole (see p. 319). The characters are vividly human, and speak for themselves; and they are often delineated in ways we might not have expected to find. That the mighty commander-in-chief of the greatest legendary exploit of the Greek race should be a weak leader, insecure and the first to give up hope: that the unfaithful wife who caused all the suffering should be a remorseful and grief-stricken woman, as well as one who yields too easily to her passion for a man she despises: this seems unlikely to be a traditional portrayal, and is very probably due to the imagination of the poet. In fact, many of Homer's characterizations were not continued by later authors, especially that of Odysseus (see Stanford 1954). The most interesting aspects of the characterizations are mentioned in Part Two, and need not be repeated here.

The individual qualities of language and style in which characters express their views have not yet been studied in detail. One recent article, however, has compared the style and language of Achilles' speeches with those used by other men in his presence, and concluded that they show relatively more sustained and cumulative images, more abruptness and nonlinkage of sentences, more use of two emphatic particles (*ê* and *dê*), and a tendency to greater use both of formal titles and of vivid language of abuse (Friedrich and Redfield 1978). It is especially interesting that Achilles uses "but now . . ." (*nun de*) twenty-six times compared with the seven times it is used by others in his presence; the authors suggest that this "is consistent with his combination of imagination and realism; his mind goes out into a world of possibility, and then abruptly returns to the situation before him." (283). This is the feeling he expresses so strongly in his words "In equal honor are coward and brave man" (9.319). It is certain that in his outraged speeches against Agamemnon, Achilles uses a high proportion of short, often enjambing sentences, and his words to his mother, Thetis, after the news of

Patroclus's death are composed with superb skill (see p. 272).

Bassett insists (1938.78f.) that Hector uses especially picturesque language, referring to the "tunic of stone" he wishes Paris had put on (3.57), the "bowl of freedom" he hopes Troy will one day offer to the gods (6.528), the picture he paints of a young man and woman whispering together (22.127–28), and a few other examples. Generally, however, individual habits of speech are not easy to detect. But it is abundantly clear that the uniform dialect, the formulae, and the conventional forms of expression do not prevent the poet from presenting superb delineations of the emotions and motivations—the practical, self-restrained Diomedes, the likable but infuriating Paris, the jealous and malicious Hera, the innocently wily young Nausicaa, and the other immensely believable people of these old epics.

Further Reading

ON THE SPEECHES. Fenik 1968 identifies the various types of speeches occurring in the battle scenes (see his index); Latacz 1977 discusses the form, content, and function of *paraineseis* (exhortations) and gives a complete list (21ff., 246–50). Lang 1984 makes illuminating comparisons between the speeches in Homer and those in Herodotus. Lohmann 1970 analyzes the construction of speeches in a way I have not attempted to summarize.

ON SOLILOQUIES. Fenik 1978 is now the fundamental work; see also Scully 1984, Russo 1968, and Hentze 1904.

ON CHARACTERIZATION. Griffin 1980 ch. 2 gives a good account, closely tied to the texts of the poems. Bassett 1938.77–80 and Lattimore 1951.45–52 have good descriptions of the major characters. Beye 1974 is particularly good on female characters. Willcock 1978, in a sensible explanation of some apparent inconsistencies in the *Iliad*, points out that they often arise from the words of characters who say what fits their situation and attitude, not from the words of the poet. Stanford 1954 deals with the characterization of Odysseus down through the centuries.

Paradigms and Aphorisms

The commonest Homeric means of expanding a persuasive speech, in order to give the occasion the needed weight, is the use of a paradigm. In the narrow sense, a paradigm (the rhetorical *paradeigma*, in Latin *exemplum*) is an example of behavior, drawn from the past, that justifies a certain course of action. An excellent example is Diomedes' account of the fate that befell Lycurgus, the attacker of the god Dionysus, to justify his own refusal to fight with gods (6.130–40). Alternatively, advice or counsel may be supported by a briefer appeal to an aphorism: "Love your guest while he stays; when he will go, make no delays" says the hospitable Menelaus when young Telemachus wants to be off (*Odyssey* 15.74). As both are means of persuasion, it is natural that paradigms and aphorisms occur only in the direct speech of the characters, not in the voice of the poet (with one exception, mentioned below).

Paradigms, as Austin (1966) has pointed out, are used not only to encourage someone toward (or dissuade him from) a course of action, but also to justify the speaker's right to give advice ("hortatory" and "apologetic" [that is, defensive] paradigms, respectively). Nestor's many tales of his youthful exploits are the best examples of this, though it is possible that they are given by the poet at such length not only to emphasize his high status but partly for humor. Nestor sums up the purpose of the paradigm well at the conclusion of his first one: "When they took counsel they heeded me and were persuaded" (1.273–74). Diomedes similarly justifies his speaking in opposition to Agamemnon by telling at some length of his noble genealogy (14.110–27). The same tale served another purpose when Agamemnon himself related the exploits of Diomedes' father, Tydeus, in order to urge Diomedes to fight in the forefront (4.370–400). A very poignant example of a paradigm, which simultaneously justifies a claim to be heard and supports a proposed course of action, is Andromache's recital of her sad history and her total dependence on Hector, in an attempt to persuade him not to return to the battle (6.414ff.).

The tale told in a paradigm may have very considerable emotional effect, as well as giving amplification and affording a brief change of topic for the audience. In the great scene between Priam and Achilles, the pathos is deepened by Priam's description of old Peleus, alone and defenseless at home, but still gladdened by the hope of Achilles' eventual return, which we know will never come about (24.486ff.). Achilles' tale, a little later, of Niobe's acceptance of food despite her sorrow, is profoundly relevant to the killing of the many sons of Priam by the one son of Peleus (24.602ff.; see p. 311). This characteristic alteration of a conventional motif for a deeper purpose appears often. A superb example is the modification of what was probably a standard consolation motif from mythology, "*Even Heracles* died, dear as he was to Zeus." It is used once by Achilles (18.177ff.), then changed to the much more poignant "Death took *even Patroclus,* who was a much greater man than you," and then to the still more powerful "*Even for me* there is death and harsh fate" when he consoles the doomed young Lycaon (21.107ff.; see p. 140). Other changes made by the poet in the myths he uses are described on pp. 67–69.

Aphorisms are a feature of anyone's spoken language, and it is impossible to know in any particular case whether the poet is using the phraseology of a predecessor, shaping a traditional expression into his verse, or inventing both the idea and its phraseology. One expression in particular has a markedly proverbial or Hesiodic tone and may well be older than Homer: "A fool can see it, when it's done," says the angry Menelaus as he threatens to kill Euphorbus if he does not retreat (17.32), and Achilles repeats the threat to Aeneas (20.198). "Say 'Iron itself drives a man on,'" Odysseus says to Telemachus, telling him how to explain to the suitors why he is removing the weapons from the hall (*Odyssey* 16.294 = 19.13). Less epigrammatically, the angry Achilles piles up three end-stopped verses all saying "brave and cowardly die alike" (9.318–20). One suspects that Odysseus's striking four-verse metaphor likening harvest and fighting (19.221–24) may also have a proverbial foundation.

Naturally piety toward the gods often takes sententious form. "All men need the gods" says the well-brought-up young Peisistratus as he welcomes Telemachus to a sacrifice (*Odyssey* 3.48), and "Gods always like to be listened to," Menelaus says to him later on (*Odyssey* 4.353). "If a man obeys the gods, they listen to him," says Achilles in grudging assent to Athena's advice (1.218). Less concisely, the swineherd Eumaeus tells his unknown guest "The gods do not love a man's harsh actions, but rather honor justice and lawful deeds" (*Odyssey* 14.83–84). Particularly interesting are the words of Hector to Glaucus after the deaths of Sarpedon and Patroclus: "Zeus' will is always the stronger; / he terrifies even a brave man, and takes away his victory / easily, after he has himself urged him on to fight" (17.176–78). The same verses occur in the poet's own voice when he reflects on Patroclus's folly in pressing on the battle and thus bringing on his own death (16.688–90), but the manuscript authority for the second and third verses here is weak (they may have been copied from 17.177–78) and it is uncertain if the repetition is intended to be significant. This is the only instance I have noticed of an aphorism in the voice of the poet himself, although of course he often injects his own views into the narrative in other ways (see pp. 35–38). This is in contrast to the practice of Herodotus (see Lang 1984.65) and of the Icelandic sagas (see Andersson 1976.157).

Many of the aphorisms are simply homely wisdom, statements and warnings about the basic and unchanging facts of human existence. "Rebukes from princes are nasty" (*Odyssey* 17.189); "A king is the stronger when he is angry with a lesser man" (1.80); "It is the habit of kings to hate one man and favor another" (*Odyssey* 4.692); "Victory changes sides" (6.339); "Ares is on both sides, and kills the killer" (18.309). Some are contradictory: "Better to run from trouble than be caught by it" (14.81), but "A bold man is better for everything, even if he is a foreigner" (*Odyssey* 7.51–52). Some are pessimistic: "Few sons are like their fathers; most are worse, few better" (*Odyssey* 2.276–77). Some are merely sententious: "One man likes one thing, one another" (*Odyssey* 14.228); "It is hard for one to fend off many" (*Odyssey* 20.313). A few have a neat English equivalent: "God always brings like man to like" (*Odyssey* 17.218) is comfortingly like our "birds of a feather," and Kirk (1962.175) quotes 12.412: "With more men, the work goes better," which is close to "many hands make light work." Old Nestor once delivers himself of three memorable *dicta* in a row: "Art makes a better wood-cutter than strength; / art steers the helmsman's swift ship / over the sea, battered by the winds; / art makes driver defeat driver" (23.315–18).

Further Reading

ON PARADIGMS. Austin 1966 is now the basic statement of the types of paradigms and their use. Willcock 1964 studies the mythological content of paradigms. Pedrick 1983 examines Nestor's long speech in Book 11.

ON APHORISMS. Ahrens 1937 is the basic source. Russo 1983 gives a good account of the structure and content of ancient Greek proverbs. Kirk 1962.174–75 and M. L. West 1978.211 give some Homeric examples. Lang 1984.58–67 discusses the topic with special reference to Herodotus. Pellizer 1972 collects the Hesiodic examples.

Similes

Homer uses two kinds of simile. One is the short simile of two or three words: "like a god," "like a lion," "like a storm-wind," "like man-slaying Ares." These are common both in Homer and in some other kinds of epic poetry, and often they seem to be used with no more special effect than a standard epithet. They add emphasis, but usually little or no significant description.

Very different are the second kind, the long similes, which are almost unknown in other early epics. These presumably developed from the short simile, for one common type uses a short simile as jumping-off point. At 21.29 the Trojans are frightened "like fawns"; whereas at 4.243–45 the Greeks are said to be frightened "like fawns, / which weary of running over the wide plain / stand still, and there is no courage in their hearts." "Like a lion," which often occurs alone, is continued at 20.165–73 into a nine-verse picture of a wounded and furious beast attacking the hunters, at 5.137–42 into a description of the lion's slaughter of the sheep of a frightened shepherd, and at 17.133–36 into an account of the animal protecting his cubs against hunters. There are many other such cases.

Often, however, there is a different form of the long simile, which begins as a separate entity in a new verse; after the picture is completed, a final verse rounds off the simile and returns to the narrative. For instance: the Greeks march silently into battle, and "As the south wind spreads the mist on the mountain-peaks, / no friend to the shepherd, but better than night for the thief, / and one can see only a stone's-throw ahead, / so the dust arose in clouds under their feet as they marched" (3.10–14). Both these forms are usually self-contained, in the sense that they can be removed from the text without interrupting the continuity.

Though there are some two hundred of these long similes in the *Iliad* and about forty in the *Odyssey*, all but six in the *Iliad* and two in the *Odyssey* are unique in wording. This variety contrasts sharply with the repeated phraseology that often occurs in the commoner type-scenes, and with the usual verbatim repetition of a message. Besides being different in wording, a great number of them are unique in content, too, sometimes appearing to be drawn from something the poet has just seen or thought of. These indications of originality are confirmed by the language, which is often untraditional and closer than usual to the language Homer himself spoke. It is hard not to think that in these long similes one can see the personal eye and thought of the poet.

The world depicted in the similes is different from that of the heroic narrative. The time is the present, not the legendary past; the place is not the battlefield before Troy but the Greek home or countryside, occasionally recognizable as that of Ionia, not the Greek mainland (for example, at 2.460–61 waterfowl cluster "in the *Asian* meadow beside the river Caÿster," and at 9.5 the *west* wind comes from Thrace); the people are ordinary men and women, not heroes, kings and deities, and the way of life is familiar, everyday, and humble. Warriors attack not like gods or giants (with one exception, 13.298ff.), but like lions or wolves falling on a sheepfold, or (more humbly still) like wasps or persistent flies. A mass charge is like a windstorm, or the rolling sea, the picture sometimes including (like a Japanese painting) a tiny, powerless human figure (the moon, stars, and hills dwarf the shepherd, 8.555ff.). The setting is the universal one of hills, sea, stars, rivers, storms, fires, and wild animals, and against it the lives of shepherds, plowmen, woodcutters, craftsmen, harvesters, donkeys, oxen, housewives, mothers, and children go on as they always have. Once there is a powerful vision of the punishment of Zeus for mankind's wickedness (16.384–93), a conception strange to the heroic *Iliad* but much like that of the everyday Hesiod. In the rest of the *Iliad* bronze is the heroic metal, but in the world of the similes, the world the poet lived in, iron is familiar for felling trees (4.485) and the hardening of it in water is used as a comparison for the sizzling of the Cyclops's eye as the heated stake is thrust into it (*Odyssey* 9.393). Perhaps one of the reasons there are fewer similes in the *Odyssey* is that its setting is closer to this everyday life than that of the *Iliad* and similes afford less contrast.

The observant reader will find his own favorites among these vivid, homely pictures, gleaming out from the tragic narrative of the heroic past. Apollo, at the head of the Trojans, overturns the Greek rampart like a boy kicking over a sandcastle (15.362ff.); the hands of weaving and spinning women flutter like the leaves of a poplar tree (*Odyssey* 7.106); the weeping Patroclus looks imploringly at his leader, Achilles, like a little girl tugging at her mother's skirt and begging to be picked up (16.7ff.); the sleepless Odysseus twists and turns like a great sausage cooking over a fire (*Odyssey* 20.25ff.); Hera travels from Mount Ida to Olympus as swiftly as a much-traveled man recalls one place or another in his thoughts (15.80ff.); Iris plummets through the sea to visit Thetis like the lead sinker of a fisherman (24.80ff.); Athena brushes Pandarus's arrow away from Menelaus (4.130ff.) as easily as a mother brushes away a fly from her sleeping child (an ancient critic commented, "The mother indicates Athene's favor towards Menelaus, the fly suggests the ease with which it is swatted away and darts to another place, the child's sleep shows Menelaus being caught off guard and the weakness of the blow"; quoted by Richardson 1980.279); the Trojans plunge into the river to escape Achilles as locusts swarm into the air to escape a fire (21.12ff.); Euphorbus of the beautifully dressed hair falls to earth beneath Menelaus's spear like a carefully watered olive sapling that bears its pale blossoms and then is blown to the ground by a tempest (17.53ff.); Menelaus stands guard over the body of Patroclus as a mother cow stands over her first calf (17.4ff.); the battle is as evenly balanced as the scales a poor widow uses to weigh out the wool she spins to support her children (12.433ff.); Ajax leaps from ship to ship to defend them from the Trojan attack as a skilled rider jumps from one horse to another as they gallop (15.679ff.).

But Homer's art works at several different levels, and we miss much if we simply note the beauty of the little picture and pass on. Often there is a deeper poetic meaning beneath the surface, bringing added intensity or pathos to the narrative. Some of the most interesting examples follow, grouped according to features they share.

In many similes the obvious point of comparison overlies a deeper and more significant, unstated meaning. As Achilles charges toward Troy, Priam sees his divinely made armor glittering like the brightest of all stars, Orion's dog Sirius; but that star (the simile continues) brings great evil for mortals, and we know Achilles will do the same for Priam and Troy (22.26ff.). Odysseus weeps as he hears the tale of the wooden horse and the fall of Troy, and his weeping is said to be like that of a woman over the body of her husband, slain fighting for his city, as the victors drive her away to a life of slavery; Odysseus's grief is thus likened to that of a victim of his prowess (*Odyssey* 8.523ff.). Patroclus's immortal horses stand motionless in the midst of the battle, mourning their dead driver; their stillness is likened to that of a monument set over the tomb of a hero, which in fact they *are* at that moment (17.434ff.). After his battle with the sea, the naked, weary Odysseus, ignorant of where he is and totally alone, heaps leaves over himself for warmth as a man in the remote countryside preserves the spark of fire—or the spark of Odysseus's life. Achilles, returning to battle after the loss of Patroclus, is like a lion that at first ignores the hunters, but when wounded by one of them attacks them all in a fury—a neat summary of the present action (20.164ff.). The round dance of men and girls on the rim of Achilles' shield runs as lightly as a potter's wheel, and one thinks of the friezes of figures around a Geometric-style pot, which must have given the poet the idea of placing such a dance on Hephaestus's artifact (18.600ff.).

Eumaeus the swineherd welcomes Telemachus home as a father welcomes his only son when he (the father) returns from ten years in a distant country; of course the simile both suggests Eumaeus's surrogate fatherhood and foreshadows the coming reunion with Odysseus (*Odyssey* 16.17ff.). Immediately after the suitors depart to ambush Telemachus on his return voyage, Penelope wonders whether he will escape them, as a lion trapped by a crowd of men "in a treacherous circle" ponders in fear (*Odyssey* 4.791ff.). Perhaps the most evocative of all are the instances where the disguised Odysseus praises his wife Penelope to her face for being as famous as the good king who rules his country prosperously (*Odyssey* 19.109ff.), and where Penelope welcomes her husband as a shipwrecked voyager (which Odysseus was in Book 5) welcomes the sight of land (*Odyssey* 23.233ff.); in both cases the lives and identities of husband and wife seem to be intentionally intertwined, and in the latter the simile in fact first appears to be describing the joy of Odysseus rather than that of Penelope. Both have been lost at sea, both now sight land.

The poet may use a simile as one means of foreshadowing the future and so increasing the tension and emotion. In his first lament over Patroclus, Achilles is compared to a lion whose cubs have been stolen by a hunter and who sets off angrily in pursuit, as will Achilles himself (18.318ff.). The doomed Hector and the doomed Patroclus are both compared to a lion that turns at bay and refuses to run, and "it is his own courage which kills him" (12.41ff.; 16.752ff.). Sarpedon is likened to a hungry lion that attacks a well-defended sheepfold and "either seizes a sheep, or is himself wounded by a spear from a swift hand" (12.299ff.); one suspects that the poet already has in mind Zeus's dilemma whether to save his son or let him die beneath Patroclus's spear (16.431ff.). When Athena rouses Achilles to send his terrifying cry against the Trojans who are fighting round the body of Patroclus, two similes within a few verses tell of beleaguered cities, one sending up a blazing signal fire for help, the other hearing the trumpet call of its attackers (18.207ff., 219ff.). As the Trojans see the body of Hector dragging behind Achilles' chariot, a wailing arises as if all Troy were burning, which it soon will be now that their main champion is gone (22.410ff.); similarly Achilles inflicts upon the fleeing Trojans a sorrow like that which arises from a city burning because of the gods' anger, which again befits Troy (21.522ff.). Achilles mourns Patroclus as a father mourns his son, "who dying grieved his unhappy parents" (23.222–25), and one thinks of the grief of Priam and Hecuba for Hector and that of old Peleus for Achilles. On a lighter note, Nausicaa leads her maidens in the dance as Artemis leads the nymphs, and not many lines later Odysseus will ask her ingratiatingly if she *is* Artemis (*Odyssey* 6.102ff., 151ff.).

The picture developed in long similes often has its own action, which is sometimes carried through until its relevance to the point illustrated disappears. Hector charges at Achilles like an eagle that dives to carry off a lamb or hare; but unlike these helpless victims, Achilles charges in return (22.308ff.). Menelaus hunts for his friend and ally, Antilochus, as an eagle looks for a hare cowering in the undergrowth; but Antilochus is not cowering harelike, he is "encouraging his companions and urging them into the fighting" (17.674ff.). Achilles' Myrmidons, preparing to follow Patroclus into battle, are like wolves full of battle fury, but these wolves have just killed a stag and with full bellies are drinking at a spring, which hardly fits Achilles' battle-starved followers (16.156ff.).

In cases like these it has been thought that the poet has pursued the simile at the expense of the main narrative. This may sometimes be the case. But occasionally it seems that a simile that does not parallel the narrative intentionally develops a strong contrast with it, attracting the audience's attention by a kind of shock effect. In the longest of all the similes, a snowstorm picture is introduced for a comparison between the number of stones hurled at the Greek wall and the innumerable snowflakes that fall in a storm, but the simile passes on into a long description of a quiet snowy landscape, and the silence of the muffling snow contrasts sharply with the thundering din of the flying stones when we return to the narrative (12.278ff.; see

Damon 1961.262ff.). The Greeks stand fast, like clouds that hover motionless above mountaintops when the winds are asleep—but the Trojans are not asleep, they are vigorously pressing their attack (5.522ff.). There is a similar kind of shock effect in the reversal of roles when Priam enters Achilles' shelter and kisses the "murderous" hands of the hero, "like a disaster-stricken man who has *murdered* another man in his own country" (24.480ff.). In many other cases the poet seems to dwell on the peaceful aspects of his picture before returning to the savagery of the battlefield; but, since similes are a typical means of describing a general battle scene, it would be going too far to say that they occur primarily to give a relief from battle.

Sometimes the poet develops the picture within the simile and then turns some feature of it to good advantage when the narrative resumes; the independent life of the simile contributes a new idea to the vividness and color of the main tale. Agamemnon sees the Ajaxes and their "cloud" of troops as a goatherd watches a black storm cloud move over the sea before the wind, and a few lines later the blackness of the cloud is repeated in the description of the close ranks of soldiers (4.275ff.). The two Lapiths lead the attack on the Greek gates like two wild boars who tear up trees at the roots with a great *crashing* of their tusks; such was the *crashing* of the weapons hurled at the bronze breastplates of the two heroes (12.146–52). Ajax is immovable as a donkey in a cornfield, though the children *break many sticks* beating him; and then the narrative returns to the Trojans *stabbing vainly with their spears* against Ajax (11.555–65). Hector leads a Trojan charge like a huge boulder rolling down a rock face, thundering down through the forest, and finally stopping in the plain; a few lines later Hector's charge is stopped, too (13.137ff.). A second point of comparison may be brought out more fully than the first; Paris runs swiftly as a stallion that glories in its strength and beauty, and it is the beauty of Paris in his glittering armor that matters, not his speed (6.506ff.). A lion kills a deer's young and the mother dashes away in fear, and similarly Agamemnon kills two sons of Priam and the rest of the Trojans flee (11.113ff.). As men pursuing a stag or goat turn in flight when a lion suddenly appears, so the Greeks give up their pursuit when Hector is seen (15.271ff.).

Sometimes this close association of the simile with the narrative is taken even further, and an idea or action is developed in the simile and then transferred back to the main narrative, so that if the simile were to be removed there would be a break in

the thread of the narrative. These cases are a particularly interesting and sophisticated development in artistic technique.
The Trojans rush against the Greeks like dogs attacking a
wounded boar, but the boar turns on them and they scatter; so
the Trojans gave ground before the two Ajaxes (17.725ff.). In two
successive similes at 15.524ff., Hector charges the steadfast
Greeks as a storm wave falls upon a ship, and the hearts of the
seamen are frightened; so the Greeks are frightened. Then his
attack is compared to that of a lion on cattle under a nervous
herdsman, which stampede as he kills one of them; and so the
Greeks take to flight, except for the one Hector kills. Here the
whole weight of the narrative of the battle turning is carried by
the movement of the two similes. Diomedes charges like a
storm-swollen river that crumbles its banks and the vineyard
ditches; and so the Trojans broke before him (5.87ff.). The Trojans follow Aeneas as sheep follow the ram who leads them to
drink, and the shepherd's heart rejoices; so Aeneas' heart was
gladdened as he saw them follow him (13.492ff.).

Finally, there are two ways in which the actual language of a
simile merges with that of the narrative, forming an unusually
close bond. The ancient critics perceived this occasional exchange of terminology between narrative and simile, and it has
been the subject of a recent book (Silk 1974). When the contingents of Greeks coming to assembly are likened to swarms of
bees, the collective noun *ethnea*, "companies," is used both for
the bees and for the Greeks (2.87ff.). In a few cases a metaphor
cues a simile. A "cloud" of soldiers is compared to a storm cloud
over the sea (4.274ff.); Achilles' "brazen" voice blares out like a
trumpet (18.219ff.); a wave to which the Greeks troops are being
compared "helmets" (*korussetai*) itself into a crest (4.422ff.); and
Penelope's cheeks "melt" into tears like melting snow (*Odyssey*
19.205ff.).

The interconnection between simile and narrative can be so
close that it is impossible to be sure if what is being described
is a simile or a metamorphosis. Humans are often straightfor-
wardly compared to birds, especially the eagle; but sometimes
when a deity is so compared it is unclear whether the proper
translation should be "like a bird" or "as a bird." Poseidon, disguised as Calchas, reinvigorates the two Ajaxes, and then departs like a hawk pursuing another bird, and as he does this he
is recognized by his feet and so cannot actually be in bird shape.
But when Athena leaves Telemachus "like a soaring bird" (*Odyssey* 1.320), the meaning is not clear; not is it when she leaves

Nestor's palace "like a vulture," astonishing the beholders (*Odyssey* 3.372ff.). Athena descends to the Trojan plain with the speed of a meteor, but the spectators are as amazed as if they have actually *seen* such a portent (4.75ff.). Another time she comes like a rainbow, sent by Zeus as a sign of war or storm, but the phrasing "so, wrapping herself in a bright colorful cloud she mingled with the tribes of Greeks" (17.547ff.) suggests that she actually takes the form of the gloomy portent. Thetis, coming to visit the sorrowing Achilles, emerges from the sea like a mist from the gray water (1.359), and this too seems more than just a simile. It has been thought (for example by Bowra 1930.115) that these ambiguous, evocative cases were the origin of the simile; it could also be argued, on the other hand, that they are a very sophisticated artistic development of it.

What prompts the poet to introduce a simile? Ancient critics said that similes were used for amplification, vividness, clarity, and variety. A modern scholar (Coffey 1957) has summarized their functions as illustration of movement (especially mass movement), sudden appearance of a character or thing, noise, measurement of time, space and number, various narrative situations, and inward feelings. Fundamentally, a simile, like a detailed description of an artifact or of an artifact's history, is a technique of expansion, a means of creating a pause in the forward movement of the narrative. The action is held still for a moment and the focus of attention changed, and new thoughts or contrasting emotions can be added. For example, Hector's flight before Achilles (22.136ff.) is interrupted by a number of similes and also by the description of the washing pools where the Trojan women gathered together in the old days of peace. After these and the other expansions in that episode, our attention returns to the two heroes and we find them still racing over the plain, the situation unchanged, and so the long duration of the pursuit is brought out again and again. Similes regularly occur in passages describing general movements, where other elaborating techniques would be difficult to use, and to call attention to the sudden appearance of a new hero, who needs to catch our eye immediately. It is the presence of these techniques, not boredom of poet or audience, that accounts for the large number of similes in battle scenes.

Similes often occur in pairs, illustrating or contrasting complementary aspects of a scene. A famous example is the comparison of Ajax to a baffled lion for fury and courage, and to a donkey for obstinate resistance (11.545ff.). The poet is not afraid of overusing the technique; indeed, for very special emphasis, massed similes are used, to herald the display of forces and the beginning of the great catalogues in Book 2, to introduce the major and successful attack of Hector (15.592–637), and to describe the agonized struggle of the Greeks over the body of Patroclus (17.722–61). The effect is impressive and adds much to the visual color of the scenes as well as their emotional impact.

A long simile, by its very presence, shows that the poet wishes to attract notice to something; attention to its content adds much to the pleasure and involvement of the audience, filling in a good deal of the background of ordinary life that cannot otherwise appear in the heroic narrative. A close study of them makes possible an appreciation of the poet's eye for a striking scene and for a comparison, and also of his skill in welding the simile to the narrative and exploiting the possible interactions between the two. One may doubt if any predecessor developed the device so effectively; and few would claim that any successor has.

Further Reading

Fränkel 1921 is still the most detailed examination of the content of the similes. Coffey 1957 discusses their purposes and effects. W. C. Scott 1974 categorizes similes by content, type, and placement within the narrative. Moulton 1977 finds a building up of effect in sequences of similes (see also Moulton 1974). Damon 1961.261–71 has a good chapter on the kind of simile that seems to stray from the narrative. Mueller 1984 has a sound general chapter. Bowra 1930.114–28 has some good points, but a view that would now be thought rather superficial. Shipp 1972 finds linguistic lateness in the language of the similes.

13

Metaphors

Homeric language is full of metaphors. Many are obviously traditional and probably retain little effective meaning; a few are probably original coinages: and between these limits there are a host of others whose metaphorical force it is hard to assess. Doubtless the effect of a metaphor on members of Homer's first audiences varied, just as nowadays no group of people could agree which are the really "dead" metaphors in speech or literature. Much must therefore be left to the taste of the individual reader of the poems. Some of the commoner examples and commoner sources of metaphor are indicated here and a few of the most striking occurrences discussed.

Some of the commonest formulaic expressions in Homer include a metaphor, which may have retained little real meaning for poet and audience except perhaps an air of dignified archaism; "shepherd of the people," "winged words," "the barrier of the teeth," and the obscure "bridges of war" catch our attention because of their strangeness, but Homer's original audience would hardly have found them strange. Probably many of the metaphorical uses of "iron" and "bronze" (discussed below) were the standard fare of epic battles and had lost a good deal of their force. Perhaps that was also the case in the many instances of personification of a weapon, when a spear (for instance) "longs to glut its taste for men's flesh"; but since the same words for "eagerly" and "attacked, pressed on" are used both of men and of weapons (so Griffin 1980.34), something at least of the vividness of metaphor may have survived.

On the other hand, the "stone tunic" (stoning) that Hector says should have been Paris's fate (3.56–57) must have had a powerful impact; was it perhaps a picturesque popular expression in common speech, like "he ought to be strung up"? A little less vividly, Achilles calls Agamemnon, "You there dressed in shamelessness!" (1.149). Heracles "widowed" the streets of Troy (5.642), and the word retains its literal meaning elsewhere for a young wife whose husband has been killed. The earth "laughs" at the glitter of armed men (19.362), and there is certainly a striking effect, though the expression recurs in the *Hymn to Demeter* 14 (earth laughs at the marvelous flower) and the *Hymn to Apollo* 119 (earth laughs at the god's birth) and may well be traditional. Similarly, the sea "rejoices" at Poseidon's passage (13.29). These are perhaps personifications rather than metaphors; closer to metaphor is the "trumpeting" of heaven as the battle of the gods begins (21.388).

The variety of usages can be seen when some of the common sources of metaphor are grouped. "Iron" characterizes the strength (*menos*), mind (*thumos*) and heart (*êtor*) of many a warrior. It also describes the sky overhanging the wicked suitors (*Odyssey* 15.329, 17.565) and the fury of the fire that burns the victims slain at Patroclus's funeral (23.177). In a striking, surely self-conscious passage of battle description, the "iron" tumult rises to the "brazen" sky (17.424–25). The sky is also of bronze ("much-brazen," literally) in the midst of the battle (5.504), but since the same epithet is used when Telemachus arrives in peace to visit Nestor (*Odyssey* 3.2), it may not have any special military connotation.

Bronze, the invariable material for Homeric weapons, is one of the standard epithets for the war god Ares, and is (like iron) used for the hearts of fighting men and (more effectively) for the "bronze sleep" of a warrior killed by Agamemnon's sword (11.241; Virgil used this twice, translating it as "iron": *ferreus urguet / somnus; Aeneid* 10.745–46, 12.309–10). Bronze is the great voice of Achilles as it terrifies the Trojans (18.222), and before the mighty catalogue of the Greek troops the poet declares, "Not if I had ten tongues, ten mouths, an unbreakable voice, a *bronze* heart, could I tell" (2.489ff.). In one unusual passage, which one would think an original invention, it is used in a kind of double metonymy for both weapon and reaping hook: "Suddenly a satiety of battle comes upon men, / when most thickly the bronze has scattered the straw on the ground / and the harvest is smallest when Zeus has poised his balance" (19.221–24; see Combellack 1984). The same image of lines of reapers for battle lines is used in a simile at 11.67ff., but that passage has nothing of the compression and war-weariness of this.

A "cloud" of soldiers, mentioned both at 4.274 and 23.133, is in the former case followed by the simile of a storm cloud, which suggests the image is still alive; use of the cloud image for a flock of birds (17.755) shows that the ideas of number and similarity predominate. Ajax speaks of Hector as a "cloud" of war that covers everything (17.243). A dark cloud of grief covers Hector (17.591) and Achilles (18.22) at the news of the death of a beloved companion, and several times a dark cloud of death ends a man's life. Light and fire are the source of other occasional and effective metaphors.

Further Reading

Moulton 1979 is now the fullest treatment of Homeric metaphors. Milman Parry's fine article (A. Parry 1971.365–75) gives an account of the praise ancient writers gave to Homer's metaphors and his influence on English poetry, and shows that many of the Homeric examples must be traditional.

14

Symbolism

At the end of his long description of the shield Venus gives to Aeneas, on which Vulcan has depicted the triumphs and the glorious heroes of the future Romans and Octavian's victory over the fleet of Antony and Cleopatra, Virgil writes: "[Aeneas] marvels at these things on Vulcan's shield, his mother's gift, and knowing nothing of the events, rejoices in the pictures of them, raising upon his shoulder the fame and fated future of his descendants" (*Aeneid* 8.729–31). The symbolism here is effective and obviously intended by the poet. It is of two kinds; the object (the shield) represents the destined future greatness of Rome; and Aeneas's action in shouldering it symbolizes his willing acceptance of the burden of warfare that will make this future possible.

The same kinds of symbolism are often found in Homer, and Part Two draws attention to the major examples. Some are limited to a single scene: Hector's infant son squalls at the sight of his father's warrior helmet, and the doomed man lays it aside while he takes up the child and prays for a glorious future for him (6.466ff.; see p. 211). Achilles, wondering whether to kill Agamemnon there and then, half draws his sword, and thrusts it back into the sheath when he decides against such a rash act; a little later he dashes to the ground in disgust the staff held by the speaker in the assembly, the staff that symbolizes the civilized norms of behavior that have now fallen in ruins (1.188ff.; 245ff.: see pp. 180 and 181). Just before Patroclus's death, the helmet he is wearing, Achilles' own, made by a god, falls from his head and rolls in the dust, and the poet's own voice speaks of the event as a sign both of the disgrace his friend's death brings to Achilles and of the transient nature of Zeus' favor to Hector (see p. 264). In the *Odyssey*, just before the climactic recognition of Penelope and Odysseus (*Odyssey* 23.177ff.), she orders that their marriage bed be moved from their bedroom, to the fury of her husband, who knows that it secretly incorporates a living tree; and on a deeper level, there is the suggestion of violation of the marriage bond, and of the married couple's knowledge of the secret intimacies of physical union. On a more abstract level, the unbridgeable gulf between mankind and the gods is often driven home by the association of the mortal Achilles with his goddess mother, Thetis, and that of the lifeless Patroclus with the immortal horses he used to drive (see p. 139).

Such clear uses of symbolism suggest that the same technique should be recognized in the motif of Achilles' divinely made armor, which is important in many scenes in Books 16 to 22. The disguise of Patroclus in the armor given to Achilles by Peleus is hardly employed at all by the poet for any practical use (see p. 255), except that the loss of the armor when Patroclus is killed provides a convenient reason for Achilles' not entering battle immediately to seek vengeance, and of course leads up to the magnificent description of Hephaestus's making the new shield. But this divine armor was the gift of the gods to Achilles' human father, Peleus, at his marriage to the goddess Thetis, and by its very existence suggests the great gulf between mortals and immortals, not satisfactorily bridged by this shortlived and not very fruitful union; and Hephaestus's making the new armor in Book 18 is juxtaposed to Achilles' decision to seek vengeance even at the cost of his own death (see p. 269). So the old and new sets of armor constantly function as symbols of the contrast of mortals and gods, form a visible link between the deaths of Patroclus, Hector, and Achilles, and bring out the irony that the invulnerable armor cannot preserve the life of any of the three who wear it in the *Iliad* (see pp. 264 and 296).

When Patroclus puts on the armor, it identifies him as Achilles' surrogate in battle and in death (since Achilles will not die in the *Iliad*), and acts as a symbol of the concession Achilles is making to the Greeks. When Hector puts it on after it has been stripped from the dead Patroclus, his action shows arrogance and *hubris* (for Hector has no divine parent), and Zeus comments explicitly upon this: "Poor fool! death is not in your mind, / but it is close beside you; you put on the immortal armor / of a great man . . . / whose companion you have killed . . . / and his armor improperly from his head and shoulders / you have taken" (17.201–6).

At the final duel, the armor Hector wears is the visible sign not only that he killed Patroclus, but that Achilles himself sent him to battle wearing it; we feel that Achilles' guilt intensifies his longing for revenge. There is even more than this; for Achilles accepted that his killing Hector would bring his own death closer (see p. 273), and so when he sees Hector wearing the armor he recognizes as his own and kills him, he is symbolically (and to the eye of an observer) killing *himself*. The contrast between mortals and immortals is powerfully before our eyes, for both heroes in this final confrontation are wearing god-given armor, which did not save Patroclus in the past, does not save Hector now, and will not save Achilles in the future.

There is another different intensifying effect we should note, a kind of symbolic anticipation by which the foreground action casts a huge shadow of events to come. Hector's parting from his wife and son in Book 6 must be seen in the larger context of his later death at Achilles' hands, his wife's enslavement at the sack of Troy, and his son's murder by the victorious Greeks, all of which are directly or obliquely referred to in the scene. In his grief at the death of Patroclus, Achilles lies in the dust with his head in his mother's hands, and the tableau strongly suggests his own death and funeral (see p. 271). The renunciation by Achilles and the other heroes of the simple happiness of everyday life is suggested by the depiction on the shield not of heroic scenes but of the ordinary, familiar Greek existence. Perhaps this representation of human life through art by the smith god suggests the poet's own recreation of the human condition (see p. 285).

Further Reading

Wilson 1974 is good on the symbols of Achilles' mortality. J. T. Kakridis 1949 gives the first detailed account of the deeper meaning of the scene of Achilles' grief. P. J. Kakridis 1961 very perceptively draws attention to some of the symbolic significance of the exchange of armor.

15

Sound

Ancient Greek was a euphonious language, with a high proportion of vowels, less collocation of consonants than many languages, and no heavy stress accent. One Homeric line contains eighteen vowels and only nine consonants (*huiees huiônoi te biês Hêraklêeiês*, 2.666), and Hermes finds Calypso "singing in her lovely voice" (*aoidiaous' opi kâlêi, Odyssey* 5.61). Ancient critics were very interested in this aspect of literature, and praised the Homeric poems highly for artistic use of the sounds of the language. Their work on Homer has been conveniently collected and appraised by recent scholars, and the computer has made it possible to prepare accurate statistics on the usage of vowels and consonants, which have on the whole borne out the observations of the ancients (see Packard 1974).

Since most of these effects cannot be carried over in translation, only an outline of some of the instances of onomatopoeia, specially effective arrangements of vowels and consonants, and obvious rhythmic effects will be discussed here, to give an idea of the poet's skill. In the transliteration below, an accent (like ó) indicates the metrical stress in Greek; long vowels are indicated by the circumflex (like ô); the Greek *chi*, an aspirated *k*, is transliterated as *ch*.

Perhaps the best example of onomatopoeia is the very common and almost certainly traditional formula for the sea, *polúphloisbóio thalássês*, of which Ezra Pound wrote: "the turn of the wave and the scutter of receding pebbles. Years' work to get that. Best I have been able to do is cross cut in *Mauberly*, led up to: . . . *imaginary / Audition of the phantasmal sea-surge* which is totally different, and a different movement of the water, and inferior" (Paige 1951.364). In one case it is preceded by the splashing of *páphlazónta* (13.798). Water splashes again in the verbs *prosplázon* (12.285) and *kelarúzei* (21.261), and waves are heard breaking in *éklusthê de thalássa* (14.392) or crashing against a cliff in *kluzéskon* (23.61).

The lowing of cattle is a *múkêthmos* (18.575), goats can be heard bleating in their formula *mékades aíges*, and so too the Cyclops's uncomfortable unmilked ewes in the long *ês* of the

line *théleiái d' ememékon anémelktói peri sékous* (*Odyssey*
9.439). Perhaps the shrill voices of the girls playing ball with
Nausicaa are heard in the phrase *amphéluthe thélus aütê,*
"women's voices re-echo" (*Odyssey* 6.122). The Cyclops's eye siz-
zles (*síz', Odyssey* 9.394), a bow twangs (*língxe,* 4.125), a child re-
gurgitates (*apóbluzón,* 9.491). The noisy clangor of the word root
klanggê appears both in nouns and verbs, and the harsh cluster-
ing of consonants is particularly apparent in the phrase *tríchtha
te kái tetráchtha* "three times, four times," used once for the
shattering of a sword on a helmet (3.363) and once for the tearing
of a sail by the wind (*Odyssey* 9.71). There is a particularly noisy
passage for the din of the battle at 16.102–5, including four uses
of the root *ball-,* "hurl," and the expressive word *kanachê,*
"clanking."

Many verses are praised by ancient commentators for their
harmonious arrangement of vowels. Perhaps the most famous is
the description of a riverside meadow, *pár potamón keladónta,
pará rhodanón donakéa* (18.576), where the rhythm of the many
short syllables is also suggestive. The first words of Patroclus's
ghost to Achilles are full of the dipthong *eu,* perhaps imitating
a wail; *heúdeis, aútar emeío lelásmenos épleu, Achílleu* (23.69;
could *emeio* have been pronounced *emeu* here, compare *meu* in
the next verse, in spite of its being unmetrical?). With such
effects one may compare Virgil's verses describing Orpheus's sad
song, *té dulcís coniúnx tê sólo in lítore sécum | té veniénte dié
tê décêdénte canêbat* (*Georgics* 4.465–66), or Tennyson's own
favorite among his own verses, "The mellow ouzel fluted from
the elm."

The rhythm of the verse, the arrangement of short syllables
and word end, may be used for special effect. In antiquity this
verse describing galloping mules was much admired: *pólla d'
anánta katánta paránta te dóchmia t' élthon* (23.116), in which
the effect comes partly from the repeated -*anta* sound (the verse
has the highest number of *a*s in the poem), partly from the uninterrupted dactyls (two short syllables after every long one, with
word end between the first four pairs), and partly perhaps from
the six successive acute pitch accents (so Stanford 1976.220). A
similar effect can be seen in the phrase describing horses,
rhímpha pherón thoön hárma . . . (11.533, 17.458). (Virgil produces
much the same effect in order to imitate horses: *quádrupedánte
putrém sonitú quatit úngula cámpum* [*Aeneid* 8.596].)

On the other hand, when Achilles calls on the shade of Patroclus as the funeral pyre burns, the verse consists only of long

syllables: *psúchên kíklêskón Patróklêós deiloío* (23.221). Such verses are very rare in epic hexameters, but Terpander uses long syllables alone for a libation prayer (frag. 3) and Aristophanes for a solemn procession (*Frogs* 372–82), and it is clear that the Homeric verse has an intentionally solemn and religious effect. Rhythm and sound combine to produce effects much admired by ancients and moderns alike in the account of Sisyphus and his rock, which he rolls uphill to jarring juxtapositions of identical vowels, *láan anó ôthéske,* and which subsequently rolls back in swift dactyls, *aútis epeíta pedónde kulíndeto láas anaídês* (*Odyssey* 11.596, 598).

One other unique sound effect should be mentioned. When the terrible news of Patroclus's death is brought to Achilles, he lies groaning in the dust; his mother, Thetis, hears him from the sea depths, where she sits surrounded by the sea nymphs; and Homer tells us all their names, filling the following ten verses. The lines are musical, with many long vowels and repetitions of sound, and it has been suggested that the passage is included simply for the effect of lovely sound to cover the harshness of Achilles' grief. "It is just the relief and release of feeling that was needed; the strain of thought is for the moment completely lifted, and the mind finds rest and refreshment in sheer beauty that requires not the slightest effort to apprehend it" (Owen 1946.157). A translation of the lines by W. Arrowsmith is quoted in Part Two (p. 271).

Further Reading

The most detailed works on the sound of Greek are Stanford 1967 and 1976. Packard 1974 surveys the collocations of vowels and consonants in Homer, with accurate statistics. Richardson 1980.283–87 discusses the views of ancient scholars.

16

Word Play and Significant Names

Like any poet, Homer sometimes enjoys playing with words. A common occasion for this is the need to invent names for his characters, for he loves to give names to the host of warriors who appear only to be killed and even to otherwise undifferentiated individuals; for instance, the seven elders on the wall of Troy (3.146–48) and the nine sons of Priam who prepare the ransom wagon (24.249–51). And, in a fashion common to all poetry, in many verses word is matched against word in an artfully balanced construction.

The best-known and most elaborate play on a name, of course, occurs when Odysseus tricks the Cyclops by giving his name as "Nobody," so that the Cyclops' neighbors fail to help him when he complains that Nobody is killing him (*Odyssey* 9.408). The trick itself may not have been invented by Homer, though the evidence seems to show that in folk tales "Myself" is a much commoner version of the name than Nobody and neither is found in combination with the giant-blinding tale (see Page 1955.5–6). But not only has Homer exploited the pun to the full, he has added another, an exclusively Greek one. Odysseus gives his name as "Outis," repeating it immediately in the accusative case to make it sound like a real name, and the Cyclops repeats it once more (*Odyssey* 9.366, 369). This of course is the form he uses when he howls that Outis is killing him, and the others misapprehend it as *outis*, "nobody" (with acute accent instead of circumflex). But Greek has two negatives, *ou* and *mê*, and good grammar leads them to respond, "If *mê tis* [nobody] is harming you . . . " (410). The poet has prepared for this by having them use *mê tis* twice in their previous questions: "Surely nobody (*mê tis*) is driving off your sheep? Surely nobody . . . ?" (405–6).

Then a few lines later the poet drives home another joke, for Odysseus rejoices that he has fooled them by his name and his "superb *guile*" (414); and the Greek word for "guile" is again *mêtis*, with circumflex instead of acute accent but clearly intended as a further pun on the second form of "Nobody." The same word for "guile" is soon brought in again (422). The poor Cyclops's last words to his beloved ram are "all the evils which no-use Nobody [*outidanos Outis*] has brought upon me" (*Odyssey* 9.460). Even when he lies sleepless in his home, wondering how to overcome the suitors, Odysseus thinks again of the Cyclops and his own *mêtis* (*Odyssey* 20.20). The point is all the neater because Odysseus's standard adjective is "guileful," *poly-mêtis*.

Most Greek names have an obvious meaning, and meaning can be wrung even from the few where it is not immediately apparent; this meaning is often interpreted very seriously, as an omen of the person's position or fortune. Twice Homer emphasizes that Hector's son Astyanax, "lord of the city," is named for his father's prowess (6.402–3, 22.506–7), and twice Hector's own name seems to be punned upon as "holding" (that is, defending) the city and its womenfolk (5.472, 24.790). Agamemnon's daughters, Chrysothemis, Laodice, and Iphianassa, are named for kingly qualities ("Golden right," "Justice for the people," "Rule strongly"; of course they may not have been invented by Homer). In the *Iliad* many of the names of the insignificant characters who are to be killed on both sides are made up from place names, and others from the general qualities of soldiers. In a few lines Patroclus kills Tlepolemos ("War-enduring"), Ipheus ("Strong"), Euippos ("Well-horsed"), and Polymelos ("Sheep-owner"). A craftsman's father is named Harmonides, "son of Carpenter" (5.60). Agamemnon was given a horse by Echepolos, "Horse-owner" (23.296–99). The disguised Hermes has a little fun (and relieves the tension for a moment) by telling Priam he is the son of "Much-possessor" (instead of Zeus), and the joke was quietly anticipated when Priam told the elegant stranger he must come of "blessed" parents (24.397, 377). The melodious Nereid names that expand the scene of Achilles' grief (18.39–49) naturally describe aspects of the sea; Hesiod provides a much longer list (*Theogony* 243–62; the Homeric list is translated on p. 271).

This invention of names is carried further still in the *Odyssey*. Here in one extravagant tour de force, no less than thirteen young men of the sea-loving Phaeacians are given names ostentatiously connected with ships and the sea, one of them complete with genealogy ("Sea-girt the son of many-ships the son of Ship-wright," *Odyssey* 8.111–16). The queen to whom Odysseus makes his supplication is Arêtê, "She-who-must-be-implored," (*not* Aretê, "virtue"), the bard in his palace in Ithaca is Phemios Terpiadês, "Praiser, son of Delight," and there are many others.

There are instances closer to what we could term a pun,

though with a deeply meaningful rather than a frivolous connotation. Athena, worried about Odysseus, asks, "Why are you so
angry, Zeus (ôdusao Zeu)?" and the last two words sound much
like Odysseus's name (Odyssey 1.62; see also Dimock 1956). Only
Achilles can wield (pêlai) the spear of Pêleus, given him on
Mount Pêlion (16.141ff. = 19.388ff.). Peleus gave his armor to his
son Achilles as a prize of honor (gêras), but Achilles did not grow
old (egêra) in it (17.197). The dreams that emerge from the underworld through the gate of ivory (elephantos) deceive (elephairon-
tai), whereas those that come through the gate of horn (keraôn)
come true (krainousi) (Odyssey 19.563ff.). There is a kind of unspoken double pun in Patroclus's reproach to Achilles that the
hard-hearted hero is the son not of Peleus and the sea-goddess
Thetis, but of the precipitous rocks (compare Mount Pelion) and
the gray sea (16.33ff.). Less seriously, we find "Prothoös the swift"
(Prothoös thoös) (2.758); Tlêpolemos is watched by Odysseus's
tlêmôn ("enduring") spirit (5.668–70); and "Eupeithes / they obey
(Eupeithei / peithonto)" Odyssey 24.465–66). The syllable dus-,
"unhappy," can be prefixed to a word in another kind of word
play; Paris in Hector's insulting address becomes Dusparis (3.39,
13.769), Telemachus calls Penelope "Mother, my unhappy
mother" (mêter emê dusmêter, Odyssey 23.97), and the grieving
Thetis gives herself the striking compound dusaristotokeia,
"unhappy-hero-mother" (18.54).

The most striking example of skillfully matched word against
word is the twice-used couplet: "locking spear to spear, shield to
shield-face, / buckler to buckler pressed, helm to helm, man to
man" (13.130–31 = 16.215–16). This kind of construction occurs
also in Hesiod ("potter angers potter and craftsman, craftsman; /
beggar envies beggar and bard, bard"; Works and Days 25–26) and
may well be traditional. There is a similar pattern, again in an
unwarlike context, in the description of Alcinous's garden: "pear
on pear ripens, apple on apple, / grape-bunch on grape-bunch, fig
on fig" (Odyssey 7.120–21).

Slightly less contrived forms are found: "Arrange your men by
clans, by tribes, Agamemnon, / so that tribes tribes may assist,
clans clans" (2.362–63); "Foot-soldiers foot-soldiers killed as they
were driven to flee, / horsemen horsemen" (11.150–51). This kind
of thing is also found in the martial songs of Tyrtaeus (11.31–33
West), in Ennius (premitur pede pes atque armis arma teruntur;
frag. 584 Skutsch), and with less ostentation (as would be expected) in Virgil: haud aliter Troianae acies aciesque Latinae /
concurrunt; haeret pede pes densusque viro vir (Aeneid 10.360–

61). Not surprisingly, it also turns up in erotic poetry. Archilochus, perhaps a century after Homer, sang "to throw belly on belly, thighs on thighs" (frag. 119 West; see O. Murray 1980.127), and a later poet picks up the idea: "chest leaning on chest, breast on breast, lips pressing on sweet lips" (Marcus Argentarius, *Greek Anthology* V.128 = Loeb vol. I. p. 188).

One further kind of balancing of words may be mentioned — switching from active to passive in the various expressions meaning "kill or be killed." The most complex instance, a double one, is found as Hector vows to fight Achilles himself if need be; "I will stand, to see if he wins great glory, or if I win it [*ê ke pherêisi . . . ê ke pheroimên*]; / Ares is with both, and has killed the killer [*ktaneonta katekta*]" (18.308–9). There are many other examples, using different verbs, though Sarpedon's famous discourse on this theme ends pithily but without actual wordplay (12.328).

There are many instances in Homer of the careful juxtaposing of words that an inflected language makes possible. "Ill-fated he, evil-fated me [*dusmoros ainomoron*]," says Andromache of her father and herself in her lament (22.481). *Megas megalôsti*, "mightily in his might" is reserved for fallen heroes on special occasions: for Hector's charioteer, killed by Patroclus immediately before Patroclus's own death (16.776), for Achilles in the first shock of grief (18.26; see p. 270), and again for him after his own death (*Odyssey* 24.40). There are four verses in Homer made up of only three long words, and twice virtuosity is shown by filling the second half of the verse with a single hyper-polysyllabic word (*duôkaieikosipêchu*, "twenty-two cubits long"; 15.678, cf. 23.264). Homer may well have been composing without the aid of writing, but that did not prevent the careful construction and memorization of especially neat expressions.

Further Reading

ON WORD PLAY. Stanford 1939 ch. 7 is the basic source; most recently see Haywood 1983 and his references. Durante 1976.147–54 deals with some kinds of verbal repetition and paronomasia.

ON SIGNIFICANT NAMES. Hoekstra 1981.57–66 examines them closely and concludes that some go back to a period earlier than Homer. Stanford 1965 comments on many of them (see his index under this rubric); Clarke 1981.64ff. has a brief account. Beye 1964 has a detailed treatment of the names of heroes who fight and die in the battles of the *Iliad*. Seymour 1981.15–16 lists examples of parechesis, onomatopoeia, and plays on proper names.

Gods, Fate, and Mortality

No subject is so full of contradictions and inconsistencies as the subject of religion. To discuss "the religion of Homer" leads immediately to insoluble questions: Does "Homer" mean an individual who composed the poems, or an average Greek of the eighth century B.C.? Can one speak of the religion of an "average Greek" any more than an "average American"? What is meant by "religion"—the nature of the divinities who appear and act in the poems, the cult practices represented, the beliefs of the characters, the religious purpose of the poet, the myths invented by a creative folk? How can divine power and perhaps foreknowledge be reconciled with the power of fate and with human responsibility for individual actions? What is the association (if any) between religion and morality? Individual modern readers are likely to have very different answers; in fact, often we do not even identify the question clearly.

Nor can logical answers to questions like these be expected, then or now. A recent program announcement for a TV movie on the passion of Christ declared, "Meanwhile, aware of the danger he faces, Jesus prepares for his appointed destiny." Probably few who read this were perplexed at the confusion of thought between "appointed destiny," divine foreknowledge, and the freedom of choice that Jesus (as God, man, or both) might well be thought to possess. Should Greek epics be expected to be any more logical than this?

In Homer, Hesiod, and the early *Homeric Hymns*, the functions, genealogy, and family arrangements of the gods and the heroes descended from them are already stabilized and consistent. Minor discrepancies are not hard to explain; for instance, Hephaestus is married to Aphrodite in Demodocus's song in *Odyssey* 8 but to Charis, "Grace," in *Iliad* 18, probably because Aphrodite's well-known pro-Trojan bias would complicate Thetis's reception and making the new armor for Achilles. This is a considerable achievement and, in the absence of a priestly caste in Greece, must be attributed to the bards, to the pan-Hellenic festivals, and to close associations between Greek cities both on the mainland and in Ionia.

The development of a standardized poetic language (see p. 42–44) is probably a good parallel. Bardic tradition also developed different genres of poetry, such as epic, hymns, catalogue poetry or genealogies, cosmogonies, and so on, and it is likely that the attitude toward the gods may have been different in the different genres. In the poetry that survives, considerable differences exist. The *Odyssey* attributes to the gods a care for just men and women and (in the case of Athena) a comforting readiness to assist their favorites; the *Hymns*, together with the song of Ares and Aphrodite in *Odyssey* 8 and the "Beguiling of Zeus" in *Iliad* 14, present intensely human divinities whose adventures are entertaining, undignified, and often comic; Hesiod's *Theogony* and *Works and Days* give them authority and concern for morality among men but little personality (except perhaps in the Prometheus tale, which may derive from a *Hymn*); and the *Iliad* presents a complex and possibly unique picture, which will be discussed in detail below.

Our purpose here is not to give an account of early Greek religion, or of the significance of Greek myth, but to attempt to assist appreciation of the Homeric epics. The following discussion, then, will deal primarily with two questions: What common human religious needs do the gods of the epics fill for the human characters? In what ways does the poet use his "divine machinery" as a compositional device, as a convenient means (usually denied to a modern novelist) of assisting the telling of his tale and of producing desired effects? A final section will deal with the ever-present contrast of human mortality and the carefree eternity of the gods. Where necessary, differences between the *Iliad* and the *Odyssey* will be indicated.

The Gods as the Religion of the Characters

For the characters in the poems, the gods are omnipresent, always observing mankind's actions, their power as real as the government's is to us—and even more important. The roles they play may be divided for convenience into a number of categories, though these are of course artificial and may overlap.

1. They function as a higher power, and provide an explanation of otherwise inexplicable events. These include natural phenomena: Zeus sends the thunder (7.478–79) and the mountains tremble in earthquake under Poseidon's feet (13.18–19, 20.57–58). Their sheer size is awe-inspiring; Olympus shakes when Zeus nods his head, when Ares is wounded by Diomedes he yells like

ten thousand men (6.860) and when knocked down by Athena he covers seven acres (21.407), Poseidon's war cry is like that of nine or ten thousand men (14.148–49), and as the gods all advance to war Hades fears the earth may break open beneath them (20.61ff.). Since there is no accident or random chance (see below, part 4) every unusual occurrence is attributed to them, from a fighter's sudden feeling of strength (17.210–11), to Hector's lopping off the head of Ajax's spear (16.119–20), and even to Odysseus's forgetting his cloak (*Odyssey* 14.488–89).

They act as patrons of crafts and technology (Hephaestus, Athena), and personify certain abstractions, such as warfare (Ares) and sex (Aphrodite; see pp. 143–47). Zeus, king of the gods, personifies authority, and human authority figures like Agamemnon are under his protection (1.278–79, 2.101ff.). They wield power in a certain sphere, but usually the Greek love of anthropomorphism does not envision them in the *form* of that power; Sleep is not at all drowsy but is interested in women like any other male god (14.231ff., see p. 249), and the winds feast and ogle Iris like any obstreperous gang (23.200ff.); but Hephaestus boils the waters of the river as a fire would (21.343ff.), and the river god Scamander sometimes seems incarnate in his watery element (21.211ff.).

As the superiors of humans, they provide an object for human tribute and awe, and serve as the recipients of the sacrifices mankind feels obligated to make to some higher power. Human piety consists of the plentiful provision of these sacrifices, and Hector and Odysseus are specifically honored for this by the words of Zeus: "My heart is grieved for Hector, who has burned the thighs of many oxen for me" (22.169–70 and, at greater length, 24.66–70; *Odyssey* 1.66–67).

2. In return for human tribute, the gods are a potential source of help in trouble, the objects of prayers either to obtain something (strength, success, helpful action on one's behalf) or to avert something (the plague, the mist over the battlefield). Particularly noteworthy are the detailed accounts of the prayer of the Trojan women to Athena and that of Achilles to Zeus (6.269ff., 16.220ff.; see pp. 207 and 260). Approach to the gods, both by words and by sacrifices and gifts, is normally direct, not through the intermediacy of a priest. Very often a prayer includes a reason why the request should be granted, or an account of its purpose. On one occasion Glaucus states explicitly that a god can hear a prayer wherever he happens to be at the moment, a neat accommodation of the necessity of their presence at their

cult centers to the fiction of their active participation in the Trojan War (16.514–16).

3. Guidance about the future can be obtained from the gods by means of omens, dreams, and oracles. The longed-for security of a destined future, however, is provided for the Greeks not by the Olympians but by fate (usually *moira* or *aisa*, both probably meaning "portion"). Fate is hardly ever personified in Homer and is given no genealogy. In the *Iliad* its power is shown primarily in the determination of the length of a man's life; the day of his death is set at the time of his birth (20.127–28, 23.79, 24.209–10). Even divine foreknowledge usually means only foreknowledge of a man's death. The decrees of fate cannot be swayed by prayers, as can the much more human gods, and *moira* often takes the place of a grim god of Death. A warrior like Hector, however, like all soldiers facing the uncertainties of battle, derives comfort from a fatalistic outlook (6.487–89; see p. 212). Fate does not affect his actions or the good and evil sent by the gods. Agamemnon's coupling of fate with Zeus and the Fury as jointly responsible for his unwise behavior [19.87] is exceptional, and may be due to the association of fate with men's deaths.

In the *Odyssey* the characters attribute a wider power to fate. It is said to be fated that Odysseus and Menelaus shall reach home again (*Odyssey* 5.114–15 and elsewhere; *Odyssey* 4.475–80), that Troy should fall (*Odyssey* 8.511), even that Odysseus should escape from his trials to sanctuary among the Phaeacians (*Odyssey* 5.288–89). This more benign attitude of fate is in harmony with the generally more optimistic tone of the poem. In both poems the expression "beyond fate" is sometimes used; see below (p. 136).

Accident and "luck," in our sense of random chance (the "Russian Roulette" of the movie *The Deer Hunter*), are unknown in Homer. This absence is characteristic of early Greek thinking, for random chance appears almost nowhere before the philosophy of Epicurus; the only significant mention is in the words of Sophocles' Jocasta as she proclaims the falsity of oracles ("Best live at random, as well as one can!" *Oedipus Rex* 978), and the error of her thinking is overwhelmingly apparent to the audience. It must not be forgotten that the tale is being told by a poet who knows what the future has in store for its characters, either because he is following tradition or because he has himself created character or plot; and he obtains emotional effects by revealing the future to the audience, and sometimes to the characters, before it comes about. In addition, it is natural for him to fulfill the audience's universal desire to find reason, not random chance, behind the chaos of human experience. Both these inducements may produce a heavier emphasis on fate in the poems than was normal in the poet's society.

4. The gods provide the characters with a source of good and evil beyond human comprehension. The most explicit depiction of this appears at the final emotional climax of the *Iliad*, in Achilles' description of the two jars from which Zeus gives either mingled good and evil or evil alone (24.527ff.), without any reference to his motives in the distribution. Achilles has said previously that the quarrel between him and Agamemnon came about because Zeus wished death to come upon many of the Greeks (19.273–74), though the poet did not suggest this in Book I. Even more frightening to a thoughtful audience would be the conversation between Zeus and Hera at the conclusion of the theme of Achilles' withdrawal (18.356–67), where all the suffering of the Trojans, past and future, is attributed to the personal spite of the mean-spirited Hera. Before the battle really begins there is a prelude (4.30–67) in which Zeus speaks of his love for Troy and Hera offers to sacrifice her own favorite cities in return for Troy's destruction; the traditional reasons for her hatred—the judgment of Paris and Zeus's love for the Trojan boy Ganymede (given by Virgil, *Aeneid* 1.25–28)—are left unmentioned, perhaps to make her anger—and thus the causes of man's suffering—seem even more irrational.

For the human characters in the *Iliad*, irrational evil comes from the gods; for the poet, who presents to us what is in the minds of the gods, human troubles are not irrational but all too easy to comprehend if one believes in gods like these. But there is, of course, a difference between religion and artistic creation.

The same idea that evil and good come from the gods occurs in the *Odyssey*, but the tone there is rather different. Though the gods bring upon a man good days and bad, this is said in the context of man's misconduct, and Odysseus explains the troubles that came upon him as caused by his own violence and folly and predicts that disaster will come to the suitors because of their own similar behavior (*Odyssey* 18.130–50). In fact, the gods themselves walk the earth to see which men are good and which are not (*Odyssey* 17.485–87). Indeed Nausicaa tells the naked vagabond, Odysseus (*Odyssey* 6.187–90), that good fortune and bad come to a man from Zeus, and he must endure it, much as Achilles said to Priam in *Iliad* 24; but this may be attributed (such is the poet's care in psychological depiction in this scene) to her courtesy, for it is neither tactful nor consoling to tell one obviously afflicted by the gods that he must have done something to deserve it. Helen, too, in order to remove blame for human suffering from the present company, says lightly that Zeus gives out good or evil as he wishes (*Odyssey* 4.236–37). But at the conclusion of this poem, as old Laertes proclaims when he recognizes his long-lost son, the gods are not dead but obviously taking good care of human affairs, since the suitors have paid for their misdeeds (*Odyssey* 24.351–52).

5. The gods are the source of specific gifts to certain individuals. The most detailed statement of this is Odysseus's lecture to the ill-mannered Phaeacian Euryalus, who has been given good looks but not the graces of speech (*Odyssey* 8.167–77). In the *Iliad*, another dignified enunciation of the principle is put in the mouth of Polydamas, who claims greater wisdom than Hector, though the latter is better at warfare (13.729–34). The idea is very much a commonplace; to the gods' gift are attributed the size, strength, and good sense of Ajax (7.288–89), the prophetic power of Calchas (1.72), the technical skill of the craftsman Phereclus (5.61), the inspiration of the poet (*Odyssey* 22.347), and many more distinctions.

Often a different angle is given by emphasizing that the gifts cannot be refused, as does Paris when Hector reproaches him for his sex appeal (3.65ff.); Nestor speaks of the gift first of youth, then the unwelcome one of old age (4.320–21); and Agamemnon jealously declares that since Achilles' strength comes from the gods, it does him no personal credit (1.178). Later poets repeat the idea that the gods' gifts are inescapable (Solon 13.64 West, Theognis 133–34, 1189–90). For the heroes of the epics, any successful shot, any victory in a race is due to the favor of a deity, usually that of an unspecified *daimôn*, for mortals cannot always know which god is helping them or their enemies.

Forces that we would consider psychological may also be attributed to an external and divine power. Aphrodite, the goddess of sexual desire, is the clearest example; when she afflicts men or women, they may act in total disregard of their better judgment and their own best interests. Less familiar to us, at least by name, is *Atê* ("Ruin," "Delusion," "Blind Folly"), the daughter of Zeus, of whom Agamemnon gives a full account (19.91–136). She it is who makes one do something foolish, counterproductive, against one's best interests, something which afterward cannot be understood as the choice of the individual and which is therefore attributed to an external power (see pp. 145–46).

6. The gods preside over certain standards of social behavior, rewarding those who observe them and punishing those who do not. Usually this is done not from ethical principles but because of some infringement on an agreement or relationship under the god's protection. Apollo in *Iliad* 1 avenges the insult to his priest, and so to his own honor. Helios insists on punishment for those who have killed his cows (*Odyssey* 12.376ff.). And Zeus can be relied upon to avenge the breaking of the oath sworn in his name (3.276ff., 4.160ff.), Paris's outrage to him as god of guest and host (3.351–54, 13.620–27), and any wrong done to stranger or suppliant (*Odyssey* 9.269–71); heralds, and beggars too, are dear to him (8.517; *Odyssey* 14.57–58). The gods also disapprove of Achilles' unrelenting rage against Hector even after he has killed him to avenge Patroclus's death; mortals are supposed to endure the deaths of those they love, and Achilles' fury verges on a challenge to the gods (24.46ff.). But only in one place in the *Iliad*, and in the untraditional circumstances of a simile, is Zeus said to be angered by the wrongdoing of men and to punish them with natural disasters (16.384–93).

In the *Odyssey*, however, the gods are much more concerned with morality, and they wander in disguise over the earth, watching men's conduct (*Odyssey* 17.485ff., 7.199–206). A man's sufferings are partly the result of his misdeeds, not simply the will of the gods. This is stated firmly in the proem of the poem, where Odysseus's companions are said to lose their day of homecoming because of their own wickedness in eating the cattle of the Sun (1.7–9). A little later, Zeus makes an almost explicit refutation of Achilles' account of the jars of good and evil as he carefully clarifies the theodicy for the present audience, using the example of Aegisthus (1.32–43). Aegisthus, he says, was *warned* not to do wrong, but nevertheless seduced Agamemnon's wife and killed him on his return home, and so he suffered for his wickedness "beyond fate," that is, in addition to any sufferings fate ("fate" as in the *Odyssey*, see part 3 above) or the gods might have sent upon him. Similarly, before the punishment of the suitors they are warned many times that their behavior will lead to trouble: by the omen of Zeus (2.146ff.), by Telemachus's threats of Zeus's punishment (1.378ff., 2.143ff.), by the disguised Odysseus (18.125ff.), and by the frightful vision of Theoclymenus (20.350ff.).

The poet's point is not so much that the gods are kind enough to warn mankind; he is presenting the beginning of the idea that men are responsible for their own misfortunes, that their

troubles arise because they *knowingly* do wrong, a view that is
eloquently proclaimed a century or so later by Solon the Athenian (4 West). The gods of the *Odyssey* are beginning to support
the indignation we all feel at willful and successful wrongdoing,
and to satisfy our sense of justice by punishing it; they do not
irresponsibly (or even inscrutably) dispense good and evil as in
the harsher world of the *Iliad*.

7. The gods are thus in many ways an upward projection of
(and justification for) the human social hierarchy, exercising a
power that often seems, to the lower orders, more or less arbitrary. They do not present an ideal for human conduct, as Jesus
did; instead, they adopt the privileges of the powerful and trans-
gress many of the standards they expect their inferiors to follow.
Only as patrons of seers, craftsmen, and others, and as suppor-
ters of courage and cleverness, do they represent objects of imitation or admiration. On the other hand, they do not yet suffer
from jealousy of human achievements, from *phthonos*, as the
gods do later in Greek thought; the divine jealousy of which
Calypso complains is merely that of male sexuality (*Odyssey*
5.118ff.). Herodotus insists in one example after another that the
gods delight to bring low any human who rises to preeminence,
just as he also stresses jealousy among men themselves (7.236.1).
But there is no hint in Homer that the gods cause suffering to
Achilles, or bring about his early death, merely because of his
superhuman greatness.

The Gods as a Compositional Device

In a work of fiction the gods and Fate are as much in the power
of the poet as are the characters; it is he who determines their
actions, their motivations, and probably to some extent their
powers. We can never know what is traditional, what is drawn
from common belief of the poet's own time, and what is essentially his own contribution. But by identifiying certain areas that
clearly belong to creative imagination rather than to the facts of
the religious belief of a historical society, we can avoid some
misapprehensions.

1. In the *Iliad* most of the gods who appear, with the exception
of Zeus, are either pro-Greek or pro-Trojan. For our benefit, and
in proper epic style, Homer gives a catalogue of the gods arrayed
on each side as they go to war after Achilles has returned to
battle (20.31–40). On the Greek side are Hera, Athena, Poseidon,
Hermes, Thetis, Hephaestus; for the Trojans, Apollo, Artemis,

Aphrodite, Ares, Leto, and of course the local river god Xanthus. It is remarkable that at such an early period in Greek history their gods are already the universal gods of the world, and it seems likely that this is the result of the long existence of the epic tradition before Homer. Conflicts between gods were known in Greek myth, and representations of the mighty battles of the Olympians against the Giants and the Titans were popular in epic and art. But all the Olympians are subject to Zeus, and though his power has been threatened by other superhuman powers in the past, by the time of the Trojan War all human affairs, Greek and Trojan alike, are under his sway.

The fact that both the warring nations worship the same universal gods makes it easier for the poet to portray the human qualities of Greeks and Trojans. It is hard to imagine the *Iliad* being so great a poem if the Trojans (like the Saracens in *Roland*) worshipped barbaric gods; Virgil was aware of the dehumanizing effect of such gods when he pictured the animal-headed deities of Egypt backing Cleopatra on the shield of Aeneas (*Aeneid* 8.698–700). Occasionally a reference to mythology is given as a reason for the divine lineup. The judgment of Paris explains the hatred of Hera and Athena for the Trojans, and Aphrodite's favor toward them (24.25–30); the ill treatment of Poseidon and Apollo by the former Trojan king Laomedon accounts for Poseidon's hostility toward the Trojan people (21.441–57). The poet even draws attention to the oddity of the support given to the Trojans by these Greek gods, when Athena tells Ares that his mother, Hera, is cross with him for deserting the Greeks (21.412–14), and above all when Poseidon roundly condemns the aid given to the Trojans by Apollo, the god of Delphi, Delos, and much of Greek national identity and culture (21.441–60). It may well be that the epic tradition has preserved a reflection of the origin of Apollo in Asia Minor, not fully understood by Homer.

In the *Odyssey* the situation is, as usual, rather simpler. No god supports the wicked suitors, and the hostility of Poseidon toward Odysseus is explicitly accounted for, at the beginning of the poem, by the tale of the hero's injury to the god's son Polyphemus (*Odyssey* 1.68–75). Zeus and Athena support him because he provides the gods with many sacrifices and because they admire his intelligence (*Odyssey* 1.60–62, 65–67; with humorous self-consciousness the poet makes Athena admire the good sense he has given to Odysseus, *Odyssey* 13.330–36).

2. The major divinities form an extended family, living together on Olympus with second residences in the centers of

their cult. Zeus is father and patriarch, and his adult children are still subordinate to him. He is also a ruler who maintains his power not by wisdom or justice but by force, and does not hesitate to boast of it (8.450–56, 15.162–67). His brother Poseidon claims equality in rank and supreme power in his own sphere of the sea, but Zeus declares that he is elder and greater and Poseidon does not press the point (15.158–217); Zeus's wife and sister, Hera, yields unhappily but of necessity to his threats of violence (1.565–67, 8.415–31), which have been actually carried out in the past (15.18–25; this passage may be post-Homeric). It is noteworthy that the goddesses join in the councils of the gods as equals with the males, and in both epics Athena is in practice the most powerful figure after Zeus. In view of the exalted positions of Penelope, Helen, and Arete in the *Odyssey*, one feels that powerful female figures may not be unknown to Homer and his audience in human ruling families.

Naturally there are alliances and quarrels within the family. Hera, Athena, and Poseidon unite against the Trojans; Ares and Aphrodite assist them. Ares and Athena are constant antagonists, like a boy with a bossy elder sister, and the unpopular Ares always suffers ignominy as well as defeat (5.827ff., 15.121ff., 21.391ff.). In their relations with each other they embody—or parody—the frailties of ordinary human nature (see p. 252). Zeus and his wife Hera squabble continually. Hera, in a furious temper because she cannot get her way, derives a disgustingly mean satisfaction from telling Ares of his son's death (15.110ff.). When hurt, Aphrodite, Ares, and Artemis in turn wail to a parent, "He hit me!" (5.370ff., 872ff., 21.505ff.). Thetis has a mother's uncritical love for her magnificent son Achilles, but is not bright enough to realize that it is hardly tactful to say to him with smug satisfaction, "Haven't you got just what you asked for?" when he has just heard of Patroclus's death (18.74ff.).

In the *Iliad* the intensely human interrelationships of the divine first family enable the poet to present a picture of the less serious side of human life that circumstances as well as the dignity of the human characters make impossible in any other way. They bring needed humor and relaxation to the grim tragedies of the poem. Besides all the minor humorous scenes in which they are involved, their brawling in the Battle of the Gods (21.385ff.) is like a parody of a *War of Gods and Titans* (Zeus himself is vastly amused by it; 21.388ff.) and ends at about the level of Offenbach's *Orpheus in the Underworld*. The long and brilliant episode of the beguiling of Zeus in book 14 (see pp. 247–50) adds pure entertainment to the long-drawn-out defeat of the Greeks before the entry of Patroclus.

Such tales provide light relief from the troubles and anxieties of the human characters; inventing and gossiping about the undignified behavior of our superiors is an appealingly human method of getting our own back on those who live as we would like to live ourselves but cannot. Already by the late sixth century Homer's fun and the Greeks' religion had become confused, and a thoughtful man was much offended by all this ungodly behavior: "Homer and Hesiod have attributed to the gods everything that is thought a shame and reproach among mankind: theft, adultery, deceitfulness" (Xenophanes, fragment 11. Diels-Kranz).

3. The presence of the gods often facilitates the smooth working of the plot. The Greeks can be beaten, without losing too much face, because it is the will of Zeus; and the will of Zeus can be brought into play against them not because of any wrongdoing or offense on their part, not as a punishment for Agamemnon's treatment of Achilles, but because Thetis has requested it in the name of her beloved son.

Duels between important heroes can occur without wasteful fatalities because a god, like modern Superman, can swoop down in the nick of time to rescue the weaker combatant (Paris from Menelaus in Book 3, Aeneas from Diomedes in Book 5 and from Achilles in book 21). Assistance to the stronger man can be direct, and brings him additional honor (Athena returns Achilles' spear in Book 22, Diomedes' whip in book 23). The duel of Hector and Achilles, fought without either the courteous conventions of a truce or the fear of intervention by other heroes, can be arranged by the help of Apollo (Books 21 to 22); and the meeting of Priam and Achilles, impossible to arrange at the realistic level without harsh straining of human probability, becomes simple with the introduction of Hermes (Book 24).

Sometimes the gods are employed to bring out the psychological weaknesses and strengths of the human characters. It is Aphrodite who leads Helen to go to bed with Paris in Book 3, yielding to sex despite her contempt for her partner; Athena who encourages the foolish Pandarus, proud of his bow and his archery, to shoot the arrow that breaks the truce (4.89ff.), and who suggests to Achilles that it would not be wise to kill Agamemnon (1.206ff.). Reckless actions of Automedon (17.469ff.) and Glaucus (6.234ff.) are attributed to the hand of the gods, even when the spirit of Blind Folly, *Atê*, is not mentioned. They help heroes on the human level: even when assisted by a god, heroes on the battlefield do not become invisible or slay dozens at a blow; they achieve their successes on the plane of human greatness, not the supernatural.

Characteristically Homeric is the notion of "double motivation," by which many decisions and events are given one motivation on the divine level and one on the human. Often this is explicit: Ajax says that Achilles has "placed a savage temper in his breast" and goes on in the same breath to say that the *gods* put it there (9.629, 636); similarly Diomedes says Achilles will return to the battle "when his inclination [*thumos*] and the god drive him" (9.703). Odysseus's poor oarsman, Elpenor, attributes his fatal fall from the roof to "the evil fate of the gods and too much wine" (*Odyssey* 11.61).

A dramatic example is Achilles' great cry to terrify the Trojans away from Patroclus' body, magnified by Athena (18.217–18); it has been compared to the relief from the temple of Zeus at Olympia, which shows Heracles straining to support the burden of the sky while behind him Athena effortlessly lends a hand to make the feat possible. The dying Patroclus says to Hector, "Deadly destiny [*moira*] and Leto's son [Apollo] have killed me, and of men it was Euphorbus; you are the third to slay me" (16.849–50). Zeus drives on Hector "though Hector himself was in a fury" (15.604). This "over-determination," as it has been called, allows the poet to retain the interest of human characterization and action while superimposing upon it, for added dignity, the concern of the divinities.

4. The gods can be used by the poet to foretell the future (though for purposes of the plot they may sometimes be unaware of even the present). Before we have even met Odysseus, we can be told by Zeus in some detail of his journey to the Phaeacians and his eventual return home with many gifts (*Odyssey* 5.31ff.). A prediction from a god can add greater pathos and foreboding than if it were given in the poet's own voice. Thetis can tell Achilles, as he vows to kill Hector in revenge for Patroclus, that it is fated that his own death will follow soon after Hector's, and so Achilles makes a conscious decision to ignore his own coming doom (18.94ff.). Also particularly effective are Achilles' knowledge, from Thetis, that he may choose a short life with glory or a long life in obscurity, and his decision at that point in the tale to abandon the quest for glory (9.410–16; a rather similar prophecy occurs in the case of the minor figure Euchenor [13.663–70], which suggests a traditional motif adopted for Achil-

les by Homer). Zeus's foreknowledge enables the poet to create much pathos as the god sadly contemplates the deaths of Sarpedon and Hector (16.431ff., 22.168ff.; see also p. 35).

Fate, of course, is the will of the poet, limited by the major features of the traditional legends; its power is great because, to one looking back on history, the outcome of events can always be seen as the result of prior decisions, and because the poet needs to satisfy his audience's desire to find an order and rationality in human experience. In an obviously artistic, not religious, motif, Zeus holds up his scales to determine the decree of fate (see p. 294), and the gods act to ensure the fulfillment of such a decree; Poseidon rescues Aeneas for this reason, as it is fated that through him Dardanus's line shall continue (20.300–308). On two occasions Zeus considers the possibility of saving a hero from the death that fate has decreed (his son Sarpedon, 16.433ff., and the beloved Hector, 22.167–81), but both times another deity declares this to be exceptional and a bad policy, and Zeus gives up the idea.

The episodes should be considered a device for increasing tension and pathos by raising the possibility of a last-minute rescue, which is then abandoned, not a means of determining whether Zeus could actually overrule fate (if he had decided to try). They are elaborations of the common emphasizing motif that something would have come about "beyond fate" (*huper moron*) if a god had not intervened: the Greeks would have returned home if Hera had not taken action (2.155ff.), Achilles and the Greeks are on the point of storming Troy and must be stopped (20.30, 21.517), and Odysseus is nearly drowned when saved by Athena (*Odyssey* 5.436). In fact, Homer does not concern himself with the theological problem of the relationship of the gods and fate. Hesiod, probably his contemporary, dodged the issue by providing two different answers, at one place making the *Moirai* ("Fates") daughters of Night, coming into existence before Zeus himself and so superior to him, and at another the daughters of Zeus and Themis ("Order") and so under his patronage (*Theogony* 217–22, 904–6).

5. It has already been said that the gods' interventions lend dignity and status to their favored heroes (see p. 6). They are success-boosters. Ajax, mighty hero as he is, is not supported by any deity and always comes second. Hector and Antenor, when faced by the overwhelming might of Achilles, each say that sometimes even the weaker man may win (20.430–37; 21.566–69), but in practice this does not happen. As with so many other as-

pects, the poet seems to make a character comment on his technique. Aeneas complains bitterly of Athena's help to Achilles, but admits that he is a good shot even without such help; if the gods would only stand aside, however, Achilles would not find it quite so easy (20.98–102; Aeneas has just said that only Zeus's help saved *him* from Achilles on an earlier occasion).

6. Homer sets very firm limits to divine interventions and to supernatural phenomena generally in the *Iliad* and the *Odyssey*, in contrast to what we know of the fantastic occurrences in other epics about Troy (see Griffin 1977). There are no invulnerable or invisible warriors, no magical weapons, not even a mention of the Palladium, the image of Athena that must be removed from Troy before the city can fall, or the bow of Heracles that must be brought to Troy by Philoctetes. The bizarre has no place in these poems. A god may save Paris from Menelaus, during a duel that could only have been inconclusive, given the force of the traditional tale; but no god causes or intervenes in the quarrel between Agamemnon and Achilles, or influences Achilles' decisions in books 9, 16, and 18, or takes part in the encounter when Achilles and Priam are face to face in Achilles' shelter. The divine armor of Peleus, and that made for Achilles by Hephaestus, are not said to be invulnerable during the battles; the divinely made shield fends off a spear (21.164–65), and so does the greave (21.592–94), but ordinary bronze might do as much (though the idea of invulnerability must underlie the poet's mockery of Achilles' fear that Aeneas would pierce his shield; 20.261–72).

No hint is given of the tale of Achilles' own personal invulnerability (see Young 1979), and in fact he is wounded once in the arm, which is unprotected by his armor (21.166–67); by contrast, Ajax seems to have enjoyed invulnerability in the *Aethiopis* (Griffin 1977.40). It is not hard, in the context, to accept the immortality of Achilles' horses and their mourning for their driver Patroclus (17.426ff.); it is harder for us to regard with solemnity the conversation Achilles has with one of them before he enters the battle, but perhaps any incongruity felt by Homer's intended audience would be satisfied with the explicit termination of this unnatural happening by the Furies (19.404ff.; see p. 287).

Homer also ignores many aspects of contemporary religion with which he must have been familiar. There are no fertility cults, no cult of dead heroes, no bizarre cult figures like the horse-headed Poseidon, the black Demeter, the Aphrodite in armor. Mystery religions, one of which is celebrated in the

Hymn to Demeter, composed not much later than Homer's time, are not mentioned. There is no punishment of children for the sins of their fathers, an idea that appears a century or so later in Solon.

Homer's divine personalities, imposing but intensely familiar in their human qualities, acting just as we do or would like to, have contributed much to art, literature, and entertainment; though it may seem odd to us, the tale that Pheidias's mighty statue of Zeus at Olympia was inspired by the Zeus of the *Iliad* (1.528–30) shows that they could also contribute to religious belief.

Mortals and the Gods

Mortals hate death and old age, and long for immortality. This longing appears in literature from the earliest times; it is the prime motivation of the hero in the Sumerian/Assyrian epic *Gilgamesh* (see Renger 1978.36ff.), and still features in modern movies. Those who are doomed to death feel that those who they imagine are not, must be free from all care, and resent their happiness; and so they make the world of those who are without death, age, and suffering full of frivolities, as in the *Iliad,* or full of the apathy and boredom of spoiled children, as in the 1970s movie *Zardoz.*

"So the gods have assigned to unfortunate mortals, / to live amid griefs, but they themselves have no cares," says Achilles in his great consolation speech to Priam (24.525–26). The formula "the gods who live at ease" (*theoi rheia zôontes*) occurs three times, always with some pertinence: when the gods punish the attack by the mortal Lycurgus on one of their number, when they resent the love of the goddess Dawn for the mortal Orion, and when they comfort the anxious Penelope with assurances of their care for good men (6.138, *Odyssey* 5.122, *Odyssey* 4.805).

By contrast, a common formula for humanity is "miserable mortals" (*deiloisi brotoisi*). At the end of Book 1 of the *Iliad,* after the plague brought by Apollo, the disastrous quarrel of Agamemnon and Achilles, Achilles' withdrawal from the Greek army and Zeus's promise that they will be made to regret it bitterly, the gods feast blithely, and Apollo sings delightfully for their pleasure. In the *Hymn to Apollo* (189ff.) the song he and the Muses sing at a similar feast tells of "the eternal gifts of the gods, and of mortals / the sufferings, enduring which at the hands of the immortal gods / they live senseless and helpless, unable / to find healing against death or help against old age." It is Apollo, too, who firmly states to Diomedes the distinction between men and gods: "Never are the races alike, / those of the immortal gods and of men who walk upon the earth" (5.441–42).

This distinction between mortals and immortals is constantly asserted, the common Homeric terms for each class being as transparently opposed in meaning as are the English words. And in the *Iliad* it is not merely the traditional language that brings out the great difference between the two races, for both in his main plot and in many small and inessential scenes the poet dwells on this fundamental limitation of his splendid heroes. Most of these are discussed in detail in Part Two, but a summary of the most significant passages is given here.

Achilles himself is a constant and highly concentrated symbol of the mortality of even the greatest human prowess; not only is he—goddess' son though he is—doomed to die, but his life will be even shorter than that of most men, and he is already aware of it; and he himself chooses to bring his end closer to avenge the death of his friend (see p. 273). With superb irony, immediately after this decision he is given magnificent armor made by the god Hephaestus, armor that, though perhaps invulnerable, will not save him from death (see pp. 115–16). His immortal mother is often with him; she herself personifies the great gulf between them, and her words never fail to dwell upon it. At their first meeting she mentions that, magnificent though he is, his life will be shorter than that of most men (1.415ff.); and the last time they meet, the poet avoids the usual departure element of a visit scene in order to leave them "saying much to each other" (24.141–42), for little time remains and his death will mean their eternal separation.

Even Achilles' horses are immortal, and Homer four times makes use of this traditional fact for pathetic effect. As he goes into battle Patroclus yokes a mortal horse beside the immortal ones, symbolizing his own vulnerability despite his divinely made armor, and later its death foreshadows his own (16.152–54, 467–69). Zeus sees the immortal horses grieving for their dead driver and reflects: "There is nothing anywhere more pitiable than man / of all things that breathe and walk upon the earth" (17.446–47), and in the context it is man's awareness of his mortality that makes his race so wretched (interestingly, when Odysseus expresses the same thought in similar words, it is man's blind optimism that makes him pitiable; *Odyssey* 18.130–35). When Achilles himself sets off for battle, there is a further startling reminder of his coming death from the mouth of one of these horses, and Achilles acknowledges in response that he will never see his home again (19.408–23). Finally, at the beginning of the funeral games for the dead Patroclus, Achilles states that these horses will not compete in the chariot race because of their grief for their former driver (23.279ff.).

During his great speech in reply to the embassy in Book 9 Achilles reflects on the death which will come to him despite his mighty deeds (9.319ff., 400ff.). Even more powerful is the scene between him and the terrified young Trojan Lycaon, where he offers him the solace that the death he faces comes even to the greatest of men (21.106–13):

Die, my friend, you too; why lament like this?
Death took even Patroclus, who was a much greater man than you.
Do you not see how splendid *I* am in beauty and size?
My father was a hero, and a goddess bore me;
Yet even for me there is death and harsh fate;
There will be a morning, or an afternoon, or a noontime,
When someone shall take the life even from me in the fighting,
Either with a spear-cast or an arrow from the bowstring.

The passage seems to be a brilliant double adaptation of the trope "even Heracles died" (18.117ff.), with first Patroclus and then Achilles himself substituted for the paradeigmatic Heracles. His frequent references to his coming death (in addition to the poet's repeated foreshadowings of it) culminate in his instructions to mingle his bones with those of Patroclus after his funeral (23.243–48); and when his last rites are described by Agamemnon, as the *Odyssey* draws to a close (*Odyssey* 24.43ff.), it is fitting that there is no hint of the version in which Thetis carried him away to immortality (*Aethiopis* fragment 1 Evelyn-White).

The poet also brings in the theme in other ways. The simile of the falling leaves symbolizes the death of the individual and the continuation of the race, immediately before Hector predicts his own death to his wife (6.146ff., 21.462ff.; see pp. 202–5). Sarpedon meditates aloud about honor as the only solace for mortality, and sees the inevitability of death as the only reason for seeking honor (12.310ff.), in much the same tone as the traditional military exhortation "Do you want to live forever?" The poem ends not with the triumph of Achilles in Book 22, or with his magnanimous restoration of the body of his enemy, but with a funeral; not the funeral of the hero of the epic, Achilles, but that of his defeated enemy, Hector. We know that Achilles, Priam, and many other Trojans are soon to die. Only the gods will continue their same routine of feasting.

In the *Odyssey* the distinction between mortals and immortals remains, but the resentment does not appear. Odysseus, in an almost visible contrast with the *Iliad*, is offered the opportunity of an immortal life beside the lovely goddess Calypso, and rejects it in favor of a return to his middle-aged wife and his obscure island kingdom of Ithaca (*Odyssey* 5.203–13). Menelaus will live forever in the Elysian fields, but this eternal continuation of his rather acid relationship with Helen is hardly held up as an ideal (*Odyssey* 4.561–69). The afterlife portrayed in book II is dismal indeed, but there is little sign of revolt against it; in Odysseus's meeting with his mother the note is entirely one of pathos, and the dead Agamemnon complains not of death itself but of the way he was killed.

Only in the case of the dead Achilles, fittingly enough, is there a protest. Though reunited with his dear friends Patroclus and Antilochus, Achilles speaks of Hades as the place where "the senseless dead dwell, the images of mortals who have died" (*Odyssey* II.475–76). In answer to Odysseus's well-intentioned (if unwise) consolation, "When you lived the Greeks honored you like a god, and now here you have great power among the dead," he makes the famous reply, "I would rather be the farmhand of a poor peasant with no land of his own than rule over all the dead" (*Odyssey* II.484–86, 489–91). He still worries about his old father, Peleus, as he does at the end of the *Iliad*, and only Odysseus's lavish praise of his son Neoptolemus cheers him. Though one may wonder how well Achilles' pride would endure a farmhand's lot, his rejection of any comfort in honors among the dead recalls the tone of the *Iliad* perhaps more than anything else in the *Odyssey*.

In Homer's time the mystery religions were already offering the comfort and hope of a happy eternity, another kind of protest against death. They are not mentioned in Homer. But neither poem has a tone of pessimism or despair; courage and endurance are the glory of mankind, and in these the gods have no share at all (see Afterword). The pervasive melancholy of so much of mediaeval literature (despite its Christian surface), the mournful *ubi sunt* ("Where are these heroes now?") of Villon and others, and the foreboding misery of the end of *Beowulf* are totally alien to the glory-seeking realists before Troy.

Further Reading

The bibliography on the gods in Homer is enormous; Combellack 1955.45–47 lists some of the still useful older works. Dodds 1951, Fränkel 1973.53–93, Greene 1948, and Guthrie 1950 are standard authorities. Among recent publications, the *Cambridge Ancient History*, vol. II part 2 ch. 40, gives a brief survey, and there are chapters on the gods in Griffin 1980, Mueller 1984, and Schein 1984. On the relationship of gods and mortals, see especially Willcock 1970, Griffin 1978, Thalmann 1984.78–112, and Clay 1981. Wilson 1974 makes excellent points about Achilles' divinely made armor, his immortal horses, and his goddess mother. Rubino 1979 emphasizes the importance of the imminence of death to the heroic ideal.

18

Personification and Psychology

The strong anthropomorphic colors of the Homeric gods appear also in the vivid personifications of some of the abstract conceptions introduced into the poems. A good example of the usage and the problems is the case of Sleep, who with his brother Death bears Sarpedon away to his far-off home after his slaying by Patroclus (16.681–83). Nothing more complex is involved here than a sympathetic evocation of the last long sleep and perhaps a picture of a pair of young and beautiful winged gods, as on the Euphronius crater in the New York Metropolitan Museum. But Sleep, his name a transparent personification in Greek as in English, also plays an important part in the subplot of the beguiling of Zeus.

Hera wishes him to perform his own proper function, putting Zeus to sleep so that her plan can work, but the bribe she offers is a throne and footstool (14.231ff.), aimed at a fully anthropomorphic deity. He demurs, nervously remembering a former occasion when Zeus's anger forced him to ask old Night for protection. So Hera offers him a further gift, even more anthropomorphic: the nymph he loves. Sleep now agrees, and conceals himself in a tree, taking (as the Olympians themselves sometimes do) the form of a bird. Zeus makes love to Hera; then follows: "So the Father slept peacefully on the top of Gargaron, / by sleep and love overcome." Or should it be "by Sleep and Love"? Most editors and translators reject capital letters for both abstractions here (14.353), but why? Sleep is very much a person in this scene, and Love here is *Philotês*, present on the girdle of Aphrodite, which has brought about Zeus's seduction (14.216), and personified again in Hesiod in a sinister context, with Deceit, Old Age, and Strife (*Theogony* 224–25). In the next verse Sleep dashes off to Poseidon to give him the news like any other messenger.

All this, of course, is straightforward storytelling, not really likely to raise ontological problems in a reader's mind. Nor is the personification of Dream, Zeus's messenger to Agamemnon in 2.6ff., even though he adds something of his own to Zeus's words. But in some cases the question of what kind of existence such abstractions as sleep, fear, justice, actually have in the poet's mind is important, if essentially unanswerable. In modern editions and translations the perplexity often shows itself in inconsistent capitalization. Personification of abstractions with moral associations raises the question of allegory, and the question of internal feelings requires a brief account of Homeric psychology.

The same kind of treatment as that given to Sleep, essentially Hesiodic but often with more dramatization, is frequent in Homer. Fear and Terror (*Deimos, Phobos*) not only accompany Ares into war (4.440) but can be sent like equerries to harness his horses (15.119–20; fittingly, they live on as moons of Mars). The final familiarly Hesiodic touch of personification is assigned to Terror when he is given a genealogy and made the son of Ares (13.299ff.; this is in the less traditional circumstances of a simile). Panic (*Phuza*) is his companion (9.2). Another of Ares' associates, his sister Strife (*Eris*), receives more philosophical development, for she is said to be first a small creature as she puts on her helmet (that is, as men arm themselves), but then to tread the earth and tower to the sky, spreading hostility and pain among men (4.440–45). She is given a big role in restarting the battle after the intermission of Books 9 and 10 (11.3–14). It is she who embodies the quarrel of Agamemnon and Achilles (1.8), and later in his great grief Achilles wishes she would disappear from among gods and men (18.107). Another vivid figure is Rumor (*Ossa*), who "flames" among men as Zeus's messenger (2.93–94) and (with less drama) tells the Ithacans of the killing of the suitors (*Odyssey* 24.413–14). It has been pointed out (by Fränkel 1973.62) that in the tragedy of the *Iliad* there is no place for Hesiod's "lovely-ankled Victory" (*Theogony* 384).

The poet's visualization of these abstractions leads him to portray Fear and Terror on the shield of Agamemnon (along with the Gorgon's head); Strife, Tumult (*Kudoimos*), and Doom (*Kêr*) appear in the battle presented on Achilles' shield, described vividly (18.535–38). An even more threatening troop is depicted on the *aegis* worn into battle by Athena (Terror, Strife, Prowess [*Alkê*], and Onslaught [*Iôkê*] as well as the Gorgon; 5.739–41). Presumably the same idea lies behind the figures of Love (*Philotês*), Desire (*Himeros*), and "Sweettalk-Persuasion" (*Oaristus Parphasis*), which appear on the girdle of Aphrodite (14.215–17), though here again editors and translators are reluctant to capitalize them.

Rather different from these personifications is the kind of

animism of physical objects that adds vividness; this may well be part of the traditional language of the poet. Spears long to taste flesh (11.574 and elsewhere), an arrow is eager to fly through the mob of men (4.125–26), the bronze of the weapons is formulaically "pitiless" (nêleï chalkôi). An even more imaginative example is Sisyphus's "shameless" rock (Odyssey 11.598). Many other examples give perhaps not only vividness but also a feeling of comprehension and control of these impersonal forces.

Perhaps surprisingly, fate is barely personified in Homer. Moira "spins" a man's fate once, in Hecuba's words (24.209–10), and so does Aisa in Hera's (23.127–28); Aisa is also once coupled with the otherwise unknown "Spinners" (Klôthes) in the same phrase (Odyssey 7.196–98, Alcinous speaking). Usually the image is that of weaving, and is reserved for the plans of the gods (24.525 and elsewhere). Similarly, the Hesiodic Shame and Indignation (Aidôs ánd Nemesis), who don their white gowns and leave the company of mankind so dramatically at the end of the Iron Age (Works and Days 197–200), find only an impersonal existence in Homer ("Fix aidôs and nemesis in your hearts"; 13.121–22). Justice (dikê) is honored by the gods and cast out by wicked men (16.388 [in a simile]; Odyssey 14.84), but remains an abstraction.

The most difficult, and most interesting, cases of all involve Atê, the personification of blind foolishness and ruin. At his reconciliation with Achilles, Agamemnon says (19.87ff.) that Zeus, Moira, and Erinys ("Fury") cast savage atê (not capitalized by most editors and translators) into his heart in that disastrous assembly in Book 1. Then he goes on to personify that "Folly" very vividly, calling her the elder daughter of Zeus and describing at length an occasion on which she overcame the wits of Zeus himself and led him to hurl her out of Olympus by the hair, to dwell thereafter among men. The poet is expanding Agamemnon's speech to emphasize the importance of the occasion, not relating a fact in his own voice, and it is a plausible move on Agamemnon's part to relieve the embarrassment of the whole situation by telling a story (he can even recount the actual words of Zeus and Hera). But it is not necessarily the poet's intention that Atê should carry all the blame, though he may have contributed to the "soft feet" that enable Atê to approach undetected, a neat allusion to the fact that no one (not even the poet) mentions Atê's activity until it is too late. We cannot be sure what the poet would say if asked whether he actually believed in a being who inflicts foolishness upon mankind, or even if he would understand the question.

In an even more remarkable passage (9.502ff.), old Phoenix tells of a strong, swift-footed *Atê* who visits every land to harm mankind; far behind her, to heal the trouble, limp the lame, wrinkled, squinting daughters of Zeus called Prayers (*Litai*). If a man listens to them, they help him and will listen to his own requests; but if rejected, they pray to Zeus that *Atê* pursue and punish him. The ideas are not completely clear: is *Atê's* first attack unconnected with any wrongdoing; does the rebuffed suppliant pray again to Zeus, or does Zeus automatically receive rejected prayers; would not a Fury make a better executor of Zeus's wrath than the apparently irresponsible *Atê*? Also, the physical characteristics of the Prayers seem to derive from different participants in the tale: they are "lame" obviously because repentance comes too late; are they "wrinkled" because of the sorrowful appearance of the wronged, or of the repentant wrongdoer, or because of the old age of wise men like Phoenix; do they "squint" because the repentant wrongdoer cannot look his victim in the face? But in spite of these uncertainties, the description is vividly dramatic, and the application to Achilles' present situation, with the suppliant Greeks before him, is obvious enough.

It seems reasonable to suppose that this picture is the poet's invention, and if so it is the most Hesiodic thing in the *Iliad* and the *Odyssey*. The tale is not an allegory (though it is sometimes so called) because the characters do not represent anything other than themselves ("allegory" is best reserved for such examples as Hesiod's fable of the hawk and nightingale [*Works and Days* 202–12] and Archilochus's ship of state). It is a paradigm, presenting an ideal of conduct not through actions of past heroes, but through actions of the poet's personifications. It may be significant that this passage, like Agamemnon's tale of *Atê* and Zeus and like other paradigms, is in the voice of a character and not the poet's (see pp. 318–19). Its detailed development, however, makes it unique both in the epics and in Hesiod.

Certain aspects of Homeric psychology verge on personification and should be mentioned, though the whole topic is too complex and confused to treat fully here. Homer's psychological terminology is heavily linked to physical organs, many of which, of course, actually do react to the force of emotions; in English we speak of "losing heart," "having the guts to. . . ," "having no stomach for . . . ," and so on, and in Homer this usage is carried much further. The *kradiê* is the heart, which can be transfixed by a spear (13.442), but is also the seat of emotion and swells with anger (9.646); the *phrên* (or plural *phrenes*) is the midriff or diaphragm, holding in the liver (*Odyssey* 9.301), and also the organ of wisdom and intelligence; the *thumos* is breathing—often abnormal breathing—which one loses when unconscious or dead, and also the home of anger, desire, courage, and so on; the *psuchê* is the warm breath of life that leaves the body when unconscious or dead, the "spirit" or "soul" of later language, and the only entity that survives death; and the *noös* is the mind, the thoughts, plans, and way of thinking, not associated with any physical organ.

As the disguised Odysseus lies sleepless in his hall, furiously resenting the foul behavior of the suitors and maidservants, his *kradiê* "barks" or "growls" within him "like a dog," and he addresses a few lines of reproach to it by name, reminding it of its endurance in the past (*Odyssey* 20.13–22). Since the passage is a simile, it is likely to be the poet's own extension of the usual usage. One's *thumos* may be seized by anger and grief, and it is often addressed by a worried hero in a standard formula: "So, perturbed, he spoke to his mighty *thumos*," for example when Achilles sees Antilochus approaching and suspects bad news (18.5). It may well talk back; the regular verse for concluding a mental debate and reaching a decision attributes the thinking to one's *thumos* (for example, 22.122), and Hector's *thumos* once orders him to "speak his mind" (7.68). After Odysseus has decided "in his mighty *thumos*" to stab the Cyclops, another *thumos* holds him back, lest they be trapped in the cave (*Odyssey* 9.299–302). The *psuchê*, though during life it has nothing to do with emotion, thought, or personality, is all that remains after a man's death and so becomes his ghost in the underworld, assuming all that survives of his individuality. When the poet presents an interview between Achilles and the ghost of Patroclus (23.65ff., see p. 302) the ghost has normal intelligence and memory (for good artistic reasons), but eludes Achilles' grasp when he tries to embrace it, and he complains that it is only a *psuchê* and *eidôlon* ("image") and has no *phrenes* in it at all (23.103–4). The poet clearly means to depict a continuing personality with sensibility but without physical substance, as he does in the underworld scenes in *Odyssey* 11, and here at least common belief and artistic creation seem to coincide.

Further Reading

ON PERSONIFICATION. Dodds 1951 and Fränkel 1973.53–85 are standard works on the attitudes of the early Greeks to what we consider abstract conceptions. On *atê* in particular: Adkins 1982 includes a discussion of Phoenix's paradigm, and disagrees with the views of Lloyd-Jones 1971; Vlastos 1975.13–17 disagrees with Dodds 1951; Wyatt 1982 and Doyle 1984.7–22 examine various aspects, with some interpretations I would disagree with.

ON HOMERIC IDEAS OF PSYCHOLOGY. Harrison 1960 is a sound general treatment; Redfield 1975 includes studies of *nemesis, aidôs* ("shame"), *psuchê,* and *noös* ("mind"); and Russo and Simon 1968 survey the field from the viewpoint of oral poetry and give a bibliography. Vermeule 1979.145–78 deals with the ideas of sleep, desire, and death in Homer. Kokolakis 1980 collects and discusses interesting examples of animism in Homer.

19

Honor, Proper Behavior, and Warfare

The *Iliad* and the *Odyssey* are works of art, not necessarily an accurate record of the ideals of a society, either the society of the poet's own time or that of the earlier age in which the story is set. But the prime ideas and aims that underlie the actions and words of the epic characters continue to appear in later Greek literature and life, and may be considered fundamental principles of ancient Greek society.

The strongest force is competitiveness, which finds expression almost everywhere in ancient Greek literature. In Hesiod there are no warrior heroes, but he declares that the cruel Strife who produces warfare has also an elder sister, another Strife, much better for mankind, who urges a man on to rivalry with his neighbor; so "potter struggles with potter, craftsman with craftsman; beggar is jealous of beggar, singer of singer" (*Works and Days* 25–26). A century or so later, Solon warns the Athenians that the contest for wealth is causing turmoil in the state. Pindar declares, "There is a divine presence in a test of human strength" and almost immediately continues to the warning, "Do not expect to become Zeus" (*Isthmian* 5.11, 14; quoted and translated by Young 1982.167). Sophocles in his *Ajax* portrays a hero of the old Homeric kind who ends his life because he has failed to win the honor he desires and instead has been plunged into dishonor. Aristotle asserts that the "great-souled" or "high-minded" man (*megalopsuchos*) will be primarily concerned with honor and dishonor (*Nicomachean Ethics* 4.3.17) and suggests Achilles and Ajax as examples of this type, along with the real-life Alcibiades (*Analytica Posteriora* 97b15). The famous warnings against presumption ("Nothing in excess"; "Know yourself [mortal]") were not given because it was easy for Greeks to observe them.

The same spirit is obvious everywhere in the culture. The ancient Greek love of athletic competition is familiar to everyone, and appears in Homer in the games at the funerals of Patroclus and Achilles and in the festivities in Phaeacia. Cultural activities like singing, oratory, and dramatic productions were usually competitive, too, for honor both to the gods and to the winners. In fifth-century Athens, the constitution even provided for the legal removal (by ostracism) of overpowerful and dangerously ambitious persons. Such an intense and universal competitiveness is not so widely acknowledged in our own society, and we must make an effort to understand it if we are to appreciate (for instance) Achilles' reaction after he has been publicly insulted.

In this section the main ethical principles of the Homeric heroes will be discussed under three headings: the meaning of honor; the proper way to behave; the attitude toward warfare.

Honor

"Always be the best, and superior to others." This sums up the heroic code; it was the counsel with which Peleus sent his mighty son Achilles off to fight with the Greeks at Troy, and so too Hippolochus sent his son Glaucus to fight on the other side (Iliad 11.783, 6.208). Less aphoristically but with more pathos, Hector tells his wife he would be ashamed before the Trojan men and women if he did not fight in the front ranks of the Trojans (6.441ff.), and the same shame keeps him facing Achilles in his last duel (22.105ff.). "Let us kill or be killed, win glory or let it go to others," says Sarpedon as he begins the battle in which he will die (12.328); Odysseus, in a tight corner, says, "Only cowards retreat; a man who wants honor in battle must stand fast and kill or be killed" (11.408ff.); and the theme is repeated by Idomeneus (13.321, 486) and Hector (18.308). It is a zero-sum game, as Gouldner has pointed out (1965.50), in which one must lose what the other gains.

The winner's prize is honor, the public acknowledgment of his superiority. It must be marked by material tributes and gifts. Sarpedon links the wealth in land ownership, the seats of honor, choice meats, and full winecups with the obligation of fighting in the forefront (12.310ff.); Agamemnon as commander-in-chief has the pick of the booty (1.166–67); and Achilles is honored for his leadership by a gift from the army (1.276). The gods, too, must have their superior honor recognized by proper offerings from mankind (see Motto and Clark 1969.119 and n. 22.).

The honor a hero achieves endures after his death. If Achilles stays and fights at Troy, he says his glory will be everlasting (9.413). The idea is amplified in Hector's words about the tomb of his potential victim (7.87–91):

And men will say, even those who come long after us,
Sailing in their ships over the gleaming sea,
"That is the tomb of a man who died long ago,
Who once, fighting bravely, was killed by brilliant Hector."
So men will say one day, and my glory will not be lost.

Honor such as this conquers death and recompenses a hero for his mortality. Sarpedon argues that honor is all that matters because life itself is short and death is certain, always at hand (12.326–28). In both poems death is the enemy, and the hero conquers it by accepting it, by refusing to attempt to escape or postpone it, by ranking other things ahead of it and so overwhelming it. Achilles chooses to take vengeance on Hector at the cost of his own life, and the poet adds the superb scene with Lycaon to allow him to say in his own words that he has overcome death by accepting its necessity (21.107–12; see p. 140). Hector retains some hope even when he stands to face the approaching Achilles, but in his last isolation, after the disappearance of his apparent supporter Deiphobus, he too knowingly confronts death and consoles himself with his everlasting honor: "But now my death comes upon me. / Let me not die tamely and without honor, / but after some great deed which men to come will hear of" (22.303–5). Though they are of second rank, Sarpedon and Patroclus likewise see and speak of their death before it overwhelms them (16.495–500, 844–46).

In Sophocles' *Ajax* this choice of death is pushed further still, as the hero meditates aloud before the audience and then kills himself when his claim of honor has been denied and his revenge frustrated. Plato's Socrates chooses death rather than surrender his convictions, and associates his decision with that of Achilles (see p. 317). Much of the significance—or insignificance—of the gods derives from their exclusion from this greatest of all choices.

Modern admirers of this ethic sometimes go too far in attributing such a consciously courageous, clearsighted outlook to the heroes. It is of course the *poet* who is creating and depicting it, perhaps from observation of the warriors of his own time, but more probably from his admiration for the superhuman greatness of the heroic past and his sympathy for the sadness of human life and the gulf between man's hopes and aspirations and his inevitable end. The dramatization of the conception is the art of the poet; almost certainly it is peculiar to these two poems and did not occur in the more superficial adventure stories of the epic cycle (see Griffin 1977). Among other epics, *Beowulf* in particular, despite its Christian surface, shows the same heroic desire for praise and glory.

The Proper Way to Behave

The quest for honor is the result of the wider principle of recognizing, and ensuring that others recognize, one's proper status, and in turn recognizing the proper status of others. This means behaving in a way suitable for one's standing. Agamemnon and Achilles quarrel because of differences of opinion about their respective amount of honor; Thersites (2.211ff.) claims too much and is chastized for it; Eumaeus the swineherd, through born a prince, is now a slave and behaves properly for that status by displaying the qualities of fidelity to his master in his absence and devoted care for his master's property (*Odyssey* 14.524ff.). The maidservants in Odysseus's palace who fail in this duty die for their misbehavior (*Odyssey* 22.417ff.).

Besides claiming proper treatment for oneself, one must show it to others. This includes showing proper honor to the gods by sacrificing to them; Zeus expressly compliments Hector and Odysseus on their diligence in this respect (22.169–72; *Odyssey* 1.66–67). If someone refuses to show proper respect to others, he must be reminded of his duty, as both Agamemnon and Achilles are by Nestor (1.275ff.), Thersites by Odysseus (2.246ff.), Diomedes and Patroclus by Apollo (5.431ff., 16.702ff.). Besides failing to behave in the proper way toward Achilles, Agamemnon also fails to give proper respect to the priest Chryses and, on a wider scale, to public opinion, represented by the army, which thinks that the ransom offered by the priest should be accepted (1.22–23).

Achilles, on the other hand, behaves with proper respect to all except Agamemnon; Athena's suggestion that he should not kill Agamemnon, and Thetis's that he restore Hector's body, he accepts, though curtly and reluctantly (1.216–18, 24.139–40), and the heralds of his enemy he treats with respect (1.331ff.), as well as the suppliant Priam. Women show their proper virtue by properly performing their household duties (as Andromache is bidden to do by Hector, 6.490–92) and by being faithful to their husbands (Penelope is promised undying fame in song for this; *Odyssey* 24.194–98). Violators of these codes of behavior are few: Agamemnon in the *Iliad*, Achilles in his treatment of Hector's body (24.22, cf. 22.395, 23.24), the suitors in the *Odyssey*, the steward of Menelaus who attempts to turn away guests and is sternly rebuked by his master (*Odyssey* 4.26ff.), the disloyal maidservants in Odysseus's palace.

Much of the practical code of behavior is reinforced by being placed under the protection of a divinity, so that any infringement by a mortal is an insult to the godhead and brings punishment. Agamemnon's rejection of the suppliant priest and Apollo's swift retaliation begins the *Iliad,* and Achilles is warned by Phoenix not to make the same error (9.510–12). The Trojans break the oath of truce, which Agamemnon declares an offense to Zeus (4.157–68). In the *Odyssey,* as mentioned, the gods' watchfulness over the way humans behave is even closer (see p. 128).

A man has duties to the community, too, especially to fight bravely beside his fellows in defense of his family and his country: "It is no disgrace, fighting for one's country, / to die; for his wife will be safe and his children after him, / and his household and estate will be unharmed," says Hector to his troops (15.496–98). Nestor appeals to the Greeks to remember their wives and children, their property and their parents, and so to stand their ground in the battle (15.659–66). At the more personal level of the simile, the poet shows his respect and sorrow for a slain warrior in this picture of a woman weeping over the body of her husband: "who fell before his city and people, / warding off a pitiless day from his city and children" (*Odyssey* 8.524–25). A man must assist his allies (17.142ff.) and stand his ground in the battle; "it is cowards who leave the battle," says Odysseus (11.408), and Idomeneus gives an oddly vivid description of a coward's pallor, pounding heart, and chattering teeth (13.278–83). Duty to one's fellows, however, falls far short of the responsibilities to the future shouldered by Virgil's Aeneas, as C. S. Lewis indicated (1942 ch. 6).

The standard of conduct is common opinion and social precedent (see Long 1970). Respect for this is *aidôs,* proper feeling, and failure to observe it is likely to be *hubris,* arrogance or violence. The sanction against violators is *nemesis,* righteous indignation and public disapproval, such as that meted out to Thersites and (less conspicuously) to Agamemnon. This is encapsulated in Achilles' rebuke to the unseemly quarreling of Ajax and Idomeneus at the funeral games: "Stop this exchange of bitter words, / you two; it is unfitting. / You would strongly disapprove of [*nemesaton*] anyone else who behaved like this" (23.492–94). Young Nausicaa concludes with the same phrase as she explains to Odysseus why she must keep her distance from him to avoid scandal (*Odyssey* 6.273–88). If human sanctions fail, Zeus and the other gods may be watching and show their disapproval (see p. 130). "Justice" is a legal term rather than a moral conception of equity; it is the settlement between disputants normally made by a king, council, or arbitrator (see p. 281; the formidable Queen Arete sometimes takes over this duty, *Odyssey* 7.74). If the king is himself a party in the dispute, as Agamemnon is in Book 1, it must be settled by Zeus, as the *Iliad* demonstrates.

Warfare

The *Iliad* must be considered a war poem, as its setting is the siege of Troy. But like other great war stories, it ranges far beyond the battlefield; it deals with human life and emotions, and the war itself is both a setting and a kind of microcosm of life generally, as is the search for a husband or wife in many novels. Warfare is accepted, like mortality, grief, and suffering, as an inevitable part of human life, arising partly from human weakness and partly from the will of the gods. It is the field for the struggle for honor, a battleground not only for opposing forces but for rivals on the same side.

Hector's spirits rise as he sets off for the battlefield (6.526ff.; see p. 212), and the simile of the splendid stallion making for the river meadows where the mares are is applied to him as well as to the thoughtless Paris (15.263–70). The kindly Menelaus feels a fierce joy as he scents a chance to fight Paris (3.21ff.), and the gentle Patroclus falls into a maddened fury in his victorious charge against the Trojans (16.686ff., 784ff.). Other victorious warriors also enjoy their triumphs over lesser mortals (see p. 93). This is natural enough. "When a young man lies dead, killed in battle, everything is proper," says Priam (22.71–72; on the elaboration of the idea in Tyrtaeus, see Willcock 1976.241). War provides a young man with the opportunity not only to achieve honor but also to die nobly and escape the indignities of old age. The phrase describing the passing of the soul of Patroclus and Hector, "lamenting its fate, leaving young manhood behind" (16.857, 22.363), may convey not simply pathos, but also a kind of triumph and satisfaction.

Aristophanes has his Dionysus say, "What did the divine Homer receive honor and glory for, if not for teaching us noble things like the marshalling of battle-ranks, fighting valor, the arming of heroes for war?" (*Frogs* 1034–36). But it is not the poet's purpose to glorify war. Again and again the heroes joyously vaunt over a fallen enemy; and again and again the poet himself adds a few verses explaining the sorrow this victory will bring to the dead man's parents and wife. The proem to the *Iliad* speaks not of glory but of suffering. The tragedy that the fall of Troy will mean for its people, some of whom we come to know and admire, is evident throughout; and though the Trojans are in the wrong in weakly agreeing to the continuing presence of Helen and the property Paris seized with her, though they are responsible for the breaking of the truce in Book 4, still Hector, his family, and his people could not have seemed to be villains even to a Greek audience. Here the *Iliad* is far different from *Beowulf* with its Cain-descended monsters, and from *Roland's* conflict between Charlemagne and the devil-worshipping Saracens. The tone is not far removed from that of Virgil's *Aeneid*, where the poet must show respect for both components of the Roman race, both the indigenous Latins and the Trojan invaders, and where he must have evoked sympathy even from the Romans for Dido, queen of their Carthaginian enemies.

Though they may glory in victory, the characters are not said to approve warfare itself. Achilles, Priam, and Alcinous all consider it an affliction sent by the gods (24.547ff., 3.164ff.; *Odyssey* 8.579–80). Ares the war god is admired by no one; his father Zeus says bluntly, "You are the most hateful to me of all the gods on Olympus; / for always strife is dear to you, and wars and battles" (5.890–91), and the second verse is also used by Agamemnon as a reproach to his best warrior, Achilles (1.177). The Greeks en masse show their distaste for the war early in the poem, when they run joyously to launch their ships after Agamemnon's unwise command to set sail (2.142ff.), and they and the Trojans alike rejoice at the proposed duel in Book 3, which ought to end the dispute by personal conflict between Helen's two husbands (3.111–12, 320–23). The Trojans are often said to hate Paris (especially 3.453–54), their elders long for Helen to be given back (3.159–60), and even the Trojan herald who bears their offer to give back the goods stolen by Paris declares his hatred for him (7.390). Several standard epithets describe the misery of war, and the characters speak of it with distaste; Odysseus, complaining of Agamemnon's weakness, says: "[Would you did not rule over] us, for whom Zeus / from youth has appointed even to old age the accomplishing / of harsh wars, until we all are dead" (14.85–87); and Menelaus, vaunting over a foe he has killed, is made to complain three times over that the Trojans are never glutted with war (13.621, 635, 639).

The brutality and bloodiness of warfare is often brought out. The theme of maltreatment of the dead begins in the *Iliad* proem with the mention of bodies left for dogs and birds, and often recurs, even Athena and Hector speaking of it enthusiastically (8.379–80, 13.831–32; see Segal 1971b.9ff.). Hector threatens the dead Patroclus with decapitation (17.125–27), as a part of the buildup for Achilles' outraging of Hector's body. Gory wounds are often described, especially in Book 13 (there is a good summary in Griffin 1980.91). Usually such wounding is credited to minor heroes, perhaps to counterbalance their insignificance. There is a good example of this at the beginning of Book 5 (37–83), where the first killings by Agamemnon, Idomeneus, and Menelaus are limited to bare statements of weapon and wound (though as usual with personal details of some of the victims), and the next three, by the much less important Meriones, Meges, and Eurypylus, all include the bloody details. Meriones, in particular, specializes in dealing out painful wounds in the groin (5.65ff., 13.567ff., 650ff.; see Fenik 1968.144). In many cases a spear is driven through a man's face or mouth and the destructive effect described (16.345–50 is a sufficient example).

Occasionally, though not often, the description is physically impossible: a nonexistent blood vessel running up the back is torn away (13.546ff.), a still-beating heart shakes the butt end of the spear that penetrates it (13.442ff.), a man's eyeballs fall into the dust before his feet (13.616ff.). The sometimes gruesome realism seems, however, to arise not from any delight in gore, but from the poet's desire to parallel the vividness of other physical descriptions, such as Hector vomiting and sweating after he has been struck in the chest by a huge rock (14.437ff., 15.241ff.), and Diomedes sweating beneath his shield strap (5.796–97). There is one unrealistic convention: if seriously wounded, heroes do not suffer long agonies but always die immediately.

In contrast to this bloody realism stand the many details (too numerous to list) of pathos when a hero dies. Again and again they tell of brave young men dying far from home, deprived of their hope of happiness, leaving behind defenseless, aged parents whose care they cannot repay, a lonely young wife whom they had given much wealth to win. Like the similes, these vignettes are not standardized but always different, and thus are likely to be the poet's own thought. As with the similes, every reader will find his own favorites. (On this pathos, see Griffin 1976 and 1980 ch. 3 and 4.)

To mention a few such characterizations from a single book (Book 5): Scamandrius, coached in hunting by Artemis herself, who cannot help him now (49ff.); Phereclus, gifted by Athena, who built the ships that took Paris to Greece, "since he did not know the gods' plans" (59ff.); Pedaeus, a bastard brought up by a man's legal wife (69ff.); Hypsenor, the son of a much-venerated priest (76ff.); the two sons of an aged dream-interpreter, who failed to expound his sons' dreams as they left home (148ff.); the two sons of old Phaenops, who could not hope for other sons to inherit his wealth, so it went to remote kinsmen (152ff.); the noble ancestry of two powerful young Greeks, who are dignified too by a simile before they are killed by Aeneas (541ff.).

From other books, one remembers the tale of Axylus, renowned for his hospitality but undefended now by his many former guests (6.12–19); the sons of a skilled prophet, who tried in vain to hold them back from the expedition (11.329–34); the priest of Zeus from Mount Ida (16.603–7); the miserable death of Priam's youngest and most beloved son, Polydorus, whom he worries about, unaware of his death, even as he tries to call Hector back from facing Achilles (20.407–18, 22.46–48).

Homer sees warfare as a necessity in human affairs, and as a field on which to play out the unrelenting struggle for honor, even at the cost of one's life; but it is one of the evils the gods have decreed for mankind, not a glorious opportunity for heroism.

Further Reading

ON HONOR AND PROPER BEHAVIOR. Only a few of the many relevant works can be mentioned here. Dodds 1951 is a pioneering and influential study of the value systems of Homeric and later Greek society. Adkins 1982 is "concerned with the values, goals, emotions, and behavior of some of the principal characters of the Homeric poems and with the relationship between the respective values of the characters, the poet or poets, the original audience or readership, audiences in the fifth and fourth centuries B.C., and readers in the twentieth century A.D." (p. 292); he concludes that Homeric values were in general admired uncritically by the Greeks, and are "essentially the values of the modern nation-state" (p. 323). Adkins 1960 had already studied heroic ideas of merit and responsibility, and followed this up by many later articles on related topics; his views are challenged by Long 1970, and the issues reviewed (with bibliography) by Rowe 1983.

Whitman 1958 and 1982 paints a very bright picture of the heroic ideal; Rubino 1979 emphasizes the importance to it of the imminence of death. Gouldner 1965.41–77 is very good on the competitiveness of early Greek society; Stigers 1981 shows the highly significant *absence* of it in Sappho's poetry, compared with the work of male poets. Lloyd-Jones 1971 deals with the relationship of religion and morality. Redfield 1975 examines many aspects of the cultural system depicted in Homer. Sale 1963 and Claus 1975 discuss Achilles' actions in particular. There are good statements of the heroic approach to life in Schein 1984.67–88, Mueller 1970, and Lewis 1942 ch. 5 and 6.

ON WARFARE. Simone Weil's well-known account of the violence in the *Iliad* (1945) presents only one side of the picture; most of the brutal statements she quotes are made by the characters, not by the poet, and she says nothing of the words of pathos and sympathy that follow so many of the killings. Griffin (1976; 1980 ch. 4) deals especially with these pathetic comments. Bespaloff 1947 has a short but interesting chapter comparing the ideas of the *Iliad* with those of Tolstoy's *War and Peace*. Segal 1971b includes much about the bloody side of the fighting as well as the mutilation of corpses, and Mueller 1984 ch. 3 includes sections on the *ethos* of fighting and on the descriptions of injury and death. Redfield 1984 points out that Homer presents war not as a historical event but as a personal experience, and that the Greeks see war as hateful but admire those who are good at it; for Homer, battle and the songs about it give the only real immortality. In an interesting short article, O. Murray 1985 suggests that, in Homer, death in battle is tragic because it means a failure for the individual, whereas after the rise of the city-state it becomes a necessary and glorious sacrifice for the city, no longer simply tragic.

20

History and Society

Asked to name the first historian of his race, the first author to record his past, any Greek would have replied without hesitation: Homer. The fifth-century historians Herodotus and Thucydides treat the Trojan War as fact; even the proudly unromantic Thucydides uses figures from the Homeric catalogue of ships to show that "even allowing for a poet's exaggeration" the size of the Greek expedition to Troy must have been small compared to those of his own time (I.10). Whether in fact a Greek expedition was ever the cause of one of the numerous destructions of the successive settlements at Hissarlik is still a matter of controversy, and does not matter for the appreciation of Homer. How far the society depicted in the poems reflects an actual historical society is no less controversial, and of considerable interest to readers of the poems. It is also desirable to know something of Homer's conscious archaisms in order to understand the inconsistencies that occur in his descriptions of the use of weapons.

Three historical periods are involved. It is generally agreed that Homer lived and the poems took their present shape in the eighth century B.C., in Ionia, the Greek settlements on the western coast of Asia Minor and the adjacent islands. If the Trojan War ever took place, it was in the Late Bronze Age, which ended at the close of the thirteenth century B.C.; during this period Agamemnon's kingdom of Mycenae was rich and powerful and a united Greek expedition against the city of Troy was possible. Between these two periods fall the so-called Dark Ages, the intervening period of decline and depopulation from the twelfth to the ninth centuries, during which the immensely significant colonization of Ionia occurred.

Our inadequate knowledge of both the Dark Ages and eighth-century Ionia makes it difficult, even impossible, to distinguish features that belong to just one of these periods; and the changes in social order that must have taken place—the dying-out of kingship and the rise of the new kind of city-state, the change from a mainly pastoral to a mainly arable economy—happened at different times in different states. But it is obvious that the eighth century was marked by a renaissance, a new prosperity, a revived freedom of interest in Greek nationalism and the heroic past. Of this the Homeric poems were the most memorable result.

The following sections give an account of what is known of the society of eighth-century Ionia and the preceding Dark Ages; then summarize Homer's consciously archaizing use of traditional material from the much older time of Mycenaean greatness; and finally describe the main features of the (at least partly) artificial society presented in the poems and the nature and use of the heroes' weapons.

Ionia in the Time of Homer

From references in the poems it is clear that Homer was an Ionian, perhaps from Smyrna on the coast of Asia Minor or the offshore island of Chios, where later the Homeridae ("descendants of Homer"), a guild of bards, were centered (see p. 26). Similes describe birds gathering in the meadow beside the Ionian river Caÿster (2.459ff.) and the northwestern winds blowing from Thrace (9.5). Greek colonization of the west coast of Asia Minor began two centuries or more before this time, around 1000 B.C. (even earlier settlements are possible, but left no trace in legend). Stories told that the movement consisted of refugees from many parts of Greece who had collected in Athens and set off under the leadership of the sons of Codrus, the Athenian king. The uniformity of dialect and religious festivals in the Ionian cities suggest that there was in fact probably some common base for the migration.

The destruction that struck Mycenae and the other great cities between 1250 and 1150 B.C. ended their power and began the Dark Ages, a time of massive depopulation, great diminution of wealth, and loss of the knowledge of writing and the art of working stone and ivory. Local kingdoms took the place of the centralized Mycenaean bureaucracies (one of Odysseus's lying tales depicts the kind of man who might become such a regional chieftain; Odyssey 14.199ff.), and for some time there were no sizable towns either on the mainland or in Ionia. Iron took the place of bronze, not so much from technological advance but because reduction in trade made copper and tin unobtainable.

The kings used their wealth (and what they could squeeze out of lesser folk, as Alcinous recommends; Odyssey 13.14–15) to attract and hold their retainers, and to establish ties of guest friendship with their peers, based on reciprocal gift-giving. This custom is particularly common in the *Odyssey*, and is explicitly described at the end of the conversation between Telemachus and the disguised Athena (*Odyssey* 1.310–18). Telemachus describes the situation in Ithaca as one with many potential kings, all ready to aim for the position once Odysseus is firmly out of the way (*Odyssey* 1.392ff.), and in Phaeacia there are twelve "kings" besides Alcinous (*Odyssey* 8.390–91).

The society then gradually passed from one based upon strong households, with one household dominating the others, to the new development of the *polis* (city-state); it was centered on a city but united town and surrounding country with no political distinctions between the residents of either.

Familiarity with what it was like to establish a colony is evident in the description of Phaeacia. Its founder, Nausithous, had led an expedition to the site, founded and built a city and temples, and divided up the farmland (*Odyssey* 6.7–10); Nausicaa describes it as a walled city on a promontory linked to the island by a causeway, with two harbors, a well-built assembly place and a temple (*Odyssey* 6.262–65). This is an accurate description of the site of more than one Ionian city. Odysseus's own eye for a promising site appears in his wistful description of the uninhabited island off the Cyclops's shore, a prize for a colonizing expedition (*Odyssey* 9.116–41).

The Ionian colonies thrived, and from 900 on their prosperity increased. The founders had become kings and were given honors as heroes after their death, but monarchy did not become hereditary and fairly stable oligarchies were the norm. (Rather later than Homer's time, in the seventh and sixth centuries, rising population caused problems, which led to further colonization and often to the strongman rule the Greeks called "tyranny.") Power was usually held by a council of elders, the heads of the noble families; the executive consisted of magistrates, perhaps chosen for annual terms, whose powers were limited by the elders in council. There would also be an assembly of adult males, which was subordinate to the council but heard the debates of the leaders and gave or withheld their assent.

Life in Greece and Ionia in the eighth century must have been similar to that depicted on the shield of Achilles (18.483–607; see pp. 280–83). The year's work was divided among plowing, sowing, and harvesting, with the vintage in the autumn and the year-long herding of cattle and sheep. As in Hesiod, the later staple, the olive, is not yet of importance. Kings were small-scale land-owners (18.556–57), there was a formal judicial system, and warfare with neighbors was (as always) very common. Festivals and dancing gave relaxation. The cities described on the shield are already very much like the classical Greek city-state, the *polis;* a city is walled, with a marketplace, a tract of territory, and its own independent institutions.

In the eighth-century renaissance trade and communications improved, an alphabet modified from the Phoenician script was adopted, and fresh colonies were sent out to the western Mediterranean. In mainland Greece the pan-Hellenic importance of the Olympic Games and the Delphic Oracle increased. The Ionian cities, traditionally twelve in number, instituted the joint celebration of the Panionia at Mykale, a promontory close to Samos and Miletus. This was probably similar to the festival on the island of Delos, vividly described in the *Hymn to Apollo* (146–55), composed not much later than the Homeric poems:

> But in Delos, Apollo, you most delight your heart;
> there the long-robed Ionians gather,
> they and their children and their modest wives,
> and with boxing and dancing and song
> they honor and delight you, whenever their gathering is held.
> One would say they are immortal and ageless forever
> if he came upon the Ionians when they meet together.
> For he would see the beauty of them all, and would delight his
>   heart
> looking upon the men and the well-dressed women
> and their swift ships and all their wealth.

At such festivals bards must have been prominent figures (see pp. 16–19). This is a period of great self-confidence, of renewed national pride, and of curiosity about cities and minds of other peoples (*Odyssey* 1.3). Recent archaeological work has also demonstrated a sudden resurgence of interest in the heroic past, displayed in the dedication of new offerings to age-old tombs from the Mycenaean period and in the appearance of lavish funeral rituals like those described in Homer. Clearly this new pride in the present was accompanied by an admiration for the heroes of the past, and with this the Homeric epics must have been intimately associated.

In important respects Homer consciously archaizes. This is partly by omission; he never gives a hint of Greeks living in Asia Minor where the *Iliad* is set (Miletus, a major Greek site, is even described as a city of the Carians; 2.868), of cities without kings, of writing, of the use of iron weapons. Conversely, he retains without exception certain features that could not have been familiar to him in ordinary life and must have survived as part of the tradition of song and legend from the age of the great and wealthy cities of the Mycenaean period. This is the period in which the power, organization, and easy communications of the mainland cities made possible (whether or not it ever took place) a Trojan War—an attack by a unified Greek force, owing service to one especially powerful king, on a powerful, well-defended city near the coast of Asia Minor. At this time there were many wealthy centers on the mainland of Greece in addition to Mycenae, among them Athens, Thebes, and Pylos.

In Mycenae society was highly centralized, possessing much wealth and an enormous amount of gold, and organized by a highly developed bureaucracy. This is the origin of the account of the power and wealth of Agamemnon, though in Homer his position is modified by the addition of a council and assembly belonging to a later time. From this time, too, comes the use of bronze for armor and weapons, with iron known for its hardness but rigidly restricted in use. The use of chariots in warfare, described unrealistically in the Homeric poems, must also be derived from this period. Descriptions of a few artifacts unknown in Homer's own time must have survived in the oral traditions: the helmet made of boars' tusks (10.261ff.), Nestor's great cup (11.632ff.), the technique of metal inlay on the shield, which can be seen on daggers of the Mycenaean period, and the semicylindrical shield of Ajax (on these, see Kirk 1962.179ff.).

The tradition must also have preserved some old words, old names, the magnificence of the walls of Troy, and some at least of the geographical details of the catalogue of ships, for some places are mentioned that were not inhabited after the Mycenaean period. Any historical facts, any characters, genealogies, and deeds underlying the great sagas of the Trojan War and the battles for Thebes must derive from his period, developed into legend during the Dark Ages.

Why this powerful civilization came to its catastrophic decline is still not understood. New defensive works had been added to the great palaces, but nevertheless they were burned, baking for our information the soft clay tablets on which their records were kept. It might have been an influx of non-Greek raiders (at this time destruction was widespread in the eastern Mediterranean), or of a different race of Greeks, the Dorians; or an uprising of the local population, perhaps under stresses caused by some natural disaster such as plague, drought, or famine. No new culture appears. The Dark Ages begin, and a century or more later there comes a further great change in the Greek world, the large-scale settlement of the Asian coast known as Ionia.

Society and Weapons in the Homeric Poems

Just as with the epic dialect and the family of the gods, the bardic tradition has produced the depiction of a society that is a fairly uniform and consistent but essentially artificial amalgam, a combination of elements deriving from different historical periods. The weaponry also shows a mixture of different practices.

Agamemnon is "the lord of men," the great king of Mycenae; but he has lost the mighty bureaucracy, the retainers and subordinate ministers, the tax collectors such a king must have had in historical fact. Only his heralds are left. He leads to Troy an expedition of troops from many mainland cities and some of the islands, each division headed by a subordinate king. The muster roll of participants on both sides is given at the parade before the first battle of the poem (2.494ff.), though this list is not entirely consistent with the rest of the poem and is better considered a record of the contingents that set sail from Greece years before (see p. 188).

Agamemnon's motive was not conquest or profit, but the recovery of his brother's wife, Helen, abducted by the Trojan prince Paris. Homer does not make clear exactly why the other national leaders follow him. According to the legend, they joined him (in some cases reluctantly) because they were compelled by the oath exacted from Helen's suitors by her father, Tyndareus, before he gave her away in marriage, that "if anyone should carry her off by force, and thrust aside proper behavior (aidôs) and fear of public opinion (nemesis), they should all together set off after him to take vengeance" (Hesiod frag. 204.81–84 M.-W.). This tale, like that of the judgment of Paris, Homer keeps somewhat at a distance.

Agamemnon's supremacy is asserted by Odysseus as he rallies
the fleeing troops: "Not all we Greeks are kings here. / It is not
a good thing for many to rule; let there be one leader, / one king,
to whom Zeus gave / scepter and judicial power, so that he may
be king over us" (2.203–6). Achilles (too young to have been one
of Helen's suitors, and so not bound by Tyndareus's oath) is told
by Nestor: "Do not try to contend with the king / in strength,
since he has no equal allotment of honor, / he the scepter-
wielding king, to whom Zeus has given glory. / Though you are
the stronger man, and a goddess was your mother, / yet he is the
greater, since he is lord over more" (1.277–81). It is possible that
this expressed preference for an autocrat reflects not so much
the views of surviving kings of Homer's own day, as a commoner's preference for one overlord rather than the more
numerous demands of an oligarchy. As the highest leader, Agamemnon receives the largest share of booty, even though he has
not himself taken part in its acquisition, as Achilles bitterly
complains (1.163–68; 9.332–33). In return, he must give feasts for
the others; as Nestor reminds him, "All entertainment is your
responsibility, for you rule over many" (9.73).

But his power is far from absolute. "In 'Homeric' society the
kings do not consistently make political, judicial or even military decisions on behalf of their people" (Geddes 1984.28). Important public business is discussed by a council of chiefs, whose
advice Agamemnon is told by Nestor to follow (9.74–75), and is
then taken to a general assembly, which can be called by anyone,
not just the king, and includes stewards, helmsmen, and commissariat workers (19.42–45). Here the king's scepter is held by
whoever desires to speak. There is freedom of speech for the
chiefs, as Diomedes claims (9.33ff.), though for the less eminent
it is not wise to displease one's betters, as Calchas fears he will
do if he identifies the cause of the plague (1.78–83). Thersites is
incautious, and speaks not only rudely but without holding the
speaker's staff (which is in Odysseus's hands), and he suffers for
his impropriety (2.211ff.). He is a nobleman, not a commoner
(later writers say he was the son of Agrius, who was brother of
Diomedes' grandfather, Oeneus, and he claims to have captured
Trojans for ransom; 2.231), but he is unpopular and has spoken in
assembly too often before (221, 276–77).

Skill in debate is as important for the hero as superiority in
battle; he must be "both a speaker of words and a doer of deeds"
(9.443; see also 2.273, 18.105–6, 252), and the assembly can receive
the attribute "where men win glory" (1.490). The assembly votes

by acclamation (2.394) and breaks up without formal ceremony. At the beginning of the poem Agamemnon overrules the assembly, perhaps because a personal matter is in question (like Paris's refusal to accept the will of the Trojans; 7.357ff.) and also, of course, for the sake of the story. But in the assembly he is contradicted by Achilles, Thersites, and Diomedes, and it is not he who decides if the army shall stay at Troy or return home, or who shall be its champion against Hector (7.107ff.). Apart from his wealth, Agamemnon's power resembles that of an eighth-century magistrate or executive rather than that of a Mycenaean "lord of men."

In Ithaca the assembly summoned by Telemachus similarly includes nobles and others; it has not met since Odysseus left, but the questioning about who called them together implies that he was not the only one who could do so (*Odyssey* 2.26ff.). There are many problems in the position of Telemachus, who does not automatically inherit Odysseus's kingship in the case of his death, though willing to do so; as he says, "There are indeed other chiefs of the Greeks too, / many of them, in Ithaca, young and old, / who might hold this rank, since Odysseus has died" (*Odyssey* 1.394–96; the whole discussion [386–401] is full of difficulties; see Geddes 1984.29). There are further problems in the position of Odysseus's father, Laertes, who apparently resigned long ago in favor of his son and did not resume the kingship when Odysseus left for Troy.

Marriage with Penelope may possibly confer some right, or at least power, of kingship upon her husband, as Aegisthus ruled at Mycenae after seducing Clytemnestra and Oedipus at Thebes after marrying Epicaste (*Odyssey* 3.304–5; 11.275–76); the leading suitor Antinous is said by his companion Eurymachus to desire the kingship rather than the marriage itself (*Odyssey* 22.49ff.). But it is clear that the requirements of the story and the influences of other tales—the suitors' quest for Penelope's hand resembles that of the heroes who sought to wed Helen (see p. 65)—confuse the situation to such an extent that no very logical situation can be deduced. Perhaps Homer was not very familiar with hereditary monarchy.

The society depicted is in other ways artificial and incomplete. There is a military hierarchy, outlined in Achilles' power over his five subordinate captains, who give orders under his overall direction (16.70–71). There are heralds, bards, and other professional craftsmen (see p. 16). There are also slaves. But there is no clear term for an intermediate free proletariat class, though of course the "people" or "host" (*plêthus, laos, dêmos*) are often mentioned. When Odysseus recalls the fleeing army (2.188ff.), he makes what seems to be a distinction between officers and other ranks ("men of the *dêmos*"), but Hector's constant counselor Polydamas, a Trojan noble, seems in a perplexing passage to include himself among the latter (12.211ff.; neither Lattimore nor Fitzgerald translates the words). Homer's world must have known richer and poorer, upper and lower classes, but his poems do not attempt to represent this consistently.

Weapons and armor are uniformly of bronze, which had been used for two millennia before the zenith of Mycenae. It is durable, noncorroding, easy to work, can readily be remelted and reworked, and takes a good edge. The military uses of bronze, preserved in the tradition, pass over into vivid metaphors: Achilles' battle cry is "brazen" (18.222), and so is the voice of the famous herald Stentor (5.785); once a dying hero lapses into a "brazen sleep" (11.241).

Iron, however, is often mentioned in nonmilitary uses, for knives (18.34, 23.30), axes (4.485, 23.851), plowshares (23.835), and metaphorically for hardness of heart (*thumos*, 22.357) and moral courage (24.205; Camps 1980.65–66 gives further examples). Some of these uses for iron may derive from the Mycenaean period, but are more likely to come directly from the poet's own experience, as does the description of the quenching of red-hot iron in the horrifying simile used for the destruction of the Cyclops's eye (*Odyssey* 9.391ff.). His awareness of the use of iron for weapons is betrayed in the proverb "iron itself drives a man on" (*Odyssey* 16.294, 19.13), and in the "iron tumult" that "rises to the brazen sky" in the struggle over Patroclus's body (17.424–25). The tradition of the Bronze Age died hard; even in the fifth century Herodotus calls a blacksmith forging iron a "bronzeman" working in his "bronze-shop" (*chalkeus, chalkêion,* I.68.1).

Conflict between tradition and later practice often causes inconsistency in use of weapons. Most heroes carry a smallish round shield with a boss (a convex projection) in the middle. Ajax has an older type, semicylindrical and "like a tower," tall enough to stand on the ground and protect the entire body of the warrior; but Hector's "bossed shield," obviously the round type, in one memorable detail touches his neck and ankles as he runs to Troy with it slung behind his back, as only a tower shield would do (6.117–18). Periphoetes once trips up on a similar shield, which "reached to his feet" (15.645–46).

One long thrusting spear is the oldest form of armament, dignified by its use to describe Peleus and Priam; but two shorter throwing spears are a later development, and often there are inconsistencies—Paris as he arms picks up one (thrusting) spear (3.338), though earlier in the book he brandished two (throwing) spears (18), and then throws it (346). On the other hand, Agamemnon when arming picks up two (throwing) spears (11.43), and thrusts with one of them (95). Patroclus, who cannot manage Achilles' great spear, takes two smaller ones instead (16.139). The ambiguity of how many spears a warrior has available is turned to good account in the final duel, when the mighty spear of Peleus has been returned to Achilles by Athena but Hector, after throwing a spear in vain, "has no spear" and calls vainly for one to the supposed Deiphobus (22.293ff.). Chariots are very often mentioned, but the Greeks seldom use them (Achilles' is mentioned only at 20.498ff.), and when used they are mainly transportation to the fighting, not a vehicle for a charge or a raised platform for wielding weapons more easily.

The constant references to the power and wealth of Mycenae—a tiny village in Homer's time—and the use of bronze weaponry contribute to the air of remote ancient greatness surrounding the names of the traditional heroes. This remoteness makes it easier to accept the gods' intervention, and adds a little of the emotional appeal of *ubi sunt?*—"where are these great figures now?"—which reinforces the *Iliad*'s emphasis on human mortality. In some ways the *Iliad* and the *Odyssey* depict different worlds, but this is mainly a matter of viewpoint rather than of chronology. The *Iliad*, like the heroic funerals of the late eighth century, reflects a reactionary aristocratic view, where the important values are territorial defense, expansion, acquisition by seizure, and personal military success and the resultant honor (see pp. 150–52). The *Odyssey* shows an interest in exploration, colonization, and trade, in resourcefulness and the advancement of an unprivileged individual, and in personal family relationships.

Both poems foster the idea of a national Greek identity, a community of language, religion, festivals, and traditions, brought about by a new ease of communication and acquaintance with other, non-Greek peoples; the one through its record of a great united Greek action against non-Greeks, the other by its narrative of the adventure of travel in foreign lands and the joy of a return home after a long absence. Neither of these exploits would have been possible during the Dark Ages; the first belongs to the long-past age of Mycenaean greatness, the other to the renewed confidence and expansion of eighth-century Ionia. It is this new national spirit, more than political or material changes, that sets Homer's own period apart from the Dark Ages that preceded it.

Further Reading

Many of the topics of this section are very controversial, and different views will be found in the sources mentioned here. O. Murray 1980, Austin and Vidal-Naquet 1977, Andrewes 1971, and Finley 1970 have manageable, up-to-date, clear, and very sound chapters. Luce 1975 gives a good overview of the archaeological evidence with many excellent illustrations (though few scholars share his confidence in Homer's knowledge of Ithaca). Finley 1978 is well known and of much value, but may perhaps draw too consistent a picture of an actual society from the poems, placing it one or two centuries before Homer's time; Snodgrass 1974 holds that the Homeric society could not actually have existed at any period. Geddes 1984 examines the place of the common people and the position of the king in Homer, concluding (after a most interesting study) that Homer had no experience of overlords who were very wealthy at the expense of the masses, that in fact the masses hardly exist at all, and that the kings seem to have no real function. Kirk 1962 is still a good general guide, and Kirk 1976 ch. 1, 2, 3, and 9 gives a good background to the poet and his society. Among the most important major works devoted to the period between the Mycenaean Age and Homer's are Snodgrass 1971 and 1980, Coldstream 1977, Jeffery 1976, Vermeule 1972, and Webster 1958. The *Cambridge Ancient History* vol. II part 2 ch. 27, 36, 38, 39(b), vol. III part 1 ch. 16, 18a–b, 19, and vol. III part 3 ch. 39a, 45a is a basic guide. Snodgrass 1967 is the standard work on Homeric weapons. Donlan 1982 is good on gift-giving. On the historicity of the Trojan War see Foxhall and Davies 1984.

Commentaries

II

21

Iliad Book I

This will be a tale of legendary heroes of the past, united in a mighty Greek achievement against a foreign foe, the siege and sack of Troy. But it is also much more. From the very first lines Homer will raise the question of the origins of human suffering, and the first episodes will present scenes of very human men reacting in human emotional ways to an ordinary human situation. He does not depict good men fighting to overcome the wicked (as in the *Odyssey*), or a grand hero struggling against forces of evil (as does *Beowulf*). He will show a man of superior rank who holds his position by hereditary right and is unequal to its demands, whose insecurity makes him overassertive in the face of an apparent challenge. He will show another man, ranked below the first in the hierarchy but with much greater gifts as a fighter and a leader and greater strength of character, who has become resentful, bitter, and frustrated by the inadequacies of the officer to whom he must submit. Both of them prize, above all else, their honor and the status they know they deserve, the one by hereditary right, the other by merit. And in this potentially explosive situation, familiar in any organization where one person is placed above another, a spark ignites a flame and both men resort to angry words, take up ill-considered positions from which they will find it hard to retreat, and involve themselves in a confusion of conflicting duties and responsibilities to their position, their peers, their dependents, and themselves. Amidst all this, the voice of common sense and order is heard but disregarded.

The spectators of this human conflict are the gods; the characters turn to them for help and for explanation of phenomena beyond human knowledge and control, and the poet employs them to glorify particular heroes, to foreshadow the future, and (surprisingly to us) to introduce the element of comedy (see p. 133). Their head, Zeus, must accept ultimate responsibility for everything that happens, though often he seems not to cause it: human weakness and human strength do that. And underlying the affairs of gods and men alike, emerging more and more clearly as the Trojans enter the tale and wider human situations and emotions appear, is the ultimate and dominating fact of man's mortality, the essential and inevitable limit to his achievement. This limitation is illuminated by the carefree immortality of the gods, and brought to a sharp focus on the hero Achilles, born of a goddess and a human, superhuman but mortal, doomed to die even before the usual human lifespan, and fully aware of all this as he consciously chooses actions that will bring about his end. The poet accomplishes all this within the framework of traditional characters, a traditional setting, and traditional techniques of structure, exposition, language, and verse, shaping them all by his personal skill to produce the grandeur of the poem.

After a brief introduction to the complete epic, the first book describes the events leading up to the quarrel of Achilles and Agamemnon, Achilles' angry withdrawal, and Zeus's decision to have the Greeks defeated until they realize they must recall Achilles to their ranks. We learn a great deal about these two men, and also meet a few of the other characters, in particular Nestor and the divinities Athena, Thetis, Zeus, and Hera. In addition, we note the voice of the poet himself and some of the themes he will use in the poem: human folly, resentment, and anger, which bring suffering for many who were in no way involved; human wisdom and self-restraint; and also humor and light relief.

For convenience of discussion, this book will be divided into five parts: the short proem; the priest's appeal and the plague; the assembly and quarrel; the meeting of Achilles and Thetis; and the assembly of the gods. As usual in Homer, the successive scenes are actually closely connected.

The Proem (1–12a)

The word "anger" begins the poem: Fitzgerald's "Anger be now your song, immortal one, / Akhilleus' anger . . . " is a much better representation of the forcefulness of the Greek than Lattimore's version. The theme is immediately illuminated with further colors of suffering, the death of warriors, and the dishonoring of the fallen. This will not be a song of the glories of a Greek victory and the defeat of those hated by the gods, but of the weaknesses of human beings and the troubles that result from them.

Already the poet's use of the tradition he inherits can be seen, for he is introducing traditional motifs but refusing to elaborate most of them in order to pass as quickly as possible—though without the appearance of haste—to the action of the plot. In other poems, and later in this one, these motifs are handled in much greater detail when amplification is desirable. There must be a call to the Muse, who is the source of the poet's skill and the guarantee of the truth of what he tells, but here it is limited to her name and a word of command ("sing!"); later, when more expansion is needed to introduce on a fitting scale the massive catalogue of the forces marching out to battle, there will be a much fuller summons and explanation of the poet's dependence on her (2.484–94). On this occasion, it is the suffering that is amplified, by means of the motifs of "sending souls to Hades" and "giving men's bodies to dogs and birds."

"The will of Zeus was fulfilled." There is a question about the meaning of this. Did Zeus will all the suffering just described, or is this only an allusion to his agreement with Thetis later in this book? It is wiser to take the words as a general acknowledgment that nothing happens without Zeus's general agreement, a kind of weaker form of Hesiod's praise of Zeus's power at the beginning of the *Works and Days* (3–8). Hector says, "Zeus's will is always the stronger; / he terrifies even the brave man, and takes away victory / easily, after he has himself urged him on to fight" (17.176–78), and the words are repeated in the poet's own voice (16.688–90). Achilles in one of the final scenes of the poem describes the two urns from which Zeus dispenses good things and bad to mankind (24.527–33). On one occasion Zeus's deliberations are described at some length, in a more serious vein than we shall see at the end of this book (16.644–55). The characters hold Zeus responsible, and perhaps the poet too in his ordinary life; but within the poem it is, of course, the poet who manipulates the events, and as he presents the tale Zeus consents to what goes on but cannot be blamed for the quarrel of the two leaders or the resulting sufferings of the Greeks.

Then the time of the action is set; it will begin with the quarrel between the two heroes. The cause of the quarrel is first identified in a question to the goddess: "Which god set them at loggerheads?" (a question to the Muse is standard in an invocation, as can be seen at 2.487). The poet skillfully helps his audience grasp the immediate situation by slipping into the future (Apollo's anger and the plague) and then moving back from that point, through Agamemnon's rebuff of the priest, to the present time; the action begins almost imperceptibly as the priest approaches the ships of the Greeks. The same technique of rapidly summarizing a situation by jumping forward in time and then moving back can be seen in Phoenix's autobiography (9.447ff.), where he recounts first his flight from his home, then his father's hatred, then the seduction of his father's mistress, which caused it.

The proem is very short. That of the *Odyssey* is of similar length (though different in tone) and so, by conscious imitation, is that of the *Aeneid*. This is in contrast to the great double proem of Hesiod's *Theogony*, with its two long invocations of the Muses (first on Helicon [1–21], then on Olympus [36–93]), and the account of the poet's relations with them (again twice over, 22–35 and 94–103). Hesiod does not reach the proposed subject of his song until about a hundred verses after it has begun (104–15). Homer's method is very different.

The Priest's Appeal and the Plague (12b–52)

The priest approaches. Only the essentials are given. We hear the purpose of his coming—the return of his daughter—but nothing of the circumstances of her capture (this is filled in later; 1.366–69). He is said to be bringing ransom, to show he is behaving in the proper way of a suppliant, but there is no detailed description of it (compare the account of the ransom for Hector at 24.229–37; the absence of attendants, or even a means of transporting the ransom, not only speeds up the story but intensifies the priest's isolation). Above all, he is bearing the staff and insignia of the god Apollo; not simple visual color, but a highly significant identification of a priest who has the power of the god behind him. The introduction to his speech makes it clear not only what his purpose is, but that he is addressing all the Greeks; the poet has not delayed to tell us of the summoning of the assembly. Within these few verses the poet has outlined most of the elements that occur in a hugely expanded form in the preliminaries of Priam's appeal to Achilles, which covers nearly 350 verses (24.142–485). At that point, the poet is slowly building up to the great climax of the poem; here he is moving swiftly into the great quarrel scene. The scenes are identical in shape but very different in scale (see pp. 71–77).

The priest's speech is short but formally complete, including a benediction, a request, and an offer of ransom. He does not touch Agamemnon's knees or chin, as is usually done by a suppliant, perhaps because of the speed of the narrative, or because this would be unfitting for a priest in full regalia. (Odysseus's modest clutching of a leafy branch to hide his nakedness from the young princess causes another exception at *Odyssey* 6.141ff.) All present want to respect the priest and think the ransom adequate; all except Agamemnon, and the introduction to his words forewarns us of his displeasure. His tone is bullying and unnecessarily brutal, combining disregard for Chryses' suppliant status, his old age, his sacred office, and his feelings as a father. He also ignores the will of the assembly and (some of the audience may reflect) the opinion of his strong-minded wife, Clytemnestra, for to take a concubine into one's house is to dishonor a wife (9.450, *Odyssey* 1.430ff.). In a very few lines—his speech is little longer than the priest's—he has defied both the proper way to behave and the will of the people for whom he is responsible, and has characterized himself in most vivid fashion.

The rejected suppliant goes to the seashore, which is not primarily a topographical reference but a symbol of desolation and misery; later in this book Achilles will carry his sorrows to the seashore, and so do (among others) Telemachus and Odysseus in their times of greatest despair (*Odyssey* 2.260, 13.220). Line 34 is also well known for its sound, the initial monosyllable of the verb leading on to an imitation of the waves breaking on the wide beach: *bê d' akeôn para thîna poluphloisboio thalassês,* "went silent beside the shore of resounding seasurge" (see pp. 117–19). He prays to his god (hailing him as "lord of the silver bow," a bow we shall soon see in action) and claims help, as usual on the basis of past services rendered. Apollo hears and comes at once. Journeys of gods to men are common in Homer, and if the occasion is important he often dignifies it with some fitting simile or other decoration, such as the long wave-skimming journey of Hermes to Calypso's island (*Odyssey* 5.28–75), the harnessing of the golden chariot for Hera and Athena (5.720ff.), Poseidon's imposing progress from Samothrace to Troy (13.17–38), and later in this book, Thetis's highly individual appearance from the sea mist to speak with her son. Here Apollo's reaction is most important and must be expanded, but instead of using a simile, the poet describes him as a hunter striding over the mountains, arrows "clanging" (*eklanxan*) in his quiver; of course he is always the archer god, and the tone here is full of menace. Then comes the simile "like the night." It now sets him apart from a mere human hunter, and its effective imprecision conveys speed, suddenness, silence, and doom, for "darkness hid his eyes" is a standard Homeric euphemism for death. He kneels, as Greek bowmen in sculpture always do, and lets fly with his arrows. In the Greek, the single-syllable verb (ball'), placed at the beginning of the line, seems to imitate the sound of the bowstring.

If we compare the description of the plague with Achilles' account of it to his mother later on (382–84), we notice a significant difference. There Achilles simply says that the Greeks die. But here the poet avoids the plain statement and, in a striking phrase, pictures the funeral pyres smoking all over the plain: "The mules first he struck and the swift dogs, / but then against the men themselves loosing his piercing dart he / shot; continually the pyres of the dead were burning, everywhere." Apollo attacks the nameless Greeks, not Agamemnon or the other leaders. Of course the plot demands this, but the first few lines of the poem told how many men die when leaders make a mistake; as Horace put it, *quidquid delirant reges, plectuntur Achivi* (see p. 317). In just fifty-two verses the poet has shown Agamemnon's first mistake and its disastrous results for his army. He has shown one way to receive an apparently helpless old suppliant who seeks to ransom his child; the final book of the poem will show a different way.

The Assembly and the Quarrel (53–305)

The action flows smoothly on, with the standard link "for nine days . . . then on the tenth" (the parallel to the nine days' grieving for Hector before his burial on the tenth, in the last book, may not be accidental); and there begins the longest episode in the book, the monumental quarrel between Achilles and Agamemnon. An assembly must be summoned; it might be inartistic to have Agamemnon call it, since it is his action that will have to be discussed, and in any case it is a good opportunity to thrust Achilles into a leading position. So now the spotlight shifts to him, characteristically taking a bold action. As a contributing agent the poet introduces the goddess Hera, who will play a large part in the plot of the epic and will be brought in again at the end of the quarrel theme (18.356–67). But the action is still moving swiftly; the summoning of the troops is much more rapid than it will be in the second book, or at the reconciliation meeting at 19.40ff., where the tense situation leads to the poet to build up his climax with the gathering of the ship crews, the stewards, the individual wounded chiefs, and finally Agamemnon himself.

Achilles opens the debate and proposes a course of action. The army's official prophet, Calchas, is introduced by the poet, who tells us that the seer has been reliable in the past and perhaps hints at his terrible prophecy about Agamemnon's daughter at Aulis, which the audience is probably intended to recall later when the king abuses the prophet (106–8). Calchas's revelation is foreshadowed by his timid request for reassurance, and Achilles' forceful words reveal a suspicion that Agamemnon's action may be the cause of the problem (as well as giving the audience a hint of the exciting conflict ahead). This is then made explicit by the prophet, and the king flashes out at him in anger. But he reluctantly agrees to return the woman, putting the good of all before his own preference. Finally, however, his pride takes over, and he demands a replacement to confirm the mark of honor she represented. Achilles' aggressive initiative may have provoked this, but Agamemnon's proposal would have been better made by someone else, and Achilles' reaction is characteristically vigorous.

He leads off with an insult. His speech begins with the regular "most honored son of Atreus," but instead of concluding the verse with the usual "lord of men, Agamemnon" he goes on, "greediest of all men" (122). The rest of his speech is more reasonable in tone, but the damage has been done; Agamemnon knows the discomforts of having a better man as outspoken subordinate, and with a weak man's anger goes on to make his second big mistake. It would have been tactful to ignore Achilles' thinly veiled truculence on this occasion, but instead he presses hard on the issue of compensation—thus providing support for Achilles' insulting phrase—and he goes on to threaten to seize another chief's prize. His anger is shown by his fractured syntax: something like "or do you wish, so that you yourself may keep your prize, but that I like this / sit here without one, and you tell me to give this one back?" (133–34). Then, perhaps seeing Achilles' furious face (we are close to the theater here), he backs away into the security of giving orders for the woman's return, with one final thrust at Achilles; saying in effect, "you go do it, since you started all this" (146–47).

Too late. Beginning with further insults, Achilles voices his long-standing disgust, resentment, and frustration at his unsatisfactory commander-in-chief. It is for Agamemnon's quarrel that they are at Troy, to maintain *his* honor, and now he threatens to destroy the honor of his loyal subordinates; Achilles has always done the hard work of fighting, Agamemnon got the pick of the profits. If there is to be no honor for Achilles, only wealth for Agamemnon, he will quit right now.

The situation is not irretrievable, if Agamemnon were wise enough. But he is not; he begins with worse than name-calling ("Run away then!") and lets loose his own old personal dislike of this troublesome subordinate. Finally, consolidating his mistake and cutting off his own retreat, he announces his decision to seize Achilles' prize as substitute for his own. The challenge is issued, the needless duel made inevitable, the superb son of a goddess is locked in conflict with the unwise king who holds his authority under Zeus. For a while Homer holds them still, face to face, as he shows us Achilles' thoughts.

Achilles wonders whether to kill the man who is dishonoring him or to hold back. This kind of decision scene is common in Homer, and as usual two possible courses of action are laid out, of which the hero will eventually choose the second. In this case, the internal dilemma of the hero is dramatized by a quasi-physical description—"his heart within his hairy chest was torn two ways" (Homer probably thinks of a physical effect upon the organ)—and by a visible action, as Achilles half draws his sword. It will remain half drawn until his decision is taken, a character-istically Homeric physical representation of a mental state (see pp. 114–16, and see also T. S. Eliot's "objective correlative," a physical counterpart of an emotion; quoted by Booth 1961.97).

Suddenly his perplexity is resolved by the arrival of a divinity. This is common enough in decision scenes, but here the abrupt-ness and unexpectedness of her appearance is mirrored in the verse itself. Achilles is drawing his sword (194), and as the end of the verse approaches the experienced hearer expects it to be concluded with the usual decorative epithet "stúdded with sílver" (see pp. 52–53). But the crisis is acute, and Athena loses no time; not only does she dispense with similes, sandal-donning, and the usual appurtenances of a divine journey, she brusquely shoves aside the patient old epithet and bursts into verse, which ends "Cáme then Athéna / . . . ." (A similar effect of abruptness and disruption of the usual formulaic ending of a verse is found at her sudden appearance to Diomedes, 10.507.) She stands behind Achilles and again the usual proprieties are violated, for instead of addressing him she takes him by the hair (once again emotions are expressed by a physical action). He whirls around in amazement, and a third time the usual conven-tions are rejected, for instead of listening to what the visitor has to say (the normal type-scene element) he accosts her first.

He intentionally ignores the obvious reason for her presence and invites her to witness his punishment of Agamemnon; the same aggressive dissimulation appears later when Patroclus appears in tears and Achilles ignores the obvious reason for his distress (the sufferings of the Greeks) and asks if he has had bad news from home (16.2ff.). Athena urges him to stay his hand, if he will be persuaded by her (Lattimore's "but will you obey me?" for line 207 makes her sound much too uncertain of the outcome), and promises that in the end it will be much to his advantage. He wisely, though reluctantly, assents (he will give the same brief, grudging response to Thetis's request at 24.139–40) and confirms it with the symbolic action of resheathing his sword.

It is important to note exactly what the poet has Athena do here. She does not put anything into the hero's mind, or exercise any superior power over his thinking. She assures him of Hera's loving care for both himself and Agamemnon, urges him not to strike Agamemnon but to vent his anger in insult, and tells him that at some future time he will be amply compensated for what he is putting up with. There is no threat. Neither is there logical argument, which is one reason why she should not be taken as a kind of projection of Achilles' own better judgment; what she says does not sound at all like what is going on in Achilles' mind. He is not persuaded by reason; he chooses to follow her advice because of respect for the gods and a sensible man's knowledge that one defies them to one's cost. But the decision is his.

So Achilles turns back to Agamemnon (as usual during divine interventions, he and the army have been ignored while our attention is on Athena and Achilles) and taunts him with cowardice. He also blames the rest of the chiefs for weakness in not resisting him (231–32), a charge that helps explain his attitude to them in Book 9 (see p. 233). He swears by the speaker's staff that one day the Greeks will long for his return, and throws the gold-studded staff to the ground. Again this is a symbolic action displaying his inner feelings, for the staff is (as he says, 237–39) the symbol of Zeus-given law and order, which the "scepter-holding" (279) king should maintain. The young Telemachus, in his first assembly of chiefs on Ithaca, similarly hurls down the staff in frustration (*Odyssey* 2.80). The staff, once held by Zeus himself (2.100ff.), should be held high to call him to witness a pledge (as at 7.412); instead Achilles throws it down, showing how all the normal proprieties have been violated by Agamemnon's proposed action against him. The code of behavior by which the society lives has been broken by its supreme leader, and now Achilles himself will refuse the duty of service to his superior.

At this crisis a mediator arises: Nestor, ceremoniously introduced to give his words weight and to give us the same relief that his hearers must feel. In a beautiful speech, he voices experience, wisdom, and moderation. He deplores the present situation, and then, addressing both adversaries, claims the right to be heard in a lengthy account of an occasion on which even the great heroes of the past welcomed Nestor among them and listened to his counsel. Nestor often recounts such tales. They are not just senile rambling or self-glorification, but establish the credentials of the speaker, to show on what grounds he claims a right to be listened to, and is a usual preliminary to offering advice (see pp. 98–99). Then he delivers his opinion on the present issue: both parties are in the wrong, and the claims of good order must be reaffirmed; Achilles must show proper respect to the king, and the king must respect his subordinates, Achilles in particular.

But the contestants remain unmoved (a further error on Agamemnon's part), and the disastrous assembly ends, as usual without formal dismissal. Homer does not himself apportion the blame for the outcome. Achilles will now withdraw in anger; later he will be said to have the sympathy of his fellow chiefs (in Book 9, and also at 13.107–10, 14.49–51, 19.85–86). Agamemnon will soon be obliged to admit his mistake publicly.

Achilles and Thetis (306–492)

Several scenes now pass swiftly, without elaboration. Achilles returns to his dwelling, accompanied (we are significantly told) by Patroclus, whose death will result from this quarrel. Agamemnon dispatches a ship to restore Chryses' daughter to him, and completes the purification of the army from the god's wrath. It is noteworthy that this purification takes place *before* the priest has been reunited with his daughter and asked the god to end the plague; presumably the poet wants to finish off the plague episode now, so that after the return of the mission to Chryse he can turn our eyes to Achilles, not to the army.

Then comes a more elaborate scene, the dispatch of heralds to bring back Achilles' prize. They are sent off abruptly, not with a message (as is usual) but with an order. They go reluctantly, their unhappiness illuminated by a reference to the desolate seashore, and when they arrive, they stand speechless instead of going through the normal procedures of a messenger (entering the house, going up to the recipient, and delivering the message). This is so that Achilles can show courtesy, in contrast to Agamemnon's brusqueness, by welcoming them as guests and taking the initiative as host with the greatest politeness ("Welcome, heralds, messengers of Zeus . . . come in."). He blames not them but Agamemnon, his words reminding us of Agamemnon's threat that he would personally take the woman away (185). Actually, of course, Agamemnon's presence would be impossible, as either Achilles would have to kill him or our conception of the characters would be ruined, and the poet takes the idea no further than this. After a few more words of foreboding, the woman is led unwillingly away.

The following scene between Achilles and his mother, Thetis, is of great importance for the plot of the poem, as it leads directly to the defeat of the Greeks and the death of Patroclus. It is also important because it introduces for the first time in the poem one of its major themes, the frustration and sadness of man's biggest limitation, his mortality. Achilles in his grief goes to the shore of the desolate sea and calls upon his mother the sea goddess. In his prayer, the normal claim to the divinity's favor takes the unique form of an appeal on the grounds that his life is to be so short. Thetis emerges from the waters like a mist, in an effectively vague mingling of simile and metamorphosis — we must imagine not an anthropomorphic figure shooting up from the waves, but a sea mist gradually congealing into a figure beside the weeping hero. He tells her of his sorrows at considerable length, for we must feel the immensity of his grief before he vanishes offstage for so many books; and on the human level, it is good psychology for him to pour out his woes to his loving mother. Finally he asks her to seek Zeus's aid to defeat the Greeks while he is absent. She agrees, and her first words intensify the pathos of his situation by repeating that he is not only mortal like all men, but doomed to die young: "But now both short-lived [literally 'swift-doomed'] and wretched beyond all men / you are" (417–18). She departs; but the poet's words do not lead the audience with her back to her home, as in the ending of most divine visits, but hold our attention there on the shore with the grieving Achilles.

The poet now describes the journey of Odysseus and his men and the restoration of the captive woman Chryseis. He does it at considerable length. A number of standard type-scenes, all elaborated to some extent, follow one after another—the tying up of the ship on its arrival, the handing over of Chryseis as a gift (since no ransom is given for her now), the prayer and sacrifice, the meal and entertainment (the song of Apollo), retiring for the night, the departure and return journey by sea, and finally the beaching of the ship again by the Greek camp. Only one description of a sacrifice is longer than this: Nestor's extravaganza for the eyes of young Telemachus (*Odyssey* 3.418–76), which adds the preliminaries of catching the cow and gilding its horns and includes the only occurrence of the cry of the womenfolk. The joyful return journey is also given full treatment, including Apollo's provision of a fair wind, indicating that his favor is now restored.

Why is there so much detail? Not just to fill in time while the gods are away on the twelve-day vacation Thetis mentioned, for that period too is not fact but must be the poet's invention. Partly it is because of the importance of the mission, the cost of satisfying Apollo's honor and that of his priest. Probably, too, it is to lead up to the short description that follows, for when the scene returns to the Greek encampment the poet again paints a picture of Achilles, just as we left him—grieving, lonely, and furious by his ships (488–92). We are made to feel that days and days of battle and other activity have been going forward without him, not just the twenty-four hours or so that have actually passed (the journey to Chryse involved only one night away from camp); and the long series of type-scenes has given the impression of a long lapse of time during which the hero has been grieving. The twelve-day absence of the gods was invented for the same purpose, and we feel that for all these long days Achilles had been left alone, bereft of his prize of honor, apparently abandoned by the other chiefs, and longing for the fighting which he is denying to himself. He will be waiting like this until Book 9; and then the long loneliness will play a part in his decisions.

The Assembly of the Gods (493–611)

Thetis goes to Zeus and approaches him in the usual way of a suppliant, embracing his knees and raising her hand to his chin (Athena's remark that she *kissed* his knees [8.371] is just her malicious exaggeration). She does not detail her claim to his favor, as Achilles suggested she should; perhaps Homer knew, as Aristotle did, that a great man does not like to be reminded of favors done him by others. Nor does she repeat in detail the wrongs done to her son; doubtless a real pleading mother would be more eloquent on her son's behalf, but here the poet condenses the material we already know to bring out the interaction of the divinities. She *does* refer again, however, to the shortness of his life: "my son, most short-lived of all men" (505).

We await Zeus's majestic decision. It does not come; the poet, in a unique instance of repetition of this part of the type-scene, has Thetis timidly renew her request in order to increase our anticipation. Then finally he answers; his shrewish wife is the problem, and nervously he pushes Thetis away from his knees before Hera can see what is going on. His tone is one of comical harassment; he has not been pondering the claims of justice, or the long-range results of his decision, or any unalterable decrees of fate, but the reactions of his strong-minded consort. Nevertheless, he gives his assent, with words of impressive dignity, seconded by a few lines in the poet's voice about the majesty of the occasion. The verses were famous in antiquity, and were said to have inspired the sculptor Pheidias as he fashioned the mighty ivory and gold statue for the temple of Zeus at Olympia. But it is hard to avoid the feeling that by building up the tension of the decision, and then introducing the bathos of such mundane domestic considerations, the poet is playing with the disparity between the mighty ruler of the Greek universe and the henpecked husband of his epic.

Human troubles are then forgotten in the quarrel of the First Couple. Zeus, late because of his interview, makes an imposing entrance, but Hera's jealous eye has not missed what was going on and she demands to know who was asking what and with what result. He tries ineffectually to stall, but she attacks again and now reveals that she knew all the time who the visitor was and has guessed exactly what happened. Hera is sharp-witted, and she knows (as we should) that once in the past Zeus had a romantic interest in Thetis—to which perhaps Thetis herself is supposed to allude in her earlier words (516; the story is told in Pindar *Isthmian* 8.27ff.; see Young 1982.164–65). Zeus, overmatched in argument, must resort to the threat of violence, which he has actually used in the past (15.18–30); and the resulting social embarrassment of all present is relieved by Hephaestus, who takes the mediator's role and offers advice to his mother, indirectly urging Zeus too to be more gracious. He offers her a toast and brings back her smile; and then the lame, ugly god bustles about pouring drinks for them all in the role of Ganymede or Hebe, and they all break into laughter—not perhaps at his deformity but at the contrast with the usual beautiful cupbearers, and in relief, too, at the end of the social awkwardness. So the divine quarrel, unlike the human one, is patched up for the present; but we have not heard the last of Hera's insubordination and troublemaking.

After the feast, the party continues, with Apollo as the entertainer, in very different guise from that which he presented to mankind at the beginning of the book; *nec semper arcum tendit Apollo.* They retire for the night in standard fashion, the scene elaborated by a word or two about their dwellings; and as usual in this type-scene we are told that host and hostess sleep together, perhaps with special point here because of their recent quarrel. The tone of the episode has been much lighter and more humorous than that of the scenes on earth; a dreadful thing it would be, as Hephaestus said, if the gods are to quarrel like this for the sake of mortals (573–74). Dryden goes rather beyond Homer in his translation of the end of the scene, but his tone is accurate enough (quoted by Mason 1972.59):

Drunken at last, and drowsy they depart,
Each to his house; Adorn'd with labour'd Art
Of the lame Architect: The thund'ring God
Ev'n he withdrew to rest, and had his Load.
His swimming Head to needful Sleep apply'd;
And *Juno* lay unheeded by his Side.

Apollo brought the plague because Agamemnon's rejection of his priest was an insult to his godhead, and Greek gods were as sensitive about their honor as Greek heroes. But no god made Agamemnon insult a priest. No god caused the hot words between him and Achilles, for it is not suggested that Apollo intended the plague to lead to the quarrel. No god told Agamemnon to take away Achilles' prize, or advised Achilles to withdraw from his service to the supreme commander. Zeus has ordained, with his majestic nod, that the Greeks shall be defeated until Achilles returns; but this is what one would have expected to happen anyway on the purely human level.

The conflict that has broken out is not between Greeks and their enemies, but between Greek and Greek. Just as it broke out from human motivations, so it will somehow have to be resolved through human means, for the gods presented to us, though impressive for their deadly power, have shown no superior conception of justice, no concern for mankind apart from a demand for men's respect and an affection for their particular favorites, and no interests beyond their own honor and their wonderful parties. The questions of a man's rights and his duty to himself and to others will have to be worked out at the human level, not by decree from the divine, and the unforeseeable and disastrous outcome of the mishandling of a minor issue will not be effortlessly corrected by a god but will cause sufferings to be endured by many who were not to blame. This is an uncompromisingly real world.

Further Reading

Kirk 1985 gives a detailed commentary on Books 1 to 4. Edwards 1980b examines the type-scenes in Book 1 and compares other occurrences of similar scenes. Griffin and Hammond 1982 give a careful appreciation of the first fifty-two verses. J. T. Kakridis 1971.125–37 analyzes the Chryses scene. De Jong 1985 makes an interesting comparison between the implied author's narrative of the quarrel and Achilles' account to Thetis.

22

Iliad Book 3

In the second book Homer has broadened the scope of the tale. First comes the episode of Zeus's false message to Agamemnon and the latter's unwise testing of the army, resulting in the joyous rush to the ships, which makes clear how unwilling the army is to be besieging Troy and how much it wants to go home. Odysseus, introduced again as a man of reliability and resource, makes an encouraging speech to the assembly, reminding us of the distant days at the beginning of the expedition and of the portent as they embarked, which predicted victory in the tenth year of the war (2.301–330). Agamemnon admits he was wrong to alienate Achilles, but urges them into battle, and there is a big preliminary sacrifice.

Then, after a flourish of massed similes and a dramatic appeal to the Muse, the poet begins the mighty catalogue of the Greek and Trojan forces. The Greek catalogue contains a great deal of very archaic material inherited by the poet, and was clearly designed to record not the troops moving out to battle at Troy but those who embarked on the ships at Aulis at the start of the expedition nine years earlier; it is slightly updated by references to the absence on the present occasion of the aggrieved Achilles (2.686–94), of Protesilaus, who was the first to leap from his ship at Troy and in so doing was killed (2.699–710), and of Philoctetes, still lying wounded on Lemnos (2.721–25). The poet has thus set his plot against the background of the whole length of the war by giving a reprise of the omen predicting eventual victory and the great embarkation nine years ago. In Book 3 he continues this reprise, and as the poem progresses will introduce the future as well as the past as he foreshadows the events lying beyond the end of his tale, the death of Achilles, and the fall of Troy.

At the beginning of Book 3 the two armies have marched out and all is ready for a mighty conflict; but instead the poet mounts a single combat between the two rivals for Helen—her husband, Menelaus, and her Trojan seducer, Paris. Such a duel, in all common sense, ought to have taken place long before this, and it fails to decide the issue in any case; why is it introduced here?

Because the poet is now turning to the original cause of the war, of which this book will be a reenactment. What was the reason for all this suffering, past, present, and still to come? What could bring about, what could (or can) justify all the grief, agony, and death of warfare? In the *Iliad*, not the ambition and aggression of a powerful king; nor, as in Virgil's *Aeneid*, the eventual ending of a nation's foreign and civil wars in the peace and good order brought to the world by the rule of Augustus in Rome. The Trojan War, as represented in Homer's epic, was caused by the selfish action of an irresponsible young man and the character weakness of an intelligent, sensitive woman who realizes only too well the calamities their uncontrolled passions have caused but is still unable to resist her lover. Of course the gods must want it this way, but that does not make the tragedy of the humans any less futile, or any less their own fault.

Achilles has already explained in contemptuous terms why he is at Troy (1.152–60), and his feeling of the senselessness of the war runs through his great speech to Priam at the poem's emotional climax (24.518–551). The Greek troops showed in Book 2 how much they long to go home, and in this book both armies are overjoyed at the thought of settling the war by a single combat; the old Trojans are made to say how they wish Helen would depart (159–60), and after the duel no Trojans would be willing to conceal Paris from Menelaus's vengeance (3.451–54). But the ordinary man's common sense is not always sufficient to prevent warfare.

However, the Trojans are admittedly in the wrong, for the abduction of Helen by Menelaus's guest is an affront to Zeus and their toleration of it cannot be approved; and this awareness of their false position will add much depth to Hector's character and words later on. In this book the poet not only rehearses the old wrong done by Paris, but prepares for a new wrong against the Greeks by another Trojan, a new insult to the godhead of Zeus. For a truce must be called for the duel to take place, and much care is devoted in this book to describing the oath-taking that establishes it. This is not just digression, for in the following book the truce will be broken by the Trojan Pandarus during the awkwardness and uncertainty that follows the inexplicable disappearance of one of the combatants. Menelaus will be wounded by Pandarus's arrow, and Agamemnon's grief-stricken and furious denunciation of the action reinforces the sense that the doom of Troy is inevitable. Zeus cannot overlook such an insult as the breaking of the oath so laboriously sworn in his name.

So a second time the Trojans are placed in the wrong by the actions of one of their number.

The book may be divided into four parts: the challenge to the duel; Helen and Priam on the wall of Troy; the duel and the rescue; and the scene between Helen and Paris.

Challenge to a Duel (1–120)

The two armies advance toward each other, each pictured in a five-line simile. There are many examples of such a scene, usually including similes; a major instance occurs at 4.422–56, where the buildup is a good deal longer as a major battle is actually going to begin, and the same motifs—the silence of the Greeks and the polyglot clamor of the Trojans and their allies—are even further emphasized. It seems to be a way of contrasting the basic unity of the Greeks with the diversity of nations and languages of Asia Minor, with which Homer, as an Ionian, would naturally be familiar (see p. 160). It is an early example of the Greek habit of differentiating clearly between Greeks and all non-Greeks. Then the plot of this book is introduced with Paris and Menelaus, one rashly and impetuously aggressive (but not really equipped for hand-to-hand dueling, as his bow and lack of body armor show), the other grimly glad at the chance to get at his hated enemy. Paris, abashed, draws back; the verse (32) is elsewhere used only when a man has been wounded or has launched his weapon uselessly, not (as here) when he is just afraid to begin the encounter.

This show of cowardice is noted by Hector, and his rebuke vividly characterizes Paris, from the line of insults that replaces the usual titles to his reproach for the abduction that began the agony; he concludes with a striking metaphor for stoning to death, "you should be wearing a cloak of stones for the wrong you did" (57). Paris is often verbally chastised by Hector, and once by Diomedes (11.384ff.), always with the same contrast between the works of war and those of Aphrodite; Diomedes even has a chance later on to taunt the goddess herself with this contrast (5.347–51). There seems to be a pun in the Greek here, for when Hector says, "The gifts of Aphrodite will not help you when you are *coupled* with the dust" (54–55) he uses a word (italicized) that is also used for sexual union. Paris replies with disarming amiability, which we later come to see is invariable with him when under attack. The gods have given him different gifts from Hector's, and he must live with them as best he can. The notion of a man's special qualities being the gift of the gods, which he must needs accept, is already a commonplace in Homer (see p. 129); so Paris has tradition on his side, though Hector is hardly likely to be mollified.

He goes on, however, to offer to fight Menelaus, taking up again the challenge motif of his first appearance; whoever emerges the winner of the duel shall take Helen and her possessions, and the Greeks shall return to "Greece, the land of lovely women"—the epithet is traditional, but possibly applied, too, with a touch of humor here. The relieved Hector calls a parley and suggests a duel on the terms stated, though when the oath is actually sworn, the poet, foreseeing the inconclusive ending the combat is bound to have, alters the wording to "if A *kills* B or B *kills* A" (281–87). Menelaus accepts, and his demand that Priam participate initiates the heavy stress on the oath-taking, in preparation for the later violation of the oath, and leads on to the old king's appearance in the following episode. The troops on both sides gleefully strip off their armor, hoping in vain that the *Iliad* will come to an end here without slaughter, and the heralds set off for the city.

Helen and Priam on the Wall (121–244)

While the heralds are on their way (Homer often changes to a new scene to cover the time elapsing in another), Helen makes her appearance, before us, before the old men clustered on the wall of Troy, and—symbolically at least—before the two contestants. The episode is simple and rigorously limited in scope, in the poet's fashion. Logically, it is rather absurd, for Helen, summoned to the wall of the city to view the contest, names the major Greek chiefs at Priam's request, as if he had not had nine years already to learn who was besieging his city. When the duel begins, she is kept off-camera, and we see nothing of her emotions as she watches the struggle and its mysterious conclusion.

Visible beneath the surface of the action, and contributing unobtrusively to its effect, are old narrative patterns (see pp. 64–66). An alluring woman appears (with veil and women attendants to affirm her modesty) before an admiring group of men, as Penelope does before her suitors (*Odyssey* 1.328ff., 18.206ff.) and Hera before Zeus (14.292ff.); a prize is displayed and admired before the contest for it begins, as happens before each competition in the funeral games in Book 23 and with Penelope before the bowstring test (*Odyssey* 21.63ff.). It may well have been traditional to place a catalogue of the attackers in the mouths of the besieged, as there are examples in Aeschylus's *Seven against Thebes* and Euripides' *Phoenissae*. (Anchises' presentation of the souls of future Romans to Aeneas may owe something to this pattern [*Aeneid* 6.756ff.]; there is a modern descendant in the naming of athletic team members one by one as they emerge from the tunnel into the stadium.) From these traditional plot ideas, Homer fashions a scene that superbly depicts Helen's wretched situation and her feelings of guilt.

Helen is summoned to the wall by Iris, the messenger of the gods. For once, we are not told who dispatched her on this errand; what deity could plausibly do so here? Iris is really the messenger of the poet. That Helen receives a summons is, however, normal, for there are several parallels to the summoning of a woman by a goddess in a sexual context (Athena calls Nausicaa, *Odyssey* 6.13ff.; Athena calls Penelope, *Odyssey* 18.187ff.; and of course Aphrodite herself summons Helen later in this book). As always in a messenger type-scene, the occupation of the person sought is described. Helen is employed in weaving, the proper work of a chaste housewife. The picture she is working is a fitting one, the struggles of the Greeks and Trojans for her sake, and indicates what is always on her mind. As she comes into public view on the wall, her care for propriety is stressed again by the mention of her attendants and their names (143–44). Admiration is voiced not by a group of suitors, but by the old city fathers; in famous words they not only wonder at her beauty but lament her presence and the grief she has brought to their city. As so often in Homer, a regular element of a scene is turned to a new and poignant use.

Priam's reaction is different, and is perhaps intended to show why Helen has not been returned to the Greeks. Instead of turning aside he calls her to him, draws her attention to the array of her Greek kinsfolk and friends, and immediately softens any implied reproach (has he seen her expression change? the superb characterization invites thoughts like this) by absolving her of blame for the war. He attributes it to the gods, though we need not agree with him (see p. 318). Swiftly leaving the delicate topic (again, the poet's skill here makes a psychological interpretation irresistible), he asks her about the distinguished figure at the head of the Greeks; and she responds to his kindly thought before she answers his words, expressing her appreciation of his graciousness and her own self-reproach, loneliness, and grief.

Then she names Agamemnon. Priam comments on his good fortune and power.

Then the formal shape of this catalogue of the leaders of the attackers continues with a second question from Priam and a further response by Helen; and this time the comment, by Antenor, describes a famous episode of the past, the visit of Menelaus and Odysseus to Troy. The tale is interesting in itself, giving rare physical descriptions of the two heroes and commenting on their respective styles of oratory. It prepares the way for the choice of Odysseus as an envoy in Book 9. Moreover, for those who know the history of Troy well, it is also a further allusion to the guilt of the Trojans, for on the occasion of this embassy a Trojan leader had suggested diplomatic immunity should be violated and both Greeks murdered (the story is told at 11.138–42). Antenor's speech is also interesting as a major example of the linear style sometimes found in Homer, where thoughts are added one after another with parallel syntax ("once when . . . but when . . . but when . . . but when . . . but when . . . then indeed"; 205, 209, 212, 216, 221, 224).

A third time Priam asks a question, and Helen's reply trails off into a soliloquy, as she forgets her Trojan companions and looks over the rest of the Greek host for her two brothers, the heroes Castor and Pollux. She cannot find them, and in the way we have now learned to expect from her, she turns their absence into a reproach to herself. This time the comment that completes the formal shape of the dialogue comes in the voice of the poet himself, as he tells of the death of Helen's brothers at their old home in Sparta. This kind of irony is found elsewhere, notably in Priam's appeal to Hector from the wall, where he looks vainly for two of his other sons who we know have already been killed by Achilles (22.46–55, see 20.407ff. and 21.34ff.).

Here the two verses brilliantly drive home not only the self-reproach but also the utter loneliness and isolation of this unhappy woman (see A. Parry 1966.197ff.). Her brothers lie dead in the "life-bearing earth" (*phusizoös aia*, 243). The poet could have used the commoner alternative formula *zeidôros aroura*, "grain-bearing land," but here and in two other passages where the earth is said to hold the dead (21.63, *Odyssey* 11.301) the poet substitutes the more ironic adjective contrasting life and death. (The significance of the phrase has been much discussed; I have no doubt that the above view, most recently supported by Kirk 1985.300–301, is correct.)

The heralds now arrive to fetch Priam, and the oath for the truce is sworn in the midst of the armies with a good deal of elaboration (for its violation is to be important). Priam withdraws, saying that he cannot bear to watch his son fight with Menelaus; his love for Paris helps us understand why Paris is allowed to retain Helen at such cost to the Trojans, and of course for the poet Priam's presence would be an embarrassment later on when the duel is aborted and the truce broken. Twice in these scenes the thoughts of the mass of Greeks and Trojans are mentioned, almost as if they were a dramatic chorus (297ff., 319ff.), and it is noteworthy that the same technique is used (again twice) before the duel between Hector and Ajax (7.178ff., 201ff.). In a similar way the contrasting thoughts of each side are given during the struggle over the body of Patroclus (17.414ff., 420ff.). The technique serves to emphasize the moment by reminding us of the presence of the onlookers and showing us their thoughts, too; and the longing for the war to end, which the soldiers on both sides feel, is placed effectively before the combat that should have realized their hopes.

A Homeric warrior, like a western gunfighter or a football hero, must equip himself for combat with impressive dignity and in a certain sequence. Identical verses regularly describe the donning of greaves, corselet, the straps supporting sword and shield, the helmet, and the final grasping of the spear. But the amount of expansion given to the scene varies according to the circumstances (see pp. 71–77). Paris, the center of attention, receives an arming scene, but there is only one item of elaboration; in the circumstances, more would perhaps come too close to parody. The one item is the information that the corselet he put on belonged to his brother Lycaon (with whom we shall later have a memorable meeting, 21.34ff.), and it serves not merely to personalize the scene a little but to remind us that Paris is by preference an archer, shooting at his enemy from a safe distance, rather than a hand-to-hand fighter in heavy armor; the point was stressed in the description of his attire on his first entry in this book. (The Greek bowman Teucer must similarly don armor when he drops his bow in order to fight, 15.471ff.) The same type-scene is not usually repeated too soon, and Menelaus receives only one verse for his arming; though he will be at least the moral victor, it is Paris who is the focus of attention now and requires the expansion.

The actual duel is made of the same kind of actions as the encounters in the main battle scenes (see pp. 78–79). The failure of the first throw, the prayer to a god and the more successful throw by the antagonist, the charge, the fruitless attack, and the lament are all standard elements, though as usual in Homer there is no precise parallel to their arrangement here (the closest is 13.601–17). Even the grip on the helmet of the defeated opponent is found elsewhere (13.527). The duel of Hector and Ajax in Book 7 is also interrupted before a casualty can occur, and several times in the general fighting episodes a deity intervenes to prevent a death the poet must not permit to happen, particularly in the case of Aeneas, saved by Aphrodite and Apollo (5.311ff.) and by Poseidon (20.288ff.). So Aphrodite's rescue of Paris is not unusual; but the following scene comes as a surprise.

Helen and Paris (383–461)

Gods usually disguise themselves when they talk to mortals. Not uncommonly the poet makes them careless and they are recognized, as is Poseidon by Ajax (13.66ff.) and Apollo by Aeneas (17.333ff.). So Helen's recognition of the disguised Aphrodite when the goddess tells her to join Paris in his bedroom is not surprising; but the tone in which she speaks to the goddess *is*. She begins with a very familiar form of greeting, *daimoniê*, used (for example) by Zeus to Hera preceding his threat of physical violence in the first book (561); by Andromache to her husband, and by him to her (6.407, 486); by Priam to Hecuba (24.194); and also by a warrior taunting his opponent (13.448, 810). Its tone is one of familiarity and sometimes remonstrance. In the words that follow, Helen goes beyond reproach to direct insult, suggesting that Aphrodite become the wife of Paris if she loves him so much—or his concubine, if he does not think fit to marry her. This goes beyond Diomedes' taunt to the goddess after wounding her (5.348–51), beyond even Achilles' furious words to Apollo after the god has tricked him out of his slaughter of the Trojans (22.15–20). It is a powerful demonstration of Helen's strength of mind and her contempt for Paris and for her own past folly. It is also very good psychology. I have heard Helen's words summed up as "the almost inevitable, compulsive response of a woman to another woman (usually a mother-in-law or a rival) who has hinted that she ought to treat her husband better. What else can one say except, 'If you think he's so marvelous to live with, you're welcome to try it.'"

But Aphrodite is a goddess, and, as we have been told before, the favor of a deity cannot be refused. Helen is cowed by the divine threats and follows Aphrodite to Paris's bedroom, "silently, and no Trojan women saw them; for a goddess led her" (420). It is as if Paris had won the duel and the bride, and the love goddess were escorting her to the marriage chamber. The goddess herself then places a chair for her, as would the maidservant she is pretending to be; in the Greek there is careful stress on this ("she, the goddess," 425) and perhaps also on Helen's descent from Zeus (426). Brides are conventionally shy and hesitant before the marriage's consummation, and Hera similarly adopts a pose of reluctance before she achieves her planned seduction of Zeus (14.330ff.). Here the poet replaces coyness with scorn, and in this our first sight of them together Helen taunts Paris with weakness and in very human fashion asserts the greater prowess of her first husband. But Paris, amiable as ever, philosophically hopes for better luck next time, and turns to the more important matter of lovemaking; and the poet slips into a seduction motif, in which the seducer impresses upon his quarry how much his passion for her exceeds anything he has felt before. Its most lavish and brilliant use is at Zeus's seduction of his wife Hera, where for purely comic effect the poet leads him into obviously inappropriate detail about his extramarital affairs (14.315–28; see p. 249). Without another word, Helen yields.

The episode thus concludes, by masterly technique, with a reenactment of the original seduction. Here, as at that time long ago, Helen knows that she is doing wrong, and despises herself and her lover for it; but she is unable to resist Paris. Conscious of shame at her past actions and contemptuous of the irresponsible, oblivious young stud to whom she has united herself, denouncing him to his face for his weakness, she nevertheless joins him again in bed at this suggestion. Aphrodite, the goddess of sex, dominates her; but the goddess herself has vanished from the scene before Helen goes to Paris's bed, and it is Helen's choice and not the goddess's threat that brings about this conclusion. She bears the responsibility for her action, just as Agamemnon and Achilles do for their quarrel in Book 1.

While the two make love, the poet returns us to the battlefield, and with effective juxtaposition describes the victorious Menelaus searching in bafflement for his vanished opponent, whom we alone know is happily in bed with Menelaus's wife. The situation may be outrageous or humorous, depending on the observer's outlook. Agamemnon seeks to decide the issue by demanding that Menelaus be declared the victor and the bargain fulfilled; and the book ends in this perplexity, with a further reminder by the poet of how much the Trojans hate Paris and the war he has brought upon them (453–54). Of course the duel has not settled the issue of the War, and we always knew it could not. What the book has done, besides laying the foundation for the Trojan breaking of the oath in the next book, is to repeat before our eyes the seduction that begins the tale, making comprehensible (and very human) Helen's combination of proper feelings and irresistible weakness for Paris. It has shown the folly of the two sinners, and it has shown how others became entrapped into suffering and dying for such an inadequate cause.

Further Reading

Kirk 1985 gives a detailed commentary on Books 1 to 4. Hooker 1979 is also useful. Kirk 1978 compares the duels in Books 3 and 7, and Edwards 1980a considers the Helen/Priam scene as a development of a catalogue of heroes. J. T. Kakridis 1971.25–53 and Clader 1976 consider the character and situation of Helen in the *Iliad* and the *Odyssey*.

23

Iliad Book 6

After the abortive duel of Book 3, quarrels on Olympus at the beginning of Book 4 foreshadow the trouble to come for some of the immortals. The truce is broken by the arrow of the Trojan Pandarus, whose pride in his bow makes him an easy prey for the disguised Athena's persuasion, and the wounding of Menelaus allows Agamemnon both to show his love for his brother and to remind us in solemn words that Troy's iniquity must ensure her eventual fall (4.157–68). Then as a prelude to the resumption of battle there is a new catalogue of warriors, a form of the pattern also seen in the great catalogue of Book 2 that introduces the first parade and the catalogue of Myrmidons when Achilles' men first enter the battle (16.168ff.). In this catalogue, Agamemnon visits his captains one by one, dispensing praise and blame in a series of encounters that are similar in form and serve to show both his own nature and those of the other leaders. The last hero he speaks with is Diomedes.

Though Achilles has withdrawn from the battle, the Greeks must not be defeated too soon, and at this point the poet uses Diomedes to spearhead a Greek attack; this will motivate the return of Hector to Troy for the domestic scenes there, and also lead up to the reversal of Greek fortunes in Book 8, when Zeus takes steps to aid the Trojans. Diomedes must therefore be emphatically brought to our attention, and so Agamemnon irascibly upbraids him for no good reason, his diatribe glorifying Diomedes (unconsciously, as far as the speaker is concerned) by reminding us of the mighty deeds of his father Tydeus (4.372ff.). Agamemnon is answered angrily by Diomedes' second in command, but Diomedes himself, a very different character from Achilles, keeps his temper and rebukes his comrade, speaking (as Shakespeare's Henry V will do) of the awesome responsibilities of the commander-in-chief (4.412ff.).

For the moment Diomedes is a surrogate Achilles, and his domination of the battle here is identical in pattern with that of Achilles in Books 20 to 22; both fight a number of Trojan warriors, then the gods themselves, and finally engage a single opponent in a lengthy scene. In both cases the combat with gods emphasizes the hero's prowess and his divine support, allows him lengthy duels while avoiding the difficulty of providing enough important Trojans who can become his victims, and also (as will be explained below) brings out the contrast of mortal and immortal and the frustrations of human transience.

As Book 5 begins, Athena strengthens Diomedes, and there is a foretaste of coming episodes (in Homer's way) as Hephaestus rescues the son of his priest (as Aphrodite will later save Aeneas) and Athena chats with her later opponent, Ares. She intervenes again to reinvigorate Diomedes after he has been wounded by Pandarus, and the poet prepares the way for the coming encounters by having her give him the power to recognize the gods and instruct him to fight only with Aphrodite. Pandarus and Aeneas attack Diomedes together—all his fights here are with two opponents, to indicate his superior prowess—and he kills the truce-breaker and attacks Aeneas. But this Trojan must not be killed, as emerges more specifically later when he faces the furious Achilles (20.158ff.; especially 302ff.), and Aphrodite picks him up in her arms. This is what the poet was waiting for, and Diomedes, recognizing her and fortified by Athena's permission, wounds her in the hand. She screams and drops her son (who is fortunately scooped up by Apollo before he hits ground) and the scene drifts off into the usual frivolity of the gods as she is comforted by her mother, like a child. Here too, however, there is a reminder of the gulf between human and god, for Dione utters a warning that a man who fights against the gods has no happy homecoming; and the legend tells that during Diomedes' long absence, his wife fell victim to Aphrodite and was unfaithful to him. Diomedes again attacks Aeneas, and is repulsed only by the mighty voice of Apollo.

On the other side, Ares lends heart to the Trojans, and Diomedes, always well under control, sees him and wisely withdraws. The combined power of Hector and Ares forces back the Greeks, and the battle narrative pauses for a moment for the elaborate departure of Hera and Athena for the front, complete with description of the yoking of their chariot and Athena's arming scene. In the climax of this encounter of god and man, Athena assists Diomedes to wound the mighty god of battles himself. Like any school-story bully (and totally unlike a wounded mortal), Ares yells and collapses immediately, and in a repetition of Aphrodite's complaint scene, he bewails his woes to his father, Zeus. Besides the obvious humor of the scenes, the poet has contrived a kind of parody of the love-war opposition, with the divinities who preside over both spheres behaving in precisely the same undignified way. (They both suffer other indignities at a poet's hands elsewhere; see the song of Demodocus, *Odyssey* 8.266ff.)

The action of Book 6 is divided between Diomedes' exploits and Hector's encounters within Troy. Each of these parts is subdivided into an account of several different actions followed by one long and important conversation between two characters. In the following commentary these four subdivisions will be retained.

The Battle Continues (1–118)

After a few verses of general battle description, which are often used for transition between series of duels, a typical sequence of single combats takes place, Diomedes participating as one among others. Characteristic too of the poet's technique in battles are the few pathetic lines about such a figure as Axylos (12–15), who was rich and offered hospitality to all men, but now dies beyond the help of those he befriended. This passage, and the following account of Aisepos and Pedasos (20–28), are good examples of the conventional structure (found in the catalogue in Book 2 and everywhere in the battle scenes) — (1) basic information on who the victim is; (2) an anecdote about him (often, as here, the circumstances of his birth or his genealogy; 21–26); (3) what happens to him in the present context. Genealogies are common in Homer, and may be given by the poet, as in this instance, or by the hero himself, as will occur at great length in the case of Glaucus later in this book. A similarly lengthy example is given for Aeneas (20.213–41).

Then follows a supplication scene, in which Menelaus has the Trojan Adrestus at his mercy and is inclined to spare him, but yields to the savage words of the still furious Agamemnon. On several other occasions a character pleads for his life, but all are slain; there is a specially close parallel at 11.122ff. — the supplication is in identical words and the refusal again comes from Agamemnon. The most elaborate and most moving of all these scenes is that between Achilles and Lycaon (21.34–135), which shares with the scene in Book 11 the startlingly impersonal, objective phrase introducing the response to the suppliant's plea, "but he heard the pitiless voice . . . ." Here the brutal episode serves to remind us of the Trojans' responsibility for breaking the truce, and of the savagery, as well as the love for his brother, often apparent in Agamemnon. It also sets off the extreme civility of the coming encounter between Diomedes and Glaucus, and Achilles' own honorable behavior toward Andromache's father (6.416ff.).

Then Nestor delivers a short *parainesis*, or speech of encouragement of the kind common in battle scenes (see pp. 92–93), to lead up to a very brief statement of the desperation of the Trojans (73–74) and the conference scene between Hector and his brother Helenus. The basic pattern of the action is found elsewhere; after a Greek success, there is rebuke, advice, or persuasion between one Trojan and another, and eventually they rally. Here Helenus is given the role of adviser to Hector, more often taken by his other brother Polydamas. So Helenus suggests that the commander leave the struggling Trojan army and return to the safety of the city to seek the prayers of the noblewomen of Troy. It is hardly a sensible action in terms of the army's morale — Helenus himself could have been better spared with the message — but the poet, of course, wants to show Hector with the women of his family. Before he goes, Hector — as he does when he withdraws to put on Patroclus's armor (17.183–87), and as Agamemnon and Eurypylos do when disabled by wounds (11.276ff.; 586ff.) — delivers a short speech of encouragement to his men; diplomatically he includes the elders of Troy among those he intends to confer with, as well as the women suggested by Helenus. As he goes, the poet puts in the single touch of description he loves to insert, here Hector's tall shield, now slung on his back, knocking against his neck and heels. A similarly naturalistic note was struck earlier at 5.796–97, where Diomedes' shield strap galled his shoulder.

Diomedes and Glaucus (119–236)

A challenge between two heroes before they begin to fight is quite common; there was one between Tlepolemos and Sarpedon at 5.632–54, and there is an especially long one between Achilles and Aeneas at 20.176–258 (see p. 288). They are quite unrealistic interludes in the midst of a battle; epic is not drama, after all, despite the long sections of direct speech, and these conversations are an example of something the epic poet can get away with that writers for theater or film cannot. Why this long scene here? In the first place, it covers the time Hector needs to run from battlefield to the city. This technique of covering the time taken for action in one scene by means of action in another is not invariable in Homer but is quite common; a good example occurs when the battle over the dead Patroclus continues while Antilochus makes his way to Achilles' shelter (17.700ff.). Secondly, it enables the poet to leave Diomedes in a mood of calmness after his superhuman feats against the gods, and it bridges the difference in tone between the killings on the battlefield and the emotional meetings within Troy. Most important of all, the episode gives the poet an opportunity to continue and reaffirm, on a more serious note, the emphasis on the distinction between gods and men that has been in the foreground of Diomedes' light-hearted attacks on Aphrodite and Ares. This emphasis on human mortality falls appropriately before Hector's farewell to his wife and return to the battlefield.

As Diomedes and Glaucus come face to face, the mighty Greek asks the name of his opponent, adding a few words of compliment to his valor in daring to oppose him; a less elaborate example of this kind of preliminary to the duel can be seen in the encounter of Achilles and Asteropaeus (21.150ff.). He follows this up with an appropriate threat: "But unhappy are those whose children come against my might!" (This line, too, recurs in the example in Book 21, at 151.) Then his words pick up the present context by his declaration that if Glaucus is a god he will not fight with him, a reminder that Diomedes is above all a sensible man and knows that he has lost the power Athena gave him to distinguish gods from men (at 5.127ff.) and without her support must not continue his attacks on divinities.

To justify and emphasize his view, he uses a paradigm, a mythical tale which supports the course of action he is taking (see pp. 98–99). This is the story of Lycurgus, king of Thrace, who attacked the god Dionysus and his attendants and was punished with blindness and premature death. It is told in complex ring form, beginning and concluding with the threat to his enemy (127 and 143), within which are the three matching statements: (1) "If you are a god . . ." (128) and "If you are a man . . ." (142); (2) "I will not fight with a god" (129 and 141); and (3) "Lycurgus, who did so, did not live long" (130–31 and 139–40). At the center of these rings is the narrative itself (132–39). Coming from Diomedes, this caution recalls Dione's sinister words about his prospects to the wounded Aphrodite (5.406–15).

Glaucus's response begins, "Why do you ask about my descent?" The same words are used by Asteropaeus in his reply to Achilles (21.153), and there the speaker continues without pause to recount his origins. The significance of the question is made clear in the encounter between Achilles and Aeneas, where the same introductory words "But if you wish to be instructed in this too, so that you may know my descent well, many men know it" (20.213–14, 6.150–51) are prefaced a few lines earlier by "We know each other's descent and parents" (20.203). The normal implication thus seems to be "Why do you need to ask what everyone knows?"—perhaps a standard boast about the fame of one's progenitors. But instead of continuing immediately with his ancestry, as Asteropaeus does, Glaucus goes on to reflect on the transience of human generations, shifting the sense of the word *geneê* from "race, descent" to "generation of men" and leading on to the famous simile of the annual fall and rebirth of the leaves. The effect is startling in the context; it has been suggested that Glaucus is terrified and is spinning out time in talk, but if this is his intent he is running a big risk; a large, aggressive cop demanding to know your name is unlikely to be soothed by a philosophical "What's in a name? A rose...." What exactly is the thrust of the comparison with the leaves here, and why does the poet insert the passage?

One of the encounters during the Battle of the Gods is between Apollo and Poseidon (21.435ff.). The older god challenges the younger, reproaching him for his folly in fighting on behalf of the city whose former king cheated them both. Apollo replies, ignoring his words but declaring it would be foolish for him to fight so senior a god for the sake of mortals, "wretched as they are, who like leaves at one time / live in brightness, eating the fruits of the earth, / and at another fade away and perish" (21.464–66). Here the point is simple, the transience of mortals compared to the deities' everlasting life, and there is no place for the mention of regeneration of leaves or of men. This is the idea taken up by later poets. Mimnermus (frag. 2 West) virtually quotes the phrasing of Book 6, but his thought is that we flourish as leaves grow in the spring sunshine, and for a short span enjoy the flowers of youth with no thought that both good and evil come from the gods; then come the dark fates of old age and death. Simonides (frag. 8 West) quotes the first line of the simile (6.146), calling it the best thing in Homer, and goes on to complain that young men forget their mortality. Horace, among countless others, saw the changing seasons as a symbol of death, not rebirth, for mankind: "The changing year's successive plan / Proclaims mortality to Man." (*Odes* iv 7.7–8, tr. Samuel Johnson, quoted by Mason 1972.III–12). Memorable passages in the Old and New Testaments contrast this human transience with the

permanence of the love of God (*Psalms* 103.15–18; *I Peter* 1.24–25),
but of course this love was not available to classical poets.

Glaucus's words similarly assert the inevitable death of individual humans, and probably the unimportance of the individual
amidst these countless hordes, since leaves are used in similes
for thousands of troops (2.468, *Odyssey* 7.105). But the words also
assert the rebirth of new generations to replace those who die.
This connotation of the simile is irrelevant to Apollo in Book 21,
and brought no comfort to Mimnermus or Simonides. The passage closest in tone to Glaucus's words is the startlingly Greek
passage in *Ecclesiasticus* 14.14–15, 17–18:

> Do not miss a day's enjoyment
> or forgo your share of innocent pleasure.
> Are you to leave to others all you have labored for
> and let them draw lots for your hard-earned wealth? . . .
> Man's body wears out like a garment:
> for the ancient sentence stands: You shall die.
> In the thick foliage of a growing tree
> one crop of leaves falls and another grows instead;
> so the generations of flesh and blood pass
> with the death of one and the birth of another.

The idea of rebirth is also included in three hexameters attributed to the legendary singer Musaeus (frag. 25 Kinkel), whom
Homer was said to have paraphrased in the Glaucus passage
(though of course "Musaeus'" verses may well be based on the
Homeric ones): "In the same way the life-giving earth puts forth
the leaves too; / Some die away on the ashtrees, others come to
birth; / So both the race of man and the leaves come and go."

The appropriateness of the passage is clear. Human mortality
has just been emphasized by the contrast between men and gods,
which has played so large a part in Diomedes' recent career, and
the poet continues the theme by appending it to the request to
state one's parentage by means of a kind of play on the word
geneê, which means both "descent" and "generation." Glaucus's
meditation on death as the common lot of men is appropriate as
he faces the invincible Diomedes; and of course it actually *is* his
genealogy that saves Glaucus's life, when he and Diomedes discover a former guest-friendship relation between their families
and Diomedes calls off the fight. But Glaucus is not a meditative
man elsewhere in the poem, and essentially the verses prepare
for the scene of Hector's parting from his wife, and mark the
poet's own consciousness of the mortality of human greatness

and of the consolation of the continuance of the human race, long generations after the mighty tale he is here relating.

Then Glaucus tells of his ancestors. After two generations the list is interrupted by the long history of one of them, Bellerophon, after which the "begats" resume. The story is notable for its obscurities and its folk-tale elements. It has the air of being condensed from a much longer narrative; one would like, for instance, much more detail on Zeus's part in backing Proetus (159), on the "noble escort of the gods" (171), on the "portents of the gods" that enable him to overcome the chimaera (183), and especially on the "hatred of the gods" that later afflicted him (200).

Among the components of the Bellerophon tale that are found in other stories, and that suggest folk tale, are: the virtuous man falsely accused by a lustful woman (cf. Hippolytus, Peleus [Pindar *Nemean* 5.25–34], Joseph and Potiphar's wife [*Genesis* 39.7–23]); the letter demanding that the bearer be killed (cf. Uriah, 2 *Samuel* 11.14–15); the hard tasks completed with supernatural help (this must be the meaning of "the portents of the gods," which resulted in his acquisition of Pegasus); and the offer to the hero of the king's daughter and half his kingdom after his eventual triumph. Finally, we are told, Bellerophon was hated by the gods and wandered a vagabond over the earth, and two of his children are killed by the gods. No explanation is given, but his fault must have been his *hubris*, his refusal to accept his mortality, in his attempt to join the gods on Olympus by means of his winged horse Pegasus (Pindar *Isthmian* 7.42ff.: "For we all die alike . . . . For winged Pegasus threw his master Bellerophon when he wished to enter the halls of heaven and the company of Zeus."). The allusion is driven home by the words "but when he *too* was hated by the gods" in line 200, which links him with the Lycurgus of Diomedes' paradigm and with the god-wounding Diomedes himself. (It is also probably relevant that Diomedes' father, Tydeus, with whom he is so often linked [e.g., 4.372ff., 5.125ff., 800ff., 6.222ff.], was nearly offered immortality by Athena, but at the last moment his bestial ferocity made her change her mind.)

So Glaucus's tale demonstrates the results of the favor and disfavor of the gods, with implications for the future of Diomedes himself, and once again emphasizes the chasm that separates mortals and immortals. At last Glaucus reaches the name of his father, and ends his tale with the advice his father gave to him as he left for war. The lines (207–10) are a memorable summary of the heroic code, and the heroic motto in 208, "to be always the bravest and to rise above others," was urged by Peleus on Achilles himself at his departure (11.784).

The scene ends with the mollified Diomedes gladly recognizing a hereditary friend and exchanging armor with him. The gesture is the same as the exchange of gifts between Hector and Ajax at the conclusion of their duel (7.299–305), and perhaps also echoes the usual ending of exploits such as those of Diomedes, stripping the armor from a corpse. The poet, however, comments in his own voice about the inequality of the exchange. This seems to be a touch of humor, not perhaps aimed at any foolishness in Glaucus, for after all he got away with his life and can have nothing to complain of, but at the traditional heroic motif of armor exchange as a mark of friendship. The intrusion of the poet's voice, as Bassett has suggested (1938.107), helps to defuse the dangerous situation and eases the transition from the battlefield colloquy to Hector's arrival in Troy.

So the episode, and the battlefield scene, and Diomedes' divinely inspired exploits come to an end in this courteous colloquy. We have seen Diomedes behaving with perfect propriety in different situations—with the insulting Agamemnon, with Athena, in the midst of battle, and with his hereditary friend Glaucus. The poet has shown us the civilized standards possible in human life, in contrast to the savagery of the preceding slaughter, and has set the inevitable death of the individual, however heroic, against the immortality of the gods and of the human race as a whole. This has well prepared us for the deep emotions of the scenes that follow.

Hector with Hecuba and with Helen (237–368)

The rest of the book is devoted to the character of Hector and to the feelings of women when their menfolk are at war. The scenes have always been regarded as a masterpiece of the poet's art. In fact, some may feel that, with their universality of action and emotion, expressed by the words of the characters rather than the poet's description, they need no exposition, amplification, or commentary. But the detail is so rich and so deep, the thoughts underlying the words so carefully suggested, that new implications and allusions appear with every reading.

As soon as Hector enters the city, the tone of the coming scenes is set by the ordinary women of Troy, who surround him and ask about their husbands, their sons, and others in the bat-

tle; the poet's voice is mournful: "sorrows fell upon many." As
Hector walks through the courts of Priam's palace, the poet, in
his usual way, describes the scene that met his eyes, and indicates the splendor and size of both the buildings and the family
of the Oriental monarch.

The first person Hector meets is Hecuba. Like any mother, she
worries that he must be tired and thirsty, and like the other
women later she tries to detain him. He declines her offer of refreshment, discharges the ostensible purpose of his mission by
urging her to sacrifice, and concludes with exasperated words
about the impossible Paris; one must think that only to the
mother of them both would he allow himself such free condemnation. She does not reply, but sets about the sacrifice; it is
normal for a person to whom an order is given to carry it out
without a word, so there may be no particular implication in her
silence.

The sacrifice is an important matter, and so is described at
some length, and the poet takes the opportunity to bring in once
again the wrongdoing of Paris and his city: the robe Hecuba
chooses for the goddess was acquired on the same journey on
which he carried off Helen. Naturally Athena does not accept it.
(Virgil copies this use of ill-omened gifts when he has Aeneas
present Dido with adornments that Helen took to Troy "and her
impermissible marriage"—Dido herself will seek another such
marriage—and when Latinus, doomed to lose his kingly authority, is given the scepter of the dead Priam; *Aeneid* 1.647ff.,
7.246ff.) The universality of the Homeric gods, which enables
the poet to present Athena as a goddess worshipped in Troy,
gives a considerable emotional effect to the prayer of the Trojan
women and its inevitable rejection; the poet of *Roland*, opposing
the Christian God to the devils of the heathen, had no such opportunity.

Hector then goes on to the house of Paris, handsomely described as befits the husband of Helen. As he enters it the poet
gives him one item of description, the spear he holds (see p. 85).
This description is unusual for a visitor, and reminds us that
Hector is in full armor, straight from the battlefield, and a striking contrast to this brother. For as always in visit type-scenes the
poet tells what the person sought is doing: Paris is handling his
bow and his armor, but with no indication that he plans an immediate return to the field. Hector rebukes him once again, and
Paris amiably apologizes (333) and denies that he is angry with
the Trojans (335–36; there may be a hint here of a tale in which

Paris once withdrew from the battle because of hostility toward his fellows, as did others besides Achilles, but Bassett's explanation [1938.134–35] that the last we heard of Paris was how much the Trojans hated him [3.453–54] seems adequate]. He agrees to rejoin the battle. Helen, he says, had been urging this too, "with gentle words" (337), and in view of the way she usually speaks to, and about, Paris, the formulaic expression may hide a touch of sardonic humor here on the part of Paris—or the poet.

The tone becomes more serious as Helen speaks. She reproaches herself, condemns Paris, and attempts to detain and comfort Hector just as his mother did. In conclusion she says their ill-starred lives will be sung of by generations to come; perhaps a standard thought, as it also comes from the lips of Alcinous of Phaeacia ("The gods brought this about [the fall of Troy], and wove destruction for men, so that there might be song for men to come"; *Odyssey* 8.579–80), but it is unusually effective in the mouth of Helen. Hector declines courteously; speaking as if Paris were not there (363–64), he treats Helen as respectfully as Priam did, and she will remember this in her lament over his corpse (24.767–72). His parting words carefully prepare the way for his meeting with his wife and son, of whom we still know nothing, and also reveal his gloom and uncertainty whether he will ever return. We do not see the face of Helen, the cause of all this, but the poet has said enough to suggest the effect of these words upon her.

Hector and Andromache (369–529)

The following meeting and leave-taking of Hector and his wife establish him as a loving husband and father; as an honorable, thoughtful, and articulate man who describes his feelings as he goes into the dangers of battle, a battle that he knows his country will lose and deserves to lose; and as a very human person who goes through a rapid series of different feelings in a situation of enormous emotional tension. For much of the remainder of the poem he will appear as the warrior leader, sometimes brutal, sometimes ill-advised, sometimes arrogant; just before his death his thoughts will be shown again as he faces his last fight with a superior enemy (Book 22). The coming scene is an actual dramatic presentation of the material of the anecdote that so often individualizes a dying fighter by mentioning his young wife or aged parents. Sarpedon the Lycian said to Hector, not long before this, "I myself came to be your ally from far away; /

for Lycia is far off, by the eddying Xanthus; / there I left my beloved wife and my infant son" (5.478-80); his own farewell must
have been like this, and so must that of innumerable other
soldiers.

The setting of the scene draws into clear focus some of the
strongest and most universal of human emotions; the young
husband leaving his wife to go to war, his sharing of his inner
thoughts with her, his intense anxiety over her future if he dies,
his pride in his son, his attempts to comfort her distress, and his
recalling the reasons he must leave her and join his companions
in the battle. On her side, there is her love and fear, the attempt
to detain him, which she cannot resist making but which she
knows must be fruitless, her concentration on what his loss will
mean to her and to their son, and her sudden practical advice.
The single touch of immediate detail the poet loves appears in
the brief distraction caused by the baby's fright at the sight of his
father's glittering helmet, and the loving amusement that unites
the young parents. Within the poem, the family picture serves to
predict, through the words of Hector, the fall of Troy, and shows
what that fall will mean to Andromache, her son, and all the
other wives and mothers of the city. On the wider scale, it depicts the leave-taking at the onset of battle that took place time
and again, year after year, in Greek families of every age and at
all times and places since. No comparable examples of such
leave-takings are found in surviving ancient literature, but the
frequency with which these scenes occur in Greek vase painting
indicates their appeal.

Hector leaves the barren, loveless household of Paris and
Helen and seeks his wife in his own home. But she is not there;
instead of the regular picture of the person sought, in this case
dutifully occupied with weaving amid the household women (as
Helen was in Book 3, and Calypso and Circe are when visitors
arrive, *Odyssey* 5.61-62, 10.221-22), Andromache is not in her
home. The standard scene is interrupted, the effect one of shock
and tension. A similar technique will be used again, even more
impressively, after Hector's death in Book 22, when Priam and
Hecuba burst into successive laments from the city wall but
Andromache is absent, at home preparing for Hector's return. Besides the increase in tension produced by the postponement of
their meeting, the poet may wish to avoid too close a parallel to
the conjunction of Paris and Helen at home while he should be
on the battlefield, and to set their colloquy in the more dramatic
circumstances of Hector's imminent departure for the battlefield

through the city gates. Somehow everything goes awry within Troy—the libation Hector refuses to make, the rejection of the ill-omened offering to Athena, perhaps even the wailing of Hector's son—and his failure to find his wife may repeat the same sinister tone.

They meet beside the Scaean gate of the city. Both Andromache and the infant are introduced by the poet, since we knew nothing of them, and Hector's silent smile at his son is a preparation for the later part of the episode. Her words speak primarily of her utter dependence on her husband; of course this was normal for every woman in Greek society, but (in Homer's way) it is intensified in Andromache's case because she has no male relatives left to take her in after her husband's death. Andromache's mother, she tells us, after her own husband's death returned to her father (428), but Andromache has no father or brothers living. All have been killed, and killed by Achilles, and of course we are aware of the irony that the same fate awaits her husband, too.

There is a further irony here, if we observe it; for Achilles honored Andromache's father with a funeral and a tomb, but he will outrage Hector's body; until at the end of the poem Priam's appeal and grief will induce him to show similar respect even to the man who killed his great friend. Her demonstration of her utter dependence on Hector thus also foreshadows future events. Immediately she goes on to offer practical advice about the defense of a weak point in the wall. Perhaps this is a sign of her common sense, or a natural turning aside momentarily from the strain of an emotional appeal to the relief of a practical problem; or perhaps she thinks this will keep her husband in a safer position than back in the front line. Or is it the poet's hint at the eventual breaching of the city wall in the last days of Troy?

Hector replies; throughout the scene the barest of formulae introduce the speeches and all the color is given by their content. This is drama, not the narrator's voice. He repeats the code of honor by which he must live; one verse, "I would feel ashamed before the Trojans and long-robed Trojan women" (442), he will use again when he wonders whether to retreat before Achilles in his last soliloquy (22.105). His duty is to himself above all, and his place as a prince of the Trojans is at their head in battle. But his mood (after her words) is despairing, and the intimacy between them does not allow him to pretend otherwise; repeating Agamemnon's words after the treacherous wounding of Menelaus (4.163ff.), he predicts the eventual fall of the city and pictures her fate as the slave of a Greek. Vaunting words will be said to her about her defeated husband; "She is the wife of Hector, who was the bravest in battle / of the horse-taming Trojans, when they fought at Troy" (460–61) would not be spoken sympathetically in Greece. She will be toiling at the loom and carrying water for her Greek master, and more—for though Hector does not say it, we know from Agamemnon's words at 1.31 and Nestor's at 2.354–55 that she will also be sharing her master's bed. Few women in ancient Greece could consider themselves safe from such a fate.

Hector does not mention his son. Instead, Homer has him turn to take the child from the nurse, and the infant squalls at the sight of the glittering helmet and the high waving crest. The incident is totally natural, but it is hard not to take it as symbolic too, for the helmet is Hector's most personal and characteristic martial accoutrement, given him by Apollo (11.353), source of his standard title "bright-helmeted Hector," and mentioned twice in descriptions of his battle fury (13.805, 15.608–10); and Hector will die fighting Achilles. (Virgil has a similarly poignant effect when Aeneas, fated to a life of warfare, kisses his son farewell through his helmet as he leaves for the final duel; *Aeneid* 12.434.) There is also a masterly manipulation of the traditional formulaic language. As Hector takes off the helmet and lays it on the ground, instead of ending the verse with the formulaic epithet for the earth, "mother of many," which would be normal in these metrical circumstances, the poet replaces the expected adjective with another most significant one, "glittering brightly," which qualifies not the earth but the helmet that lies upon it. The unexpected effect, startling to anyone familiar with the usual formulae, directs attention both to the sight of the helmet lying on the ground and to its glitter, the reason for the child's fright. The poet violates the traditional methods of composition for a shockingly appropriate effect.

With his son, the hope of the future, in his arms, Hector's mood abruptly changes, and he joyfully prays that the child may become a better fighter even than his father. Of course this is inconsistent with his recent dismal prediction to Andromache, but it is very natural. It is also heavily ironic, for the legend tells that Hector's son was intentionally killed by the Greeks at the sack of the city, to prevent him from avenging his father; the murder is explicitly foretold by Andromache in her last lament over her husband (24.734–35). The usual indication of the gods' response to the prayer is omitted; the audience knows it only too well.

Hector hands the boy to his mother, and is moved more than ever by the love and anxiety they share. So now he gives her what comfort he can, though again it is inconsistent with what has gone before. He takes the fatalistic view, common with those constantly exposing themselves to dangers, that the time of his death has long been fixed and may come soon or late, and that in either case concern about it is useless. This deterministic idea gives a kind of security; it is quite different from the random chance that may strike at any moment, vividly symbolized by the "Russian roulette" scenes in the movie *The Deer Hunter*. Nothing comes about by chance in Homer; one of the few proponents of it in Greek literature is Sophocles' Jocasta as she triumphs in what she thinks is the defeat of the oracles about her husband-son Oedipus, and there the irony of her wrongness is overwhelming (*King Oedipus* 979). Then Hector sends his wife home to wait, the traditional fate of women, and picks up again his helmet and his own fate. She departs, and the lament that follows foreshadows the death to come in Book 22. Hector will actually sleep another night in Troy, but the fact is handled as lightly as possible (7.310) as we are to consider this their archetypal and final farewell.

Paris has been totally forgotten. But he turns up again, described as returning warriors usually are, by a simile, and the stallion he is compared to characterizes well his beauty, enthusiasm, speed, and thoughtless sexuality (this simile is, oddly, repeated for Hector himself after his strengthening by Apollo, 15.263ff.). He comes upon Hector "as he was about / to turn away from the place where he had talked with his wife" (515–16); an indication of the contrast between their married lives, and perhaps a suggestion that Hector is standing looking back at the departing Andromache. He apologizes for delaying his brother, with the poet's delicate irony—Hector's thoughts had been far from Paris. In his turn Hector, his mood gentler now, amiably explains his earlier irritation. With yet another natural change in his feelings, he brightens as he leaves behind him the emotional struggle of the parting and goes on to the relief of vigorous action beside his cheerful brother. So his final words give a note of hope, and as the next book begins the two of them advance side by side to rejoin their companions.

Books 5 and 6 show a sequence of different aspects of the gulf between gods and men: Diomedes' physical attacks on Ares and Aphrodite, the warning tales of the *hubris* of Lycurgus and Bellerophon, the philosophical simile of the death and new birth

of leaves and of mankind, and the courage of the doomed, resigned Hector. Besides this, Book 6 begins the striking achievement—whether original with Homer we cannot tell—of the portrayal of the gentlest and most attractive sides of a man's
character not in the person of a Greek hero, but in that of an
enemy, a "barbarian" or foreigner, a man of a race that Homer
himself (as an Ionian) as well as later generations of Greeks must
have regarded as their hereditary antagonists in Asia Minor, and
probably in most ways as their inferiors. In most great epics
(especially in the *Aeneid*) there is some sympathy shown for the
losing side, even when they fight against fate or the true god as
well as against national heroes; but Homer's humanity goes far
beyond this. Through this irresistibly moving presentation of
the family of the doomed opponent of his Greek heroes, he
shows the emotions of parting before battle, overshadowed by
our awareness of the death and misery that will inevitably come.

Further Reading

Kirk 1983 comments extensively on the handling of the episodes
in Books 5 and 6. Gaisser 1969 gives a fine analysis of the poet's use
of traditional material in the Diomedes-Glaucus episode. Fenik 1968
has a chapter on the fighting in Book 5.

24

Iliad Book 9

In Book 7 Hector and Paris return to the battle and the slaying briefly resumes, with Glaucus playing a part but with Diomedes offstage. But before the Trojan victories that Zeus has promised come about, the poet inserts two further abortive attempts to end the war. At the gods' suggestion a duel is set up between Hector and a Greek champion, Ajax winning that role after lots are drawn. Nothing comes of the duel, which is called off when the evening light descends. The episode is in some ways similar to the duel of Paris and Menelaus in Book 3 — the truce-breaking at its conclusion is now ignored — but it is not meaningless padding of the poem. The emphasis on the courtesies of the formal duel, the promise to return the corpse of the loser after stripping his armor, and the exchange of gifts when the affair is over, must be contrasted with the duel between Hector and Achilles in Book 22, where Achilles refuses such civilized agreements. The account also gives additional fighting stature to Hector, especially by the initial reluctance of the Greeks to take up his challenge, and this is particularly appropriate after the picture presented in Book 6 of the family and city he is fighting for. It also introduces Ajax, who is to be important in the embassy to Achilles (Book 9) and the battle at the ships (Book 15). The whole episode, of course, is possible only in the absence of Achilles, whose anger overshadows all these books and is referred to explicitly by Ajax (226–32).

In the second half of Book 7 the Trojans attempt to end the fighting by handing back Helen and the property of Menelaus that Paris had taken off with her, but Paris vetoes the return of Helen and the Greeks reject the offer of the property alone. Diomedes voices their thoughts, that the offer is made only because Greek victory is approaching. There is heavy dramatic irony in this scene, because very soon Zeus will hand the Greeks a severe setback (Book 8). The future action is also prepared for by the building of a mighty wall around the Greek camp; it is emphasized by the concern of Poseidon that it will eclipse his own handiwork on the walls of Troy (7.446ff.), and will become important in the battles of Books 11 to 15. The dead on both sides are burnt and lamented (7.421ff.), and the book concludes with a glimpse of the Greek commissariat (467ff.).

Zeus's thunder has threatened the Greeks at the end of Book 7, and as Book 8 opens he warns the other gods not to assist either side in the human struggle and reminds them of his mighty strength. Of course they will take no notice. As the battle continues, the Greeks find themselves in trouble and Nestor has to be rescued by Diomedes. Hector is inspired by thunder from Zeus, and despite the efforts of Agamemnon and Teucer, in particular, on the Greek side, the day comes to an end with the Trojans in the ascendant. Interwoven with the human conflict are less serious scenes among the gods. Hera tries to incite Poseidon to intervene on the Greek side, but he begs off. She has better success with Athena, and the two of them set off after a fine description of Athena's arming (384ff.), but Zeus summons them back and administers a stiff rebuke, his words including a forecast of Achilles' eventual return to battle after the death of Patroclus (473ff.).

This change in the Trojans' fortunes is strongly marked by the poet, for it leads up to the attempt to have Achilles rejoin the Greek forces (Book 9). So at a Trojan assembly Hector makes a long speech giving instructions for them to make camp on the plain instead of withdrawing within the city as usual, and the poet impresses the picture upon us at the end of the book with a famous simile describing their campfires burning between the city and the ships, as men and horses await the next day's fortunes (see p. 86). The campfires are as numberless as the stars on a clear night, but we are warned that the Trojans' triumph will not last, for their sacrifices are not accepted by the gods (550–52; the verses are found only in a quotation by Plato and may not belong here, but they are quite appropriate).

Many episodes in Homer are presented virtually in the form of drama—the confrontation of Achilles and Agamemnon in Book 1, the farewell of Hector and Andromache in Book 6, the meeting of Priam and Achilles in Book 24—and Book 9 is the most sustained achievement of Greek epic in this respect. In dark, outdoor, firelit settings, it begins and ends with tense, emotional scenes of the Greek chiefs in council, and its heart is the long drama of the speeches of the envoys and Achilles' responses, the four speakers motionless but for the intensity of their successive declamations, with the doomed Patroclus silent in the background. As in Greek or French classical theater, the brilliant characterization and on-stage conflict of minds offers the audience more excitement and involvement than any violent action could. No gods appear; everything is left to human persuasion and decision. The book would afford magnificent scope for actors, and in ancient Greece no doubt called into play all the powers the reciting bard or rhapsode could command.

The main turning point in the plot has now come. In answer to Achilles' request, Zeus has at last brought about the defeat of the Greeks, and they are forced to send envoys to their greatest warrior to ask him to return. The offer of compensation for his hurt feelings is large, and Achilles might well give up his anger, charge into battle, and bring a triumphant end to the poem—or rather, since the old traditions cannot be too blatantly contradicted, die gloriously before Troy. That might produce a first-rate poem. But this poet is working on a larger scale, and plans a much more complex portrayal of human character and the causes of human events, of the fundamental conflict between one's duty to oneself and one's social responsibilities.

Though gradually mollified, Achilles will not yield after the third speech of supplication here, though in most tales the third appeal would be effective. Only after a fourth, which is unobtrusively prepared for but will not come until Book 16, will he take pity on the sufferings of his fellow Greeks. Despite the magnificence of the compensation offered for his hurt, and the overwhelming need for him the Greek leaders admit, Achilles feels that his honor is not yet properly satisfied. In his words, and in those of the friends who seek to persuade him, the poet not only brings out his character and theirs, but portrays a situation of conflicting feelings, duties, and principles that has sometimes been seen as a challenge to the entire system of values in the heroic society. Until now, Achilles has had the tacit support of his fellow chiefs; but after he has rejected the compensation offered in this book, he stands alone.

This commentary will fall into six parts: the decision of the Greeks to approach Achilles; the three envoys and their reception; the speeches of Odysseus and Achilles; the speeches of Phoenix and Achilles; and the speeches of Ajax and Achilles, followed by the return of the envoys to the Greek council. A final section will review the significance of Achilles' decision.

The Greeks Decide to Approach Achilles (1–181)

After their victorious onslaught, the Trojans are encamped on the plain before Troy, waiting to make a further attack the next day. Frightened, the Greeks are summoned to assembly by the despairing Agamemnon, who reproaches Zeus for deception and recommends that they abandon the expedition and return home immediately. Agamemnon has a genius for poor timing; he chose the wrong time to assert his primacy over Achilles in Book 1 and the wrong time to test the army's morale in Book 2 — perhaps it is not just the conventions of Homeric diction that make him repeat here the disheartened words of his foolish testing of the army (18–25, 26–28 = 2.III–18, 139–40) — and now he proclaims his demoralization much too soon and much too publicly. He will make the same mistake again when the wounded chiefs gather during Hector's victorious onslaught (14.74ff.). He is no coward physically, as his achievements in battle show (especially in Book II), and his desire to end the slaughter by a withdrawal may well be thought to show admirable qualities in him; but it is not good for an army's morale for the commander-in-chief to be the first to declare he has given up hope.

The embarrassed silence is ended by the strong, sensible young Diomedes. It was he who spoke for the majority in reply to the Trojan herald's offer to return Menelaus's possessions but not Helen (7.400ff.), he will make the concluding comment when the dejected envoys return (697ff.), and he will speak up again against his commander's despondency (14.110ff.). Diomedes has not forgotten Agamemnon's unjustified slight on his courage, though he did not protest at the time (4.365ff.), and with the freedom of speech allowed in the assembly he accurately identifies Agamemnon's lack of moral strength (Lattimore's rendering "heart" for this [39, 41: Greek *alkê*] is regrettably ambiguous). Even if all the others go, he and his squire will stay and fight to the end; the naive simplicity and directness of the statement, and Diomedes' uncomplicated principles, may be contrasted with the similar words of Achilles later on, when in a confused torment of emotions he wishes all the Greeks and their agonizing problems would disappear and leave him and Patroclus to get on with the work of sacking Troy (16.97ff.). The same idea is used to convey very different states of mind.

Diomedes' pinpointing of Agamemnon's inadequacy as a leader is unseemly before a general assembly of the troops, and Nestor intervenes to end it, not denying Diomedes' good sense but implying that an older man might show more tact. He proposes that men be sent off to guard duty (a reminder that this was not necessary while Achilles was fighting and the Trojans were pinned within the city), and that the chiefs adjourn to Agamemnon's dwelling to decide in greater privacy what is to be done. (It is interesting that Agamemnon had addressed this assembly using a formula normally reserved for the chiefs alone ["leaders and councillors," 17], which may show confusion in his mind, or the poet's, or possibly in the text.) Agamemnon shall give a feast for them, says Nestor; this will do something to restore the prestige his lack of resolution has damaged, for he is, after all, their commander (73). So Nestor gets the situation back under control, and diplomatically prepares to grasp the opportunity the crisis offers. With his usual skill, in their fairly short speeches the poet has given brilliant and consistent characterizations of Agamemnon, Diomedes, and Nestor.

After the feast, Nestor continues at some length to try to put some backbone into Agamemnon. Others may give counsel, he says, but the achievement of any proposal depends upon Agamemnon alone (102). After this diplomatic boosting of the commander's self-confidence, he goes on to say that the seizure of Briseis was a mistake, as indeed he said at the time (1.275ff.), and that the time has now come to admit this and persuade Achilles to return, "propitiating him with friendly gifts and soft words" (113). Already in Book 2 Agamemnon had admitted that he had been the first to lose his temper in the quarrel (2.377ff.), and now he agrees that he must have been "beside himself with folly" or "controlled by *atê*" when he angered such a man (116; see p. 145). He counts off a magnificent list of reparations, some to be given now, some at the sack of the city, some after their return to Greece. Characteristically, he partly spoils the effect by demanding in conclusion that Achilles acknowledge his superiority; this is the wrong time for this, and not at all what Nestor meant by "soft words." (Odysseus has the sense to omit this ultimatum when he repeats Agamemnon's words to Achilles.) Nestor rapidly nominates the envoys to carry these terms to Achilles (with heralds to make it official), and after proper formalities and some quiet words of advice from Nestor, they depart.

The Three Envoys and Their Reception (182–221)

Like the unhappy heralds sent to fetch Briseis in the first book, the envoys go along the seashore; the reminder of nature's impassiveness emphasizes their worries and reminds us of the earlier scene. The three are Odysseus, whose oratorical powers have been described for us by Antenor the Trojan (3.216ff.); Ajax, whose high standing among the Greeks has been recently reaffirmed by their choice of him for the duel with Hector (7.178ff.);

and Phoenix, one of Achilles' retainers whom we have not heard of before, and for whose presence at Agamemnon's council no explanation is given. From this point to and including Achilles' welcome of them, the poet refers to the envoys in the dual number instead of the plural; that is, the grammatical forms mean "the two of them." The Alexandrian scholar Zenodotus held that the dual could be used interchangeably with the plural. This idea is not now accepted, but nevertheless it is likely that the dual was not used in the ordinary Ionic dialect of Homer's time; in the *Homeric Hymn to Apollo* the second person dual is three times used for the plural (456, 487, 501), and a singular verb is sometimes used after the dual *osse*, "eyes," on the analogy of the alternative neuter plural form *ommata*, which (like other neuter plurals in Greek) always takes a singular verb. It thus seems possible that the dual forms conveyed to the poet not so much a rigid grammatical duality as an air of honorable antiquity, so that the solecism was not so apparent to him and his audience as it is to us; just as after a certain amount of "he knoweth" and the like, many of us would not be too perturbed by an ungrammatical "thou knoweth."

Another view proposed in antiquity is that Phoenix was sent on ahead of the other two to prepare for their coming (see Nestor's "Let Phoenix go first," 168), though Achilles' surprise at their arrival hardly supports this. Others consider that Phoenix was added later to an earlier version in which only two envoys were sent, but this involves a considerable carelessness on the poet's part in not altering the dual forms to accommodate him. In recent years scholars unwilling to accept the later addition of Phoenix have proposed that the duals intentionally recall the two heralds who visited Achilles to bring back Briseis in Book 1 (Segal 1968), that Phoenix is not of equal rank with the other two and so is not included with them (Köhnken 1975), that Odysseus is a traditional enemy of Achilles and so is an outsider here (Nagy 1979.49–55), or that the duals refer to two *groups* of people, either Phoenix on the one hand and Odysseus plus Ajax on the other (Thornton 1978), or the envoys as one group and the heralds as another (Gordesiani 1980)—though in either case Achilles' greeting to them is peculiar (197–98: "Welcome, you two groups! beloved friends have come in two groups!"). Further considerations are urged below in the discussion of the Meleager paradigm, but the difficulty remains, and it seems unlikely that anyone will ever be convinced by anyone else's explanation.

The envoys reach Achilles' camp; as always on the arrival of messengers, they find the person sought and we hear what he is doing. Usually he is feasting, and we might expect Achilles to be found preparing or enjoying his dinner. But this would be too great a contrast with our last view of him in Book 1, as he sat moping miserably on the seashore; we must not think that his anger and grief are over. So he is playing the lyre and singing of the famous deeds of heroes. This is a striking and unexpected scene; perhaps the poet is violating realism to produce this effect, for a king would hardly control the techniques of oral composition (see p. 21; the passage in *Beowulf* [2105–17] where Hrothgar the king is sometimes said to play the harp and sing is ambiguous; see Opland 1980.199–201). The tone is not cheerfulness but pathos, for Achilles ought to be *performing* such deeds, not singing of others who have done so, and soon he will be forced to give up all hope of continuing his heroic career. The unexpected picture also reminds us of Achilles' past victories, for we are told that the lyre is booty from the city of Andromache's father. (Alternatively, it has been thought that the picture is a peaceful one, and Achilles is confident that Agamemnon will in time come to his senses and make good his loss of honor; this seems to me much less probable.) Patroclus is introduced as his companion, and plays a large part in the preparation of the coming meal, for the friendship between them must be stressed.

The envoys come forward, but before they can begin to deliver their message the type-scene changes to that of the reception of guests, for Achilles sees them with surprise, invites them to enter, and offers them hospitality. This indicates that he considers them his guests, not the messengers of Agamemnon (the point will be important), and obscures the minor issue of when they actually enter Achilles' dwelling (messengers enter and stand beside the person sought, whereas guests wait in the doorway to be invited in; the envoys here seem to do both).

So Achilles receives them: "Welcome! My good friends have come. *And so you should!* For even in my anger you are my best friends among the Greeks" (197–98). The meaning of the italicized phrase (*ê ti mala chreô*) is not clear, and it can be taken as "and greatly I need you" (Lattimore and Fitzgerald) or "some great matter must bring you" (*nec dubium est quin serii quid agatis*, van Leeuwen 1912, note to 197), but it is best to retain the ambiguity in the translation. A few lines later he again refers to them as his beloved friends and guests (204). Then at great length the hospitable meal is prepared by Achilles himself and Patroclus; this is probably intended to show special honor to the guests, and avoids the distraction of bringing on other retainers. The description is lengthy (the equally important meal for Priam, 24.621ff., takes much less time), because the host-guest relationship thus established has much significance both for Achilles, who may well think his friends are still on his side, and for Ajax, who will later say that the relationship gives them an additional claim on his consideration. Probably the poet also wishes to dignify the occasion by the elaboration and to protract the suspense of both characters and audience. The silent but busy Patroclus can also be further brought to our notice.

Odysseus's Speech and Achilles' Response (222–431)

Ajax looks to Phoenix to open the business of the meeting. This is surprising, since Nestor was said to have relied most on Odysseus, the renowned orator and councilor (180). It has been suggested that Ajax makes a stupid mistake, or that Homer "defines the personalities of three individuals in seven words . . . the ponderous Aias, the unassertive Phoenix, and the quick-witted Odysseus" (Willcock 1978.17–18), but perhaps he even intends an ironic hint that Odysseus will overreach himself and his contribution will not be a success. Odysseus moves in quickly, and his speech is a model of skillful, well-constructed, persuasive oratory. He drops in Agamemnon's name casually and early, then passes swiftly on to refer to the distress of the Greeks and give a long and vivid account of the fury and pride of Hector, who prays (like the French in *Henry V*) for dawn to come so that he may destroy ships and troops together. This leads up to the first climax: come and kill Hector!

Then, more quietly, he speaks of Achilles' anger, and paints a picture of old Peleus at his departure urging his aggressive son to keep his temper and avoid quarrels—advice that Odysseus could hardly venture to give to Achilles in his own voice. Agamemnon is offering most generous gifts if he will only give up this anger, and Odysseus relays the list virtually as it was proclaimed by Agamemnon, with once a direct word of address to Achilles (*anax*, "O King"; 276) to stress the fact that Agamemnon has refrained from the additional insult of sleeping with Achilles' concubine. He has the sense, however, to omit Agamemnon's closing words about the need for Achilles to admit his inferior status, and instead asks Achilles to pity the Greeks even if he cannot forgive Agamemnon; and he concludes with a further mention of the grand opportunity of killing Hector. In this beautifully composed speech, painting vivid oratorical pictures of Hector's victory and Peleus's parting admonitions, he has offered Achilles glory and splendid gifts, and has urged him to control his anger; but he has said not a word in censure of Agamemnon's behavior or of his admission that he was in the wrong (115ff.), not a word of any support or sympathy for Achilles from the other chiefs, nothing of any anger on their part at the insult done to him. They need his help, that is all. He will be well paid for it.

Odysseus's speech was a good example of skillful oratory. Achilles' response, in contrast, is a long and furious outburst of feeling, with many powerful rhetorical questions but with none of the paradigms that normally serve to expand a speech that must be of impressive length. Again and again he circles back to the overwhelming fact of his hurt. He begins very formally. In a long series of heavily end-stopped lines, delivered perhaps with the slowness and pauses of extreme self-restraint, he carefully explains that he must say exactly what he thinks, that he hates deception. In Book 1 it was this clarity of thought and directness of expression that brought the quarrel with Agamemnon to a crisis before cooler heads, like Nestor's, could intervene. There is, of course, also an implication that Agamemnon is attempting to cheat him and that Odysseus has not said all that is in his mind. (The audience, and the poet, may be thinking of the lying Odysseus of the *Odyssey*.)

He explains the situation as he sees it, still in slow, end-stopped, often aphoristic statements. He has received no honor in return for all the heavy fighting he has endured, and death comes alike to brave men and to cowards (316–22); so what is the sense of going through all this hardship for the sake of other men's wives? He becomes more specific: he has sacked twenty-three cities, brought back the plunder to Agamemnon (who had stayed safe in his tent), and Agamemnon gave away a little of it but kept the major part for himself. And this leads to the worst thing of all, for in Achilles' case alone even this small reward, the prize of honor, has been snatched back—and it was not just a precious object, but a woman dear to his heart. His furious indignation bursts out here in a series of short, vehement rhetorical questions, running over the end of the verse and stopping after the first word of the next (336–41):

Let him lie with her
enraptured! Why must fight with Trojans
Greeks? Why has he collected and led here this host
Atreus's son? Was it not for lovely Helen?
Alone do they love their wives among mortal men
Atreus's sons?

There is nothing like this anywhere else in Homer.

His anger turns from Agamemnon to those who follow him, and he taunts Odysseus with their inability to defeat Hector even with the help of the great wall they have built. Achilles alone could control Hector (355); and not only is Achilles now not on the battlefield, he will soon leave Troy altogether, for his fury drives him on at this point to resolve to return home at once. There he has wealth enough without Agamemnon's gifts—but the reference to the prizes he has won brings back the thought of the one taken from him, and again he bursts into furious denunciation of Agamemnon, again in the short sentences with the explosive runover word "Atreus's son" (368–69). Many of the sentences begin with *oude*, "not [even], nor":

Not even would he
dare, shameless dog though he is, to look me in the face!
Nor will I join him in any counsel, *nor* in action.
For he deceived me and hurt me. *Nor ever* again
will he cheat me with his words. Enough of him. Let him as
  he chooses
go to hell! For Zeus has taken away his wits.

(372–77)

Then in a contrasting sentence that runs on for ten verses (a mighty priamel), he rejects any gifts that Agamemnon might offer and says he will not be persuaded until Agamemnon has atoned for his soul-destroying insolence. Only Agamemnon's humiliation, it seems, not his gifts, will satisfy Achilles, and this will not come in full measure while he is still supported by the other chiefs.

Marriage with a daughter of Agamemnon he also rejects indignantly—"let him find someone *more kingly!*" (392; this is the word Agamemnon had used in 160 to describe himself)—and the thought takes him back to his home and his future life there. There he can marry any woman he pleases, and live a normal life in the enjoyment of his wealth. And now this leads to the philosophical climax of the mighty speech, for he proclaims in powerful language (another huge priamel) that his life is worth more to him than all the prizes that honor brings (410ff.). This is stated with enormous emphasis, beyond the capacity of normal English to reproduce: "*Seize* I can cattle and sheep, / *Win* I can tripods and horses, / *man's life* however cannot be seized again / or won, once it has passed out through the mouth" (406–9).

He has been told that he must choose glory or long life, and if his prowess at Troy is to lead only to booty, and if his glory (for a distinction is now made between the two) can be destroyed by Agamemnon's insult, long life is clearly preferable. The prophecy that he says gives him this choice (410ff.) is not mentioned elsewhere and may well be an innovation by the poet for this occasion, but the idea is not unparalleled: Heracles is fabled to have been offered a life either of ease and delight (by Evil) or of nobility and hardship (by Virtue: Xenophon, *Memorabilia* 2.1.21–34), and Gilgamesh was counseled by the ale-wife Siduri to give up his search for immortality and enjoy the ordinary pleasures of feasting, dancing, and family life (Pritchard 1973.64). A long, inglorious life is now Achilles' choice, and he concludes with advice that the rest of the army should abandon the expedition too, "for Zeus has stretched out his hand over Troy" (419–20), exactly as Achilles himself had requested in Book 1. Let them do that, or try some other plan, for their present attempt to inveigle him into fighting has utterly failed. As a final reassertion of his decision, he tells Phoenix to be ready the next morning to leave with him if he wishes.

Odysseus's words have brought disaster. Achilles had thought his friends were on his side, coming perhaps to ask him to kill or supplant Agamemnon and save the Greeks. Instead, they are supporting Agamemnon, offering gifts on his behalf with no word of complaint about his insolence, no word of condolence for Achilles after all he has suffered. There is therefore no hope of restoring Achilles' proper honorable status with the army, and more wealth from Agamemnon's gifts or from Troy's sack he does not need, so he can only give up hope of fame and return home to a long, inglorious life in the obscurity of Phthia.

Phoenix, Meleager, and Achilles (432–622a)

An appalled silence falls, broken at last by Phoenix. He speaks first of his personal need of Achilles, with whom he had been sent by Peleus as a tutor, to make Achilles "both a speaker of words and a doer of deeds" (443). Then at considerable length he tells his own life story. It is the first of the three paradigms that

form his speech (see pp. 98–99), a respite from the tension caused
by Achilles' passionate rejection of Odysseus's terms. His account is a claim to the right to influence Achilles, an appeal to
his emotions, to his memories of his childhood and the hopes his
father had for him, and it establishes Phoenix as a surrogate
father for Achilles, parallel to the parents and sisters who make
the second appeal to Meleager (see below).

No clear parallels have been adduced for the tale of Phoenix's
quarrel with his father over his seduction of his father's concubine, but Paul fulminates against intercourse with a father's wife
(*I Corinthians* 5.1) and the curse of childlessness, presumably im-
potence, sounds like a symbolic form of the castration of an adul-
terer. (Intercourse with the same woman as one's father seems
not to have been considered incestuous in Greek thought; there
are several examples in the tales of Heracles of his giving his
former wives or concubines to his sons, and Hyllus's opposition
to the idea in Sophocles' *Trachiniae* seems based only on his
hatred for the woman who caused his father's death.) The impo-
tence motif has obviously been adopted by the poet as a reason
for Phoenix's exile, because it accounts for his having no children of his own and for his devotion to the only son of Peleus,
which intensifies his dependence on Achilles (492–95).

Exile would be the normal result of a father's curse; but the
murder of one's father in retaliation would not, and it may well
be that the verses telling of his threat to his father's life (458–61)
did not belong to the original *Iliad* (on this, see Scodel 1982 and
Apthorp 1980.91–99). His ineffectual imprisonment by feasting
kinsmen is hard to account for, but their presence may be a reflection of the kinsmen who are sometimes mentioned as driving away an exile (2.665–66, *Odyssey* 15.273–75, 23.119). The number of lines devoted to Phoenix's imprisonment and escape,
which seems needless to the tale, may be intended to suggest
that he was not considered the guilty party in the episode. It is
interesting to note that nursing and feeding a king's infant son
did not (for Homer) make a man unfit to be a leader of warriors.

Having established his right to give advice and be listened to,
Phoenix urges Achilles not to be inflexible, for even the gods can
be moved by prayers and offerings (496–501). He justifies his
opinion in the usual way, by a "hortatory" paradigm, an example
of conduct that should be followed. The content of this second
paradigm is unique, for instead of characters of legend its actors
are the personifications of Prayers and Blind Folly (*Atê*, see

p. 146). The application here is very clear; the first cause of all this trouble was the swift-footed *Atê*, as Agamemnon himself admitted to the chiefs just before the envoys left (115ff.), and now the limping Prayers have arrived at last and are trying to heal the wounds; if Achilles rejects the prayers of his friends, Zeus will hear them and send *Atê* to bring about his punishment. This indeed is a possible view of what happens when Achilles sends Patroclus to battle in his place and so causes his death, though it is never explicitly said that this caused his action. Concluding this part of his speech, Phoenix reaffirms that Agamemnon is making a generous offer of gifts and has sent Achilles' best friends as envoys, though unfortunately he does not actually say that Agamemnon had admitted to them that he was in the wrong.

Then as a further example of right conduct to be followed, Phoenix recounts a third paradigm, a tale from the old days of heroes, the story of Meleager (524ff.). His purpose is to show that even great heroes were "appeasable by gifts and persuadable by words" (526); at the end of the story the moral has been narrowed slightly to "*With gifts promised* / go, and the Greeks will honor you like a god. / But if *without gifts* you enter the deadly fight, / not so great will be your honor, though you beat back the battle" (602–5). Some scholars have thought that the story of Meleager's anger and withdrawal is the model for the plot of the wrath of Achilles in the *Iliad*, and certainly it may well be older. It is probably best, however, to consider both the Meleager tale (as told here) and the *Iliad* plot as modified and expanded versions of the same basic plot structure, of which some idea may be gained by observing where the two versions coincide.

The basic pattern is "withdrawal-devastation-return" (see p. 62). The first envoys sent to persuade the hero—both Meleager and Achilles—to return offer him gifts on behalf of the city or king; the gifts are rejected. A second supplication is made by the parents and sisters of the hero (in Achilles' case, Phoenix takes the role of surrogate father, by virtue of his biography; 438–95); this appeal is also rejected. The danger increases, and finally the hero's wife, the highest in the scale of affections (so J. T. Kakridis 1949.19ff., 152ff.), implores him to come to the defense of his people; he does so, and beats back the enemy. It may well be that in many versions of the tale the hero, though victorious, is also killed; this idea may underlie Meleager's return to battle and most certainly does Achilles'.

In Phoenix's version of Meleager's tale, one of the adaptations to fit the tale to the situation is probably the addition of the hero's "best friends" to the list of envoys, after the official city delegation and the hero's parents and kinfolk (585–87). Their presence in the third place in the rising scale of affection seems implausible, and they are likely to have been included to parallel more closely the third appeal to Achilles by Ajax, speaking as one of his "best friends" (630–31, 640–42). Another addition may well have been the name of Meleager's wife, who is brought to our attention in no less than ten verses (556–65), just as Achilles' companion Patroclus has been earlier in this book. The poet carefully explains that she has two names (561–64), and it has been observed that the word roots that make up her second name, Cleo-patra ("of famous ancestors"), are the same as those of Patroclus's name, in reverse order (this is more obvious in Greek, since some forms of Patroclus's name show the *kle-* root clearly). This odd correspondence may well be not coincidence but the result of the poet's invention, for Patroclus, too, Achilles' best-loved companion, will be the successful suppliant, appealing tearfully to the hero's sense of pity for his people (16.2–47).

That the gifts are never given to Meleager (598–99) is probably invented to suit Phoenix's attempt to persuade Achilles to take the gifts *now* and return immediately to the battle; or possibly there is a hint at Meleager's death in the battle, which is reported by Hesiod (frag. 25.12–13 M.-W.) and in the *Minyas* epic (frag. 5 Kinkel; in both accounts he is killed not by the Fury summoned by his mother [566–72] but in more heroic fashion by Apollo). The tale of the firebrand with which Meleager's life was linked, which was burned by his mother to avenge his killing of her brother, seems to be alluded to in the mention of her anger, but is ignored later when she is included among the suppliants.

In the *Iliad* the successful supplication is made when the danger is extreme and the Greek ships are about to be set on fire, as was Meleager's city before his wife's appeal (589); but before this happens an *Iliad*-scale episode is inserted, the surging of the battle around the Greek wall and its eventual penetration by Hector (Books 11 to 15). It may be partly because of this long postponement of the final appeal that three supplications instead of two precede it in Book 9, and besides the official offer of gifts by Odysseus and the supplication of the "parent" Phoenix there is a final appeal by Ajax on the grounds of friendship. This addition is so closely connected with the plot of the *Iliad* that it may well be (like the matching appeal of Meleager's best friends) an innovation on the part of the poet; Ajax's simple emotion and sincerity can naturally bring about a display of the better side of Achilles' character, and he can be made to yield a little further in response, but he can still impose a qualification that will prevent his return in Book 16 and will link on to the vengeance theme (see below).

The surprising and unexplained presence of Phoenix at Agamemnon's council suggests that his joining the embassy dispatched to Achilles is in some sense an innovation, too, and perhaps in some way this gave rise to the use of the duals for the journey and Achilles' welcome, or at least to their retention from an earlier version. For Phoenix, though speaking as surrogate father to Achilles, is also a kind of doublet of Patroclus, and would have been expected to be beside Achilles in his camp. Both were fugitives taken in by Peleus (9.478ff., 23.84ff.), both are said to have been sent with him to Troy to guide him in the ways of heroes (9.438ff., 11.784ff.), and both make emotional appeals to him to give up his anger with the Greeks (such character doublets are common in both the *Iliad* and the *Odyssey*; see Fenik 1968.148ff. and 1974.172ff.).

Placing him in Agamemnon's council has many advantages, which the poet exploits: it distinguishes him from Patroclus; it means his appeal can be unsuccessful (the successful appeals come from persons who are actually living with the hero, though for reasons of the plot Patroclus is not actually beside Achilles in Books 11 to 15); it means he can more convincingly worry about being left behind if Achilles actually goes home to Phthia (434–38); and Achilles' perplexity and irresolution can be dramatized by his inviting Phoenix to stay overnight in case he decides to depart the next morning (617–19). But the oddity of his not being with Achilles already, as Patroclus is, remains, and may well be related in some way to the use of the dual number for the journeying envoys. Modern explanations that "doubtless his years gave Phoenix the freedom of the Greek camp so that he could remain where he chose" (J. A. Scott 1912.74) or "the great concern of Phoenix for the suffering Achaeans (9.431) would certainly lead him into the assembly and the council" (Thornton 1978.3) are hopelessly realistic.

Another major adaptation follows Achilles' yielding to the final supplication in Book 16, for because of the final statement the poet has him make to Ajax in Book 9—that he will not return until Hector threatens to set fire to his own ships (650–53) he cannot himself immediately rejoin the battle. So Patroclus goes as surrogate, preparing the way for the vengeance theme that will follow his death at Hector's hands. The gifts are later handed over to Achilles, though by then he does not care if he gets them or not (19.147–48), and the return of Briseis is presented not as a solace to him but as further reminder of the greatness of his loss (see p. 287). His actual return to battle at the end of Book 19 is a kind of doublet of his yielding in Book 16, but his motive is by this time the urge for vengeance; and both then and afterward the fact that his own death will result directly from his killing Hector is brought forward (see p. 288), perhaps reinforced in the minds of the audience by their feeling that the hero's death, as in Meleager's case, is the proper ending of this tale.

The lesson Phoenix draws is clear: yield to persuasion, and take the gifts while you can. Achilles is moved by his old friend's distress more than by his advice, which he ignores. Addressing Phoenix with a term of affection (Fitzgerald's "Uncle" is good), which is used elsewhere in Homer only by Telemachus to the swineherd Eumaeus and by Menelaus to Athena when she is disguised as Phoenix, he says that he does not need the honor of Agamemnon's gifts, for he will always be honored among the Greeks because of the strength Zeus has given him. This is no more than the truth: both Nestor and Agamemnon said as much at the Greek council (9.110, 117–18).

He is hurt that Phoenix is taking Agamemnon's part, and says so in simple words, without the furious resentment he had shown in his reply to Odysseus: "You must not / be friend to him, so you may not become hateful to me your friend. / Best for you with me to harm whoever harms me" (613–15). In an emotionally violent overstatement he expresses his regard for his old mentor: "Be king equally with me and share half my honor" (616). Then he urges him again to stay the night there, but not necessarily so that they may depart together the next morning; now Achilles' emotions are too strong and too diverse for him to know what to do, and he postpones the decision for the morrow. He has had enough of this emotional turmoil, and he nods to Patroclus to make up Phoenix's bed as a broad hint to the others to take their leave.

Ajax and Achilles, and the Envoys' Return (622b–713)

At last Ajax puts in a word. Addressing Odysseus, he refers to Achilles as if he were not there, using words he might hesitate to apply to him directly; indeed they might as well leave, he says, since Achilles has become impossible to deal with, oblivious to the affection and honor he used to receive from his friends. Yet most men are willing to accept compensation even for the death of a brother or son. "But *you*"—here he turns and speaks directly to Achilles (636ff.)—"will accept no recompense for just one woman!" He concludes with a last appeal, using the powerful and irrefutable arguments that he has been received as an honored guest in Achilles' dwelling, that they are envoys not just from Agamemnon but from the whole Greek army, and that they are his best friends.

Ajax speaks briefly and simply, but with emotion and obvious sincerity. For him, Achilles' honor will be amply restored by acceptance of the gifts and return of the woman, and he fails to understand what Achilles is still making so much fuss about. This must be considered the opinion of the ordinary, down-to-earth Greek captain. It has an impact all the greater if the audience thinks of the events lying in Ajax's future: he himself will feel his honor slighted when Achilles' armor is awarded as the prize of honor to Odysseus instead of to himself, and the insult to his pride will lead to his death (the story is referred to at *Odyssey* 11.543–64, and was told in other poems of the Trojan cycle).

Achilles thinks Ajax's words over, and replies slowly. First, Ajax's titles. Then an acknowledgment of his own regard for Ajax and his good sense: "All you have said seems in some ways [*ti*] to be in accord with my own wishes" (*kata thumon*, cf. 1.136) (645). He is glad of their friendship and wishes he could do what they ask. But Agamemnon's insult still stands in the way (he will recall it again later on, 16.55–59), and Agamemnon must be punished so that he will admit his mistake. So he will act as Meleager acted; he will not return to the battle until Hector reaches the ships of Achilles' own men and throws fire on them (this will be exactly the situation he requested from Zeus in the first book, that the Greeks be penned up by their ships; 1.408). It is not that Achilles is willfully doing what he knows to be wrong; his nature and feelings prevent him from assisting Agamemnon until he can be confident that his commander realizes his mistake.

Patroclus has Phoenix's bed made up at last and they retire, and the other two envoys (in the plural number!) make their way back to the waiting Greek chiefs. Odysseus reports the answer Achilles gave to *him*, which must stand as Achilles' official reply to Agamemnon's offer; it is important for the plot that the embassy be represented to the army as unsuccessful, and it would be an anticlimax here to have Ajax qualify Odysseus's account by telling of Achilles' later response. Agamemnon and Nestor, their plan a failure, say what is appropriate: nothing.

Diomedes, as before, eventually breaks the gloomy silence, and as always he speaks with insight and good sense. "Leave him alone. He'll come back when he wants to and the god moves him. We can carry on without him." Thus in typically Homeric fashion, Achilles' will and the stimulus of the god are mentioned in parallel, tending toward the same end (703); Ajax too had blamed both Achilles and the gods (628–29, 635–36; see p. 135). Diomedes concludes with words of encouragement to Agamemnon, which prepare the way for the latter's great deeds when the battle resumes in Book 11. But it is thanks to Diomedes, not to Agamemnon, that morale is to some extent restored.

The Significance of Achilles' Decision

The view taken of the motives for Achilles' decision here is crucial for the interpretation of the *Iliad* as a whole and the tragedy of Achilles. All thoughtful readers of the poem will form their own opinions about why the hero acts as he does, and whether he is acting rightly or wrongly, and those opinions may well change with rereading and reconsideration. It is characteristic of a supreme and "classic" work of art that no single interpretation is likely to satisfy generally or for long, and every society, every individual, every experience of the work will be, and should be, different. Every reader brings to a work his or her own presuppositions, preferences, and philosophy, just as every actor will interpret a role in a great drama differently; and if Book 9 were produced as a drama, much of the particular force of each production would depend on the nuances brought out by the individual actor.

Achilles may be viewed in this book as the supreme hero whose ideals rise above those of his peers and who challenges the accepted norm of the society in which he lives; as a spoiled and sulky child who is holding out for more coaxing than he has yet received; as a victim of *Atê*, blind folly, who makes a decision that must bring disaster for himself and others; as the incarnation of *hubris*, the arrogance that almost automatically brings retribution and ruin: as the model for Aristotle's conception of the hero destroyed by some *hamartia*, or his picture of the *megalopsuchos*, the "great-souled" man who must demand the full measure of honor from his associates. Furthermore, it must never be forgotten that the book is not a record of the words and actions of a person in a particular situation, but the invention of an artist who has certain purposes and certain inherited conventions, and who is composing for an audience that has expectations to which he must to some degree conform. Again, the views of the poet may not be the same as those expressed by his main character. The following discussion is an attempt to interpret the poet's intention by examining the construction of the plot, the recurrent features of the characterization, and common patterns of action in Book 1 and Book 9.

If the *Iliad* is intended to be a whole in the form in which we have it, Achilles must reject the supplications at this point; and if the poet is planning to send Patroclus into battle instead of Achilles (in Book 16), he must produce a reason for so doing. Then the "withdrawal" pattern, instead of ending with the hero's return in Book 9 or Book 16, can be linked to the "revenge" pattern, which in turn will be joined to the "ransom" pattern in Book 24. The poet must therefore find reasons for Achilles to refuse to return in Book 9, and to be unable to enter the battle himself in Book 16, when the Greeks' situation is desperate enough for him to send Patroclus and his troops instead. The question then becomes, not "Why does Achilles reject the envoys in Book 9?" but "Has the poet produced reasons consistent with the characterization and plot? Are they connected with events and situations that come before and after? Is the motivation of significant interest as an aspect of general human reasoning or emotion, as a credible reaction to a recognizable situation in human society?" We are not divining and passing judgment on the motives and actions of an ancient Greek king, but interpreting the design of a creative artist.

It will be helpful to list the forces the poet has presented as acting upon Achilles at this point:

1. His own quick-tempered, uncompromising nature. This is demonstrated in his swift resentment against Agamemnon in Book 1. Agamemnon claimed that strife was dear to him (1.177), Peleus warned him to control his temper (9.255ff.) and to follow the advice of Patroclus (11.788ff.), and he himself boasts that he hates to disguise his feelings (9.312f.). Even when magnanimously granting Priam's request in Book 24, he has difficulty keeping himself under control (see p. 311), and his offer of a truce for Hector's funeral takes no account of the views of his commander-in-chief.

2. His dislike of Agamemnon, and his resentment at his own inferior status. This is suggested by his first offer to protect Cal-

chas against Agamemnon if necessary, his swift insult when Agamemnon demands a substitute prize (1.122), and his sarcastic suggestion that Agamemnon can find a "kinglier" man for his daughter to marry (9.392). Agamemnon's constant insistence that his superior position be recognized of course makes this hostility worse; his demand for a replacement prize is followed by repeated demands that Achilles admit Agamemnon's higher rank (1.185ff., 287ff., even 9.160ff.). Achilles' dislike is brought out again in their encounters in Books 19 and 23, and in his reference to Agamemnon in 24.653–55.

3. His still unsatisfied demand that Agamemnon be made to recognize the wrong he has done him. Thetis was to ask Zeus that the Greeks should be pinned back against their ships, so that "even Agamemnon may know his folly [*atê*] in not honoring the best of the Greeks" (1.409–12). This has not yet happened. Agamemnon has in fact admitted that he was the first to lose his temper (2.378), and that he was incredibly foolish (*aasamên*, 9.116, 119), but this has not been conveyed to Achilles, and he has no reason to suspect that the Greeks' difficult situation at the beginning of Book 9 has made Agamemnon appreciate his mistake. It is a feature of Homeric technique, well illustrated by Bassett (1938.103–37), that "in matters of slight importance what the listener knows, because the poet has told him in the preceding narrative, the character may be assumed to know" (p. 131), but it need not be presumed here that Achilles knows of Agamemnon's repentance. (Glaucus knows that it was Patroclus, not Achilles, who killed Sarpedon [16.543], because *we* know it; on the other hand, Achilles knows nothing of the death of Patroclus until he is told by Antilochus.) When the reconciliation is finally made in Book 19, there will be a public admission by Agamemnon of his error, as well as the restoration of Achilles' prize of honor and a recompense for the insult he has suffered; but no such admission has been made to Achilles yet. "He doesn't even dare to look me in the face, shameless dog though he is!" (9.372–73).

4. His feeling that he is not being supported by his friends. The army supported Chryses' attempt to ransom his daughter (1.22–23), but Achilles has had no open support since. Agamemnon at first threatens others besides Achilles ("I shall take your prize, or Ajax's, or Odysseus's" 1.138), but they say nothing, and the angry Achilles wonders "why any of the Greeks obeys you so willingly" (1.150). Agamemnon retorts that even if Achilles goes home the others will stay (1.174–75), and Achilles can only repeat that "you rule weaklings, or they would end this behavior" (1.231–

32), tell him to "order *others* about" (1.295–96), and ask his mother
that "they may *all* reap the benefit of their king" (1.410). None of
his friends visits him during the long days he spends alone on the
shore before his mother makes her appeal to Zeus (1.488–92; see
p. 184). They come to him at last, when the envoys arrive in this
book, but not because of their sympathy with him or in revolt
against Agamemnon, but as the obedient spokesmen for his
hated antagonist. His hurt feelings emerge in his taunt to Odysseus that he and the others should get together with Agamemnon and plan how to cope with Hector (9.346ff.), and his open
rebuke to Phoenix for siding with his enemy (611ff.).

The arrival of the envoys and Odysseus's speech thus present
Achilles with the worst possible situation; all the above pres-
sures are operating on him with full force. If this *were* a historical occasion, one might speculate how different the outcome
would have been if Agamemnon had come himself to Achilles,
or had summoned him to an assembly and publicly admitted his
mistake, as is normal in an apology (Agamemnon does this to
Odysseus after his undeserved reproach to him at the ordering
of the army [4.356ff.], the Phaeacian Euryalus does so to Odysseus after his insulting remark that he looks like a merchant, not
a gentleman [*Odyssey* 8.406ff.], and Agamemnon will do so to
Achilles at last at their reconciliation in Book 19). Or how different it might have been if the chiefs had come without gifts,
ignoring Agamemnon, and had asked him to return out of friendship to themselves!

Disguised as a Greek, Poseidon will say, as he rallies them
later on, that Agamemnon is in the wrong (13.111–14), and Agamemnon will speak twice of their anger against him (14.49–51,
19.85–86), but nothing of this is conveyed to Achilles by the envoys. As it is, everything we have seen of Achilles' character and
feelings has prepared us for his violently antagonistic response.
Odysseus's speech reveals to him that his friends not only have
no comprehension of the enormity of the wrong he has suffered,
but come to him as mouthpieces of the hated Agamemnon; no
wonder his quarrelsome nature breaks out and he speaks his
mind without disguise! This is perfectly consistent with all that
we know of him. The poet has prepared the way well.

The resulting sequence of reactions in Achilles' mind has also
been foreshadowed in the pattern of the quarrel in Book 1. There,
in his first outraged fury, he threatened to go home at once
(1.167–71), then after Athena's soothing intervention he changed
this to the more moderate "you will feel the need of me"

(1.240ff.), and finally he agreed to hand over Briseis but warned Agamemnon against seizing any other property of his (298ff.). In Book 9 he first decides to go home immediately, then after Phoenix's emotional appeals he postpones a decision, and finally he says that he will return to battle only when his own ships are threatened. The pattern of action is identical and the characterization beautifully consistent.

In Book 1, however, Achilles valued highly the army's gift, the prize of honor, which he had received from the booty captured from the ravaged city of Thebe: is this consistent with his disdain for Agamemnon's gifts in Book 9? Yes; because the prize given by the army conveyed honor to Achilles, and it was the honor that mattered to him and that he lost when the prize was removed. The gifts offered by Agamemnon in Book 9 would also bring honor to Achilles, as all the Greeks see, but they can be removed as easily as Briseis was (or never handed over). Moreover, munificence on that scale does great honor to the giver, too — like mercy, it blesseth him that gives and him that takes — and it is Agamemnon's humiliation that Achilles desires, not an increase in his stature. Gifts of that value would reaffirm in the strongest way Achilles' subordinate status to Agamemnon. Achilles does not need more wealth; he does not want gifts of Agamemnon's giving, gifts that would honor his enemy as much as himself. Still less does he desire to be linked to Agamemnon by marriage with his daughter. What he wants is honor among his fellow Greeks, the kind of honor that comes from affection and esteem. This, after Ajax's words, he knows he has retained; but it will be made complete by Agamemnon's acknowledgment of his mistake, not by his splendid gifts.

Achilles' decision to go home, when he feels that he has been deserted by his friends, is thus the only possible one. He can win nothing further at Troy, if he cannot see Agamemnon's humiliation. He must accept, and make the best of, the long life with wife and children, in obscure prosperity and ease, which Siduri recommended to Gilgamesh. Gilgamesh did not stop to consider it, and how contented an actual Achilles would have been with it may be left to the imagination.

Sarpedon's reflections on honor (see p. 151) show that the poet is capable of examining the principles upon which the heroic society he depicts is founded. But in Achilles' case there is little indication of a higher conception of honor, above material wealth, or of a rejection of the conventions of his society. Achilles is dissatisfied with the framework of his society not because he sees the vanity of the importance it attributes to honor and its physical trappings, but because its emphasis on power and wealth ranks above him, forever and unchallengeably, the weak, insecure, and inadequate Agamemnon. Confronted with the familiar conflict betwen one's duty to one's own integrity and the claims of one's friends, in Book 9 (as in Book 1) Achilles places first his desire to make Agamemnon admit his inferiority.

But it is the poet's great achievement in constructing his plot that Achilles will also be seen placing the welfare of his fellow Greeks before his own interests, when he yields to Patroclus's supplication in Book 16. Similarly, he also both *rejects* supplication in Book 9, which (as Phoenix has said) will lead to disaster for him, and also *yields* to it, when he agrees in Book 16 to assist his friends by dispatching Patroclus. Between these two books he is alone with his anger against Agamemnon (the theme announced at the beginning of the poem), misunderstood by his uncomprehending friends, an outsider in his society. When Achilles first appears in this book, he is singing of the great deeds of heroes. In this book he, and we, learn that it is not a simple thing to be a great hero: there is more to it than killing men in battle.

Further Reading

ON BOOK 7. Kirk 1978 analyzes and compares the duels in Books 3 and 7, concluding that probably a single poet composed both scenes, basing them on a general narrative idea.

ON BOOK 8. Fenik 1968 analyzes the battle scenes, finding that familiar elements form a background for a number of untypical incidents.

ON BOOK 9. Page 1959.297–315 vividly presents cases for considering Phoenix an addition to the embassy and the embassy an addition to an existing *Iliad.* This is an extreme form of the view taken in the commentary, that the basic plot structures of both Book 9 and the entire *Iliad* have been adapted and enlarged by the poet for the present poem.

ON THE DUAL FORMS FOR THE ENVOYS. Segal 1968 sums up the main explanations to that date, and gives an interesting idea of his own; the major discussions since that date are mentioned in the commentary above.

ON PHOENIX'S AUTOBIOGRAPHY. Rosner 1976 discusses the speech as a whole, with references to earlier work, and finds thematic parallels with other parts of the *Iliad;* Scodel 1982 surveys previous work on Phoenix's life history, and finds links between his tale and the Meleager and Achilles stories.

ON THE MELEAGER STORY. Willcock 1964 (adding to J. T. Kakridis 1949) is the basic work, with a bibliography of previous studies; his view is a little different from that put forward in the commentary above. Petzold 1976 examines it as an example of early Greek historical consciousness.

ON ACHILLES' DECISION. The views are too numerous and too varied to summarize. Schein 1984.104–16 takes a sound view, with good accounts of other scholars' ideas; so too Redfield 1975.3–23, 103ff. Adkins 1982.302–12 (see p. 157) deals in detail with Achilles' decision; he concludes that Achilles is not angry with the other leaders for not taking his part, and that the others cannot censure his behavior in terms of Homeric values but do censure that of Agamemnon, for it has led to an ignominious failure. On Achilles' idea of honor, see especially Segal 1971a and Claus 1975. Whitman 1958.181–200 and 1982.19–43 is the main proponent of the idea that Achilles' ideals transcend those of his society. Eichholz 1953 stresses the lack of any apology to Achilles; Lloyd-Jones 1971.8–24 discusses the morality of the issue. Willcock 1978 has a good discussion of Achilles' choice of fates. On aspects of gift-giving in Homer, see Donlan 1982.

25

Iliad Book 13

At the conclusion of Book 9 Diomedes reflects somberly on the failure of the embassy to Achilles, and urges Agamemnon to lead them vigorously into battle again the next day without him. Before that time comes, however, a further episode (Book 10) is added to the night's activities. Odysseus and Diomedes undertake a spying expedition against the Trojans, which results in the capture of the Trojan spy Dolon, the killing of some of the enemy, and the seizure of the splendid horses of Rhesus, the newly arrived Thracian king. The adventure is lighthearted and well told (after a rather slow start, as Agamemnon and Menelaus, both sleepless, get dressed and round up the rest of the chiefs), and the participants on both sides are well characterized, but the main plot is not affected in any way and the usual interconnections and foreshadowings are absent. There are also a number of peculiarities in language and style. It is likely that the book, whether by the same poet as the *Iliad* or not, was composed independently, after the completion of the rest of the *Iliad* (since it presupposes the situation at the end of Book 8), and added to the main poem.

The Greeks must now suffer further defeat; and the description of it must last for a long time, to be in proportion to the magnitude of Achilles' resentment and the scale of the events of the remainder of the poem, the death of Hector and the ransoming of his body. However, the dignity and heroic standing of the Greeks must somehow be retained, for they must remain the better men, and their major leaders must not be killed, for tradition cannot be violated too greatly (Hector in fact kills only one major hero, Patroclus, in the whole of the poem). How are these apparently incompatible aims to be achieved?

Naturally the gods provide a solution, and the defeat of the Greeks is divided into two climaxes, one at the end of Book 12 and the other concluding Book 15. In the first part of the action (Book 11), the Greeks rally under the leadership of Agamemnon, but he is finally wounded, and so are Diomedes and Odysseus; Ajax alone holds the line valiantly after they have withdrawn. At this point Achilles sees Nestor conveying the wounded

Machaon away from the fighting line (11.598ff.) and summons Patroclus, who begins the sequence of events leading to his death: "He came out, a warrior like Ares, and this was the beginning of his trouble" (11.604). Achilles claims that the Greek defeat will bring them to him in supplication, and dispatches Patroclus to find out the identity of the wounded man. His concern and his dispatch of Patroclus prefigure, in Homer's way, the much more detailed account of his sympathy and his sending out of his army with Patroclus at its head in Book 16.

The scene in Nestor's dwelling is to be of the greatest importance, and so it takes up a great deal of time. No less than twenty-six verses (11.617–42) describe his arrival and the refreshment prepared for the returning warriors, and his speech to the polite but restive Patroclus is the longest he has in the poem. He begins with a long paradigm, which both justifies his right to give advice and sets a model of behavior to follow. First he tells us of his prowess in leading a successful cattle raid against the Eleians (11.669–706), complete with details of the division of the booty; then just as if it looks as if the tale is over and Patroclus can at last get away, he passes on to another story of how he killed the enemy leader and a hundred men besides when the enemy in retaliation laid siege to his city (11.706–60). At last he comes to the point, contrasts his own services to his people with Achilles' withdrawal, and after telling Patroclus it is *his* duty to provide Achilles with wise advice, he presents his brilliant idea: if Achilles will not come, let him send Patroclus as substitute in his own immediately recognizable armor. To allow time for the battle to continue, Patroclus's return to Achilles is further delayed by his assistance to another wounded man, Eurypylus. He will remain with him until 15.390, and our suspense over the outcome of Nestor's plan helps to bind these central books together.

Book 12 recounts the battle at the Greek wall, the first great triumph of Hector. The building of this wall was suggested by Nestor after the inconclusive duel between Hector and Ajax (7.337–44) and built (rather improbably) in one night (7.436–41). Poseidon expressed reservations at that time, fearing the comparison with the walls of Troy that he and Apollo had built (7.446ff.), and Achilles poured scorn on its value as a substitute for his own strong arm when the envoys came to him (9.349–50). Since so much depends upon this wall in these central battle books, the poet devotes some thirty verses to it at the beginning of Book 12, explaining in a long direct address to his post–Trojan

War audience how it was later destroyed by Poseidon and so can no longer be seen on the Trojan plain (see p. 31). The attack on it is heralded by the first of several similar scenes between Hector and his friend and counselor Polydamas and by a short catalogue of the Trojans (12.88–104). The scene of struggle around the wall is further dramatized by a short apostrophe by the poet himself about the burden of attempting a description (12.176).

While Hector still waits by the ditch, a sinister omen is seen, an eagle (the bird of Zeus) unable to complete its victory over a snake and wounded by its intended victim. Polydamas points out the likely parallel with the imminent Trojan attack, and we may recall the explicit words of Zeus when he promised Hector success only until the end of this day (11.207–9). But Hector trusts Zeus (12.241–42), as Agamemnon did when the lying Dream was sent by Zeus to him in the second book, and says defiantly, "One bird-sign is best, to fight in defense of one's country" (12.243). He will show a similar overconfidence again later, when he puts on the immortal armor of Achilles and refuses Polydamas's cautious advice to withdraw within the city wall now that Achilles is likely to reenter the battle (see p. 275).

The Ajaxes try to rally the Greeks and the struggle continues; its duration, as well as its intensity, is conveyed by the long and well-known simile of the snowstorm, which fills the air with its flakes as it is now filled with stones hurled by the fighters, while the silence of the peaceful winter scene throws into startling contrast the huge din of the battle (12.278–89; see p. 106). Then Sarpedon takes the stage, to continue the building up of his character in preparation for his killing by Patroclus in Book 16, and after the compliment of a short description and a simile he delivers his famous exhortation to Glaucus (12.310ff.; see p. 150). Sarpedon's attack on the wall is seen by Menestheus, the rather unimportant leader of the Athenian contingent, who summons help from the two Ajaxes. It is this removal of the Ajaxes from the part of the wall facing Hector that allows him to break down the gate a little later. The two drive back Sarpedon, who is (for the moment) defended by his father, Zeus (12.402–3).

Then after another description of the general battle, including two similes, Hector's great moment comes; with Zeus backing him (12.437) he calls to his men, seizes a great rock (which is enlarged by eight verses of description, 12.446–53), and destroys the gates with it. As he enters, the poet draws the colors of darkening countenance, glittering bronze armor, and fiery eyes with unusual detail (12.462–66). The Trojans pour in behind him and sweep the Greeks back toward their ships. This is the gravest crisis yet for the Greeks.

The long Book 13 describes the fighting inside the Greek wall after Hector's incursion and before the rally of Book 14; it is a kind of interlude between the Greek-dominated Books 11 and 14 and the Trojan victories of Books 12 and 15. At its end the situation has changed little: the major Greek heroes are wounded and offstage during its length; no major hero on either side is killed; most of the action is devoted to heroes of the second rank (Idomeneus, Meriones, Deiphobus) who play no role in the main plot; the only divinity active is Poseidon, and that only at the beginning of the book. Though it contains some passages of much interest, a reader who finds uninterrupted battle scenes boring might well consider it the dullest in the poem.

The book provides, however, an excellent opportunity to observe the poet's techniques in presenting a long struggle that has no major heroes and effects no real change in the overall situation. In the following schematic analysis, key words identifying the techniques or type-scenes are italicized. Type-scenes, descriptions, similes and word play are further explained in Part One chapters 7, 9, 12, and 16 respectively; duels, woundings, and a hero's exploits (*aristeiai*) in chapter 8; exhortations, vaunts, challenges, rebukes, conferences, and calls for help in chapter 10. To show the alternation from one army to the other, the names of those fighting on the Greek side are printed in capitals. The analysis owes much to Fenik's work (1968.115–58).

1 *Description* of Zeus's inattentiveness (a shorter instance of the motif that appears at greater length in Book 14; see p. 247).

10 Divine journey *type-scene* for POSEIDON; expanded (because he will play a large role in this and the following book) by his viewing of the scene, his impressive march to his stables, and his picturesque chariot ride. (His intervention was prepared for at 8.198ff.)

39 *Description* of the Trojan charge, with two short *similes*.

43 POSEIDON delivers an *exhortation* (or *parainesis*: p. 92) to the two AJAXES, whose reaction is expanded by direct speech.

81 *Description* of the discouragement of the Greeks.

91 In a repetition of the earlier theme, POSEIDON *exhorts* other Greek leaders. His long speech contains a striking criticism of Agamemnon's cowardice, the resulting poor morale of

the Greeks, and the dishonoring of Achilles (107–14).

125 *Description* of the reforming of the Greek ranks, including a striking *word play* (130ff.).

136 *Description* of Hector's charge; the *simile* (137ff.) draws a parallel not only to his onrush but also to his halt as he encounters the Greek ranks. He gives a short *exhortation*.

156 *Duels*. (1) Deiphobus and MERIONES (both will be seen again in this book); (2) TEUCER and Imbrius; (3) Hector, TEUCER, and the AJAXES.

206 POSEIDON *exhorts* IDOMENEUS. The same pattern is found at 5.800ff. and 20.83ff. (Fenik 1968.128–29).

240 The *exploits* of IDOMENEUS begin. He dons his armor, which glitters as usual in this pattern (see p. 79), but before entering the battle meets MERIONES and has a long *conference* with him, including a remarkable description of the physical characteristics of "the Coward" (279–83). MERIONES receives an unusual *simile* drawn from mythology instead of from ordinary human life (298ff.), and they hold a second *conference*. Fenik (1968.129) finds the whole episode untypical.

330 *Description* of general battle, including a *simile* (334ff.), a direct address of the poet to the audience ("Boldhearted would he be, who might rejoice to see . . ." 343–44), and an omniscient statement by him about the thoughts of Zeus and POSEIDON.

361 The *exploits* of IDOMENEUS continue with his charge and his five *duels*: with Othryoneus, over whom he makes a sarcastic *vaunt* (374ff.; see p. 93); with Asius, whose pride in his horses was shown at his earlier appearance (12.110ff.) and who by the poet's careful touch has them close behind him still (385–86; the horsey Antilochus [23.301ff.] gets them later [400–401] as he does those of Pylaemenes [5.589]); with Deiphobus (subsequently a husband of Helen, so he must survive until the sack of Troy); with Hypsenor, who seems to be killed (412ff.) but by a slip in use of a formula is borne away "groaning heavily" (423); with Alcathous, who is bemused by POSEIDON (434ff.) as Patroclus will be by Apollo (16.790ff.) and over whom IDOMENEUS *vaunts* about his genealogy (450ff.), as others do before battle (6.150ff., 20.213ff.). Fenik finds parallels for all the incidents of these duels (1968.130ff.).

455 Deiphobus, the son of Priam, features in a decision-making *type-scene*, and has a *conference* with Aeneas.

469 Aeneas charges, and IDOMENEUS *calls for help.*

489 Aeneas also *calls for help.*

496 A short *description* of general battle.

502 *Duels* of Aeneas, IDOMENEUS, Deiphobus, and their victims. Ares' son ASCALAPHUS is killed fighting on the Greek side, though Ares fights with the Trojans (5.846ff.); later Hera will maliciously taunt Ares with his death (15.110ff.). The poet inserts a reminder that Zeus has told the gods not to intervene in the battle (521ff.), as a preparation for Hera's later distraction of his attention (14.153ff.).

527 MERIONES *wounds* Deiphobus, who is rescued by Priam's son Polites (who will be killed by Achilles' son Pyrrhus [or Neoptolemus] before Priam's eyes in Virgil's *Aeneid* 2.526ff.). Fenik points out (1968.24ff.) that the structure from 455 on is similar to that at 12.310ff., where Sarpedon consults with Glaucus, they charge against the wall, MENESTHEUS calls for help, and in the fight that follows Glaucus is wounded.

540 *Duels* of Aeneas, ANTILOCHUS, MERIONES, Helenus, and their victims.

581 MENELAUS *wounds* Helenus, who is helped by Agenor. This help to an injured man is common; Diomedes is so helped both by Sthenelus (5.112ff.) and by Odysseus (11.397ff.).

601 *Duels* of MENELAUS; his *vaunt* over Peisandrus (620ff.) is unusually significant, rebuking Zeus for his support of the Trojans, whose seizure of a host's wife should have outraged him, and the Trojans for their love of warfare. His encounter with Harpalion (643ff.) is exactly the same in structure as that of ANTILOCHUS and Adamas (560ff.): both consist of an insignificant Trojan striking an important Greek after a slaying, the failure of his spear to pierce the Greek's shield, his attempt to withdraw to safety, and his unusually bloody death (Fenik 1968.143). By a famous slip on the poet's part, the father who walks in tears beside the dead Harpalion (658) was killed at 5.576ff.

660 *Duel* of Paris, who kills EUCHENOR, whose fate gave him a choice of deaths, reminiscent of the choice claimed by Achilles (9.410ff.).

674 *Description* of Hector's lack of awareness, in the center of the line, of the Greek successes on the left.

685 *Catalogue* of the Greek forces facing Hector. Major renewals of the battle are introduced by catalogues of the forces, such as the huge listing of Greeks and Trojans in

Book 2, the roundup of Greek leaders by Agamemnon in Book 4, the account of Achilles' troops when they return to fight in Book 16, and the lineup of the gods before their conflict in Book 20. There is no such purpose here, and this catalogue may well be un-Homeric because of its irregular position, its peculiar structure, its unparalleled mention of the Ionians, and the geographical and other problems it presents (see Fenik 1968.152ff., Edwards 1980a.100, Willcock 1976.154ff.).

723 *Rebuke* of Hector by Polydamas, who declares that Hector has the gift of preeminence in battle but not that of wisdom, and counsels a strategic retreat, together with a significant warning that Achilles might come upon the scene. Hector agrees, as he did in the similar scene at 12.61ff. (but not at 12.211ff.).

754 *Description* of Hector rallying his forces (without a direct exhortation). He *rebukes* Paris, who amiably rejects it.

789 *Description* of the Trojan charge. Fenik (1968.154) points out that the Polydamas-Hector scene at 12.61ff. includes an identical structure of advice, agreement, rally of forces, catalogue, charge, and defense by the Greeks (here AJAX; at 12.127ff. the two LAPITHAE).

809 *Challenge* by AJAX, who blames Zeus for the Greek repulse and predicts that his favor will soon change. An omen confirms this before Hector replies to him.

833 *Description* of general battle. This breaks off the confrontation between Hector and AJAX, which is not resumed until 14.402. Fenik (1968.156ff.) finds no parallel to this interruption in a developing action of this kind, but Whitman and Scodel (1981.6) suggest two parallels and consider the insertions emphasize the importance of the confrontation.

Like this episode, the book ends inconclusively, but with a promise of excitement to come. Hector's mighty and apparently successful attack on the Greek wall at the end of Book 12 has been defused, and the scene will be repeated with even greater impact after two more books have passed. Now, with one of Homer's careful transitions, the uproar of the battle is heard by Nestor in his shelter, and as we listen to his words it fades away in the background.

The most important recent work on Book 10 is Fenik 1964. Books 11 and 13 are analyzed by Fenik 1968. Latacz 1977.101ff. analyzes the battle from the beginning of Book 11 to the rescue of Patroclus's body in Book 18, on structural principles rather different from Fenik's. Schadewaldt 1938 is a still-useful study of Book 11 and its interconnections with other books of the poem. Whitman and Scodel 1981 show the elaborate structure and time sequence in Books 13, 14, and 15.

26

Iliad Book 14

The previous book ended with an abortive confrontation between Hector and Ajax. After a council of the Greek chiefs, the major part of the present book is devoted to the so-called Beguiling of Zeus, Hera's plot to distract Zeus's attention from the battle so that Poseidon can go to the help of the Greeks. The episode is brilliantly told and deserves detailed comment. In the final part of the book, Poseidon seizes his opportunity, rallies the Greeks, and the Trojans retreat. Zeus's awakening and the subsequent activities of the gods occur in Book 15, but will be treated as the fourth part of this chapter.

There is no special break between Books 13 and 14, though the scene changes, nor between 14 and 15, though again the book division has been placed at a change of scene. The duel between Hector and Ajax runs over from 13 to 14, and the two parts of the encounter of Zeus and Hera from 14 to 15.

The Greek Council (1–152)

Nestor has not been seen since Patroclus left him at the end of Book 11, before the disasters the Greeks suffered in the following book. Aroused by the clamor, he meets with Agamemnon, Odysseus, and Diomedes, all of whom were wounded in Book 11. The following informal council of chiefs gives scope for further characterization: Agamemnon is as usual despondent, fearful that the Greeks will turn against him as Achilles has (49–51), and recommending abandonment of the expedition as he did at the beginning of Book 9; Nestor seeks a plan of action (but says nothing about his suggestion to Patroclus); Odysseus is outspokenly impatient with his faint-hearted commander, and is as determined to stay to the end as he was in his long address to the troops after their flight to the ships (2.284–332) or in his soliloquy when cut off in the battle (11.404–10); Diomedes is (as ever) conscious of his youth, and justifies his right to express an opinion by reciting his pedigree—its length lends the needed weight to his words—and finally gives the best advice of all, that they should go out to encourage their troops despite their wounds. As they return, Poseidon (oddly disguised as an unidentified old man) consoles Agamemnon, and with the gigantic battle cry of a god he reinvigorates the Greeks. Hera is watching, and the poet now turns our attention to her.

The Beguiling of Zeus (153–353)

At the beginning of Book 13 Zeus withdrew his attention from the struggles on the Trojan plain, either to observe the larger affairs of mankind or because he has a short attention span, and Poseidon was able to reverse the course of the battle in that book. Now the poet repeats the motif in much more elaborate form in this famous episode, in which Hera takes her own measures to distract her husband. Her intervention is not essential to the plot, for Zeus could have been left blissfully oblivious for any length of time the poet wished. Homer must have inserted the scene as an intermission in the long course of the battle, and for the delight of presenting so amusing and skillfully crafted a vignette of the lighter side of life. What is more likely than that the mind of an unoccupied male, especially one with Zeus's reputation, should turn to sex? Tales of a similar tone are found in the song of Demodocus (*Odyssey* 8.266ff.) and in the *Homeric Hymn to Aphrodite*, but the humor, insight, and careful detail of the Beguiling are hard to equal. Though much of its charm is obvious, the poet's skill here, as in the superb human scenes of Books 3 and 6, deserves a thorough examination.

Hera comes into view, and we watch her expression change as she looks first at her brother Poseidon, who is assisting her own favorites, and then at her husband, Zeus, unconscious of all this turmoil. A brief deliberation type-scene tells us of her plans, for as usual the Greek poet would rather whet our eager expectation of what we know is about to happen than keep us in the dark. Then Hera begins the three stages of her preparations.

First her adornment (165–86). Other examples of this type of scene survive. In the *Hymn to Aphrodite* the goddess decks herself out before setting off to seduce Anchises (58–65), but with considerably less elaboration; an even shorter version, though still with the three elements of bathing, anointing, and clothing, is found in the song of Demodocus, placed for structural reasons *after* the seduction instead of before it (*Odyssey* 8.362–66). The bedecking of Pandora before her seduction of menfolk in Hesiod (*Works and Days* 72–76, *Theogony* 573–84) is naturally limited to the last element, since she is newly made and needs no bathing, and the details are different (a crown of flowers, or of gold, instead of a veil). A seven-line fragment of the *Cypria*, one of the epics of the Trojan cycle, describes the flower-decked garments Aphrodite wore, probably to the Judgment of Paris (frag. 4 Allen, 6 Evelyn-White). The present example, extended not by overdoing the bathing or clothing elements but by adding the account of the boudoir, the fragrance of her cosmetics, and her earrings, brooch, and sandals (none of which occurs in other examples), is both the fullest and the best balanced. (In the seduction scene of Helen and Paris in Book 3 this part of the episode is, for obvious reasons, omitted.) In the martial context of the *Iliad* the comparison of Hera's preparations for overcoming her husband to the arming scene of a warrior before battle comes naturally to mind.

Next she visits Aphrodite (187–223), to make certain her mission is successful. Of course the beguiling could have been contrived without Hera borrowing Aphrodite's special girdle, but the poet wants the additional amusement of outwitting the love goddess, who is usually a target for his fun and who of course supports the Trojans, not the Greeks. In form their meeting is a supplication type-scene. Hera's address is informal and affectionate ("my dear child"), and she openly and affably admits their opposed interests in the war; the official titles that begin Aphrodite's response perhaps indicate her wariness of this unexpected charm. Hera tells her false tale, which does much credit to her amiability, and the unsuspecting Aphrodite is willing to help; the reason she gives for her deference, "for you lie in the arms of supreme Zeus," is not a simple statement of Hera's conjugal status but befits the love goddess's special interests, and also amusingly foreshadows the actual outcome of the loan she is making. The bewitching girdle is described—the phrase "on it is . . . , on it is . . . " and so on, is reminiscent of the description of the *aegis* worn into battle by Eris (5.740ff.)—and Aphrodite hands it over with the innocent wish that Hera's plans may work out. Hera "smiles" (222), and "smiling" (223) stows away the girdle: one grateful smile for Aphrodite, one satisfied smile for herself.

Finally Hera begins her journey, but the poet has still further plans for her. She goes not to Zeus but to the god Sleep, to make another supplication for aid. He demurs (the only example of the supplication type-scene in which this happens), and explains his reluctance by a paradigm, demonstrating how cooperating with Hera in her mischievous plans against Zeus and his favorites has got him into bad trouble in the past. (The tale of Heracles' sack of Troy is well known [5.640–42]; Hera's attack on him afterward, and Zeus's punishment of her, are described more fully at the end of this episode [15.18–30], but this and Sleep's role in the affair may well be the poet's invention.) So Hera must make a second offer, this time one of the Graces whom the anthropomorphic Sleep has had his eye on for a long time, and he enthusiastically agrees.

Now the climactic scene can begin. The conspirators draw near to Zeus as he sits on Mount Ida near Troy, and Sleep, anthropomorphic as ever, disguises himself as a bird to avoid his eye (291–92). The seduction begins. Zeus sees and desires Hera, and accosts her, asking where she is going and why she does not have her chariot. (This is a good question, since the gods' chariots are often mentioned as a means of elaborating upon their journeys; for instance, Aphrodite needs one to get back to Olympus when she has been wounded [5.357ff.], Hera and Athena twice take one to the battlefield [5.720ff.; 8.382ff.] and so does Poseidon [13.23ff.], and Zeus took his to Mount Ida [8.41ff.]. Are we to think Aphrodite's girdle shows to better effect on a walking figure?) She repeats her false tale, leaving out a few unnecessary details (lines 202–4 and 208–10 in the version told to Aphrodite are omitted here), and with proper wifely piety claims that she wished to tell him the reason for her absence.

Zeus cannot wait. Like Paris persuading Helen in the parallel scene (3.442ff.), he tells her that his passion is greater than ever before, but instead of mentioning their own past embraces as Paris does, the poet has Zeus launch into a catalogue of his former mistresses and their offspring (317–27). Scholars ancient and modern have been scandalized, and have removed the list from the text: van Leeuwen (1913, note to 317) writes with dignified brevity: "*Uxori nomina pelicum enumerare neque decorum neque aptum ad persuadendum*" ("To enumerate to one's wife the names of one's paramours is neither proper nor likely to persuade her"). But surely the inappropriateness is just the point, the climax of the humor of the passage. For Hera is traditionally jealous of Zeus's extramarital affairs, and now she is confronted with them by her errant husband himself and cannot afford to protest for fear of spoiling her plan. If only one could see her face as his list continues! The circumstances bring a piquancy that goes far beyond Leporello's catalogue of Don Giovanni's affairs, or the Wife of Bath's account of her successive husbands.

Somehow Hera manages to control herself, and she assumes a

fitting modesty; in the present circumstances she may be attempting to lure Zeus as far as possible from the Trojan plain, but of course it is in character for a bride to be hesitant (Helen is, too, before she goes to bed with Paris; 3.328f.). Her shame at the danger of being seen making love recalls the ending of the song of Demodocus, when the young male gods make ribald jokes when Ares and Aphrodite are trapped in bed together (*Odyssey* 8.325ff.). But Zeus takes precautions, and the two make love within a golden cloud, on the carpet of flowers the earth provides. Finally, the poet describes Zeus as overcome by sleep and love (*philotêti*). Or should it be Sleep and Love? The former is very much personified and present, and in fact leaves immediately to take to Poseidon the message the poet has omitted to have Hera give him; but the latter was represented on Aphrodite's girdle (216), and perhaps should also be capitalized here as a reminder of her presence and irresistible effect (see p. 144). Sleep's journey returns the action to the battlefield, after this exquisitely handled relief from the arena of human effort and suffering.

Poseidon Rallies the Greeks (354–15.4a)

Given the go-ahead by Sleep, Poseidon yells out an exhortation, which turns into instructions for the peculiar exchange of armor that follows. What appearance he has adopted is not mentioned. Somehow in the midst of the fray the fiercest fighters receive the replacement of their armor, doubtless a sound idea after the long trauma of the battle but difficult to achieve in the actual circumstances (I know of no satisfactory explanation or parallel). Then Poseidon leads them forward, and his element the sea itself lends its support (392). Hector's rally of the Trojans balances this, and three powerful interconnected similes – sea surf, forest fire, and storm wind (394–401) – describe the renewed clash of the two armies.

At last the duel between Hector and Ajax, interrupted at 13.833, is resumed. The themes are familiar, but amplified more than usual: Hector launches an ineffectual spear, tries to withdraw, and is wounded. He is carried off half-conscious, and the poet does not hesitate to use the formulaic phraseology to describe him vomiting "dark-clouded" blood (437). He will be incapacitated until revived by Apollo at 15.239. Then the duels resume, with Greek and Trojan alternately victorious and an unusual number of joyful vaunts from the winners (Polydamas 454ff.,

Ajax 470ff., Acamas 479ff., Peneleos 501ff.). Then a short invocation of the Muse by the poet (508–10), like that before Agamemnon's exploits (11.218–20) or before Hector hurls fire on the Greek
ships (16.112–13), suggests that a major turn in the tide of battle
is coming, and builds up expectations that will be soon be
thwarted by Zeus's awakening. A rapid list of Trojan casualties
shows the effect of the Greek charge; a similar onrush of deaths
will soon mark the Trojan counterattack (15.328ff.).

Zeus Awakens (15.4b–261)

The Trojans are thrust back over wall and ditch and stand terrified; but suddenly, at the end of a verse, "wakened was Zeus"
(15.4), and the following scenes among the Olympians show the
same superb characterization as the Beguiling. Zeus sees
Poseidon rampant on the plain, the Trojans in flight and Hector
wounded, and he chides Hera, guessing immediately that she is
responsible: no titles, but "surely then this wickedly-planned
trick of yours, you utter fool, Hera, / has stopped Hector" (15.14–
15). He reminds her (in a kind of paradigm) of the violent punishment he had inflicted on her for her previous persecution of
Heracles, the same violence he threatened all the gods with
when he forbade them to interfere in the fighting (8.527ff.).
Daunted, Hera swears a long and terrible oath that she did not
incite Poseidon; in her last line Zeus's abbreviated title, "dark-
clouded," sounds almost like an endearment (it is used alone like
this elsewhere only by Poseidon in a friendly dialogue, *Odyssey*
13.147; Odysseus once addresses Athena with the similarly
familiar vocative "Owl-eyes [*glaukôpi*]," *Odyssey* 13.389).

Zeus's anger vanishes in amusement and postcoital amiability; he knows that Poseidon would not have gone so far without
her implicit support, and says so to her with friendly irony: "If
you then would share my views, even Poseidon would have to
agree with us at once!" (15.49–52; see Whitman and Scodel
1981.12). Then as a mild retribution for her insubordinate behavior, he makes her the unwilling agent of the reversal of her de-
signs, sending her off ("if you are *really* not responsible," 15.53) to
bring Iris and Apollo so that he can dispatch them to remove
Poseidon from the field and to heal Hector. This instruction
passes into a prediction of the future, more detailed than hither-
to, including the deaths of Patroclus, Sarpedon, and Hector himself and the eventual fall of Troy. This will, after all, bring some
comfort to his vexed consort.

Hera departs in a flash, her speed described by a remarkable simile (as fast as one's imagination or memory can picture a place, 15.80–83); no doubt she is accelerated both by her fear that Zeus's mood may change again—she has gotten off very lightly—and by irritation that her plot has ceased to work. She joins the other Olympians, and before she delivers her message from Zeus the poet puts in a kind of epilogue to the preceding action (so Fenik 1968.228). The poet likes this kind of elegant conclusion of an action, and similar postludes follow the abortive expedition of Hera and Athena to the battlefield (Zeus teases the angry pair, 8.442ff.), the wounding of Aphrodite and Ares by Diomedes (Dione comforts her daughter, 5.370ff., and Zeus gruffly heals Ares, 5.868ff.) and Artemis's manhandling by Athena (Zeus comforts her, 21.505ff.). So on this occasion Hera's disgust at the end of her plot shows on her face, and Themis comments on it. After Hera's tight-lipped response the poet himself describes how "she smiled / with her lips; but her forehead and knitted brows / were not warm" (15.101–3). "Damn him!" she goes on, in effect (15.104–9), and wanting to hurt others as she has been hurt herself, she nastily tells Ares of the death of his son. (The poet carefully informed us when he was killed that Ares did not know of it, 13.521ff.)

Everyone looks at Ares, who with sorrow and furious bluster orders his chariot and gets on his armor. Athena rises to the crisis and stops him, "fearing for all the gods" (15.123), but her brisk removal of his helmet, shield, and spear (not to mention her language) is strongly reminiscent of the behavior of a bossy elder sister. The two were matched against each other in Books 4 and 5, and will be again in 20.48ff. and in the formal Battle of the Gods (21.391ff.). So Ares is quenched; Hera in brief, surly fashion sends Iris and Apollo to do what Zeus wants (15.145–48); and so ends this entertaining glimpse of family life on Olympus.

Iris is sent to recall Poseidon, just as she was to Hera and Athena when they set off for the battleground in Book 8 (397ff.). Unlike them, Poseidon rebels, saying Zeus may keep his orders for his offspring; but Iris, like a good secretary who knows her boss's moods, waits and quietly suggests that he might like to give the matter a little more thought. He does so, and is courteous enough to thank her for it (15.206–7). So he leaves, with a threat that there will be big trouble if Zeus tries to spare Troy itself. We all know this is a meaningless threat, but it doubtless makes him feel better.

Zeus now turns to Apollo. It is usually said that in real time his instructions to his second messenger ought to follow directly upon those he gave to Iris, but that the convention which demands that simultaneous events be described as successive here requires that Iris's actions be completed before Apollo's can begin. This is true enough, but the poet diminishes any awkwardness, almost as if apologizing for the conventional mechanics, by making Zeus explain that Apollo can act now that Poseidon has taken himself off the scene (15.222–23) so that no direct clash will occur. In fact, Zeus is human enough to declare at some length his relief that Poseidon gave in so quickly (15.224–28). Apollo asks Hector, now beginning to recover, what happened to him, and like Achilles when his mother asks the same question, Hector expresses surprise that the god does not know (15.248–50; cf. 1.365). Apollo then reinvigorates him for his great triumph, and after the unfortunate (but highly entertaining) interlude Zeus's master plan for the Greek defeat again becomes operative.

Further Reading

Sowa 1984.67–94 analyzes six seduction scenes in the *Iliad*, the *Odyssey*, and the *Hymn to Aphrodite*. Whitman and Scodel 1981 show the elaborate structure and time sequence in Books 13, 14, and 15. Frazer 1985 argues that the council of chiefs at the beginning of this book demonstrates a leadership crisis that is resolved by Poseidon's intervention.

27

Iliad Book 16

After the respite given them by Zeus's inattentiveness and Posei-don's assistance in Book 14, the Greeks are again driven back in Book 15, and the poet extends the episode to very considerable length while giving major prominence to only two heroes, the furiously advancing Hector and the unshakable Ajax. Twice Apollo leads a charge together with Hector, once when the Greek heroes begin a rear-guard action on the advice of Thoas (15.306ff.), and again when he demolishes the Greek ditch and wall, as easily as a child does a sandcastle, and leads the Trojans through (15.355ff.). This brings the situation back to where it was at the end of Book 12, and soon it becomes worse still for the Greeks, who climb on to their ships to hold off the Trojans with long pikes (15.387–89). There the action stays until the end of the book, in a deadlocked and interminable turmoil of struggle.

There is one forward movement of the main plot. Patroclus, still tending his wounded colleague Machaon, sees that the Greeks are close to total disaster and darts off to carry his en-treaty to Achilles (15.390–405). The effort to set fire to the ships begins, and is thwarted by Ajax. From this time on the firing is mentioned again and again, once as a part of Zeus's plan (15.596ff.), but it will not succeed until the poet brings it about before Achilles' own eyes so that it can inspire him to immediate action (16.122ff.). Noteworthy in the course of the struggle in Book 15 are the balancing exhortations of Hector and Ajax, one magnificent pair after Zeus has saved Hector by breaking Teucer's bowstring (15.486ff. and 502ff.), the other a part of the splendid excitement of the end of the book (15.718ff. and 733ff.; see p. 92). The last few verses picture the mighty Ajax striding from ship to ship, desperately fending off the attackers with a huge pike.

In Book 16 the main plot moves forward rapidly, as Achilles allows his great friend Patroclus to put on his own armor and lead his troops to the rescue; Patroclus drives the Trojans back but is finally killed by Hector. Like Book 9, this book could have brought the end of the wrath of Achilles, for the Greeks have been defeated as he demanded and Achilles could have been made to return with honor. The book begins with a fourth supplication to him by Patroclus, corresponding to the successful appeal of Meleager's wife Cleopatra (see p. 227). But because of the stand Achilles took after the three supplications in Book 9, he can yield only to the extent of dispatching Patroclus as his surrogate, as Nestor suggested (11.793ff.), and so before the withdrawal part of the main plot has ended with Achilles' return, it has been meshed with the new theme of revenge for Patroclus's death. That theme will continue until it in turn merges into the ransom and consolation at the end of the poem. In addition, sending Patroclus as surrogate brings in the theme of Achilles' armor, which is seized by Hector at Patroclus's death and must be replaced before the return of Achilles himself to battle.

The possibilities introduced by these advances in the plot are fully exploited by the poet. Achilles' perplexity, his misgivings about allowing his friend to go to battle, and his love for Patroclus are movingly conveyed. Patroclus wins great glory for himself by beating back the Trojan attack and killing Sarpedon, whose stature is much amplified by the concern of his father, Zeus. Hector kills Patroclus, but his glory is shaded somewhat by the manner of the slaying and the forebodings of his own death.

Less obvious as a part of the plot, but contributing immensely to the depth of feeling and allusion in this and later books, is the disguise of Patroclus in Achilles' armor. The ostensible purpose of this, as old Nestor planned in Book 11, is to deceive the Trojans into thinking that Achilles himself has returned. In fact, however, this intended result is almost ignored; indeed, the Trojans are once said to think that Achilles had abandoned his anger (281–82), but no other mention is made of this until Sarpedon declares that he will find out *who it is* that is causing them such heavy losses (424–25), and not long afterward the Trojan ally Glaucus is well aware that it was *Patroclus* who killed his friend (543). No Greek is ever said to believe that Achilles has returned. The reason seems clear enough; the effect of Patroclus's death, and its significance for the feelings of Achilles and the fate of Hector, could only be spoiled by Hector's discovering, as his victim lies at his feet, "It's not Achilles at all, it's only Patroclus!"

The idea of the exchange of armor does not recur in this form in Greek tales, and may be the poet's own invention. Divinely made armor was probably in origin a magical device given by a helper to the hero to make him invulnerable, like Hermes' gift of the herb moly to Odysseus (*Odyssey* 10.302ff.; see p. 62). But

Homer is careful to avoid the question whether the armor is invulnerable, both at the deaths of Patroclus and Hector and while Achilles is wearing it in battle. In the *Aethiopis* Achilles was killed by Paris's arrow in his unarmored ankle, but we do not know how far the invulnerablity of his armor was emphasized (on this see Young 1979.22 note 34).

The ramifications of the exchange of armor, however, extend far beyond the momentary deception of the Trojans. It may reflect the usual disguise of the absent hero upon his return (see Odysseus's return in the *Odyssey*; Patroclus returns in place of the absent Achilles). The armor identifies Patroclus as Achilles' surrogate, and acts as a symbol of the concession he is making to the Greeks; it is also a symbolic reminder of the contrast between the immortal gods and the mortal heroes whom it will not save from death (see p. 115). Its loss at Patroclus's death brings dishonor as well as additional grief and guilt to Achilles himself (as becomes clear in Book 18.) Hector's donning of the divinely made equipment is portrayed by the poet as a sign of arrogance and *hubris* (especially at 17.198ff.), and an indication of the misjudgments that will lead to his own doom. At Hector's own death it is insistently stressed that he is wearing the armor he took when he killed Patroclus, so that the reason for Achilles' mercilessness is visually present before us (especially at 22.321ff.). (Virgil uses the same technique, more obviously, when Aeneas kills Turnus, the slayer of Pallas; *Aeneid* 12.940ff.)

Practically, the loss of Achilles' armor provides the poet with an acceptable reason for not having him dash into the battle to kill Hector immediately upon hearing the news of his friend's death, and so avoids crowding the climaxes one upon the other. It also leads up to the magnificent scene of the decoration of the great shield made by Hephaestus at the end of Book 18, and the ironic juxtaposition of Achilles' decision to seek vengeance even at the cost of his own life with the making of the armor by the immortal god. The purely practical reason for Patroclus's disguise is minor compared with the symbolism and emotional depth it allows the poet to invoke in later scenes.

The commentary on Book 16 will be divided into four parts: Achilles and Patroclus; Patroclus's preparations for battle; Patroclus and Sarpedon; and the death of Patroclus.

This is the first time the poet has shown us Achilles and his friend speaking together at length; it is the last time they will be together while Patroclus is alive. When Patroclus enters, both he and Achilles have long forgotten the mission on which he was sent (11.601ff.). He is in tears, and Achilles, instead of waiting for his message, addresses him first, showing the same aggressive impatience he did when Athena interrupted him in Book 1. He regards his friend's distress with pity (5), but—just as he did with Athena—he ignores the obvious reason for it and mockingly compares him to a little girl crying to be picked up. Has Patroclus alone heard bad news from home? Then he drops this pretense and comes to the point, asking if Patroclus is upset because the Greeks are reaping the reward of their own mistreatment of himself. His tone has hardened, for Patroclus begins his response, "Do not be angry" (22).

Patroclus is bitterly reproachful; Achilles was born of a harsh mountain and the gray sea, not Peleus (whose name recalls Mount Pelion) and the sea goddess Thetis (a kind of reversal of personification). He goes on to make the request suggested by Nestor, that if Achilles himself will not return, he will let Patroclus wear his armor. The wording (36–45) is precisely the same as that of Nestor's original suggestion (11.794–803), with a few necessary grammatical changes; this is Homer's habit in the case of messages and carries no special significance (but see p. 23). The prophecy of Achilles' death, which it is suggested he may have heard, is a foreshadowing of the circumstances under which Achilles will eventually return (18.95–96), possibly a reminiscence of the choice of glory or long life Achilles spoke of to the embassy (9.410ff.), and perhaps partly a euphemism for "if you are impossibly intransigent" (compare also the fate of Meleager; p. 227). The poet then adds, as he did when Patroclus's mission began (11.603–4), a grim reminder that his sympathy with the sufferings of his fellow Greeks will bring about his own death (46–47).

Achilles is much upset, and his confused emotions are revealed in a long response in which they are presented one after another. No prophecy holds him back, but continued resentment over the humiliation he suffered from Agamemnon; his words are similar in tone to his reply to Ajax in Book 9. This is the general reason, but he goes on to say that it is not now compelling and he could be mollified (60–61); this is the essentially good-hearted man who gave honorable burial to Andromache's father (6.417ff.) and comes to terms with Agamemnon in Book 19 and with Priam in Book 24.

The problem is the position Achilles took up at the end of Book 9, that he would not return to battle until the Trojans reached his own ships. He would look a fool if he were to go back on this, and his pride will not allow that. It is his own words, rather than Agamemnon's insult, that now stand in his way. So he consents to Patroclus's going in his stead, wearing Achilles' own armor; and after this concession his mind moves over the whole stupid situation—the Trojans forcing the Greeks back to the ships, Hector triumphant, Diomedes and Agamemnon unable to hold him, all this unnecessary "if only great Agamemnon would treat me well" (72–73).

He instructs Patroclus carefully. He must save the ships; but Achilles himself must have an opportunity to win glory and to achieve the return of Briseis and gifts as recompense, so Patroclus must come back after that limited victory. He repeats this (the point is very important); if Patroclus is too successful, it will reduce Achilles' own chances of honor. Then a further concern comes to the forefront, and he unconsciously predicts exactly what will in fact happen; if Patroclus in the heat of the battle attacks Troy itself, the Trojans' patron, Apollo, may destroy him. So, once more repeated, Patroclus must come back as soon as the ships are safe.

Then in a final superb touch Achilles, weary of all this unnecessary complication and worry and all the tedious problems of human relationships, hating the world, wishes in heartfelt exasperation that all Trojans and Greeks alike would vanish and he and Patroclus, alone and side by side, could get on with the straightforward job of sacking Troy. We should remember these words when, shortly before Patroclus's death (707–9), Apollo declares that neither Patroclus nor Achilles himself will conquer the city.

Achilles is torn between concern for the battered Greeks, sympathy for Patroclus's grief, longing to return to battle himself, desire for restoration of his own honor, need to stand by his own words, and above all fear for the safety of Patroclus. Some scholars have felt that his references to the abduction of Briseis (56ff.) and his desire for her restoration with compensatory gifts (85ff.) require the assumption of a version of the *Iliad* without the offers made to him in Book 9. This risks oversimplification, for Achilles' final decision in Book 9, that he would not fight until Hector reaches his own ships, is given by him here as the prime reason for not returning to battle now (61ff.).

Though not explicit in the text, it is reasonable to suggest that the root of the problem is the same as it was in Book 9, that Agamemnon himself has not come to ask Achilles' help and offer restitution. So far as Achilles is concerned, nothing has changed since his decision at the end of Book 9, for Hector has not yet reached his ships, and Patroclus has no new argument or new offer. But if Agamemnon had come himself to ask his help, a mollified Achilles would in huge relief and joy have surged back against the Trojans. Instead, his goodheartedness leads him into taking a quite illogical position, for by allowing Patroclus to drive back Hector from the ships he is removing the best chance of fulfillment of the conditions under which he said he himself would return; only if Patroclus is killed will Achilles be called upon now.

So whatever the outcome, Achilles must lose his hope of restitution or his beloved companion; and in fact he may even be in danger of losing both friend and gifts, for in the paradigm of Meleager, recounted to him by Phoenix, after the hero has yielded to the pleas of his wife and driven away the attackers, his townsmen renege on the gifts they had previously offered (9.598ff.). Achilles is now in a situation in which he cannot but lose; but it is compassion, not intransigence, that has brought him there.

Patroclus Prepares for Battle (101–256)

The scene cuts abruptly back to the ongoing battle at the ships, with a few very noisy lines (102–6; see p. 118) and a sympathetic description of Ajax's physical exhaustion. Then a short invocation of the Muses hails Hector's disarming of Ajax, by Zeus's design, and suddenly, anonymously, fire blazes up from a Greek ship—fire mentioned in three successive verses. Then in the last section of the verse attention leaps back to Achilles, calling excitedly to Patroclus to hasten: "They threw unwearying fire / on a swift ship. At once unquenchable raced the flame! / So its stern the fire seized! *But Achilles* / slapping his thigh called to Patroclus" (122–25). This has all happened rapidly. But now at this climax of the action the standard Homeric technique takes over, and the importance of the scene demands several pages of expansion while the poet ceremoniously prepares Patroclus and his troops for their entry into the battle.

First Patroclus puts on the armor. The standard verses (see p. 72) repeat the regular sequence of actions, particularized first by the reminder that the corselet is Achilles', then more significantly by the explanation that he does not take up Achilles' spear, gift of the centaur Chiron to Peleus at his wedding, for only Achilles can handle such a weapon. On the practical level Hector must not capture this spear, which will be used by Achilles for his massacre of the Trojans and for killing Hector himself, but primarily perhaps the motif is included because at this vital instant of Patroclus's disguise as Achilles it indicates that he is far from being Achilles' equal in battle, with or without Achilles' armor.

There are other signs too. "The element of the shining of the armor is lacking. The *Patrocleia* is the only one of the five great *aristeiai* [the exploits of Diomedes, Agamemnon, Hector, and Achilles are the others] in which this element of the preparation is lacking. . . . If the hero is arming for his last battle, his arms do not shine" (Krischer 1971.29). For further amplification of the arming scene, the harnessing of the horses is described, and again the poet adds a symbolic reminder that Patroclus, hero though he is, is unequal to the burden of assuming Achilles' identity and his divine armor; for beside Achilles' immortal horses is harnessed the mortal horse Pedasos. Harnessing of a trace horse beside the two attached to the chariot pole is found elsewhere (8.81ff., *Odyssey* 4.590), but there seems to be special significance here, for the mortal horse, like Patroclus, will die in this battle (467ff.).

The Myrmidons arm themselves, too, during the elaboration of a long simile (which rather oddly describes the satiety of successful wolves, not their hunger for the hunt), and their formal entry at last onto the battlefield of the *Iliad* is celebrated by a catalogue, as the first array of the armies was in Book 2. A good deal of personal anecdote is given for the first leaders, then as usual in catalogues it diminishes toward the end. Achilles delivers a short exhortation, and there is a description of the closeness of their ranks; this fills the place of a general description of the march into battle, like that at the beginning of Book 3.

All is set for the departure. Homer, however, is working at deeper levels than simply that of the approaching conflict, and there is a further protraction of preparations—the fire blazing all this time on the Greek ships—while Achilles prays to Zeus for his friend's safe return. A comparison with Virgil's adaptation of the scene to the departure for battle of Pallas, the doomed young son of King Evander (*Aeneid* 8.558–84), shows up the very different characteristics of the Homeric technique. Virgil gives his old king a passionate appeal to the gods, demanding immediate death in preference to ever hearing the news of the loss of his son. Achilles' appeal is very formal and matter-of-fact, befitting his dignity and the solemnity of prayer, but Homer shows the depth of his anxiety by the long description of his meticulous preparation of the chalice that he reserves for Zeus alone (220–29). All the time that we are watching his careful unwrapping and cleansing of the chalice, we are coming to realize the agony of worry in his mind. As usual the divinity's response is mentioned, in this case the reaffirmation of the death sentence on Patroclus. The departure ends with a final picture of Achilles again watching, with even greater yearning, the battle he has barred himself from joining (255–56).

Patroclus and Sarpedon (257–683)

With a further simile and a second exhortation, this time from their leader Patroclus, the Myrmidons charge into the battle, and the Trojans retreat, thinking that the armor-clad figure at their head is Achilles himself (278ff.). Patroclus begins the series of duels by wounding the well-named Pyraichmes ("Fire-spear" or "Fire-armed"), and the flames on the ships are extinguished. Then a number of other Greek leaders have successful encounters, the tide of battle turns, and after a temporary rally Hector retreats (358–63 and 367ff.; see Fenik 1968.193ff.). There is no clear indication that he thinks he is facing Achilles. After further triumphs for Patroclus, Sarpedon emerges from the throng; in a short exhortation to his followers he wonders aloud who this dominating figure is. Aeneas did the same (in the same verses) during Diomedes' victories (5.175–76), and the motif seems to be conventional, not a pointed reference to Patroclus's disguise in Achilles' armor. It is clear that Sarpedon does not fear it is Achilles himself whom he is facing. He then joins battle with the unknown warrior (419ff.).

The killing of Sarpedon, the son of Zeus himself, is to be Patroclus's greatest achievement, and in the poet's way he has been quietly brought before our eyes long before this. During the exploits of Diomedes he rebuked Hector, mentioning his own history and the wife and infant son he had left behind in Lycia (5.471–92), and a little later in that battle he is wounded and again mentions wife and son in his appeal for help (5.684–88). His most memorable moments come when he reflects on honor and the reasons why men must go into battle, in his colloquy with his friend Glaucus (12.290–328; see p. 150).

Now, to bring out the importance of the coming duel and glorify both heroes, Homer holds the scene on earth still for a moment and moves to Olympus, as he will do again before the final struggle between Achilles and Hector in Book 22. Zeus wonders if he could save his doomed son after all, and is promptly chided by his loving wife: no exceptions are allowed for mortals, but at least they may have magnificent funerals. (The poet intends no theological dispute over the respective power of Zeus and of fate, any more than he does a little later when the Greeks are successful "beyond fate" [780]; see p. 136.) Zeus unhappily agrees, and the poet concludes the Olympian scene with a phrase about Sarpedon's death "in fertile Troy, far from his homeland" (461) that evokes more sadness (formulaic though it is) than the deities can.

Patroclus kills Sarpedon's squire, and Sarpedon kills Patroclus's mortal horse Pedasos, whose death foreshadows that of Patroclus himself. Then rapidly, as usual, the duel concludes and Sarpedon receives his death wound. His last words are not addressed to his killer, as are those of Patroclus and Hector, perhaps to avoid raising the unwanted issue of the identity of the figure in Achilles' armor; they are to his friend Glaucus, with whom we have seen him before, and his request for protection of his dead body prepares for the ensuing struggle for it and for its exceptional rescue by the orders of Zeus himself.

Glaucus complains to Apollo, with a bitter reproach to "Zeus, who does not even protect his son" (522). Then, healed, he rebukes Hector, saying firmly that Sarpedon has been killed by *Patroclus* (543), putting an end to any lingering idea of the disguise. This is the first example of the six-times-repeated rebuke-charge-repulse pattern that will carry the narrative to the end of Book 17 (Fenik 1968.205). Patroclus encourages the two Ajaxes — no Greek ever seems to have been deceived by his disguise as Achilles — and the battle sways back and forth over the dead body. The foreshadowing of Patroclus's death, now close at hand, is accelerated by Zeus's further reflections on how best to bring it about (644ff.), and Patroclus is granted the honor of stripping Sarpedon's body.

But the body itself is not left in the dust, for Zeus, like that other father Priam later in the poem, takes measures to ensure proper burial. In a superbly peaceful and musical passage, spoken by Zeus and repeated by the poet as his wish is carried out, Apollo himself attends to the washing, oiling, and clothing of the dead body of Zeus's son, and the twin brothers Sleep and Death bear it away to his home in Lycia. This lovely, idealized picture of funeral rites sets human mortality beside the godhead of Zeus himself, and the quiet funeral rites beside the tumult of the conflict still raging on the Trojan plain. (Both Patroclus and Hector, at certain points in the poem, seem unlikely to obtain the honor of funeral rites.) The smooth and musical flow of the lines is carried forward by the repetition of *ambrosiêi . . . ambrota* ("immortal") and *heimata hesson* ("with clothing clothe") in one verse and *pempe . . . pompoisin* ("attend . . . with attendants") in the next (670–71). A roughly isometric translation is given above (p. 46). Much more effective in sound is Christopher Logue's rendering:

> And God turned to Apollo, saying:
> "Mousegod, take my Sarpedon out of range
> And clarify his wounds with mountain water.
> Moisten his body with tinctures of white myrrh
> And the sleeping iodine; and when the chrysms dry,
> Fold him in minivers that never wear
> And lints that never fade,
> And call my two blind footmen, Sleep and Death,
> And let them carry him to Lycia by Taurus,
> Where his tribe, playing stone chimes and tambourines,
> Will consecrate his royal death as fits a man
> Before whose memory even the stones shall fade."
>
> *(Arion* 1.2 [1962]: 23)

The Death of Patroclus (684–867)

The long scene of Patroclus's death now begins, and the poet introduces it with a characteristic passage of "double motivation." Though all danger to the ships has long passed, Patroclus continues to pursue the Trojans, and *meg' aasthê* — "he is overwhelmed by madness" or even "by *atê*," though this spirit of blind folly is not clearly personified here (685; see p. 145). Then the poet comments, "Fool! If he had kept the command of Achilles / he might have escaped black death," and goes on to say that Zeus's will is all-powerful and this is his work. In fact, Zeus planned all this before our eyes not long ago (644–55); but part of the responsibility seems to fall upon Patroclus, and indeed it is natural enough for anyone to go too far after the winning streak he has been enjoying. In conclusion, the poet directly addresses his favorite character (691–92; see p. 37), using an adapted formulaic expression, "Then who first, who last did you kill, Patroclus?" and the pathetic phrase, used only here and by Hector of himself (22.297): "as now the gods summoned you [me] to death."

Apollo, the ally of the Trojans, against whom Achilles had specifically warned Patroclus, now moves into action. He drives Patroclus back from the Trojan wall, the poet using the same expression, "Three times . . . but the fourth time," he had employed when Apollo held the triumphant Diomedes away from Aeneas (5.431ff.). There the god reminds Diomedes of the great gulf between men and gods; here, even more significantly, the poet makes him warn Patroclus that he is not so mighty as Achilles, and that even Achilles will not live to sack Troy. The audience will be aware that Apollo will assist at Achilles' slaying, too. The god goes on to rebuke Hector and urge him against Patroclus, for the disguise of the armor is now long forgotten. Before the final encounter, Patroclus kills Hector's charioteer Cebriones (this expansion technique was also used before Sarpedon's death), and the struggle over his body is a microcosm (more accurately, a less amplified version) of that which will fill Book 17. It is held still for a moment by a simile and a short general description; and in the midst of the tumult of fighting the dead man lies quiet and still (775–76; see Parry 1971.liii).

The sun sinks toward the day's end; three times Patroclus charges, and in an impressionistic, unparalleled phrase, each time kills nine men; the fourth time brings Patroclus's own end, for Apollo approaches, "terrible" (789; the word is emphatically placed at the beginning of the verse) but invisible, and dashes away his armor and weapons. There is symbolism here, for divine armor is not proper for Patroclus, who has no divine ancestry; there is also the poet's skill, for armor made by Hephaestus has overtones of invulnerability, which might produce awkwardness if it were said to be pierced. There is also added sympathy for the now unarmed hero, who is not only half-stunned by the god's stroke but is wounded by another man before being killed by Hector. Beyond all this, the poet uses the action to depict, behind the imminent death of Patroclus, the future doom of Hector at the hands of Achilles; for as we watch the magnificent plumed helmet rolling in the dust, we hear "Before that time it had not been allowed / to befoul the horsehair-crested helmet in the dust; / but of a godlike hero the head and handsome brow / it had guarded, Achilles'. But then Zeus granted to Hector / to wear it on his head, and disaster was close to him" (798–800; see p. 35). This superb technique of combining the present action and the future result it symbolizes is repeated when Achilles mourns Patroclus (see p. 271).

Hector stabs Patroclus, already wounded by the unimportant Euphorbus; "he falls heavily," and since he already has been stripped of his armor, the poet carefully replaces the rest of the standard verse "and his armor clanged about him" with the more effective "and the Achaean warriors were greatly grieved" (822). (The word for "grieved," *êkache*, may have been connected by the poet with the name of Achilles and with that of the Achaeans; see Nagy 1979: Index *s.v. akhos* "grief.") Then Hector delivers the conventional vaunt over his fallen enemy, and betrays his total misunderstanding of the situation, for he thinks that Achilles contemptuously sent his friend to battle as a match for Hector. Patroclus's death speech denies Hector the glory of his victory, which belongs to Apollo and after him to Euphorbus, and again foretells Hector's own death at the hands of Achilles; his last words are the name and honorific titles of his king, friend, and avenger Achilles. Hector's boastful response foreshadows the arrogance and folly he will show (in Book 18) in deciding to keep his army on the plain when Achilles himself returns to fight.

Even when we lay aside our modern ideas of sportsmanship, it seems clear that Apollo's intervention against Patroclus, besides his prior wounding by Euphorbus, deprives Hector of much of the glory of his slaying, for Patroclus's last words are used to draw attention to the point. This is not at all the same thing as the intervention of Athena in the duel between Achilles and Hector, which glorifies the victorious hero (see p. 6). It is not the poet's purpose here to glorify Hector, since there will be plenty of opportunity later on to do this before he in turn is slain. At the moment Patroclus must claim our attention and our sympathy, and after him Achilles, for it is *his* feelings that must be in our minds for the next several books. The following book continues not with the exploits of Hector, as is usual after a hero's victory, but with the slaying of Euphorbus, whose participation in Patroclus's killing has already prevented our giving too much glory to Hector.

Further Reading

Eichholz 1953 is good on the reasons for Achilles' decision in this book. Fenik 1968 analyzes the battle scenes. Kirk has identified the type-scenes (1962.78–79) and studied the verse structure and emjambment (1966.105–52). P. J. Kakridis 1961 very perceptively draws attention to some of the symbolic significance of the exchange of armor; on other aspects of the armor J. I. Armstrong 1958 is still useful. Wilson 1974 makes good points on the armor as a symbol of the mortality/immortality contrast. Thalmann 1984.45–51 is good on the interconnections of the deaths of Sarpedon, Patroclus, Hector, and Achilles. Krischer 1979.147–49 very acutely points out the contrast between Sarpedon's reflective words on life, death, and honor before a battle that he will survive (12.310ff.) and the desire for revenge and victory he expresses before the duel in which he will be killed (16.422–25), comparing Virgil's different practice. Clark and Coulson 1978 are the most recent scholars to support the theory that the Sarpedon tale is based on the Memnon story in the *Aethiopis*, and hold that it also influenced the magnificent depiction of the removal of Sarpedon's body by Sleep and Death on the Euphronius crater in the New York Metropolitan Museum of Art.

28

Iliad Book 18

Patroclus died at the end of Book 16, and the victorious Hector pursues his charioteer and the immortal horses of Achilles. It is the poet's way to space his climaxes—or more accurately, to build up to them carefully. Before the news of the tragedy is brought to Achilles, an entire book intervenes. But Book 17 is not digression or padding, for part of the honor paid to a dead warrior is a struggle to recover his corpse for proper burial, as in the case of Sarpedon (16.531ff.), very obviously in the case of Hector (Book 24), and eventually in the case of Achilles himself: "You in the whirling dust / lay mightily in your might, your horsemanship forgotten; / but we the whole day long struggled [over you]," says the shade of Agamemnon to Achilles' shade in Hades (*Odyssey* 24.39–41). And in this particular case the poet must emphasize two things: the armor Patroclus was wearing, Achilles' armor, must be captured by Hector, so that new armor can be made for Achilles by Hephaestus (and also so that he cannot immediately charge into the battle and kill Hector); and his corpse must not be lost, both because of the dishonor and because if the Trojans were holding Patroclus's body the return of Hector's could not be treated as it is.

The book-long struggle over the body is structured by four repetitions of one of the standard patterns of battle scenes, the rebuke and incitement of a warrior by a companion (or a god), which lead to a drive forward on his part (Fenik 1968.158ff.). The heroes of the struggle are Hector and Aeneas on the Trojan side and the two Ajaxes on the Greek side, but the most interesting character development is that of Menelaus, who plays a much larger role in this book than in any other. He and Patroclus are exceptional in the number of times they are directly addressed by the poet (see pp. 37–38), and he gives to both of them attractive qualities of gentleness and good feeling.

As Book 17 begins, the aftermath of Patroclus's death is presented not in the form of the further triumph of Hector, as would be normal, but in a duel betwen Menelaus and Euphorbus, who shared in Patroclus's death. With a good deal of pathos in the speeches and a moving simile (53–60), the duel ends in

Euphorbus's death. (In the second century A.D. Pausanias saw in the temple of Hera at Corinth the shield that Menelaus took from Euphorbus. Pythagoras the philosopher saw this shield and claimed to recognize it as his own in a previous incarnation as Euphorbus; the story is referred to by Horace, *Odes*, 1.28.9–15.)

At first Hector is kept offstage; but then Apollo rebukes him and he returns to the scene, frightening the weaker Menelaus (whose soliloquy includes the moving line "Patroclus, who lies here for the sake of *my* honor," 92). Ajax comes to protect the body, and Hector, after another rebuke from Sarpedon's friend Glaucus (who does not know Zeus took care of Sarpedon's corpse in Book 16), puts on the immortal armor of Achilles, given by the gods to his father, Peleus (192ff.; see pp. 115–16). This is arrogance in Hector, who has no divine parent, and the poet draws attention to it with words from Zeus that foreshadow Hector's death and remind us of his farewell to Andromache (198ff.).

As the struggle continues, Zeus drifts a mist over the scene (268ff.), which is mentioned again at the beginning of an extended passage of general description (366–459; see p. 85). A part of this passage is an unusual view of the unsuspecting Achilles and his thoughts, given at some length (401–11). Before returning to the battle, the poet presents the powerful scene of the immortal horses, mourning for their dead driver Patroclus "like the monument over a tomb" (434–35), and Zeus's reflections on the wretchedness of the death from which he and they are free, aptly placed in the midst of the tragedy and struggle going on before Troy (see p. 139).

Then the fortunes of the battle sway from one side to the other, and finally the usually laconic Ajax has an exasperated speech in which he reproaches Zeus with his transparent favoritism toward the Trojans, demands that a messenger be sent to Achilles himself for help, and calls upon Zeus to clear away the mist: "At least kill us in daylight, if killing us is what you want" (647). Menelaus, with a few words calling on the Greeks not to forget the gentleness of poor Patroclus (669ff.), finds Antilochus, the companion of Patroclus and Achilles, and after breaking the news to him sends him off to Achilles; on his return to the Ajaxes he refers to Achilles' lack of armor, to foreshadow the actions of the following book. The body is raised from the dust and the rescue begins amidst a furious Trojan attack. The scene remains thus, held still in a great cluster of noisy, straining similes, until the book ends.

Book 18 is of exceptional artistry, the work of a poet who is both a genius in structuring a story and also brilliant in the small touches that give emotional impact to individual scenes. It is one of the turning points of the poem. It concludes Zeus's plan for the defeat of the Greeks and Hector's domination of the battlefield. It marks the transition from the story pattern of Achilles' anger and withdrawal to his revenge against the slayer of his best friend, and prepares the way for his reconciliation with Agamemnon and his killing of Hector. The different scenes of the book are carefully alternated to emphasize the actions of Hector and Achilles that will eventually bring them together in the final duel in Book 22.

Beyond this, the deeper themes of the poem appear as huge shadows behind the action in the forefront; the first rites for the dead Patroclus at the beginning of the book are heavily evocative of the death and funeral of Achilles himself, which is the direct result of his killing Hector; and the killing of Hector is again the result of Hector's killing of Patroclus. Behind the making of new armor for Achilles at the end of the book appear the scenes depicted by Hephaestus upon the shield, the pictures of the ordinary life of mankind which Achilles has renounced and Troy has lost forever, superimposing the happy days of peace upon this grim tale of war.

The many scenes of the book, powerfully evocative in different ways, are united by one theme running through the whole: Achilles' need for new armor and, at the book's conclusion, its forging and decoration by Hephaestus. The loss of Achilles' armor when Patroclus died, and the necessity for its replacement, is probably a major reason for Patroclus's impersonation of Achilles. It brings the additional advantage of providing a natural reason for Achilles not to charge immediately into the battle when he hears the news, rescue the corpse, and kill Hector on the spot. Such a realistic development would unbearably overload the action of this already long and calamitous day. As it is, the unavoidable delay allows for the reconciliation with Agamemnon and the rout of the Trojans by Achilles before the climax in his duel with Hector in Book 22; it also gives the poet opportunities to enrich the significance and depth of the action. With the irony we have seen in Homer before, the immortal armor is fashioned by a god precisely at the time when the approaching death of the mortal who will wear it is being so heavily foreshadowed.

The book falls into six parts: the mourning of Achilles; the recovery of Patroclus's body; Hector in the Trojan assembly; the lament over Patroclus's corpse; Thetis's visit to Hephaestus; and the description of the new divinely made shield and armor.

The Mourning of Achilles (1–147)

The first scene moves swiftly. The messenger Antilochus arrives—by an unusual and perhaps accidental grammatical change, he receives Achilles' own conventional description, "swift-footed"—and finds Achilles sitting reflectively beside his ship. As usual we hear what the person a messenger seeks is doing, and the poet gives Achilles' thoughts in a short monologue. Much the same technique is used at other times of great emotion, for instance when Odysseus realizes the storm means his shipwreck (*Odyssey* 5.299ff.), Hector sees the gods have doomed him (22.297ff.), and Andromache guesses the reason for the burst of lamentation from the city wall (22.447ff.). To sharpen Achilles' foreboding he is made to recall a prophecy that he would live to see the death of the best of the Myrmidons. Remembering a prophecy too late is a common folk-tale theme, and occurs three times in the *Odyssey:* Polyphemus had been told he would be blinded by Odysseus, Circe that Odysseus would visit her island, and Alcinous that Poseidon would eventually lose patience with the Phaeacians' kindness to shipwrecked sailors (*Odyssey* 9.506ff., 10.330ff.; 13.171ff.). The poet uses a traditional motif to make Achilles, in very human fashion, guess the bad news before it is announced; still, this does not prepare him for the shock.

Antilochus's brief words tell not only of Patroclus's death but of the loss of the armor he was wearing, Achilles' own armor, which though made by a god for Peleus could not save the life of Patroclus (and will not save that of its present wearer, Hector). Achilles is overcome with grief; and the poet composes a scene of startling effect. Achilles pours dust over his head, as do Priam and Laertes in their grief (22.414, *Odyssey* 24.316–17), and the poet continues: "in the dust, mightily in his might, he lay stretched out" (26). These last expressions are used elsewhere in the *Iliad* only of *dead* men (for example, 16.775–76, 485), and in the *Odyssey* describe Achilles' own *death* (*Odyssey* 24.39–40). Furthermore, the slave women, captured by Achilles and Patroclus together (a reminder of their lifelong companionship) wail around him, as if around a corpse.

The shadow of Achilles' own death grows darker still as Thetis and her nymphs join the lament, for her words (52ff.) are introduced by the regular phrase for a funeral dirge and speak of the lost homecoming of Achilles, not of the death of Patroclus. When she arrives on the shore, she takes Achilles' head in her arms in the mourning gesture of the Trojans and Andromache around dead Hector (24.712, 724). She is, as Beye notes (1974.91), the *mater dolorosa*, and the tableau is that of Achilles' own funeral rites rather than those of Patroclus. As is made clear in the next scene, Achilles' death will result directly from Patroclus's, and the poet, in a manner few artists have achieved, has brilliantly shaded in the future behind the present, the greater sorrows to come behind those of the moment.

When Thetis first heard Achilles' cry of grief, the poet gave us all the names of her companions the nymphs, in a passage that has much exercised both commentators and translators (39–49). Perhaps they have been carried over from a description of Achilles' own funeral, to emphasize the still deeper shadow in the background (in the account of his funeral they wail beside Thetis; *Odyssey* 24.47ff.); or better, it may be the poet's way of holding the scene still for a few moments, as a simile does, in order for us to appreciate the tableau he is presenting of the mourning of Achilles for Patroclus, and of Thetis for Achilles. The names are melodious and meaningful; Arrowsmith's rendering conveys more of this than most:

Seagreen and Shimmer, the goddess Blooming and Billow
and those who are names of the islands, those who are called
for the caves,
and She-who-skims-on-the-water, and Spray with the gentle
eyes
like the gentle eyes of cattle, naiads of spume and the shore,
the nymphs of marshes and inlets and all the rocks outjutting,
and Dulcet too was there and Wind-that-rocks-on-the-water
and Grazer-over-the-sea and she whose name is Glory,
and the naiads Noble and Giver, and lovely Bringer, and
Nimble,
and Welcomer too, and Grace, and Princess, and Provider,
and she who is named for the milk, the froth of the curling
breakers,
glorious Galateia, and the famous nymphs of the surf,
and Infallible and Truth, true daughters of their father,
and goddesses over the sands, and she who runs from the
mountains

and whose hair is a splendor, and all the other goddesses
who are daughters of Nereus along the deep floor of the sea.
                                                (*Arion* 6.3 [1967] 347–48)

The first remarks of the loving but not over-intelligent Thetis
drive home relentlessly the irony of the situation: "What's the
matter? Hasn't Zeus done what you wanted?" (73–77). Patroclus's
death has been brought about by Achilles' request for the defeat
of the Greeks, now fulfilled all too well. Even the meeting of
mother and son inevitably suggests this, for it was at their last
encounter in Book I that the request was made; Thetis, goddess
mother of a mortal son, always and inevitably incarnates the
gulf between mortal and immortal, and her motherly concern
for him leads her to talk of little else. Achilles' response (79–93)
is masterly, conveying much in a few words and with immensely effective word order: his wish has been granted, but

> What joy for me in that, when my beloved friend is dead,
> Patroclus, whom I honored above all my friends,
> as much as my own life? I have lost him. His armor Hector
> killing him has stripped off, [armor] huge, wonderful to see,
> lovely, which the gods gave to Peleus, a splendid gift,
> when they married you off to a mortal.

His thought runs from his dead friend to a superb juxtaposition
of his divine armor and the goddess-mortal union that denies
him immortality.

He goes on to declare that he will not return home unless he
can kill Hector; in response, Thetis tells him (in a prophecy probably invented for this occasion) that his own death is fated to
follow soon after Hector's (95–96). Achilles accepts these terms,
again reproaching himself for not protecting Patroclus and the
other Greeks, too, and his thoughts run on again (98–105) into a
curse on Strife (*Eris*), who embroiled him with Agamemnon.

In this way the idea of the reconciliation that will come in
Book 19 is introduced. He will kill Hector and then accept his
own death when Zeus wills; he will repeat the same verses, not
just because of formulaic repetition, when he replies to the dying
Hector's warning of his own death (115–16 = 22.365–66; Virgil
rather oddly gives them to his wicked Mezentius, *Aeneid* 10.743–
44). As an example of a mighty hero who nevertheless had to face
death he names Heracles; later on, to the terrified young Lykaon,
he will take Patroclus and himself as even more pertinent examples of the humbling of human greatness by death (21.105–

13). (The idea is found again at 15.139–40, and became a familiar *topos*; see Curtius [1953] 80–82.)

Achilles thus joins the company of those who do what they feel they have to do although they know it will accelerate their own death. There are many others in Greek myth who knowingly give their lives for what they think is right, among them Amphiaraus and Eteocles (Aeschylus, *Seven against Thebes*), Menoeceus (Euripides, *Phoenissae*), Iphigenia (Euripides, *Iphigenia in Aulis*), perhaps Megistias the seer who died at Thermopylae (Herodotus 7.228), and perhaps Meleager, the paradigm for Achilles in Book 9 (see pp. 226–29). The origin of the story pattern may lie in a sacrifice to ensure success in war, or in times of special crisis (see Versnel 1981, and Lloyd-Jones 1983.88–89). It is a master stroke on Homer's part to introduce it into the *Iliad* to enrich the characterization of Achilles. Socrates admired it, and saw his own conduct in the face of the threat of death in the same light (see p. 317).

Thetis in her reply speaks again of the loss of Achilles' armor, predicting once more that Hector will not live to wear it long; and the theme of its replacement by a new gift from Hephaestus is stressed three times over in the next few lines. In 144 the poet carefully replaces the regular epithet for armor, "decorated with bronze," with "all-glittering," for the god's work will be of gold. She goes off to Olympus and the nymphs return to their home.

The Recovery of Patroclus's Body (148–242)

All this time the struggle for the body of Patroclus has been continuing, and with a jolt we return to it. Hector is still attacking triumphantly, and is on the verge of success when Iris reaches Achilles and warns him that unless he takes action the corpse will be beheaded by Hector (this is not just Hera's malicious invention, but has been anticipated in the poet's own voice, 17.125–27; a dead Trojan is so treated by the lesser Ajax, 13.202–5). Achilles' response appears surprisingly composed—"Who sent you?"—but Iris's urging is directly contrary to Thetis's instructions to wait for the new armor (134–35, 189–90), and it is wise for him to inquire on whose authority she is speaking. His question brings out the fact that Zeus does not know of this (167–68, 185–86), for we are to think of him as still supporting Hector.

Finally there comes a kind of epiphany of Achilles, with all the light and splendor the poet can contrive. He rises up at last, heralded by a significant "beloved by Zeus" (203); in place of armor, his shoulders are covered by the divine *aegis*, worn to battle by Athena herself (5.738–42), and in place of a helmet crest, flames tower from his head (as with Diomedes when he was glorified by Athena, 5.4–7). The vision is held still for a moment, while we watch, by the suggestive simile of signal fires rising from a besieged city (207–14). He shouts aloud, and his cry is magnified by Athena, just as she is portrayed assisting Heracles to bear the sky on the well-known metope at Olympia. Apollo himself once terrified the Greeks with the *aegis* and a mighty cry (15.318–27), but here the cry is expanded by another simile, and the ensuing rout of the Trojans is described in some detail (222–27). Then cry and rout are repeated by the poet, this time using the familiar "three times" motif (used also at 155f.). And at last the body is rescued by the Greeks.

At this point there are only a few verses about Achilles' grief at seeing the body of his friend, for the poet wishes first to insert the coming scene with Hector, so as to place Hector's decision to continue the battle between accounts of Achilles' grief and rage. The verses are, however, effective, given in the poet's own voice as he invites us to watch and reflect on the scene (235–38). Then follow the verses describing the ending of this long day, significant not only because they add to the picture of the sad procession returning to the Greek camp as the sun sets, but because (as the coming scene will show more forcefully) this is the end of the day of Hector's triumph: "I grant power to him / to kill, until he reaches the well-benched ships / and the sun sets and holy darkness comes," said Zeus as this battle began (11.191–94, repeated 206–9, reaffirmed 17.201ff.). So the poet signals that Hector's day of triumph is now over, and significantly he introduces Hera, implacable enemy of Troy, to cause the sun to sink and end Hector's glory. The next scene will be devoted to Hector.

Hector's Decision (243–313)

The following Trojan council prepares the way for the massacre of their troops by Achilles in Books 20 and 21, and thus for the confrontation of Hector and Achilles in Book 22. The preparation involves more than plot; it contributes to our understanding of Hector's character, leading up to his later self-reproach and his refusal to face the taunts of lesser men (22.99ff.).

The Trojans, terrified by Achilles' reappearance, are addressed first by Polydamas, who is given a careful introduction; he has often appeared before this, but now the introduction heralds the special importance of his words, for his advice gives Hector his last chance of saving his life. He speaks wisely: "Go back, and stay within the city walls." Polydamas's advice has twice been accepted by Hector (12.80ff., 13.748ff.), and once rejected (12.230ff.). Faced with the decision that will decide the fate of his city as well as his own, Hector rejects his friend's advice now, confident that the glory Zeus has given him that day will continue (293–95) and hoping for victory even over Achilles himself; in unconscious foreshadowing of his flight before the duel in Book 22, he declares he will not run away from Achilles (306–8). Patroclus, too, had overestimated his success, and before he had to pay for it the poet forewarned us: "Fool! If he had only kept the command of Achilles" (16.686ff.). He does the same thing here, though here the Trojans are in assembly and it is they who are "Fools!" for listening to Hector instead of to Polydamas (311–13). Hector had flung the word "Fool!" at Polydamas (295), and he will accept the responsibility for this decision when he comes face to face with Achilles.

The Lament for Patroclus (314–67)

Now the poet juxtaposes the action on the other side—the immediate result of Hector's prowess, and a foreshadowing of the long-term outcome. The formal rites for his victim Patroclus begin, and Achilles leads the lament; the lion simile that introduces the scene emphasizes not only his furious grief but also his future quest for the killer, as the lion hunts out the man who has captured its cubs. He speaks with much pathos of his own coming death and the grief of Thetis and old Peleus, and promises revenge. (In these lines [334–35] Hector's name is unusually placed, for emphasis, in the verse ahead of that in which its controlling nouns stand ["Nor will I bury you, until *of Hector* I bring here / the armor and the head, killer of you greathearted"], and the adjective "greathearted," which technically should qualify "killer," as in Lattimore's translation, should probably be taken irregularly and emphatically with "you," as does Fitzgerald.) In conclusion he speaks of the lament of women—the captive women, who serve also as a reminder of their past exploits together. It is noticeable that the lament is very closely tied to the narrative situation, unlike that of David for Jonathan, which expresses praise, sorrow, and love in very general terms (2 *Samuel* 1.19–27). Then follow the washing, anointing, and clothing of the body, amplified a little by the kindling of the fire to heat the water.

Suddenly Zeus and Hera begin to speak, in a violent change of scene from the Greeks mourning on the Trojan plain. Perhaps the abruptness is an intentionally sharp juxtaposition, for their short conversation signals the end of the plot that began in Book 1, the withdrawal of Achilles and Zeus's agreement to bring about the defeat of the Greeks. This he has done, at the cost of Patroclus's life, and Achilles is now only too eager to return to the battlefield. Zeus mocks Hera's favoritism for the Greeks, just as he teased her with a suggested end to the war before the main fighting of the poem began (4.5–19). At that time she responded with a frightening offer to allow her own favorite cities in Greece to be destroyed without protest if only she might contrive the ruin of Troy; here she contents herself with remarking that even men like to get their own way, so it is only natural for her, as queen of the gods, to bring sorrows to the city she hates.

Homer seems as conscious as Xenophanes, a couple of centuries later, that men make gods in their own image, but in this poem human hatred will not be carried so far as that of the gods. Taken with Hera's earlier words in Book 4, the poet is anticipating Herodotus's conception of the rise and fall of cities (Herodotus 1.5.4). This shocking little scene of implacable divine anger marks the end of Zeus's aid to the Trojans and the doom of Hector.

Thetis Visits Hephaestus (368–477)

After all the sorrow and anger depicted in this book, the pleasant scene between Thetis, Hephaestus, and his wife is welcome, and it also provides a properly ample introduction to the massive description of the shield (so Austin 1966). Her visit is described with careful detail, observing, amplifying, and sometimes adapting the traditional formalities of the visit type-scene. She draws near the house; a cluster of adjectives describe what she sees (370); and of course the smith god built it himself (371). There he is, the person she seeks, and as usual we hear what he is doing, this time naturally with more interesting detail than usual (another standard item, description of the companions with him, is saved for later on).

Then there is an interruption, for the sweaty Hephaestus can hardly receive his lady visitor properly, and so the poet brings forward (and perhaps invents) the wife of the craftsman of lovely ornaments (400–401), the suitably named Charis ("Grace"). (Of course there is no place for the pro-Trojan Aphrodite here, to whom he is none-too-happily married in Demodocus's song; *Odyssey* 8.266ff.) In the usual way of the type-scene the hostess expresses surprise and pleasure, invites the visitor in for refreshment, and gives her a chair. She calls to her husband, and Hephaestus confirms the welcome with a paradigm explaining how much he owes to Thetis; the tale of the unkindness of his "dog-faced" mother, Hera—some prim ancient critics preferred to read her conventional "ox-eyed"—was a part of the story of his banishment, revenge, and recall by the skills of the wine god Dionysus, which featured so often in later vase-painting. He bids Charis offer Thetis refreshment while he tidies up the forge and takes a shower. Then he joins his guest, assisted by his female robot attendants (this is the postponed element describing his companions, 417–21), and speaks the formal words of welcome. But since the scene has continued so long, and has been complicated by the double welcome by Charis and Hephaestus, the "refreshment" element of the type-scene (which normally follows) is abandoned, and we jump directly to the after-dinner conversation.

Thetis seizes the opportunity to relate her sorrows to a kindly ear, and confides to her fellow deities that she was always unwilling to marry the mortal Peleus (434) and that it was Apollo, not Hector, who is responsible for Patroclus's death (454–55). She pours out Achilles' tale from the beginning, including his rejection of the embassy in Book 9 and of course the loss of the armor he gave to Patroclus in Book 16. This is good psychology, and also a suitable summary of the quarrel theme now that it is about to be superseded by the revenge theme; it is also, of course, a further juxtaposition of Achilles' mortality and the divinely made armor. (Those interested in Homer's oral technique might note that the two verses in which she describes the taking of Briseis by Agamemnon [444–45] also occur in Achilles' complaint about Agamemnon's action, but with more vehemence added by an extra verse of outrage after each of hers [16.56–59].) So she asks for new armor for him, and Hephaestus willingly consents, goes off to the forge, and begins his preparations. Then the poet begins the largest amplification in the poem; it is not a digression but a delineation of the ordinary human life of which his heroic tale is an exceptional part.

The Shield of Achilles (478–616)

Structurally, the description of the shield can be considered part of a hugely expanded arming scene, glorifying Achilles before he begins his mighty deeds of battle; the remainder comes at the end of Book 19. Like an enormous simile, the scenes on the shield hold the narrative still for a while as we gaze at them; and the content is like that of a simile, too — it is the ordinary life of mankind that we observe, not that of heroes or gods.

This is an unusual decorative motif for epic armor. Agamemnon's shield bears a terrifying Gorgon head, together with Fear and Terror, and his corselet and shield strap are decorated with fearsome serpents (11.25ff.); Athena's *aegis* has similar figures (5.739–41); the baldric worn by Heracles in the underworld (*Odyssey* 11.610ff.) has worked upon it fierce beasts, battles, murders, and killings; the shield of Heracles, described at length in an account of his fight with Cycnus, attributed to Hesiod but probably composed in the sixth century, borrows some peaceful motifs from Achilles' shield but carries mainly a "Pandemonium" (as it has been called) of frightful forms — Fear, Strife, Slaughter, and their kin, described in gruesome detail (*Shield of Heracles* 144ff., printed in Evelyn-White 1936). Such pictures perform the proper work of a shield device, to inspire terror in the enemy; the predominantly peaceful, even happy scenes on Achilles' shield would not do that.

Human craftsmen of a later period loved to depict the wars of the Olympians against the Titans and Giants, and Hesiod gives a lurid account of the struggle of Zeus against the monster Typhoeus (*Theogony* 820ff.). One might have expected some such awe-inspiring picture of this from the god's hands. Instead, he presents the everyday life of the ordinary Greek, and the repeated adjective for the scenes is "beautiful." This is not the straightforward symbolism by which Virgil lays upon the shoulders of Aeneas the "glory and fate of his descendants," the achievements of later Roman history that depend upon his victory (*Aeneid* 8.626–731). It is hardly likely that the poet's purpose was to suggest that the future fate of the ordinary Greek depends upon Achilles. After an examination of the construction of the shield, and of the separate scenes, the general question of the poet's choice of decorative motifs must be addressed.

The construction of the shield is reasonably clear. Like most shields in the *Iliad* it seems to be round (there is some support for this from 19.373–74: "its radiance shone far off like the moon's"), and it is made of five layers (481). Ajax's shield (7.219ff.) is a "bronze, seven-ox" one, and Hector's spear strikes it "on the bronze, on top, the eighth [layer]," pierces six layers (presumably of oxhide), and is stopped in the seventh. Achilles' spear strikes Aeneas's shield "at the outer rim, where the bronze runs thinnest, and thinnest is the oxhide laid" (20.275–76) and rips through, penetrating two "circles" of it (20.280–81). In these cases the shield seems to be made of several thicknesses of oxhide with a surface covering of bronze; this is confirmed by the description of the making of Sarpedon's shield (12.295–97). In a twice-repeated phrase the bronze is explicitly said to be "beaten out" (*epelêlato*, 13.804, 17.493) on top of the oxhides. If concentric circles of hide of diminishing size formed the outer, convex face of the shield, the appearance would be like a modern-day archery target, and if the bronze surface of a hero's shield were beaten out on top of the oxhide circles, or imitated the all-leather face of a lesser man's equipment, it would be natural to decorate it in concentric bands corresponding to the layers of hide that lay behind it. Decoration in concentric bands like this appears on bronze shields from Crete and bronze bowls from Cyprus at a date not far removed from that of Homer (see Fittschen 1973.7–9).

Two other passages are relevant. Agamemnon's shield (11.33) has ten bronze "circles" around it, and this can be taken to mean either an unusually heavy shield, with ten thicknesses of hide, or an exaggeration upon the bronze of the number of hides backing it. The remaining passage is very hard to understand. During his fight with Aeneas, Achilles fears that his enemy's spear will pierce his shield, and the poet mocks him for not realizing that the gifts of the gods will not yield to a mortal thrust; and in fact "the gold, the god's gift, warded off" the spear (20.268). Four subsequent verses explain that the spear penetrated the two outer bronze layers but was stopped by the next layer, that of gold, which was backed by two further layers of tin. Gold is, of course, the specially divine metal, but nevertheless this seems an incredible way of constructing a shield, unserviceable both for appearance (since only bronze would be visible, not the more decorative metals) and for practicality (layers of gold and tin would not stop a bronze-headed spear). At 21.165 (the same verse as 20.268) "gold" simply refers to the whole shield of Achilles, and it seems best to take this as the sense in 20.268 too. The obscure following lines (20.269–72) are a muddle based on 18.474ff. and 481, arising essentially from a bard's difficulty in imagining a shield made from layers of different metals instead of from oxhides. They must surely be an addition by a later bard.

One should therefore think of this "five-layer" shield as based on one made of five thicknesses of oxhide, diminishing regularly in size on the outer face and covered with a bronze surface that retained the appearance of five concentric bands, like a target. How Hephaestus adapted a technique designed for leather to an artifact made of three or four different metals remains his secret. The poet clearly thinks of the bronze, tin, gold, and silver as forming the scenes on the shield, perhaps together with *kyanos*, niello or black glass-paste (18.564). There may be a memory here of the inlaying of metals familiar to us from Mycenaean daggers. The arrangement of scenes in concentric bands, however, as indicated above, is a technique roughly contemporary with Homer. The design is thus essentially different from that portrayed on the reconstruction of the shield by John Flaxman (in 1821; there are examples at the Ashmolean Museum in Oxford and at the Huntington Library Art Gallery in San Marino, California), on which one wide frieze, extending from the center boss (chariot of the Sun, and stars) to the rim (waves) includes all the scenes in juxtaposition.

The first line of the description—"He wrought upon it the earth, the sky, and the sea" (483)—seems to encompass the whole field, from the heavenly bodies in the center through the scenes of human life to the ocean that surrounds the rim. Then the poet, following the hands of the craftsman, defines the pictures one by one, working outward from the center to the rim; in practice the crowded scenes of the two cities are thus located on the smallest band but one, but for the poet's narrative this is hardly a serious objection.

The center of the shield, perhaps surrounding the boss (if the poet thinks of it as having one), depicts the eternal heavenly bodies that order all human activities; for the sun determines the day, the moon the month, and the constellations the changing seasons. The constellations named are significant. The poet's world is not the heroic age but that of the farmer Hesiod, in which they proclaim the agricultural year: "When the Pleiades, daughters of Atlas, rise, begin your harvest"; "When the Pleiades, and the Hyades, and strong Orion sink, then remember it is the season to plow" (*Works and Days* 383ff., 614ff.). The Bear is well chosen, too, for though he does not rise or set, and so is of no use for the calendar, he provides a guide for seafarers; Odysseus watches the constellations in the sky and keeps the Bear on his left as he sails away from Calypso's island (*Odyssey* 5.272ff.), and the Bear's circumpolar habit (and the mythology in which the constellations play a part) is neatly explained by his need to keep a wary eye on the hunter, Orion. So first the orderly annual sequence of human life and work is established.

The next band is full of movement, and divided into two contrasting parts. The first shows a city at peace, its orderly social life represented by the happy ceremonies of marriage and the formal judicial procedures of the lawcourt. There may be further contrasts between the youthfulness of marriage partners and the seniority of the elders who sit in judgment, and between the social ceremonies of consummating a union and reconciling dissension. The contrasts suggest the poet's deliberate attempt at comprehensiveness. Alternative translations are possible for some of the verses describing the legal case, and it is not clear to us if the dispute concerns whether or not compensation for the killing of a man has been handed over, or whether it should be accepted at all. If it is not accepted, the killer would be forced into exile (so Murray 1980.62). This latter situation corresponds well to Achilles' refusal to accept the offered recompense in Book 9, and in fact Ajax says there that even for a brother or son a blood price is accepted (9.632–33); and of course the recompense will be accepted by Achilles in the following book (so Andersen 1976).

The alternative interpretation (that of Gagarin 1973) is that one man claims to have paid restitution for a man's death, and the other denies that he has received anything. They therefore go to find an arbitrator for a decision (in the midst of a typical excited Greek crowd). The elders on their formal seats, holding their speaker's staffs, in turn propose settlements; and two talents of gold (the amount of the fourth prize in the chariot race, ranking next above the clay jar; 23.269–70) will be given to the elder whose opinion is considered the fairest by the surrounding people. This procedure is much like that which follows the dispute between Antilochus and Menelaus after the chariot race (23.566ff.), where Menelaus invites the Greek leaders to decide between them (573–74) and then goes on to propose a settlement himself, either as participant or as elder (579ff.), which Antilochus is ready to accept; if he had not accepted it, presumably Achilles or someone else would have made another proposal. Whichever interpretation is correct, a civic adjudication is taking place, a better solution to disagreement than vendetta or exile; and it is possible that by presenting this scene here the poet intends an allusion to Achilles' refusal to accept Agamemnon's offer of compensation and the dreadful results of his inflexibility, which became apparent to him at the beginning of this book.

Opposite to this is the scene of a city at war. The poet presents not just a battle line, as is often seen in later art, but a much wider picture. There is a city under siege, with armed forces on either side; it is uncertain if they belong to one army and are depicted on either side of the city, or to two different armies, as in Nestor's account of the Pylian border town besieged by an Epeian army and rescued by another from Pylos (11.710ff.). The attackers are undecided whether to sack the city or to allow the citizens to surrender their possessions for equal division, as Hector muses that the Trojans might do (22.111–21).

But the townspeople send out a foray, led by the larger-than-human figures of Ares and Athena; and after an ambush they capture cattle and sheep for the besieged. With the same small touch of pathos that marks the death of so many inconsequential warriors in the poem, Homer shows the unsuspecting herdsmen happily playing on their pipes just before they are killed (526). A battle with the other army ensues, and a bloody picture is painted, full of hateful personifications of war's miseries. These four verses (535–38) are found also in the Hesiodic *Shield of Heracles* (156–59), where they are more at home, and it is probable that they do not belong here. Warfare was, of course, a constant feature of Greek life, and the depiction of a happy pastoral life destroyed by it befits the *Iliad*; the same note is sounded in the brief reference to the long-abandoned washing pools of the Trojan women, as Hector passes them in his flight from Achilles (22.147ff.).

The next band shows gentler agricultural scenes, gentler too than the toil-laden pictures painted in the *Works and Days* by the dour Hesiod. There is no bitter class struggle here; plowmen work together on a larger field (perhaps common land) and are well cared for; reapers and binders harvest while a king watches in satisfied silence and a meal is prepared; youthful vintagers, men and women together, work and dance at the same time to the music of the lyre. This is the same picture at that of the good king in the *Odyssey* (19.109ff.), who "ruling a numerous and powerful people / upholds good government, and the black earth bears / barley and wheat, his trees are laden with fruit, / his sheep always bear young, the sea provides fish / from his good government, and the people prosper under him."

So the seasonal work of the year is complete. The next band

adds the ongoing care for the animal stock, and according to the most probable reconstruction is again divided into two parts, one depicting the very active scene of cattle, lions, dogs, and herdsmen, the other the flocks of sheep. Friezes of lions and other animals are very common on pottery of the poet's period, and this must be in his mind here. And of course the subject fills in the unchanging background of Greek country life, the same world as that of the similes, in which wild animals attacked cattle and frightened dogs made a lot of noise (585–86).

The last of the bands is again filled by a frieze, this time one of young men and maidens dancing. This again is a popular subject on pottery of Homer's time, and perhaps this is subtly hinted at in the simile of the potter at his wheel (600–602). As before, the poet has included a good deal of action and added items that would be hard to present on an actual shield. He may possibly have included a bard in the scene, a counterpart to himself (as Pheidias modeled himself as Daedalus on the shield of his Athena in the Parthenon), for a late writer (Athenaeus) quotes 604–5 as "happily; among them sang an inspired bard / plucking his lyre; and two acrobats" (the lines occur at *Odyssey* 4.17–18.) But these verses are not found here in *Iliad* manuscripts.

Finally, on the rim itself the poet places the mighty ocean that embraces the lands of men, doubtless indicated (as on pottery) by sporting dolphins. (In fact one papyrus of the first century before Christ has extra verses here, similar to verses 207–13 of the *Shield of Heracles*: "On it he made a harbor of fine tin, / as if with breaking waves; and two spouting / silver dolphins were feasting on [?] the mute fish, / and beneath them bronze fishes were trembling; and on the shore / . . . .")

The rest of the armor is completed quickly—even the corselet is dismissed in a line, though it might have borne decoration as Agamemnon's did (11.19–28) had the poet not known where to stop—and without more ado Thetis delivers it to Achilles. It is now dawn (19.1–2); it was already after sundown when the Trojans assembled and the Greeks mourned for Patroclus (18.239–41, 354–55), before Thetis reached Olympus, but the poet has not troubled us with concern that Hephaestus was working all night long. Despite its beauty, or perhaps because of it, the Greeks dare not look at the god's handiwork; only Achilles can do so, and he feels a dreadful joy. He alone can match its terrifying splendor.

This description of the shield is part of an immensely elaborated arming scene, intended as always to honor a hero going into battle; and its scale is fitting for a hero like Achilles, for a poem the size of the *Iliad*, and for such a climax. Just as the massive catalogues of Greeks and Trojans in the second book appropriately introduced the conflict that fills the poem, so this mighty *ecphrasis* fittingly proclaims the entry into battle of the mightiest hero of all. Within the framework of the plot and themes of the *Iliad* itself, the ordinary life that Achilles' shield depicts appropriately represents the human life he has just resigned in this book for the sake of taking vengeance on Hector, the long life in obscurity that in Book 9 he described, and for a while chose, as the alternative to the short life with everlasting glory that he now knows will be his lot. Achilles thus bears into battle with him an ever-present symbol of his own mortality, a divinely made reminder that even armor made by a god will not save his life, just as it failed to save Patroclus's life and will not save Hector's. This theme of mortality (see pp. 138–42), which pervades the *Iliad*, appears in another way, too: the shield (unlike the *Shield of Heracles*) is made before our eyes by a god, one more example of the constant observation of human activities by the immortals, whose eternal lives would seem otherwise to be even more trivial than they are.

Besides this pertinence to the poem, one can only guess how far the shield represents the feelings of the poet himself. The parallel with the world of the similes (see pp. 103–5) suggests that the poet desires to include pictures of the ordinary life that he cannot well fit within the plot of the *Iliad*, the familiar world of farmer-citizens that Hesiod describes in his *Works and Days*. But comparison with Hesiod's picture immediately shows the peculiarly Homeric characteristics of the scenes on Achilles' shield. Here there is nothing of Hesiod's insistence on unremitting and wearisome labor, or of his complaints against the inadequacies of justice under the rule of corrupt kings. Instead, the tone is one of delight in the ordinary routines of the year, in festivals, in feasting after labor, even in labor itself (as in the vineyard scenes). Weddings are shown, not funerals; this is the world of Nestor's Pylos and Menelaus's Sparta in the *Odyssey*, not too far from the idealized happiness of the Phaeacians. Suffering there is, in the scene showing the city at war, but this too is an essential part of life, accepted (as it is in the *Iliad*) as a thing that must be endured. And in the battle on the shield, as in that in the *Iliad*, no victory is shown, only acceptance and endurance of warfare. Except in the scene of war no gods appear on the shield, perhaps because, omnipresent though they are in the fictional world of the *Iliad*, they do not so directly affect the life of ordinary men.

The fundamentally optimistic attitude toward human life, despite the follies and suffering that beset it, seems identical in tone to that of the *Iliad* as a whole (see p. 321); and the portrayal of the continuity of the human race beneath all the individual human tragedies and triumphs has already appeared in the famous simile of the dying leaves and their rebirth in Book 6 (146ff.; see pp. 202–5). Similar, too, to the superbly sophisticated construction of the rest of the poem are the juxtaposition — or rather, superimposition — of scenes of peace on the equipment of war, and the depiction of the life of the poet's own time, just as the decisions have been taken that will result in the deaths of the greatest legendary heroes of Greeks and Trojans and the sack of the famous but now vanished city. This is the same kind of depth of field the poet achieved with the mourning for Patroclus, and for Achilles too, at the beginning of this book.

It has been plausibly suggested that one may go beyond this and draw a parallel between the two artists, the smith god and the poet, the one traditionally lame (397, 411, 417), the other traditionally blind (as are Demodocus [*Odyssey* 8.63–64] and the singer of the *Hymn to Apollo* [172]), but both given as a compensation the skill to depict the whole of human life through the medium of art; the one on the shield, the other in the great poem itself. In the *Odyssey* the poet seems to delight in the presentation of the bards, his counterparts, and strongly stresses their contribution to civilized life. "For among all men on earth bards / are given honor and respect, since to them / the Muse has taught her tales, and she loves their guild," says Odysseus (*Odyssey* 8.479–81) as he sends Demodocus a specially rich hunk of meat; and the highest praise Alcinous can heap upon Odysseus for his magnificent story is to say, "The beauty of words is in you, and good sense is in them, / and the tale, like a bard, you have told skillfully" (*Odyssey* 11.367–68). It would not be surprising if Homer thought to symbolize in this way the power and the immortality of his craft, which shaped in the *Iliad* itself a masterpiece "such as any / of the host of men shall wonder at when he sees it" (466–67).

Further Reading

There is an analysis of Book 17 in Fenik 1968. J. T. Kakridis 1949 makes excellent points on the scenes of Achilles' mourning; it is also discussed in Edwards 1986. Edwards 1968 examines the manipulation of formulae for special effects in Book 18. Segal 1971b discusses the references to mutilation of corpses in this and previous books.

ON THE SHIELD. The most detailed study, including archaeological evidence, is Fittschen 1973. Willcock 1976.209–14 gives a good summary account. Taplin 1980 studies the content of the shield scenes in relation to the rest of the *Iliad* and *Odyssey*, with good bibliographical notes. Reinhardt 1961 and Schadewaldt 1965 have valuable chapters. On the trial scene, see especially Gagarin 1973 and Andersen 1976. There is a good brief treatment of the Hesiodic shield in Thalmann 1984,62–64.

29

Iliad Book 22

Thetis brings the new armor to Achilles at the beginning of Book 19, but there are still further actions to be taken before he can return to the battlefield. An assembly of the Greeks is called, with much expansion because of its importance. Achilles announces the end of his anger and withdrawal. Agamemnon again admits, this time publicly and before Achilles, that he must have been afflicted by *Atê*, Blind Folly, and tells a long tale about how even Zeus himself was not immune to her attacks (see p. 145); finally he offers to hand over the gifts he promised in Book 9. Achilles cares little about the gifts and wants only to get back into battle immediately, but Odysseus asserts that those who have been fighting all along need food (his words about the toil of battle and the need to eat even amidst grief are very moving; 221–33); the lengthy speeches about the issue may be designed to lead up to the gods' care to infuse ambrosia into the still-fasting Achilles before he arms himself (19.352ff.).

The gifts are handed over, Agamemnon takes an oath that he did not sleep with Briseis, and her return is skillfully emphasized by her lament for the dead Patroclus, which avoids any suggestion that Achilles' sorrows are eased by her presence; Patroclus's life has in a sense been exchanged for hers, and at this moment Achilles wishes he had never seen her (19.59–60). As she and the other captive women lament around the corpse, Achilles himself with the warriors utters a further lament, speaking sadly of his long absence from his father and his son and his realization that he will never return to his home. There is now a good deal of subtle emphasis laid on the loneliness and pathos of Achilles, mighty though he is; the poet notes that sorrow is a very personal and isolating thing when both the captive women and the Greeks, lamenting for Patroclus, each weep for their own sorrows (19.302, 339).

At last Achilles dons his new armor, with much elaboration and repeated stress on its dazzling glitter, which besides the visual effect is a sign of his coming victory (see p. 79). The final item of the amplification is a short conversation with one of his immortal horses as he mounts his chariot. This is closer to the fantastic than Homer usually approaches in the *Iliad*—and he very properly has the Furies swiftly put an end to such abnormal behavior—but the reminder given by the horse's words of Achilles' own approaching death is particularly effective at his departure for battle, and gives the hero a further chance to assert his knowledge and acceptance of it. Probably such warnings occurred in other epics when Achilles or other heroes entered their last battle, and the poet has adapted the scene for the present occasion.

Now that Achilles and Agamemnon are reconciled, Zeus is no longer bound by his promise to Thetis, and at the beginning of Book 20 he turns the other gods loose to intervene as they see fit, so that Troy may not fall immediately to Achilles' onslaught. A short catalogue (as usual) lists the participants for us as they set off for the battlefield (20.33–44). Homer wants to build up slowly to the climactic duel of Achilles and Hector, but an unrelieved massacre of unknown (even if named) Trojans could not be protracted for long, and in order to magnify the grandeur and the isolation of Achilles he does not wish to bring other Greeks on to the stage. As usual the gods are used to fill the need, and their activities take up a good deal of the space in this book and the next. So a cosmic conflict (which may owe something to such conflicts in the mythologies of Asia Minor; see West 1966.20ff.) is introduced (20.47ff.).

A duel with Aeneas occupies Achilles for some time and significantly introduces the history of Troy, which his reentry into the battle brings closer to its unhappy end (20.215–40), until it is ended in conventional fashion by Poseidon's intervention. After exhortations by Achilles and Hector, the slaying of the Trojans at last begins, the most noteworthy victim being Priam's son Polydorus (20.407ff.), whose death will be mentioned again later. A preliminary encounter between Achilles and Hector is aborted by Apollo, and after further killing the book ends with a general description of the havoc on the battlefield.

This continues into Book 21, focusing on the panic as the fleeing Trojans try to cross the river Xanthos (or Scamander). Achilles takes twelve prisoners who will later be sacrificed on Patroclus's pyre (21.27ff., 23.175ff.); and then, to let us see into his mind again, the poet puts in the supplication scene of Lycaon, son of Priam and a former captive of Achilles. Shortly before this Achilles killed a suppliant without listening to him, as a forerunner (in Homer's manner) of this scene (20.463ff.), but to Lycaon he offers no pity but a kind of consolation, a reminder that he is only suffering the fate that has already seized Patroclus and will soon grip Achilles himself for all his magnificence (21.106–13; see p. 140).

The slaughter continues, over the repeated protests of the river god, whose stream is dammed up by Trojan corpses, until the two rivers of the plain unite and nearly drown Achilles, who is rescued (at Hera's prompting) by Hephaestus. This unusual conflict of the elements was lightly foreshadowed during the introduction of the divine combatants (20.73–74), but nevertheless it is a shock for us to pass from the chattering, squabbling people on Olympus to these powers of nature, the irresistible forces of flood and forest fire. Owen, usually a very sympathetic and sensitive critic, admitted his distaste for this scene, and thought it might be intended to appear grotesque and weird (1946.186ff.). He speaks of "an alien atmosphere . . . this discordant note . . . partly horrible and partly amusing" and seems on the verge of evoking *King Lear* ("the earth is filled with strange signs and commotions. Nature seems confounded. It is as if a howling storm swept down upon the battlefield, or rather as if some ghastly nightmare were abroad"; 187). This is exaggerated, and overlooks the fact that to Homer and his society, natural forces *were* the work of the gods; it is Homer's portrayal of the deities as such intensely human characters that might more fittingly be called grotesque, and appeared so to at least one thoughtful Greek (Xenophanes) as early as the sixth century (see p. 134).

Then the usual divine frivolity takes over again, and the cosmic conflict, which was interrupted after their march to battle (at 20.75), is resumed, much to Zeus's amusement (21.389ff.). It is a parody of a battle scene. Athena and Ares engage in a real Homeric duel, complete with a fall of victim in the dust and vaunt of the victor, but the regular stripping of armor from the "corpse" is replaced by a ludicrous episode with Aphrodite, who is once again unlucky in warfare (see p. 199). The other "duels" are entertaining but of course abortive, each broken off after the "challenge." The whole lighthearted episode is a characteristic Homeric contrast to the mighty confrontation of the two merely human warriors that is to come.

The scene is then prepared for the great duel of Book 22. Priam opens the gates of Troy to receive the fleeing army; to allow them to escape the pursuing Achilles, Apollo encourages a captain named Agenor, who has appeared occasionally without being of any special significance, to win his place in literary history by standing his ground to face the invincible Achilles. In a type-scene the poet has used before, and will use again to immense effect when Hector himself faces Achilles, Agenor's thoughts emerge in a soliloquy (see pp. 94–95). He wonders whether to run to the city, and probably be overtaken and killed by Achilles, or to desert his companions and try to escape to the mountains, in which case again he will probably be caught. Desperately he decides to stand and face Achilles, knowing that even the goddess's son is mortal. So he summons up his courage, challenges Achilles, and hits him with a spearcast. Before Achilles can go into action, Apollo removes Agenor from the scene, takes his place in disguise, and runs off to lure Achilles away from the rest of the Trojans, who escape into the safety of the city. Agenor and Apollo have saved them, and Homer has contrived, without obvious improbability, that Hector and Achilles will face each other alone, and without the protection of the formalities of an agreed-upon duel.

Like the other duels in the *Iliad*, the final combat between Achilles and Hector will be short, its action limited to the ineffectual hurling of a spear by each warrior, a charge by each, and the mortal wound delivered by the spear of Achilles. This is probably the normal convention of heroic duels, adhered to consistently in this poem. So this short exchange must be extended by the poet in order to raise it to the necessary grandeur. And it is this that gives the episode its universality and its greatness; for a long account of the physical actions of the two fighters, even if their emotions during the battle were presented, could not give as much tension, color, and involvement as the various accessory actions, pictures, and devices the poet employs to enlarge his scene. It is not simply the culmination of the plot and the finality of the action that make this book so affecting; it is as always the elaboration on the bare structure that shows the poet's genius and deepens and enlarges the emotional impact on the audience.

Book 22 may be divided into five parts for the purpose of this commentary. After the preliminaries, the confrontation of Achilles and Hector falls into three stages, ending with Achilles' boast of victory over the corpse; then the lamentations of Hector's family come as conclusion.

Preliminaries to the Duel (1–91)

The initial lines set the scene with Trojans, Greeks, and the solitary and doomed Hector. Apollo reveals his true identity to

Achilles, and once more reminds us of the hero's mortality. Achilles' response to the taunt is strong and rude, a fitting answer to the god's mocking tone. As so often when the levity and immunity of the gods are set beside the self-reliant courage of struggling mortals, one has little doubt which condition is the more admirable. Helen took the same harsh tone with Aphrodite (3.399ff.).

Achilles' advance on the city and the solitary defender standing before it is expanded to more than a hundred verses (21–137). First come two similes. The first shows his speed; the second, in which the poet (with superb technique) sees him through Priam's eyes, brings out both the glare of his divine armor and the evil it portends (25–32). Then Priam appeals to his son to withdraw, his words holding irony and pathos as he mentions two of his other sons whom he cannot see but who we know have already been slain by Achilles (Lycaon 21.134ff., Polydorus 20.407ff.). The structure is the same as that seen in Helen's vain search for her dead brothers (3.236ff.), and the presentation of the thoughts of a character as another draws near is used when Antilochus brings the news of Patroclus's death to Achilles (18.5ff.). Finally Priam makes a personal appeal, much as Andromache did in Book 6, portraying his own sufferings if Hector is killed and the city falls. This emphasizes the identification of Hector's fate with that of Troy, which will continue to the end of the poem.

Hecuba laments, too, baring her breast in the archetypal gesture of a mother supplicating her son (which is also seen when Clytemnestra begs Orestes for her life in Aeschylus's *Choephoroe*). Like Priam's, her words are prophetic, describing the maltreatment to which Hector's body will be subjected. Andromache is absent. Perhaps her presence would overload the situation, and make it impossible for Hector to reject the supplication; another hero, Meleager, resists the appeals of his father and his mother, but yields to his wife (9.590ff.).

Hector's Soliloquy (92–130)

Hector remains, awaiting the approach of Achilles. He is given a simile, compared not (as most fighters are) to a lion or boar but to a snake, fierce but probably unheroic; no other warrior is so compared. The poet adds his typical single item of description: Hector turns and leans his heavy shield against a buttress of the wall. Then we hear the inner thoughts of the brave and lonely soldier. There are other examples of this structure—besides the recent one of Agenor, a similar situation overtakes Odysseus (11.401ff.) and Menelaus (17.90ff.)—but the thoughts of each hero are different (see Fenik 1978.68ff.). Like the others, however, Hector explores possible avenues of escape, for he does not wish to die.

To withdraw within Troy would mean humiliation before lesser men—his words repeat those he used to Andromache when he left the city (6.442)—for it was he who urged the Trojans to remain outside the walls and face Achilles after his return (18.284ff.), and as a result many Trojans have died. Death would be better than that. Shall he put aside his armor and offer terms of surrender? The thought trails on, line after line, as his mind strays away from the present into imagined details of division of the city's wealth and oaths of honesty, reminders of Troy's guilt.

Suddenly he pulls himself together, with the standard line of decision in these soliloquies: "But why do I think about all this?" (122). It is too late; impossible to talk to Achilles now, after he has killed Patroclus (and he is right in this, as the poet has carefully foreshadowed in the case of Lycaon). No way to talk quietly to him now "as a young man and a girl talk together" (127–28). The half-verse phrase is repeated at the end of one verse and the beginning of the next, an unusual effect to stress the reminder of the old days of peace, perhaps even of Andromache (a substitute for her missing appeal?). So, like Agenor, he sees no alternative and resolves to stand his ground. He has faced Achilles before (9.355, 20.364ff., 419ff.), and has said that sometimes the gods allow even the weaker man to prevail.

By skillful double use of the soliloquy type-scene, with Agenor and now with Hector, Homer has contrived to bring the two leaders together, alone, in position for a duel but without the formal dueling conventions that appeared in Books 3 and 7. No true or chivalrous agreements will be made between these two. So Hector waits, his courage bright but his peace of mind dimmed by his reflections on the guilt of his city and his own unwise past decisions. We feel more sympathy for him than we would for a more perfect knight.

Hector's Flight before Achilles (131–213)

Hector has decided to stand his ground. Achilles approaches, a simile showing him dazzling and threatening like an incarnation of war itself (132). Hector turns and runs. While another simile illustrates his flight, we think about what this means. There is no parallel to this in the other instances of the type-scene. Agenor did not run, he hurled a spear at Achilles and was then promptly rescued by Apollo. But no god comes to rescue Hector, and the only explanation of his flight must be drawn from the simile, that he is frightened as a dove is by a hawk. His panic is a vivid shock to the audience, the sharpest shock in the poem, and it comes as suddenly as fear overwhelmed Hector.

It has been said (by Owen 1946.197) that Hector has not overestimated his courage, he has underestimated what his courage had to meet. When he faced Achilles before, and launched a spear at him (20.419ff.), he was in the heat of battle, surrounded by his companions; now he is isolated on the plain, facing Achilles alone. And this is not the formal duel of chivalry, but the fury of revenge. What Achilles is thinking we do not hear. The poet's bold innovation has set a man with human weaknesses and merely human courage against a remote, invincible, and deadly power.

The following account of the flight and pursuit is the fullest display of the poet's techniques of expansion. Normally for extended presentation of a scene he resorts to the direct speech of the characters; a good example of this is the long description of the chariot race at 23.362ff., a good deal of which consists of the speeches of contestants and spectators. Here the poet chooses not to give speeches of either Greeks or Trojans, so that all our attention is directed at the scene on the plain. A parallel, on a smaller scale, can be seen in the buildup for Hector's final assault on the Greek ships (15.592–637).

After the initial simile, from the world of wild animals, comes a rare topographical description of the fig tree, the wellsprings, and the washing troughs. It brings in the world before the war, the days that the women of Troy will not see again; instead of chattering together as they work beside these springs, they will, not long after the death of the hero now running past the spot, be dispersed into slavery among the victors. Then the narrative voice shifts, and the poet himself comments on the importance of the action—no foot race, but life or death. A simile likens their speed to that of racehorses, superhuman.

Then the focus moves to the watchers; not the Trojans, who are left out here (probably so that their appearance solely at the beginning and end of the book may frame the whole), but the gods peering down. Perhaps they add dignity, certainly they add concern and regret, even pity; this occurs elsewhere, when Zeus worries over Sarpedon (16.431ff.) and Poseidon over Aeneas (20.291ff.), and more generally in Zeus's memorable words of sorrow for the human lot as he speaks to the grieving immortal horses of Patroclus (17.441–47). It is not only the modern reader who sorrows for the death of Hector the Trojan, but the Greek gods and the Greek poet, too. Hector's doom is confirmed by Zeus's regret, Athena's quick anger (exactly like that of Hera when Zeus daydreams of saving Sarpedon), and his consent to her intervention against Hector. She takes off for earth, and our eyes return to the plain before Troy, where a third simile, that of a dog hunting a fawn, shows us the chase still going on.

It is Hector running desperately; no god has taken his place. He repeatedly attempts to seek shelter beneath the city wall, but Achilles prevents it. Then the fourth simile takes us into Hector's mind, into his nightmare, bringing out the interminable agony of this pursuit. It is interminable because Achilles cannot gain on him, and the poet's voice tells us why, in a rhetorical question suggesting that Apollo's aid must still be with him; a similar rhetorical question from the poet stresses a like climax of the action as Odysseus slays the leader of the suitors (Odyssey 22.12–14).

There is one more closeup of the action, as Achilles waves off the other Greeks; and then on the fourth circuit of the city, the poet moves again to Olympus and the scales of Zeus, which signal the end of Hector's life and his final abandonment by the gods. The scales are an indication of what will happen, an artistic means of creating tension, not a real decision-making device. They have been brought in before, to indicate the turning of the general battle against the Greeks (8.68ff.), and two shorter mentions of "the balance-beam of Zeus" (16.658, 19.223) suggest the unelaborated, quasi-metaphorical form of the motif. Apollo gives up his support, Athena arrives from on high, and Achilles ceases his pursuit.

The long chase has expanded and dignified the action, and has brought before our eyes the visual setting (with a reminder of the peaceful past) and the loneliness of Hector, isolated first from his people and finally even from the gods. Achilles is seen only through Hector's eyes, inscrutable and inhuman. Again and again the poet takes our eyes away from the agonizing pursuit into a simile or to Olympus, and when we return it is still continuing, interminably.

Athena tells Achilles to stop the chase, promising him victory; her intervention, though adding honor and dignity to the hero she chooses to help, does not contravene ordinary probability, for Achilles (for all his "swift feet") has been unable to catch his victim, and it is natural for him to stop. Then she appears to Hector in the form of Deiphobus, who has been offstage since he was wounded by Meriones (13.527ff.), and Hector's relief at this brave and well-timed support by a beloved brother pours out in a final irony. The joining up of two fighters against an opposing hero is common (among other examples, Aeneas and Pandarus join forces against Diomedes' mighty rage [5.166ff.], Deiphobus sought out Aeneas to help him against Idomeneus [13.455ff.], and Hector had asked Aeneas to assist him in capturing Diomedes' horses [17.483ff.]). But the irony is unique, and Homer plies it heavily as he has Athena describe how "Deiphobus," like Hector himself, rejected the prayers of their father and mother in order to come to assist his brother.

Emboldened, Hector addresses his opponent, as many other combatants do before a fight, and in anticipation of what is to come in the last two books, asks for respect for the corpse of the loser. He is attempting to return to the chivalry of the duels in Book 3 and Book 7. Of course it is too late now, and Achilles refuses and hurls his spear to begin the duel. A selection of standard battle elements follows, though there is no exact parallel to this particular collocation of them, and as always the exchange is quickly over. Hector ducks and shouts to Achilles in triumph: a normal response, given added point here by his reference to his previous flight. *Now* he can face his attacker.

He hurls his own spear, but (as often) it does not pierce Achilles' shield; Homer is careful here not to suggest that it could not do so because the shield was made by a god. Hector is now without a spear, whereas Achilles', as the poet has carefully mentioned, was returned to him by Athena. Achilles hardly needed such specific practical help, but the incident prepared the way for what happens now. Hector (uniquely) calls to his brother for another spear (there is no direct speech to him, perhaps to bring out the coming monologue), and discovers Athena's trick.

As he did with Achilles, the poet has contrived that Hector faces death knowingly. He fled before Achilles not long before; but now, with even less hope, knowing he is deserted by the gods, he stands and faces him. The verse that introduces his speech is formulaic (296), but this is the only time the poet presents a doomed hero's thoughts like this (296–305). Hector recognizes the hand of Athena (anti-Trojan, and perhaps as guileful as she claims to be in the *Odyssey*; 13.298–99) and the will of Zeus; but at least his death can be glorious. This, though he does not say so, is really the doing of the gods who stopped his flight, and of course of the poet. In this soliloquy there is no choice of options, only the courage that realizes the absence of hope but still goes on—the courage that Andromache said would destroy him (6.407), that destroys the wild animal at bay to which Hector was once compared (12.41–48). The structure of the short speech is familiar, particularly close to Achilles' at 20.344ff., where again a sudden clearing of vision is followed by a final resolve; but the combination of courage, isolation, and hopelessness is unmatched.

They charge simultaneously, a regular motif; Hector is like an eagle swooping, but Achilles' terrifying splendor is glorified by the description of his magnificent divine armor and a comparison to the evening star, brightest and fairest of all. As Kirk points out (1976.216–17), in both similes the background is darkness. At last the poet lets us into Achilles' thoughts, as he looks for the vulnerable place in the armor that he knows—for it is his own, taken from his dead friend. In this way we are reminded that both heroes are wearing divinely made armor, though both will die soon and both are well aware of it.

The armor is a visible symbol of the contrast between mortality and immortality, but the poet does not want to raise the less realistic issue of whether it is invulnerable to mortal weapons, and he dexterously avoids it by having Achilles stab Hector in the throat, where the armor gives no protection. Here, as the poet has said (325), death comes most swiftly; but Hector must speak before he dies, and with some awkwardness the poet explains how this will be possible (328–29). Hector falls, and Achilles taunts him, guessing more accurately at the earlier thoughts of his enemy than Hector did when he killed Patroclus. Achilles' threat to dishonor the dead body, Hector's request that he accept ransom, and Achilles' rejection of this all foreshadow events to come later in the poem.

The deaths of Hector, Patroclus, and Achilles are bound one to another by the divine armor, and Hector's death in the "gift" of his enemy is (like Patroclus's) a surrogate for the death of Achilles himself, foreshadowed but not accomplished within the plot of the *Iliad* (see p. 115). The poet brilliantly and movingly reinforces this interconnection in the next lines. Hector's last words foretell the fate of Achilles, recalling the prophecy Thetis related before Achilles set out for his revenge (18.95–96); they also recall Patroclus's death, for Patroclus had similarly foretold the fate of his conqueror, Hector, and his last words were the name and dignified title of his beloved Achilles (16.854). Moreover, the three moving verses describing the flight of the dead man's soul to Hades, "lamenting his fate, leaving the prime of manhood behind," are the same in both scenes (363; 16.857) and occur only there. They may be formulaic, but even if they are the poet has reserved them, through the innumerable deaths in the poem, for these two instances alone, and the repetition must be as significant as it would be in any later poet. (One may compare the reservation in *Beowulf* of the common "beasts of battle" trope for the lament at the end of the poem; 3025–27.)

In both scenes the living hero rejects the warning (his words introduced by the same verse, "Dead though he was, Achilles [Hector] spoke to him"). Hector arrogantly expressed his hope for victory even over Achilles himself, which we knew to be impossible; and Achilles here, with perhaps the most effective repetition in the poem, repeats the words he had spoken when he decided to avenge Patroclus even at the cost of his own life: "I will accept my fate at the time when Zeus and the other gods wish to accomplish it" (365–66 = 18.115–16). Hector's boast was natural enough for a victor; but Achilles' words, on both occasions they are used, summarize not only his acceptance of his own death as the price of vengeance on Hector, but acknowledgment of his mortality despite his magnificence; the theme is most fully expressed in his scene with Lycaon (21.108–13). The solemnity of this scene allows no place for the gods, who have now withdrawn.

Achilles strips the armor from the corpse. There is no mention now that it is Peleus's armor, for that could not deepen our emotions here. Instead the formulaic phrase "he stripped off the armor" is followed (for the only time in its six occurrences) by the "runover" participle *haimatoent'*, "bloodied," for divinely made though it was, it had not saved its wearer; this is a fine example of the powerful individual effects possible within the formulaic language (see p. 52). The Greeks run up and join him, stabbing the corpse in their immense relief and joy—an action natural enough, if reprehensible—and Achilles begins a speech of victory, calling for a final assault on the city.

But he breaks off; in the midst of his triumphant exhortation to the army the poet suddenly puts in the verse that is used only to introduce the decision-making in a soliloquy, used by Hector and Agenor not long before: "But why do I think about all this?" (385, cf. 122 and 21.562). The verse shows that he is suddenly caught up in his own thoughts, that his joy is interrupted by his remembrance of Patroclus, still lying unburied and meaning more to him than the capture of Troy. Then he turns back to his men and tells them to march back in triumph to the ships. No other speech has this insertion of a soliloquy within an address to others, and the juxtaposition of Achilles' public triumph and his personal sorrow is another masterpiece of technique within the formulaic conventions.

Then the poet turns back again to the pathos of the dead Hector, as Achilles drags his body off in the dust behind his chariot. The action is not perhaps shockingly barbaric, compared with Hector's own intention of cutting off Patroclus's head and giving the body to the dogs (17.125ff., 18.177), but Homer makes it clear that disapproval is not confined to our modern taste. The act is "shameful" for Hector, and possibly "wrong" for Achilles to carry out (395; the Greek may mean either or both), and the lines describing the fouling of Hector's beauty in the dust of the land he died attempting to protect (401–4) show the poet's compassion for the character he has created, enemy though he was to the Greeks.

The First Laments for Hector (405–515)

As the chariot drags the corpse off toward the ships, a wailing arises from the city wall. It seems (says the poet) as if Troy were already blazing with the enemies' fires; and the simile beautifully superimposes the fall of the city on the death of its greatest defender. Then the focus closes down on old Priam. His longing to supplicate Achilles for the return of the body looks forward to his appeal to Achilles in Book 24, and his lament foreshadows the appeals he will use then: the old age of Achilles' own father, Peleus, the number of sons Priam has lost, the lack of the solace of weeping over the corpse of the dearest of them all. Hecuba in her turn bewails the loss not only to herself but to all the women of Troy.

And Andromache? The poet delays our expectation, as he did when Hector sought her at his home in Book 6; she is not on the wall with the others but at home weaving among her women. The delay increases the tension and avoids too close a parallel with the three more formal laments over Hector at the end of the poem. Beyond this, the poet intensifies the pathos by showing her constant thought and care for her husband, as she begins preparations for him to wash on his return from the blood and dust of battle. There is, of course, irony here, too; for Hector is now "far from warm baths" (445), and there is little hope at the moment that his corpse will ever receive the usual washing of the funeral rites. Perhaps, too, the poet has in mind that the washing of Hector's body, when it comes, will be performed by the servants of Achilles, not by Andromache, and so the association of loving wife and funeral washing is used at this point instead.

Andromache hears the wailing, guesses the truth—that Hector's courage has killed him, as her first words to him in the poem foreshadowed ("Your own courage will destroy you," 6.407)—and dashes to the wall. Before her lament begins, a physical action both describes her agony of mind and symbolizes the magnitude of her loss; the headdress that falls from her head as she faints away was a gift from Aphrodite on the day she wedded Hector, and is the sign of a married woman's modesty, to be violated when the city falls; perhaps too by a play on words it refers to Troy itself, for the Greek word signifies both a woman's veil and the ramparts of a city (see Nagler 1974.44ff.). The phrase used for her fainting, "dark night covered her eyes" (466) is normal for warriors dying in battle, so perhaps there is another hint here that her life ends with her husband's.

Andromache's lament reminds us of their parting in Book 6, first by its words about the death of her father and her utter dependence on Hector, then by its long picture of the wretched fate that now awaits their infant son, whom we still remember. There is irony again, for her description of the dismal future of the fatherless infant barely mentions (487) what we know will actually happen to him at the sack of the city. At last she turns back to the present misery, the loss of the consolation of proper burial and the contrast between the love and comfort of Hector's life and his death in the dust. Her words about burning his clothing, since it is now useless to him, conflict (perhaps intentionally) with the notion that precious objects burned with the body will be of use to the dead man in the next world (as horses, dogs, and Trojan captives are burned with the corpse of Patroclus; 23.171ff.). Perhaps, too, (as with the washing preparations earlier) there is a substitution here for the future dressing of the corpse, to be done by Achilles' women, not by Andromache.

Achilles' vengeance is complete. But the book has shown us little of Achilles' thoughts, much of Hector's. It has shown his decision to face his superhuman enemy and his very human panic; but thanks to Athena's intervention, he later faces death bravely and honorably, though alone. In the plot of the poem, Hector's death represents the accomplishment of Achilles' revenge for the killing of Patroclus and the fulfillment of the results of the quarrel between him and Agamemnon, which began the poem so long ago; it also foreshadows, as Homer clearly indicates, the fall of Troy and the death of Achilles himself, both to come about beyond the end of this poem. And on the wider scale, Hector's resolution and courage, and his fear, and the agony of his family over his death and the failure to recover his body, would be familiar to every Greek, and a part of universal human experience.

Further Reading

Fenik 1978.68–90 analyzes Hector's soliloquy and three others based on the same pattern. Krischer 1979.148–49 makes interesting points about Hector's flight and his speeches in this book. Nagler 1974.44–51 shows the depth of meaning in the description of Andromache's swoon, and Segal 1971c examines the use and modification of formulae in her lament; Edwards 1986 also discusses this lament. Segal 1971b shows the development and interconnections of the ideas of defilement and mutilation of the dead in this and previous books.

30

Iliad Book 24

The tale of Achilles' loss and his vengeance might have ended with his killing of Hector in Book 22, or with the magnificent funeral he gave his dead friend in Book 23. This is the usual conclusion of such tales, and has ended many western movies. The killing of a friend must be avenged, and the Greeks would be satisfied when this had been done. But it is the special greatness of the *Iliad* that Homer was not content with this, and in the final book he added a further episode to the completed vengeance pattern. Vengeance does not relieve Achilles' grief; only when he overcomes his fury against Hector through sympathy for old Priam, and sees his own loss as a part of universal human suffering, can he return to an acceptance of life on human terms. Then the poem ends quietly with Hector's funeral, honoring the dead hero and foreshadowing the death to come for Troy and its people and for Achilles himself.

The conclusion of the poem has not been overtly foreshadowed by the poet. After it has happened, however, it may appear that this had always been his plan, and discreet indications can perhaps be identified. The poem began with a ransom scene, in which the suppliant was rudely rebuffed, and ends with another in which a suppliant is treated with great courtesy. Andromache told of Achilles' slaughter of her father and brothers, but remembered his courteous treatment of her father's corpse (6.416ff.); and at the end he behaves in the same way toward that of her husband. Her lament that she cannot care for the corpse of her husband (22.508ff.) perhaps foreshadows that these duties will be performed at the order of Achilles himself (see p. 311). The importance of a proper funeral has been stressed by Zeus's care for the body of Sarpedon in Book 16, as well as the magnificent honors for the dead Patroclus. The emphasis on Achilles' continuing maltreatment of Hector's corpse in Book 23 perhaps looks forward to its eventual restoration, and the gracious side of Achilles' character is much in evidence during the funeral games of Book 23. Above all, Achilles' unique and lonely decision not to do as other men would and accept the recompense offered him in Book 9 needs to be balanced by a similar act of superhuman scale before he leaves the scene.

Book 23 has been devoted to Patroclus's funeral and the games with which the honors to the dead hero concluded. Achilles holds a splendid funeral feast—though after it still "his heart is angry for his companion" (23.37)—and then reluctantly attends the official banquet signifying his reconciliation with Agamemnon. This was predicted at the time the reconciliation was made (19.179–80), but Achilles' continuing grief is shown by his refusal to wash until Patroclus's funeral is completed, by his juxtaposing the feast with the further preparations for the funeral (23.49–53), and by his subsequent falling asleep on the seashore, which the poet marks as a breach of the normal order of things (58–61). Neither reconciliation feast nor funeral feast brings him any relief, and the poet dramatizes further his agony of sorrow and self-reproach by bringing in the ghost of Patroclus.

The ghost requests speedy burial, a preparation for the remainder of the funeral, but its purpose is to increase pathos by recounting their past life together, to remind us once more of Achilles' own approaching death by a further prediction of it (23.80–81) and by a request that their bones lie together in the same urn. All this is, as has been pointed out, an expression of Achilles' own feelings, and by the skeptical can well be taken as a dream rather than an apparition. The transient reunion ends with the vain embrace showing the gulf between living and dead. As the rites continue, the poet takes another opportunity to remind us of Achilles' own death, as the normal cutting of the mourners' hair to lay upon the bier (23.135–36) is amplified in Achilles' case into the sacrifice of the lock he had once dedicated to celebrate his own homecoming, which is now a lost hope (140–53).

The deaths of Patroclus, Hector, and Achilles have been interwoven since Book 16, and the poet continues to evoke emotion by effective juxtapositions. The contrast between the honor shown to Patroclus's corpse and the maltreatment of Hector's began directly after Hector's death, and was repeated at the beginning of the rites for Patroclus (23.19–26); and later in the rites the poet inserts a passage describing the preservation of Hector's body by the gods (184–91). A simile likening Achilles' grief for his friend to that of a father for his son points forward to Priam's supplication (23.222–25). The summoning of the Winds to speed the burning of the pyre—and dignify the occasion by divine participation—is elaborated with the relief of very human interactions between Iris and the boisterous male gods, and afterward Achilles again sleeps exhausted in the open air; this repeated deviation from normal behavior is continued when the other chiefs awaken him and he addresses them from a sitting position (23.235ff.).

The funeral games show Achilles and the other Greeks at their most civilized. Achilles is master of ceremonies and the dominant figure, a quality that has been called essential for the tragic hero, showing "that charisma of personality which in literature as in life is part of the magnetism of the heroic character, and which properly belongs to the tragic hero as hero if not as tragic" (Krook 1969.39). He skillfully smooths over a quarrel in the bleachers between the excitable lesser Ajax and Idomeneus. He copes graciously with the dispute between Antilochus and Menelaus, a superb scene that shows both Menelaus's natural resentment of an affront and his appreciation of all that Antilochus and the others are suffering on his behalf (23.607ff.)—how different from the inflexible stances of Book 1! He behaves with delightful courtesy to old Nestor, whom the poet gives one last chance to recall the feats of his youth, when he won four of the contests and was beaten in the fifth only because his rivals were Siamese twins (23.634ff.; he also has a chance to give long-winded advice to his charioteer son on how to drive, 23.306ff.).

Achilles also avoids the possible embarrassment of a defeat for the touchy Agamemnon by giving him the prize for spear-throwing without bothering to hold a contest, and does *not* recall (though we may do so) his old complaint that Agamemnon always gets the best prize without doing anything to earn it (1.165ff., 9.332ff.). Antilochus, who will take on the role of Patroclus in the later story (the *Aethiopis*) and will be killed by Memnon and avenged by Achilles, receives a good deal of space, and so does the kind-hearted and considerate Menelaus. Of course the gods cannot resist interfering from time to time, except when the competition is inconclusive (the wrestling and armed-battle contests). Patroclus is repeatedly mentioned (279ff., 618ff., 746ff., 800), as he is always in Achilles' thoughts.

The structure of Book 24 consists basically of three type-scenes: a divine visitation of Thetis to Achilles, a suppliant scene of Priam to Achilles (enormously expanded by the inclusion of other type-scenes) together with the response of the person supplicated, and Hector's funeral. In the following discussion the long central scene will be divided into two parts: Priam's preparations and journey, and his actual meeting with Achilles.

After the funeral of Patroclus the Greeks disperse to take up normal life again. But Achilles cannot; his grief has not been assuaged by his vengeance on Hector or the splendid burial he has given Patroclus. "I might put an end to the wailing [of my dead brother's wife and parents] if I could bring back your head and your armor and toss them into their hands," said Euphorbus to Menelaus (17.38–40), but the poet devotes many lines (3–22) to describing how Achilles' continuing mistreatment of Hector's corpse does *not* help him overcome his grief. He remains sleepless in his misery, thinking only of their past companionship (the direct description of his thoughts is paralleled in Odysseus's wretched night, *Odyssey* 20.9ff.); he roams on the seashore, the usual sign of desolation, and the poet makes the scene more vivid by omitting the conventional adjective for the sea, "barren," at the end of the verse (12) and adding instead the description of the dawn breaking over sea and beach before his wakeful eyes. But Apollo protects the body of Hector, "dead though he was" (20) — the phrase is in an emphatic position, to show that ill treatment of a dead body is offensive to gods and men alike, inert clay though it is (54).

After nine days of this, the concern of the gods bursts out; nine days is the same length of time as the plague in Book 1, and is probably conventional for "many days", but the balance of the two periods of divine displeasure is hardly accidental. Apollo voices his dislike for Achilles' actions and describes his character in a way the poet would not do in his own voice; his hostility is based not only on his support for Hector and Troy but probably also on the tale that Achilles killed young Troilus, Priam's son, in the temple of Apollo (Apollodorus, *Epitome* III.31; Virgil, *Aeneid* 1.474–48.). Achilles must learn that "*enduring* is the temper [*thumos*] the fates have set in mankind" (49). Hera sourly reminds him that he sang at the wedding of Achilles' mother and father: Aeschylus said (perhaps imitating a lost epic the audience should have in mind here) that he sang of the long life of her future son (Plato, *Republic* 383a)!

This is the last divine assembly in the *Iliad*, and though Zeus is sympathetic to both sides, the others do not show themselves to good advantage. Apollo, the god of the great Greek religious sites of Delos and Delphi, is bitterly opposed to the greatest hero of the Greeks, the hatred of Hera and Athena for Troy is underlined by the account (in the poet's voice) of the judgment of Paris,

Poseidon is associated with their prejudice, and even Aphrodite's gift to Paris for his favor is described not as the beautiful Helen but as "lustfulness" (*machlosunê*), a word used twice by Hesiod of women's inordinate sexual desire. During this book the better side of human nature will become evident, but nothing seems likely ever to mitigate the vicious antagonisms of the deities. The effect is not too far from that produced by the self-centered and cruel Aphrodite and Artemis in Euripides' *Hippolytus*.

Zeus, however, shows some sense of propriety and tact. He vetoes the idea of stealing away Hector's body on the polite (and untrue) pretext that Thetis's presence beside Achilles makes it impossible, and when she comes from the sea depths (where she actually is) to Olympus, he tells her that his motive was respect for her and the desire to grant glory to Achilles. This glory, of course, will be that brought about by the ransom he receives from Priam, not that which we may feel he gains by his compassion for the old king's sorrow; that would hardly occur to a Homeric god. The appearance of the black-robed, mourning Thetis among the Olympians dramatically reintroduces the imminence of Achilles' own death, and this, of course, she immediately refers to herself when she journeys down to speak with him (131–32). This is why the poet sends her as messenger, instead of Athena or Iris; her visit to Olympus is also a dramatic reminder of how much the situation has changed since her first journey (in Book 1) to ask Zeus to help Achilles.

Achilles is still mourning, while for contrast his men are preparing a meal he presumably will not share; and Thetis wails that he is neither eating nor sleeping. He accepts Zeus's will, much as he did Athena's suggestion in Book 1, with a few grudging words. At this point we do not see far into his mind. Instead of departing, as is usual at the conclusion of a divine visit, Thetis remains with him; a sympathetic touch on the poet's part, for they must make the most of the short time now left to Achilles. Zeus then dispatches Iris with instructions for Priam. It is not made clear how Zeus knows that Achilles has agreed, and in fact it could be argued that though related consecutively, in Homer's way, Thetis and Iris are actually sent simultaneously, like Iris to Poseidon and Apollo to Hector (15.157ff., 220ff.) and (in more complex fashion) Athena to Telemachus and Hermes to Odysseus (*Odyssey* 1.96ff. and 5.44ff.; see p. 34). It would be foolish to seek to determine whether he assumes, or foreknows, Achilles' agreement.

Preparations for the Ransoming (143–321)

The long, richly decorated scene of Priam's supplication to Achilles begins with a divine visit, Iris bearing the message from Zeus. As usual when a messenger or visitor arrives, the sight seen by the visitor is described, and here the scene element is used to present, with powerful effect, the terrible lamentations in Priam's palace. There are many others to be mourned besides Hector (166–68). After Zeus's message has been delivered, the poet binds the following actions closely together by means of a ring-form structure: (a) Priam orders the wagon prepared; (b) he goes to the storeroom for the ransom; (c) he speaks to Hecuba; and (d) she responds, voicing her fear of the dangerous proposal and her hatred for the killer of her sons. Then the order of the items is reversed: (c) Priam tells Hecuba that he is determined to go; (b) he collects the ransom, which is described in detail (for the poet is moving unhurriedly here, giving weight to so important a matter; the chalice receives a special flourish of historical association); and (a) finally the wagon is prepared, again with great detail (there is a shorter version at *Odyssey* 6.71–73, and one shorter still at 24.690), and the chariot more briefly (for the poet knows where to stop).

Between the two last items Priam lashes out in anger, first at the surrounding Trojans, then at his sons in particular, a vivid and very human touch that also reminds us of the other sons he has lost besides Hector. Ares has destroyed the brave and spared the useless (260), a reproach repeated even more neatly in an epitaph attributed to Anacreon: "Ares spares not the brave but the cowards" (*Greek Anthology* 7.160).

For further expansion and dignifying of the preparations—and of course to build up further the tension of waiting—Priam's departure is preceded by a libation and an omen, as is Telemachus's departure from Menelaus's palace (*Odyssey* 15.147ff.). The detail extends even to a simile to picture the majesty of the eagle of Zeus, whose appearance signifies the divine approval.

Priam's Journey to Achilles (332–468)

Priam whips up his horses and drives "rapidly" (327) out through the city; the adverb seems improbable, in view of the laden mule cart and following company of lamenting kinfolk, and must be due either to habit on the poet's part (chariots always drive swiftly) or perhaps to the desire to convey Priam's eagerness for his mission. The poet, however, is still telling the story very slowly and impressively, with much elaboration of the type-scenes. So Zeus gives his instructions to Hermes, who in turn takes his time in donning sandals and grasping his wand, and then descends in disguise to the plain.

His arrival to deliver the message is technically very interesting. Instead of having him stand beside Priam and address him, as would be normal, the poet elaborates the usual description of what the person sought is doing into the warning of Hermes' arrival given to Priam by his companion Idaeus, and the usual surprise of the host becomes Priam's fright at the appearance of the newcomer (and his divine aura?). This results in an unusually abrupt jump in narrative plane, from Hermes to the travelers, between 348 and 349.

Priam has forgotten that Iris told him he would be escorted by Hermes, and this allows the charming scene between them, illustrating what Zeus meant when he said Hermes loved to be a companion to men (334–35). There is even a hidden joke or two: Priam declares the delightful youth must come of "blessed" parents (*makarôn* [377], a word usually used of the gods), and Hermes (son of Zeus) gives his father's name as Polyctor, "Much-possessor" (397). One overlooks the chronological problems caused by this still very young man (347–48) who seems to have left home for the front nine years ago (396). The care of the gods for Hector is brought out once again in the long account of the preservation of his corpse (411–23), and gains additional depth on the lips of the god who is now caring for Priam.

As Achilles' dwelling meets their eyes it is given a full description, based on an account of its construction (like Pandarus's bow and Achilles' shield; see p. 83); when Agamemnon's heralds (1.328) and the Greek envoys (9.185) approached it, the weight of the scene was on Achilles' feelings, not those of the approaching suppliants, and so the description was not appropriate there. Now, however, its great size begins the building up of Achilles' dominance in the coming scene. To comfort Priam, Hermes reveals who he is, and then departs.

The availability of this supernatural guide has enabled the poet to bring Priam and Achilles face to face without distracting problems of human probability, for the supernatural is much easier to believe than the merely improbable; Odysseus's blinding of a one-eyed cannibalistic giant seems less unlikely than his slaying of 118 suitors with a handful of helpers. The convenience of the technique is encapsulated, as if intentionally, by Hermes' effortless opening of the gate, which normally took three men to unbar (453–57). But a god would be out of place at the intensely serious meeting of mortals that is to come, so Hermes now goes his way.

Priam and Achilles (469–676)

The following scene between Priam and Achilles is as famous as the farewell of Hector and Andromache in Book 6, and it may be thought (as with that scene) that no commentary is required to explain its emotional impact. But the effect is produced by art, and the techniques of that art are not simple; and a careful study of the choices the poet has made, the allusions that lie in the background, and the appropriateness of the treatment of traditional motifs will probably, for most readers, further enrich their appreciation of this superb episode.

Priam enters Achilles' dwelling and finds him inside; as usual on the entry of messenger or guest, the poet describes what he sees, the companions and occupation of the person sought. Achilles has just finished a meal, two of his retainers are clearing away, and the table is still beside him. This is the standard single item of description usually given (see p. 85), but after the poet's insistence, as recently as Thetis's visit that day, that the grief-stricken hero is still refusing to eat, some explanation is called for. After the meal Achilles and Priam share later in the scene, the old king says that he has eaten nothing until then since Hector's death; would it not be more effective if Achilles too first broke his long fast at the meal that formalizes their mutual understanding? Two recent commentators (Nagler 1974.186; Macleod 1982.125) have noted the question and considered that the poet intends to show that Achilles' attitude has softened since the message from Zeus, that his grief is no longer so intense. This is very possible.

As an alternative, however, it may be suggested that Achilles is described as eating because he must be viewed here not as another grief-stricken sufferer like Priam, but as the lordly figure who dominates the situation, who has Priam's life in his hands as well as the power of granting or withholding his request. This is conveyed by presenting him as the noble chief whose retainers have just served him as he presides at a meal in his halls. This has been prepared for by the recent description of his impressive halls and compound (448ff.) and by the epithet "dear to Zeus" given him when his name is first mentioned here (472; probably more than a conventional use).

Just as his sleeping in the open air after Patroclus's funeral, and again after the games, signified an abnormal state of affairs (his exceptional grief for Patroclus), so here his dining amidst his retainers presents him as the all-powerful, inscrutable figure that Priam sees; and the motif of fasting is interrupted for this now more important purpose. In the same way King Alcinous has just concluded a feast when the suppliant Odysseus appears (*Odyssey* 7.136–38, 188), Nestor when Patroclus calls in (11.640–41), Menelaus when Telemachus turns up (*Odyssey* 4.3–19), and so on. The significance of the poet's handling of this scene can be appreciated if one thinks how different the tone would be if Priam came as suppliant to Achilles and found him lying in agonized grief on the seashore.

The usual gesture of the suppliant, taking the knees of the person supplicated, is strengthened by Priam's kissing Achilles' hands; the poet's own voice drives home the effect in the following verse: "terrible, man-slaughtering hands, which had killed so many of his sons" (479). There is a complex irony here too, for "man-slaughtering" is the conventional epithet for *Hector*, and besides this passage it is applied only to the hands of Achilles as he lays them on the chest of the dead Patroclus (18.317, 23.18). The normal surprise of a host at a new arrival is here introduced by a simile (480–83), which holds the scene still for a moment; it startlingly compares Priam to an outcast murderer, and reinforces the dominant position of Achilles by placing him in the position of the rich man whom the suppliant of the simile approaches.

Priam begins, not formally with Achilles' titles, but directly with the main note of his appeal: "Remember your own father." As he continues, his picture of old Peleus deepens into the heavy irony of Peleus's still living hope for the return of his doomed son Achilles. His tale of his own lost sons culminates in the name of Hector, postponed to the emphatic and pathetic position at the beginning of the verse (501); and he concludes the quite brief speech with a reminder of the moving gesture of supplication that preceded it.

Achilles' response is introduced not by a spare speech-introduction, as are most of the speeches in the Hector-Andromache farewell, but by the poet's description of the lamentations of both men. His speech does not immediately refer to Priam's request, but instead takes the form of a consolation. He begins with the welcoming phrases of a host, preceded (in place of titles) by a few words about Priam's suffering and his courage. Then he sums up the human situation with the famous image of the jar of evils and the jar of blessings, from which Zeus distributes at his will the fortunes of mankind, drawing either a mixture from both urns or from evils alone.

The fundamental idea is probably traditional, as it is enunciated with the air of a cliché by Helen at the dinner party for Telemachus (*Odyssey* 4.236–37), and so probably is the image, for the evils brought to mankind by Pandora in Hesiod's tale are also contained in a jar (*Works and Days* 94ff.). The Greek is ambiguous enough to allow the interpretation (sometimes taken both in antiquity and in modern times) that there are *two* jars of evil compared with one of blessings, but this is not necessary and seems overly subtle; Plato [*Republic* 379d] quotes a slightly different version of 528 meaning "[jars] full of fates, one of good, the other of evil," which supports the normal interpretation. No mention is made of Zeus's motives in assigning the fortunes. This seems to imply that he has no necessary concern with justice and the reward of merit; on the positive side, however, there is no implication that the sufferer must have done something to deserve his loss, which is out of place in a consolation (*pace* Job's comforters). The only alternatives in life are a mixture of good and evil, or unmixed evil, such as the wretchedness of the starving, homeless wanderer, despised by men and gods alike (531–33).

Then Achilles justifies this view, in the normal way, with a paradigm; and the poet draws its subject not from old legend, but much more effectively from the case of Achilles' own father, Peleus. This brilliantly repeats the parallel Priam has drawn between his old age and that of Peleus, for in the past both men could have been considered the most favored of mortals, Priam for his power and his many sons, Peleus for his wealth and his goddess wife. But both alike have drawn from the jar of evils, for Priam now suffers the losses of warfare, and Peleus's only son (540) is far away at Troy and will never return to him. In this way the poet also introduces the contrast between the many sons of Priam and the only son of Peleus, which he will bring in again a little later in the Niobe paradigm.

Finally comes the conclusion of the consolation: Priam's suffering is not exceptional, for he has received good as well as evil; it is the universal lot of mankind, the will and work of Zeus, and like all men he must have the courage to endure it, for only further sorrow lies ahead. "Enduring is the temper the fates have set in mankind," says Apollo early in the book in his protest against Achilles' behavior (49), and now Achilles himself makes the same statement to another victim of the gods. Perhaps one should recall, as the two mourners face the trouble still to come, that soon another of Priam's sons (Paris) will kill Achilles, and Achilles' own young son Neoptolemus will kill Priam; the father-son relationship stressed so heavily here will link them even more closely.

Priam, however, can think only of seeing the body of his son, and Achilles' momentary irritation ("Don't push me!" 559–60) reminds us of the restraint he is imposing on himself. This is no sentimental swearing of eternal friendship, but still a situation of extreme tension. He has the body washed by his servants and clothed in robes from the ransom (so that Hector should not lie in his enemy's gift), and again the poet explains that Achilles might be angered beyond his control if Priam were to lament over the corpse. Homer here wants to show the controlled acceptance of grief by both men, and to confront Priam with the corpse could ruin this. By now the emphasis has shifted from Priam's feelings to those of Achilles, and to dramatize the depth of his emotions and the effort he must make, the poet has the hero himself lift the body of his enemy onto the bier with an apology to his dead companion (594). In this way Achilles himself begins the funeral rites for Hector.

He returns and invites Priam to eat, persuading him by the paradigm of Niobe, who "thought again of food when worn out with weeping" (613). Of course her eating was no part of the usual story (see p. 67). The poet has chosen that myth because of the parallel of Niobe's many children killed by Leto's two, just as Priam's many sons have died at the hands of Peleus' only child; he has used this contrast before (for example, at 495 and 540 above). In addition, the poet extends the motif of petrifaction from Niobe to her people, so that the bodies can lie unburied for nine days until the gods take charge of the matter; this corresponds to their similar concern for the corpse of Hector at the beginning of this Book. And of course the pattern of Niobe's proud achievement giving way to disaster can be applied too to Priam, Peleus, Troy, and the short-lived Achilles himself. For his own purposes the poet has adapted the usual version of the tale as freely as the tragedians of the fifth century altered the inherited myths.

The meal is then prepared and eaten. No washing is mentioned—though Priam's befouling himself with dust during his days of grief has ben stressed three times—because he is still in mourning, and we recall that Achilles, too, in his grief refused to wash before his feast with Agamemnon (23.38ff.). There is no prayer, no libation, no conversation; instead, the poet has the unique and immensely effective idea of having the two of them gaze silently at each other in admiration.

Priam asks for a place to sleep; his words emphasize that this meal has ended the fasting that symbolized the grief of both men, and their sleeplessness will now end, too. The regular retiring for the night type-scene begins, and Priam's bed is prepared on the porch. This is also the arrangement made for young Telemachus in Menelaus's elaborate palace (*Odyssey* 4.296ff.) and is presumably normal; it is also convenient for Priam's later unobserved departure. Achilles, however, offers an explanation, saying that some Greek may come to talk with him inside the dwelling and might report Priam's presence to Agamemnon with subsequent trouble.

A problem arises because the line that introduces this speech (649) includes the participle *epikertomeôn*, which in its two other occurrences in Homer is used of a speaker mocking an antagonist who is at his mercy, and would be translated "jeering" (16.744, *Odyssey* 22.194). This does not suit the tone of Achilles' speech here, and some commentators understand Agamemnon, not Priam, as the implied butt (so Fitzgerald's translation, "defiant of Agamemnon"). Others take the participle in the weakened sense of "deceptively" (the related adjective *kertomios* has this sense at *Odyssey* 24.240, where Odysseus begins his rather cruel deception of old Laertes) and suggest either that Achilles is not really worried about reports to Agamemnon but has had enough of this strained companionship, or that he wants to facilitate Priam's departure with the god who guided him there (cf. 563–64) but is too polite to say so (so Macleod 1982.142–43). Either or both of these interpretations may be right.

We may reflect, however, that the poet's purpose in these two speeches is to prepare for Hector's funeral by arranging for the truce; but he does not wish to risk any impression that warfare and hostility have come to an end with the agreement of Achilles and Priam, and so Priam's speech ends sadly "and on the twelfth day we will join battle, if indeed we must" (667). Achilles' mention of Agamemnon reminds us of this unchanged background of the war, and the participle *epikertomeôn* introducing his words may be intended to convey that he and Priam, though recently united in hospitable meal and understanding of each other's grief, must remain formal enemies. Just as Achilles' first burst of sympathy with old Priam was held back a little by his irritation at Priam's too-swift wish to see the corpse (559ff.), and his lifting of his enemy's cleansed body onto the bier was followed by his agonized cry to Patroclus's ghost (591ff.), so too the recent mutual sympathy and admiration of Greek and Trojan must be kept within bounds, and the poet does this with *epikertomeôn*. The proper stage direction might be "distantly"; translation should not perhaps be more specific than "curtly" or "gruffly."

Both men retire. Regular retiring scenes conclude with a mention of the host sleeping beside his wife: Menelaus with Helen (*Odyssey* 4.305), Alcinous with Arete (*Odyssey* 7.347), Nestor with his wife (*Odyssey* 3.403), Achilles and Patroclus with captive women (9.664–68). So here Achilles sleeps beside Briseis. This may be simply the usual convention of the type-scene, but it is hardly fanciful to suggest the poet presents it as a sign not only of the restoration of Achilles' prize, but of his reconciliation to life on ordinary human terms. Not only the wrath and the withdrawal of Achilles have now ended, but also his uncontrollable grief; and it has been ended not by revenge, but by understanding of the universal nature of human suffering and endurance.

The Funeral of Hector (677–804)

Sleep links the scene in Achilles' dwelling to the gods and to Hermes' wakeful care, and with a further warning about Agamemnon, who has been completely bypassed by the still-dominant Achilles, he swiftly moves the cortege back to Troy. It is first seen by Cassandra, presumably because of her prophetic power (though that is not mentioned here), and she summons the city to the first spontaneous lamentations over Hector. Then, within the palace, begin the formal dirges of the singers (720–22; these later become a literary genre) and the more personal laments of the kindred women. Here these, too, are given a formal cast, for the introductions are similar (though not identical), and after each of the three individual laments there follows a verse (again similar but not identical) describing the general mourning.

The three individual laments are from the women whom we saw meet with Hector in Book 6. Andromache's is the first. The verse of introduction (723) would normally end "began the loud lament," as in 747 and elsewhere, but instead of the adjective "loud" the poet inserts "white-armed," a traditional epithet referring to Andromache, and adds a verse saying that she was holding the head of Hector in her arms: it is hard not to think that the change of the adjective is intended to evoke more vividly the picture of her bare arms around the corpse. For her, Hector was husband, father, and protector of the families of Troy.

She speaks of her son, predicts more clearly than ever the fate of the women and children of the city now that its main defender has gone, and in particular foretells the actual fate of Astyanax. Among the few remaining verses of the *Iliad's* continuation, the *Little Iliad*, are those that tell how Achilles' son Neoptolemus "led off Hector's wife to the ships; / his son he took from the bosom of the lovely-haired nurse / and seizing him by the foot hurled him from the tower; and falling / he met dark death and harsh fate" (see Evelyn-White 1936.519). Andromache's own later life is related by Virgil (*Aeneid* 3.294ff.).

Hecuba's lament stresses not so much her personal loss as the care of the gods for Hector even after his death, and his beauty despite the attempted defilement. This is the immensely natural and appropriate pride of the mother in her splendid son. Helen's is the most personal of all, and perhaps the most moving, for she speaks not of Hector's martial prowess but of his "gentle mind and gentle words" (722), of his unfailing courtesy to her in her loneliness and distress. As in Book 3 and 6, Helen still thinks of herself and her own sorrows first, but the pathos of her situation and her consciousness of her own responsibility bring her some sympathy despite her selfishness. It is appropriate that she appear thus at the conclusion of the poem, mourning over one of the many whose deaths are the result of her action, and in the company of a weeping wife who will one day be a slave.

Dignity and amplitude are given to the remaining preparations by Priam's directions for the gathering of wood for the pyre and the completion of the task in nine days; his short speech also reminds us of Achilles' kindness and of the fearfulness of the Trojans. After the burning of the body, the collection of the bones, and the building of the tomb and barrow there comes another reminder of their nervousness and of the imminent resumption of the warfare (799–800). There has been no washing, oiling, and clothing of the body of Hector, as there was for Patroclus (18.343ff.), as this part of the rites has already been accomplished by the orders of Achilles. The poet also omits here the armed parade, the cutting of their hair by the mourners, the calling of the dead man's name, the sacrifices at the pyre, and (for obvious reasons) the funeral games. The last scenes must be given the proper weight but not overburdened with detail.

Finally comes the funeral feast. The feast for Patroclus took place beside his bier, and before the pyre had even been built (23.29ff.), but Hector's is placed in Priam's palace and at the conclusion of the funeral and of the poem. Perhaps this implies again the Trojans' fear of a Greek attack, but more probably it is to enable the poet to concentrate his ending not only upon the dead Hector but also upon the living but doomed Trojans and their city. For even after Hector's death, life—with its struggles and its deeds of glory—must continue.

The quiet ending of the poem is like that of many fifth-century tragic dramas, or the close of Plato's account of the death of Socrates. In form the ending of *Beowulf* is similar, with its final laments for the dead warrior and its predictions of disaster to come now that his protection has gone. But the uniqueness of the *Iliad* lies in its exceptional design and the superb way in which that design embodies and dramatizes the final significance of the work; for the *Iliad* ends neither with the victory of the hero over his opponent nor with the hero's death, but with both suffering and the honor of noble deaths continuing through past, present, and future. The ending of the *Song of Roland* is a little like this, for there too the hero Charlemagne is still alive (like Achilles) and the angel Gabriel's summons to fresh battles evokes from him only a lament for the weariness of his life.

In the *Iliad* the insistent foreshadowing by the poet of the death of Achilles himself and the fall of Troy means that nothing is complete at the end of the poem, and men will continue to fight and either win glory for themselves or yield it to others, as Sarpedon (12.328) and others have said. Achilles himself carries on, not as the splendid hero who has defeated all opponents, but as a man who knows that in the rest of his short life he will find no more real happiness, and for whom the honor he has won in the world, as the words given to him in the underworld appropriately maintain (*Odyssey* 11.488–91), has now little value.

The final view the poem describes, however, is the gathering of the Trojans to feast in honor of their own mighty hero, whose eternal tomb appears in the distance. The proud celebration of individual greatness, combined with the symbol of the continuity as well as the transience of human life, well epitomize the *Iliad* itself.

> After piling up the tomb they went back to the city. Then
> gathering gladly together they held a splendid feast
> in the palace of Priam the consecrated king.
> So they performed the funeral of Hector, tamer of horses.

Further Reading

Macleod 1982 gives a good introduction and a detailed commentary (on the Greek text). Nagler 1974.167–98 is a most interesting analysis of the theme of consolation in this book; Nethercut 1976 argues that Priam's journey to Achilles is a journey to the lodge of Death. Segal 1971b discusses mutilation of corpses and refusal of burial in this and preceding books of the *Iliad*. Edwards 1986 examines the poet's treatment of the funerals of Patroclus and Hector and the meeting of Priam and Achilles. Bespaloff 1947 has a good chapter on the Priam-Achilles scene.

Afterword: The World-view of Homer

Socrates at his trial, according to Plato, praised Achilles for retaining his honor by avenging his friend even at the cost of his own life (*Apology* 28c). The day before his death, Socrates even dreams that a figure addressed him in Achilles' words, saying that he was to "go home" (*Crito* 44a–b; *Iliad* 9.363). He obviously admired Achilles for his decision to do what he thought right and avenge his friend, even at the cost of his own life, and sees in the same light his own refusal to abandon what he thought the right way of life even if it led to his execution. He says nothing of Achilles' quarrel with Agamemnon, his prayer for the defeat of his fellow Greeks, his rejection of Agamemnon's offer of recompense, or his sending Patroclus to battle in his place. Nor does he mention Achilles' restoration of his enemy's corpse. Aristotle takes Achilles as an example of the "high-minded" or "great-souled" man, primarily concerned with his honor, but does not discuss his actions in detail (see p. 150).

In the intellectual world of the Romans, Horace, rereading Homer in the quiet of the country, concluded that the poems showed, better than the philosophers did, what was right and wrong, expedient and not. "The story of Paris' love . . . is full of the passions of stupid kings and peoples. . . . Whatever follies the kings commit, the people suffer for it; insubordination, deceit, crime, lust, anger—such wrongs are committed on both sides of the Trojan wall" (*Epistles* I.2.1–16). He takes the *Iliad* as a picture of the darker side of life, not as the glorious deeds of Greeks against barbarians or as the individual tragedy of Achilles, and he censures mankind, not the gods.

Many other opinions about Homer's intent and views have been held, as can be seen in a recent book (Clarke 1981), and of course no interpretation of a serious classic will remain canonical for long. The following discussion expresses a view that I have held for many years.

Horace's view of Homer is reasonable enough, but one-sided; like Socrates, he pays no regard to the events of Book 24, and describes only the dark side of the *Iliad*, human folly but not human strength. Certainly Homer calls upon his Muse to sing of Achilles' wrath, not his immortal fame, and his Helen says that it is her misdeeds, not her beauty, that will be sung of by men of the future (6.356ff.). Certainly the characters of the *Iliad* live in a harsh world and blame the gods for it. But what the characters say and believe is not necessarily the whole view of the poet.

In his magnificent consolation to Priam, Achilles declares that Zeus distributes evils and blessings among mankind at his will (24.527ff.); this is doubtless true, but the great quarrel between Achilles and Agamemnon at the beginning of the poem, which the poet declares brought such suffering and losses to the Greeks, is presented not as the work of Zeus, but as the outcome of a human clash of wills. Both heroes in turn blame the spirit of *Atê* for their quarrel (19.85ff., 274ff.), but not a word was said by characters or poet about her activities at the time the quarrel took place. The poet's own view is likely to be more clearly shown when Achilles inveighs against Eris, "Strife," without implying that she is sent by the gods (18.107ff.).

Priam in his fatherly and comforting speech to Helen says that he blames not her, but the gods, for the war against the Greeks (3.164–65); but the rest of that book shows the weakness and lust of Paris and Helen, and it is not Zeus but Paris whom the rest of the Trojans are said to blame (3.453–54). Two passages suggest that the Trojan assembly is at fault for refusing to compel Paris to return her to her husband (7.345–97; 22.114ff.). Helen herself blames the gods for her destiny (6.349, 357ff.), but when she sleeps with Paris at the end of Book 3, after Aphrodite has departed, it seems to be by her own will. Hector blames Zeus for his approaching death at Achilles' hands, though when he killed Patroclus he had no fear of Achilles' revenge and was more optimistic about the future than Zeus was (22.301ff.; 16.859ff.).

In the poems, it is of course the poet who fashions mankind's destinies, not Zeus; and often when humans declare that an event was Zeus's doing, it is the human motives that the poet portrays as the dominant factors. This is the "double motivation" or "over-determination" often pointed out by scholars (see p. 135). Zeus is ruler of gods and men, and everything that happens must, in the widest sense, have his agreement ("The will of Zeus was accomplished", 1.5); but the prologue of the *Odyssey*, in which Zeus declares that mankind suffers not because of the gods but from their own transgressions, explicitly states the problem about the origin of evil that occupied the poet throughout the *Iliad*. In the *Odyssey* the presentation is much simpler

and less realistic, but the ideas are not essentially different. The
differences between what the characters say about their responsibility for their lives and the way the poet portrays the causes
of human troubles, the discrepancy between (for example) the
realistic clash of personalities the poet presents in *Iliad* I and the
way they later blame *Atê*, brings depths of moral ambiguity and
irony to the poem.

If this difference of viewpoint between characters and poet
seems too sophisticated a conception for an oral epic, compare
the heavy irony at the end of *Beowulf*, where the old and dying
king rejoices in the gold that his slaying of the dragon has made
available (2794ff.), but his doomed people treat it as useless and
destroy it with his corpse (3010ff.). In the Homeric epics, remember the many instances where it may be plausibly suggested that the poet is transcending or intentionally violating
the tradition of poetry he inherited. Formulae are passed over in
favor of new phrases, type-scenes and narrative patterns are used
for new purposes, myths are adapted and invented.

Much of the characterization may be original with Homer, including the attractiveness of Hector and Priam, and probably the
frivolity of the gods in the *Iliad* (which is not found even in the
Odyssey). The questioning of the code of honor by Achilles in
Book 9 and by Sarpedon in Book 12, and the structuring of the
plot so that (in both poems) the tale does not conclude with the
execution of vengeance, are almost certainly due to the original
genius of the poet.

Such questioning of heroic decisions and traditional values is
not unexpected in a prosperous eighth-century Ionia, where the
beginnings of philosophy were to arise a century later. It can also
be matched in other great epics. The questionable decisions of
Achilles in Books 9 and 16 are paralleled by that of Aeneas in the
killing of the suppliant Turnus at the end of the *Aeneid*, by
Beowulf's fatal decision in his old age to fight the dragon alone,
and by Roland's refusal to blow his horn, which causes the death
of all but sixty of his men and for which he is sternly rebuked
by Oliver (1705ff.).

There is much violence in the *Iliad*, as Simone Weil's well-
known *The Iliad: or, The Poem of Force* asserts (1945). But the
merciless remarks she quotes are spoken by the characters, not
by the poet, and most of the brutal triumphs of the heroes are
immediately followed by the poet's sympathetic account of what
the victim's death means to his wife, children, or parents (see p.
156). The sufferings of Andromache and all other women at the

sack of a city and the sorrows of their lives in slavery are often foreshadowed (for example, 1.29–31; 6.450–65; *Odyssey* 8.523–30). Nabokov remarked that "in a first-rate work of fiction the real clash is not between the characters but between the author and the world" (*Speak Memory* [New York 1966] 290, quoted by R. Eisner in *Arethusa* 12 [1979]: 153), and the *Iliad* certainly presents a world with many faults, which the gods do little to put right. One is reminded of Stephen Crane:

A man said to the universe:
"Sir, I exist!"
"However," replied the universe,
"The fact has not created in me
A sense of obligation."

The poet's sympathy for the sufferings he portrays is made much more obvious than (for instance) Hemingway's. Sometimes Homer seems to protest; Hera's terrifying fury against the Trojans is given no motive other than her personal hatred, and no justification (4.31, 18.361–68). Even a god complains of the unmerited sufferings of humanity: Poseidon sympathizes with Aeneas, who "suffers sorrows though he is guiltless, / because of the wrongdoings of others, though he sacrifices properly to the gods" (20.297–99). Human characters, of course, blame the world's unfairness directly on the gods, as in Menelaus's protest against the flagrant favoritism of Zeus toward the wrong side (13.620–39).

But the poet's consciousness of the world's shortcomings falls far short of (for instance) the defiance shown by Captain Ahab in *Moby Dick*. In the *Odyssey*, justice is done in the end. The *Iliad* is not so romantic, but its tone approaches tragedy not only in its suffering but also in its strong affirmation. Krook (1969.8ff.) has listed the following as the four elements of tragedy: (1) the act of shame or horror, which directly precipitates the central spectacle of suffering; (2) the suffering, properly tragic only if it generates knowledge in the sense of an understanding of man's fundamental nature or the fundamental human condition; (3) knowledge, in this sense; and (4) "some kind of affirmation, or reaffirmation, of the dignity of the human spirit and the worthwhileness of human life."

This affirmation is powerfully felt at the end of the *Iliad*. Priam and Achilles, Trojan and Greek, weep for their dead, but they weep *together*: "The two of them remembering, the one [remembering] Hector the manslayer / wept loudly as he crouched before the feet of Achilles; / and Achilles wept for his own father, and then again / for Patroclus; and their lamentation rose through the dwelling" (24.509–12). Afterward, Achilles controls his grief and rage in order to relieve the sorrows of the other man, and in so doing overcomes his own; and after they have shared a meal they gaze at each other with admiration (24.628ff.). They poem ends not with the satisfaction of vengeance, as it might well have done, but with this mutual consolation in grief and with the honorable funeral of a brave man. This is far from the gloom and hopelessness of the ending of *Beowulf*.

This positive note of affirmation is diffused throughout the poems, because though the circumstances of life may be harsh and inequitable, life is never futile or insignificant. It is given significance by the courage and endurance that accept and thus triumph over the hardships of life, which enable Priam to go on, awaiting the destruction of his city, and Achilles to take up life again without Patroclus, knowing his old father is far away and in need of him, until his own end comes. This courage and endurance is what Achilles holds up to young Lycaon just before he kills him (21.99ff.).

There is nothing to look forward to in life but similar troubles, and certainly death will bring no reward or consolation, as the afterlife of *Odyssey* 11 shows. These are the conditions of human life, dramatized by the poet's stress on mortality (see pp. 138–42), and there is dignity in accepting them. One cannot overcome these conditions, any more than Achilles can defeat Apollo or Helen can resist Aphrodite (22.15ff.; 3.399ff.); but just as the two mortals rise in our opinion because of their bold demeanor in these encounters, so too we admire those who without fear or illusions rely on their courage to face the unavoidable sufferings of life. The tone is close to that of William Faulkner in his Nobel Prize acceptance speech: "It is easy enough to say that man is immortal simply because he will endure. . . . I refuse to accept this. I believe that man will not merely endure: he will prevail. He is immortal, not because he alone among creatures has an inexhaustible voice but because he has a soul, a spirit capable of compassion and sacrifice and endurance. The poet's, the writer's, duty is to write about these things."

In the case of Virgil, a knowledge of the ideas of the Stoics and Epicureans and the writings of Cicero can provide us with an intellectual background that helps us understand his viewpoint. For Homer we do not have this. We can say that his attitude toward life is considerably different from the famous phrases of

Greek pessimism: "Best not to have been born" (Theognis 425–28, Sophocles *Oedipus at Colonus* 1224–25); "Call no man happy until he is dead" (Solon, in Herodotus 1.32.7). In some ways its self-reliant strength anticipates existentialist ideas, as does also the isolation in which Homer places Achilles between Book 9 to 16 and 20 to 22, and Hector in Book 22. Camus wrote of his Sisyphus: "At each of those moments when he leaves the heights and gradually sinks toward the lairs of the gods, he is superior to his fate. He is stronger than his rock. . . . All Sisyphus' silent joy is contained therein. His fate belongs to him. His rock is his thing" (1956.314–15).

C. S. Lewis saw something of this independent spirit in the *Iliad*, and was appalled by it: "Before any event can have that significance [of a profound change in the history of the world], history must have some degree of pattern, some design. The mere endless up and down, the constant aimless alternations of glory and misery, which make up the terrible phenomenon called a Heroic Age, admit no such design. . . . No achievement can be permanent: today we kill and feast, tomorrow we are killed, and our women led away as slaves. . . . Much has been talked of the melancholy of Virgil; but an inch beneath the bright surface of Homer we find not melancholy but despair. . . . It is all the more terrible because the poet takes it all for granted, makes no complaint. . . . For Homer it is all in the day's work" (1942.29–30). This view is incomplete, because Lewis is looking for the kind of purposeful Grand Design he finds in Virgil and in Christianity. In Homer there *is* a design, but it is unchanging and permanent, always renewed but always the same, like the leaves in Glaucus's simile (6.146ff.), not moving toward some mighty end; and it is not being woven by a divinity, but has always been there in the threads of human life.

Gilbert Murray was intensely aware of the positive note in the Homeric poems: "The feeling in [the *Iliad* and *Odyssey*] that the day of the heroes was a great and wonderful day seems to lie deep in the structure of both poems. . . . There is a sense of exhilaration in the narrative, as if in the presence of a beautiful and inspiring world. . . . There is a sense of joy in the world, except when definite disasters come from the gods or your enemies, or, of course, from your own Ate" (1927.201). This goes too far; this exhilaration belongs to the devoted scholar rather than to the poet or the characters. But joy there is, and pride in both the past and the present—the heroic past of their Greek ancestors, and the present that appears so clearly in the similes and on the shield of Achilles. For Homer does not look on the present as the ruins surviving from a mighty past, as many Anglo-Saxon poems do. The present has its hardships, as had the past, but they can be endured as were those of Priam and Achilles. And the present is a time for pride and joy, too, as the poet of the *Hymn to Apollo* felt (151–52):

You would say they were immortal and ageless always,
if you came upon the Ionians when they meet together.

Further Reading

For a history of interpretations of Homer, see the fine study by Clarke 1981. Most writers on Homer put forward a view about his attitude to "man's predicament"; besides those already referred to in this section, see the listing on p. 158. Damon 1980 discusses the complexities of meaning in *Roland* and *Beowulf* but unfortunately only outlines in a sentence (which it seems unfair to quote out of context) his view of the *Iliad*.

Bibliography

This listing consists mainly (but not entirely) of works referred to in the text and in the suggestions for further reading. I have tried to include standard authorities and recent significant studies, giving preference to works in English, but I am unable to include all the works I have profited from. The following abbreviations are used:

AJP	*American Journal of Philology*
CJ	*Classical Journal*
CP	*Classical Philology*
CQ	*Classical Quarterly*
CW	*Classical World*
G&R	*Greece and Rome*
GRBS	*Greek Roman and Byzantine Studies*
HSCP	*Harvard Studies in Classical Philology*
JHS	*Journal of Hellenic Studies*
TAPA	*Transactions of the American Philological Association*
YCS	*Yale Classical Studies*

Adkins, A. W. H. 1960. *Merit and Responsibility*. Oxford.
——. 1971. "Homeric Values and Homeric Society." *JHS* 91:1–14.
——. 1972. "Homeric Gods and the Values of Homeric Society." *JHS* 92:1–19.
——. 1982. "Values, Goals, and Emotions in the *Iliad*." *CP* 77:292–326.
Ahrens, E. 1937. *Gnomen in griechische Dichtung*. Halle.
Allen, T. W. 1924. *Homer: The Origins and the Transmission*. Oxford.
Andersen, Ø. 1976. "Some Thoughts on the Shield of Achilles." *Symbolae Osloenses* 51:5–18.
Andersson, T. M. 1976. *Early Epic Scenery*. Ithaca, N.Y.
Andrewes, A. 1971. *Greek Society*. Harmondsworth.
Apthorp, M. J. 1980. *The Manuscript Evidence for Interpolation in Homer*. Heidelberg.
Arend, W. 1933. *Die typischen Scenen bei Homer*. Berlin.
Armstrong, C. B. 1969. "The Casualty Lists in the Trojan War." *G&R* 16:30–31.
Armstrong, J. I. 1958. "The Arming Motif in the *Iliad*." *AJP* 79:337–54.
Auerbach, E. 1953. *Mimesis: The Representation of Reality in Western Literature*. Trans. W. Trask. Princeton.

Austin, M. M., and P. Vidal-Naquet. 1977. *Economic and Social History of Ancient Greece*. Berkeley and Los Angeles.

Austin, N. 1966. "The Function of Digressions in the *Iliad*." *GRBS* 7:295–312. Reprinted in Wright 1978 (see below).

———. 1975. *Archery at the Dark of the Moon: Poetic Problems in Homer's "Odyssey."* Berkeley and Los Angeles.

Bassett, S. E. 1938. *The Poetry of Homer*. Berkeley and Los Angeles.

Bespaloff, R. 1947. *On the "Iliad."* New York.

Beye, C. R. 1964. "Homeric Battle Narrative and Catalogues." *HSCP* 68:345–73.

———. 1966. *The "Iliad," the "Odyssey," and the Epic Tradition*. Garden City, N.Y.

———. 1974. "Male and Female in the Homeric Poems." *Ramus* 3:87–101.

Block, E. 1982. "The Narrator Speaks: Apostrophe in Homer and Vergil." *TAPA* 112:7–22.

Booth, W. C. 1961. *The Rhetoric of Fiction*. Chicago.

Bowra, C. M. 1930. *Tradition and Design in the "Iliad."* Oxford.

———. 1962. "Metre." In Wace and Stubbings 1962 (see below).

———. 1972. *Homer*. London.

Braswell, B. K. 1971. "Mythological Innovation in the *Iliad*." *CQ* 21:16–26.

Brooks, Cleanth. 1947. *The Well Wrought Urn*. New York.

Burkert, W. 1972. "Die Leistung eines Kreophylos: Kreophyleer, Homeriden und die Archaische Heraklesepik." *Museum Helveticum* 29:74–85.

———. 1979. "Kynaithos, Polycrates, and the Homeric Hymn to Apollo." *Arktouros, Hellenic Studies Presented to B. M. W. Knox*. Berlin.

Calhoun, G. M. 1933. "Homeric Repetitions." *University of California Publications in Classical Philology* 12.1.1–26. Berkeley and Los Angeles.

———. 1962. "Religion and Mythology" and "Religion and Ethics." In Wace and Stubbings 1962 (see below), pp. 442–50.

Cambridge Ancient History (3rd ed., 1975) vol. II Part 2: vol. III. Cambridge.

Camps, W. A. 1980. *An Introduction to Homer*. Oxford.

Camus, A. 1956 "The Myth of Sisyphus." Trans. J. O'Brien. In *Existentialism from Dostoevsky to Sartre*, ed. W. Kaufmann. New York.

Chantraine, P. 1952. "Le Divin et les Dieux chez Homère." *Entretiens Hardt* 1:47–79.

Chatman, S. 1978. *Story and Discourse*. Ithaca, N.Y.

Clader, L. L. 1976. *Helen: The Evolution from Divine to Heroic in Greek Epic Tradition* (*Mnemosyne* Supplement 42). Leiden.

Clark, M. E., and W. D. E. Coulson. 1978. "Memnon and Sarpedon." *Museum Helveticum* 35:65–73.

Clarke, H. W. 1967. *The Art of the "Odyssey."* Englewood Cliffs, N.J.

————. 1981. *Homer's Readers*. Newark, N.J.

Claus, D. B. 1975."Aidôs in the Language of Achilles." *TAPA* 105:13–28.

Clay, J. S. 1981. "Immortal and Ageless Forever." *CJ* 77:112–17.

————. 1983. *The Wrath of Athena: Gods and Men in the "Odyssey."* Princeton.

Coffey, M. 1957. "The Function of the Homeric Simile." *AJP* 78:113–32.

Coldstream, J. N. 1976. "Hero-cults in the Age of Homer." *JHS* 96:8–17.

————. 1977. *Geometric Greece*. London.

Combellack, F. 1955. "Contemporary Homeric Scholarship: Sound or Fury?" *CW* 49:17–26, 29–55.

————. 1965. "Some Formulary Illogicalities in Homer." *TAPA* 96:41–56.

————. 1984. "A Homeric Metaphor." *AJP* 105:247–57.

Culler, J. 1981. *The Pursuit of Signs: Semiotics, Literature, Deconstruction*. Ithaca, N.Y.

Curtius, E. R. 1953. *European Literature and the Latin Middle Ages*. Princeton.

Damon, P. 1961. *Modes of Analogy in Ancient and Medieval Verse. University of California Publications in Classical Philology* 15.6.261–334. Berkeley and Los Angeles.

————. 1980. "The Middle of Things: Narrative Patterns in the *Iliad, Roland,* and *Beowulf.*" In *Old English Literature in Context,* ed. J. D. Niles, pp. 107–16. Cambridge.

Davison, J. A. 1963. "The Transmission of the Text." In Wace and Stubbings 1963 (see below), pp. 215–33.

Dihle, A. 1970. *Homer-Probleme*. Opladen.

Dimock, D. E. Jr. 1956. "The Name of Odysseus." *Hudson Review* 9.1.52–70. Reprinted in *Homer,* ed. G. Steiner and R. Fagles (Englewood Cliffs, N.J.: 1962), 106–21.

Dodds, E. R. 1951. *The Greeks and the Irrational*. Berkeley and Los Angeles.

Donlan, W. 1982. "Reciprocities in Homer." *CW* 75:137–75.

Doyle, R. E. 1984. *ATH: Its Use and Meaning*. New York.

Duckworth, G. E. 1966. *Foreshadowing and Suspense in the Epics of Homer, Apollonius, and Vergil*. New York.

Durante, M. 1976. *Sulla Preistoria della Tradizione Poetica Greca* II (*Istituto per gli Studi Micenei ed Egeo-anatolici: Incunabula Graeca* vol. LXIV). Rome.

Edwards, M. W. 1966. "Some Features of Homeric Craftsmanship." *TAPA* 97:115–79.

————. 1968. "Some Stylistic Notes on *Iliad* XVIII." *AJP* 89:257–83.

————. 1975. "Type-scenes and Homeric Hospitality." *TAPA* 105:51–72.

————. 1980a. "The Structure of Homeric Catalogues." *TAPA* 110:81–105.

———. 1980b. "Convention and Individuality in *Iliad* 1." *HSCP* 84:1–28.

———. 1982. "Philology and the Oral Theory." *Pacific Coast Philology* 17:1–8.

———. 1986. "The Conventions of a Homeric Funeral." *Studies in Honour of T. B. L. Webster* I, ed. J. H. Betts, J. T. Hooker and J. R. Green. Bristol.

Eichholz, D. E. 1953. "The Propitiation of Achilles." *AJP* 74:137–48.

Evelyn-White, H. G. 1936. *Hesiod: The Homeric Hymns and Homerica* (Loeb Classical Library). Cambridge, Mass.

Fenik, B. 1964. *"Iliad X" and "Rhesus": The Myth*. Collection Latomus 73. Brussels.

———. 1968. *Typical Battle Scenes in the "Iliad."* Hermes Einzelschriften 21. Wiesbaden.

———. 1974. *Studies in the "Odyssey."* Hermes Einzelschriften 30. Wiesbaden.

———. 1978. *Homer: Tradition and Invention* (ed.). Leiden.

Finley, M. I., J. L. Caskey, G. S. Kirk, and D. L. Page. 1964. "The Trojan War." *JHS* 84:1–20.

Finley, M. I. 1970. *Early Greece*. New York.

———. 1974. "The World of Odysseus Revisited." *Proceedings of the Classical Association* 71:13–31.

———. 1978. *The World of Odysseus* (2nd rev. ed.). Harmondsworth.

Finnegan. R. 1977. *Oral Poetry*. Cambridge.

Fittschen, K. 1973. *Der Schild des Achilleus* (Archaeologia Homerica II Kap. N. Teil 1). Göttingen.

Fitzgerald, R. 1961. *Homer: The "Odyssey"* (trans.). Garden City, N.Y.

———. 1975. *Homer: The "Iliad"* (trans.). Garden City, N.Y.

Foxhall, L., and J. K. Davies. 1984. *The Trojan War: Its Historicity and Context*. Bristol.

Fränkel, H. 1921. *Die Homerischen Gleichnisse*. Göttingen.

———. 1973. *Early Greek Poetry and Philosophy* (trans. of *Dichtung and Philosophie des frühen Griechentums*, by Hadas and Willis). New York.

Frazer, R. M. 1966. *The Trojan War: The Chronicles of Dictys of Crete and Dares the Phrygian*. Bloomington, Ind.

———. 1985. "The Crisis of Leadership among the Greeks and Poseidon's Intervention in *Iliad* 14." *Hermes* 113:1–9.

Friedrich, P., and J. Redfield. 1978. "Speech as a Personality Symbol: The Case of Achilles." *Language* 54:263–87.

Gagarin, M. 1973. "*Dikê* in the *Works and Days*." *CP* 68:81–94.

———. 1974. "*Dikê* in Archaic Greek Thought." *CP* 69:186–97.

Gaisser, J. H. 1969. "Adaptation of Traditional Material in the Glaucus-Diomedes Episode." *TAPA* 100:165–76.

Geddes, A. G. 1984. "Who's Who in 'Homeric' Society?" *CQ* 34:17–36.

Gordesiani, R. 1980. "Zur Interpretation der Duale im 9. Buch der Ilias." *Philologus* 124:163–74.

Gouldner, A. W. 1965. *The Hellenic World: A Sociological Analysis.* New York.

Gransden, K. W. 1984. *Virgil's Iliad: An Essay on Epic Narrative.* Cambridge.

Greene, W. C. 1948. *Moira: Fate, Good and Evil in Greek Thought.* Cambridge, Mass.

Griffin, J. 1976. "Homeric Pathos and Objectivity." *CQ* 26:161–85.

———. 1977. "The Epic Cycle and the Uniqueness of Homer." *JHS* 97:39–53.

———. 1978. "The Divine Audience and the Religion of the *Iliad.*" *CQ* 28:1–22.

———. 1980. *Homer on Life and Death.* Oxford.

Griffin, J., and M. Hammond. 1982. "Critical Appreciations VI: Homer, *Iliad* 1.1–52." *G&R* 29:126–42.

Griffith, M. 1985. "What Does Aeneas Look Like?" *CP* 80:309–19.

Gunn, D. M. 1970. "Narrative Inconsistency and the Oral Dictated Text in the Homeric Epic." *AJP* 91:192–203.

———. 1971. "Thematic Composition and Homeric Authorship." *HSCP* 75:1–31.

Guthrie, W. K. C. 1950. *The Greeks and Their Gods.* Boston.

Hainsworth, J. B. 1966. "Joining Battle in Homer." *G&R* 13:158–66.

———. 1970. "The Criticism of an Oral Homer." *JHS* 90:90–98.

———. 1978. "Good and Bad Formulae." In Fenik 1978 (see above), pp. 41–50.

———. 1982. "Sul Testo e sull' Apparato Critico." In *Omero: Odissea* vol. II, ed. J. B. Hainsworth, xvi–xxx. *Scrittori greci e latini.* Milan.

Hansen, W. F. 1977. "Odysseus' Last Journey." *Quaderni Urbinati* 24:27–48.

———. 1978. "The Homeric Epics and Oral Poetry." In Oinas 1978 (see below).

Harrison, E. L. 1960. "Notes on Homeric Psychology." *Phoenix* 14:63–80.

Haywood, M. S. 1983. "Wordplay between θέω/θοός and θεός in Homer." *Papers of the Liverpool Latin Seminar* 4:215–18.

Hellwig, B. 1965. *Raum und Zeit im homerischen Epos.* Hildesheim.

Hentze, C. 1904. "Die Monologe in den homerischen Epen." *Philologus* 63:12–30.

Heubeck, A. 1958. "Zur inneren Form der Ilias." *Gymnasium* 65:37–47.

Hoekstra. A. 1981. *Epic Verse before Homer: Three Studies.* Amsterdam.

Hölscher, U. 1978. "The Transformation from Folk-tale to Epic." In Fenik 1978 (see above), pp. 51–67..

Hogan, J. C. 1979. *A Guide to the "Iliad."* Garden City, N.Y.

Hooker, J. T. 1979. *Homer: "Iliad" III.* Bristol.

Janko, R. 1982. *Homer, Hesiod and the Hymns.* Cambridge.

Jeffery, L. H. 1963. "Writing." In Wace and Stubbings 1963 (see below), pp. 545–59.

————. 1976. *Archaic Greece: The City-States c. 700–500 B.C.* New York.

Johnson, W. R. 1976. *Darkness Visible: A Study of Vergil's "Aeneid."* Berkeley and Los Angeles.

de Jong, I. J. F. 1985. "*Iliad* 366–392: A Mirror Story." *Arethusa* 18:5–22.

Kakridis, J. T. 1949. *Homeric Researches.* Lund.

————. 1971. *Homer Revisited.* Lund.

Kakridis, P. J. 1961. "Achilleus' Rüstung." *Hermes* 89:288–97.

Kiparsky, P. 1976. "Oral Poetry: Some Linguistic and Typological Considerations." In *Oral Literature and the Formula*, ed. B. A. Stolz and R. S. Shannon. Ann Arbor, Mich.

Kirk, G. S. 1960. "Objective Dating Criteria in Homer." *Museum Helveticum* 17:189–205. Reprinted in Kirk 1964 (see below).

————. 1962. *The Songs of Homer.* Cambridge.

————. 1964. *The Language and Background of Homer.* Cambridge.

————. 1965. *Homer and the Epic.* Cambridge.

————. 1966. "Studies in Some Technical Aspects of Homeric Style." *YCS* 20:75–152.

————. 1968. "War and the Warrior in the Homeric Poems." In *Problèmes de la Guerre en Grèce Ancienne*, ed. J.-P. Vernant. Paris. Reprinted in Kirk 1976 (see below).

————. 1970. *Myth: Its Meaning and Functions in Ancient and Other Cultures.* Berkeley and Los Angeles.

————. 1974. *The Nature of Greek Myths.* Harmondsworth.

————. 1976. *Homer and the Oral Tradition.* Cambridge.

————. 1978. "The Formal Duels in Book 3 and 7 of the *Iliad.*" In Fenik 1978 (see above).

————. 1983. "The *Iliad:* The Style of Books 5 and 6." In Winnifrith et al., 1983 (see below).

————. 1985. *The "Iliad:" A Commentary. Vol I: Books 1–4.* Cambridge.

Kitto, H. D. F. 1966. *Poiesis: Structure and Thought.* Berkeley and Los Angeles.

Köhnken, A. 1975. "Die Rolle des Phoinix und die Duale im I der Ilias." *Glotta* 53:25–36.

Kokolakis. M. M. 1980. "Homeric Animism." *Museum philologicum Londiniense* 4:89–113.

Krischer, T. 1971. *Formale Konventionen der homerischen Epik.* Munich.

————. 1979. "UnHomeric Scene Patterns in Vergil." *Papers of the Liverpool Latin Seminar* II:143–54.

Krook, D. 1969. *Elements of Tragedy.* New Haven, Conn.

Lang, M. L. 1969. "Homer and Oral Techniques." *Hesperia* 38:159–68.

————. 1975. "Reason and Purpose in Homeric Prayers." *CW* 68:309–14.

————. 1983. "Reverberation and Mythology in the *Iliad.*" In Rubino and Shelmerdine 1983 (see below), pp. 140–64.

———. 1984. *Herodotean Narrative and Discourse.* Cambridge, Mass.

La Roche, J. 1866. *Die homerische Textkritik im Altertum.* Leipzig.

Latacz. J. 1975. "Zur Forschungsarbeit an den direkten Reden bei Homer (1950–1970)." *Grazer Beiträge* 3:395–422.

———. 1977. *Kampfparänese, Kampfdarstellung und Kampfwirklichkeit der Ilias, bei Kallinos und Tyrtaios.* Munich.

Lattimore, R. 1951. *The "Iliad" of Homer* (trans.). Chicago.

———. 1969. "Nausikaa's Suitors." *Illinois Studies in Language and Literature* 58:88–102.

Lee, M. O. 1979. *Fathers and Sons in Virgil's "Aeneid."* Albany, N.Y.

Lesky, A. 1966. *A History of Greek Literature* (trans. of *Geschichte der griechischen Literatur,* 2nd ed. 1963). London.

Lewis, C. S. 1942. *A Preface to "Paradise Lost."* London.

Lloyd-Jones, H. 1971. *The Justice of Zeus.* Berkeley and Los Angeles.

———. 1983. "Artemis and Iphigeneia." *JHS* 103:87–102.

Lohmann, D. 1970. *Die Komposition der Reden in der Ilias.* Berlin.

Long, A. A. 1970. "Morals and Values in Homer." *JHS* 90:121–39.

Lord, A. B. 1951. "Composition by Theme in Homer and Southslavic Epos." *TAPA* 82:71–80.

———. 1960. *The Singer of Tales.* Cambridge, Mass.

———. 1974 (trans.). *The Wedding of Smailagić Meho* by Avdo Mededović. Cambridge, Mass.

Lord, M. L. 1967. "Withdrawal and Return: An Epic Story Pattern in the Homeric Hymn to Demeter and in the Homeric Poems." *CJ* 62:241–48.

Luce, J. V. 1975. *Homer and the Heroic Age.* London.

MacCary, W. T. 1982. *Childlike Achilles: Ontogeny and Phylogeny in the "Iliad."* New York.

Macleod. C. W. 1982. *Homer: "Iliad," Book XXIV.* Cambridge.

Mason, H. A. 1972. *To Homer through Pope.* New York.

Matthews. V. J. 1980. "Metrical Reasons for Apostrophe in Homer." *Liverpool Classical Monthly* 5.5:93–99.

Mondi, M. 1983. "The Homeric Cyclopes: Folktale, Tradition, and Theme." *TAPA* 113:17–38.

Motto, A. L., and J. R. Clark. 1969. "Isê Dais: The Honor of Achilles." *Arethusa* 2:109–25.

Moulton, C. 1974. "Similes in the *Iliad.*" *Hermes* 102:381–97.

———. 1977. *Similes in the Homeric Poems.* Göttingen.

———. 1979. "Homeric Metaphor." *CP* 74:279–93.

Mueller, M. 1970. "Knowledge and Delusion in the *Iliad.*" *Mosaic* 3:86–103. Reprinted in Wright 1978 (see below).

———. 1984. *The Iliad.* London.

Murray, G. 1927. *The Classical Tradition in Poetry.* Oxford.

Murray, O. 1980. *Early Greece.* Fontana.

———. 1985. "Ancient Greece." *Times Literary Supplement,* May 19, 1985, p. 546.

Murray, P. 1981. "Poetic Inspiration in Early Greece." *JHS* 101:87–100.
————. 1983. "Homer and the Bard." In Winnifrith et al., 1983 (see below).
Nagler, M. N. 1974. *Spontaneity and Tradition: A Study in the Oral Art of Homer*. Berkeley and Los Angeles.
Nagy, G. 1974. *Comparative Studies in Greek and Indic Meter*. Cambridge, Mass.
————. 1979. *The Best of the the Achaeans: Concepts of the Hero in Archaic Greek Poetry*. Baltimore.
Nethercut, W. R. 1976. "The Epic Journey of Achilles." *Ramus* 5:1–17.
Nilsson, M. P. 1932. *The Mycenaean Origins of Greek Mythology*. Berkeley and Los Angeles.
Oinas, F. J. 1978. (ed.) *Heroic Epic and Saga*. Bloomington, Ind.
Opland, J. 1980. *Anglo-Saxon Oral Poetry*. New Haven, Conn.
Otis, B. 1964. *Virgil: A Study in Civilized Poetry*. Oxford.
Owen, E. T. 1946. *The Story of the "Iliad."* Toronto.
Packard, D. W. 1974. "Sound-patterns in Homer." *TAPA* 104:239–60.
Page, D. L. 1955. *The Homeric "Odyssey."* Oxford.
————. 1959. *History and the Homeric "Iliad."* Berkeley and Los Angeles.
————. 1972. "The Mystery of the Minstrel at the Court of Agamemnon." *Studi classici in onore di Q. Cataudella* 127–31. Catania.
————. 1973. *Folktales in Homer's "Odyssey."* Cambridge, Mass.
Paige, D. D. 1951. *Letters of Ezra Pound, 1907–1941*. London.
Palmer, L. R. 1963. "The Language of Homer." In Wace and Stubbings 1963 (see below), pp. 75–178.
Parry, A. 1966. "Have We Homer's *Iliad*?" *YCS* 20:177–216.
————. 1971. *The Making of Homeric Verse: The Collected Papers of Milman Parry* (ed.). Oxford.
————. 1972. "Language and Characterization in Homer." *HSCP* 76:1–22.
Peabody, B. 1975. *The Winged World*. Albany, N.Y.
Pedrick, V. 1983. "The Paradeigmatic Nature of Nestor's Speech in *Iliad* 11." *TAPA* 113:55–68.
Pellizer, E. 1972. "Metremi proverbiali nell 'Opere e i giorni' di Esiodo." *Quaderni Urbinati* 13:24–37.
Petersen, L. 1939. *Zur Geschichte der Personifikation*. Würzburg.
Petzold, K. E. 1976. "Die Meleagros-Geschichte der Ilias." *Historia* 25:146–69.
Pfeiffer, R. 1968. *History of Classical Scholarship*. Oxford.
Powell, B. 1977. *Composition by Theme in the "Odyssey."* Meisenheim.
Pritchard, J. B. 1973. *The Ancient Near East* I. Princeton.
Propp, V. 1968. *Morphology of the Folktale* (2nd ed., trans. Scott). Austin.
Quiller, B. 1981. "The Dynamics of the Homeric Society." *Symbolae Osloenses* 61:109–55.

Redfield, J. M. 1975. *Nature and Culture in the "Iliad."* Chicago.

———. 1984. "Warfare and the Hero in the Classical World." *Laetaberis: Journal of the California Classical Association* n.s. III:1–16.

Reinhardt, K. 1961. *Die Ilias und ihr Dichter.* Göttingen.

———. 1966. "Personifikation und Allegorie." *Vermächtnis der Antike* 7–40. Göttingen.

Renger, J. M. 1978. "Mesopotamian Epic Literature." In Oinas 1978 (see above), pp. 27–48.

Richardson, N. J. 1980. "Literary Criticism in the Exegetical Scholia to the *Iliad:* A Sketch." *CQ* 30:265–87.

Rosner, J. A. 1976. "The Speech of Phoenix: *Iliad* 9.434–605." *Phoenix* 30:314–27.

Rowe, C. J. 1983. "The Nature of Homeric Morality." In Rubino and Shelmerdine 1983 (see below), pp. 248–75.

Rubino, C. A. 1979. "'A Thousand Shapes of Death': Heroic Immortality in the *Iliad.*" *Arktouros: Hellenic Studies Presented to B. W. M. Knox.* 12–18. Berlin.

Rubino, C. A., and C. W. Shelmerdine. 1983. *Approaches to Homer.* Austin, Tex.

Russo, J. 1968. "Homer Against His Tradition." *Arion* 7:275–95.

———. 1983. "The Poetics of the Ancient Greek Proverb." *Journal of Folklore Research* 20:121–30.

Russo, J., and B. Simon. 1968. "Homeric Psychology and the Oral Epic Tradition." *Journal of the History of Ideas* 29:483–98. Reprinted in Wright 1978, see below.

Sale, W. 1983. "Achilles and Heroic Values." *Arion* 2:86–100.

Schadewaldt, W. 1938. *Iliasstudien.* Leipzig.

———. 1965. *Von Homers Welt und Werk* (4th ed.). Stuttgart.

Schein, S. L. 1984. *The Mortal Hero: An Introduction to Homer's "Iliad."* Berkeley and Los Angeles.

Scholes, R. 1974 *Structuralism in Literature.* New Haven, Conn.

———. 1982. *Semiotics and Interpretation.* New Haven, Conn.

Scodel, R. 1982. "The Autobiography of Phoenix: *Iliad* 9.444–95." *AJP* 103:128–36.

Scott, J. A. 1912. "Phoenix in the *Iliad.*" AJP 33:68–77.

Scott, W. C. 1974. *The Oral Nature of the Homeric Simile.* Leiden.

Scully, S. 1984. "The Language of Achilles: The *ochthêsas* Formulas." *TAPA* 114:11–27.

Segal, C. 1968. "The Embassy and the Duals of *Iliad* 9.182–98." *GRBS* 9:101–14.

———. 1971a. "Nestor and the Honor of Achilles." *Studi Micenei ed Egeo-anatolici* 13:90–105.

———. 1971b. *The Theme of the Mutilation of the Corpse in the "Iliad."* Leiden.

———. 1971c. "Andromache's *Anagnorisis:* Formulaic Artistry in *Iliad* 22.437–76." *HSCP* 75:33–57.

Seymour, T. D. 1902/1981. *Introduction to the Language and Verse of Homer*. New York.

Shipp, G. P. 1972. *Studies in the Language of Homer* (2nd ed.). Cambridge.

Silk, M. S. 1974. *Interaction in Poetic Imagery*. Cambridge.

Snodgrass, A. M. 1967. *Arms and Armour of the Greeks*. Ithaca, N.Y.

———. 1971. *The Dark Age of Greece*. Edinburgh.

———. 1974. "An Historical Homeric Society?" *JHS* 94:114–25.

———. 1980. *Archaic Greece: The Age of Experiment*. London.

Sowa, C. A. 1984. *Traditional Themes and the Homeric Hymns*. Chicago.

Stanford, W. B. 1939. *Ambiguity in Greek Literature*. Oxford.

———. 1954. *The Ulysses Theme*. Oxford.

———. 1965. *The "Odyssey" of Homer*. London.

———. 1967. *The Sound of Greek*. Berkeley and Los Angeles.

———. 1976. "Varieties of Sound-effects in the Homeric Poems." *College Literature* 3:219–27.

Stigers, E. S. 1981. "Sappho's Private World." In *Reflections of Women in Antiquity*, ed. H. P. Foley. New York.

Suerbaum, W. 1968. "Die Ich-Erzählungen des Odysseus." *Poetica* 2:150–77.

Taplin, O. 1980. "The Shield of Achilles within the *Iliad*." *G&R* 27:1–21.

Thalmann, W. G. 1984. *Conventions of Form and Thought in Early Greek Epic Poetry*. Baltimore.

Thornton, A. 1978. "Once Again, the Duals in Book 9 of the *Iliad*." *Glotta* 56:1–4.

Todorov, T. 1977. *The Poetics of Prose*. Trans. R. Howard. Ithaca, N.Y.

Turner, E. G. 1968. *Greek Papyri: An Introduction*. Oxford.

van Leeuwen, J. 1912. *Ilias*. Leiden.

———. 1913. *Ilias: Pars Altera. Libri XIII–XXIV*. Leiden.

Vermeule, E. 1972. *Greece in the Bronze Age* (2nd ed.). Chicago.

———. 1979. *Aspects of Death in Early Greek Art and Poetry*. Berkeley and Los Angeles.

Versnel, H. S. 1981. "Self-sacrifice, Compensation and the Anonymous Gods." *Entretiens Hardt* XXVII 135–85. Geneva.

Vivante, P. 1985. *Homer*. New Haven.

Vlastos, G. 1975. *Plato's Universe*. Seattle.

Wace, A. J. B., and F. H. Stubbings. 1963. *A Companion to Homer*. London.

Walsh, G. B. 1984. *The Varieties of Enchantment*. Chapel Hill, N.C.

Webster, T. B. L. 1952–1953. "Language and Thought in Early Greece." *Memoirs and Proceedings of the Manchester Literary and Philosophical Society* 94:1–22.

———. 1958. *From Mycenae to Homer*. London.

Weil, S. 1945. *The Iliad: or, The Poem of Force.* Trans. M. McCarthy. New York.

Wender, D. 1977. "Homer, Avdo Mededović, and The Elephant's Child." *AJP* 98:327–47.

West, M. L. 1966. *Hesiod: "Theogony," Edited with Prolegomena and Commentary.* Oxford.

———. 1973. "Greek Poetry 2000–700 B.C." *CQ* 23:179–92.

———. 1978. *Hesiod: "Works and Days," Edited with Prolegomena and Commentary.* Oxford.

West, S. 1967. *The Ptolemaic Papyri of Homer (Pap. Coloniensia III).* Cologne.

———. 1981. "Sul Testo dell' Odissea." In *Omero: Odissea vol. I,* ed. S. West, xxxix–LIX. Scrittori greci e latini. Milan.

Whitman, C. H. 1958. *Homer and the Heroic Tradition.* Cambridge, Mass.

———. 1982. *The Heroic Paradox: Essays on Homer, Sophocles, and Aristophanes,* ed. C. Segal. Ithaca. N.Y.

Whitman, C. H., and R. Scodel. 1981. "Sequence and Simultaneity in *Iliad* N, Ξ and O," *HSCP* 85:1–15.

Willcock, M. M. 1964. "Mythological Paradeigma in the *Iliad.*" *CQ* 14:141–54.

———. 1970. "Some Aspects of the Gods in the *Iliad.*" *Bulletin of the Institute of Classical Studies* 17:1–10. Reprinted in Wright 1978 (see below).

———. 1976. *A Companion to the "Iliad."* Chicago.

———. 1978. "Homer, the Individual Poet." *Liverpool Classical Monthly* 3:11–18.

Williams, G. 1983. *Technique and Ideas in the "Aeneid."* New Haven and London.

Wilson, J. R. 1974. "The Wedding Gifts of Peleus." *Phoenix* 28:385–89.

Winnifrith, T., P. Murray, and T. W. Gransden. 1983. *Aspects of the Epic.* New York.

Woodhouse, W. J. 1930. *The Composition of Homer's "Odyssey."* Oxford.

Wright, J. 1978. *Essays on the "Iliad": Selected Modern Criticism.* Bloomington, Ind.

Wyatt, W. F., Jr., 1982. "Homeric ATH." *AJP* 103:247–76.

Young, D. C. 1979. "The Diachronic Study of Myth and Achilles' Heel." *CCA-NS Journal* 4.1:3–34.

———. 1982. "Pindar." In *Ancient Writers I,* ed. T. J. Luce. New York.

New York

Index

Page references to the main treatment of a topic are italicized. Except in the case of similes, line references to passages in the *Iliad* are not given here, as they can easily be found in the table of contents. Line references to discussions of passages in the *Odyssey* are listed at the end of that entry.